I0656319

# The Eyes Below

## Book 10

### Of The Warrior Series

By

Sandra J Yearman

**Seraphim Publishing LLC**

**We Will Bring Light To All The Dark Places**

Registered trademark-Sandra J Yearman

Seraphim Publishing
438 Water St
Cambridge, WI 53523
sandrajyearman@gmail.com

Library of Congress Catalog Number: 2016903562

ISBN: 978-0-9890263-8-3

First Edition

# About The Author

Sandra J Yearman is a native of Wisconsin, where she currently resides. She graduated from the University of Wisconsin with a Bachelor of Arts degree in Journalism. Sandra was a member of the United States Army Reserves for over twenty years. She retired from the Dane County Sheriff's Office in Madison Wisconsin as a sergeant.

Sandra is a cancer survivor. And it is on this journey that she says she found her voice and began to write. She established Seraphim Publishing LLC in 2008. Sandra has spent decades supporting and working with rescued domestic animals.

Books written by Sandra:

### Novels

Brother Kings
The Scroll And The Sword
Song Of The Second Son
The Faces Of The Damned
A Single Lion Roars
Stand Before The Children
Tyrants, Dictators And Kings

Politicians And Kings
Armada Of The Dead
The Eyes Below

## Poetry

A Gathering Of Angels
I AM Who You Seek
A Celebration Of Angels
The Time Of Angels Is At Hand
The Warrior On Bended Knees
Celebration of God
On His Wings
The Voice Of An Angel
If I Had Wings
Souls On Fire
As Angels Hover Over
From The Mist The Angels Came
You Are The Song
Be Still
Walking With Angels
When Angels Smile
Angel Dreams
An Angel's Touch
Dancing With Angels

To The Homeless

Children

Everywhere

May Love Find You

# Contents

# Contents

# Contents

# The Kingdom
# Of Inferus

## Elods

A race as old as time itself, the Elods lived deep within the bowels of the World of Nunc. They hid when the Old Ones first came to that world. When the Elods saw the horrors that the demons brought they choose to separate themselves from the others, the ones who called to the demons.

The Elods first hid in caves but as the darkness in man called to the darkness of the demons, the Elods' terror grew. They followed the teachings of an ancient prophesy, the Prophesy of Isto, and burrowed deeper and deeper within the world until they found a level where they determined no one else would go. They burrowed eight levels within the ground, farther than any other human or animal had ever gone. Here on the eighth level they built a new world, they named it Inferus which means 'below' in the old language.

The Prophesy of Isto told of a paradise, a promised land, deep within the World of Nunc. After centuries of digging through rock the Elods found a world like nothing they had ever seen before. Lush jungles that were inhabited with strange creatures. Crystal waters and a sun that shone brightly on the landscape.

The Elods were a race of brilliant people. Their intelligence set them apart from the many tribes of barbarians that terrorized the World of Nunc in the early ages. The Elods would send spies to the world above to observe the many races and species that populated that world. They swore oaths to themselves that they would never fall to the greed and depravity that they thought motivated these other peoples.

But for all of their good intentions and brilliance they could not fight their own humanity. Over the centuries they grew more like the peoples who lived above the ground. They sought the same pleasures, they had the same needs and desires and they too called the Old Ones in.

# Chapter I
## Lost Children

A baby cried and Thedes ran to the closed door of his bedroom. "Can I come in?" he yelled.

"Just give us a few minutes," said Princess Zada, wife of Lakin. "Then you can meet your daughter."

"Daughter, did you hear that? We have a daughter," Thedes said. The pride and awe was evident in his voice as he turned and spoke to everyone in his parlor and yet to no one in particular.

King Manu and Queen Delilia got out of their chairs and stood next to the door as did Prince Lakin, Prince Gael and Prince Hadar. Their wives were in the bedroom with Ibula helping to deliver the newest member of their family.

Princess Paj, wife of Hadar, opened the bedroom door and Thedes rushed in. He ran to the bed where Ibula was sitting up and holding a baby who looked exactly like her. "She looks Ruala," said Ibula and tried to hand the baby to Thedes but he kissed his wife over and over before he took his daughter.

Thedes walked to the doorway and addressed all of the people in their home. "Meet Clea, Delilia, Renya the first girl born into this new race. Clea was my mother's name, Delilia is Ibula's mother and Renya is our adopted mother. This baby binds our races and as the Sanuri would say, 'She ushers in the Prophesy of The Seven Sons."

When Lieutenant Collins and the caravan he was leading got close enough to the monastery that was north of the City of Leven in the Kingdom of Ganz, they saw that the monastery was not burning but the forest behind it was.

Collins gave the order to move forward but the Sanuri repeatedly yelled, "Wait!" as he drove his boca to the front of the caravan. "This makes no sense." The Sanuri said to the leaders.

"The lands we have traveled are soaked from the storms. That fire was deliberately set and something is feeding it. We well wait for the Enrops to return."

The group did not have to wait long before they discovered the trap that was set for them. As a flock of Enrops flew from the caravan towards the monastery, a Huta spear flew into the air narrowly missing one of the giant birds.

"Hutas are so arrogant that they don't hide," said Thaos. "They are taking orders from someone."

"Would anyone care to join us?" the Sanuri called out to the heavens.

"The priests inside of the monastery are alright, at least for now," said the Angel Daniel as he appeared at the front of the caravan. "The fire was set to get your attention and if that did not work, Hector was prepared to kill all of the priests and destroy the monastery. It is his demon who controls the Hutas. Your mission now is to protect this monastery until Claudius' army arrives."

"What about General Amundsen?" asked Lieutenant Collins. "The fort is closer than the General from Lentz."

"This is true, but Amundsen's men are tied up trying to keep the citizens of Port Friada safe from the warring factions of the Insidiae. The city has become a battle zone. Samael added more fuel to the fire there so that you would not have anyone to rescue you."

"How many Hutas are surrounding the monastery?" asked Sorren.

"Considerably more than you are capable of fighting," said Daniel.

"Then will you help us?" Sorren asked.

"I have been waiting for you to ask," Daniel said.

"Wait; you mean the priests inside the monastery haven't asked for help?" asked Dominic.

"They are safe for now," Daniel said. "But there is a lesson to learn here." Although the Angels had appeared to many of the people in this group before, they had never appeared to Drake, Tally, Zeke and his men and the soldiers who accompanied them. Now as Daniel spoke all of the people in the caravan saw and heard the Angel.

"There are many kingdoms in these worlds besides the ones you are familiar with. Most people go through their lives being aware of nothing more than what appears before their eyes. Most of you here have increased your awareness greatly and you have chosen to do so but there is so much more for you to understand. The Prophesy of The Seven Sons is unfolding and doors to worlds beyond your imaginations are opening. Some doors will open to allies and others to foes. Do not be short-sighted."

"The Great Ruler has given life to many things. Yet mankind believes they are the center of the universe." Daniel turned and looked at the fire as he spoke. Huge clouds had formed over the forest fire and heavy rains now stopped the flames. "A living forest is a home to many creations. Sorren if someone set your home on fire what would you do?"

"Stop them, kill them. Hunt them down if I have to," Sorren replied.

"The Sanuri will tell you when it is safe to proceed forward," Daniel said and disappeared.

While being in the presence of an Angel is emotional for anyone, the men and women of this group who had never seen an Angel before were particularly affected. These hardened and in some cases brutal people were unable to control their emotions. Some were laughing, others crying and some just stood in awe. But the sounds of battle soon brought them back to their realities.

Roars, screeches, screams, growls and thunderous groaning sounds filled the air. Ashley grabbed Cassidy and turned his head away as the people in the caravan watched nature destroy the army of Hutas.

"What is that groaning?" asked Edward.

"The trees," said the Sanuri. "They too are alive."

"You mean the trees are fighting with the Hutas?" Gideon asked in disbelief.

"It is not just the trees," replied the Sanuri. "Mankind ultimately fears nature because they know they cannot control it. But you are thinking of storms, floods and earthquakes. Battles like the one you are watching happen in these worlds but most of the time there are no witnesses to tell of them."

Raul and Simon led their troops northward in the Kingdom of Lentz. They were far enough south in that kingdom that to turn west would take them into the Kingdom of Stordt, and that would be considered an act of war. Their plan was to travel north until they reached Langer. They would stop at the castle of King Mathas then turn west and possibly stop at the castle of Claudius before entering the Kingdom of Wetpr. The Princes planned these stops because of the wounded priests who traveled with them.

Nyla and Saran rode on horses but Nina wanted to ride with Raul on his horse. Simon had already sent Enrops to give Michael the verbal message that his sisters were safe. "We are going to have to stop in Castor for supplies," Matthew said. "We left everything at the campsite. "Angelina, maybe you could help the girls buy some clothing."

"I was already thinking about that," she replied. "Actually they, well we all could use baths. What if we spend the night in Castor?"

"That's fine with us," Raul said as he looked at Simon. "Girls, when we get there you should write letters to Michael; he has been so worried about you."

"I don't mean to insult you but do you know how to write, because we can help you," said Simon.

"Mother taught us," said Nyla. "I can help Nina if she needs it."

"We are going to write to our family," said Raul. "You are more than welcome to write to them too."

"What would we say?" asked Saran.

"Anything you want. You could tell them about the journey you have been on and how you escaped your tribe," said Simon. "How did you escape?"

"An old woman helped us," said Saran. "We never saw her before but she came to us one night and led us away from the tribe. She stayed with us until the soldiers found us. She was really nice."

The adults smiled as they listen to Saran's story. "Was her name Ruth by any chance?" asked Gabriel.

"Yes, how did you know?" asked Nyla. "Did you send her?"

"She sent us," said Raphael. "Ruth is an Angel."

"What is an Angel?" asked Nina.

"Since we have two high priests here, why don't one of you take the lead on this," Simon said to Gabriel and Raphael with a grin.

It took over an hour for the grisly battle around the monastery at Leven to subside. When it did, it was the Sanuri who led the caravan forward. Ashley made Cassidy ride in the carriage and wouldn't allow him to look at the battlefield they traveled through.

While almost everyone in the caravan had battle experience they rode in silence as their minds could not fathom what their eyes were seeing. Two thousand Huta soldiers were dead but their bodies were tangled in trees and vines, torn apart by animals and partially swallowed by the ground.

As the group drew closer to the monastery they could hear the voices of the priests yelling, "The Sanuri is here! The Sanuri is here!"

The huge wooden gates in the stone wall that surrounded the monastery creaked and a groaned as they opened. High Priest Barnabas stood in the forefront with a group of priests behind him.

Most of the priests were on top of the walls of the monastery for they believed they would have to do battle with the army of Hutas that had surrounded them.

"This is not over," said the Sanuri as the caravan entered the courtyard. "Lieutenant Collins have your men join the priests on the walls."

The Sanuri turned to Barnabas and said, "The Angel Daniel told us to stay here and protect you until an army comes for us. We have much to discuss."

"Excuse me padre," said Sorren. "How many ways can someone enter this monastery?"

"There are gates at the front and back," said Barnabas.

"I am putting my warriors on the gates," Sorren said and left the group.

"We will get you all settled in rooms and care for your horses," said Barnabas. "Then we will have a meeting. Sanuri how large a room will you need?"

"Large; your priests should be part of this too."

The war in Port Friada took on new proportions after the demon Samael became involved. He wanted to keep all of General Amundsen's soldiers and Admiral Wainburst's sailors so occupied that they could not send anyone to help either the monastery or the caravan that the Sanuri was traveling with. Because of this, Samael was not giving Hector's men an easy victory. The chaos and fear caused by this war increased Samael's power; it fed him as all wars do.

With the healing and the increased powers that Samael gave to Hector, he was able to work on multiple strategies simultaneously. Besides commanding his troops in Port Friada, Hector had sent the demon Negal to the monastery at Leven to create a trap for the Sanuri. Hector was a controlling commander and did not leave the details of the ambush to Negal. When Hector told the demon to massacre the priests and burn the monastery the demon argued.

"When the Hutas did that at Avaide all of the world took notice," Negal said. "You know that I have no issue with the orders other than you and everything you do from this day forward will be exposed. Are you sure you are ready for that?"

"You make a valid point but Samael wants the Sanuri at all costs," said Hector as he thought about Negal's words.

"I am certainly not telling you to go against Samael but Hector you have worked so hard and gone through so much and you may lose everything with this one decision. I think you can ambush the Sanuri without destroying the monastery."

"Just do what I tell you!" Hector said angrily. He wasn't mad at Negal for speaking his mind. Hector was angry because he realized that Negal was right with what he was saying.

The Sanuri wanted to keep the meeting with the priests fairly short since he expected another attack on the monastery. He told them of the war in Port Frida and the words of the Angel Daniel. The Sanuri told the priests very little about the mission in Port Friada but he did tell them that General Claudius was leading over five-thousand troops from Lentz to the monastery.

"I am a little confused," said High Priest Barnabas. "Does the Angel Daniel mean that there will be no more threats to the monastery after the army from Lentz arrives? Because we have others here who we protect and with the war in Port Friada more may come here for shelter also."

"You make a very good point but I don't have an answer to your question," said the Sanuri. "Who is here now besides workers and the priests?"

"We are giving shelter to some families, after the Hutas destroyed their farms. The only reason these families survived is because they were not home at the times of the attacks. They were here for a service," explained Barnabas. "And we have some orphans. And that Sanuri brings up an issue which I need to speak with you about."

"By all means," said the Sanuri and nodded.

Barnabas looked at the members of the caravan who were in the room before he spoke. "We have a Ruala child."

"What?" asked Dagon loudly. "How can that be?"

"There were three Ruala criminals who terrorized this area. Several women were raped and one of them conceived. She killed herself shortly after giving birth and her family brought the baby to us. She is a beautiful child and very good natured but we don't know if she should be with her tribe."

"We will take her," said Nana and stood up. "One of us can take her to the Ice Caves. We will find her a home."

"Perhaps the Sanuri should look at the child to make sure she has no evil in her," Sol said.

Barnabas nodded to a priest who stood up and left the room. "She is about a year old and has already started to fly. Which I don't mind telling you gave us all quite a scare. The family didn't name her so we did. Her name is Amelia."

"I want to remind everyone in this room that a child should not suffer for the sins of its father," said the Sanuri. "Many of you have strong opinions and emotions about Bruno, Morgan and Nada. This child is innocent."

As the Sanuri spoke a priest carried a little girl with dark curly hair and big brown eyes to the Sanuri. She held out her arms and the Sanuri took her and stared into the child's eyes. After a few moments he said, "There is no evil in her. Dagon write to your parents about her."

"You think that is wise?" Dagon asked. "They may want to take her."

"And what if they do?"

"Misha."

"Perhaps you need to write to them so they can help Misha work some things out."

Risa and Nana walked up to the Sanuri together. "We will make sure she gets a home," Nana said and took Amelia who laughed and played with Nana's long hair.

The priest who had carried the little girl into the room looked at Risa and said, "She has some things if you would like to follow me."

"I'll help you," said Ralf as Nana walked back to her seat where people surrounded her to look at Amelia.

"Edward, I hope you aren't mad," Nana said. "But we need to take her home."

"I'm not mad at all. But I am a bit concerned about traveling with a little one when we may have to fight our way home," Edward said then looked at the Sanuri. "Should we send them to the Ice Caves now?"

"While that sounds practical, I just feel like we need to take her back to Wetpr. But that doesn't mean she will live there." The Sanuri now turned back to Barnabas. "Is she the only Ruala child you have?"

"Yes. But we have three other orphans, two boys and a girl," replied Barnabas.

"Where did they come from?" asked Thaos.

"People just leave the children at the front gates and ring the bell. At least Amelia's grandparents brought her inside. We aren't really sure with these children."

"What do you mean?" asked Sorren. "Are they too young to talk?"

"I am sorry, I am not doing a very good job of explaining this," said Barnabas. "It always breaks my heart when children are left like that. Two nights ago Padre Bishop heard the bell and went to the gates. He found the three children shivering and starving. They were filthy and crying. They have spoken little since they arrived. And to think, those precious children could have been out there when the Hutas came; thank The Great Ruler that He got them to us in time."

"Why don't you bring them in here also," suggested the Sanuri. While some of the people in the room questioned why the Sanuri wanted to meet the children, no one said a word. Risa and Ralf returned to the room with Amelia's belongings moments before one of the priests walked in with the three children; a little girl about six years of age and two boys ages nine and ten. The priest led the children to the Sanuri who was standing in the front of the room.

"Do you know any of them?" Thaos asked Cassidy.

"No," Cassidy replied in a whisper. He didn't understand why he felt so upset seeing the homeless children.

"There is nothing to be afraid of," the Sanuri said in a soothing tone as he squatted down so he could look into the faces of the children. "Are you brothers and sister?" Both of the boys shook their heads from side to side to indicate 'no'. The little girl merely stared at the Sanuri. "What are your names?"

"She's Chasity, I'm Logan and he is Marty," said the oldest boy.

"Chasity!" yelled Joao as he and Dack jumped out of their seats and walked up to the children. "Sanuri can you tell if she is Joey's and Tommy's sister?" The little girl swung around and looked at Joao as he spoke.

"I'll bet she is," said Dack in disbelief. "But how did she get here?"

"Chasity do you have brothers named Tommy and Joey?" asked the Sanuri. She smiled and nodded.

"I don't believe this," said Rachel as she, Dagon, Batina and Ratri also walked to the front of the room.

"Chasity, my sister and her husband Elan, adopted Joey and Tommy and they have been looking for you," said Joao as he squatted down in front of the little girl.

"They made Tommy leave because he couldn't stop crying," said Chasity.

"Who did?" asked Dack.

"Those bad men," Chasity said and started to cry.

"Honey don't cry," said Joao and picked her up. "We're going to take you home and you can live with Tommy and Joey." Chasity put her arms around Joao's neck and hugged him tightly. "I might cry too," Joao said with a smile, although he was only half joking.

Rachel saw the looks on the faces of Logan and Marty. "Dagon, we can't leave the boys here," she said. "Let's take all the children home and well, with our family we will figure out something."

"I agree," said Sorren as he too walked to the front of the room. "We'll get them all homes." Sorren looked at Logan and Marty. "I have boys about your ages. We will take care of you until we sort all of this out." Sorren put his arms around the boys as he spoke. Then he looked at the Sanuri and said, "I guess I owe the Angels an apology, I thought they wanted us to hide from Hector's men. I didn't even think there would be more to it."

# Chapter II
## Healing

"Ratri, I am sorry. I do feel sorry for those children but I don't think I am ready for a family yet," said Batina as the two were walking around the monastery grounds. "So do you really want to adopt one of them?"

"Actually I am not sure but we have never really talked about a family. The good thing for us is that there are plenty of people at the house to help care for the children so we can still work on missions."

"And my family is close too, although Father is still healing. I guess I don't really know what to say."

"Batina, I am not trying to pressure you into anything. I just think we should talk about it. Remember what happened to Koby and Bekka when she got pregnant. They went crazy because they never even thought that could happen. We've been married for over a year and when I saw those children I realized there is a lot we haven't talked about."

"Ok, what is on your mind?" Gideon asked as he and Ashley were unpacking some of their things in their room at the monastery.

"I am just thinking about those children," Ashley said.

"I knew it," Gideon said and turned so he could look at her. "Which one do you want to adopt?"

"Actually I am not sure that I want to adopt just yet. I mean we still need time to get to know each other but with all of these wars there are just so many homeless children. When we get to Langer, I want to volunteer to work at the orphanage and I would like to be a benefactor."

Gideon walked over to Ashley and hugged her. I very much like those ideas. Ashley, I certainly am not against having a family and I don't care if we adopt or have our own."

"But right now we both have so much going on that it wouldn't be fair to the child or either of us to adopt one of those children now. Let's wait a year; that should give us both time to get set up in our jobs and establish a household. Then we can start talking about a family. What do you think?"

"I think that is the perfect idea," Ashley said as she put her arms around Gideon's neck and kissed him on the lips. "And it is good that we are discussing this now because I can set the house up for children." Gideon laughed and kissed her again.

"Dagon, I don't know what you are so mad about," said Rachel. "That baby isn't Bruno or Morgan, it's not going to hurt anyone."

"I am not mad; I am just concerned about Misha. You and I weren't in Nora when he killed those two, but the others told us how bad he got. I just wish he could forget about all of the abuse and pain and move on with his life."

"Well, it certainly seems to me like he is moving on."

"He's my brother. I know him better and I am telling you he isn't over all of this."

When Raul's group reached Castor, the five hundred soldiers made camp outside of the city but they were given free time to enjoy themselves. Raul and Simon got rooms for the family members and the Patronus priests on the same floor of the Tides End Hotel. All of the rooms were on the fourth floor, some faced the street and others the beach. This was an exclusive hotel and the rooms as they were called were actually chambers. Each chamber had two or three bedrooms, a bathing room and a small parlor. They all had balconies which had small tables with chairs on them besides plants and statues.

Angelina and Matthew took chambers that were closest to the one the wounded priests would be in. Gabriel and Raphael shared a chambers as did Raul and Simon. Nyla, Saran and Nina had their own chambers but as Raul and Simon were unpacking there was a soft knock at their door.

Simon opened it and saw Nyla, Saran and Nina standing in the hallway. "We want to stay with you," said Saran as all three girls walked into the parlor.

"Don't you like your chambers?" asked Simon.

The girls did not answer the question. "Are you afraid to be by yourselves?" asked Raul. Nina nodded. "Then let's do this. Your chambers has three rooms, we will move in there. Can all of you share a room?"

"Our house wasn't as big as these hotel rooms," said Nyla. "We are sorry if we are troublesome."

"You aren't troublesome," said Simon. "But to save time why don't Raul and I clean up here and you girls do the same in your chambers then we will move our things in."

All of the girls smiled. "Ok," said Nina and all three girls returned to their chambers.

"We should let Mother know about this," said Raul. "You know she is preparing rooms. I think these girls aren't ready for separate rooms yet."

"I think she should put the girls right next to Michael's chambers," said Simon. "Maybe they will all help each other heal."

Joao and Dack excitedly wrote a letter to Cassandra and Elan, telling them about Chasity. After Dack and Joao told Chasity that they were her new uncles she clung to both of them. If she wasn't holding one of their hands she was sitting on one of their laps.

"I don't know if we should move her in here or leave her in the room with Marty and Logan," Joao said. "If there is a battle I don't want her alone in this room."

"Well, Nana can't leave the baby. Let's ask her to watch Chasity if we are attacked," said Dack.

Gideon and Ashley had just finished unpacking when there was a knock on their door. Gideon opened it and saw Stephan. "Seems like I am always disturbing you," Stephan said with his normal grin.

"We were just unpacking. Come in," said Gideon.

"I came to ask a favor," Stephan said. "No one has figured out what we are going to do with Marty and Logan but right now they are playing with Cassidy. Thaos, Sorren and I are taking turns watching the boys. But if we get attacked; will you watch them Ashley?"

"Of course I will. In fact, why don't you take me to them now and introduce me. If we get attacked are some of us supposed to stay in our rooms or go to a central meeting place?"

"I don't know," said Stephan. "Let's ask one of the priests."

The demon Negal was a powerful demon who had existed in the World of Nunc for hundreds of years. Although Negal did not see the Angel Daniel when he appeared to the Sanuri's caravan, Negal sensed the strong presence of holiness.

Integrity never was nor will it ever be a trait of demons. Negal abandoned his Huta army to fight the forces of nature. When he materialized it was not in Port Friada as he had planned but in the hell domain of Samael. Negal bowed before the powerful demon.

"Why do you run?" bellowed Samael. "I want the Sanuri!"

"My Lord, didn't you see what happened?" asked Negal with confusion as he assumed that Samael could watch everything in the world above.

"See what!"

"I felt the presence of Angels then the forest came alive and attacked the Hutas. My Lord, I can fight the Sanuri but I cannot fight Angels. Unless you want to increase my powers."

"Let me think about this," said Samael angrily.

"My Lord if I would not have escaped there would be no one to tell Hector what happened."

"Yes, yes, yes," said Samael as he was deep in thought. "Negal, I might have another job for you."

"Ladies, oh I am sorry and Lords," Mathas said with a big smile as he walked into the parlor where Rosa, Fahron, Isadore and Bella were meeting with Spooner, the architect for the orphanage. No one had seen Mathas smile since the death of his sister so they welcomed whatever news he brought.

"Bella there is a letter for you here also," Mathas said as he walked towards her. "Matthew, Angelina, Raul, Simon, Gabriel and Raphael somehow found Michael's sisters. I don't know all of the details but the girls were traveling with a group of Patronus priests when they were attacked by a war party of Hutas. The Angel Ruth sent our people to help. Some of the priests are badly wounded so Matthew and the others want to stop here and at Bella's home on their way to Wetpr."

"Matthew says they all expected the girls to be terrified of them. But once the girls saw Raul and found out they were all family they are so happy they can't stop talking."

"Oh, this is wonderful," said Rosa happily. "When will they be here?"

"Sounds like tomorrow if they don't run into any problems," said Mathas.

Bella was reading her letter as she listened to Mathas speak. "Angelina wrote my letter," said Bella. "She says the same but she added that the girls are very thin, filthy and wearing rags. She said they all seem like sweet girls and the youngest, Nina, won't let go of Raul. Fahron, Isadore, I believe I will leave so I can prepare for our guests. There are twelve priests and all of them are wounded but three have serious wounds."

"I am going to also," said Rosa excitedly. "And I am sending a letter to Renya and Sudfad."

Raul, Simon, Matthew and Angelina took Michael's sisters shopping and all four adults were touched by the wonder and awe the girls experienced in seeing many things for the first time.

"This reminds me of the first time I took Annabelle shopping," Simon whispered to Raul as they walked down the main business street of Castor.

"Why are we going to so many stores?" asked Saran.

"We are getting gifts for our families too," Matthew said.

The girls had their arms full of packages when Nyla suddenly dropped hers on the walkway. Saran and Nina started to laugh until they saw the look on their sister's face. "Nyla what is it?" asked Saran. Now all of the adults turned and looked at the girls.

"I just saw one of his men," Nyla said fearfully.

"Where?" asked Raul.

"He was watching us and when he saw me looking at him he ran down that alley," Nyla said fearfully and pointed to an alley that was to the left of the walkway a few hundred yards away. Both Matthew and Raul ran in that direction. Simon and Angelina ushered the girls into a store.

Raul and Matthew ran down the alley which led to another busy street which was filled with people. Neither man knew how Karzman's man was dressed or what he looked like. Both Princes stood for a few moments and watched the crowd to see if anyone was acting suspiciously. They turned and walked back down the alley and to the street they had previously been on.

Simon saw Raul and Matthew first and called them into the store. "Nyla said the man was tall and thin with dark wavy hair and a pock-marked face. But he wasn't wearing anything different to identify him from anyone else," explained Simon. "If they followed us they know about the soldiers. So they will probably make their move while we are in the city."

"Where are Gabriel and Raphael?" asked Raul.

"I don't know; they might be shopping," said Simon. "Why? What are you thinking?"

"That maybe we should leave for Mathas' castle."

"We won't make it before dark," Matthew said. "Let's just bring some of the soldiers to the hotel."

The men turned and walked to the back of the store where Angelina was guarding the girls. "We are going back to the hotel," Simon said. "Girls if you see any of Karzman's men, you tell us right away. Shout it out if you have to."

The group walked out onto the walkway in a formation. Nyla, Saran and Nina were in the middle of the group. Raul and Simon walked in front of them and Matthew and Angelina walked in the rear.

"The hair on the back of my neck is raising," Simon said to Raul.

"I know; we are being watched; I just don't know by who," Raul said as he continually looked around.

"Wait," said Angelina and waved to some Enrops she saw flying overhead. Four of the giant birds landed on a hitching post near the group.

Raul spoke to the birds. "The Warlord Karzman sent some of his killers after these girls. One of them was just watching us. We don't have descriptions of any kind. Will you keep an eye out for anything suspicious?"

"There's Gabriel and Raphael," Nina yelled and pointed to the two men as they were walking into a store on the other side of the street. Raul's group stayed in formation as they crossed the street and entered a large store. They found Gabriel and Raphael in the back buying toys.

"Girls look around but stay together," Simon said. Raul, Simon and Matthew walked up to Gabriel and Raphael and told them about Nyla seeing one of Karzman's men. Angelina stayed with the girls.

Although Angelina had just met Michael's sisters that day, they had already touched her heart. She remembered the horrible stories that Michael told of his family's existence and Angelina wanted to protect these girls from ever returning to such a life. "You can have that," Angelina said to Nina when she saw the little girl staring admiringly at a rag doll.

"Really?" Nina asked. "She's so beautiful."

"Yes, in fact why don't all of you pick something out."

The men watched as Nyla, Saran and Nina walked up to them. Each of the girls was holding a rag doll as if it was a priceless object. "I don't think they ever had toys," Angelina whispered to Matthew. "Look at them."

Matthew looked at the clerk and said, "Add those dolls to our bill."

"Are there more of those dolls?" Gabriel asked.

"Yes," Saran with a big smile. "I'll show you."

"I'll get some for our girls too," said Raul and he and Gabriel followed Saran. Simon was watching the back door of the store as Matthew watched the front door.

All of the girls started to giggle as Gabriel and Raul walked to the counter. "We're buying them all," Gabriel said and both men were smiling.

Four Wetprian soldiers walked into the store. "Some Enrops told us about Karzman's men," said Sergeant Carlson. "Most of our men are in the city shopping and seeing the sights. I sent Private Norge to round a few of them up and take them to your hotel."

"Thanks," said Raul. "Did the Enrops see anything suspicious?"

"No, but as you can see there must be a couple of thousand people on the streets," Carlson said. "Do you want us to stay with you while you finish shopping?"

"Yes," said Simon. "And if you see anything you want for your families just put it on our bills."

Negal never made it to Port Friada. Samael sent him back to the monastery at Leven. The demon walked around the grounds outside of the monastery and looked at the remains of the Huta army he had led.

Samael was enraged when Negal told him of the presence of Angels at the monastery. First, he felt that the Angels had no right to interfere with his business and secondly, he knew the Angels had blocked his sight. Samael had been watching the monastery and never saw any of the things which Negal had described. Negal was now assigned to watch the monastery and to follow the Sanuri's caravan if it left the monastery. Negal was to wait for further orders.

Samael was a demon as old as time itself. He originated on the World of Orantho. A world that he conquered and dominated for centuries. As both his powers and boredom increased, Samael turned his sight to other worlds. The World of Nunc both intrigued and infuriated him. He was enraged that the humans, who he despised, would stand up to the demons of this world. Then as Samael watched the battles unfold in Nunc; he saw humans winning their battles against the dark lords and the demons.

Every world had its period of dark ages and while some people would rebel, the fear and chaos of these times always fed and empowered the demons. But never before had men overcome their fears, broken down their walls and stood against darkness as one. And all of this was being done by a handful of people. The news of the rebellion on Nunc spread to all of the worlds in the Astrum Solar System and beyond. The demons didn't think this was a danger until the races of their worlds were inspired by this tiny army of warriors. Soon rebellions started in the other worlds.

The demons of all worlds decreed that no one should talk about these rebellions yet the stories soared and hope, that had been long forgotten in many worlds, was given a rebirth.

Spirits that had been broken were healing and finding courage. And suddenly people who never knew of or believed in The Great Ruler were calling Him and His Angels in.

While great numbers of peoples in every world do not worship The Great Ruler and even larger numbers question His existence, the irony is that the demons know He exists. The demons know their adversaries. And the war between the darkness and Light has been played out in every world, in every solar system since mankind started to call to demons.

Samael came to Nunc for many reasons but the strongest was to destroy the rebellious people and to force them to understand their place in the worlds.

The Enrops who had been traveling with the caravan, flew over the monastery grounds and spotted Negal as soon as he appeared. "That demon has returned," Othro the Enrop told the Sanuri. "But he is alone. He is looking at the men he left to die."

"Are you sure he is by himself?" asked Sorren.

"Yes but he has a great darkness around him," Othro said.

"I don't understand what that means," said Sorren.

"It means he is very powerful," Erebus said. "Othro, does he have more darkness than he did before?"

"Yes."

"Only an Old One can increase the powers of another demon that quickly," Erebus explained. "He's not here just to do a headcount of the dead. I would expect another attack fairly soon."

# Chapter III
## Memories

"I should kill you," Nethers said angrily as he slapped Voss across the face with the back of his hand. Two of Karzman's men held Voss up as their boss beat him. "Now they have a damn army in that hotel."

"I got the hell out of there as soon as Nyla saw me," Voss said then spit a mouthful of blood on the ground.

"You know we can't go back without those girls," Nethers yelled. "The old man will have us all killed." Nethers stared at Voss for a few moments. The he looked at the two men who were holding Voss' arms. "Let him go. We're gonna have to keep following them until we get our chance but we don't have money for supplies. Your jobs tonight are to get us the money; just don't get your asses caught. Chances are they will leave early in the morning so get the money and the supplies and be ready to head out."

A small flock of Enrops flew past the priests and soldiers on the wall that surrounded the monastery at Leven, they flew around the monastery until they found Michael. The Sanuri saw the birds fly in and followed them. "Eat and take rest," the Sanuri said to the Enrops as he found them in a corner of the monastery.

Michael was sitting on a bench with a handful of notes and tears filled his eyes. He looked up at the Sanuri but did not speak; he handed the Sanuri the letter from Raul. Michael laughed and cried as he read the three short letters from his sisters. As he completed each one he handed it to the Sanuri to read. When all of the letters were read Michael said, "They sound so happy. I can't remember the last time they sounded happy."

The Sanuri smiled. "Michael, you are such a complicated man. In some ways you excel at everything you do and in other ways you have had such difficulties adjusting to your new life. Your sisters need you to help them adjust because only you really understand what they will go through."

"You do know you can come to me if you need help or have questions but also know that Sudfad and Renya are there for all of you." Michael nodded but did not speak.

"This is making me nervous," Thaos said to Stephan. "We know there is a damn demon out there. What the hell is he doing?"

"Maybe just spying on us," Stephan said as he stared into the darkness of the forest that surrounded the monastery.

"Wouldn't you think he would use his damn ravens for that?"

"What's eating you?" asked Stephan. "I've never seen you like this before."

Thaos paused before he spoke. "I think it's the kids and this damn place; brings back too many memories."

"I saw the look on your face when Daniel said that Nikki told the family about your past. Are you mad at her?"

"I don't even know. Sometimes I feel like Michael. There are just things you can't talk about."

Raul's army had been on the road for almost two hours the following morning, before his family in Wetpr received the letters about Nyla, Saran and Nina. Enrops flew into the family dining room as the Royal Family ate their breakfast. Sudfad read the first letter from Raul and Simon out loud. Then he read the short letters from each of the girls to his family.

"They sound precious," said Renya and took one of the letters to reread it.

"I am surprised about how they are acting," said Laurel. "I too thought they would be terrified of the boys."

"The terror is still within them," said Vitomas. "But the realization that they don't have to be afraid anymore is overwhelming. I don't think anyone can truly understand that unless they have lived through hell."

When the sun rose, the soldiers and priests who guarded the wall of the monastery at Leven expected to see an army of monsters but they saw only the forest.

"Something isn't right here," Gideon said to Sorren.

"I know. I can feel it too."

The priests and soldiers were being rotated off from their guard posts so they could eat breakfast. Rachel walked up to Nana and said, "I'll hold her so you can eat. Has she eaten?"

Nana handed Amelia to Rachel and said, "Yes. She is really good but I am not used to having a baby around so I didn't get any sleep because I was afraid she would get out of bed."

"Get some sleep. I will watch her."

"Rachel, remember she flies," Nana said.

"I know, we have Lily in the house at home. It's always a mad dash to make sure the windows are closed." Rachel saw Dagon walk into the dining room and walked up to him. "I'm babysitting for a few hours so Nana can get some sleep. Besides I need practice with Ruala babies."

Dagon laughed and kissed Rachel on top of her head. "Don't get too attached to her because we don't know what will happen when we get home."

"Do you think Misha will hate her?"

"I think she will make him relive things he is trying to forget."

During the previous night, Michael had somewhat come to terms with his emotions after reading the letters from Raul and his sisters. Michael found Sorren, Thaos, Stephan, Cassidy, Marty and Logan sitting together eating breakfast. He joined them at their table and handed out his letters to the men.

"I have never heard my sisters sound happy before, they sound so happy," Michael said with a broad grin.

"I am happy for all of you son," Sorren said and exchanged letters with Stephan.

"Now you know why Ruth had us stop you," Thaos said and smiled. "You're tough but you couldn't take on a whole Huta war party."

"What are you talking about?" asked Cassidy.

All of the men looked at Michael, then Sorren spoke. "Michael's stepfather is a very bad man who hurt his wife and children a great deal. Michael's little sisters ran away and some of Michael's new family has them and are bringing them home."

"You'll meet them when you come to Wetpr," Michael said.

"We ran away too," said Logan. This was the first time any of the children had spoken about their circumstances.

"Those men that killed our parents," Marty said. "They sell kids at auction. Logan, Chasity and me were locked in the same cage and they must have forgotten to lock it. When we found out the door wasn't locked we ran as fast as we could until we got here."

"Was this in Port Friada?" Thaos asked angrily.

"No, but they steal kids from Port Friada too," Cassidy said.

"It's not far; between here and Leven," Logan said. "We've been afraid they are going to find us."

"Don't worry; no one is taking you from us," Thaos said. "I know the kind of operation you are talking about. I was a victim of one too, when I was young. Do you boys think you can take us there?"

"Show them a map," Miranda's voice said in Thaos' ear.

"Stephan watch them, I am going to get a map," Thaos said and left the table. When he returned he had most of his team members as well as the Sanuri, Erebus and Lieutenant Collins with him.

"They said there were lots of kids there when they escaped," Stephan said.

"We ran away at night," Logan said as he watched Thaos unfold a map and place it on the table. "But there was a full moon."

"The moon isn't full this time of month," said Gideon.

"It may not have been the moon that was guiding them," the Sanuri said. "Logan, Marty would you let me look into your eyes? It's hard to explain but sometimes I can see the things that you've seen. It won't hurt you."

Logan looked at Sorren who nodded. "Alright, what do you need me to do?"

"Just sit still. You can look at me while I am looking in your eyes," the Sanuri said and sat down near the boy.

Marty kept looking between Logan and the Sanuri and the map on the table. "There was a pond that Chasity fell in. She can't swim; we had to pull her out," Marty said.

"It doesn't show it on your map but there is a large fishing pond here," Lieutenant Collins said and pointed to an area about four miles southeast of the monastery.

High Priest Barnabas walked up to the group. "What is going on?" he asked.

"The boys are telling us about a place where children are sold at auction. Their families were killed and the children were stolen," said Stephan.

"Marty do you remember which direction you came from before you found the pond?" Thaos asked.

"It was right outside of the barn we were kept in. That's why Chasity fell in."

"Marty can I look into your eyes now?" the Sanuri asked.

"It doesn't hurt at all," Logan said to Marty. Logan and Marty switched chairs.

"Logan this is important," said Joao. "Chasity has other brothers and sisters. Two of them are in our home. Do you know what happened to the others?"

"We were already in the cage when they put her in," Logan said. "We didn't see anyone with her."

"How long where you there?" asked Rachel.

"Not long, a couple of days. Marty was there first, then me, then Chasity."

"Miranda, we are going after those kids," Thaos said angrily.

"Miranda's voice was heard by the adults. "That is a fine choice. But there are things the children did not see. The Sanuri will now see them."

"The farm is in a small valley," said the Sanuri. "There are men guarding it who are stationed all along the ridge that surrounds the buildings. There are at least five buildings; that appear to be filled with cages. I couldn't count how many children were there but there were a lot."

"Miranda will you protect the priests from that demon while we rescue those kids?" Sorren yelled as he started to stand up.

"My priests do not hide from this world," said High Priest Barnabas calmly. "You have no idea how many children or killers there are. Some of us will go with you."

Before anyone else could speak Dagon said, "This is the same type of setup that Shanksaw had in Salar. The men on the ridge were supposed to warn the men in the buildings if strangers came up the road. Then the men in the buildings had orders to kill all of the hostages. We, I mean the Rualas will have to silence those guards first."

"Miranda," said Edward. "It is no coincidence that we are here and I am willing to bet those children had help escaping. Is there anything you want to tell us?"

"Who are they talking to?" Logan asked. Cassidy shrugged his shoulders.

"What would be a better question?" Miranda's voice asked.

"Miranda will you help us?" Batina asked. "Help us to save all of those children without any of them getting killed."

"Now that is the way you ask a question," Miranda said. "Dagon is right. This is a very similar situation as Shanksaw's. But Shanksaw had one building and forty guards inside. There are five buildings and one hundred guards. Even if the Rualas silence the guards on the ridge you still need a diversion."

"What if I rode up to the farm?" asked Barnabas. "They would be able to see my robes; certainly they would not hurt the children."

"And what would you say to them?" asked Miranda.

"I would tell them about the Hutas and offer them shelter in the monastery."

"Well, you can't ride in there alone; especially after you tell them a war party of Hutas are on the loose. You will need others to go with you," said Sorren. "And that may distract some of the men but not all of them. And what about that demon?"

"That demon is acting as they eyes and ears of Samael," explained Miranda. "If you destroy him, Samael will send more, at least you have eyes on this one."

"So we should do nothing about him?" Gideon asked incredulously.

"I did not say that," said Miranda.

"He wants me," said the Sanuri. "I will deal with him."

"You can act as a distraction but Samael has given him so much power that you cannot kill him."

"Then why hasn't he done something?" asked Sorren.

"Because he senses the Angels," Erebus said. "So you have been here all of the time?"

"Do we ever really leave you?"

"Then what do you want us to do?" asked Thaos irritably.

"Make your plans and save those children. You will have your diversion and I will take care of the demon."

"Wait, none of this makes any sense," said Erebus. "First, Samael is strong enough to see us unless you are blocking him. And you are right that demon is in the open. Why would one demon expose himself unless there were more that we cannot see?"

"Erebus, you are the Overseer of these teams now," said Miranda. "You must learn to take control of that position."

"What the hell!" yelled Ratri as he stood on top of the wall around the monastery. "There's an army of demons out here. They just appeared." Although Ratri was outside his voice carried throughout the buildings.

"Your friends would have run out to save those children and would have been butchered," Miranda said to Erebus. "What you take for granted the others do not understand. No longer can you stand back and wait for them to figure it out."

"You are right," Erebus said. "Did you remove the cloak that prevented us from seeing them?"

"Yes," said the Angel.

"So is that farm real?" asked Stephan. "Or is it a trick?"

"Both, and that is one of the reasons that Daniel told you to come here. But you see the demons understand you better than you understand them. They know you will do anything to save others. Hector runs that kidnapping ring and it was his men who unlocked that door and allowed those children to escape. He knew that if the Hutas didn't get you that you would go to that farm to save those children. Those guards are expecting you."

"And now you understand how ruthless Hector is. Many of you have viewed him as another of Juleta's victims. The monster in her fell in love with the monster in him. When Sarah was born, for a brief moment in time, Juleta was allowed to see herself as others did."

"That is when she put the baby in this monastery. You have learned a great deal this morning," Miranda continued. "Now my brave warriors what is your plan?"

"How many Angels are here?" asked the Sanuri.

"Enough," said Miranda.

"Then we are free to go after the children?" the Sanuri asked.

"Yes."

"What will be our diversion?"

"Erebus what do you always say about the Sanuri's aura?" asked Miranda.

"That it is like staring at the sun; it is blinding."

"Sanuri, today others will see your aura."

"Miranda wait," said Sorren. "Are you going to be the only Angel fighting those demons?"

"Why? Do you want to join me?"

"I would hate for you to have all of the fun. I will fight at your side. Will you touch my sword?"

"What is he talking about?" asked Gideon.

"The Angels touch our swords with holiness so we have the power to kill demons," Stephan said.

Now Miranda materialized in the room. "How many swords will I be touching?"

Gideon knocked over his chair in his haste to get to Miranda. "I failed you once, never again."

"Everyone who is going to fight with Miranda on this side of the room," yelled Sorren. "And everyone who is going after the children on the other side of the room. We will keep the demons off you."

"Boss which battle are you going to?" Sam asked as he walked up to Thaos.

"I'm going after the kids."

"I'll get the boys and we'll ride with you."

"Lieutenant Collins," said Miranda. "Take your men to the farm and afterwards take the criminals to the fort. The children should come here."

"Miranda are you saying it is a coincidence that Chasity is here?" asked Dack.

"I am not saying that at all. But all of you should leave now. Daniel will explain the rest."

"We're going with you," Drake said as he and Tally caught up with Michael. "Are you going after the kids?"

"Yeah, did you hear that we are riding into an ambush?" asked Michael although he kept walking to his room to get more weapons.

"Why do you act like you always think we are going to run?" Tally asked with annoyance. "There's a lot that we ain't but we ain't no yellow bellies."

"Listen, you can stay here and do nothing or fight with an Angel which will give you better chances than coming with us," Michael said angrily.

"Ok, what are you really saying?" asked Drake.

"Those kids are in the same situation I was with Karzman. You never did anything to help me. Sure you won't act the same now?"

"Michael, screw you!" yelled Tally. "We ain't those guys no more and we're gonna prove it to you."

"We don't have time to fight about this; grab your weapons and mount up," Michael said angrily and ran into his room.

# Chapter IV
## The Auction

It had been a couple of days since Madeline and Javier spoke with the children in Gabriel's home. Joshua, Luca, Misha, Maxwell and Elan continually searched the grounds but saw no sign of the intruders. Sudfad too, increased security at the castle and at both homes the children were not allowed to play outside without adult supervision.

"Hurry up Vivian; we want to go out," Adrone said impatiently.

"Boys, you haven't even finished your breakfast," Maxwell said. "Clean your plates then you can go out."

"Why are we being punished?" asked Paul. "We didn't do anything wrong."

"We are just trying to keep you safe," Joshua said. "Now finish...."

"Enrops!" screamed Christopher and all of the boys jumped up from the table to feed the birds.

One of the birds handed a letter to Maxwell while another spoke to the family. "Everyone from Port Friada is at the monastery in Leven. The Angel Daniel told them to go there. I don't know why but the demon Samael has been setting traps for them."

"Is everyone alright?" asked Natasha.

"They are unhurt but Dagon said you might be upset after you read this letter. We will wait if you want to send one back." Now everyone looked at Maxwell. He had been holding the letter so that Emeral could read it with him.

"What is going on?" asked Hannah.

Before Maxwell could speak, more Enrops flew into the dining room. "This is for Cassandra and Elan," one of the birds said. "They found Chasity."

41

"What!" gasped Cassandra as Elan tore the letter open. Now all of the boys gathered around Elan's and Cassandra's chairs.

"There were orphans at the monastery and one of them is Chasity. The Sanuri looked into her mind and said she is Joey's and Tommy's sister," Elan said excitedly. "Joao and Dack are bringing her home. She is about six with long blonde hair and brown eyes. And she won't let go of Dack or Joao for a minute."

"Did you hear that boys?" Cassandra asked and hugged Joey and Tommy. "Your sister is coming home."

After Joey hugged both Cassandra and Elan he turned to the other boys and said, "You'll like her. She is really nice."

"We are all very excited about Chasity," Emeral said. "But we need to discuss this other letter as a family."

"High Priest Barnabas told the Sanuri that they had a Ruala baby at the monastery," Maxwell started to explain.

"What? How can that be?" asked Luca.

"Please, let your father explain this," Emeral said.

"The High Priest said that three criminal Rualas had terrorized that area and several women had been raped. One of them gave birth to a baby girl then killed herself afterwards. Her parents took the baby to the monastery. The little girl is about a year old and very cute. Her name is Amelia and she looks all Ruala. The Sanuri told Dagon to write to us because he feels the baby should be brought to Wetpr although that doesn't mean she will live with us. Nana has offered to take her to the Ice Caves."

Diana looked at Misha then asked, "Why does the Sanuri think she should be brought here?"

"You can read it for yourself," Maxwell said as he handed her the letter. "Dagon doesn't say and that is probably because the Sanuri didn't explain it. Misha, Dagon is concerned about how this will affect you."

"What do you mean?" asked Misha.

42

Before Maxwell answered Diana said, "The Sanuri looked at the baby and said she doesn't have any evil in her." No one at the table spoke.

"What are you all looking at me for?" asked Misha. "That poor baby didn't do anything wrong. That's like someone hating one of our boys because of something I did."

"But will having her around make you remember?" Emeral asked.

"Mother, I never forget."

The demons that surrounded the monastery were as surprised as the humans that their cloak had been removed. The front gates of the monastery creaked and groaned as they opened. Miranda walked out of the monastery with warriors, soldiers and priests behind her. This meager group was greatly outnumbered by the tens of thousands of demons that surrounded the monastery. Yet the demons took pause for every human glowed as brightly as the Angel.

But this pause was momentary then the demons attacked. "Now!" yelled the Sanuri and Thaos led the second group out of the back gates of the monastery. Thaos, Stephan, Michael, Drake, Tally, Zeke and his men sped ahead of Lieutenant Collins and his troops and the Ruala warriors flew ahead of them all. The Sanuri was driving his boca in case the children or wounded needed to be transported. Both Erebus and Harlow sat in the front seat with him. Four other priests also drove bocas. These wagons moved considerably slower than the warriors on horseback and trailed behind the others.

High Priest Barnabas was conflicted as to whether he should fight with Miranda or save the children. The Angel made his decision for him and told him to go to the farm. Miranda said that as a leader of that monastery and the community he needed to see the darkness that had been allowed to take hold and grow. Barnabas and the other priests prayed the entire way to the farm.

They did not pray for their own safety. They prayed for the safety of the children, the success of the mission and the eradication of darkness.

"There's a group of twenty-five men following you," an Enrop told Raul and Simon as they led their troops to Mathas' castle.

"A group that small won't attack the troops," said Simon. "They will wait in ambush for the girls."

"Then let's give them a surprise," said Matthew. "You continue forward. I'll take some men and double back. I know this area better than you do."

"Raphael and I are coming with you," said Gabriel. "In case they travel with a demon"

"I'm coming too," said Angelina.

Matthew called out one hundred soldiers and the group broke away from the main body and turned to meet Nethers and his men.

The demon Negal was many things, a leader of troops was not one of them. The powerful demon watched as the illuminous group of humans and the powerful Angel fought Samael's legions of demons. Negal had an inherent fear of Angels that even his newly acquired powers could not overcome.

"Master, we need you here," prayed Negal to the demon Samael. He repeated this prayer until it became a mantra but Samael did not respond. Fear consumed Negal as he watched his soldiers being slaughtered by the handful of humans. It was at that moment that Negal realized he no longer saw Miranda on the battlefield. He quickly turned and saw the Angel standing behind him.

"Your master cannot hear you Negal," said Miranda. "But you will feel his wrath soon. What your eyes have been watching has been transmitted to every world and every hell domain."

"Your cowardice and the inability of your demons to defeat these humans is being played in every solar system. I will not destroy you because your fate is much worse."

Miranda disappeared as did the legions of demons. Sorren, Gideon, Edward and the others were momentarily disoriented as the holiness left them.

"Miranda, you healed us," Edward said as the Angel reappeared on the battlefield. "Thank you."

"You are welcome. Now go and help your friends. That battle will be more disturbing. The demons can scare you, the darkness in man can tear you apart."

Nethers and his men saw the dust cloud produced by the horses of the group that Matthew led before they saw the army. "I think they turned back," yelled one of Nethers' men, but he stated the obvious to them all.

"Damn it! Damn it!" yelled Nethers. "There's no turning back now boys. Charge!"

The Ruala warriors had killed most of the hired killers on the ridge surrounding the farm when Thaos and the others arrived. Thaos and his men stopped and surveyed the scene before them without exposing their presence to Hector's men. "Zeke, take your boys and meet up with Collins. All those soldiers are causing dust clouds. Slow them down and have them circle the complex. No one goes in until I say so," said Thaos.

"Sure nuf boss," Zeke said then he and his men turned and rode towards the troops.

"They've got a good set-up," Stephan said. "No one can enter that valley without being seen."

"We have to wait for the Sanuri since he is the distraction," Thaos said. "I want each one of us to be in charge of a building because we all know things can get real crazy when the fighting starts."

"The building next to the pond is number 1, Stephen that is yours. The one to the right is number 2; that's yours Michael. To the right of that is Tally's and the right of that is Drake's. I will take that farthest one. Our job is to make sure all of those kids get out safely. Let the soldiers do most of the fighting to begin with. Any questions?"

"The kids are gonna be scared," said Drake. "Do we just tell them to run to the bocas? Because you know we will be fighting too."

"I'll have a priest go in every building too," Thaos said.

"Didn't Miranda say that Daniel would be here?" Stephan asked. "Daniel where are you?"

"I am pleased with your plan," said Daniel as he materialized. "But you are receiving another gift. Hector's foreman was planning on having weekly auctions but with our help circumstances kept preventing them from taking place. We have watched over those children more than you realize and I know that is a question you all have been thinking."

"An auction is scheduled for today, in two hours. Because of the previous delays you should expect all of the monsters to attend who are customers of Hector's. The rest I will leave up to you. And Thaos you will see some familiar faces."

"Is Kagen coming?" Thaos asked in a hoarse whisper.

"He is the auctioneer," Daniel said and disappeared.

"Who's Kagen?" asked Stephan.

Thaos could not answer right away as he was trying to control his exploding emotions. The men with him could see this. "Kagen was to me what Karzman was to Michael."

"Then we save him for you," Tally said.

Nethers knew it was suicide when he ordered his men to charge the army of soldiers coming at them.

What Nethers or any of his men did not expect was that the soldiers would take them all captive. Matthew wanted these men interrogated. While most of Nethers' men were wounded in the brief battle only one was killed.

Matthew sent two soldiers to tell Raul and Simon that they had Karzman's killers and would be taking them to the dungeons for interrogations. No one wanted the girls to ride in the same group as Karzman's men. Matthew said his group would travel behind Raul's and go straight to Fort Langer.

After Daniel left, Drake rode out to meet Lieutenant Collins and tell him about the auction and how Thaos had divided up the buildings. Drake did not have to ride far and returned to his group in ten minutes.

"They are breaking into groups and surrounding the compound now," Drake told Thaos and the others. "And I saw the bocas. Do you want me to bring them here?"

"Yes," Thaos said.

It was another twenty minutes before Drake returned with the Sanuri, Erebus, Harlow and the priests. Drake had briefed these men on the plans and Daniel's visit. High Priest Barnabas assigned a priest to each building then he turned to Thaos. "Before you attack the auction I need to see the faces of the men. Miranda told me to come to understand this."

"Well, don't take too long padre," Thaos said. "Cuz we're stopping these bastards today." Then Thaos looked at the Sanuri. "Ready to get this show on the road?"

The Sanuri smiled. "Miranda tells me that while all of you will be able to see, the others will not and that includes the children. You will have to lead them out of the buildings." The Sanuri started the descent into the valley. The other bocas followed him.

"Did you see how pale Thaos looked?" Erebus asked. "What is going on?"

"He is fighting his demons today," the Sanuri said. As the Sanuri's boca traveled into the valley it started to glow and the aura that normally existed around the holy man now expanded to his boca then to all of the bocas then it filled the valley.

"Now!" Daniel's voice was heard by all of the rescuers. What the rescuers did not hear were the chains and locks falling from all of the cages simultaneously. Neither the rescuers nor the guards heard Daniel's voice tell the children to stay in the cages until the men and women came who would be saving them. And no one but The Great Ruler heard Daniel pray.

"What the hell is going on?" yelled one of the guards as he walked out of the building to try and see what was causing the intense light. Michael ran his sword through the guard then pushed him aside and ran into the building.

Hired killers were running out of the buildings as they heard the sounds of battle but they were blinded by the light. The children also heard the sounds but Daniels' voice kept them calm. The children too were blinded by the light so they would not witness the bloody battle taking place around them. But the children could see the men and women who now ran into the cages and led them out of the buildings and to the bocas.

The battle took less than an hour and when it was over the Sanuri's aura returned to normal. "Daniel do we have all of the children?" Stephan yelled.

"Yes," said Daniel's voice. "Take them now to the monastery. Your friends have finished their battle and are coming to help you. Do not underestimate the monsters who will come to the auction."

High Priest Barnabas did not return to the monastery. The old priest walked inside of each building that had been used as a prison and wept.

Most of the hired killers had been killed; several dozen were wounded and Lieutenant Collins had half of his soldiers take these men to Fort Friada. Collins was staying at the compound to arrest the people who would hold and attend the auction.

"Collins! Collins wait!" yelled Thaos. "We found wagons with bars on them behind one of the buildings. You can transport your prisoners in them."

Collins' soldiers had just started out and were still in the valley. He had them return and load the prisoners into the wagons. The rescuers who remained at the compound broke into groups. Some took care of the wounded. Others searched the buildings and grounds and the third group moved the bodies and tried to clean up the signs of a battle.

"Just dump buckets of dirt on some of these blood stains," Stephan told the soldiers.

Sorren and his group arrived and helped with the tasks. With all of them it took only forty minutes. "Some of us are going to have to play the parts of Hector's men," said Edward. "Or the scum coming to the auction will get suspicious. Thaos, you are not going to play a part; you're too involved with all of this. Be mad at me if you want."

"I think we all agree with Edward," said Stephan to Thaos. "You can have any of them but let the rest of us get them in place."

"I'm not arguing," said Thaos.

"We can't let them see the soldiers or the priests," Edward said loudly.

Dagon flew over the group and announced, "Riders are coming. About a dozen."

"Edward, you might have to show them a sample of who is going on the auction block," said Kate. "Use me."

"And me," said Batina and pushed her way to the front of the crowd.

"I don't look like a child but me too," yelled Rachel and walked up to the front of the group.

"You girls are right," said Edward. "We will tell them you are our special feature."

"Edward since you are the best actor among us you should act as the foreman," Sorren said. "Gideon, you and I will act as customers. The rest of you who aren't in uniform will act as thugs. Remember Hector had one hundred men out here."

"I'll act as a customer too," said Erebus.

"They are almost here," yelled Joao as he flew over the group.

Everyone dispersed among the buildings. Michael and Stephan locked Kate, Rachel and Batina in cages in the building closest to the road.

"You girls need any weapons?" Drake asked.

"Trust me, we have them," said Kate. "And I hope we get a chance to use them." Drake laughed and walked out of the building.

"Edward, your girl is a mean one," Drake said with a grin.

"Don't you know it," Edward said and laughed as they watched the first group of men riding towards them.

Tally walked out of one of the buildings with four bottles of whiskey and set them on a table that Edward was standing next to. "This should keep them busy," Tally said. "I'll see if I can find some glasses."

Thaos was standing in one of the buildings and wanted to scream with rage and pain when he saw Kagen dismount. It took Thaos a few moments to get control of himself then he stared at Kagen in wonder. When Thaos was a boy, Kagen seemed like an old man but now he didn't look that old. Thaos wondered if his view of the world was different in his youth. Then he quickly walked out the rear door of the building and found the Sanuri.

"That man in the black hat. He kidnapped me when I was nine. He looks exactly the same. He must have sold his soul or he is a demon," Thaos explained and both the Sanuri and High Priest Barnabas peered at Kagen from their hiding place.

"That first one's aura is as dark as night," Erebus whispered to Sorren and Gideon.

"Is he a demon?" Sorren asked.

"I don't think so but he's a dark lord or a warlock."

Edward offered Kagen a drink as the two discussed how Kagen wanted the area set up. "Tally, Drake get your asses over here," yelled Edward. "Set this area up the way he wants. I'm going to bring out some furniture."

Within minutes another group of men rode up to the compound. Then another and yet another. In less than half an hour over forty men and women had arrived at the compound. The Ruala warriors were on the ridge when they heard Daniel's voice. "You have three more coming and that is it." Edward and the rescuers at the compound also heard Daniel speak.

"How long before the rest of them get here?" Edward asked Kagen.

"Should be soon. Why? Are you in a hurry?"

"No but we have a special surprise for you and I don't want to take them out of the cages any too soon."

"What are you talking about?" asked Kagen suspiciously.

"Don't know how he did it but Hector got his hands on three young female warriors. Everyone is a beauty but they fight like wildcats. He wants them sold."

"Really?" Kagen asked with a salacious grin. "I might just save them for me. You say they're beauties."

"I could bring them out but like I said they fight like wildcats. It will delay the auction," Edward was facing the road and saw three more riders coming towards the compound. "Course your taste may be different from mine. Why don't I bring them out and show you?" Kagen nodded.

Edward walked to the building where Kate, Rachel and Batina were in cages. Stephan, Michael, Tally, Drake and six Nordes warriors were also inside the building. "Everyone is here now," Edward said. "I want to bring the girls out so they can distract everyone so they don't see the Rualas. So you girls put on a show."

51

"Gladly," Batina said and let out a war cry.

Within minutes all three women were being led to the auction block and they were giving their captors a fight. The group of men and women who had come to the auction were captivated by the scene before them.

"Let's give them more of a show," Stephan whispered and let go of Kate's arm. She punched him then kicked him in the stomach then turned on Tally who was holding her other arm. None of spectators saw the Rualas land in the compound.

"I'll take all three," Kagen called excitedly.

"Now you just wait a minute," yelled a man in the crowd. "Start the bidding."

"I'll buy them all," said High Priest Barnabas and walked up to the crowd and stared in the faces of darkness. The people were so shocked to see him that no one spoke for several moments.

"What the hell is going on here?" yelled Kagen.

"Its judgement day," Thaos said as he was now behind Kagen.

Kagen swung round and stared at Thaos. "Remember me?" Thaos asked. "Remember Derek? We were some of your kids." Before Thaos finished speaking he punched Kagen in the face twice then in the stomach. Now all of the rescuers attacked the group at the auction. The Ruala and Nordes warriors and the soldiers came out of hiding. Most of the people who had come to purchase children tried to run; they did not get far.

Thaos just focused on Kagen. The dark lord's powers did him little good against the rage that surged through Thaos. Faces of the children who had died because of Kagen filled Thao's mind and every time he saw a face he struck the murderous pedophile. All of the people at the auction had been captured and Thaos was still beating Kagen.

## Chapter V
## Young Princesses

The demon Negal cursed Miranda as he transported through time fields trying to escape the death squads that were sent after him by the Old Ones. He had no place to hide for the transmission he unwittingly sent angered demons in all the worlds; it ignited uprisings and above all else it gave hope to all those who were slaves to demons.

"Come on son," Sorren said softly as he and Stephan pulled Thaos off from Kagen's body. It was then that Michael realized that Thaos was crying.

"Everybody back, I am sure you have work to do," Michael said as he blocked anyone from coming near Thaos, Sorren and Stephan. The three men walked into one of the buildings. Within moments Dagon walked in and handed Thaos a bottle of whiskey.

"I won't stay long," Dagon said. "But I wanted you to know that when Misha killed Morgan and Bruno it was like he was lost for a few days. He said that he was so filled with hatred for them that afterwards he felt empty. Don't be surprised if you don't feel the same way. If you need anything just let me know." Thaos nodded and Dagon left the building but Michael had been standing in the doorway listening.

"That is exactly how I felt after I found Sudfad and he claimed me for his son. I think sometimes I still feel empty," Michael said and took the bottle that Thaos handed him. All four men drank from the bottle without saying another word.

Simon sent Enrops ahead to tell Mathas and Rosa that the group expected to arrive by noon. Gabriel and Raphael felt no presence of demons around Nethers' men so they rode forward and rejoined Raul and Simon. Both priests sensed that they needed to protect the girls.

Raul and Simon had been telling Nyla, Saran and Nina about their new family. "I am still confused," said Nyla. "Both King Mathas and King Sudfad are Matthew's fathers. And he is your brother and your cousin?"

"Every word of that is true," Raul said and laughed. "So what does that make Rosa and Mathas to you?" None of the girls answered.

"Your aunt and uncle," Raphael whispered with a grin.

"We've never had an aunt and uncle before," Nina said. "At least not that I know of."

"And they have a daughter Margarit who is almost Saran's age. She is a young princess as are all of you," said Simon. "But she is at our home in Wetpr visiting now. So you won't meet her until we get home."

"All of you have been so nice to us," Nyla said. "But I, well our lives have been so different from all of yours. I hope you understand there is so much we don't know. We don't want to make you mad or disappoint you but you are going to have to explain things to us."

"Honey, we don't expect you to know about our lives here," said Raul. "But don't worry, Father and Mother will get you tutors for your education and the Patronus priests will give you your religious education. Then when you are ready you can all go to the university if you want."

"What is a university?" asked Nina.

"A school for more advanced learning," said Gabriel. "For example my wife went to a university to learn how to become a physician. Personally I would suggest that all of you go when you are ready, since you are princesses."

"That's what I mean," said Nyla. "Everyone is telling us that we are princesses but what does a princess do?"

"That is a good question," Simon said. "But the answer will take a while and we are almost there. I will tell you tonight."

"The good princesses like Angelina and Raul's and Simon's wives do all sorts of things to take care of the people in their kingdoms," Raphael said. "And all of the princesses look up to your stepmother Renya because she is not only a great mother and queen but she is a mighty warrior too. Did you know that?"

"No," said Nyla in awe as all three girls stared at Raphael.

"Now, when you meet your Aunt Rosa in a few minutes she is a wonderful person and a great mother and queen also, but she is not a warrior," Simon explained. "You will have the choice of what you want to be."

"Are you saying we can become warriors too?" asked Saran. "Really?"

"Yes, you can become anything you want," Raul said. "Margarit wants to become a physician like Gabriel's wife Hannah. But we can tell you more about that later."

"Looks like you are getting a royal welcome from your new aunt and uncle," Simon said as an honor guard of soldiers from Lentz rode up to them.

The Captain leading the honor guard stopped the procession and said, "Prince Raul and Prince Simon, King Mathas has sent gifts for the princesses with you." Three soldiers now rode to the front of the procession and each was leading a white horse with a beautiful saddle. Each horse had flowers braided into their manes.

"Girls, it's time to switch horses," Simon said with a huge grin.

"You mean those are ours?" asked Saran.

"Yes," said Raul then he looked at Nina who was sitting in front of him on his horse. "Nina do you think you can ride a horse?"

"They are very gentle and well trained," said the Captain.

"I know how to ride; I just like to be with you," Nina said to Raul.

"Nina that horse is a gift to you," Nyla said. "You should ride it."

As the two older girls dismounted a soldier rode alongside of Raul so he could set Nina on her horse. All the men smiled as they watched the faces of the girls light up. "Now ride behind us," said Simon, only two horses can fit through the gate at a time."

When the procession rode into the courtyard people cheered. "Who are these people?" Saran asked Gabriel.

"I know some of them, we will have to wait for introductions."

The procession stopped and Raul and Simon dismounted then they helped Nyla and Saran off from their horses. Raul picked Nina up and carried her. They walked to Mathas and Rosa.

"Uncle Mathas and Aunt Rosa, let us introduce your nieces, Nyla, Saran and Nina." The two older girls curtsied before the King and Queen.

"Should I curtsy?" Nina asked.

"How about a hug," said Rosa and held her hands out to Nina, who hugged both Rosa and Mathas. Then Nyla and Saran hugged their new family.

"I don't mean to be rude," said Simon but we have some injured men here."

"Of course," said Mathas. "We have rooms prepared for them. Please follow us."

All three of the girls walked in silence as they stared at the splendor inside of the castle. As always, Nina held Raul's hand but Simon was surprised when Saran and Nyla held his hands.

The wounded priests were taken to their individual chambers where they were checked by physicians. The priests who felt up to it joined the rest of their group in the Great Hall for a celebration.

After twenty minutes of introductions the girls were clearly overwhelmed. Nyla, Saran and Nina had already been introduced to Bella's family. Now Nikki, Ingr and Ryan walked up to them.

"Raul, Simon, why don't we take them outside for a few minutes they look like they could use some air," Nikki said.

"Good idea," Raul said and looked at his sisters. "We will be right here." Ingr held out her hand and Nina took it.

As soon as they all walked into one of the gardens that surrounded the castle, Nikki said, "We grew up poor so we know how you feel when you see all of this."

"This is such a different world," Nyla said. "I feel so stupid. I don't know what to say or do and everyone is looking at us like they expect us to do something."

"They don't expect you to do anything," said Ingr. "But everyone here is family or close friends and they know Michael. He is loved and respected and..."

"What Ingr is trying to say is we all know about your family and everyone is just so happy that you escaped and are safe now. We didn't know this until today but Mathas said that Sudfad has been waiting for some missions to end then he was going to your tribe and get you."

"Really? Why would he do that?" asked Nyla.

"Sudfad didn't know that any of you existed before Michael confronted him. You see Sudfad wanted to marry your mother but she told him she was going to marry someone else. So he left and met Renya and married her. All of Sudfad's family was horrified when Michael told them about Karzman. And they all consider you family," Nikki explained.

"But Karzman would kill him," said Saran.

"You haven't met Sudfad yet," said Ingr. "He is a mighty warrior and a very good man. Both Sudfad and Renya will be good parents to you; just give them a chance. They both love Michael very much."

"I wish he was here," said Nina. "We miss him."

"He's with our husbands working on a mission. Hopefully they will be home soon," said Nikki.

"People have talked about missions. We don't understand what they mean?" said Nyla.

"That's a long story," said Ingr. "For now let's just say they save people."

Nikki started to smile when she saw the way that Ryan was staring at Nyla. "Do you girls know how to dance?" Nikki asked.

"No, are we supposed to know?" asked Nyla.

"There will be dancing later; why don't you have Ryan teach you. He is a very good dancer. You will like it."

To the shock of both Nikki and Ingr, Ryan who was normally so shy around women that he couldn't talk; now stepped forward and asked, "Who wants to learn first?"

"Nyla, you go first and we will watch you," said Saran.

"Will you excuse me a moment," Ingr said and returned to the Great Hall where she grabbed Bella's hand and pulled her to the garden door. Both women stood in the doorway and smiled as they watched Ryan dancing with Nyla.

That afternoon and evening were both chaotic and sad at the monastery. Fifty-six children had been rescued. All of them had the same stories, that their parents had been killed and they had been stolen. When all of these children were eating in the main dining room, Dack and Joao took Chasity around the tables. They wanted to find her brothers and sisters.

Chasity was anxious and excited at first but burst into tears when they reached the last table because she didn't see any of her family. Dack carried her into the courtyard where they found Cassidy crying.

"Cassidy are you hurt?" asked Dack. Cassidy shook his head from side to side to indicate no. "Do you want to talk about it?" Dack asked as he and Chasity sat down next to the boy.

"Before I found your friend's house, I was living on the street with some other kids. Two of my friends disappeared and we all knew they got stolen. One of the kids in there told me they are dead. They got killed fighting."

"Did you tell Thaos and Stephan this?"

"No," Cassidy said as he wiped the tears from his cheeks.

"Come on," Dack said and held out his hand to Cassidy. They walked around the monastery until they found Thaos, Stephan and Sorren talking with Harlow.

"Cassidy what is the matter?" asked Stephan as he was the first of the group to see the boy.

"He just found out that some of his friends from the streets that were with all these kids were killed in some kind of fighting," Dack said.

Thaos picked Cassidy up and hugged him. "See that is exactly what I mean," Harlow said. "If you let me write your story then we can expose these kind of crimes and stop them. Thaos, think of the children you will be saving."

"Thaos what is he saying?" asked Cassidy as he looked into Thaos' eyes.

"I was one of those kids once and a lot of my friends were killed too."

"How did you get away?" asked Cassidy.

"A friend and I escaped like Marty and Logan did."

"Where are they? I thought they were with you Cassidy," asked Stephan.

"They're still with Ashley."

"Let me think about this," Thaos said to Harlow. "Part of me agrees with you but you have to understand that the only person I've ever told is my wife and that was difficult for me."

"Well, Barnabas I believe you just started an orphanage," the Sanuri said as the two men walked through the crowded dining room looking at the children.

"This just makes me sick and to think all of this horror was happening just a few miles from here."

"Barnabas, you are a loved and respected man in this kingdom. You know that Miranda wants you to lead the fight against these kind of crimes and to protect the children."

"I understood her but she didn't have to tell me my responsibilities. I realized what I had to do when I saw that compound."

Did you know that Thaos was a captive in Kagen's compound? That is why he killed him."

"I was told. I plan to find him this evening and see if he wants to unburden his soul."

"I have looked into his mind and I believe you would benefit from hearing about his life."

"I wish Nikki was here," Thaos said to Stephan as they walked into a meeting room at the monastery.

"Guess you will just have to settle for me," Stephan said and both men laughed. Thaos welcomed the laughter.

When they entered the room, Sorren and Gideon were carrying bottles of wine and whiskey. Nana, Rachel and Risa were carrying in trays of glasses.

The members of Edward's, Dominic's and Gabriel's teams were in the small room as were Michael and Harlow. Thaos looked pale as he walked in front of the group. "Is everyone here?" he asked.

"Ashley is helping with the children," Gideon said. "So she won't be coming."

Edward stood up and closed the door but as soon as he returned to his seat the door opened and to the surprise of many High Priest Barnabas walked in and took a seat in the back of the room.

Thaos took a big gulp of his whiskey and said, "I have worked and fought alongside of most of you in this room for years and today is the first time many of you learned of my life. I don't talk about it because it is difficult. In fact, Nikki is the only person I have ever told and then I had to do it over several days. And I wasn't going to tell her but she said she couldn't marry a man she didn't know."

"Harlow wants to write my story, to expose places like we attacked today. He believes people don't believe places like that exist. He thinks most people are afraid to realize that monsters like Kagen live among us and I agree with him. I have agreed to his request but I don't believe you should have to find out about me in a newspaper. You deserve to hear it from me. If anyone doesn't want to listen to this please feel free to leave. It is not going to be a pretty story."

Barnabas stood up. "Thaos, we can all see this is emotional for you but you must understand that you are truly giving us the information we need to stop these horrors. After today the priests of this monastery have a new mission. Our mission is to protect the children."

Thaos talked long into the night. His audience were on a roller coaster of emotions. Horror, anger, disgust and sadness were surging through them. Some of the women cried at times and when Thaos was done speaking every person in that room felt drained.

Batina ran up to Thaos and hugged him. Edward stood up and said, "Thaos at times you seemed humiliated by what you told us. But none of us saw that. We are all amazed that you could survive that and turn into the man and the warrior you are. I believe every person in this room respects you even more than we did before." Then Edward turned and said, "And Michael that is what we have all been trying to tell you too."

Michael didn't speak, he just wiped the tears from his cheeks.

# Chapter VI
## Change of Plans

The courtyard of the monastery was illuminated by torches. After Thaos finished telling his story, few people stayed in the meeting room. The majority returned to their rooms to get a couple of hours of sleep. When Gideon was about to open the door to the room that he and Ashley shared he saw a note hanging from a nail.

*Gideon the boys are sleeping on the floor. Wake me when you come in.*

*Ashley*

Gideon smiled and slowly opened the door. The room was small and he didn't want to wake Marty, Cassidy and Logan. Ashley had kept several candles lit so Gideon could see when he returned to the room. She awoke when he crawled into bed with her. They kissed for several moments then he said, "It is good you didn't go. I thought I had seen and heard everything but people were crying listening to Thaos talk. Sometimes I think people are worse than the demons."

"I don't know his story but I do understand how dangerous the streets are and not just for children. Many adults are just as abused."

"Did Cassidy tell you about his friends?"

"Yes, it is so sad. I am glad that Thaos and Stephan are taking him home with them. He is such a sweet child."

"Are they taking Marty and Logan too?"

"With everything that has happened, I don't think they have had time to really think about that. Why?"

"With Cassidy and Chasity both getting homes, I don't..." Gideon did not finish his sentence.

"Gideon what are you saying?"

"After listening to Thaos I don't want to leave any of those kids behind. I am not really sure what I am saying. I am just thinking out loud."

"Are you considering adopting some of these children?" Gideon didn't answer. "I thought we had everything planned out."

"You know when we get to Langer we will be living in Claudius' castle for a while."

"Gideon, I know you are exhausted but I really am not following what you are saying."

"Honey, like I said I am just thinking out loud. I haven't made any decisions. This morning when we talked everything sounded so logical. You and I are both going to be tremendously busy for at least the next year. Do you really want to have a child that is raised by nurses? But now I am thinking, well, you are going to love Claudius' family and the castle is filled with children and now Cassidy is going to add to the mix."

"You really are considering adopting some of these children," Ashley said with surprise.

"At this point it is only considering and maybe I am too tired to even know what I am saying. How do you feel about this?"

"I think that our original plans are perfect. But life isn't perfect and we could save lives here. My suggestion would be to adopt children that are a little older because you are right we both will be very busy. Then later we can have our own babies or adopt babies."

Gideon sat up in bed and looked at Ashley. "Well then, what do you think about adopting Marty and Logan? They seem like fine boys and look at how they took care of Chasity and they didn't even know her. And they are already friends with Cassidy."

"I would say you have been giving this more than a little consideration," Ashley said and kissed him. "I agree with every word you said. But you should talk to Thaos, Stephan and Sorren tomorrow before we say anything to the boys."

"How did everyone sleep?" asked Mathas with a smile as his family and the priests gathered around the breakfast table.

"The girls moved in with us," Simon said and winked at his new sisters.

"Why, did something happen?" asked Rosa.

Nyla and Saran looked embarrassed but Nina said innocently, "We get scared. We like being with Raul and Simon." Nina looked at Gabriel and Raphael who were grinning at her. "Oh, we like being with you too."

"We're glad to hear that," Gabriel said with a big smile. "When we get to Salar you will have to come to our home and play with the children. You can't believe all of the toys they have."

"And dogs," Raphael said.

"We would like that very much," Saran said sincerely. "We could never have pets. But now we have those beautiful horses. How can we ever thank you enough?"

"You already have," said Mathas then he looked at Rosa and smiled.

"Mathas are you going to ruin the surprise?"

"I am thinking about it."

"What surprise?" asked Nina with a big smile.

Mathas looked across the table at Raul and Simon. "We have no idea of what you are talking about," Raul said.

"Renya will kill me," Mathas said as he looked at Nyla, Saran and Nina. "Have the boys told you about Petra?" The girls nodded. "And our daughter Margarit?" The girls again nodded without speaking. "And Kyra?"

"No, is she a sister?" asked Nyla.

"She's the sister of our cook and she has been Petra's playmate for years. And now that they are older, well I think they are boyfriend and girlfriend but they won't admit to it," Raul said and laughed.

"Well those three children are excited that you are moving in with them and they wanted to do something for you," Mathas said.

"Oh, I know where this is going?" Simon said with a smirk.

"Where?" asked Saran.

"They already bought each of you a puppy," Mathas said and laughed at the looks on the faces of the girls. Nina's mouth fell open and Nyla and Saran got big smiles.

"I can't believe this," said Nyla then to everyone's surprise she started to cry. "This is like a dream; I am afraid I will wake up."

Raul looked shocked and said, "That is exactly what Vitomas said when we brought her home."

"Why?" asked Saran.

"A man like your father stole her when she was young and he stole Simon's wife Annabelle too."

"How did you find them?" asked Nyla.

"Actually that is a really long story," Raul said. "Maybe we should save that for the ride back."

Gideon met with Thaos, Sorren and Stephan early in the morning then all four men went to the dining hall for breakfast. The dining hall consisted of long tables with benches. Most of the team members were sitting at two tables they had pushed together. Ashley, Cassidy, Marty and Logan were sitting at these tables. Gideon smiled at Ashley and nodded and she got a smile that lit up her face.

"Boys, Gideon and I want to talk to all of you," Ashley said as Stephan pulled another bench up to the table and the four men sat down.

"First, you should know that Ashley and I are starting new jobs in Langer. That is where Thaos, Stephan and Sorren live and where Cassidy is going to be living," explained Gideon.

"We haven't bought a house yet and we haven't had time to plan our wedding so for the next year I expect that our lives are going to be pretty crazy. Now that you know that," Gideon said. "Logan, Marty, we were wondering if you would like to come home with us and be our sons? You don't have to give us an answer right away."

All of the team members started to laugh at the reactions of the boys. Marty, Logan and Cassidy all looked shocked. They kept looking back and forth at each other with grins on their faces.

"You know Gideon and Ashley will be living at our castle until they find a home," Thaos said. "So all of you can play together. That is if you want them for your parents."

"Oh yes," Logan said. "We are just so surprised."

"Does that mean you are going to be our mama and papa?" asked Marty. "And Logan and I will be brothers?"

"Yes," Gideon and Ashley said in unison.

"Really? Are you telling us the truth?" Marty asked.

"Yes, do you want to be our sons?" asked Gideon. Both Logan and Marty got very excited and nodded their heads.

"Yes," Logan said. "When do we start?"

Everyone at the two tables broke out in laughter. "How about right now," Gideon said with a grin. First Marty then Logan got off the bench and hugged Ashley and Gideon. Ashley started to cry.

The war in Port Friada ended midmorning, mostly because Samael stopped feeding it. He was so enraged by the battle at the monastery, which had been transmitted to other worlds, that he stopped sending mercenaries and demons to the city. Samael wanted Hector to focus all of his attention on the Sanuri and not to be distracted by a war.

Hector was not aware of the transmissions until Samael pulled him into hell. "I don't understand what is happening," Hector said as he stared at the scenes. "Why are those people glowing? And what is that really bright light?"

"You disappoint me every time I talk with you," Samael snarled. "That bright light is an Angel who surrounded those men with holiness. The holiness gives them power to kill demons."

"Are you telling me the truth?" Hector asked. "I didn't think anything could kill demons besides other demons."

"You really are a fool," Samael yelled. "Too much of a fool to do this mission."

"I'll do it! I'll do it!" Hector said. "I've never believed in things like Angels. Maybe you need to catch me up."

Thus far Claudius' journey to Leven was uneventful. So uneventful that everyone was becoming paranoid. They had been making good time but they still had at least four days of travel to get to the monastery. Daniel had warned them that Samael would soon turn his eyes upon them. Claudius and all of his leaders wondered why Samael was taking so long.

Commanding General Amundsen was livid when Lieutenant Collins told him about the child trafficking ring they had broken up outside of Leven. Words always came easily to Amundsen except this afternoon when Collins described in detail the presence of the Angel Daniel and the actions taken at the farm where over fifty children were held captive.

As Collins spoke, the veins were protruding from Amundsen's throat and forehead, his face was turning red and he started to pound his desktop. "Collins, I hope you realize I am not angry at you but this situation," Amundsen said. "You did well and will be rewarded. Since you started this mission so to speak, I want to keep you on it. Interrogate the prisoners then execute them. You know there are more people involved with this filth."

"Sir, does that mean I am at liberty to arrest Hector?" asked Collins.

"I have already sent men to his compound. I want to see that animal burn."

"Sir, I am sure that High Priest Barnabas will be contacting you if he hasn't already but he is taking on a new mission to protect the children of Port Friada."

"How is he going to do that?"

"Understand that the last time I spoke with him was at that farm and we were all enraged at what we saw. I don't believe he has worked out the details yet. But he has taken all of the children to the monastery. They may be giving the priests more information about Hectors' operation."

"I think it is time I saw all of this for myself. As soon as the troops return with Hector I am going to the monastery."

Five thousand soldiers attacked Hector's compound as soon as the sun set that day. While most of Hector's hired killers were Second Sons and thus enabled with superior strength, they were also exhausted and wounded from the war they had been fighting day and night for over a week.

Major Strong led the troops that first surrounded the compound. Strong sent one hundred of his best men in to kill the sentries on the wall of the compound and to open the gates of the massive wall.

Hector had lost over half of his men in the war and the ones who remained were so weakened that the battle was won before it really started. The hired killers who were not killed were taken as prisoners. Strong had the compound searched twice but Hector and his head lieutenant Clev were not found. Strong went to Amundsen's home and woke him to report the results of the raid. "Strong, you did well and I will reward you. I want all of those animals interrogated and have wanted posters of Hector and Clev made. We are going to flood the kingdom with them."

Hector and Clev were in Samael's hell domain when he showed them the scene of the raid on their compound. "I need to get back!" screamed Hector.

"Can you not see that you lost that battle?" sneered Samael. "But not the war. We have a change of plans."

As soon as the sun rose the following morning, Amundsen and one thousand soldiers started a journey to the monastery at Leven. Although the concept of talking birds still confounded the General, he sent Enrops ahead to tell High Priest Barnabas and the Sanuri that he was coming and why. Amundsen said he also wanted to see the farm where the children had been held captive.

Claudius' army was just about to break camp when two flocks of Enrops descended on them. One group was from Wetpr and the other from the people taking shelter in the monastery. Enrops told Claudius and his men about the battle with the army of demons that had taken place at the monastery and the kidnapped children before anyone opened a letter.

Claudius received letters about the battle and the auction. He received a letter from Gideon telling him about adopting Logan and Marty and apologizing for any inconvenience that might cause. But the letter that shocked Claudius was the one he received from Stephan explaining Thaos' decision to talk about his past.

Claudius knew his son well and could tell that Stephan was upset by Thao's revelations. Claudius immediately wrote letters to both Thaos and Stephan, then one to Bella.

As the group talked among themselves about their letters it was Jared who got everyone's attention. "Zoya had, well apparently she has had a couple of visions," he said loudly as he stood up. "She says she keeps seeing eyes from underground watching us and she feels danger but she has no idea what she is seeing."

"She also says that she sees a connection between Hector and these eyes but that too confuses her. She thinks they are enemies. She says the eyes are old, very old and they aren't demons, at least not in the sense that we are used to. And she keeps seeing images of Thaos and books. She told Sudfad about her visions and he told her that Thaos had gotten some of Juleta's spell books and ledgers."

"Zoya said that as soon as Sudfad told her this she felt that Thaos was in great danger. She sent him a letter telling him about this and wants Archetenus and me to watch over him. She says that normally when she sees her visions she is just looking at things but with these visions she feels all kinds of emotions. Strong emotions but they aren't hers."

Gideon and Ashley were walking out of the dining room of the monastery with their arms around each other's waists. "You know when I left Langer I never imagined that I would be returning with a family," he said with a warm smile.

"I know. Everything is happening fast but yet it doesn't seem like that. It seems right," Ashley paused and smiled. "You know we had met before this mission; at parties in Port Friada."

"Oh believe me, I remember. I thought you a beauty and so did the men who were always surrounding you."

"Is that why you never asked me to dance?"

"Partly that and fear."

"Fear! What on earth are you afraid of?"

"Ashley, you are an intoxicating woman. Not the kind of woman you want to leave at home when you are at sea chasing pirates. I needed to have my head in the game."

"So if you wouldn't have taken the job in Lentz, we probably would never have fallen in love," she said almost more to herself than to Gideon.

Mathas' Court Physician told Raul and Simon that the wounded priests needed a couple of days of bedrest. This news was welcomed by Mathas and Rosa who were greatly enjoying their newly found nieces. On this day Rosa, Angelina, Nikki and Ingr were taking the girls shopping then meeting Bella and Isadore for lunch. Raul, Simon, Matthew, Raphael and Gabriel were returning to Fort Langer to continue the interrogations of Karzman's men.

Each of Karzman's men was separated from his comrades and given the truth potion. This morning, Gabriel did something he had never considered before; he prayed to be showed the questions to ask.

Just before noon, Ryan heard the front door to his shop open. He was in the back of the shop with twenty other men. They were creating the furniture for the new orphanage. "I'll be right there," Ryan yelled.

"We are giving the girls a tour," Bella said loudly and Ryan dropped the carving blade he had been holding.

Artis winked at Ralph and asked Ryan, "Are those the girls you were talking about?"

"Yes," Ryan said with embarrassment. "Do you want to meet them?" The three men started to walk towards the front of the store when all of the women walked into the workshop. All of the men except for Ryan were shocked to see the Queen walking among them.

"We can't believe you make all of these things," Saran said loudly.

"Well, if you see anything you like take it," said Ryan.

"We can't do that," said Nyla. "But you make beautiful things."

"We just finished the first pieces for the orphanage," Ryan said proudly. "I was going to bring them home to see if they were what you wanted. We'll get them."

71

"Oh I am sorry, this is Artis and Ralph and this is Nyla, Saran and Nina. They are the sisters of Prince Michael."

"We are very proud to meet you," said Artis. "Ryan has been telling us about all of you. How long are you going to be here because we could make you a cradle for that doll you are holding," Artis said to Nina.

"Really? I think she would like that," Nina said of her doll then she looked at Rosa. "Aunt Rosa how long are we going to be here?"

"Maybe two more days at our home but then they are going to Bella's," Rosa said.

"Well that is plenty of time," Ralph said. "Would you girls like one too?"

"Yes," said both Nyla and Saran with big smiles.

"Artis, Ralph can you bring them back here?" Ryan called out.

When the women walked to the back of the shop they were delighted. Ryan and the other carpenters had arranged furniture into room groupings. "As you can see these beds, cradles and dressers are for the children. I don't know how you have decided to set up their rooms but here are little chests, cupboards and tables and chairs. We can paint them whatever colors that you want."

"Ryan these are absolutely wonderful," Isadore said as she opened the drawers of one of the dressers.

"We are all working on them but me, Artis and Ralph are doing most of the carvings."

"Who are these people?" Nina asked as she pointed to the carvings on a headboard.

"They are Angels," said Artis.

"Our Angel didn't look like that, she was a lot older," Nina said. "She helped us escape. She was really nice."

"What is she talking about?" asked Rosa.

"The Angel Ruth," said Angelina. "She walked the girls out of their village and stayed with them until soldiers came and took the girls to a monastery."

All of the carpenters were staring at the women, most of them in disbelief. Ingr and Nikki saw the looks on the men's faces and grinned. "Ryan is one of these Miranda?" Ingr asked.

"Can't you tell?" asked Ryan as he walked closer to her.

"Oh my god! Bella, Nikki look at this," Ingr was pointing to one of the carvings of an Angel. "It looks just like her."

"Ryan can you carve other things with her face?" asked Bella.

"Actually Ralph carved that one. Sure we can; what are you thinking of?"

"I'm not sure yet."

"Gentlemen, can you take this entire room setting and deliver it to the castle?" asked Rosa. "I want Mathas and Fahron to see it. We are still designing the rooms. And what is this other furniture?"

"Those are some ideas that we had for the adults," Ryan said.

"We didn't even consider offices and chambers for adults," Isadore said. "I am so glad we saw all of this."

"Ryan can you join us for lunch?" Bella asked.

"Go, we will watch the shop," Artis said with a grin.

After Ryan and the women walked out of the workshop one of the carpenters said, "If they are Prince Michael's sisters than their daddy is Chief Karzman. I'll bet he is wondering where those girls are."

Both Artis and Ralph felt uneasy as they listened to the man speak. "First, that is none of our business," said Ralph. "And second, how do you know so much about Karzman?"

"I don't. I am just thinking out loud," said the carpenter and returned to his painting."

Raul and the others did not return to Mathas' castle until dinner time. When they walked into the dining room, Nina got out of her chair and ran up to Raul who picked her up. "You can't believe the things we saw today," she said excitedly.

Raul laughed and said, "We want to hear all about them."

"Is anything wrong?" asked Angelina. "You all look so, well I guess mad."

"Disgusted would be a better word," Matthew said as he kissed her on the cheek. "But we can talk about it later."

"My Lord, My Lady you have company. They said they need to tell you something," said one of the housekeepers.

"Thank you," said Mathas. "Please show them in."

"Why, Artis and Ralph, what a surprise," said Rosa. "Would you like to join us?"

Both old men looked uncomfortable. "We are really sorry to intrude but My Lady after you left the shop something happened and the more that Artis and me thought about it, well, we don't know if it is important but we don't want to take any chances of anything happening to those little girls."

"What are you talking about?" asked Simon.

"We would just a soon not tell you here," said Artis and glanced at Nyla, Saran and Nina.

"In my study," Mathas said and all of the men and Angelina left the dining room."

"Like Ralph said this might not be anything at all," said Artis. "It's just that this really bad feeling has been gnawing at us both. As soon as all you ladies and Ryan walked out of the workshop, one of the new carpenters, his name is Ted, we don't really know him. Well, Ted says 'if those girls are Prince Michael's sisters then their daddy is Chief Karzman and I'll bet he is wondering where they are."

"We only knew about Karzman because Ryan told us about the girls. We've never heard that name before," said Ralph. "So how would this Ted know so much? And it's hard to explain but it was just the way he said it that gave both Artis and me the willies. We don't want to scare you none for no reason but we felt we should tell you."

"We are glad you did," said Matthew. "We will pay a visit to the shop tomorrow. Did you tell Ryan or Bella?"

"We thought about telling Ryan but, now we don't mean no disrespect cuz we love that boy, but he ain't no fighter and Ted looks like he is," said Ralph.

"I know exactly who you are talking about," said Angelina. "Ralph is right, Ted looks like a fighter and I mean one who is trained like all of you. I wondered why he was painting children's furniture."

"And we didn't tell Bella because the girls are here," said Artis. "We were going to go out there next."

"No, that is a long ride and it is getting late," said Mathas. "You were right to come here and tell us. Please won't you join us for dinner? Claudius loves your stories about the sea; perhaps you can tell us a few."

"There is something else," said Artis. "And now we feel real bad. We asked the girls how long they are going to be here because we are making cradles for their dolls and Queen Rosa said a couple of days then they were going to Bella's. We don't know who all heard that."

"We aren't stupid," said Nyla challengingly when Mathas and the others returned to the dining room. "Are more of his men here?"

"We won't lie to you," said Simon. "We don't know. One of the carpenters talked about Karzman after you left and it made Artis and Ralph suspicious. So we are going to talk to the man tomorrow."

75

"Was it that big guy who was painting furniture?" asked Saran.

"Yes," said Angelina. "Why? Did he say something to you?"

"No, he kept staring at us," Saran replied.

"I know who you are talking about," said Nyla. "I noticed him too because he didn't look like the other men."

"What do you mean?" asked Raphael.

"He looked like a soldier. The way he carried himself and well just everything about him," said Nyla.

"Girls, no one thinks you are stupid," said Mathas. "You have to understand that all of us are so happy you are here and we want to protect you. But I think we are realizing that all of you are wise for your ages."

"Girls, do you know how to fight or use weapons?" Angelina asked.

"No, the women of our tribe were not allowed such things," said Nyla.

"Tomorrow let's visit my tribe. All the men and women are warriors and if you would like to learn we can start teaching you these skills," Angelina said. All three of the girls smiled.

"We would like that," said Saran.

"Why don't all of you come?" offered Angelina. "Artis, Ralph have you ever been to my village?"

"No My Lady," said Ralph. "And we would be honored but we have to work."

"Perhaps tomorrow isn't a good day for you to go in," said Matthew. "We'll explain to Ryan that you had a change of plans. He will understand."

# Chapter VII
## Mercenaries

The next morning Gabriel and Raphael returned to the fort to interrogate Karzman's men. Matthew, Raul and Simon rode into Langer. They arrived at Ryan's store just as he was opening it. Nikki, Ingr and Bella were setting up the treats and coffee; no one else was in the building. Matthew quickly told Bella's family about Ted, Artis and Ralph, while Simon and Raul looked around the shop. They were looking for hidden weapons and doors.

"Do you know anything about this Ted? Who hired him?" Matthew asked both Bella and Ryan.

"I do all the hiring," said Bella and now that you mention it he did look like a soldier but he seemed nice enough."

"He doesn't really talk so I am surprised about what he said yesterday," said Ryan. "Why didn't Artis and Ralph tell me?"

"Because they were afraid that you would confront Ted and get hurt. It sounds like they think of you as a grandson and they want to protect you," Matthew said.

"I really like those two," said Ingr. "Bella, let's get the babies and all go to our village with Angelina and the girls. It will be fun."

"I think I would enjoy that," Bella said. "But first I want to see what goes on here. I would hate to think I hired a terrorist."

"Bella, how would you know," said Nikki and put her arm around her mother-in-law.

"We didn't find anything suspicious," said Raul. "But you have some beautiful things here. We want to place some orders."

"Let's do that now," said Ryan. "Do you want some cake and coffee first?"

"No wonder you do such good business here," Simon said and grabbed a handful of cookies. Between the food and the workmanship you're going to make a fortune."

"You better get a pen and paper," said Raul as he grabbed a piece of cake. "We are remodeling Father's study. Claudius showed us what you made for his study and we were impressed."

"And we are going to need seven of those big jewelry boxes with the music," Simon said. "Then we will start on the toys."

"We'll need more than seven," said Raul. "We should get them for Emeral and Hannah and the others too."

"Alright, give us three dozen and if there are any leftover Mother can give them as gifts," Simon said.

"Bella, you are going to have to hire more workers," said Ingr with a big smile.

Bella started to speak but stopped when they heard some of the carpenters in the back room. Ryan looked in the work room and whispered "He's not here yet."

This morning, shortly after Sudfad's meeting started there was a knock on the door. Joshua was the closest and opened the door. Micha and Thomas entered the study.

"Is anything wrong boys?" Joshua asked.

"We are sorry to intrude but we wanted to tell all of you something," said Thomas.

"Please join us," said Sudfad. "And boys you are welcome to attend these meetings."

"Thank you," said Micha. "Thomas and I and our wives have been staying at Erebus' house while he is gone. We are watching the place and overseeing the workmen he hired. This morning Bianca took coffee to some of the workmen and they asked her if the woman found us. Bianca had no idea of what they were talking about so she asked a lot of questions. Apparently yesterday afternoon while we were at our home for lunch a beautiful woman with dark hair stopped at Erebus' house. The men said she was very friendly and asked for Erebus. They told her he was on a holiday and that we were watching the place."

"The men are fixing one of the barns behind the house. They said the woman walked towards the front of the house and said she was going to speak with us. The men didn't think there was anything suspicious so they didn't follow her. Bianca asked the housekeeper if the woman came to the door and the housekeeper said there weren't any visitors."

"Mother, Vivian and Emeral are with our wives now searching the place. We are going back to help them. We think it was Madeline but we have no proof."

"You were right to come here," said Sudfad. "Did you find anything at all out of the ordinary?"

"Not yet," said Thomas. "She may have just been gathering information. But the men said that she walked around the house to talk to them so they didn't see if she came in a carriage or with someone."

"And we are sure it wasn't Hecate?" asked Maxwell.

"Well, that is a possibility too," said Micha. "We've been coming home for meals maybe I should buy some food and we won't leave the house."

"We will cancel the meeting this morning," said Sudfad. "Misha take some men and check on Horace and Zelda and have men check on Zoya and Delilah. Maxwell assign troops to watch all of these homes, including Erebus' around the clock. If you want soldiers at your home assign them."

"I am getting a really bad feeling about this," said Raul. All of the carpenters had come to work except for Ted, Artis and Ralph.

"You two stay here and I am going to get some soldiers to stay here with Ryan," Matthew said and quickly left the building.

"Is Ted friends with any of the other men?" asked Simon.

"He was new and really kept to himself," Ryan explained. "But ask them."

Ryan, Raul and Simon walked into the workshop. "Listen up everyone," said Ryan. "This is Prince Raul and Prince Simon from Wetpr. They have some questions for you."

"We have reason to believe that Ted is a hired killer who may be a threat to the Royal Family here. Can anyone give us any information about him? Did he talk to any of you?" asked Raul.

"He was pretty quiet," said one of the carpenters. "He did his work and left."

"Did he ever get any visitors or did any of you see him outside of work?" asked Simon.

"You know Artis and Ralph challenged him yesterday. Did he do something to them because they never miss work?" asked another carpenter.

"Bella has them working on a project," said Ryan although what he said was a lie.

"I don't know if this is anything," said one of the men. "But about a week ago I went to the Catfish Tavern to play cards and Ted was there with some fellas. They were drinking and laughing. I didn't say anything to him and I don't know if he saw me."

"Can you describe these other men?" asked Simon.

"I really didn't look that close. They just seemed like regular fellas."

Matthew returned to the shop with six soldiers who were assigned to protect the men in the shop. Raul, Simon and Matthew went to the Catfish Tavern, which was near the docks. It was a small building but it was filled with customers even at that time of the morning.

Matthew walked up to the bartender and said, "We're looking for a guy named Ted. Big, looks like a fighter. He comes here with four or five other guys."

"Can't say anyone sticks out, My Lord. The only Ted I know died last week but he was an old fellar. But you have to understand that most people don't give their names and if they do they are probably lying about them. But I got other people who work here too. Right now everyone is in the kitchen cooking. You can go in there and ask."

Raul and Simon had been walking through the tavern looking at the patrons. Now Simon and Matthew walked into the kitchen while Raul stood at the bar. The bartender served several men then walked to Raul. He knew that Raul had walked in with Prince Matthew.

"Do you want something while you wait?" asked the bartender.

"No, but did Matthew ask you if you have heard the name Karzman mentioned?"

"No, he didn't and I can't say that I have but I usually stay behind the bar. The girls take food and drinks to the tables. They are in the kitchen now."

Raul walked into the kitchen as one of the older women was talking, "That description is pretty vague but I have heard that name before; not Ted the other one, Karzman. Just give me a minute to think. This place is always crazy. Ok, two, maybe three nights ago I had a group sitting at one of the large round tables. Five men, none of them were from around here because they kept asking me about places in the city."

"What kind of places?" asked Matthew.

"Oh, the usual stuff, general store, black smith. The only reason I remember them is because they ate like they hadn't eaten in weeks. They each ate two or three dinners."

"One of the times I walked up to the table with food I heard one of them say something like 'Karzman is going to be real pissed'. Then they all stopped talking because I was there."

"Can you describe any of these men?" Matthew asked.

"I am sorry My Lord but we must have a couple of hundred guys in here every day. After a while they all look alike."

Matthew handed every woman in the kitchen several gold coins, as he said, "If you see these men again or anyone else mentions Karzman's name please tell one of the soldiers that the King wants that information. We believe these men are threats to my family." The women were obviously surprised and pleased to receive the money.

"Thank you My Lord, we sure will," said one of the women.

"I'm not sure what is taking them so long," said Angelina. "Maybe we should get started."

"Honey, why don't you wait a little longer," said Rosa. "I would just feel better if Matthew and the boys went with you. If they are this late something might be wrong."

"If we start out too late I won't be able to show everyone the lands," Angelina said as she looked out of the window of the parlor. "A carriage just pulled up. It's Bella, Nikki and Ingr. They have all the babies." Angelina said this last sentence as she ran to the front door of the castle.

"Good, you are still here," said Nikki. "They told us you were going to the villiage so we decided to come along." Amy jumped into Angelina's arms and they hugged each other. Three nurses also got out of the carriage.

"Who told you?" asked Angelina.

"Matthew, Raul and Simon when they were at the store. That Ted never showed up and one of the other carpenters said he saw him at a tavern so they are going there," said Ingr.

Angelina escorted all of the women into the parlor. "Bella, we are real sorry that we didn't go to work today," said Artis as he and Ralph stood up.

"That is quite alright, we are just glad you told everyone about that Ted," said Bella. "He didn't come to work today so Matthew, Raul and Simon are looking for him."

"Did they tell you why we didn't say anything to Ryan?" Ralph asked.

"Yes, and as far as I am concerned you made the right choice," Bella said. "But what are you doing here?"

"I invited them to come to the village," said Angelina. "But Gabriel and Raphael are still at the fort and Matthew isn't back yet. I don't know if we should just start out."

Rosa had gone to Mathas' study to tell him about Angelina wanting to leave. Now Mathas and Rosa entered the parlor. "If you go now you are taking soldiers with you. I don't want it to be just you girls and the children." Mathas paused then said. "Ralph, Artis I didn't mean to offend you."

"My Lord, we are past our fighting days," said Artis. "No offense taken."

"I'm going to get some soldiers," said Angelina and walked out of the room.

"Where are the girls?" asked Bella.

"In the kitchen writing letters to Michael," Rosa laughed. "As big as this castle is and they like to sit in the kitchen. It took us a while to realize they probably spent time in the kitchen with their mother."

"Rosa and I have become very attached to those girls," said Mathas. "If Sudfad and Renya weren't taking them we would adopt them."

Nina ran into the room ahead of her sisters, "Ingr, Nikki, Bella," she said with a big smile. "Are you coming with us?"

"Yes," said Nikki.

"Here are the letters for Michael," Nyla said and handed three envelopes to Mathas.

"And these are for you," said Nina and handed Rosa three pieces of paper.

"They are just pictures and cards," said Nyla with embarrassment. "We didn't know how to thank you for everything."

"These are wonderful," said Rosa as she read each card then handed it to Mathas who smiled.

"We like these very much," he said.

"Saran is the best at pictures," said Nina to Mathas and Rosa. Then she turned to Amy. "Amy want to see my doll?" The girls held hands and ran out of the parlor.

"My Lords is this the last one?" asked Sergeant Henderson. He was referring to one of Karzman's men who had been interrogated.

"Yes," said Gabriel. "You can return him to his cell. We need to get to the castle."

"Actually we have orders to execute them as soon as you are done," Henderson said.

As Henderson spoke, Gabriel and Raphael were packing up their notes and vials of truth potion. Both men quickly left the dungeons at Fort Langer.

Matthew, Raul and Simon returned to Ryan's shop before they left the city. Ted had not come to work.

"I don't like this," said Simon. "We need to get back to the girls."

"You don't think that Angelina would start out before we get there do you?" Raul asked Matthew.

"You know I was just wondering about that myself," said Matthew and all three men quickened the gaits of their horses.

"Where are the girls?" asked Gabriel as he and Raphael looked into the parlor of Mathas' castle.

Rosa was walking towards the men, "They all left maybe twenty-five minutes ago. Why? Is something wrong?"

"Rosa, I don't mean to be rude but are Matthew, Simon and Raul with them?" asked Gabriel.

"No, but Mathas made them take some soldiers."

"Do you know how many soldiers?" asked Raphael.

"I am not sure, maybe twenty."

"Rosa, tell Mathas that Karzman has a number of men in the city," said Raphael. "We will explain when we get back."

"Take more soldiers," Rosa yelled as Gabriel and Raphael ran out of the castle. Rosa turned and ran to Mathas' study.

Angelina, Nikki and Ingr, decided to ride horses as did Nyla and Saran. Nina rode in the carriage with Amy, Bella, four nurses and the small children. Angelina brought one of the nurses from the castle to help with the children. Ten soldiers rode in front of the carriage and eight in back. Two soldiers sat in the front seat of the carriage, one was the driver. Artis and Ralph rode next to the carriage.

It took a little over two hours to ride from Mathas' castle to the Village of Tyger. This small caravan was forty minutes into its journey when four Enrops flew over Angelina, Nikki and Ingr.

The caravan stopped. "Gabriel and Raphael sent us," said one of the giant birds. "Karzman has a lot of men in the city because they have been spying on Michael. They have been watching your castle. As we flew here we passed a group of maybe thirty men. Some of our flock went to get help. Gabriel and Raphael are coming."

"How much time do we have?" asked Angelina.

"Ten, maybe fifteen minutes," said another Enrop. "We will stay with you."

Angelina turned to the Sergeant who was in charge of the detail of soldiers. "There's a hunting cabin about half a mile in that direction," Angelina pointed to the forest as she spoke. Take half the men and the carriage there. We will meet you."

"But, My Lady..." the Sergeant said.

"Go! We don't have time," yelled Angelina. "Half of you men stay with us. We are going to ambush them. Nyla, Saran go with the carriage. You too, Artis and Ralph."

"We have swords," said Ralph.

"Then protect the children," said Angelina. "Now all of you go!"

Nikki and Ingr rode up to Saran and Nyla. "You might need these," Ingr said as they handed the young girls knives. "Do you think you can use them?"

"Yes," said Nyla.

Nikki and Ingr dismounted and draped a rope across the road. One end was tied to a tree. Nikki hid on the other side of the road with the other end of the rope. Angelina positioned the ten soldiers in the forest along the roadway.

Bella had heard what the Enrops and Angelina said. Bella now took control of the situation. "Stop!" she yelled and climbed out of the carriage. "Saran get inside."

Bella mounted Saran's horse and rode up to the Sergeant. "No one is hurting these children," she said. "Give me a weapon." The shocked Sergeant handed her one of his knives, then they sped towards the cabin. "Miranda, if you can hear me please help us," Bella said out loud.

"Great Ruler please protect our babies," both Ingr and Nikki prayed separately as they watched a dust cloud coming towards them.

Two soldiers stood with Nikki; when Angelina yelled a war cry the soldiers and Nikki pulled the rope taunt that was on the road. The four horses in the lead tripped; two threw their riders. One fell on top of its rider and the fourth jumped and reared on its hind legs. The four riders directly behind the first row lost control of their horses. Men were yelling and horses were screaming as arrows propelled out of the forest.

Since they were so outnumbered, Angelina wanted the archers to stay hidden in the forest until they were forced to fight hand to hand. As soon as the first row of horses had tripped, Nikki and the two soldiers grabbed their bows and added to the barrage of arrows that were raining upon Karzman's men.

While Karzman was paying all of these men, most of them were hired killers who had been sent to Lentz to track down the deserters of his tribe. Only five of the thirty men were actually members of the Kozach Tribe. All of these men had battle experience. Although they were taken by surprise, the men recovered faster than their horses did. The horses were frightened when some of them tripped over the rope and their riders where desperately trying to get them under control.

One of the men was thrown from his horse. He wasn't injured and as he got up he saw the wheel tracks of the carriage. He momentarily examined the tracks then called to some of the other men. Four more joined him and they rode into the forest.

The soldiers ushered the nurses and children into the small cabin. "Artis, Ralph take Nyla and Saran and go in there too," said Bella. "How I wish Claudius was here," she said as she watched the soldiers take positions in the forest. Four of the soldiers went inside of the cabin.

As Bella entered the cabin, Nyla ran up to her. "There's weapons in here and lots of them."

"Where?" asked Bella and followed Nyla as she ran to a chest that was sitting at the end of the bed in the only bedroom. The chest was half full of weapons. Bella grabbed a sword and secured a dagger in the belt of her dress. When Bella saw that Nyla and Saran were both holding swords she shook her head and said, "God help us."

Matthew, Simon and Raul were already on the road to the Village of Tyger when a flock of Enrops appeared out of nowhere. The Princes had previously stopped at the castle and Rosa told them that Angelina and the others had left for her village.

This was before Gabriel and Raphael told Rosa and Mathas about Karzman's men.

"Quickly they are being attacked," yelled one of the birds and the three men raced down the road. "Gabriel and Raphael are behind you," one of the birds yelled. "Bella and the children are hiding in a cabin and Angelina and her friends ambushed the men."

"Of course she did," said Matthew fearfully as his horse raced down the road.

The five hired killers who were tracking the carriage were prepared for another ambush. They saw the tracks from the soldiers' horses and knew how many men they would be fighting. The men on horseback could travel faster than the carriage. The soldiers outside of the cabin were assuming their positions in the forest when Karzman's men arrived. Two of the soldiers were kill before they realized they were being attacked.

"Take the children into the bedroom," yelled Bella when she saw the soldiers fighting with Karzman's men.

"We aren't leaving you out here Bella," Artis yelled.

Two soldiers were at the front door of the cabin and two at the rear door. The two at the front door were afraid of hitting their comrades so they didn't shoot their arrows. To Bella's horror she saw Karzman's men quickly kill the soldiers. The mercenaries now turned towards the cabin. "We just want the girls," yelled one of the men.

"God, Miranda I hope you heard me," Bella said in a whisper then she moved in front of a window. "You will not touch these children!" she yelled.

Matthew, Raul and Simon had swords and axes drawn as they rode into the group of hired killers. The three Princes attacked the men from the rear. Angelina ordered the archers to stop shooting so they wouldn't hit the Princes.

Then she yelled, "Charge!" Ingr, Nikki and Angelina all screamed their war cries as they rode forward with the ten soldiers of Lentz. Raphael and Gabriel heard the war cries and pulled out their weapons. Within moments they joined the battle.

"Whatever you want Lady," yelled one of Karzman's men then spit a wad of tobacco on the ground. The five men now split up as two of them circled around to the back of the cabin.

"My Lady get back!" yelled one of the soldiers to Bella. "We'll take care of them."

"No," said Bella. "Artis and Ralph please go in with the children in case they get past us."

"Lady, we don't want to hurt you," yelled one of the hired killers and laughed. "Send the girls out." The two soldiers at the front door were waiting until the men got a little closer before they were going to release their arrows.

"This is your last chance," yelled the man as he continued to laugh, then he fell forward with an arrow in his back.

War cries were heard as a hunting party of Nordes warriors attacked Karzman's men.

Raul, Simon, Matthew, Raphael and Gabriel were all exceptional fighters. They rode through Karzman's men hacking and stabbing the mercenaries.

"Keep a couple alive," yelled Gabriel as the battle was winding down.

"We're going for the babies," Ingr yelled as she and Nikki rode into the forest. Simon and Raul followed the women.

Bella started to cry when she saw Hugo, brother of Sorren, run out of the forest and attack one of the hired killers. Karzman's men were killed in a matter of seconds.

Bella opened the door and ran out to Hugo. "How did you know we needed help?" she asked.

"Enrops got us, what is going on and how come you're out here?"

"There's tracks following the carriage!" Nikki yelled with panic in her voice. The four warriors now raced across the forest floor.

"Come inside," said Bella. "Angelina, Nikki, Ingr and I and the children were coming out to visit all of you. Michael's little sisters escaped from Karzman and are here too. Those men wanted them." As Bella spoke she and Hugo walked across the small cabin and she opened the bedroom door. "It's alright now. We're safe," Bella said as the fear was draining from her.

Artis and Ralph were standing in front of the nurses and children with their swords drawn. Nyla and Saran stood behind them also holding swords. "This is Hugo, brother of Chief Sorren and this is Artis, Ralph, Nyla, Saran and Nina. I believe you know everyone else," Bella explained then she suddenly became pale. "Hugo, the girls are fighting with more men at the road."

Hugo ran out of the cabin and yelled to his warriors. They quickly mounted and started to ride towards the road but after just a few minutes they met Ingr, Nikki, Raul and Simon.

"Hugo are the babies alright?" yelled Ingr.

"Yes, but most of the soldiers are dead. Is the battle at the road over?" Hugo asked.

"Only a few of Karzman's men were still standing when we left," said Raul. "There's soldiers and others taking care of them."

Bella was still crying when Nikki, Ingr, Raul and Simon ran into the cabin. "Thank you Miranda," she whispered.

"You're welcome," Miranda's voice whispered into Bella's ear.

# Chapter VIII
## The Journey

"Angelina!" screamed Matthew.

The terror in Matthew's voice made Gabriel and Raphael look away from the man they were tying up. "Got him?" Gabriel asked Raphael and started to run. Gabriel tore off his shirt as he could see Angelina's left side was covered with blood. Matthew had his hands covering the gushing wound as he tried to stop the bleeding. "Someone start a fire!" yelled Gabriel as he pushed Matthew to the side and pressed his shirt tightly against the wound.

Karzman's men were dead, except for the two who had been captured. A soldier ran off the roadway and quickly gathered wood. Raphael too took off his shirt and tried to make a cushion with it that he gently placed under Angelina's head.

Matthew, who had been wounded numerous times in his life was frozen with fear at seeing his wife lying on the battlefield. He looked up when he heard horses approaching. "Hugo, Angelina's hurt!"

Hugo, Angelina's uncle yelled, "We'll take care of her." His horse was still moving when Hugo jumped off with his medical bag in his hand.

Ingr and Nikki ran to their children, hugging and kissing them as Nyla, Saran and Nina jumped into Raul's and Simon's arms. Both men hugged and kissed their newly adopted sisters. "Is any one hurt?" asked Raul.

"No, Bella stopped them," Nyla said and both men now turned and looked at Bella who was hugging Amy.

Artis and Ralph went outside to help the four remaining soldiers drape the bodies of their fallen comrades over the backs of their horses. Afterwards, they searched the bodies of the mercenaries.

The nurses were just as terrified as the children and when everyone calmed down, Raul and Simon helped them all into the carriage. Nina wanted to ride with Raul but he made her ride in the carriage because none of them knew if this attack was really over. Those not in or driving the carriage, mounted their horses and led the horses of the dead. They traveled back to the roadway.

Miranda had sent numerous flocks of Enrops to help; in answers to prayers. A flock of these ancient birds were now leading King Mathas and a company of soldiers to the battleground.

As the group from the cabin neared the road they saw the littered bodies and smelled the stench of burned flesh from wounds being cauterized. They saw soldiers and Nordes warriors bandaging wounds and they saw a group of men kneeling on the ground. "What is it?" yelled Nikki fearfully for in that instance she realized she didn't see her friend, Angelina.

"It's Angelina," said one of the soldiers as he approached the group. Then in a softer voice he said, "I think she's hurt bad." Ingr and Nikki jumped from their horses and ran to the group of men who surrounded Angelina. Hugo and another Nordes warrior who had been trained in the arts of healing were working on Angelina's wound. Gabriel and Raphael were praying over her. And Matthew was crying.

"Can we help?" Ingr asked.

"No," said Hugo then he hesitated. "We need something to transport her in."

"I'll go back and get a boca," yelled one of the soldiers and turned but as he mounted his horse he saw a large dust cloud on the road. "We're getting company!" he yelled. The soldiers driving the carriage now moved it farther into the forest as the soldiers and warriors turned to face possible enemies.

"Enrops fly with them," yelled Raul and rode forward to meet the small army that Mathas was leading.

Mathas was a man of battle; he brought a physician and two bocas for the wounded and possibly to transport the women and children.

"The battle is over but Angelina is greatly wounded," Raul said as he met Mathas, whose blood ran cold when he heard the words. The group did not stop at that portion of the roadway but rode directly to the wounded.

"We need the Physician!" yelled Mathas as he jumped from his horse. "Men take care of the wounded!"

All of the soldiers who had fought on the roadway were wounded but none were killed, the casualties were the six soldiers at the cabin. Artis and Ralph stopped helping the wounded soldiers when reinforcements arrived. The two old men now walked around the dead mercenaries and searched their pockets.

The Physician worked on Angelina's wound as Ingr and Nikki stood with Matthew. The soldiers who were driving the carriage now returned to the road and Bella got out. She told the nurses and children to stay inside and she ran to the group who were kneeling over Angelina. Bella saw the look on Matthew's face before she could see Angelina and tears filled her eyes.

"There's blankets in the back of both bocas," yelled the Physician. "Someone make up a bed for her."

"I'll do that," yelled Bella and ran to one of the bocas. Nikki and Ingr followed her. Moments later Hugo carried Angelina to the rear of the boca and with the help of Matthew, Gabriel and Raphael they carefully placed her on the bedding. The Physician examined the minor wounds of the soldiers then he climbed into the back of the boca with Matthew, Hugo and Bella.

Mathas was standing with Raul and Simon being briefed about the battle when Artis and Ralph walked up to them. "My Lords, we are sorry to interrupt but there is something you should know," said Artis. "We looked at every body and Ted is not among them. We've never seen any of these men before."

93

"And this is what we got from them," Ralph said. "I put the money in this pouch but we found this on the man that was closest to the cabin. You need to read it."

"Keep the money," Mathas said as Ralph handed him the pouch and a slip of paper. The King's face turned dark red as he read the note.

"What is it?" asked Simon.

Mathas handed him the note but also explained it. "Someone was spying on the castle; they sent this note to these men. It tells exactly who was in the group, the number of soldiers, women and children."

"And they know their names," Simon said as he handed the note to Raul. Simon called Gabriel and Raphael over and showed them the note. They all decided to tell Matthew about it later.

"I was going to leave the bodies here to rot," said Mathas to the group of men he was standing with; then he yelled an order to the soldiers. "Bring those bodies, we'll string them up in the city."

"There's more at the cabin," Raul said.

Samael's power and cunning were offset by his temper and rage which often blinded him to things. So infuriated was he at Miranda's intrusion in his attack on the monastery that he failed to notice Claudius' army. It took an entire day after he returned Hector and Clev to the World of Nunc before Samael calmed enough to lose his tunnel vision.

In the same instance of clarity, the King of Demons, realized that Amundsen was leading troops from Port Friada to the monastery at Leven as was Claudius, who had entered the Kingdom of Ganz the previous night. Now Samael sat back to try and figure out what was happening. Why were two armies converging on that monastery? Was there more behind those stone walls than he realized?

Neither Zoya nor Delilah left their homes to move into the castle after soldiers told them about Madeline and Javier. But both women did allow soldiers to guard their houses. It wasn't that the women were ignorant of the threats but the Sanuri had Blue Hengers and Enrops watching both of the homes. And both women knew they could call to the Angels. It was faith that kept them in their homes; a concept that many of the soldiers guarding them could not understand.

After Ashley received the first letter from Delilah and Archetenus, asking her to live with them; the two women corresponded almost daily. Delilah and Ashley never really knew each other prior to Ashley helping Delilah to escape from Dieter. Now, through their letters, the women felt as sisters. Both women were very open in their letters about their lives, feelings and thoughts. They discovered they had many things in common. And they both came to regret that they didn't have the opportunities to become friends when they lived in Port Friada.

Delilah had not yet received the letter telling of Ashley and Gideon adopting Marty and Logan; but Delilah was busy planning an engagement celebration for her friend.

Both Jared and Archetenus had hired men to work on their properties which butted up to each other. The actual houses were less than two miles apart. Archetenus deliberately built their house close to the property line so that Delilah and Zoya would be near each other. Almost every day, Zoya and Delilah visited each other and Delilah shared Ashley's letters with Zoya. Soon Zoya started to feel an attachment to Ashley and as soon as this feeling deepened images started to appear in Zoya's mind; images she could not understand.

As soon as Mathas read the note that Artis and Ralph found, he sent half of his soldiers back to the castle to search for the spies. These men were also told to tell the Queen about Angelina.

The Physician did not want the boca which carried Angelina to move quickly over the rough road. Those who Mathas now led traveled slowly.

Hugo had sent two of his warriors back to their village to tell of the attack and Angelina's injures. Hugo and the rest of his hunting party returned to the castle with Mathas and his men.

General Amundsen was a man of honor. He held his position as Commanding General of Fort Friada not as much for power as for his genuine concern for the citizens of his kingdom. He had not received his rank by commission but he worked his way up the ranks of the army.

Amundsen grew up in the huge and open City of Port Friada. He loved its beauty and the excited energy that always seemed to fill the streets. But he was not a naïve man. He understood the dangers and the darkness that filled those same streets. Amundsen always had a heavy presence of soldiers in the city to protect the citizens and hopefully to stop problems before they got out of hand. It was because of the Generals' proactive philosophy that Hector moved his child trafficking business to Leven, a smaller and trusting community.

During his journey to the monastery, Amundsen continually chastised himself for now knowing about Hector's heinous operations. It was on this journey that Amundsen realized he needed to become more involved with other communities in the vast kingdom. As he thought about the ways in which he could accomplish this goal, he decided they needed to build at least one more fort in Ganz. Amundsen decided that he would meet with King Friada when he returned from the monastery.

King Friada was an elderly man who never had children. His family had sat on the throne of Ganz for lifetimes and the King was well aware that he was the last of his line. This King was not only very intelligent but he was a faithful follower of The Great Ruler. Friada had spent years setting up a system of governmental levels to allow his people more power in their own lives.

And he had spent decades watching the leaders of his communities looking for his successor; this was a secret that Friada shared only with the Sanuri.

The soldiers who returned to the castle in advance of King Mathas quickly briefed their officers about the battle and the spies. Major Marshal dispatched troops to search the grounds of the castle as well as to provide increased protection for the Queen. He sent soldiers to inform the officers garrisoned at the castles of Fahron and Claudius about the threat as well as sending a company of men to escort the King back to his home.

It was late afternoon when General Amundsen and his troops arrived at the monastery outside of Leven. High Priest Barnabas had rooms prepared as well as a feast. He planned to have a long talk with the General about several issues.

Amundsen was rather surprised at the gracious reception but he was all business and wanted to see the children first. The children had already eaten their dinner and were in a playground that the priests and team members had created. Although the children appeared to be having fun, Amundsen did not speak; not one word. The Sanuri and High Priest Barnabas were escorting Amundsen and now directed him to Barnabas' office.

"General, I do not know you well enough to be able to read your silence," said Barnabas. "We have much to discuss so we might as well start now. What are your thoughts about the children?"

"I am so angry that I am afraid if I speak my words will offend both of you," said Amundsen. "This whole business makes me realize that I have to expand my role. The city is my primary jurisdiction but you know as well as I that Hector moved his business to Leven, thinking that I would not find out. I plan to meet with King Friada when I return. I am going to ask him for permission to build more forts to protect our people. So if there is anything you want me to ask the King for; add it to my list."

"I know the King well actually," said the Sanuri. "I would suggest that Barnabas attend that meeting with you. Both of you are well respected leaders who care about the people; I do believe you can open his eyes." Amundsen looked at Barnabas who nodded.

"Lieutenant Collins told me you have created a mission to protect the children," Amundsen said to Barnabas. "Just how do you plan to do that?"

"Oh, I had ideas until I heard Thaos speak, then I realized I had no understanding of the real problems. I don't know if you are familiar with him, the adopted son of General Claudius of Lentz. Thaos told us about his life as an orphan on the streets of Port Friada. I cannot tell you how disturbing his words were."

"After I listened to him, I had meetings with my priests. And these are some of the things we have come up with. We will build an orphanage here at the monastery, so we can protect the children. As you know the priests routinely go into the communities to administer to the people. We plan to buy or build offices or homes, we are still working out the details, for children to come to. We will take care of them there then bring them to the orphanage."

"We will be spreading the word about our; I don't know what to call them yet, safe houses so to speak and the orphanage. We plan to start in Leven and work our way to all of the cities and villages."

"I very much like your ideas. You will need building supplies, housing supplies as well as horses and bocas. It would help for you to have some idea of numbers when we speak with the King. I will offer my men to help with the building projects and to escort your priests back and forth to the monastery but I would ask that you start in Port Friada. And I can tell you now you will need a very large building."

"Now for another matter," Amundsen continued. "My men raided Hector's compound. We arrested his men and burned the damn place to the ground."

"But we can't find Hector or his right hand man Clev. I've got wanted posters all over the city and my men are taking them to neighboring villages and cities. It is almost like someone warned him we were coming. I am now wondering if he has spies in my fort."

"While that is a real possibility," said the Sanuri. "He also has the backing of some powerful demons."

"Sanuri, you know I respect you but I just can't wrap my brain around the idea of demons or Angels. But on the other hand, I can't explain many of the things that have happened in my city. Now, Lieutenant Collins and all of his men are talking about fighting alongside of Angels here and at that farm. I really don't know what to say about any of it."

"I am about to tell you both something that does not leave this room," said the Sanuri. "At least not yet. But before I reveal that secret I must tell you General that while I too respect you and understand your skepticism, you will never be able to protect your kingdom if you do not understand your enemy. And for whatever reason; your city draws dark lords. Now let me explain that statement. Dark lords are everywhere as are ordinary criminals. But most communities don't realize who or what dark lords are and they certainly do not stand up against them as the people in Port Friada do."

"Dark lords are exposed and embattled in your city, yet they continue to come. There has to be a reason that I don't yet understand. You are a man of battle. You know you have to understand your enemy. You, my general need to open your mind and you need to pray. I am sure that Barnabas will help you with both of these matters. Now please don't interrupt until I am finished," said the Sanuri with his hand raised to stop Amundsen from speaking.

"I am an old friend as well as a spiritual advisor to King Friada. He has been watching many of his leaders for a long time as he tries to determine his successor to the throne. We have had numerous conversations about this subject and General, you are our first choice."

"But the King as I, am concerned that you will not be able to fulfill all the requirements of that position. You see Friada understands about Angels and demons and he believes strongly in The Great Ruler."

The blood drained from Amundsen's face as the Sanuri spoke. "Understand that I am not telling you what to do but you will need to make some choices not only for yourself but for the people of Ganz. I can see that this collaboration between you and Barnabas will produce great things but you must learn of each other. General, tonight let Barnabas and me tell you of The Great Ruler then you can make your choices."

Matthew spent the night sitting next to Angelina's bed. He couldn't sleep or talk and he refused to eat. He prayed and stared at his wife.

Ryan was brought to Mathas' castle and Fahron and Isadore came as soon as they were told of the battle. Mathas and Rosa wrote letters to Sorren, Shara and Sudfad. Nikki and Ingr did not want to write to their husbands about the battle until Sorren was notified. The Court Physician spent the night at the castle.

Just before dawn Angelina started to groan and move a little at first but it progressed to thrashing. Matthew ran out of the room and got the Physician who was in the chambers next door.

Bella, Ingr, Nikki, their children and their nurses shared one of the large chambers in the same hallway. They were awakened by the men's voices and ran to Angelina's chambers.

"What's wrong with her?" asked Matthew frantically.

"I don't know yet and I need to concentrate," replied the Physician as he examined the Princess. "She doesn't have a fever, that is good and her wound isn't infected."

"I wonder if there was some kind of poison on that sword," said Nikki.

"Miranda are you doing this?" asked Ingr. The Physician scowled at Ingr when she spoke so she moved into the parlor. "Miranda."

Miranda's voice was heard only by Ingr. "It is not a physician she needs. Angelina is on a journey. Hugo knows the old medicines; bring him to Angelina and tell him my words."

"Did she get pulled into hell?"

"Not in the way you are thinking. She is on Jacob's path."

"What does that mean?"

"She will tell you when she wakes."

"Can I tell Matthew?"

"You can tell anyone although do not expect the Physician to believe you."

Ingr ran into the bedroom and said loudly, "Nikki get Hugo. Matthew, I just spoke with Miranda and she said Angelina is on a journey and needs Hugo because he knows the old medicines. She said Angelina is on Jacob's path and will tell us about it when she wakes up."

"What is that dribble you are saying?" asked the Physician angrily.

"It's not dribble. Miranda is an Angel and she said you wouldn't believe me," Ingr said. Nikki and Hugo ran into the bedroom and Ingr repeated Miranda's words.

"Matthew, I need a pen and paper," Hugo said.

"Bella there is some in the desk next to you," said Matthew then he turned to the Physician. "Hugo will take over now."

"But My Lord I must protest."

"I am sorry," said Matthew.

"If she dies it is not on my head," said the Physician angrily and stomped out of the room.

Hugo wrote for several moments. "Nikki, Ingr make these tonics. If the cooks don't have any of these herbs then come to me at once. And she will need some soothing tea, whatever you can find. And I certainly will need some coffee."

"Bella will you check on the nurses and the children?" Ingr asked.

"Certainly, you just do what you need to," Bella said to her daughters then she turned to Hugo. "How can I help?"

"Bring more candles in here. Angelina may be in a very dark place and perhaps we can send her light." Hugo looked at Matthew. "I need you to move your chair to the other side of the bed. Hold her hand and tell her that we are here. Even if she can't respond she can hear you. Tell her what Miranda said then just keep talking to her until I am ready to do more."

Hugo opened his medical bag and started to take items out and arrange them on the small table next to the bed. Rosa and Mathas ran into the room and Hugo motioned for them to be quiet. He finished organizing the items then prayed over them. Then Hugo turned and walked up to the King and Queen and motioned for them to go into the parlor.

"Did Ingr tell you what Miranda said?" asked Hugo.

"Yes, but we don't really understand," Rosa said.

"It is difficult to explain but Angelina was near death; we believe that the warrior's soul goes on a journey so to speak. It is on such a journey that the warrior might speak with an Angel or ask to be in the presence of The Great Ruler. But Angelina speaks with Angels in this world and she believes strongly in The Great Ruler. Miranda said Angelina was on Jacob's path."

"A person cannot walk someone else's path without permission from the heavens. Angelina must have great concerns about something to make such a request. Do you know what that could be?"

"Well there were the concerns when they first found Jacob," said Mathas. "But the children have been in Wetpr for the last few months if something happened they did not tell us."

"Rosa please tell Matthew to come out here," asked Hugo. "Hold Angelina's hand and keep talking to her so she knows she is not alone. It really doesn't matter what you say."

Moments later Matthew joined his father and Hugo in the parlor where Hugo repeated every word he had said to Mathas and Rosa.

"I know she has been having a lot of nightmares lately but she says she doesn't remember what they are about. Angelina never had nightmares before. Are you saying she volunteered to go to hell or something?" Matthew asked as horror filled his being.

"I don't know where she is but whatever she is doing is for your son," Hugo said.

Matthew ran back into the bedroom and grabbed one of his swords; he pulled it from its sheath and placed it on top of the blankets. He wrapped Angelina's fingers around the hilt. Then he took off his crystal necklace and placed that in the hand that Rosa was holding.

"May the holiness of The Great Ruler engulf you and Jacob." Angelina started to moan louder. "Miranda give me the words," Matthew yelled.

"She is trying to save your son from a curse that the demons who killed his parents placed upon him," Miranda's voice could be heard by everyone in the chambers. Nikki and Ingr had just entered also. "To do that she needs to go back to the beginning when the curse was placed. Angelina is a healer; she understood what she must do. She allowed herself to be wounded so she could take such a journey. But she does not have to take it alone."

"What do I need to do?" Matthew asked.

"We are going too," said Nikki.

Miranda now appeared in the chambers. "This is a dangerous thing you propose."

"Why? Can't you come where we must go? I thought The Great Ruler could go anywhere," said Ingr.

Miranda smiled and everyone in the room felt her warmth. "The three of you lie on the bed next to Angelina with your swords in your hands."

"I'll get our swords," said Nikki and started to leave the room.

"Wait there are extras here," said Matthew as he handed his friends weapons. As soon as they were all lying on the bed, Miranda kissed each one of them on their foreheads and they became unconscious.

Miranda turned to Rosa, Bella, Hugo and Mathas and explained, "We had allowed Angelina to have visions of Jacob's future because of the curse. She had already sensed that something was wrong and had prayed for insight. She remembered the nightmares but she knew Matthew would never allow her to take such a journey."

"This is like the spiritual journeys of old," said Hugo. "They are being tested for their faith and courage."

"And love," said Miranda.

"May I join them?" asked Hugo.

"They will need you to lead them back," Miranda said and disappeared.

"This is terrifying," said Rosa as they stared at the four young people lying on the bed.

# Chapter IX
## A Dark Place

Matthew, Ingr and Nikki had no memory of moving between worlds. Their souls suddenly appeared next to Angelina. All four of the warriors thought they looked the same as when they were in their bodies; they could not immediately tell the differences. Matthew hugged and kissed Angelina as did Nikki and Ingr.

"Before you yell at me, I heard what Miranda told you," said Angelina. "We have to go back to destroy the demons before they set the curse in motion."

"So are we in the past?" asked Nikki.

"I think this is more than the past but I don't really understand it," said Angelina. "We are in a cave now. I jumped in here when I heard that you were coming. But this seems like a world, I mean instead of a dream or hell. You can walk on the ground and smell flowers and hear things. But I don't really know where I am yet, I mean in relation to the demons. I asked to be taken to the time I needed and I woke up here. And I think all of you are fools but I am glad you are here with me."

"So tell us how you knew something was wrong with Jacob?" Matthew asked. "I didn't notice anything."

"It is hard to explain," replied Angelina. "I am not sure there is anything wrong with him yet. You know how the Sanuri always says that his visions are like pieces of a puzzle that he has to figure out? Well, I would be carrying Jacob or bathing him and I would see images that flashed in my head but then they were gone in a second. At first I thought it was because I was tired. And as I dismissed them they seemed to come more often."

"Finally I called to Miranda and she told me to pray. After I prayed I started to have nightmares. Detailed nightmares about Jacob. I saw him turning into a monster like Roch. Then, ok I am going to make this short because I don't know how much time we have here."

"I saw Jacob when he was a tiny baby in a cradle in a kitchen with a woman who I believe was his mother. Roch rides up to the house and she offers him food. He attacks her but before he can really hurt her Miranda shows her face and tells Roch to leave. He is so scared that when he leaves he trips over furniture and runs out of the house. Later that woman finds a ring on the floor. It was one of those blood rings but I felt that it was much stronger than the others we saw people wear."

"Then I saw a man that must have been Jacob's father come home and the mother shows him the ring. He puts it on then I see Roch's face take over the man's face. Then I see, I guess the man committing crimes and beating Jacob's mother. Then I see them in that hunting cabin with two chests and demons climbing in the windows. Miranda protected Jacob so they never saw him. But those demons took Roch's ring and the chests when they left. They gave it to someone whose face I could not see. He was wearing a robe with the hood up but I see him before an unholy altar holding the ring."

"I couldn't really understand his words but somehow I knew that he was cursing Jacob with the power of that ring. Then my dreams turned to Jacob turning into a monster. I prayed for guidance and in that exact moment I remembered my mother and grandmother teaching me about the spiritual journeys of our ancestors and I knew what I had to do. Miranda explained to me how they worked then I just had to set up the situation. I was going to tell you but then we were attacked yesterday and I just knew it was time."

"We will talk about that later," said Matthew. "Don't you ever keep anything like this from me again. But what exactly do we have to do. Stop the demon's from killing his parents or get the ring from them or stop that guy in the robe?"

"I don't know. I think part of this journey is to figure that out. Or maybe it has to do with choices. All I know is that we are in the right time that we have to be," said Angelina.

"Then let's go outside and start walking," said Ingr.

They walked out of the cave and found themselves in a thick jungle. "This was farm fields when I went into the cave," Angelina said. "I wonder why the change?"

"Miranda which way do we go?" asked Ingr.

"We go that way," Matthew said as he started to walk through the foliage.

The one thing that Angelina did not tell Matthew and her friends was that she had been telling her mother, Shara, about the visions and the nightmares. Shara was a powerful healer of the old medicines and understood what Angelina must do. The two women researched everything they could find about the ancient journeys.

Now, Angelina wore two additional pouches on the weapons belt of her warrior's uniform. Both pouches contained special mixtures of herbs. One concoction was to protect Angelina and the other was to help her return to her world.

Samael was fixated on the monastery, so much so that he again pulled Hector and Clev into his domain. "Amundsen, himself led troops to the monastery," Samael snapped. "The Commanding General does not do routine patrols. And a general from Lentz leads a large army to the monastery. What is going on?" As Samael yelled he showed images of the World of Nunc to the two men.

Hector walked closer to the images and studied them. Samael was blocked by The Great Ruler from seeing inside of the monastery.

"This could be very bad," Hector said. "High Priest Barnabas and Amundsen are the two main leaders of Ganz and if they are working something out with the Sanuri...."

"Now, the human finally understands," Samael said sarcastically. "I would suggest you find out what is going on."

Hector turned to Samael and said, "My army is gone. I will need another, although it is not an army that will get us the information we need."

"Are we in our world but in a different time?" asked Nikki. "Because it seems like the same world."

"I don't know," said Angelina.

Matthew was walking slightly ahead of the women since he seemed to be the one who was given a sense of the direction they needed to travel. Now he raised his right hand into the air and closed his fist twice to signal the women to stop because there were others in the area.

The four immediately concealed themselves in the foliage of the jungle they were in. They watched as a man with short white hair rode on a white horse through the forest. He wore the robes of a priest but his saddle and the tack of his horse were trimmed with silver. No other men rode with him but he was surrounded by strange creatures.

The creatures walked on two legs like humans but they were shorter than an adult male and covered with long hair. All of the creatures were a reddish color and they appeared to be powerfully built. But what shocked the onlookers was that the faces of these creatures kept changing. Only the face of the human stayed the same.

As the warriors from Lentz watched this entourage pass, Angelina quickly covered her mouth as she gasped. This movement was not noticed by the man and his creatures who were riding in the direction of the cave that Angelina and the others had been in.

Matthew, Nikki and Ingr could see the look of terror on Angelina's face; something none of them had ever seen before. They decided to let the group pass without conflict. When they were convinced that the demonic group was no longer in the area they stood up.

"Angelina what did you see?" asked Matthew.

She did not answer her husband's question but softly called to Miranda. "Miranda, why is it that I see the face of Jacob on one of those monsters? Why have you shown us this?"

"I didn't see Jacob's face," said Ingr.

"I have seen him as an adult," Angelina said then again called to Miranda.

The Angel appeared before them. "As time passes you will see many familiar faces on those demons. They wear the masks of the souls their master owns."

"How could he own Jacob's soul?" asked Matthew.

"Because of the blood in Roch's ring. That was the blood of the demon Omnibus. The real monster in that group was the one who appeared to be human. You are no longer on your world you are inside of it?"

"I don't understand," said Matthew. "Actually, I don't understand any of this."

"Miranda, I don't know why but I am feeling there is a lot more to this," said Ingr. "We are here for more than Jacob aren't we?"

"When The Great Ruler created this world it was a paradise and all of His children lived as one family. But the seeds of darkness took hold and soon they called the demons in. Before the demons came there were no kingdoms because people did not fear their neighbors. In fact, there was no fear. There was no hatred in the sense that you know now."

"The Great Ruler wept when His children welcomed the demons with open arms. As soon as the demons took their souls the people were filled with fears, hatred and paranoia. A very dark time engulfed your world as people now killed, raped and persecuted others."

"People built walls and clung to groups for protection. You are all familiar with the Rogetts, they were once humans who moved into the dark places of this world because of their fears. Then they turned into the very monsters they sought to escape."

"They were not the only group to go underground. You are now in the Kingdom of Inferus."

"An exceptionally intelligent group of people believed there was a world within the World of Nunc. They too sought to escape the demons and horror that was filling the world above ground. They designed tools and they burrowed within your world until they came to the eighth level, which is where we are now. And they built a world that rivals the one you know."

"This race is called Elods and although they sought to flee the darkness and to build a perfect world like The Great Ruler had originally given to them their humanity could not resist temptation and they too called the demons in. This race is considerably more intelligent than most humans. And they have a great advantage in that they know your world exists. And they can travel between the worlds. They walk among you. And you have met them before."

"Is that what Madeline and Javier are?" asked Matthew.

"Yes. Like every civilization there are factions within the groups. There are many of this race who would like to once again live in the world that you know. So they pit humans against humans and humans against demons. They want you to weaken and destroy each other then they will attack."

"Can't they just live in the world with us?" Nikki asked.

"They look upon humans as you looked upon those demons that just walked past you. If they took control of your world, people would be rounded up and treated as cattle. They have been watching your world for lifetimes. They understand the fears and motivations and they prey upon them to get what they want; very much like the demons you are familiar with."

"But you and I mean all of you here and the others who stand with The Seven Sons have caused a great deal of interest and confusion in this world. There are factions in Inferus who applaud and admire what you are doing but the faction who desires the world above sees you as an obstacle to their goals."

"Javier, Madeline and others were originally sent to your world to gather information and to incite wars. Now their assignment is to find out everything they can about those who stand with you."

"They are not familiar with the prophesies and are trying to obtain information from demons as well as humans. When you return to your world you must tell the others what I have told you. Even the Sanuri does not know of this world."

"We certainly will," said Matthew. "But I don't understand how this involves Jacob."

"When many of you were in Ryed, Ruth told your group that there were prophesies that involved your children. The numbers, the sexes, the characters of your children are spelled out in ancient prophesies. And yet none of you have attempted to learn of these prophesies. Two new races have been created in your lifetime. Ruala and human and Shettee and Ruala. Some of you have named your children after Angels. And all of you have surrendered your children to The Great Ruler."

"It is no coincidence that The Seven Sons and the team members have decided to have families. Although we continue to tell you, none of you realize how powerful you are and how different you are from others because of your choices. Do you think that your children could be considered a new race? And when I say this I am talking about the children you raise, those born to you and those who are adopted."

"You are the first peoples of this world to unite for the purpose of standing up to darkness. You have torn down the walls of fear and prejudice and learned to love and respect each other. You are doing things never before done in this world and your children admire you. Don't you think they too will change this world?"

"All of those babies you care for and protect will be warriors, healers, teachers, priests, scribes, poets and kings. They are gifts to this world and more than the heavens can understand that. Zoya told you that Jacob would make you very proud someday and he will for he will be a mighty warrior, a leader and a faithful servant of The Great Ruler. But his path was stolen from him. And you have chosen to put him back on this path."

"The Elods have many attributes that most humans do not. In your world a seer or a prophet is not often seen. In Inferus everyone has the ability of second sight; some are stronger than others. The dark lord you just saw had sent emissaries into your world. Is was from these Elods that Jacob's father stole and it was not just gold that he stole but documentation the spies had been gathering. All of you thought the two chests that were missing from that hunting cabin contained the bounty that Juleta had placed upon you. They did not."

"As you can imagine Gilder; that is the name of the dark lord, was more concerned with retrieving the documentation than the gold. Jacob's father wore the ring that Roch lost. That ring contained the blood of Omnibus. The blood called to other demons. Gilder knew this and as he searched for the ring he became more familiar with Roch which led him to Sudfad's family and so on. When the ring was located, Gilder watched Jacob's family for several days before he set his demons upon them. Gilder saw the power in the child."

"You know I concealed Jacob from the demons and brought him to you. Gilder did not understand what happened to the boy but later Madeline reported to him that you had the child. Gilder took this as an opportunity. He used the ring which contained the blood of the demon but also had the blood of Jacob's father on it and he cursed your child to use as a weapon against you."

"So, does he actually own Jacob's soul now?" asked Angelina. "Because Jacob seems so normal."

"We have delayed the curse from taking hold. But Jacob is getting older and can make his own choices. You must understand that Jacob will be a powerful warrior whether he works for The Great Ruler or the demons. That is why I led him to parents who would brave hell itself to save their son."

"What must we do?" asked Matthew.

"I will return you to your world but it will not be on the same day as you left. You cannot stop Jacob's parents from being killed because of the choices they made. But you must stop the demons from delivering that ring to Gilder. The demons are low level and you have the ability to kill them without my help."

"But you are outnumbered. Pray for protection from the evil of that ring. The ring is stronger than the demons who have it. Once you have the ring pray that The Great Ruler engulf it with His Holiness, it is the only thing that can destroy the ring's power. Do not affect anything else in that time."

"How outnumbered are we?" asked Matthew.

Miranda did not answer his question. "There are others who have asked to join you on your journey. Sorren, has received word of Angelina but Shara had already told him what Angelina planned to do. Mathas, Hugo, Raul, Simon, Gabriel and Raphael have prayed to be allowed to help you. You will need Hugo to bring you back. This is your journey and the future of your son weighs upon your decisions today."

"That would give us three of The Seven Sons in addition to powerful priests and warriors," said Matthew. "Do not force anyone but if they request then we would appreciate the help." In that instance Miranda disappeared and in her place stood, Sorren, Mathas, Gabriel, Raphael, Raul and Simon. All of the men carried weapons. Sorren grabbed his daughter and hugged her while Matthew spoke.

"We have so very much to tell you but that will have to be later. Right now we are in the past. Jacob's father was wearing the ring that Roch lost, the ring containing the blood of Omnibus. This ring contains great evil so we must all pray for protection."

"We can't save Jacob's parents but we must get the ring from the demons. Only The Great Ruler can destroy the evil in that ring. The demons can be killed but there may be a lot of them. We cannot affect anything else in this time."

"I know where we are," said Simon. "We are about a mile east of that hunting cabin.

"Sorren is no longer among you," Miranda's voice whispered into the ears of the Sanuri.

"Should I join him?"

"No, your presence is needed here. The eyes of many are watching this monastery, wondering why two armies converge on it."

Simon and the others were on foot but running since they had no idea of how much time they had on this journey.

"Daughter, we will not get into this now but the next time you contemplate going into hell to save one of my grandbabies, you will discuss it with me first," said Sorren.

The men in the group all smiled as they listened to him speak. Suddenly Matthew turned around. "Sorren how did you find out about this anyways?"

"Angelina and Shara have been researching such a journey for a while. Shara told me because we both knew it was just a matter of time before Angelina would do something to get herself hurt so she could take this journey. When I got the note from Mathas and Rosa that she had been hurt I started calling to Miranda."

"So I am the only one who didn't know about this," Matthew said sternly and gave Angelina a disapproving look.

"Matthew normally such a journey is not taken as a group," said Angelina. "And one has to really understand what they are doing. Of all of you here, Father is the only one who realizes what is happening."

"What do you mean?" asked Raphael.

"I guess the best way to explain this is that it is like Miranda allowed all of you to join me in my dream. I will try to find a better way to explain..."

Raul was in the lead and now held his hand up and closed his fist twice. Everyone ducked down in the foliage. They heard screaming. Gabriel started to stand but Sorren pulled him back into concealment. Suddenly they heard a rustle in the brush to their right. Everyone grabbed their weapons as they turned but instead of seeing demons they saw an image of Miranda walking in the forest holding Jacob's hand.

Jacob appeared as he did when Angelina found him but both Miranda and Jacob had a wispy dreamlike appearance and did not respond to the group.

"I will take that as our sign," said Simon and moved towards the screaming. It was only a matter of moments before they could see the little hunting cabin. "I count eight so far," whispered Simon as they looked at demons who were standing outside of the cabin, while the screaming continued inside.

"Next time I am bringing my bow," Angelina said with a grin and looked at Matthew who scowled at her.

"Since we had a little time to prepare, we brought extra weapons," said Mathas and smiled. He untied his cape and threw it from his shoulders. He had three small cross bows and quivers of arrows over his shoulders. Gabriel and Raphael both started taking extra knives and daggers from their belts and boots and handing them to the others.

"Why don't you let the three of us take the bows," said Nikki. Angelina, Nikki and Ingr all took bows and spread out in the forest.

"Stay concealed until they come for the girls," Sorren whispered.

All Nordes warriors were exceptional archers. The first volley of arrows hit their marks with perfection. Three demons fell dead to the ground as their comrades looked into the dense forest. Three more arrows flew through the still air and three more demons fell dead. The two remaining demons who were in front of the cabin each let out a howl-like sound and dove for cover.

Three more demons ran from the rear of the cabin to the front. The women killed these three as soon as they exposed themselves to the archers. The two demons that were hiding now saw where the arrows were coming from and let out a different sounding howl. Now six more blood covered demons ran out of the cabin. Now that they had reinforcements, the two demons jumped to their feet and led a charge into the forest.

115

"Girls keep your eyes on the cabin," yelled Matthew as the seven men stood up and charged towards the demons. Nikki shot a demon as he ran past her. Then she turned her attention back to the cabin.

The demons ran on two legs like humans although they were slightly larger. They bellowed and the humans screamed war cries as the beings clashed. Sorren threw a knife that struck one of the demons between the eyes and impaled its brain. The demon fell dead. All of the demons carried weapons of some sort, clubs, axes or swords.

Simon ran up and kicked a demon behind its knee causing the demon to stumble as it swung an axe at Gabriel. "Thanks," Gabriel yelled as he thrust his sword through the stomach of the beast. The demon screamed at Gabriel and yanked at the sword as Gabriel pulled it out of the creature who was now trying to get the sword from him. Gabriel grabbed a dagger from his belt and lunged towards the demon stabbing it in the heart.

"There's howling coming from inside the cabin," yelled Ingr. The men heard her but they were all too busy fighting to look.

Angelina shot her arrow at the head of a demon as it peeked out of the cabin. She heard the demon bellow as it quickly pulled its head back but she could not see if she hit it.

The demons were not quick on their feet or agile but they were powerful. One of them punched Mathas so hard that it momentarily took his breath away. Matthew plunged his sword into the demon's back. The demon turned to see its new adversary while Mathas swung a battleaxe and crushed the demon's skull.

Sorren ran to Raul who was rolling on the ground with a demon. Raul saw Sorren and threw his weight so that he rolled onto his back with the demon on top of him. Sorren stabbed the demon in the back twice before it fell forward.

Raul pushed the dead demon off from him and ran to Simon. A demon had Simon backed up to a tree and was pounding Simon's head against it. Matthew grabbed the demon that Simon was fighting with by the arms. Allowing Simon to stab it repeatedly.

"Matthew!" yelled Angelina. "The ring!"

Raphael cut the throat of the last demon and all of the men now ran towards the cabin. Three demons were trying to escape. Two were carrying small chests and one had a pulsating dark cloud around him. The three women shot arrows at the trio. The two demons carrying chests fell dead. The arrow bounced off from the demon within the cloud.

"He must be wearing the ring," yelled Gabriel as all of the warriors now ran towards the demon. "Miranda what do we do?" One word was heard by all of the warriors, "Pray." "Great Ruler destroy the evil that is before us," Gabriel yelled and every warrior repeated his words. And they continued to repeat the prayer as they ran towards the cloud of darkness.

# Chapter X
## My Name is Adam

The spirits returned to the bodies of the warriors simultaneously. Matthew, Angelina, Nikki and Ingr were lying on the bed. Mathas, Raul, Simon, Raphael and Gabriel were lying on the floor of the same bedroom and Sorren was lying on the bed of his room at the monastery at Leven.

They each shot up to sitting positions and looked around wide-eyed as they were initially disoriented. "Did we stop it?" Matthew asked frantically. No one answered. "Miranda did we stop it?" he asked in a louder voice.

"Your prayers destroyed the ring," Miranda's voice said. "Gilder no longer owns Jacob's soul. But none of this has been erased from the memory of the dark lord. Gilder knows he lost the ring and Jacob's soul, he just doesn't understand how."

Hugo, Rosa, Bella, Nyla, Saran, Nina, Isadore, Fahron and Ryan were all in the chambers watching the bodies of their friends and family members. But Miranda stopped time for just a moment as she returned the spirits to the warriors and answered Matthew's question. Now as Miranda stopped speaking all of these people realized the warriors had returned. Tears were flowing as people hugged and kissed. After several minutes Matthew said, "We have much to tell you."

When Sorren's spirit returned to his body, the Sanuri was sitting next to his bed. Sorren too sat up and was momentarily disoriented. But he was allowed to hear Miranda speaking to Matthew. Then Miranda filled Sorren's head with the words and images that she had shared with Matthew, Ingr, Angelina and Nikki when they were in the Kingdom of Inferus.

"Sanuri, we have to have a meeting with everyone," Sorren said as he jumped off from his bed. "Wait, perhaps I should speak with Thaos and Stephan first."

"You stay here and I will get them," the Sanuri said and stood up to leave. "Drink some water, I don't know why but it always helps."

"Do you want to read these?" Michael asked as he handed letters to Rachel, Batina, Kate and Ashley. The women were in the kitchen of the monastery helping to prepare food.

"Michael, I have never seen you smile like that," Batina said. "It is nice to see you happy."

Kate smiled as she handed the letter she had been reading to Rachel. "That one is from Raul and it certainly sounds like he and Simon are attached to your sisters and they sound so cute."

"Michael, I don't mean to pry but I am reading a letter from your sister Saran. Why are men trying to attack them?" asked Ashely.

"Didn't anyone tell you?" Michael asked in surprise.

"Michael, that is your business; we didn't say anything," said Batina.

"Ashley, I don't mean to be rude but I will let the girls tell you. I really don't want to have to talk about it," Michael said. Then he looked at Batina, Kate and Rachel. "You can tell people, I don't care anymore, especially since my sisters are safe."

Selen and Hilgra walked into the kitchen. Each woman was carrying two baskets that were piled high with vegetables from the garden. "You can tell them too," Michael said and nodded towards the two women.

The Sanuri walked into the kitchen, "Michael can you come with me for a moment?" Sorren wants to have a small meeting before he holds a larger one."

When Michael and the Sanuri entered Sorren's room, Thaos and Stephan were already sitting on the bed. Sorren waited until Michael closed the door before he spoke. He first explained about the ancient medicines and the beliefs of their tribe in journeys of the spirit that warriors could take.

"Why am I getting a bad feeling about this?" asked Thaos.

"Everyone is alright so don't worry," Sorren said.

"Who do you mean by everyone?" Stephan asked anxiously.

"Just let me finish the story," Sorren said then he explained about Angelina's visions about Jacob and the research that she and Shara had done into the old medicines. Then Sorren explained the attack by Karzman's men and Angelina's injuries.

"Those stinking bastards went after our children!" Stephan said and punched the headboard.

"Stephan, truly everyone is alright but I have so much more to tell you," Sorren said and proceeded to explain the journey that Angelina started and others were allowed to join. He watched the color drain from the faces of both Thaos and Stephan as they listened in silence. Finally Sorren repeated the information that Miranda had given them about the Kingdom of Inferus."

"This shows you how damn crazy our lives have gotten that all of this is believable," Thaos said then he turned to Michael. "I don't know if Sudfad told you that he has been waiting for these missions to end so he can attack Karzman. He was going to go after your sisters and get revenge for you and Nadia. Well, now I going with him. Those bastards tried to kill my family."

"Wait!" said Michael angrily. "I didn't know anything about this. Why wouldn't he tell me?"

"Because he wants you to heal," said the Sanuri. "Even though the two of you haven't known each other long, he is your father and he cares about you as a father. It breaks his heart to know what happened to you, Nadia and your sisters."

"Well, I hope to hell he doesn't think he is going without me," Michael said.

"Without us," said Stephan angrily. "Although right now I am not sure if I am more mad at Karzman or Ingr."

"First we have to end this mission," said the Sanuri. "And all of you are letting the fear and horror of that journey keep you from realizing the gift we have been given."

"I never knew about the Kingdom of Inferus and now many things are making sense to me...."

The Sanuri did not finish his sentence because there was a knock on the door then it opened. "We are sorry to barge in like this," said Kate as six women now entered the tiny room. "But we have something to tell you. Michael showed us his letters and told us that we could tell Ashley, Hilgra and Selen about his past." Kate turned to Selen. "Selen, you explain it."

"I know the name Karzman, because it is so unusual. I heard Juleta say it several times. And one time I walked into the parlor when she and Hector were talking. They didn't seem to notice me at first and were talking about Karzman attacking both the Kings of Stordt and Wetpr. They wanted to give him men and power; I don't know what Juleta meant when she said power. Then Hector says 'Why don't you just make another Karzman and they can each lead a battle'."

"Ladies will you gather our people, High Priest Barnabas and if General Amundsen is still here get him too," said the Sanuri. "We will meet in the dining hall in ten minutes."

General Amundsen and his men were mounted and ready to leave the monastery when Batina ran up to them. Although the General acted annoyed he immediately postponed the departure and followed Batina to the meeting.

"Boy, we have been seeing a whole different side of you two," Kate said with a smile as Dack and Joao entered the dining hall and joined the women at their table. Joao was carrying Chasity and now set her on the bench between him and Dack.

"Chasity do you like your uncles?" Rachel asked.

"I love them," Chasity said with both pride and conviction. Both Joao and Dack looked at the little girl as her words touched their hearts. Kate was just about to speak when Sorren and the Sanuri walked to the front of the room.

Sorren spoke first and repeated his words from his smaller meeting. No one interrupted him. The group sat in both fascination and horror as they listened to first the story of the journey to save Jacob then to Miranda's words about the Kingdom of Inferus and the Elods.

"Michael do you and Selen want to tell the next part?" the Sanuri asked. Michael walked to the front of the room but only explained how he had been showing his letters to others and had told Kate, Batina and Rachel that they could tell people about his past. Selen was nervous speaking in front of the group and only explained the conversation she overheard between Juleta and Hector. Then she quickly returned to her seat.

The first person from the audience to speak was Edward, "We need to call to the Angels before we do anything else."

"I agree," said the Sanuri and turned to General Amundsen who was sitting at one of the front tables. The General had not spoken a word during the meeting. "The Angels don't appear to everyone," the Sanuri explained. "I tell you this only because you are at a crossroads in your belief in The Great Ruler and if they do not appear it will feed your skepticism. But also I am giving you the choice as to whether you want to be here. We will not force the heavens upon you."

The General turned and looked at the faces in the room. "Have the Angels appeared to all of you?" he asked.

"Yes," said Thaos. "And the majority of us were skeptical at first too."

"General before you make your decision know that once you have seen them your life will probably change," said Erebus seriously.

"How do you mean?" asked Amundsen.

Several people in the room started to laugh. "Erebus used to be a powerful warlock," Dagon said. "Now he is part of the family and team." The look on Amundsen's face caused others to join in the laughter.

Amundsen turned to the Sanuri and nodded. The General wasn't sure that he wanted to know if Angels existed as much as he did not want the others to think he was afraid; and afraid he was.

Although Hector had a high profile compound in Port Friada he had long ago established a series of hideouts and homes in various kingdoms of Opots. When Hector and Clev left Samael's hell domain, the demon transported them to the small coastal Village of Hafsfat in Ganz. This village was a two day ride northeast of the monastery at Leven.

Hector owned a modest home in this village. The house was on the beach and not conspicuous. He paid to have a housekeeper and a grounds man care for the house and he had six of his soldiers stationed there. The house was too small and too in the open for Hector to hide an army.

The villagers didn't know that Hector was a dark lord and many of them would not have understood what a dark lord was if they knew. He was not as reclusive in this small village as he had been in the City of Port Friada. Hector would frequent the businesses and walk on the docks to watch the fishermen unload their catches. But on this day he was looking at more than just the sights. He was looking for people to hire.

The Sanuri called to the Angels and asked if one of them would join the meeting. The people all stared at the front of the room waiting for Miranda, Daniel or Ruth to appear but they did not.

After a couple of minutes, the Sanuri again called to the Angels but this time he asked if they wanted to meet in another location. Since the Angels had previously appeared to everyone in the room except for General Amundsen the group suspected the Angels would not materialize before him.

No Angels appeared, nor did they speak to anyone in the group. "Perhaps I will go outside and try this again," said the Sanuri and took two steps towards the door when an unfamiliar voice was heard.

"Sanuri, that will not be necessary," said a deep male voice. General Amundsen swung around as he felt a presence next to him and gasped as he saw an Angel sitting beside him at the table. No one else in the room made a sound. The Angel was large and muscular and looked like a warrior. He had black curly hair and an intensity about him that everyone in the room could feel. "Tell me General; do you believe in Angels now?"

"Do my eyes betray me?" Amundsen asked meekly as he extended his right arm and gently touched the sleeve of the Angel with his fingertips. "You feel real. And there is something familiar about you; how can that be?"

"Because General, I have been talking to you for a long time. You have never asked whose voice you heard. You never questioned the moments when I allowed you to feel my presence. You never called to The Great Ruler for clarification. While The Great Ruler has infinite patience, I do not. Three Angels and an Arch Angel have appeared to these people countless times because the path of this world will affect so many others. The lives of beings in worlds you can't even imagine depend on the choices and the faith of a handful of warriors in Nunc."

"General, you have a role to play in all of this. But it is your choice as to how much of a role. The heavens listened as the Sanuri and High Priest Barnabas sat with you for hours and taught you about The Great Ruler. While your heart knew that what they said was true your mind refused to accept it. Accept it now General because we have work to do!"

The Angel stood up and walked to the front of the room. "I have been watching all of you for a long time. If you haven't figured out yet, Angels have assignments and my previous assignment was the World of Orantho which is in your same solar system. For those of you who do not understand this, the Sanuri can explain after I leave. But what you need to understand is that Orantho was dominated by the demon Samael centuries ago."

"The same demon who has conquered domains in your world. The same demon who now owns Hector's soul."

"Most of you in this room were in Ryed for the battle with Teivel. Miranda, Daniel and Ruth allowed you to see what the future held for that kingdom if Teivel completed his transformation. That is the World of Orantho. Those same individuals experienced changes in their sense of time. Those changes occurred because of the Scroll of Imari. But time affects all of the worlds as did the choices you made in Ryed."

"Many of you have been allowed glimpses of hells but there are countless worlds that would give anything for a glimpse of your world." As the Angel spoke he walked around the room in a challenging manner. "I asked Miranda, Ruth and Daniel not to come with me today because I have some questions for all of you. As individuals and as a group you have drawn not only the attention of the demons but of the heavens. You are men and women of courage, faith and integrity. You walk with Angels. You defy demons and you have chosen to transcend the limits of your humanity, even though you are doing that in baby steps."

"Notice I said you have chosen to transcend; it is all about choices. What I don't understand is while you believe in The Great Ruler and His emissaries you continually fail to grasp the significance of their words. Erebus the man who once walked with the shadows sees things more clearly than the rest of you. Is it that you want so badly to believe in the goodness of man that you are blinding yourselves? Is it out of fear that you do not listen? Who among you can give me an answer?" No one in the room spoke.

"Erebus, you once said that watching this group was like watching children trying to touch fire and the Angels keep pulling their hands back and warning them they will get burned. I am going to tell you this but once; if you get burned so do others. Because of the choices you have made your destinies have changed and you now effect the lives of worlds you will never see. But your faith, your courage, your choices will transcend the physical boundaries of these worlds. Chasity is the only child in this room and she will be blocked from what I am to show you. Behold Orantho!"

The screams of the people in that dining hall were intermingled with the screams of the people in Orantho as the Angel opened a window in time and space and allowed the people in that room to witness the true meaning of horror. The glimpse of Orantho was brief, only seconds but for the people in that room it seemed like hours; hours they would never forget. When the Angel closed the window everyone in the room was weeping and many were puking.

"Do you know how you help save a world like that?" the Angel asked. "You should; the other Angels have told you repeatedly. You give them hope and you are lighting a small path for them to come to The Great Ruler. You see many of them have never heard of Him and they do not call to us. Think of it as a man in the water and you have just thrown him a life line. They are learning of us through you."

The Angel turned and looked at Amundsen. "Now General, I am going to tell you the same thing that the Arch Angel Michael told King Mathas of Lentz. Your kingdom is a doorway into the continent. How can you protect it if you fail to acknowledge that your enemies exist? As a general you are powerful but as a king you can help to stop the darkness that is encompassing the worlds. And I don't need to explain to you that darkness takes many forms."

"I have many gifts from The Great Ruler but patience isn't one of them. I do pray for help with this but it is difficult when I have to stand by and watch a world like Orantho. General, I can tell you do not understand what I am saying. The Great Ruler gave all of His creations freedom of choice. We do not take that away under any circumstances. So General make your choices now because just north of the monastery General Claudius will be leading his army into an ambush of demons." Everyone in the room now jumped out of their seats. "Sit back down!" yelled the Angel. "General what is your choice?"

"I will fight!" said Amundsen.

"We all know that," said the Angel. "And I know that you believe in The Great Ruler. But are you willing to go the extra steps?"

"Are you willing to call to the heavens and to listen and I mean really listen to the answers? You are a powerful man, but that kind of power is fleeting in this life. Are you willing to work with the others in this room? Are you willing to call the heavens in?"

"Yes," said Amundsen in almost a whisper.

"I guess we will see before this day is over," said the Angel to Amundsen. "I too will be working with all of you now. Every one of us presents ourselves in an image that you will recognize in this world. And what image am I presenting to you?"

"You sound just like Father," said Stephan. "I mean you sound like a military commander."

The Angel smiled. "Perhaps some of you who don't really listen to the others will listen to me. You have become very attached to the other Angels you work with. You think of them as family and friends. You name your children after them. But is your love of them preventing you from really listening to them? There are many things for you to think about."

"Now, everyone who wants to go with Amundsen to help General Claudius be prepared to leave in five minutes. You will be coming from the south and coming in behind the armies of demons who will surround the General. You will be greatly outnumbered. This is Amundsen's test."

"Now just wait a gal darn minute here," said Sorren angrily. "We have all been tested in this room. But with every test we learned from experience. Amundsen doesn't even know what to ask for. You would test him while risking the lives of others?"

The Angel smiled and said, "Chief Sorren, I was wondering if you were going to speak. What should Amundsen ask for?"

Sorren looked at Amundsen, "General, we all know you are great on the battlefield but that is with men and I don't know if anyone has explained to you yet that a lot of types of demons can't be killed by us. And there are even demons that the Sanuri can't kill. To lead your men against such an army is suicide."

"In the past when we have asked; the Angels would touch our weapons with holiness because demons can't stand up to holiness. We still have to fight the bastards but it equals out the playing field."

The Angel now looked at Amundsen. "Angel, would you touch us with holiness?" asked the General sheepishly.

"That is an even better request," said the Angel as every person in the room became momentarily disoriented as holiness surged through them.

"What is happening?" asked Amundsen as he saw the men and women in the room glowing. "Sorren perhaps you should ride in front with me."

"Sorren teach him the words. You are both commanders but you have been fighting on different planes," the Angel said.

Chasity had been sitting at a table between Joao and Dack, playing with a doll. She was oblivious to the Angel's presence. Suddenly she looked up and squealed, them she got off from the bench and ran to the Angel and hugged his legs. "Thank you for bringing us here," she said as the Angel picked her up. "Joao and Dack are my uncles. They are taking me home."

"I know," said the Angel.

"Chasity, what are you talking about?" asked Dack.

"When we were lost, Adam carried me and Logan and Marty here."

"Why didn't you tell us that?" asked Joao.

"I forgot," said Chasity.

"Is that your name?" asked Sorren.

"My name is Adam."

# Chapter XI
## Angels on the Battlefield

"What the hell!" yelled Claudius and stopped his horse as Miranda suddenly appeared on the road before him. The commanders who rode behind the general gave orders to the soldiers to halt. Claudius dismounted and walked towards the Angel as did Archetenus and Jared.

"The men who will lead the teams should stand here with you," Miranda said. Calen and Koby had been flying ahead of the army but now turned back when they saw Miranda.

"Vincente, Maddox, Henrich, Ira and Angus up front!" ordered Claudius. These men didn't know why the army stopped and now as they rode to the front of the formation they saw the Angel. The men dismounted and bowed before her.

"Do not bow before me," Miranda said. "Time is short so let me speak. Samael has legions of demons prepared to ambush you two miles ahead. They are cloaked and will materialize when they surround you. You are greatly outnumbered but General Amundsen is coming from the monastery with two thousand men and Sorren is leading the other team members and warriors."

"Will that be enough?" asked Maddox.

"Can we kill these demons?" Claudius asked.

"No to Claudius' question," said Miranda. "Archetenus can you answer Maddox's question?"

"Did you touch their swords?" asked Archetenus.

"And them," Miranda said. "A new Angel has joined us and he rides with them."

"He rides?" asked Claudius. "Well be that as it may, thank you for warning us. And will you touch us also?"

"Yes and what should be your second question?" asked Miranda.

"Will you help us defeat the demons?" asked Claudius.

Miranda smiled at Claudius then turned to the new team leaders who were standing in a group. "This is my first lesson with you. Never, ever hesitate to ask the questions that Claudius just did." Miranda searched the eyes of every man standing around her. "There are many learning lessons this day, including Samael. You cannot comprehend the power he wields. He came to this world specifically to crush those of you who would stand against darkness. Claudius, we are always with you and on this day I will ride with you."

Several of the men gasped as Miranda now appeared before them on a white stallion. Her long black hair was flowing but instead of her blue dress she wore a uniform which none of them recognized. Her breast plate was solid gold and gave off such a glow as to blind the men around her. Her sword appeared to be made of gold also.

"Miranda, you look incredible," said Archetenus. "What is that uniform?"

"We don't have time to talk," she said. "You will be touched as soon as we are surrounded."

"I'm not complaining," Sorren said to Amundsen as they led their small army northward. "I've just never seen an Angel on a horse before. But guess it makes sense because they can do everything."

Adam rode ahead of the army on a white stallion. He wore the same uniform as Miranda and his breast plate and sword were also made of gold.

Thaos, Stephan and the Sanuri rode in the second row behind Amundsen and Sorren. Michael, Edward and Gideon rode in the third row. The team members followed, then the priests from the monastery then the soldiers of Ganz. "Why aren't you up front?" Stephan asked the Sanuri.

"It is not my day to learn lessons," the Sanuri replied with a smile.

"I'll tell you I like that Adam. He seems like a regular warrior," Thaos said then looked at the Sanuri. "Have you met him before?"

"No, but I have heard a great deal about him. Do you recognize him?"

"What do you mean?" asked Stephan.

"Does he look familiar to you?" asked the Sanuri.

"Don't they change their looks when they come here?" Stephan asked.

"That is what they tell me," replied the Sanuri. "But even knowing that; does he look familiar?"

"He favors Miranda," Thaos said with a grin. "Is he her brother?"

"Yes. You know how powerful the Angels are. I have been told that like humans they have certain areas of specialization or areas they excel in. Like The Lion, Adam and Miranda are warriors."

"And Ruth?" asked Stephan.

"She is a healer of souls," said the Sanuri.

"And Daniel?" Thaos asked.

"Now he is very interesting. He is a teacher and he creates songs in the hearts of people."

"Do you mean the same songs that we sing?" asked Stephan.

"I don't think so," the Sanuri replied.

The sun shining off the breast plates of the Angels caused such light that it blinded Samael from seeing the human armies until they were on the battlefield.

The men and women who rode behind the Angels were not disabled by the brightness of this light.

Miranda rode next to Claudius as they led their army southward. Adam rode in front of the men and women who were led by Sorren and General Amundsen. This army rode northward and in between the armies were legions upon legions of demons.

Samael considered many of the demons from the hell regions of Nunc inferior because they fell before the humans who called to the heavens. For this day he imported demons from other worlds to attack the army of Claudius. Samael did not know of the army that was traveling from the monastery. The demon planned to bring such horror to that battlefield that the Sanuri would rush to the aid of the humans; then Samael would have his prize.

Samael, like many other demons and tyrants believed that they could weaken humans by cutting off their connections with the Divine. Samael considered the Sanuri such a connection. But the Sanuri was also considered a scourge that interfered with the plans of demons and because of this he had many bounties on his head.

As the Sanuri rode northward he had no idea of Samael's plans for him or even the bounties that had been placed upon him. If the Sanuri would have known of these things he would not have deviated from his course. He would have still followed that Angel into battle.

Samael had distractions this day as the Old Ones of Nunc plotted against him. In the short time that Samael had been in the World of Nunc he had ordered attacks into the hell domains of the other Old Ones. He planned to expand his territory.

Information had come to Samael that a consortium had been established by the Old Ones of Nunc and powerful demons from other worlds. The reason for this association was to garner enough power to overthrow Samael from all of his holdings.

Miranda and Adam had not disseminated the information about the consortium but they planned to take advantage of the distraction it would cause.

Calen and Koby were the only two Ruala warriors with Claudius' army. They flew ahead of the group. "We must be near the demons because the hair is raising on the back of my neck," Calen said to his brother.

"What the hell!" yelled Koby and suddenly started falling from the sky.

"Miranda!" screamed Calen as he dove to catch his unconscious brother.

A Blue Henger suddenly materialized and grabbed Koby. "Come down with us," yelled Miranda. "You do not want to see what waits for you in the skies."

Calen took Koby from the claws of the Henger and flew towards the army. It was then that Calen saw the blood on the back of Koby's head. "Something attacked him. He is bleeding," Calen yelled.

"Calen put your hand over the wound and pray," Miranda called out.

"Claudius can you feel it?" asked Miranda.

"The presence of evil? Yes."

"Samael planned to make an example of you. The demons that are surrounding us are from other worlds. Tell me General do you still want to proceed?"

"Miranda, I can't believe you even ask me that question. Touch us and let us see our enemies."

"What the hell!" yelled Koby again as he regained consciousness because of the holiness that was flowing through him. "What happened?"

"Look," said Calen as he was landing with his brother. "The sky turned to night as the sun was blocked by beasts of every manner that filled the sky and the land around the army for miles.

Claudius and his army looked around them as the cloaks fell from the monsters. "Why is he showing them to us?" Claudius asked the Angel.

"Because he plans to transmit the images of your defeat as I transmitted the images of a battle at the monastery."

"Why haven't they attacked?"

"They await orders."

"Miranda, I will never shirk my duties but do you want to join me in leading this charge?"

"Claudius, I thought you would never ask," Miranda said then looked at Calen and Koby. "I love the Ruala war cry. Please do the honors."

Both Rualas took to the skies and with great pride screamed the war cry of a race once driven to the brink of extinction by darkness. Their voices carried on the wind.

"It has begun," yelled Adam when he heard the war cries. "Dagon let your brothers know we are coming."

Dagon now screamed the war cry of his people and every Ruala warrior in that tiny army followed his lead. The voices of these warriors were carried on the wind as was the voice of Adam. "Long have I waited to see humans stand up to the tyranny and horror that Samael brings to their worlds. May you fight with courage; may you walk with grace."

As the two Angels rode towards each other the brilliance of their holiness blinded the beasts from hell. The light given off by Miranda and Adam had created a type of cloak which prevented Samael from seeing them and the armies they were leading. The cloak now fell away.

"No!" screamed Samael as he watched from his window into the World of Nunc. "Attack! Attack!" His demonic armies received their commands. The earth shook from the running of hundreds of thousands of feet.

The sky was darkened and a wind arose, not from nature but from the wings of the incredible beasts that now descended on both armies.

The Angels now sped ahead of their armies; their horses running with tremendous speed. The men and women followed them but could not keep up. When Miranda and Adam were within distance of each other they held up their swords and slapped the blades together and the world itself shook.

The swords momentarily bonded and windows to all civilizations in all the worlds were opened and focused on that battlefield in Ganz. All manner of creatures watched the scene with amazement. Few of them realized where the battle was taking place or how the windows had been created.

Some creatures did not recognize the races of Rualas or humans. Most of them certainly did not recognize the Angels but they all recognized the beasts of Samael's armies. The demons and those they ruled literally stopped whatever they were doing and stared at the windows with fascination and disbelief. They watched as two meager armies of mortals did not flee from but charged towards the armies of demons that greatly outnumbered them. They watched as men and women wearing different uniforms, as priests and soldiers screamed war cries and rode, flew and ran towards the demons.

While every demon, every species and race that watched this battle believed the warriors to be insane, they screamed at them, applauded them and wept for them.

"Miranda we need Hengers!" screamed Claudius as a flying monster picked up one of his soldiers. Armies of Blue Hengers, the ancient war birds of the heavens, appeared and attacked the demonic creatures in the skies. The Rualas fought on the ground with the humans.

High Priest Barnabas had remained at the monastery with a handful of priests to protect those who took shelter within the walls. Although the battle was miles to the north, people within the monastery could feel the ground shaking.

Soon things started to fall from shelves and break upon the floors. Barnabas prayed as the priests gathered everyone and escorted them to the Hall of Worship. Most of the children were crying and everyone was frightened.

Nana was the only trained warrior in this group. She stayed at the monastery because she was taking care of Amelia and Chasity.

"Selen, will you watch the boys while I get weapons?" Ashley asked and walked Logan, Cassidy and Marty to her friend. Ashley ran out of the hall and to her and Gideon's room where they kept a chest of weapons. She hid several daggers in her clothing then grabbed as many swords as she could carry. As Ashley ran out of the room a priest stopped her in the courtyard.

"You must get into the hall, you must get into the hall," he repeated frantically and literally pulled her through the courtyard.

"Why? What is happening?"

"Please just do as I say."

"No, I demand to know."

"We are surrounded by demons," the priest said. "I don't understand why they have not attacked."

"Miranda, Daniel, Ruth, we have children to protect. Please help us," screamed Ashely. "Great Ruler please send us Angels."

"He already did," said Ruth as she materialized in the courtyard. "You wonder why they have not attacked. Perhaps you should look up."

"What is that?" asked the priest as he and Ashley were almost blinded by an intense light on the roof of the monastery.

"It is Daniel," Ruth said. "Now, please take me to the children."

The Angels maintained the size and appearance of humans. And they fought as warriors.

"I knew he was behind me," Miranda said as Archetenus killed a demon who was lunging at the Angel's back.

"I am sure you did," he said and now stood with his back against Miranda's. "I've never seen demons like these."

"They aren't from your world," said Miranda as she fought with two demons.

"You told me that if I would have stayed on the course I was on that I would have turned into a powerful demon," Archetenus said. "Like one of these?"

"Like the one who sent them."

Adam was surrounded by demons. He fought with his sword and the demons could not take him down. He was injured but elated with the hope that humans would denounce their demons. He swung his sword but stopped as Sorren jumped into the group of demons and killed the monster who Adam was about to strike. "You can't have them all son," Sorren said and fought at Adam's back. The Angel smiled.

Thor and Kate found each other on the battlefield and worked as a team. They ran up to demons and simultaneously struck them in the backs of the knees with their swords, thus severing the ligaments. Then they killed the monsters. These two warriors had practiced this type of attack since childhood training. They were quick and efficient.

Batina and Rachel had been training together and now fought back to back. Their husbands fought near them. Michael was surprised that Drake and Tally sought him out and fought next to him. The Sanuri had stopped fighting and was healing the wounded warriors.

Ira, Vincente, Maddox, Henrich and Angus had hoped to be able to observe and guide the trainees for their teams in their first battle. But in their wildest thoughts, none of these warriors ever imagined a battle as they now found themselves in.

Thaos and Stephan found Claudius and the father and his sons fought back to back. Jared ran up to Chaez, who was on the ground fighting for his life. Jared ran his sword through the back of the demon that was straddling Chaez. The demon bellowed but did not fall. The demon was trying to stab Chaez but Chaez was blocking the strike. Jared pulled his sword out of the back of the demon and came down hard with a strike to the collarbone. The demon dropped his knife and Jared split the demon's head open.

The demon's loathed the humans and Rualas but they truly hated and feared the Angels. The light that Miranda and Adam were emitting distinguished them on the battlefield. The demons flocked towards them.

As Jared was helping Chaez to his feet he felt a presence and quickly swung to the left with his sword. But the demon who was near Jared was merely running past him. It was then that Jared and Chaez saw all of the demons running towards Miranda. Without saying a word to each other, both men ran after the demons.

Samael thought that the sight of an army as vast as the horizon would cause Claudius and his army to flee or to bow down to the demons. Samael had not researched his enemies because he considered this group of humans and Rualas too inferior to be called enemies. To Samael they were insects that needed to be squashed.

Samael saw Miranda and Adam and recognized them as Angels. He wondered why they presented themselves as humans and why they did not call in armies of reinforcements. Samael now watched the battlefield with the eyes and mindset of a military commander. He was controlling his anger and focusing on the battle; it was then that Samael saw the Sanuri.

The demon laughed when he saw that the Sanuri was not fighting but was running from wounded warrior to wounded warrior. Samael saw demons running past the Sanuri and attacking the humans and Rualas. He wondered if the Sanuri was somehow cloaked.

The demon was so completely focused on the battle that he took his eye off from the monastery. His demons stood as statues around the stone walls of the ancient abbey. They were not disobeying the orders of their master; they simply could not move. The flying demons were suspended in air. Daniel stood on the highest peak of the monastery and sang. A song that only The Great Ruler heard.

Unknown to the humans and Rualas both Miranda and Adam were increasing the amount of light they gave off to distract the demons from the mortals. But the hearts of these men and women did not let fear overtake them nor would they consider leaving the Angels alone on that battlefield. The armies of Claudius and General Amundsen chased down and attacked the demons.

The Ruala warriors took to the skies since the Hengers had destroyed many of the flying demons. The Rualas hovered over the Angels and attacked the demons with their arrows. Deep within the hearts of every man and woman on that battlefield, they knew the Angels could destroy the demons but their integrity and love spurred them to protect the holy messengers.

Worlds stood in wonder as they watched this battle for it did not end easily. And when it was finally over the ground was piled with the bodies of demons and monsters. The armies of Claudius and Amundsen were exhausted, bleeding and broken. With the destruction of the last of the monsters, many of the humans and Rualas literally collapsed on the ground.

As men and women ran to their comrades to care for their wounds the battlefield was suddenly filled with noise. The warriors grabbed their weapons and prepared for another attack. But none came. There were no new adversaries within sight. The noise grew louder as the warriors looked around them in utter confusion.

"Miranda what is that?" asked Claudius as he weakly got to his feet.

"Those are the voices of humans and creatures who long ago allowed the demons to defeat them. This battle was seen by all worlds. You defeated more than the demons on this battlefield today," said Adam.

"But now more will try to stop us also," said the Sanuri. "Why didn't Samael send more reinforcements or come himself. He must have known you were transmitting these images."

"Daniel's song kept them off from us," said Miranda.

"I don't understand," said Thaos.

"You aren't meant to," Miranda replied. "Samael planned this attack for two reasons. One, he wanted to make an example of Claudius' army because demons in all worlds know that Claudius led troops into Baal's hell region. And secondly, he thought that the Sanuri would respond to such horror then Samael would get his prize. Sanuri there are bounties upon you now. We will protect you."

"What my sister has not told you is that this battle was a public humiliation for Samael. No other demons came to his aid because he has alienated so many. The Old Ones of this world are gathering support from demons of other worlds to try and topple Samael and he knows this. Not only has he been humiliated in the eyes of the demons but the inhabitants of all the worlds. He now looks weakened and already attacks are being launched against him. His eyes will be distracted from you for a while but his wrath will be incredible."

"While arrogance is a common trait among demons, Samael is defined by his. He publicly humiliated all of the Old Ones of Nunc for not being able to defeat you. He talks greatly about his superiority over other demons. While your actions this day have made many demons realize the threat you truly are to darkness, many of them enjoyed watching you embarrass the King of Demons."

The voices of other worlds yelling, crying, applauding and cursing could no longer be heard; the windows closed.

"What is happening?" yelled Amundsen who although bleeding himself was applying pressure to a wound of a soldier. "The bleeding is stopping."

"Adam is healing you," Miranda said with a warm smile. "It is his gift for you restoring his faith in mankind."

The Angel Daniel remained on the roof of the monastery while Ruth was inside healing the fears of the people. The children had swarmed around Ruth who was presenting herself as an old woman. "Do they understand that she is an Angel?" Ashley asked Erebus.

"I think perhaps on some level," he said. "I have heard that very young children can see Angels but as they grow their darkness blinds them. I don't know if that is true."

"It's a lovely thought," said Ashley. "Isn't it strange that they walk among us?"

"What do you mean?" asked Erebus.

"I guess I don't really know what I mean. It just seems like people never; I don't know, learn. You would think the Angels would just get disgusted and wash their hands of us."

Harlow walked up to Erebus and Ashley as they were talking. "You always want a good story," Erebus said to the reporter. "You should talk to Ruth. She is an Angel who looks over the peasants of Ryed. She could tell you..." suddenly Erebus started to grin. "Harlow, I never believed this when I was a warlock but since I have changed and been around the Angels I believe there are multiple reasons for everything that happens. I think you need to ask Ruth why you are with us."

Harlow didn't question Erebus, he walked up to Ruth and waited his turn to speak with her.

# Chapter XII
## Lessons to Learn

Daniel continued to hold the demons that surrounded the monastery in a state of stasis until the armies arrived. "We have one more battle this day," Adam announced. "Daniel has stopped an army of demons from attacking the monastery. He will release his hold on them when he sees us."

"Then don't let him see us until we are close," said Gideon. "There aren't enough men in there to protect the children."

"Trust me the children are protected," said Adam. "Ashley called to The Great Ruler to send His Angels to protect them." Adam's voice resounded so every warrior and soldier could hear him. "This is a day of lessons for many of us. I had forgotten what it was like to be with people who believed in The Great Ruler and whose faith was unshakable. So you see I was healed today too. For many of you, especially the leaders, you have learned that you must ask The Great Ruler to help you or you will never be able to accomplish your missions and to protect the peoples of this world."

When Daniel saw the armies he released the demons. The Ruala warriors quickly flew forward and Generals Claudius and Amundsen ordered their troops to attack. But to the surprise of all, the demon army disappeared. There was no battle or even a sign that the demons had been outside of the walls.

"Miranda, Adam are we really seeing this?" yelled Claudius as he raced towards the monastery.

"Yes, you can slow down. Samael will not endure another humiliation this day and he needs his army because his domains in multiple worlds are now under attack," said Miranda.

The armies slowed their pace and Thaos and Stephan broke out of formation and rode up to Miranda and Adam who were riding alongside of the armies. When others saw this, Archetenus, Jared, Michael and Chaez also rode up to the Angels.

"So Adam, are you joining us now?" Thaos asked.

142

Both Miranda and Adam smiled. "Why? Do you think you need the help?" Adam asked.

"We know we need the help," Stephan said. "And we don't mean anything against the other Angels but we like your style. Are you and Miranda really brother and sister?"

"Yes," replied Miranda. "Why did you ask it like that?"

"I just never thought of Angels as having families. Don't know why. Makes me realize I don't know anything about heaven," Stephan said.

"That could be because you aren't ready to know such things yet," said Miranda.

"I am more surprised that Adam said he had a lesson to learn," said Archetenus. "I thought all Angels were, well perfect. I mean you sure seem that way."

Both Adam and Miranda laughed. "Only The Great Ruler is perfect," said Adam. "We learn as we grow just as you do."

Michael was staring at the two Angels. "Miranda, I know why you feel familiar but I don't understand why Adam does. Have we met before?"

"We rotate assignments," explained Adam. "Don't get me wrong we have permanent assignments too but as you would say we wear many hats. Remember when you were eight and Karzman put you in a cage to fight?"

"He was always doing that. Any fight in particular?" asked Michael.

"Teivel was in the audience and this was another of his attempts to kill you," Adam continued. "Remember when demons suddenly filled the cage?"

"I wasn't sure that really happened," Michael said as his eyes widened. "I didn't understand about demons then and I couldn't figure out how they all got into the cage. And..."

"And what?" asked Jared as he saw the look of horror on Michael's face.

143

"Really I thought it was a dream. I don't know if I remember it right," Michael said in almost a whisper.

"Tell us what you do remember," said Adam.

"Suddenly I was outside of the cage but at the same time I was watching me inside of the cage fighting all of those demons and I won. Was that really you? Did you make yourself look like me?"

"You had a path to travel and I couldn't let Teivel know that Angels were protecting you," said Adam. "And before you yell at me, yes we were protecting you and if you would ever have done as we asked and prayed we could have protected you much more. Now to answer the question that causes you so much heartache. Different cultures have terms or stories to describe the path you were on."

"But I am going to use a story that is familiar. You know that many people believe that if enough pressure is put on coal it will turn into a diamond. They don't believe that it will crack into a million pieces and fall apart. They believe it will turn into a thing of incredible strength and great beauty. Something that pleases many in the worlds of man. Michael, you are a diamond and although your friends and family try to tell you that you do not believe them."

"Every great warrior in every world has had to walk through the fire so to speak and this walk is something that is taken without the help of others of their kind. But you rejected even us when we tried to ease your burdens. I am telling you this because as Miranda said earlier, this is a day of lessons. So Michael what lesson did you just learn?"

"I don't know," said Michael angrily.

"We will talk about it later," Adam said.

"I don't want to get in Michael's business," said Jared. "But how come you could help him then but not at other times?"

"That question is actually harder to explain than you realize," said Adam. "But in the instance of that fight, all the forces against Michael the child were not of his world. And that gave me a window to jump in."

144

"What do you mean?" asked Chaez.

"Those of you who are transcending the boundaries of your humanity, and all of you here are; whether you realize it or not. Are beginning to understand that one, you are not the most powerful and intelligent beings in the universe and two, that you aren't alone. You know you are watched by demons but it seems difficult for you to believe that you are being watched by the heavens. Archetenus remember the first time that Miranda told you that?" You were so dark you were on the brink of becoming a demon yourself. Nothing scared you but my sister's words did. Why?"

"I don't know but you are right. They scared me then they angered me. But as usual Miranda put me in my place," Archetenus said and laughed.

"We can talk about that later too," said Adam. "But back to Chaez's question. Think of your world as an arena and the heavens and hells are the spectators. There are often many of us who are ready and waiting to jump into the arena but most of you call to the demons for help."

"Wow, that is really an interesting way to look at things," Chaez said more to himself than to Adam. "So then you are saying that if say Michael would have called to any of you that he would still be in the arena fighting but you would have been in there with him?"

"Yes. You will make a fine priest someday Chaez. You should not doubt your abilities. Dominic is still in formation because he too feels inadequate to be a teacher for The Great Ruler. I would like to meet with both of you this evening."

"So are you staying with us?" asked Thaos again. "Because most of the time the Angels leave after a battle. Does this mean we will be attacked again soon?"

"I don't know how long I or Miranda will be here. That usually is not up to us. But I want to make the most of my time with you as I can," replied Adam. "I can tell that all of you are thinking about Michael and that fight. You are wishing he would have prayed when we asked him to."

145

"We have made it easy for you now because you can see us in forms that you recognize and speak with us. But know that we have spoken to every one of you your entire lives and you did not answer us."

"Well, how did we know?" asked Jared.

"Think of the many times you have heard a little voice inside of you and you dismissed it because you didn't like what it said, or it was inconvenient or you were afraid," Adam replied.

"I know exactly what you are talking about," said Jared with a sadness to his voice that all could hear. "I told all of you that when I was married the first time, my wife's name was Mary and she was as sweet as the day is long. I was young and a lousy husband. I loved her but I loved drinking, fighting and playing cards more. The day she was killed I went into town to get supplies and promised her I would be home early. Well, I started playing cards and losing. It pissed me off; I was determined to get my money back."

"Now this part I have never told another living soul. The entire time I was playing cards I had this feeling that I had to get home. And it just kept getting stronger. If a feeling could be yelling at you, mine was screaming. Hutas attacked my home while I was in town. I found her body behind the house. They had raped her and skinned her alive. If I would have listened to that feeling I could have saved her."

"Jared do you realize how you changed after that?" asked Miranda.

"Hell yeah, sorry I shouldn't have said hell," Jared said and both Angels laughed. "I was filled with hate and I spent years tracking down Hutas and skinning them alive. But I hated myself as much as those damn savages because I should have gone home and protected her."

"You were so full of hate that you lost yourself," Miranda said. "You didn't start to find yourself again until you met Zoya, which was not a random act."

"What do you mean?" asked Jared.

"You didn't realize it that day but it was The Lion's voice you listened to when you followed Sophie and then again when you entered the shop that Zoya worked in. And you listened to him again when he told you to ask her to travel with you."

"I will have to thank him. Why did he do that?"

"A lot of reasons. The obvious is that you were both lost souls that needed healing. Zoya didn't realize it but she was in great danger there, more than just the normal existence in Taperia. Someone of great evil was very attracted to her. And you, well you found out your destiny. When you listened to The Lion, he merely put suggestions in your mind but by following these suggestions you chose to change the path you were on and ultimately your destiny. By listening to him you saved your and Zoya's lives."

There was great fanfare as the armies rode through the gates of the monastery. Everyone came out of the Hall of Worship to greet the warriors.

"Joao! Dack!" screamed Chasity as she watched the sky to find her beloved uncles.

Ashley was standing in the courtyard with Marty, Logan and Cassidy. She searched the crowd until she saw Gideon. "Come on boys," she said and ran to Gideon and jumped into his arms.

As Cassidy watched Gideon hugging Logan and Marty, Thaos walked up behind him and picked him up. Cassidy and Thaos hugged each other as Stephan and Claudius walked up to them. Stephan took the boy and they too hugged. "Cassidy this is our father Claudius and he is your father now too," said Stephan with a grin.

Cassidy stared at Claudius then held out his had to shake. "How do you do My Lord?" the boy said.

Claudius laughed and took Cassidy from Stephan's arms and hugged him. Cassidy hugged Claudius back and smiled. "I have heard a great deal about you," Claudius said.

"And I have heard a lot about you," said Cassidy enthusiastically. "The Sanuri said you're a hero and a good father."

"He did, did he?" said Claudius and laughed again. "Well, I don't know about being a hero and I hope I am a good father."

"He is just being modest," Stephan said to Cassidy. "He is all those things."

"I have gifts in my saddle bags for everyone," Claudius said. "Later we need to have a meeting."

"We certainly do," said Thaos. "Do you know about the girls taking a journey with Angelina and being attacked by Karzman's men?"

"What? Was anyone hurt?" asked Claudius loudly.

"We will tell you but not in front of Cassidy," said Stephan.

"Stephan, I am not a baby," Cassidy said indignantly. "I was living on my own for a long time before you found me. I know a lot of things."

"He's right," Thaos said and chuckled.

Claudius continued to carry Cassidy as the men walked up to Sorren. "We're going to tell Father about your journey," said Stephan. "Do you want to join us?"

"Good idea. I will be telling everyone else later," said Sorren. "Do you want to go to my room it is closer?"

"We need to take care of the horses first," said Stephan. "Father why don't you go with Sorren and we'll take care of all four horses."

"Grab me my saddlebags first," said Claudius. "I have things in there for you too, Sorren." Stephan laughed loudly as he took two sets of saddlebags from his father's horse. The bags were overstuffed with items. "That's just the gifts. My gear is in the boca with the food," Claudius said with a huge grin. He was happy to be reunited with Thaos and Stephan and Claudius was surprised at how happy he was about adopting Cassidy.

148

"Marty, Logan," yelled Chasity as Joao carried her. Joao, Dack and Adam were walking up to Gideon, Ashley and their sons. "I told you. Adam is here." Both boys ran up to Adam who picked them up and hugged them.

"Ashley and Gideon have adopted us and Logan and I are brothers now and Chasity got adopted too," Marty was talking so fast he wasn't taking breaths.

Gideon and Ashley now walked up to Adam. "Thank you for saving our sons and Chasity," said Gideon. "Can we ever repay you?" Adam smiled. "I am very serious, I am not just saying this."

"Even if it means you would have to work?" asked Adam.

Gideon stared at Adam as he was trying to determine if the Angel was insulting him. "Ashley and I are very hard workers but you already know that. What do you need us to do?"

"As always you have the choice not to," said Adam. "High Priest Barnabas is planning to establish a series of temporary shelters for children in this kingdom. Places where children can be safe and cared for until they can be transported to the orphanage he will build here. Langer needs such shelters."

"I am not arguing but I have never seen homeless children in Langer," said Gideon.

"The homeless are everywhere. Most people choose to be blind to them."

"Of course we will do this," said Ashley. "In fact, I will write to Bella tonight and tell her what you said. I know she will start looking for properties."

"The orphanage that King Mathas is building will take some time and it is outside of the city. The shelters are needed now," Adam continued. "And if I may suggest, Selen, Deborah and Hilgra would be very happy working on such a mission."

"I will speak with Claudius tonight," said Gideon. "Consider it done. What else do you want us to do?"

"When you go to Wetpr for the wedding of Luca and Natalie tell King Sudfad my words, he will know what to do. The orphanage in Salar is in the center of the city so children can easily find their way there. But he has a vast kingdom and most towns and villages do not have a way to protect their children."

Adam now turned to Ashley. "You have been concerned with building trust and recognition with the people of Langer so you can set up a network there as you did in Port Friada. This mission will allow the people to get to know you and the character of woman you are." Ashley smiled.

Gideon smiled at the Angel and said, "I have a plan."

"I know what you are thinking and that is not necessary," said Adam although he smiled warmly.

"Would it be inappropriate or an insult?" asked Gideon.

"Not at all."

"Then the shelters will be called Adam's Homes so when anyone sees those signs they will know they will be protected there as you protected our children."

"Oh Gideon I love that idea," Ashley said excitedly then she looked back at Adam. "Is anything wrong? Don't you like the idea?"

"I like the idea very much. I too have had lessons to learn this day."

Cassidy wanted to remain with his new family so Claudius allowed him to sit in during the meeting in Sorren's room. Claudius sat in stoic silence and stared at Sorren. By the time Sorren had stopped explaining about the journey that Angelina and others went on and the attack by Karzman's men the veins were protruding from Claudius' neck.

"That monster attacked my family," Claudius said through clenched teeth. He was trying to contain his anger since Cassidy was sitting on his lap.

"Thaos and I are going to ride with Sudfad when he attacks Karzman," Stephan said.

"Has he set a time?" Claudius asked.

"All we know is he has been waiting for us all to return from this mission. But I would expect he will wait until after Luca's wedding. We can talk with him then."

# Chapter XIII
## The Power of the Scribe

Minutes after Sorren finished briefing Claudius a large meeting
was called. All of the team members including the new trainees
and the leaders were to attend. The meeting was held in the
dining hall and all four Angels stood in the front of the room.
When the door was closed, Miranda was the first to speak.

"You fought valiantly today and you won more than that battle.
Because your victory exposed Samael's weaknesses, he is
embroiled in the worst wars of his existence. These wars will
keep him distracted so that you can focus on other issues. But
before we explain these issues there are some things that we need
to explain to the newer members in this room."

"The battle you just fought, while not ordinary is not out of the
realm of possibility of happening again. As the demons and
criminals realize the force you are, they are throwing more of
their arsenals at you. The demons you fought today could not be
killed my humans which is why we assisted you. But you have to
remember to call us in. Also, Adam healed all of you afterwards
which is not always the case."

"I say these words because many of you are realizing the roles
you are volunteering for. These are not stories of old glory but
vicious, terrible battles. There is no shame if you change your
minds about becoming members of the teams. And that goes for
you also, General Amundsen." Amundsen was clearly angered by
Miranda's words but before he could speak a young Nordes
warrior stood up.

"I am sorry I don't really know how to address you," the woman
said shyly. "My name is Sheba and I am a member of the Nordes
Tribe. Know we will fight whatever monsters we have to but
many of the warriors and soldiers here have been talking.
Actually I think a lot of us would like to adopt some of the
children that were rescued but we don't want to take them into a
battle like that. Will we have relatively safe passage home?" All of
the Angels were smiling as Sheba spoke, so much so that she
wondered if they thought her question silly.

"We know what you are thinking and we are not laughing at you we are smiling because we approve of what you want to do," said Adam. "The demons that aren't embroiled in wars are going to plan carefully before they attack any of you again. You will have just the normal hazards of such a journey. But that doesn't mean that we won't be watching over you. Give the children homes."

"Sorren explained to you about the Kingdom of Inferus and the Elods," said Daniel. "They are a civilization as old as time in your world. The world inside of your world is like nothing you can imagine. Angelina, Matthew, Nikki and Ingr saw but a glimpse."

"The Elods resemble humans in many ways both physically and emotionally as well as mentally. But they are a strange composite of extremes. They are by far the most intelligent civilization in your world. They learned in their early existence that they could transcend their human boundaries. And in the beginning they choose enlightenment."

"They burrowed deep within the world to escape the darkness and demons they saw above. But for all of their good intentions they too called to the demons. While being the most intelligent race they are also the most brutal. They have spent centuries breeding monsters of all sorts. Many of these monsters are used for working like you would use, oxen or horses here. But many are bred for war."

"Like every civilization they have divided into factions and these factions fight among themselves. Some want to reclaim the world that you live in. Some want control of the Kingdom of Inferus. Others want enlightenment and others want to join the demons. You see they aren't so very different from the kingdoms that you know."

"The Elods do not believe in The Great Ruler because in their advancement they believed themselves to be superior to Him. This is something else you encounter in your world. But there is a small group of advanced individuals who have formed a sort of priesthood. They call themselves the Abuckto and they have abilities that others of their race do not; for example they are the strongest of seers. All Elods have this ability at some level."

"While I gave the example of a priesthood, the motivations of the members are not necessarily for good. The members of the Abuckto are extremely intelligent. Their knowledge of many things such as the sciences is vastly superior to your races. The members of this group are separated from others of their race because of their abilities and intelligence but they have the same political ideals as the different factions. They consider themselves godlike so they wear the robes of priests. Some of you have encountered them."

"While you cannot travel to their world at least for now, without our help, they travel in your world freely. Some of you encountered Madeline and Javier. They are members of a radical sect known as the Charto. This is one of the factions that wants to conquer the world as you know it. The interesting thing is that while in their worlds they appear conservative they have very dark appetites which they feed regularly in your world."

"Madeline and Javier are brother and sister and they belong to a sub-race of the Elods known as the Eto. While many members of the Elods sought to develop intelligently, the Eto sought to develop in another way. They are all seductresses. No species or race can resist them, even demons."

"Wait," said Sorren. "Gideon and Isabella's husband Josef resisted her."

"As did Matthew, Stephan and Michael," added Claudius.

"And what do all of the men you named have in common?" asked Daniel.

"They are all used to fighting demons so they can spot them," said Sorren.

"And they are all faithful followers of The Great Ruler which gives them insight," said Daniel.

"So are you saying we are impervious to them?" asked Thaos.

"No, I am saying that between your own abilities and us speaking to you that you will recognize the threat. The choice then is yours as to how you handle it," Daniel explained.

"The main reasons that Madeline and Javier are in your world is to get information and they do their jobs well."

"Isabella said that they don't cast shadows and sometimes smell like dirt. Are there other ways that we can recognize them?" asked Batina.

"Some of them wear tattoos but they disguise themselves well. They have walked in your world for centuries. And most of them merely come to observe."

"They must do more than that," said Sorren. "The dark lord that tried to steal my grandson's soul was from there. And Jacob's parents somehow stole money from that dark lord."

"How much of a threat are they to us?" asked Edward. "And how can we tell them apart from the demons?"

"Some of them are a threat to your world," said Ruth as she stepped forward. "But most of them are not. At this time I would like Harlow to step up here." Harlow reluctantly walked to the front of the room. "For those of you who do not know him, Harlow is a reporter for a newspaper in Port Friada. He has a well-earned reputation for finding the truth; not something that is easy to do in any world."

"Today Harlow and I had a very long talk. He asked me why he had never heard of many of the things that all of you encounter in the work of your missions. He suggested that if people really knew about the monsters and predators that not only could they protect themselves but protect others and he gave me the example of the citizens of Port Friada."

"Port Friada is a huge city filled with tough people and crime. But many, many good and honest people live there too. When the citizens of Port Friada discovered the atrocities that the dark lord Dieter was committing in their city, they did not hide in fear. They banded together; many unlikely companions but they came together and they stand united against that darkness. Yes, dark lords keep going to that city, but the citizens do not make their lives easy."

"The advantage that Port Friada has is knowledge. And how do they gain such knowledge? Harlow has accepted a new position. He will be the Scribe of the Teams. He will help you in your research, starting with the Elods. And he will continue to print stories to give knowledge to others. Claudius, he will be moving to your city and working with all of you and Wickfield's newspaper."

"Welcome aboard," said Claudius sincerely.

"Our time here is short and there are several of you who we want to meet with in private," said Miranda. "You have countless enemies, even if you weren't involved with these missions. It is time for you to go home and to look at your communities. Those of you who dealt with Shanksaw and Deckor know how opportunistic darkness is. Those of you from Wetpr and Lentz you will need to clean up your own backyards now. And those of you from Ganz know that Hector has not left and should not be ignored."

"We are very pleased with the love and dedication you have shown in saving the children. Remember they are your future. Teach them well. Many of you have ideas of how you can protect them and you should come up here and discuss this issue after we leave."

"Archetenus and Jared, I would like the two of you to come up here and talk about your lives. And General Amundsen this is something you need to listen to. Archetenus, bring Ashley up here with you. She never told you that after you and Delilah escaped, Dieter came to her shop and tried to force her to tell him information about you. You will find the story interesting."

"The reason we are telling all of you to share this information is two-fold, one, many of you try to rely on us for answers and two, all of you need to learn of each other and to build trust. You have some very dark times ahead of you."

While the large meeting was still in progress the Angels pulled individuals out of the dining hall and spoke with them; afterwards the Angels left the monastery.

Some of these individuals were too emotional to return to the meeting so they retired to their rooms.

It was almost midnight when the Sanuri ended the meeting because many of the exhausted warriors still had not found rooms or campsites.

Joao and Dack had just closed the door to their room when there was a knock. Dack laughed when he opened the door. Koby and Calen were standing in the doorway and Koby was holding up a bottle of whiskey. "We're moving in with you, all the rooms are full," Calen said with a grin.

Dack moved to the side so the two men could enter. "Chasity, meet two more of your uncles," Dack said.

Joao was holding the girl and walked up to Calen who held his arms out to her. Chasity went to him and gave him a hug. "We have gifts for all of you," said Calen. "And letters." As Calen spoke, Koby opened the pack he had been carrying and started to sort letters into piles.

Dack poured cups of whiskey and Joao explained, "Chasity, this is Calen and Koby. We all live in the same house together. They both have children too but they are a little young for you to play with."

"Emeral and Natasha sent cookies," Koby announced as he put a large parcel on the small table in the room.

"Great, I am starving," said Joao and grabbed a handful of cookies, giving one to Chasity.

"All these letters are for Chasity," Koby said as he smiled and handed her so many that she couldn't hold them all.

"I'll read them to you," Calen said and took the letters.

"For me," Chasity repeated several times with amazement.

"These letters are for you two," said Koby as he handed mail to Joao and Dack. "Looks like several girls from the medical class wrote to you and so did Bethany and Marina."

157

"Are they still at the house?" asked Dack. "I thought they were going to leave after the nurses came."

"We thought some more of the nurses would show up but it's just Lana and Tanya. Melinda is still healing and Hannah doesn't want her doing a lot of lifting."

"Hannah talked Bethany and Marina into helping with the medical classes and teaching her our medicine. She is paying them well, so the girls are helping with the children and chores too," Koby said.

"I am sure that Emeral put it in her letters," said Calen. "But she wanted us to suggest that you two take Bethany and Marina to Luca's wedding. But she didn't say anything to them so don't worry about hurting their feelings."

"Chasity, you get yours first," said Koby. "These are from Elan, Cassandra, Joey and Tommy." Calen set the little girl at the table so she could open her gifts. Koby handed out the rest of the gifts as Chasity squealed with delight every time she opened up a package.

"Good, now we have some clean clothes to change you into," Joao said and picked up one of the dresses from the pile of gifts.

"Rachel said that the two of you have been acting like fathers," Calen said and grinned. "That's a side of you that no one has seen."

"I guess we have," said Dack. "That whole thing just made us sick. The children were in cages...we will tell you the rest later."

"Speaking of children," Joao said. "Did you get Dagon's letter about Amelia?"

"Yeah, Emeral and Maxwell had a family meeting about it and everyone thought that Misha would have a fit but he handled the news better than anyone else," said Koby. "He said it would be like someone hating one of his babies for something he did. We're all betting that Emeral will adopt her."

"We were thinking the same thing but Nana and some of the other girls are getting really attached to the baby," said Joao.

158

"But if Nana adopts her she will probably have to get off the team."

"I don't see why," said Calen. "She could just leave the baby at our house."

"Ok, catch us up on everything," Koby said as he took the last of the items from his pouch and placed them on the table.

"You guys go ahead," said Calen. "I'm going to read some of these letters to Chasity them she needs to go to bed." The men grinned at him. "I'll admit it, I miss my kids. It will be nice having all those children join us on the way back. It sounds like a lot of them are getting adopted."

That night Matthew and Angelina got into their first fight together. When they were in the privacy of their bedroom, Matthew started to yell, "Angelina, I know you think you can handle everything by yourself but we are a family. Don't you ever do something like that again! How long were you planning that journey? And why didn't you tell me?"

"I didn't tell you because I knew you would want to go in my place. Matthew the Angels helped us so much. That is not what a journey is supposed to be like. Healers and warriors prepare for years sometimes to go on such journeys and then they don't always come back the same."

"What! What are you talking about?"

"Will you lower your voice? First, if one of us would have gotten killed in that battle, we would have really died; it wasn't like a dream. And people can experience things that are so powerful that they change when they awake. Mother told me of a man whose physical appearance changed. He was in his thirties but after he awoke his hair turned white and he looked much older. He would never talk about what he saw."

"Is that really true?"

"Yes, Mother was the healer helping him back. She said she was having difficulty getting him back to this world, she was afraid she would lose him."

"I was so scared when you got injured and then to find out that you deliberately got hurt so you could go on this journey..."

"I deliberately got hurt so I could save Jacob. And we did! Matthew, I understand why you are mad and I would be in your place but what kind of parents are we if we don't protect our children? You wouldn't just stand by."

"You are right but from this night forward you tell me everything as I will you. No more secrets!"

"I agree to that although this is the only secret I have ever kept from you. Have you been keeping secrets from me?"

"Let me think about that," he said with a grin. "I am sure I can think of something." Angelina playfully punched him on the arm. Matthew pulled her to him and kissed her passionately.

Michael couldn't sleep so he decided to take a walk. Earlier that evening he and Adam had a very long talk and Michael still felt like he was going to explode. Initially after his meeting with Adam, Michael went to his room because he didn't feel that he could be around other people. Michael's emotions were out of control, he wanted to scream, to hit something and to cry.

Although Michael understood what the different Angels had told him he still felt betrayed. His family had suffered unimaginable horrors and the Angels didn't stop it. Yes, they helped him at times but he still existed in a world of hell. To survive Michael learned at an early age to disassociate himself from the pain and humiliation that his body was enduring. But to see what Karzman did to his beloved mother and sisters tore Michael apart.

He believed that the Angels were telling him the truth but Michael could not understand how they could stand by and watch such suffering.

Adam told him about the World of Orantho and how difficult it was for him not to take away people's freedom of choice and to change that world. Michael heard the words but he did not understand the concept; he knew he could not just stand by; of that he was certain. What Michael was not certain of is if he could fulfil his destiny.

His feelings of betrayal and rage made it difficult for him to blindly follow the Angels like the others. Michael had forgiven Sudfad because he knew that Sudfad didn't know of his existence. And now that Michael knew that Sudfad was going to attack Karzman to avenge the wrongs that had been done to his family; Michael felt closer to his father. It was the Angels that Michael couldn't trust or forgive.

Soldiers, priests and warriors took turns standing guard on the massive stone wall that surrounded the monastery. High Priest Barnabas walked in the courtyard because he could not sleep. Never in his life had he imagined that he would meet the emissaries of The Great Ruler and four of them had visited the monastery and protected and blessed everyone. As exhausted as Barnabas was, excited energy surged through him.

The monastery at Leven was a huge and sprawling structure. It was built hundreds of years earlier to protect the citizens of Leven from attack. But almost as soon as the structure was completed it was turned into a monastery and the first high priest added many new buildings. The monastery covered more acreage than the City of Leven. Tonight Barnabas saw a sight he was not used to. There were so many people behind the walls that all spaces outside of the buildings were being used as campsites. The fires illuminated the night.

General Amundsen could not sleep this night either. He gulped several glasses of whiskey then left his room to take a walk. Everything that had happened in the previous days defied logic and he was a man of logic. At times he truly wondered if he was dreaming or delirious.

And all the others, they really confounded him. All of these warriors and some of them ex-criminals acted like seeing Angels and defeating demons were a daily occurrence. But what really scared Amundsen was the words of the ex-warlock who said that meeting the Angels would change his life.

Amundsen wasn't sure he wanted his life changed. He rather liked it the way it was. And all that talk about him becoming King. How could that be true? King Friada had never mentioned such thoughts to him. In fact, Amundsen wasn't really sure if the King liked him. But why would the Sanuri and the Angels lie about such a thing?

Ruth had pulled Amundsen out of the meeting and talked with him. She told him about the Kingdom of Ryed so he could learn from the mistakes of the people there.

Ruth spoke to Amundsen as if he already was the King and he found this very unsettling and he didn't understand why. As he tried to clear his head, Amundsen realized it wasn't the idea of becoming King that made him feel uneasy. It was the change to a life that he had carefully and skillfully planned out. Amundsen had everything organized and in its place and now the heavens were messing everything up.

Claudius moved into the room with his sons. It was crowded but they were all happy to be united. Claudius could see why Thaos and Stephan had taken such a liking to Cassidy. There was something about the boy that reminded Claudius of his two older sons. And the more that Claudius looked at Cassidy he realized that the boy physically favored the family. Cassidy was young but large boned and muscular. He had black hair and large brown eyes.

At times Cassidy seemed like an excited child who could not stop talking and at other times he seemed older than his years. But the one thing that surprised Claudius about the boy was that Cassidy did not seem like a lost soul, as Claudius would have expected.

Although it was late, the men decided to have a drink and read their letters before going to bed. Stephan poured the whiskey as Claudius emptied his saddlebags. "Cassidy, I am not asking this to embarrass you but can you read?" asked Claudius.

"Not really. I had just started school when my other family died."

"Then come here and I will read these to you," Claudius said. "And there are gifts."

"There are letters for me? But who would write to me?" asked Cassidy as he ran across the room and sat down on the bed next to Claudius.

"You have a family now," said Thaos. "And from what my wife wrote our daughter sent you a letter too. Amy is learning how to read and write."

"Here, why don't you start opening these while I finish sorting all of this out," Claudius said and handed Cassidy several packages.

"Bella hired a tutor for both Cassidy and Amy," Claudius said. "Then when they get older we can decide if they continue with tutors or go to school."

"I always had tutors," Stephan said. "So did Matthew. And honestly with all the attacks I'm inclined to think it is a safer way to go."

"Cassidy, you are so quiet, you're never quiet," said Thaos.

Cassidy had carefully unwrapped his gifts and organized them on the bed. He had two shirts, two pairs of pants, socks, riding boots, a belt with a very ornate sheath that held a small knife, a carved wooden horse, a leather bracelet and a pouch of hard candy. Cassidy did not speak but stared at the items as if he was afraid they would disappear. Both Stephan and Thaos stood up and walked over to the bed.

"Our wives are the daughters of Chief Sorren and they are trained as warriors," Stephan explained. "That belt and sheath are items of their tribe. See if the belt fits."

Cassidy excitedly put the belt around his waist. "It fits, it fits," he said.

"Amy is in warrior training and when they excel in an area they earn one of these bracelets," Thaos said as he picked it up. "She is giving you one of hers. Do you want to wear it?"

"Oh yes," Cassidy said excitedly and held out his wrist. As Thaos tied the bracelet on him Cassidy asked. "But Amy is little how can she be training to be a warrior?"

"In Sorren's tribe the training starts at age ten but children can start earlier. Amy is very enthusiastic and works hard so they let her train even though she is seven."

"Can I go to training too?" Cassidy asked and eagerly searched the faces of the men.

"Yes," said Claudius. "But it is a lot of hard work and you have to attend every day. And this training would be in addition to your schooling. Perhaps we should take you to the village and let you see it before you decide."

"I can work hard, really I can. Please can I go too?"

"Father, you've got another warrior in the family," Stephan said and ruffled Cassidy's hair.

"I have another son named Ryan," Claudius said as he picked up the wooden horse. "He is not a warrior but a very talented carpenter. He made this for you."

"Really? He did?" Cassidy said and touched the horse as if he was afraid it would break.

"Ryan said he will teach you some of his skills if you want to learn," said Claudius.

"I would like that very much," Cassidy said.

"Why don't you try on the clothes and boots," said Claudius. "And if something doesn't fit we will leave it for the other children and get you something else."

"Oh, I think they will fit," Cassidy said as he did not want to part with any of his gifts.

"If they don't fit we will buy you ones that do," said Claudius.

The men read their letters and opened their gifts as Cassidy tried on his clothes. "It looks like everything fits except those boots are a little big. We'll get you another pair that fits and you can save those for later or give them to one of the other children," said Claudius.

Cassidy stared at his beautiful boots. Never had he worn riding boots before. He slowly took them off and looked like he was going to cry. "I should give them to one of the others," he said.

"Cassidy, you don't have to," said Stephan.

"You already bought me shoes and some of the other kids don't have any at all," Cassidy said with sadness in his voice. Claudius picked the boy up and hugged him.

# Chapter XIV
## Ryan

The following morning Raul and Simon led their group from Mathas' castle. The previous day the Princes told Bella they were reconsidering their request to stay at her home but after she told them of all her preparations for their visit, they felt obligated to stay. Among many other things, Bella had hired nurses and a physician to stay at the castle and take care of the wounded priests.

It was only a two hour ride between the castles of Mathas and Claudius. The small army arrived at Claudius' castle while it was still early morning.

Ryan came home from his shop so he could help welcome their guests. He drove a boca that was filled with items. When he entered the castle, Bella, Ingr and Nikki were busy showing everyone to their rooms.

Amy and Nina ran out of the playroom and grabbed Ryan's hands. "Ryan look at what they brought us," Amy said and the two girls pulled him into the playroom. Ryan laughed then admired the toys that Raul, Simon, Gabriel, Raphael, Matthew and Angelina brought.

"Angelina said there are toys for you too," Amy said excitedly.

"Toys? Are you sure?" Ryan asked and grinned.

"Well they are gifts," said Amy. "We didn't open them."

Ryan walked out of the playroom which was near the parlor as he heard voices. Several people were walking down the stairs.

"Ryan good you could come home," said Bella happily.

"Artis and Ralph are minding the shop but they are coming here for the afternoon meal," Ryan said. "And I have a boca full of things to show all of you. Raul, Simon how long are you staying?"

"A couple of days," said Simon. "Why?"

"Well, I have some of the items that you ordered but I also have samples of woods and colors for Sudfad's study. I don't know if you want to look at these things now or just take them home."

"Oh, we'll look at them now," said Raul who was afraid that they would get bored during their visit. "We can help you bring the things in."

"Hi Ryan," yelled Saran as she and Nyla ran down the stairs. "There are flowers and chocolates in our room, can you believe that?"

"Well, I have some gifts for all of you too, but we should wait until Artis and Ralph get here because they made some of them," said Ryan and smiled. "So don't follow us out to the boca."

Matthew now joined the group and all of the men walked towards the front door. "Bella, you might want to clear off a table for the samples," Ryan said. As soon as the men were at the boca he explained, "Artis and Ralph are bringing gifts for Bella, Nikki and Ingr for being so good to them. They have been working on the gifts for a long time. And they made some of the toys in here. So it is only fair that they give out the things they made." Gabriel and Raphael now joined the men.

"We agree," said Simon. "Do you want us to just start grabbing or is it organized?"

Ryan was pointing out the crates that should be taken into the house. "The rest of your orders we will bring when we come for Luca's wedding."

"I can't believe you got this much done already," Raul said as he pulled a crate off the back of the boca.

"My staff works hard and most of them seem to enjoy the work. I am very lucky; Bella does a great job of hiring."

"You might want to tell her that," said Matthew. "She feels very guilty about hiring that Ted guy or whatever his name really is."

All of the items were taken to the parlor where Raul and Simon divided them by families. "Gabriel, we ordered one of these jewelry boxes for every woman in your household but they aren't all done yet," said Simon. "And we ordered some of the toys too."

"Let us pay you," said Raphael. "We were just talking about placing orders."

"No, they are our gifts, but you should visit his shop sometime," said Raul. "Ryan makes beautiful things."

Bella smiled as she listened to Raul. All of her guests knew that Ryan always felt insecure because he was not a warrior like everyone else in the family. And having a shop where he could work with wood and sell his creations was his lifelong dream. It pleased Bella that the warriors in her home were so kind and supportive of him

Ryan placed all of the samples on a table then explained the differences, benefits and drawbacks of each. All of the adults were surprised at the variety of choices that Ryan offered. After about twenty minutes Simon said, "Bella help us. You are good at this. Any idea of what you think Mother would like?"

Bella had been listening to Ryan and now asked Simon, Raul and Matthew a series of questions which made the Princes laugh. "We didn't think about any of that," Raul said. "All we know is that Mother wants something like Mathas has but she wants more meeting rooms."

"Did she tell you what fabric she wants for the chairs?" asked Bella.

"No. You see all of this was going to be a surprise from Raul, Matthew and me. We knew Ryan was a carpenter but we didn't realize the quality of his work until a few weeks ago when Claudius showed us his study," explained Simon. "That is when we got the idea to order everything from Ryan but we are all realizing that we don't know what we are doing." Simon laughed as he said this. "I guess we could just take these samples home and have Mother pick out what she wants."

"Now boys you just wait a moment," Bella said. "Ryan help me." The two walked out of the parlor and returned with bolts of material which they placed on the same table. "I have gone shopping with Renya several times and seen how she decorates. These are the three woods you want to consider and I would suggest these two colors. Now if you really want it a surprise, we can have the cushions made too."

As Bella spoke she unrolled several bolts of fabric and placed the wood samples on them. "Since you asked my opinion, I think that Renya would like this color of wood and you could have the cushions and pillows made out of these two fabrics."

"I just couldn't see any of this until you put it together," Raul said.

"I like it," said Matthew.

"So do I," said Simon. "If Raul says yes, you sold us."

"It's a sale," said Raul. "Now we just have to figure out how many tables and chairs."

As the group worked on the plans for Sudfad's study, Nikki walked into the parlor. "Artis and Ralph are here but they made us come into the house."

"Everyone take a seat in here," said Ryan with a huge smile. "I will get some soldiers."

"We can help," said Simon. "But do we need to clear some space?" The women and children gathered in the parlor and laughed as the men quickly rearranged the furniture.

"Now everyone stay right here," Ryan said and the men left the parlor. A few minutes later, they returned carrying a large ornately carved armoire. "Don't touch this yet," Ryan said and the men carried two more armoires into the room. Artis and Ralph followed them in.

"Bella, Ingr and Niki," Ralph said shyly. "Me and Artis wanted to do something to thank you for all of your kindness. These are for you and each one is a little different."

Everyone in the room jumped out of their seats to examine the finely crafted furniture. "These are absolutely beautiful," Bella said. "We love them. Thank you so much."

"Look there are mirrors inside the doors," said Ingr. "Have you ever seen anything like that before?"

Nikki hugged both Artis and Ralph and kissed them on the cheeks, Ingr and Bella followed her lead.

"Looks like we are placing more orders," Simon said as he examined the construction of the pieces.

"Me too," said Matthew. "I'll need three." He looked at Angelina and said. "One for you and our mothers." She walked up to her husband and hugged him.

"Bella, I keep telling you that you're going to have to hire more workers," Ingr said with a giggle as she was very happy at how successful Ryan's business was becoming.

"We can certainly make these but they won't be done in time for Luca's wedding," Ryan said.

"That is fine," said Gabriel. "There are several weddings coming up and we can always come and pick these up too."

"You haven't ordered anything yet," Raul said teasingly.

"That is because we are still counting," Raphael said with a grin.

Joshua marched into the parlor in Gabriel's home where many of the adults where helping the children get dressed for their Venator training. "I am coming today too," Joshua said. "I left Sudfad's meeting early because there have been five more sightings of Madeline and Javier and they have all been in the area."

"We can protect the children, Father," said Micha as he was fastening a belt around Adrone's waist.

"I know that but I just have a really bad feeling about all of this. For all we know those two have an army with them. And we don't really know if they are demons or not. Luca will be here soon to watch the house," said Joshua.

"Father, I can't remember the last time I heard you sound so worried," Thomas said. "Is there more that you haven't told us?"

"No, but if they are watching us that closely they know most of the warriors are gone. This would be a perfect time to attack."

All of the children were staring at Joshua as he spoke. "Grandpa we can help too," Christopher said enthusiastically.

"We can fight," said Paul.

"I don't think so," said Hannah as she helped Nicholas and Cerey with their backpacks.

"Actually the children have learned a lot," said Sasha then she saw the looks on Hannah's and Natasha's faces. "I mean they can defend themselves and they know how to hide and find their way home."

"We know what you meant," Emeral said soothingly to Sasha then she looked in the faces of all of the children in the room. "We know you are all brave and want to protect your families but we don't want any of you getting involved with this thing with Madeline and Javier. And when I say that I speak for all of your families do you understand?" Zack, Margarit, April and Sally all nodded their heads and said 'yes.'

Sam, Misha, Maxwell and Luca walked into the house and into the parlor. "We need to have a family meeting," Maxwell said. "So postpone the training for a little while."

"Maxwell the children are getting older and studying to become warriors," said Joshua. "Is this something they can sit in on?"

"Is this something you all want?" Maxwell asked.

"The children want to help," said Vivian. "Perhaps it would be helpful if they understood some things."

"Very well. Horace went home to get Zelda, they should be here soon and Sudfad and Renya are meeting with Shara so the medical classes may start late today too," said Maxwell. "We have increased the number of troops watching the homes. And I know several of you have appointments today but I don't want any of you leaving the house without protection."

Horace and Zelda walked into the house and everyone walked into Gabriel's study. "May I speak first?" asked Joshua. He walked to the front of the room.

"In my tribe children your ages are well into their training to become warriors and thus are allowed more responsibilities. This is the first time we are including you in one of our meetings. We expect you to act as young warriors. If we talk about anything that scares you, you may leave the room without anyone thinking badly of you. And Maxwell may not want to discuss all of the information with you. But what you do hear in this meeting you do not tell strangers. Does anyone have any questions?"

"I am really not sure if this is a good idea," Hannah said.

"They won't be in here long," said Maxwell. "None of us had received letters for several days and during our meeting Sudfad received six, so I expect more will be on the way for us. The good news is that all of our team members are safe and well but they have been in several battles which is why we haven't heard from them."

"As you know, our teams that were in Port Friada were directed to go to the monastery at Leven. Claudius' army joined them a couple of days ago. I will discuss later what they have been involved with but they are now free to return home and plan on leaving tomorrow. The Angels told them they would just encounter the normal obstacles of such a journey."

"The second group which is Gabriel, Raphael, Raul, Simon, Matthew, Angelina and Michael's sisters ran into some unexpected delays and battles also. They are alright but they have some wounded men with them so they have been delayed in returning. It sounds like we should expect them in three to four days. So you can put Luca's and Natalie's wedding back on the calendar."

172

"Children, I want to tell you a couple of things then I would like all of you to leave and go to the playroom. We have found out a great deal about the tribe that Madeline and Javier belong to. Children, all of you said that they were very nice to you. That they told you to come over and play although they did not have children and that the dogs kept growling at them. So this is a lesson that you all have to listen to. They are dangerous people who were sent here to spy on us."

"I know we have talked about this but I want to make sure you understand. As warriors what should you have questioned?"

"That the dogs were growling," said Zack. "They only growl at demons."

"Very good," said Maxwell. "What else?"

"Why would they want us to come over to play if they didn't have kids?" asked Paul.

"Again the right answer."

"Just because someone is acting nice doesn't mean they aren't dangerous," said Sally.

"Excellent. We want you to be polite to people but you have to question things and if something doesn't seem right it probably isn't," Maxwell said. "Now there is one more thing, what is it?"

"Don't go anyplace with strangers unless one of you tells us it is ok," Adrone said.

"Perfect. I will take you all out for ice cream after your training," Maxwell said with a big smile. "You know that Chasity is coming home. Well there were some really bad men in Port Friada who stole children and our teams found the children and saved them. It sounds like many of these children were orphans before they were stolen. A lot of the warriors and soldiers are adopting them and bringing them back here. So we want you to be kind to them just like with Michael's sisters."

"We will be, Grandpa," said Nicholas.

"Good, now why don't you all go into the playroom and we will get you when we are done in here," Maxwell said. As soon as the last child left the room and closed the door, Maxwell proceeded to read the letters that Sudfad had received. Letters that told of the attack by Karzman's men and the journey that Gabriel and Raphael joined. The letters told of the battles with Samael's demons and of Hector. The letters told of the Kingdom of Inferus and the words of the Angels. The group sat spellbound as they listened to Maxwell.

"I am not sure which of that is the most disturbing," said Emeral.

"I don't understand that entire thing about the journey that Angelina went on," Hannah said. "How could Gabriel and Raphael join them if it was like a dream?"

"Hannah we can tell you," said Diana. "Members of our tribe have taken such journeys but the stories are long. Do you want to hear them now?"

"Perhaps we should wait until tonight when the children go to bed," Hannah replied although a part of her really did not want to hear the stories at all.

"Well the good thing is that the demons will be occupied for a while," said Misha then he turned to Diana. "Maybe we should have our wedding ceremony soon."

Diana started to laugh. "I don't care but Emeral and Iris are planning everything. You should ask them."

"I think we can figure..." Emeral was interrupted when Margarit entered the study.

"I am sorry to interrupt but lots of Enrops are here with letters and they said some of them you need to read right away."

Late that night, Raul, Simon, Matthew, Gabriel and Raphael were in Raul's room playing cards. There was a knock on the door then Angelina, Nikki and Ingr entered. They were all carrying trays.

"We brought you some snacks," Angelina said with a big grin.

"I'll get more chairs," Raphael said and stood up.

"That's not necessary; we won't be here long," said Ingr.

Matthew was looking at the faces of all three women who were smiling. "Alright I know something is up. Why are you really here?"

"Well, since you asked," Angelina said and all of the men roared with laughter.

"We want to talk to you about Ryan," said Ingr. "He is the kindest man but he is so shy that he has never had a girlfriend."

"I have a feeling where this is going," Simon said with a grin.

"We've all seen the way he looks at Nyla," said Raul. "And don't get me wrong we would have nothing against them seeing each other but those girls have been through a lot. They sleep in our room most nights because they still get so scared. I am not sure that she is ready for a boyfriend."

"We agree with everything you said," said Nikki. "And Ryan realizes that too. But earlier tonight Saran told me that Nyla likes Ryan and that is why she is always so quiet around him. Trust us, Ryan is nothing like our husbands. It will probably take him weeks to get the nerve up to ask her to dance. We just wanted to see how all of you felt about it before we encouraged him at all."

"I don't think that Raul and Simon are the issue," said Gabriel. "I can see Michael being very protective of the girls. I would suggest that you have this exact same talk with him."

"We thought about that too," said Angelina. "But as far as all of you are concerned it would be alright if they saw each other a little? How about Sudfad and Renya?"

"Why are you making such a fuss about this?" asked Matthew.

"Because she is the first girl he has had a crush on and he is so sensitive that if any of you tell him to leave her alone, well he might not date again," said Ingr. "He is like our little brother and we are just watching out for him."

"He is also twenty years old," said Raphael. "Don't you think you are exaggerating a little?"

"They aren't," said Matthew. "Just be honest with him and tell him what we said."

"Why don't you get him and we will tell him," said Raul. "We all like him and know he is a good man."

"I'll get him," said Ingr and quickly left the room.

"After Ryan's grandfather died and before Claudius and Bella adopted him, Ryan was all alone and very lonely. He used to spend a lot of time with Thaos and me," explained Nikki. "I don't know if I have ever met anyone before who is so genuinely kind and considerate."

"But he is so shy. Having his business is making him come out of his shell. We just want to see him happy. All the rest of us are couples and he is always the odd man out. We've tried matching him up but he is always too shy to talk to the girls."

The door opened and Ingr and Ryan walked into the room. She was smiling and he looked embarrassed. "Ryan pull up a chair," Simon said while trying not to grin. "I'll just cut to the chase. We know that you and Nyla both like each other..."

"She likes me?" Ryan asked with such disbelief that it brought smiles to everyone's faces.

"Yes," said Raul. "And we certainly won't stand in the way of anything. But take it from us, dating is hard enough under normal circumstances and those girls have survived hell. It may take them awhile to get their feet on the ground. My suggestion would be to wait a while before you make your move."

"I don't think I have a move," Ryan said shyly. "I've never dated anyone."

Simon and Raul were trying hard not to grin. "Which means you might be the perfect match for Nyla," Gabriel said. "But Simon and Raul are right. I know the girls seem normal when all of you are together and I think that is because they want desperately to have a normal life."

"But they still get really scared of things and every night they ask to sleep in Simon's and Raul's room so they can feel safe."

"And they have a lot of nightmares," Simon said. "You can certainly let Nyla know you like her but you won't be able to see her often."

"You know Michael is going to be really protective of them. We can talk to him. Mother and Father would be delighted if you two started to see each other," Raul said.

"Like I said I haven't really dated anyone. I'm not sure what 'seeing each other' really means."

Angelina, Nikki and Ingr all stared at the men at the table and smiled. "Maybe you could give Ryan some pointers," Angelina said. "We'll leave you men to talk." The three women quickly left the room.

# Chapter XV
## News

Claudius was leading the combined armies away from the monastery at Leven. Thirty children now joined the group, most of them rode in bocas and some on horseback with their newly adopted parents. While every man and woman was happy to be returning home, they all felt concern for the priests and the monastery. Amundson and his men had left the monastery the previous evening. The demons would surely see that the monastery was without protection.

"You horses' ass!" Thor said loudly as he rode up to Kate and Edward, both of whom started laughing. "Why didn't you tell me you are getting married?"

"Well besides the fact that things have been a little crazy," Kate said. "Edward really wants to make a big deal out of our announcement."

"Hey, we are only doing this once, let's do it right," Edward said.

"That is fine but we have been friends since we were little. If you were going to tell anyone here it should have been me," Thor said with indignation.

"You are right and I am sorry," said Kate.

"Thor, it was me," said Edward. "I wanted to have a feast and present everyone who is going to be in the wedding with a gift. But since we are talking about it, who do you want to walk down the aisle with? Sorry but I haven't kept up with your dating. Are you seeing Melinda or Tanya now?"

"Tanya," Thor said as his demeanor softened. "Are you having a big wedding?"

"Yes," Edward said and looked at Kate and laughed. "She just isn't into any of this. I told her that we are doing this right."

"Thank you for coming," Sudfad said as High Priest Othnial walked into the King's study. "I apologize that I haven't spent any time with you since that first day you arrived."

"I am equally as guilty," Othnial said. "You know I am living in Gabriel's house, which is rather lively." Both men smiled when he said this. "By the second day, Hannah had me helping at the orphanage and hospital. And you know I am helping with the training of the Patronus priests here. I like keeping busy."

"I understand," Sudfad said as he poured two cups of coffee. "Do you know what your future plans are?"

"Only that the Angel Daniel told me to come here. I suppose I should pray for guidance as to where I need to go but right now I am enjoying my stay here and I don't want to leave until I can see Dominic, Fennel and the boys. They are like sons to me."

"Well, I have some things for you to consider," Sudfad said and sat back in his chair. "First, you have seen the Holy Vault. The Angels told us to build an altar down there besides places to study. While Gabriel and Raphael are capable they are gone a great deal. I was wondering if you would like to be in charge of the chapel we are building in the vault as well as the chapel at the Learning Center. I know you are busy so you don't have to say yes to either of these requests or you could choose just one."

Othnial looked genuinely surprised. "Why, I would be honored to fulfill both requests."

"Good, I will pay you for your services."

"That is not necessary."

"I will pay you and of course you can do with the money as you will. The Angels gave us some specific instructions as to the materials for building as well as making the material for the sacred cloths. The first shipment of wood is expected in a week. Alexander, Sam and Horace are the men you will need to speak with about that area. The material is rare and is being brought here by the teams that were in Port Friada. Laurel, Iris, Ella and Zelda are going to be making the sacred cloths."

"Of course you can have anything you want made for the chapel at the Learning Center also. Just let me know what materials and labor you will need. The chapel at the Learning Center is getting considerably more use now that the Patronus are training, but prior to that we only had a few weddings, christenings and one funeral held there. It is a beautiful building, I would like to see it get more use. I am open for any ideas."

"I will admit, this is all very exciting." Sudfad could hear the excitement in the voice of the old priest. "I believe I will go to the chapel at the Learning Center now and look around."

"I have a little free time," I will go with you. Perhaps we can put our heads together and come up with some ideas," Sudfad said.

"Come in," called Mathas as there was a knock at the door of his study. Fahron was leaving the room.

"Stay a minute," Hugo said as he walked into the room and closed the door.

"We thought you left after the meeting," said Mathas. "Did something happen?"

"Sorren asked me to check on Toni at least once a week. You know she is still in the dungeons at the fort," said Hugo.

"Actually we have talked about her," said Fahron. "We have few women in the dungeons but we consider her too dangerous to move anyplace else."

"I agree and that is part of the reason I am here. I have known Toni since she was born. The animal I am seeing in that cage is not the beautiful little girl of our village. I don't know what is happening to her. Sorren believes her to be mad and while I do not argue that point there is something else too. I would like the Sanuri to speak with her when he gets here."

"We have strict orders to the sergeants that none of our men or the prisoners are to harm her," said Fahron. "Do you suspect something like that?"

"I don't know if she is being tormented in some way or if her insanity is getting worse," said Hugo. "Fahron, I know that Timothy called to demons when he was a prisoner and I have considered that with Toni. But as you know I am a trained healer and we deal with such things. Of course I could be wrong but I don't think that is what is going on here."

"It might be a couple of weeks before the Sanuri gets here and you know that Edward and Kate are in that group. First, I don't think Toni should be given that information and secondly, is there anything you would like us to do?" asked Mathas.

"Let me go back and talk with some of the elders of my tribe. Perhaps there are some ceremonies we can try to determine what is happening to her. We have offered to help her heal many times but she always refuses. You cannot force someone to denounce their personal demons," said Hugo.

"What are you giggling about?" asked the Sanuri and smiled at the boys. Cassidy, Logan and Marty were all crammed in the front seat of the boca with him. The boys giggled louder.

"Did you know we are all going to be living in a castle together?" Marty asked. "A real castle."

"Yes. Have you ever been in a castle before?"

"No," said all of the boys. "Have you been to the one we are going to be living in?" asked Logan.

"Oh my yes. Many times. In fact, I have my own chambers there. Bella, that is Cassidy's new mother designed me special chambers because of my work."

"What makes them special?" asked Cassidy.

"Well, most chambers consist of one to three bedrooms, a bathing room and perhaps a small parlor. My chambers also have a study and a library. Logan and Marty the chambers that you are going to be living in with Gideon and Ashley are very similar."

"Thaos is married to Nikki and they have three children," the Sanuri explained. "They have an area in the castle that is an actual home as does Stephan and his wife Ingr and their three children. Claudius, Bella and Ryan live in the central wings of the castle. They have many rooms that they rarely use because they built the castle big in case people needed to take shelter there."

"Why would people do that?" asked Logan.

"If there are wars or really bad storms," said the Sanuri. "Cassidy, I would guess that your bedroom is going to be in the central wing also."

"Where is yours?" asked Marty.

"The central wing."

"There is a huge stone wall around the castle like there was at the monastery. And inside of the wall there are many buildings besides the castle because soldiers are stationed there. It is a very big place. I would not be surprised if you get lost once in a while."

"Wow," said Marty. "Really?"

"Yes," the Sanuri said and laughed. "And you know that both of your new fathers work for the King and are friends of his so you will be spending a lot of time at King Mathas' castle too."

"I didn't know that," said Cassidy.

"And King Mathas' sister is Queen Renya of the Kingdom of Wetpr; she is married to King Sudfad. Edward's and Dominic's teams and many others here work for King Sudfad. You will be meeting him in a few weeks because all of you are going to Wetpr for a wedding." All the boys smiled and their eyes widened. "So you have some real adventures ahead of you."

"We know," said Marty with a sense of awe.

"That is where your friend Petra lives isn't it?" asked Cassidy.

"Yes, and I think all of you will get along very well."

Raul and Simon were preparing their soldiers to leave for Wetpr when several flocks of Enrops landed in the front courtyard of Claudius' castle. Raul was close to the front entrance and ran up the steps and yelled inside that Enrops were delivering mail. Amy and Nina were the first two to run out of the castle. Both little girls screamed with delight and wanted to hug the birds.

Matthew was walking out of the castle with packs when Raul said, "There is a lot of mail here. Might mean something is wrong. We should read our letters first before leaving."

"Nina run in and get a basket," Simon said as his hands were filled with envelopes. When Nina returned with the basket, her sisters as well as Bella, Ingr and Nikki were with her.

"What on earth!" said Bella. "Has something happened that there are so many letters?"

"A lot of these are for the soldiers," said Simon.

Bella's family and guests all gathered in the parlor with their piles of letters. "The mission related letters we should probably pass around to make sure we all get the same information," said Gabriel. "Bella are you interested in reading some of these?"

"Why yes, I would like that. Thank you."

Many of the letters were from Claudius' group and the team members who were at the monastery. The letters told of the battles and the words of the Angels. "Boys maybe all of you should read this one," Bella said. "It is from Ashley, you know Gideon's fiancé. Well, you can read it for yourselves but Gideon wanted to thank the Angel Adam for protecting the children and the Angel said that if Gideon was sincere he could build safe houses for children; so they could be protected until they were taken to orphanages. And the Angel told Gideon to tell Sudfad about the houses, he said Sudfad would know what to do."

"Yes, let us see that," said Simon and took the letter.

"Gabriel, Raphael you won't believe this," said Saran. "We got letters from your families. They don't even know us."

"All of our families are very close," said Raul.

"Have any of you opened the letters yet about all of the sightings of Madeline and Javier around our house and Erebus'?" asked Raphael.

Matthew was the first to say, "No." Raphael handed him the letter.

"Bella do you think you can put up with us a little longer?" asked Raul. "I think we need to answer some of these letters."

"Boys, we absolutely love having you here. And as far as I am concerned we are all family too. Stay as long as you like."

"Bella, Thaos says that Claudius adores Cassidy and carries the boy all around," Nikki said with a warm smile.

"Oh, I have to read his letter next. That makes me so happy," Bella said excitedly.

Simon, got out of his seat and showed a letter to all of the men, each of them grinned when they read it. "What is going on?" asked Ingr.

"Mother is going to kill me," Simon said and laughed.

"I think we should tell them before they prepare for another long trip," said Raul.

Simon walked up to Bella and handed her the letter. "Oh my, girls, oh my," Bella said and the men started to laugh. Nikki and Ingr got out of their chairs and stood behind Bella so they could read the letter too.

"What is it?" asked Angelina and got out of her seat.

"Renya redesigned the north wing of the castle which is the second largest. She built second homes for everyone from here. She said since there are so many children and babies they don't have to bring so much when they travel," said Matthew. "That is so typical Aunt Renya."

"That is so incredibly generous of her and Sudfad," Bella said. "Really, I hardly know what to say."

"Bella, you know Mother. I am sure the places look great but she will expect that you decorate them as you want," said Raul. "So don't think about hurting her feelings if you don't like something."

"I am telling her that we told you," said Simon. "In case you want to start bringing extra things to put into your homes." He started laughing. "For years Raul and I lived out of our saddlebags. Now we practically fill a boca with all the things needed for the children. It's a big production now when our families travel."

"This sounds like she made homes for each of us," Nikki said. "Is that right?"

"That's what it sounds like to us too," said Raul. "We didn't know about this until that letter."

"Do you think I can write to her now or should I wait until she gets your letter?" asked Bella.

"Write to her," Raul said. "Mother knows us. She won't be surprised that we told you."

Claudius' group was also visited by several flocks of Enrops delivering mail. After the third delivery, Claudius had everyone stop for an early lunch break so they could read their mail.

Harlow walked up to Claudius, Sorren, Stephan and Thaos as they ate lunch. He handed Claudius a letter, who nodded and smiled when he read it then handed it to Sorren.

"I wrote to Wickfield about what the Angel Ruth told me," explained Harlow. "He set me up with an office and a couple of staff members. Exposing the tyrants, dark lords and demons will be my main assignment."

"I think we will need to assign soldiers to protect all of you," said Stephan.

"I agree," said Claudius. "Harlow, I think you should come to Wetpr with us in a few weeks and meet everyone."

Erebus and the Sanuri now joined the group. "Madeline and Javier have been visiting my home and Gabriel's," Erebus said and handed his letter to Thaos, who was the closest to him.

"Are they sure it's those two?" asked Sorren.

"Yes, because they introduced themselves to all the children at Gabriel's home and apparently tried to get the kids to come with them but the dogs wouldn't let them near the children," said Erebus.

"Now that pisses me off," said Stephan. "Remember when warriors used to fight each other instead of involving innocent people and children?"

"I don't think we will ever see those days again," said the Sanuri. "There is too much dishonor now."

It was late afternoon by time Bella's family and Raul's group read all of the letters and wrote their own. They had spread out among desks and tables in several rooms. Now Gabriel, Raul, Simon and Raphael walked around the castle until they found Bella, Nikki and Ingr. "Bella, we are going to take you up on your offer," said Simon. "We don't want to start out this late since we have the girls with us. So we were thinking; why don't all of you get dressed up and we will take you out someplace fancy for dinner. We can pick Ryan up from the shop."

"Oh, that sounds like fun," said Bella. "And I know just the spot. There is a new restaurant and they built it in such a manner that the back hangs over the ocean."

"Sounds great," said Gabriel.

"Could we be out late?" asked Ingr.

"We might. Is that a problem?" asked Raul.

"No, Nikki and I should probably leave the babies here with the nurses so they get their sleep. We'll just bring Amy."

"Couldn't help but notice how you brightened up after you got those letters," Drake said as he and Tally rode next to Michael.

"They are from my sisters. They sound so happy. I've never seen them really happy before. And it sounds like everyone is being really good to them. But Raul said they have a lot of nightmares and most nights they want to sleep in the same room as Simon and Raul because they get scared. Renya is putting them in the chambers next to mine so they can stay with me."

"Michael, you know me and Drake have done a lot of low down things but you should know that we didn't approve of what Karzman and your brothers were doing to those girls."

"But you didn't stop them," Michael said angrily. "That's as bad."

"Actually Tally and River, you remember him; big guy with one eye. Well, they did stop your step brothers one time and Karzman had them strung up and whipped. Look at Tally's back if you don't believe me. River left the tribe after that and Karzman had him hunted down and killed."

"If you're lying to me, so help me..."

"Drake ain't lying," Tally said as he unbuttoned his shirt and took it off. Michael slowed his horse and looked at Tally's back which was covered with massive scars."

"Michael the reason I am telling you this is cuz we are going back there with you," Drake said. "Karzman always had you locked up like a damn animal. But he was as bad to others as he was to all of you. He raped other men's wives and kids and killed anybody that said shit to him. You are right; most of us stood by and knew what he was doing to you but there were people who tried to stop him. He just killed them all."

Michael was shocked by Drake's words. "I didn't know anyone tried to help us."

"Don't you remember that time some of the villagers waited until Karzman was hunting and they loaded you, your mama and sisters in a boca and left the village?" asked Drake.

"What? I have no idea what you are talking about."

"Drake, he was pretty young then," Talley said. "It was an older couple, Gus and Penelope. They couldn't stand to see what he was doing to you and planned an escape. A lot of the villagers were involved and gonna lie for you but somehow Karzman found out. He skinned them both alive and beat the living hell out of all of you."

"Michael, we're telling you this because the way you always talk you thought everyone in that tribe hated you. They didn't. They didn't do the right thing because they were afraid of Karzman and it shames me to say it but that goes for me too. It ain't no type of excuse; it's just the truth," said Drake. "You know more than half that tribe was your mama's people. Karzman hired his soldiers. Tally and me were working in Stordt when he hired us."

Michael stared at Tally and Drake. "I never thought about any of that. So why did you stay? Did he pay that well?" Tally and Drake looked at each other with confusion. "Why are you looking like that?"

"Guess we are realizing that you were always in prison and didn't know what was going on," Tally said. "We told you that we left cuz he was worshipping demons and wanted the rest of us to do the same. But he always had a bunch of demons in the village and he would get visits from other demons and who the hell knows where they came from."

"You're shitting me. I never saw any demons, well there was that time they appeared in the cage." Michael was talking about the time that the Angel Adam saved him.

"Michael, Karzman had this pack of the ugliest creatures you ever done saw. They kind of looked like dogs. But they were some kind of demons. We all called them demon dogs. You fought them, don't' you remember. You were pretty little and Karzman let them at you. You must have been nine and you killed every one of those monsters. Well, of course Karzman gets more but after that none of them demon dogs would come near you." Tally said.

"I never saw those damn things," said Michael.

"Saw them, you fought them," said Drake. "We was hunting and didn't see it but everyone in the village talked about it for weeks. And Karzman was acting really strange afterwards and takes one of his long trips and when he comes back be has another pack of those things."

"He used to set those damn things on his own people," said Tally. "And if anyone left the tribe he sent the pack after them. Michael, you are the only one who ever fought those things and lived. The reason we didn't desert with the first group is cuz we wanted to see if he would send those dogs after his soldiers. But when he turned into an old man those damn demon dogs disappeared."

Michael stared at Drake and Tally for a few moments then he yelled out loud, "Ruth! Ruth!"

The Angel's voice was heard only by Michael. "I told you there was a lot you didn't know and you are so angry with me that you wouldn't believe me. As for the fight they are talking about; you will have to talk to Adam about that."

Gabriel, Simon, Matthew, Angelina, Raul, Raphael, Bella, Nikki, Ingr, Ryan, Amy, Nina, Nyla and Saran walked into the White Rose Restaurant and Raul asked for a large table with the best view of the ocean. The host escorted them to the back of the restaurant where the entire back wall was made of windows.

"This should be beautiful when the sun sets," Matthew said as he held Angelina's chair for her.

"This is a restaurant?" asked Nyla. "I have never seen any place like this before."

"Why do they have such fancy places for people to eat?" asked Nina.

"Let me think about that answer," Raul said with a grin.

"Because it is fun," said Ingr.

"Nikki, I am afraid I will hurt your dress," said Saran self-consciously.

"Nonsense", said Bella. "We are just lucky we could find things for you to wear."

"That is our fault," said Simon. "We didn't think they would need anything fancy until we got home."

"Everything worked out," Nikki said. "You know Bella bought Ingr and me our first fancy dresses. We never wore things like this before."

"Well, I am glad you brought me something to change into," said Ryan. "I doubt if they would even have let me in here." Nyla was wearing one of Ingr's dresses; it was a dark blue with tiny straps and Ryan couldn't stop staring at her.

They stayed in the restaurant for hours eating, drinking and laughing. Raul and Simon ordered all kinds of extra dishes and desserts for Nina, Saran and Nyla to try.

A platoon of soldiers waited outside with the carriages and horses. Matthew and Angelina were in the lead as the group walked out of the restaurant. As Matthew motioned to the soldiers to bring the carriages closer, Gabriel asked, "What is happening?" Everyone now turned and saw a large crowd gathering on the beach.

"Take the girls to the carriage," Raphael said. "Gabriel and I will see what is going on. It could be a diversion."

The three Princes quickly ushered all of the women and children into the two carriages. Raul and Matthew each stayed with a carriage while Simon walked towards the crowd. Simon found Gabriel and Raphael examining the gigantic body of a creature that Simon had never seen before. The rest of the crowd stood back.

"It is dead," Gabriel said as Simon walked up to them. "But have you ever seen anything like this? It looks like a lizard but it is bigger than a horse. Some of the people said that soldiers went to get the Mathas and Fahron."

"I am going back up so that Matthew and Raul can see this," said Raphael.

A few minutes later, Bella, Nikki, Ingr, Ryan, Raul, Matthew and Angelina walked up to the creature. No one in the crowd wanted to venture as close to the monster so they stood about ten feet away.

"Ingr, you should draw this," Angelina said. "Matthew, we need to get her some paper and a pen." Matthew walked up to a soldier who returned several minutes later with the items.

The crowd parted as Mathas and Fahron dismounted and walked up to the body of the creature. "This area of the beach is always busy," Matthew explained in a low voice to his father and Fahron. "People in the crowd said no one saw this thing until a little less than one hour ago. They didn't see anything else; it appears to have washed up on shore."

Fishermen had lit many torches and stuck them in the sand surrounding the creature so that everyone could clearly see it. "It has wounds," said Gabriel. "If I had to guess I would say from spears; there are five on this side. It is too heavy for us to roll over. Come closer."

When Mathas and Fahron were very close to Gabriel he said. "We didn't want the others to see this. Raphael took this off the creature right away."

"Is that what I think it is?" asked Fahron with disbelief.

"It's a bridle," said Simon in a low voice. "Can you even imagine what was riding that thing?"

## Chapter XVI
## Coming to Terms

That night Michael tossed and turned for hours. Finally he got up and walked away from the campsites and into the forest. "Adam, Ruth," he said in a whisper. After a few moments he called their names louder and a third time even louder. The Angels appeared. They did not speak and neither did Michael.

"You called us," Adam said after several moments.

Michael walked closer to the Angels. "Is what Drake and Tally told me the truth?"

"Yes," said Ruth. "And they have a great deal more to tell you. I am glad that you listen to them since you refuse to listen to us."

"Adam did you fight the demon dogs?" Michael asked.

"Adam fought every demon that Karzman and Teivel sent after you," said Ruth. "And there were many more instances than the two you have been told about."

"Thank you," said Michael sheepishly. "Did you help me when I did fight?"

"You did your own fighting but I often kept more adversaries from jumping into the cage," said Adam. "And if you really are sincere about thanking me then just for once rise above your rage and listen to us."

Michael looked back and forth between the two Angels and said in a low voice, "I will listen."

"If you didn't allow Karzman's shadow to still imprison you," said Ruth in a scolding manner. "You would see the things unfolding around you with different eyes. Michael, you are an exceptionally intelligent man. Now tell us, have you yet considered what circumstances came together that you saved Drake and Tally at the same time that your sisters escaped and Sudfad is planning his attack against Karzman?"

"No, but it is all happening together."

"Once you actually commit yourself to your destiny, your anger and fears will not run your life," said Ruth.

"What do you mean?" asked Michael angrily. "What do I fear?"

"Michael pretend that all three of us were looking at the moon but we each held a different colored piece of glass before our eyes. We would see the same object but differently, wouldn't you agree?" asked Adam. Michael nodded.

"The piece of glass that you hold up is colored by your rage and fears. While this really isn't uncommon for many people for you it is particularly dangerous because you are a Seventh Son and a Keeper of the Scrolls. The glass that you hold needs to be clear. You ask what you fear because you have already faced the horrors of mankind. Look to your heart Michael. There is a reason that you don't let anyone in. You feel that everyone you have ever been close to betrayed you and yes even your beloved mother."

"Now you are finding out the horrors they suffered to try to protect you. And why do you think you are afraid to get close to your new family? You care about them and you certainly fit in with them."

Michael was quiet for a couple of moments. "I'm afraid they are going to betray me too. I didn't realize that."

"Have any of them even remotely said or done anything that would lead you to believe you couldn't trust them?" Adam asked. "Every day you receive letters from them and pictures from the children. They don't know your sisters but they have risked their lives to protect them. Sudfad and Renya will adopt them, the papers are already drawn up. You could have a happy life if you would allow yourself. You can fight anything except your personal demons."

"There are no coincidences," continued Adam. "And these things are happening for more reasons than to have you look into a mirror. Think about what Tally and Drake told you. What did you realize?"

"I know what you are talking about. My village, even those two were victims too. I wanted nothing to do with any of them because I hated them all for not helping us. But, they need, they need us to save them; don't they?" Michael's eyes widened as he spoke.

"If you would have been looking through the clear glass you would have already realized that," said Adam. "You told me you would not stand by and allow others to be victimized and yet you are so blinded by your rage that you can't tell the victims from the monsters. You left that village as a prisoner and you will return as the conquering army. You will return as the eldest son of the King. Do you think you can help your people? And will you rise above your hatred and help them? For you, Tally and Drake will be the only ones in that army who really understand what your people have suffered and why they may act the way they do."

"What do you mean?" asked Michael.

"You could not understand how the people of Ryed allowed themselves to be victimized by the tyrants. Yet the same thing has happened to your tribe, the tribe of your mother and grandmother, both of whom suffered greatly trying to protect you and your sisters. Your people lost hope long ago. You might say they lost their spirits. We need to rekindle life in them again. But how can you do that when your spirit is in such conflict?" asked Adam.

"Michael we know your thoughts," said Ruth. "We know how you have fantasied about returning to your village and killing everyone. Do you think you can become the man that The Great Ruler meant you to be and go back and save them?"

Michael stayed in the forest after the Angels left. He did something he had not done in a long time. He wept.

"You're awfully quiet," the Sanuri said to Michael as they sat around a fire eating their breakfast. Many of the team members and Claudius' family were eating in the same area."

"Last night I went into the forest and called to Adam and Ruth," Michael said haltingly as he was still very emotional. "I wanted to ask them about some things that Tally and Drake told me..." Michael paused for a long time and no one else spoke.

"All of you know a little about my life," Michael said. "And you know I planned to kill Sudfad and that my anger was the only thing that kept me alive. Well, I was wrong. The Angels kept me alive and innocent people got hurt trying to keep me alive..." Michael was looking at the ground as he spoke. "Sudfad wasn't the only one I wanted to kill. I wanted to return to my village and kill them all."

"Then yesterday, Drake and Tally told me things I never knew and I realized that all those people I hated were as much victims as me, Mama and my sisters. Even Tally got hurt protecting my sisters and the man that helped him was murdered."

"Adam gave me an example of the three of us all looking at the moon through pieces of different colored glass. He said my glass was colored by my rage and fears so I couldn't see things the way they really are. Ruth said that part of my destiny is to save my people but she doesn't know if I can do it. I don't know if I can do it."

Jared and Archetenus were sitting on either side of Michael and could see how emotional he was. "Michael, Archetenus and me were the same way, hell a lot of us here have been at some time or other. I was so full of hatred not only for the Hutas but myself that I became worse than them. It wasn't until I met Zoya that she knocked some sense in me. Look at Thaos too. Hell if we can change you sure as hell can. And we ain't even one of you fancy boys talked about in the prophesies."

Michael laughed loudly at Jared's words. "Adam said that I had to start looking at things through clear glass or I would never be able to fulfil my destiny. I will be honest, I wasn't sure that I even wanted to."

"Then you have a lot of decisions to make," said the Sanuri. "Did he tell you anything else?"

Michael looked at the Sanuri then smiled. "Yeah, he said I expect everyone to betray me which is why I don't let any of you or my family close."

"I can understand that," said Thaos. "I felt the same way until Claudius and Bella took me in."

"Michael, you were shocked by the Angels' words yet many of us already knew those things," said the Sanuri. "I am glad that you listened to them. Look about you. There isn't a man, woman or even child in this group who has had an easy life. And many of them extraordinarily difficult like you, Thaos and Ashley. But do you see how their journeys changed when they simply chose to look through the clear glass? That is what Jared is trying to tell you."

"You know I thought that I was surrounded by enemies..." Michael said then paused. "Drake and Tally told me that the members of my tribe were my mother's people and that Karzman hired his soldiers. I thought everyone backed Karzman but Drake said they feared him. He had packs of demons but they looked like dogs and he would use them against the people of the tribe. He sent them after me once and Adam fought them. But Adam made himself look like me. Ruth said that Adam fought every one of my fights when Karzman and Teivel sent demons after me and he helped me fighting the regular men and animals."

"All this time I thought that everyone hated me but Drake said they were just too scared to do the right thing. An old couple tried to help us escape and Karzman skinned them alive. I never saw anything right."

"Michael, that is over and done with," said Claudius. "You were a child and it was your anger that kept you alive. But you are a man now so what are you going to do?"

"I am going to help my people," Michael said with conviction.

"Good," said Stephan with a grin. "Cuz we are going to kill that bastard and it would be nice to have you along."

"It should be Michael that kills him," said Thaos. "Like me with Kagen."

Instead of leaving early in the morning, Gabriel, Raphael, Raul, Simon and Matthew attended Mathas' morning meeting. They brought numerous copies of the image of the creature that Ingr had drawn. Hugo was the only man in the room who had not seen the creature.

"This is unbelievable," Hugo repeated as he studied one of the drawings.

"We've had men stationed around the beast all night," said Fahron. "They are going to move it to the fort so we can study it."

"That ought to take all day," said Simon sarcastically. "Send us any information you find."

"Ingr made a drawing of the bridle for us to take," said Raphael. "We will have team members make copies. You might want to have the Sanuri look at that when he gets here."

"Hopefully he can look at the body too," Mathas said. "Although it will be in bad shape by that time."

"The Angels said that the Elods bred strange creatures," Matthew said. "I wonder if this is one of theirs."

"But how did it get here?" asked Mathas. "If there is some kind of door that is big enough for that thing to get through, an entire army could come through."

"And maybe we could get through," said Gabriel.

Ryan was walking in one of the gardens near Claudius' castle with Nyla, Saran and Nina. "Would it be ok if I wrote to you?" Ryan asked Nyla.

"I'll write to you Ryan," Nina said loudly and they all laughed.

"Alright," he said with a big smile.

"I would like that," said Nyla shyly.

"You two act so goofy," Saran scolded. "You both like each other just admit it. Of course she wants you to write to her."

"Saran! I can't believe you said that!" Nyla said and blushed.

"Well it's true," Saran said. "And you are both shy. You know it's not like you are going to be living near each other. You need to, I don't know, talk or something."

When the army that Claudius led resumed their journey, Michael rode up to Drake and Tally and asked them to tell him about his tribe. He was so captivated by the stories that Michael didn't realize how much time had passed when Claudius had everyone stop for a midday meal.

For the first time, Michael made a campsite with Tally and Drake and the men continued to talk about Karzman and the village.

"Don't know why you sound so surprised about what that Angel said," Drake said to Michael. "We sure ain't. It makes perfect sense in a strange way."

"What do you mean?" asked Michael.

"Well first, how could a little boy fight all of those demons and win?" asked Drake. "People were starting to wonder if you were some kind of demon too. And why would the Angels go to all that work to help you if you weren't intended to do something really good? That's kind of why me and Tally were confused when you had such a jaded view of everything. I mean we know why you hate us but a lot of people in that village suffered because of trying to help your family. And here you go and tell us you wanted to kill them all."

"I don't hate you guys. I probably should but I don't. The Angels said that the three of us are going to be the only ones who understand that tribe when we get there."

"Did they say what they wanted us to do?" asked Tally.

"No and I didn't ask. I should have. I think I was in some kind of shock listening to them," said Michael.

"We'll you'll have to ask them before we get there," Tally said. "They might want us to bring stuff."

"You're right," Michael said. "I need to tell Sudfad too. I am going to write to him now."

The next couple of days were chaotic in the castle of Sudfad as the family prepared for the return of their beloved sons and husbands and for the homecoming of Michael's sisters. Because of the numerous sightings of Madeline and Javier, Sudfad greatly increased the number of soldiers guarding all of the members of the Royal Family. While everyone understood the reasoning, Vitomas and Annabelle always felt confined.

As busy as the schedules were for the two princesses, they continued their ritual of going into the city one morning a week for shopping and socializing. The event always ended with the two young women going to the Green Dragon's Inn and having desserts that were specially prepared for them by Myla, the wife of the owner.

Citizens would gather in the restaurant of the inn to talk with the Princesses. For years Vitomas and Annabelle scheduled their shopping trips on Tuesday mornings. Because of this regular scheduling the shopkeepers as well as other citizens knew in advance that the Princesses would be in the city without their husbands. It was the time when the two women felt like they could relax and mingle with the populace.

Occasionally some of the women from Gabriel's household would join Vitomas and Annabelle and on this morning it was Hannah and Natasha.

"I feel guilty leaving the baby but this has been so much fun," Natasha said as the four women entered the Green Dragon's Inn. "It sounds awful but it is nice to be without children for a couple of hours."

"Are you kidding," Annabelle said and laughed. "That is exactly why we do this."

"Although sometimes we have thought about getting a hotel room and just taking a nap," Vitomas said and smiled.

"I don't think that sounds bad at all," Hannah said. "My problem isn't as much that the children keep me awake but I can never sleep when Gabriel is gone. I am so looking forward to them returning."

"From their letters, it sounds like Gabriel and Raphael have adopted Michael's little sisters too," Natasha said. "They can't get over how normal the girls are acting after all they have been through."

"Renya says that everything is so new and exciting for them that she is afraid it will all hit them when everything settles down," Annabelle said. The women were standing in the lobby of the inn which was exceptionally crowded. "I've never seen this many people here before, I wonder if something is going on."

The soldiers who were escorting the women remained outside of the inn, now one of them entered and walked up to the women. "A body was found in the alley near the kitchen," the soldier explained. "We need to take you home now."

"Do you know who was killed?" asked Annabelle. "These people are our friends."

"All I know is that it is the body of a woman," the soldier said.

"Not Myla," gasped Vitomas. "Make way we have a physician!" Vitomas screamed several times as the four women pushed their way through the crowd. The soldier followed the women but tried to watch the faces in the crowd for signs of danger.

Vitomas and Annabelle knew the layout of the inn well. They pushed through the crowd in the lobby then turned left into the dining room which was also crowded. They forced their way through the people and entered the kitchen where they found many of the staff members crying.

"Hannah is a physician," Vitomas yelled.

Simultaneously Annabelle yelled, "Who is it?" One of the women who was crying merely pointed to the alley door and the women ran in that direction.

"Oh Myla, thank god it's not you," gasped Vitomas as the women found a small group of people standing over a body in the alley.

Rex, Myla's husband quickly turned to the women. "I don't think you want to see this," he said and held out his massive arms to block them from approaching the body.

"I am a physician," Hannah said and she and Natasha pushed past Rex.

"Oh my god!" said Natasha. "I have seen Hutas do this to people but no one else."

"Well, she wasn't killed in this alley," said Hannah. "There isn't any blood except for what is on her. She was killed someplace else and dumped here.

"But why?" asked Myla.

"Do you know her?" Annabelle asked as she and Vitomas now walked closer to the body.

"It is hard to tell," said Rex. "But she doesn't look familiar."

Hannah looked at the soldier and said, "Get the other soldiers and move this body to my office here in Salar. I want to examine her. Something is very wrong here."

Natasha looked at Myla and Rex. "Is this how you found her? I mean did you or anyone else move anything?"

"No," said Rex. "When I closed the restaurant last night I put the trash over there," he pointed to a pile of garbage that was sitting on top of a large pile of ashes. "You know me and Myla live in the inn and no one told us that they heard or saw anything unusual. Myla has been in the kitchen most of the morning. One of the cooks came out here to throw garbage on that pile and found her. No one has touched anything."

"I'm going to get a blanket and cover the poor thing," Myla said and turned to go inside of the inn. "We can't let her be seen like that."

Sudfad's morning meeting was ending when there was a knock at the door. Joshua got up to open the door but Renya and a soldier burst into the room before he could do it. "Sudfad, the girls went to the Green Dragon's Inn and, well, there was a body of a woman in the alley," Renya now turned to the soldier. "You tell them the rest."

"My Lord, I did not see the body but I was told it was cut up savagely. Hannah believes that the woman was..."

"Hannah? What was Hannah doing there?" asked Maxwell.

"She and Natasha were with the Princesses," the soldier replied. "Hannah had the body taken to her office in the city so she can examine it."

"You were saying that Hannah had some thoughts on the matter," Sudfad said.

"She believes the woman was killed someplace else and dumped in that alley. My Lord, I don't need to remind you that the entire city knows the Princesses go to the Green Dragon every Tuesday morning. I don't know if it is related but I don't believe it was just random either," said the soldier.

"Do you have anything that can link the body to the Princesses?" asked Misha.

"No, guess you could call it a gut feeling. And I don't mind saying my gut is usually right."

"Corporal Novack, I tend to agree with you," said Sudfad. "Why don't you wait and I will ride into the city with you. But first alert the men here. I will send a message to the fort."

"We're coming with you," said Maxwell.

"I assumed you would," Sudfad said then turned to Renya. "Keep the children in today and would you send a message to the Learning Center. This might be good training for the Patronus."

## Chapter XVII
## The Faces of Evil

Although the soldiers kept trying to persuade Vitomas and Annabelle to return to the castle, the women went to Hannah's medical office in Salar. Hannah had an office in her home, one in the orphanage, a third in the hospital at Fort Salar and the fourth in a building in the City of Salar.

This building was being remodeled into a hospital. Sudfad had purchased all of the buildings on a city block and was having them made into the hospital. Because this covered such a large area, Hannah and the medical students from the Learning Center could care for patients in the clinic in front of the hospital while the back was still undergoing construction.

On this day Shara was at the clinic in the city with students while Gala and her students were at the hospital at Fort Salar. Hannah had the soldiers carry the body up the back stairs so as not to alarm the patients in the front of the clinic.

"We want to see what you do," said Annabelle. "Do you need help?"

"First, I will be carefully washing her so I don't lose any evidence," said Hannah. "Would one of you get Shara? She is more knowledgeable in the torture techniques of the Hutas than I am." Vitomas turned and quickly left the examine room.

"Here," Natasha said as she handed the women large aprons. "One of the soldiers is getting us water."

"I know what the Angels said but it is too quiet," Claudius said to Sorren as they led the combined armies north to the border between the Kingdoms of Ganz and Zorta. Claudius now turned and yelled to Stephan, "Bring the Sanuri and Erebus up here."

Stephan broke out of formation and raced to the back of the caravan. "Halt! Halt!" Claudius ordered his troops. "Prepare for an attack!" The orders were yelled down the formation.

One of the Nordes warriors changed places with the Sanuri so he could respond to Claudius more quickly. The warrior now drove the boca which was filled with children and the Sanuri rode the warrior's horse to the front of the formation. Erebus had waited for the Sanuri and the two were following Stephan. "Father thinks something is wrong," Stephan yelled as the three sped towards Claudius and Sorren.

Ruala warriors were flying in advance of the army as well as in the rear. Enrops were flying overhead. Both Claudius and Sorren were searching the sky but nothing appeared out of the ordinary. "Are we riding into some kind of demon trap?" Claudius asked when Stephan, Erebus and the Sanuri stopped their horses near him.

"Nothing is moving," said Sorren. "Not a bird or a bug." Both the Sanuri and Erebus rode forward. The army was less than a day's ride from the border. They were just north of the large Village of Hadne which lay thirty miles to their west and they were west of a massive mountain range that expanded eastward to the coast. There were numerous working gold mines in this range.

"I don't feel that kind of energy," Erebus said. "But you are right, something is..."

"Look to the sky! Look to the sky!" yelled a soldier.

Six Ruala warriors were flying back to the army. One of the warriors appeared to be carrying something large. As they got closer the army recognized Sol in the lead and he was carrying a body.

Shara, Marina and eight medical students ran into the small examination room as Hannah and Natasha were cleaning dried blood from the wounds of the dead woman.

"Good you are here," Hannah said to Shara. "Perhaps we can rotate the students through here." Shara walked closer to the body as Hannah now addressed everyone in the room.

"This woman was found in the alley next to the Green Dragon's Inn. At this point no one knows who she is or how she got there. She is covered in dried blood but there was no blood in the alley. Which leads me to believe she was not killed there but dumped there. The inn is a very busy place in the center of the city so you have to ask yourselves why and how someone did this."

"And on the day that Vitomas and Annabelle always go there," said Sudfad as he, Maxwell, Joshua, Misha, Luca and Elan squeezed into the crowded room.

"Do you think this has something to do with us?" gasped Vitomas.

"We can't rule out that it is a warning or message of some kind," said Maxwell. The students moved to let the men closer to the body.

"I was in Nora when those crazy priests were trying to raise the demon Omnibus," Hannah explained. "The priests and the Hutas they commanded were stealing people to work in the mines and for sacrifices. One night a poor soul was brought to my home and he had symbols carved all over his body. I could not save him but he told us the Hutas had done that to him. With all the wounds on this woman I want to see if she too has symbols carved into her skin. So we are carefully washing away the dried blood. If there are symbols, I have to admit that I won't be able to explain them to you."

"Did you take her clothes?" asked Misha.

"No, this is how Myla and Rex found her," said Vitomas. "Actually one of their cooks saw the body first, but Myla and Rex came out immediately after the woman screamed and didn't let anyone near the body until we got there."

Shara was now assisting in cleaning the corpse. "The fact that her eyes have been cut out could have some kind of meaning but I will tell you that the Hutas are not the only animals that do things like this. I have seen people carved up just out of meanest."

"I am going back and search the alley," Misha said.

"I will go with you," said Luca and the two men left the room.

Archetenus and Jared rode to the front of the long formation. "I don't know if any of you know this," Archetenus said. But west of the river are the diamond mines which have been shut down because of Rogetts. They destroyed the entire Village of Norta."

"How far are they?" asked Sorren.

"Two, maybe three days ride to the west," said Archetenus. "Now it's been maybe six or seven years since Norta was massacred."

"So the monsters could be breeding in the mines," Claudius said as they watched the Ruala warriors approaching them. "It's not one of ours that Sol is carrying."

Sol saw the Sanuri and immediately landed in front of him. "We found a bunch of miner's shacks northeast of here," Adin yelled. "Bodies everywhere. This one is still alive."

The Sanuri as well as others dismounted and ran up to Sol and the wounded man. "I tried to stop the bleeding the best I could," said Sol. "We just missed the attack. He says it was Rogetts."

"Is he alive?" asked Claudius.

"He's been in and out of consciousness," Sol said. "We didn't have anything for the pain." Sol placed the miner on the ground and the Sanuri was kneeling over the man and praying.

"What are Rogetts?" asked Thor as he, Edward and Kate dismounted.

"You've never heard of Rogetts?" asked Thaos incredulously.

"Me neither," Kate said. "Maybe we didn't have that tribe in Ryed."

"I guess you could call them a tribe," said Thaos. "They are humans but you wouldn't believe it to look at them. They live in the earth and well, I think they kinda look like large rats that walk on two legs. They eat people."

"They eat humans! Are you kidding?" said Thor loudly as he was examining the wounds of the miner.

"Kid, they eat their own kind if they are hungry enough," said Jared. "The story goes that they moved underground thousands of years ago because everything here scared the shit out of them so they turn into worst nightmares than what they was running from."

"Is that true?" asked Kate skeptically.

"I think that is the same story that all of us have heard," said Edward.

"People call them demons," explained Erebus. "But they are humans. They sell their souls to demons so they all bear the Mark of Satan on their chests. You know the coiled red snake."

"The ones I've fought with don't wear much in the way of clothes so you can easily see the tattoo," said Thaos. "And they certainly aren't warriors. They attack the weak and defenseless first and they always attack in packs. There isn't a creature alive that has any respect for those monsters."

"It is strange to hear the way you said that," said Erebus.

"Well, we all hate the Hutas but they are well trained and tough sons of bitches," said Thaos. "And before they sold their souls they used to fight more like men. You know, man to man. It must have something to do with selling their souls that makes them fight more like stinking cowards."

"Honestly, I don't know what these marks are," said Hannah. "But they aren't normal stab wounds."

"Annabelle, start drawing them," said Sudfad as he looked closely at several of the marks.

"Wherever she was killed, there has to be a lot of blood," said Shara.

"Already have soldiers searching," Sudfad said. "Natasha can you clean this one a little more?" He asked and pointed to a cut on the woman's bicep.

"What is it Sudfad?" Hannah asked as she saw the blood drain from his face.

"Hannah please have the students leave the room for a moment. Is Marina on the team or a student?" asked Sudfad.

"She is a teacher but she isn't on the team, at least not yet," Hannah replied.

"I am going to ask you to leave the room too," Sudfad said to Marina.

"Yes My Lord," Marina said and closed the door behind her.

"We've seen that symbol before," Sudfad said and pointed to a carving on the woman's bicep. "We've seen it on the plyogram."

The Sanuri suddenly took the miner's head in both of his hands and stared into the man's eyes. The group that surrounded the miner and the Sanuri now stopped talking. After several minutes the Sanuri stood up.

"He has died," explained the Sanuri. "Which is a blessing with the injuries he had. As his spirit was leaving his body I looked into his mind. The Rogetts attacked the camp just before the Rualas got there. Which poises several questions. Why were the miners in camp at this time of the morning and not in the mines? And why did the Rogetts attack in broad daylight? I saw the image of hundreds of Rogetts running out of one of the mines and attacking the camp."

"As several of you said, Rogetts eat people. So why did they leave their meals and return to the mines just before the Rualas came? They certainly outnumbered you."

"Are they being controlled by someone?" asked Thaos.

"Is this a message or trap for us?" Claudius asked.

"I think we have to strongly consider both of those questions," said the Sanuri.

Two soldiers stood guard on each end of the alley next to the Green Dragon's Inn. Luca and Misha had gone inside to speak with Rex and Myla before they entered the alley.

"Natalie and I come here about once a week," Luca said as he was looking through a small pile of lumber. "This place is busy from the minute it opens the doors until it closes. So you've got to wonder why that body was put here. Obviously whoever killed her wanted her to be found."

"And probably wanted to scare a lot of people," Misha said. "Soldiers patrol these streets so the body must have been hidden in a boca or carriage. I am going to check the roof." Misha ascended into the air and landed on the roof of the building. He walked around the inn looking at the roof itself and the views. "Other than some bird's nests there is nothing up there," Misha said as he returned to the alley. "Did you find anything?"

"Look, there are tracks of rats and other small animals near the garbage pile but nothing where the body was. I don't think she was back here for long," Luca said. "What if this wasn't a message but a distraction of some kind? I think we need to tell Sudfad then check on the homes."

Lana and Tanya were in the play yard at Gabriel's house with the older children which included Zack and Margarit. Sam and Alexander had built a series of structures that required the children to climb them or to crawl through them. Lana and Tanya had divided the children into two teams and were having them run through the small obstacle course.

The two family dogs, Jasper and Riley were running the course with the children when they both stopped and started to growl. Both dogs were looking at the woods that lay between the house and the river. The growls became louder and louder. All of the children stopped playing.

"Lana, the dogs only growl at demons," Christopher yelled.

"Quickly, everyone in the house now," yelled Lana. "Hurry and tell the others."

"Lana aren't you coming?" asked Joey.

"Not yet. Please go inside."

"You're not staying out here," Tanya shouted.

"Go with them; I'll be in in a minute," Lana said as she searched the surrounding land with her eyes. "Miranda, what is out there?" she asked out loud.

"Not demons, but men. Very dangerous men."

"How many?"

"Seven."

"Miranda would you protect the children?"

"Always, but you would show your wisdom in waiting for your friends. In fact, you would be wise to go in and tell them what you face."

"Thanks," Lana said and backed into the front door. As she did she bumped into Vivian who was running to the door. "There are seven men in the woods watching us. Miranda will protect the children."

"As will we," said Iris.

Tanya, Melinda, Casandra, Diana and Emeral ran to the front door. And Lana repeated her words.

"Sam please stay here and protect the babies," Emeral said. "One of you girls should stay too."

The six young women looked at each other. "I'll stay," said Cassandra reluctantly.

"Tanya and Lana go back outside and act like you are guarding the front of the house. The men already know you suspect something. The rest of us will sneak out the back," said Emeral.

Emeral and Melinda took to the sky but stayed hidden by the tree tops. Diana and Vivian ran into the woods. Lana and Tanya wanted to draw the attention of the men so they walked towards the woods.

"He never said those girls were so damn pretty," said Walt and spit a mouthful of tobacco on the ground as he and six others watched Lana and Tanya walking towards them.

"He said to be careful because they is all warriors," Chuck said with a grin. "I wouldn't mind wrestling with them beauties."

"Oh looky there," said Cole. "I bet they are gonna call us out."

"We know you are there," yelled Lana. "Come out and fight like men."

"Whatever you want pretty lady," Walt yelled and the seven men rode their horses out of the concealment of the trees.

"What do you want?" yelled Tanya.

"Well now, that is changing by the minute," said Cole with a sneer.

The two Nordes warriors held their ground as the seven men rode towards them. Diana let out a war cry as her and Vivian's arrows hit their marks; two men fell to the ground. Emeral and Melinda also yelled war cries as they released their arrows. The men now turned towards their attackers and Lana and Tanya ran forward. Tanya stabbed one of the riders in his thigh then pulled him off his horse.

Lana jumped into the air to grab one of the men but quickly fell to the ground as three arrows impaled themselves in the rider.

"Leave one alive," yelled Emeral as the women all ran up to the men. Vivian snapped the neck of the man who was fighting with Tanya. Five men were dead and the two remaining men were wounded.

Sasha and Bianca were in the kitchen of Erebus' home making the midday meal when they heard Thomas yell a war cry. Since there had been spies around the property, the women had their weapons close at hand. They ran out of the kitchen door and saw Micha, Thomas and all of the workmen fighting with a group of men who looked like hired fighters. The fighting was close quarters so the women did not want to shoot their arrows. Both women grabbed their swords and ran forward.

Although the women wanted to assist their husbands several of the carpenters were losing their battles with the hired killers. Sasha struck one of the killers behind his knee, severing his tendon then stabbed him in the back. Bianca pulled another killer off one of the carpenters and stabbed him in the side then the heart. Sasha jumped on the back of one of the killers as he was choking one of the carpenters. She slit the mercenaries' throat.

Both Micha and Thomas were exceptional fighters. At first they fought back to back but after they killed their attackers they ran to help the workman who were still fighting with the mercenaries.

Three horsemen were concealed by the trees that surrounded Erebus' home. They watched their men losing the fight with disgust. "He's gonna be really pissed," said one of the men. "I hate to tell him."

"Well, I'm not going to tell him that we left anyone alive to talk," as the second man said these words. He released an arrow that struck one of his own men who Micha was tying up. Micha ducked behind the corpse and yelled a warning to his family. Three more arrows shot out of the woods and all of the attackers now lay dead.

Zoya and her son were visiting Delilah and her twins when one of the soldiers who guarded the house ran into the parlor. "We are under attack. Go to that room and I will guard the door."

As Lana, Vivian, Diana, Melinda and Tanya were tying up the two captives and searching the others, Emeral was looking around and asked, "Where are the soldiers?"

Sasha and Bianca were providing medical care to the wounded while their husbands ran into the forest to search for the men who had killed their own. A small flock of Enrops landed.

"We need help," Bianca said as she tried to stop the bleeding of one of the carpenters. "We have wounded."

Two Enrops stayed with the women as the rest of the flock flew to the King's castle. "Where are your soldiers?" asked one of the birds.

# Chapter XVIII
## Invaders

Ella and Iris had all of the children and babies in the playroom while Cassandra, Natalie and Sam patrolled the inside of the house.

"Zack, where are your parents?" asked Iris.

"They are working in Sudfad's study but they were coming home for lunch," Zack said fearfully.

"Honey, we will check on them," said Ella soothingly.

"Luca and Misha are here," yelled Natalie as she stood watch at the front door. When the two Rualas landed Natalie yelled, "Honey, they are in back."

"What are you talking about?" asked Luca.

"We got attacked," Cassandra yelled out of one of the windows.

Both Luca and Misha flew to the rear of the house. "Boys, we are alright," Emeral said. "But where are the soldiers?"

"We didn't see any as we flew in," said Misha and hugged Diana. "Who are these guys?"

"We have two to interrogate," said Vivian. "We don't know anything yet."

Cassandra landed near the group. "Now that you are here I am going to look for Zelda and Horace, they should be coming here from the castle."

"I'll go with you," said Misha. "Luca, you stay here."

Sudfad, Maxwell, Joshua and Elan had returned to the castle with the drawings of the carvings from the mystery woman's body. They were in the barn that Sudfad had rebuilt to house things of great evil. The plyogram was kept in a vault within this barn. The men were comparing the symbols when Renya ran into the building.

"All of the Enrops you sent out are returning. There have been battles at all of the homes. I already sent a physician and soldiers to Erebus' house because of the wounded. No one is injured at Gabriel's house but Misha and Cassandra are searching for Zelda and Horace. And Zoya was at Delilah's; they and the babies are alright but some of the soldiers are injured. There are two captives at Gabriel's house."

"I wonder why we weren't attacked," said Sudfad as the men quickly left the room. "Maxwell go to the fort and see if they have been attacked."

"I'll go with him," said Elan.

"I'm going home," Joshua said.

"Take soldiers, you shouldn't be traveling alone," said Sudfad.

"Wait, I am not done," said Renya. "The Enrops that flew to Gabriel's and Erebus' homes said they didn't see any of our soldiers."

"What!" yelled Sudfad. "I am going to the fort."

"No, you need to stay here," said Maxwell. "Joshua come with us then we will all go home together."

The Enrops that were leaving Erebus' home to get help saw Misha and Cassandra in the air and told them about the battle at Erebus' home and Bianca's call for help. Both Rualas changed their course and now flew to assist Bianca, Sasha, Micha and Thomas.

Thomas had started a fire to heat swords that would be used to cauterize wounds, while Bianca, Sasha and Micha were trying to stop the bleeding of the many wounds that the carpenters received.

"These poor men aren't fighters and they didn't even have weapons," Sasha screamed with frustration when she saw Cassandra and Misha land.

"Misha grab a sword and come over here," yelled Micha.

Micha removed his hands from covering a wound so Misha could press the searing blade of the sword against it. The carpenter screamed with pain then lost consciousness. "There were more in the trees," Micha said loudly so Cassandra could hear too. "They shot arrows and killed their own men so we couldn't take them captive. They got away."

"Our house was attacked too but Emeral and the girls got them. They have two captives," Misha said and moved as Bianca ran up to him with an armload of bandages that she had made from sheets.

"We were looking for Zelda and Horace," Cassandra said loudly as she was bandaging a man's wounds. "Have you seen them?"

"No," said Thomas and ran to Sasha and her patient with a heated sword.

"What happened to all the damn soldiers?" yelled Micha. "These men wouldn't be hurt if the soldiers were here. There was only about a dozen of the bastards that attacked us."

Sudfad quickly had a headcount done of the soldiers who were stationed at the castle. Renya had already brought all of the children and nurses inside. She now ran to Sudfad's study because Marie told her one of the officers had just entered the castle.

"So what happened?" asked Renya.

"Major Murdock was just saying," Sudfad said.

"First," said Murdock. "All of the soldiers here are accounted for and there are no signs that our security has been breached. I sent a company of men into the city to guard the hospital and to escort the women home. I also sent troops to Gabriel's, Archetenus', Jared's, Horace's and Erebus' homes but I have not heard from them or from the men I sent to the fort. I have the men here prepared for an attack."

"Have you heard anything about the soldiers who were supposed to be stationed at Gabriel's and Erebus' homes?" asked Renya.

"No, My Lady those men were assigned to the fort so I don't even have their names yet," replied Murdock. "My Lord, I don't believe this is over with, so we must be alert."

"I agree," said Sudfad. "Please keep me posted of even the smallest bits of information."

"Yes My Lord."

When a physician and the troops arrived at Erebus' house, Misha and Cassandra left and flew to the home of Horace and Zelda which was located between the homes of Gabriel and Erebus. They flew over the property looking for signs of invaders before they landed. They searched the house, out buildings and grounds but didn't find anything suspicious. Then they headed for the road to Salar.

Neither Misha nor Cassandra verbalized their concerns. The soldiers who arrived at Erebus' home said they did not see Horace or Zelda on the road. Misha and Cassandra now flew over the wooded areas that surrounded the road.

Maxwell was relieved that the fort had not been attacked but he was perplexed at the status of the troops who were assigned to guard the homes of Gabriel and Erebus. The soldiers assigned to guard the homes of Archetenus and Jared were all accounted for.

The home of Horace and Zelda was located on Gabriel's property so the troops assigned to guard his home were in actuality guarding two homes.

Maxwell contacted the officers who were responsible for the assignments of the day. He obtained the names of the men assigned to guard the properties. The men had left the fort at the scheduled time.

Next Maxwell found the Sergeant who was in charge of the men who had guarded the properties during the night shift. The Sergeant claimed that the men who were assigned to relieve them at dawn did indeed show up to their assignments. So what happened to over fifty soldiers in the morning hours?

There was an excited knock on the door to the exam room. Annabelle opened the door and Sally said hurriedly. "Soldiers are bringing in men who were attacked at Erebus' house. And we have already been taking care of soldiers who were attacked at Archetenus' house, apparently all of the homes were attacked but not the castle or the fort. And there are a bunch of soldiers outside that said they will take us all home."

"Who was hurt at our homes?" asked Natasha as she quickly moved towards the door.

"The only ones who have been brought in were workmen and soldiers but I don't know if there will be more," said Sally. "I will try to find out more information." Sally quickly turned to leave the room.

"Wait, I will come with you," Natasha said and the two women left the room.

"I wonder if this body was a diversion of some kind," Hannah said.

"But that doesn't really make since," said Annabelle. "Because who was really diverted besides us?"

"I think we need to get home," said Vitomas. "I'm starting to get a bad feeling."

"Renya is home; she won't let anything happen to the children," Annabelle said. "But you are right, we should go."

"Hannah do you want us to wait for you?" asked Vitomas.

"I want to go home too but let me check out front on the wounded. Will you cover the body with those sheets?" Hannah asked and left the exam room. Vitomas and Annabelle covered the body and tidied up the room.

Several minutes passed and Hannah still had not returned to the examination room so Vitomas and Annabelle walked into the temporary hospital area that was set up while the building was under construction.

Natasha walked up to the two women. "This is what I know so far; no one was hurt at the castle or the fort. Emeral, Vivian, Diana, Melinda, Lana and Tanya fought a small group of attackers at our house and killed all but two who they are interrogating."

"It sounds like a little larger group of men attacked the workmen at Erebus' house and Micha, Thomas, Sasha and Bianca ran out and saved them. The workman were unarmed and some have very serious injuries. Thomas has a good cut but nothing life threatening and the others just have bruises. One of the carpenters told me that Micha was tying one of the attackers up and an arrow flew out of the forest and killed the guy. Then arrows killed three more."

"I don't understand," said Annabelle.

"They killed their own men so they couldn't give us information," said Vitomas. "And how are Delilah and Zoya?"

"Frightened but fine because the soldiers who were stationed there fought off the attackers," Natasha explained. "No one seems to know what happened to the soldiers watching our places. And that includes Horace's and Zelda's house. Misha and Cassandra are trying to find them. Zack is at our house."

"This doesn't make any sense," said Annabelle. "First these guys attacked houses with women and children and unarmed carpenters. If they have been spying on us they would know that all of you are warriors."

"Unless it was some kind of test," said Natasha.

"Misha, I see them," called Cassandra and pointed to a small boca that was traveling towards them on the road from Salar. Both Ruala warriors quickly flew to the boca and landed in front of it.

"Are you alright?" asked Misha.

"Why wouldn't we be?" asked Horace as he stopped the two horses.

"Our places were attacked," Misha said. "And we were looking..."

"Zack!" screamed Zelda.

"He is fine, they all are," said Cassandra. "We'll tell you as much as we know but Misha and I were talking; maybe all of you should stay with us for a couple of days."

When Sudfad was convinced that both the fort and the castle had not suffered any breaches in security he took a detail of soldiers and rode to the house of Gabriel. By this time Vitomas and Annabelle had safely returned home as had Hannah and Natasha. Micha, Thomas, Bianca and Sasha arrived at Gabriel's house just as the King did.

Iris ran outside to meet her children and to check them for injuries from the battle. "Mother, we are alright," said Micha as Iris hugged them repeatedly. "But why is Sudfad here? Is something wrong? And where is Father?"

"Emeral and the girls captured two of the men and have them in the shed doing interrogations," Iris said as they all watched Sudfad dismount and start to walk towards the shed.

"I want to hear this too," said Thomas. As the four young warriors ran towards the shed, Iris called out.

"Are you staying for dinner?"

"Yes," Micha yelled back with a grin.

Diana and Vivian were pushing a man out of the door of the shed as Sudfad was about to enter. "Sorry," Diana said to the King. "We are done with this one and just starting the other."

"Don't kill him," Sudfad said to the women then turned towards his soldiers who were searching the area around Gabriel's house.

"Sergeant Morgan take charge of this prisoner. But keep him here we may need to ask him more questions."

The prisoner was a large, burly man with incredibly thick curly red hair that cascaded down his back. He had old scars on his face and neck. His wrists were bound in front of him and he swayed back and forth as if he was drunk.

"Wait!" Micha yelled as he, Thomas, Bianca and Sasha now ran to the doorway of the shed where Diana and Vivian were handing the prisoner off to Sergeant Morgan and two soldiers. Sudfad was still standing with them.

"He doesn't look like the group that attacked us," said Thomas.

"They are hired killers," Vivian said.

"But our group were all dressed alike and somewhat looked alike," said Bianca. "Like they were from the same clan."

"Well, that is going to bring up some new questions," Sudfad said.

The prisoner was grinning and staring at all of the people around him. "You are the prettiest women I ever done seen. It might be warth gettin captured." Then he laughed loudly.

"So big guy, how come you look so much different than the guys who attacked Erebus' house?" asked Diana.

"Can't tell ya that honey," said the man and laughed loudly again. "Like I's said. All I know is that we's was supposed to watch your place and grab anyone we could. He never done tells us that you all are warrior women. Damndest thing I ever seen." The man laughed again.

Sudfad nodded for the soldiers to take the prisoner and the group entered the crowded shed where the second prisoner was tied to a chair. Emeral was asking questions and Melinda was writing down the questions and answers.

Sudfad and the group that he entered with stood by the front door listening to the interrogation. "So far he is saying the same things the other one said," Vivian said in a low voice.

The group heard commotion outside and turned to see Horace and Zelda drive a boca to the house. Misha and Cassandra were landing and helping Rachel's parents to unload their things.

Joshua was sitting next to Melinda and comparing her notes to the notes from the previous interrogation. He would interject questions into the interrogation.

While one of the side effects of the truth potion was an appearance of inebriation, the second prisoner was not acting like a happy drunk as the first had. He was angry and yelling, then he started to puke on the floor.

"I'm getting Hannah," Vivian said and left the shed.

The man's face was turning dark red and he was sweating profusely. Emeral jumped away from him as his vomiting became intense. "Is he an Elod?" Sudfad yelled.

The prisoner tried to laugh but couldn't stop puking. He was starting to convulse when Hannah and Vivian ran into the shed. The man was dead before Hannah got to him.

# Chapter XIX
## New Princesses

Raul and Simon decided to make an early camp. They expected to arrive in Salar midmorning of the following day and they wanted to give Nyla, Nina and Saran time to prepare. Angelina had spied a large pond and suggested that the girls would feel better if they bathed before putting on the special dresses that Raul and Simon had bought for them.

Matthew and Angelina guarded the three girls while they took baths as the soldiers set up a perimeter and their campsites. Raul was setting up their camp as Simon cared for the horses. Loud squawking was heard as a flock of Enrops landed. Some of the birds carried letters for the soldiers but the leaders of the flock landed in Raul's campsite.

"There were multiple attacks in Salar today," Babu said as he was the leader of the flock. "Your father says you should read these letters right away. Where are Gabriel and Raphael?"

"I will call them but first was anyone hurt?" Raul asked fearfully.

"Not in your family. But the castle wasn't attacked it was the homes. Micha, Thomas and their wives all have minor injuries as do soldiers. The workmen at Erebus' home were seriously injured and could have died if Thomas hadn't come upon the attacks."

Raul turned to call to Gabriel and Raphael but they were already walking up to the campsite with Simon. "Babu was just telling me that there were several attacks in the city today. None of our families were seriously hurt but I haven't read the letters yet."

"You start them and I am bringing the girls back to camp," Simon said and walked towards the pond. Babu repeated his words to the two high priests as everyone opened their letters. Within minutes Simon, Matthew, Angelina and the three girls walked into camp. Nina squealed with delight and ran up to one of the Enrops and hugged it.

"Can we feed them?" asked Saran.

"There is grain in the back of that first boca," Matthew said and Nyla and Saran ran to that boca.

Raul stood in front of the group and read the very long letter that Sudfad had written. The letter told of the woman's body that was found in the alley next to the Green Dragon's Inn and the strange symbols that were carved into the woman's flesh. Then Sudfad described the attacks that took place simultaneously at the homes of Gabriel, Jared, Erebus and Archetenus. Lastly, Sudfad wrote about the interrogations of the two men who were captured.

"None of that makes any sense," said Matthew. "I don't doubt what the prisoners said in that someone hired them from a tavern but whoever hired them obviously didn't know what they were doing."

"What do you mean?" asked Nyla.

"First, if they were spying on my home at all they would know that it is filled with warriors," said Gabriel. "So why would only seven men try to attack a house of warriors. And some of our family members were staying at Erebus' home while he is on a mission. The two men are Venatores and their wives are Nordes warriors and they all tend to wear their warriors outfits most of the time. And in that case the attackers went after the carpenters."

"And there wasn't anyone at Jared's house, besides the soldiers guarding the place," said Matthew. "And it sounds like the soldiers guarding Archetenus' house greatly outnumbered the attackers. Mind you the soldiers are out in the open and not hiding. So why would these small groups of killers go on these suicide missions? I know you girls..."

"Us girls what?" asked Nyla indignantly. "Remember our father is a warlord and I think the three of us are the only ones that know what really happened here. And you need to warn everyone right now. Get some paper."

"I'll get some," yelled Saran and ran to the first boca. "And I will start drawing the pictures."

"I can help," said Nina and started to follow Saran.

"Nina stay with us," Nyla said. "But you can draw."

"What are all of you talking about?" asked Simon.

"Let us show you the pictures and it will make more sense," Nyla said. Saran ran back to the group and all three girls immediately started drawing while the others sat in silence. Nina giggled as two Enrops watched over her shoulder.

A few minutes later Nyla stood up and handed her sketches to Saran. "Our father, I hate to even call him that, practices all kinds of dark magics. Sometimes when he is going to attack a village or someone who he thinks might be protected by strong demons he will send villagers in to attack them. It is a distraction while his men drop things like what Saran and Nina are now showing you."

"Father calls them Juntos. The ones he makes have multiple purposes. They put curses on the people he wants to attack. He does this to weaken the power of the demons that are protecting them and he uses them as markers so later when he sends his men in they know who they are supposed to attack."

"Babu, take these drawings and tell our father everything that Nyla just said," said Raul as he was folding several sheets of paper.

"I will leave part of the flock here," Babu said and ascended into the air with twenty members of his flock.

"What does Karzman call them again?" asked Raphael.

"Juntos," said Saran.

"What does that word mean?" asked Raphael. "And what language is it?"

"We don't know," Nyla said as she looked at her sisters. "But all of those homes are going to be attacked again soon."

"Miranda!" yelled Gabriel. "Please will you speak with us?"

"Our Angel!" Nina screamed as all three girls ran to Ruth and hugged her. "I love you," Nina said to Ruth as her sisters all talked at the same time.

"Why didn't you tell us you were an Angel?" Saran asked.

"Thank you, you were right," said Nyla.

Ruth laughed and hugged each of the young girls. "Then she looked at the adults. "The Enrops are being helped in their journey. Your families are safe; no attacks will happen tonight. But listen to what Nyla, Saran and Nina tell you. They did not have normal childhoods. They had to listen constantly to a ranting maniac. They grew up with demons and weapons instead of dolls. They are young but take their counsel seriously."

"Tell Sudfad my words for he has plans that...Ruth looked at Nyla, Saran and Nina now and directed her words towards them. "You have fallen in love with those who sit before this fire. Sudfad and Renya have already drawn up the papers to adopt you and they will be wonderful parents. Sudfad had been keeping a secret from his family."

"What?" asked Simon.

Ruth looked at Simon but continued speaking to the girls. "Sudfad loves Michael very much and when Michael told him about the three of you, Sudfad's heart broke. He has been waiting for these missions to end so he can attack your father. Sudfad was going to save all of you but now he is going to stop Karzman and the poison he spreads. The three of you know a great deal of information that would help Sudfad and keep his army safe. Will you help him and tell him what you know?"

"Ingr already told us that," said Saran. "We will help."

"What does he want to know?" asked Nina.

"I think I know," said Nyla and she turned to the adults sitting near the fire. "We told you how father changed. He looks like a different man now and he got even scarier."

"He demanded that everyone in the village pray to demons or he would have them killed. Lots of his soldiers left because they weren't going to do it. Father started going crazy and he changed everything around."

"What do you mean?" asked Gabriel.

"Where he hides his weapons and demon things," Nyla said.

"I heard one of the soldiers say that Father made them dig up his treasure and hide it someplace else," said Saran. "I didn't even know he had treasure."

"We know where he keeps his demons, does that help?" Nina asked.

"Yes, all of that helps very much and I want you to start drawing pictures of your village and the land around it," said Ruth. "Draw everything that you can remember and give it to Sudfad."

Raul stood up and now walked up to Ruth and the girls. "Nyla, Saran, Nina, there is something that I need to tell you. None of us here knew if you were aware that soldiers were deserting your father's army. Michael found two of them in Langer. I don't know all the details but King Mathas hired the men and they have been helping us. Apparently Michael saved their lives and they want to repay him so they will be coming to Wetpr to help us attack Karzman."

"Simon, Raul and Michael are afraid that you will be frightened when you see these men," Angelina explained.

"Are you sure they are telling the truth?" Nyla asked.

"The Angels said they are," said Matthew.

"What are their names?" asked Nyla.

"Tally and Drake," said Simon. "Do you know them?"

Nyla suddenly looked like she was going to cry. She nodded her head and said, "A long time ago Tally and another man helped us. Father had them whipped and hung their bodies in the middle of the village for days."

228

"They both lived but the other man ran away as soon as they cut him down and Father sent his demons after him. Tally was hurt for a long time."

Moments after receiving Babu's message and the drawings other Enrops entered Sudfad's study. These birds carried the letters from Michael that talked about his conversations with Tally and Drake as well as his conversations with Ruth and Adam.

Sudfad called Annabelle into his study and asked her to quickly make copies of the drawings. Then he stepped outside and asked one of the soldiers to get Major Murdock. As he waited for Murdock, Sudfad quickly wrote down the words that Babu had told him. Murdock arrived within minutes; he was intrigued by the message from Nyla.

"My Lord that actually makes sense," Murdock said.

"I know," said Sudfad. "The girls made crude drawings of what these Juntos look like. Annabelle is making copies for you right now. You should have the grounds around all of the houses searched for these items."

"And what do we do when we find them?" asked Murdock.

Sudfad hesitated as he now realized he should have asked the Angels that question. "Miranda just said to burn them immediately and to stand away from the fire while they burn," Annabelle said nonchalantly as she continued to draw.

"That is what you do then," Sudfad said.

Fortunately for Annabelle the pictures she was drawing were simple so she could make copies quickly. She handed the sheets of paper to Sudfad who divided them up. "I am sending Enrops to Gabriel's house with drawings," Sudfad said as he handed a fist full of drawings to the Major. "These are for you to distribute."

After Major Murdock left the study, Sudfad asked Babu to go to Gabriel's home and repeat the message as well as give them the drawings. Then Sudfad sat down and reread Michael's letter.

"Annabelle when you are done will you bring Renya and Vitomas in here?" Sudfad asked.

None of the adults in Claudius' caravan slept well that night, after discovering there were Rogetts in the area. Thaos and Stephan doubled the perimeter guards and had these men relieved every two hours. The soldiers made up the exterior perimeter guards, the Nordes warriors, Ruala warriors and team members established an interior perimeter to guard the children.

Because Rogetts lived in the bowels of the earth their eyes were extremely sensitive to light, so sensitive that these monsters of humanity rarely left their dens during the daylight hours. Claudius ordered hundreds of campfires lit to deter an attack but he also understood that his people were being illuminated by the light of the fires.

The Sanuri walked among the perimeter guards as did the military officers. "Do you sense anything?" Sorren asked the Sanuri as they walked together.

"No but that attack on the miners was unusual. I think it was done for our benefit. Kind of a show of strength."

"Do you think Hector is behind it?"

"That is certainly a possibility but why give that performance and not attack us?"

Nyla, Nina and Saran were so nervous and excited about meeting their new family that none of the girls slept, which meant that others did not either because the girls talked all night. In addition, they occasionally woke Raul or Simon up to ask them questions.

"What smells so good?" asked Gabriel as he sat up on his blankets.

"Some of the priests caught fish in that pond," said Saran. "We felt bad that we kept waking all of you up so we are making breakfast."

"Actually the priests caught lots of fish," said Nyla as she poured coffee into cups. "Then they came back here and showed everyone all the fish they caught so some of the soldiers went fishing too. So everyone is having fried fish for breakfast."

"Do you need help?" asked Angelina as Nina ran up to her with a cup of coffee.

"No but you might get mad," Nyla said. "We were just too excited to sleep so when the priests gave us fish they told us about some berry bushes. We went with them and picked berries, so we could make a morning cake."

"I must have been tired because I slept through all of that," said Simon.

"Raphael is the only one who woke up," said Saran. "He cleaned the fish then went to the pond. We should tell him breakfast is almost ready."

"I'll get him," said Matthew. "I hope that all tastes as good as it smells." Matthew's words made the girls smile.

"I have to tell you that I am excited too," said Angelina. "Matthew and I have been away from our babies too long."

"Do you think you will ever tell Jacob about the journey you took?" Nyla asked as she was putting fried potatoes on the plates.

"Matthew and I discussed that," Angelina said. "If we do it will be when he is grown. So don't you girls say anything."

"We won't," said Saran. "If it was me, I would be scared to know."

Nina was singing as she handed everyone their plates and utensils. "You sure are happy today," Raul said and grinned.

"We are sorry that we kept waking you up last night," said Nyla. "But we have never met a king or queen before and we didn't know what we should do."

"You met Mathas and Rosa," said Simon.

"Is that the same?" asked Saran.

"You asked good questions," Raul said with a grin. "Although I may not have remembered them all."

"What are we supposed to call them?" asked Nina. "My Lord, Sudfad or Papa?"

"Knowing Sudfad he would prefer you call him Papa," said Gabriel to Nina then he looked up as Raphael and Matthew walked into camp. "The food is great you should get some before it's gone."

"We saved plates for you," Saran said.

"Look at all of the fish that Raphael has," said Matthew and nodded to a basket that Raphael was carrying.

"Should we clean them now and cook them up?" asked Simon "Or do you want to take them home?"

"Might as well eat them now," Raphael said.

"You eat and I will clean them," said Simon.

"Girls, everything is really good," said Raul as he grabbed another biscuit. "And as for Nina's question, I think we all agree that you should just call them Mama and Papa or Mother and Father."

"It may take a little while to get used to," said Nyla.

"I think for all of you," said Matthew. "But Renya and Sudfad make everyone feel like part of the family."

Claudius was about to drink his morning coffee when a young private ran up to him. "My Lord, the Sanuri wants you to come right away."

Claudius was sitting with Sorren and the team members, all of whom jumped to their feet. "Do you know why?" asked Claudius.

"No My Lord, he just yelled that someone should get you."

Thaos, Stephan and Calen were already standing with the Sanuri as the young soldier led Claudius and the others to the area outside of the perimeter.

"We had company last night," Stephan said and pointed to the hundreds of footprints on the ground.

"The footprints surround the entire camp," explained Calen. "And just as these here, they all look like the Rogetts were running around and acting crazy."

"I wonder why they didn't attack," said Edward as he, Thor and Kate were kneeling on the ground and examining the prints.

"Maybe because we were prepared for them," said Stephan. "They won't fight man to man."

"Unless they are being controlled by someone," said the Sanuri. "I still feel like this is a show of force."

"But why?" asked Batina.

"To scare us," said Sorren. "Fear weakens."

"I can't believe how nervous I am," Renya said as Vitomas and Annabelle were helping her wrap gifts.

"I think we all are a little nervous and excited," said Annabelle.

"I think I am more nervous about showing my feelings," said Renya.

"What on earth do you mean?" asked Vitomas with surprise.

"Don't get me wrong, I am so happy they are coming here but I also feel so sorry for those little girls and I don't want them to see that," Renya said.

"Renya, I don't think you have to worry about that. From the letters they sound like little sweeties. And just so you know, Annabelle and I plan to talk with them after things settle down. We want them to know that we lived through horror too and they can talk to us about anything," said Vitomas.

Raul had sent Enrops ahead to tell Sudfad and Renya when they would arrive at the castle. Nyla, Saran and Nina were all dressed elegantly and riding on their white horses. As soon as they reached the outskirts of the city Raul and Simon stopped the caravan and turned to their sisters. "You are getting the royal welcome," Simon said with a grin. "Just keep riding and wave at the people."

"You mean those people are there because of us?" gasped Nyla.

"You are their princesses now," said Raphael. "And the people of Wetpr love their Royal Family."

People lined both sides of the streets as well as standing on balconies and in windows to get glimpses of the Princesses. Sudfad had previously announced that they became aware of family that didn't know they had. And that Renya and Sudfad were adopting three young girls.

Although Nyla, Saran and Nina were dressed in their finest clothes the rest of the group was not and it was apparent to all the spectators that this group had been in battle. People whispered, cheered and applauded as they threw flowers at the group. The three girls smiled and waved but they were clearly overwhelmed and didn't speak.

An honor guard of soldiers met the Princes then turned around and led the group to the castle.

"This is the first time that Nina has been quiet since we found them," Simon said and winked at Raul.

"That is because they are scared to death," said Angelina in a scolding manner. "This really may be too much for them."

Trumpets announced the arrival of the caravan at the castle. As they entered the gate they heard loud cheering as the courtyard was filled with all of the student's from the Learning Center as well as team members, friends and other guests.

Sudfad and Renya stood on the platform at the top of the front steps to the castle. They held hands as they watched their children riding towards them. Vitomas, Annabelle, Laurel, Alexander, Petra and Margarit also stood on the platform. The members of Gabriel's household as well as Delilah and Zoya stood at the bottom of the steps on either side of the walkway. The formality of this meeting was for the spectators.

Raul, Simon and Matthew dismounted first and helped Angelina and the girls off their horses. Then as a family they all held hands and walked to the steps. Sudfad and Renya walked down the steps and both beamed with pride as they looked upon their children.

"Mother, Father this is Nyla, Saran and Nina," as Raul introduced them each girl curtsied. "I do believe you know the rest of your children," he said kiddingly.

When Renya and Sudfad reached the bottom of the steps Renya said, "Girls, you look terrified. This ceremony is for our audience. Why don't you give us a hug." Nina jumped into Renya's arms before she finished speaking. The two hugged each other and laughed.

"We've got presents for you," Nina said. "And we drew you pictures."

"And we can't wait to see them," said Sudfad as he took Nina from Renya's arms and hugged her. Both Nyla and Saran ran up to Renya and hugged her together then they hugged Sudfad.

"Girls turn around and face the people," said Sudfad. "Your new princesses," Sudfad announced to the crowd. "Princess Nyla, Princess Saran and Princess Nina." The crowd roared and applauded. "Please partake of the refreshment tables and enjoy the musicians," Sudfad said. Then he looked at the girls and winked. "The ceremony is over now."

When Sudfad said these words Gabriel and Raphael dismounted and ran to their wives. Simon and Raul bolted up the steps to their wives.

Renya turned to Angelina and Matthew and said, "Shara and the boys are inside with your babies. She was afraid the crowd would scare them. Matthew and Angelina ran up the stone steps and into the castle.

Sudfad carried Nina and held Saran's hand. Renya held Nyla's hand as they introduced the girls to the family and friends. As the girls were being introduced to everyone from Gabriel's house, Petra and Margarit ran up to them. "Mama, Kyra can't hold them anymore. Can't they come in?" Petra asked.

"They certainly can," Renya said. Sudfad set Nina on her feet and Petra and Margarit grabbed the hands of Nyla, Nina and Saran.

"We got you puppies," Petra announced excitedly and all of the children ran up the stone steps and into the castle. Raul and Vitomas were closest to the front door and both laughed as they heard the girls squealing with delight when they saw the puppies.

Sudfad put his arm around Renya and asked, "So what do you think?"

"They are so very precious. Now I want to kill Karzman myself."

# Chapter XX
## Childs Play

After the girls had some time to play with their puppies, Hannah, Vitomas and Annabelle entered the castle.

"That was the formal ceremony," Annabelle said. "Now you can meet all the kids."

"Don't worry, we don't have a lot of formal ceremonies," said Vitomas and laughed.

Petra, Kyra and Margarit came along as the three women led Nyla, Saran and Nina to the playroom. Annabelle opened the double doors and the three girls gasped when they saw all of the children and toys. The dogs from Gabriel's house were in the playroom as well as Petra's three dogs and Sally and April's puppies. The girls put their puppies on the floor and all of the children screamed with excitement.

"Are these all our cousins?" asked Nina.

"In a way," said Vitomas. "Our families are very close."

Hannah was leading the girls around the room making introductions when Nyla yelled, "Nina, Christopher is here."

"Christopher!" Nina said loudly. "Vitomas, Raul has his present."

"Christopher, Amy sent something for you," Nyla said.

"Come on," said Nina and held out her hand. She and Christopher ran through the castle until they found Raul.

After the children were introduced Annabelle asked, "Do you want to see all the babies?"

"Sure," said Saran. "Everyone talked about all of you so much we feel like we already know you."

The women walked down the hallway and Vitomas opened the door to the nursery. There were eight nurses with the babies. "Can we hold some?" asked Nyla.

An hour after the main ceremony everyone entered the Great Hall for a feast. Nyla, Saran and Nina quickly got over their uneasiness as they talked and played with all the other children. As soon as desserts were eaten, Petra ran up to Sudfad and Renya with Margarit, Kyra and his new sisters behind him.

"Mama, Papa can I take them out to see my pets?" Petra asked.

"First you should all change out of your good clothes," said Renya then she paused. "Girls, I am sorry we haven't even shown you your rooms yet."

"Your rooms are by Michael's but he's not home yet," said Petra exuberantly. "But you can stay in rooms next to me and Margarit too."

"Now girls," said Renya. "As you can see this castle is huge and we have many rooms but Raul and Simon told us you get scared sometimes. So I didn't know if you want to stay together or have separate rooms."

"We want to stay together," said Saran.

"We thought that might be the case, so we fixed up a couple of different rooms for you. Now, you tell me if you don't like anything. Petra find Vitomas, Annabelle and Laurel and tell them we are taking the girls to their rooms."

"We'll help," said Kyra and she and Margarit ran into the crowd.

The Great Hall was close to the hallway where Michael's chambers were. Renya led the girls to this hallway first. "These chambers are right next to Michael's and there are three bedrooms in here. Renya opened the door and the girls stood in the doorway in awe.

"You can go in," Annabelle said.

"We helped pick out the toys," said Margarit proudly.

"We have clothes for you in here but we had to guess at your sizes," Renya said. "We will take you shopping this week."

The girls were quiet as they looked at each of the bedrooms which were filled with toys. "Don't you like them?" asked Petra.

"They like them," Vitomas said.

"Since Michael isn't home yet, Petra and Margarit want you to stay near them," said Renya. "We will go to those chambers next."

"I got stolen once and I didn't want to sleep by myself for a long time afterwards," Margarit said. "So if you want to sleep in my room or Petra's that is alright."

Nyla, Saran and Nina were just as quiet when they walked into the second chambers which had been prepared for them. "I have an idea," said Annabelle. "Kyra, I'll ask Marie if you can stay then all of you can campout together in one of the rooms tonight."

"Alright," said Kyra happily.

"This will be fun," Petra said. "Let's figure out which room." All the children now ran next door to Margarit's chambers.

"They are clearly overwhelmed," said Laurel.

"Actually I am wondering if they are going to be too scared to stay in any chambers without adults," Renya said.

"It they camp out they will have all of the dogs with them so that should help," said Vitomas. "If they are really scared they can come with us."

"Girls, you and your husbands have been separated for weeks, you need your time together," Renya said. "They can stay with me and Sudfad if they need to."

It was almost an hour before Renya and the others returned to the Great Hall. "I was beginning to get worried," Sudfad said kiddingly.

239

"All the children are camping out in Petra's room tonight, then the girls are taking the chambers next to his room until Michael comes home," said Renya. "I told the girls that if they get really scared they can come to our chambers."

Sudfad smiled, "Well, we are ready here."

"Come on children," Renya said and everyone walked out one of the patio doors of the Great Hall. Sudfad led the way to the back of the castle where they found Raul, Simon and Matthew standing with three white horses. All the men were grinning.

"Since Mathas bought horses for the girls, we thought it only fair to buy horses for the rest of you," said Sudfad. "Petra, Margarit and Kyra those horses are for you."

"Me too?" Kyra asked in disbelief.

"And you all have new saddles and tack," said Raul. "The horses are gentle. We'll help you up if you need it."

"Oh thank you, thank you," screamed Margarit as the three children ran towards the horses.

"Six white horses. How in the world will the children tell them apart?" asked Laurel.

"Trust me, they will figure it out," Simon said as he helped Kyra onto her horse.

After the feast, Sudfad held a short meeting in his study. "I don't want to keep you long since many of you have been away from your families but I wanted to update you on what happened yesterday. Annabelle made copies of the drawings that Nyla and the girls made. I gave them to Major Murdock and to Gabriel's household."

"Items similar to those drawings were found on the borders of every property that was attacked. Miranda had told Annabelle that we needed to burn those things, which was done."

"Father, after we sent Babu to give you the drawings the Angel Ruth came to us. She said that the girls have a great deal of information that will be important for you when you attack Karzman. She told them to draw everything they can remember. They started the drawings last night," said Raul.

"She also said that even though the girls are young that we should listen to them," said Matthew.

"Nina did say they had drawings for us," Sudfad said and hesitated. "I hate to have those poor little things relive all that."

"Those girls are strong," said Gabriel. "And I may add, old for their years. I think we need to listen to them."

"This can wait until tomorrow too but I got a letter from Michael that was rather an eye opener. All of you can read it but Drake and Tally told him a lot of things that Michael didn't believe so he called to the Angels." Sudfad handed the letter to Raphael who was the closest to him. "Adam and Ruth told Michael the things were true and that he was so filled with hatred and rage that he didn't realize his entire village were victims of Karzman as were some of the soldiers. Part of Michael's destiny is to save his people."

"Yeah, I would like to read that now," said Simon.

"Father this is really nothing but speaking of Michael being filled with rage," said Raul. "Nyla and Ryan have crushes on each other. Of course they are both so shy they aren't doing anything but stealing glances."

"They are going to write to each other," Raphael said and chuckled. "But Nina and Saran are going to write to him too."

"We talked with Ryan and he has never even been on a date so Michael doesn't have anything to worry about but you know he will," said Simon.

"I like Ryan, he is a fine boy," said Sudfad. "But I am glad that you told me."

With the realization that Claudius' army had been surrounded by Rogetts all of the children had to ride inside of the bocas this day. The warriors knew that the Rogetts were without honor and would attack the children first.

The army crossed the border into Zorta by midafternoon, but being in a different kingdom did not make them feel any safer. Dagon led a group of Ruala warriors northward. Their task was to hire men with barges to help the army cross the tributary of the River Toba. There were many small villages along the river. Dagon, Koby and the other Ruala warriors found the people eager to earn extra money.

Claudius had the army make an early camp this night so they could cut plenty of wood for the fires. There was not a man or woman among the group who believed they had seen the last of the Rogetts.

Dagon and his group returned to the army just after sunset. "Everything is set," said Dagon as he sat down next to Claudius. "And we didn't see anything suspicious. We flew around the camps several times."

Ashley started teaching Logan, Marty and Cassidy to read and to write. The first couple of classes were held in the back of a boca. Cassidy wanted to keep it a surprise from his family and he was eager to learn. Marty and Logan both had a little knowledge of reading, writing and mathematics and helped their friend. The classes were held in the evening then the boys would practice during the day when they were riding in the boca.

Claudius, Stephan and Thaos knew that Cassidy was with Ashley and her sons but they thought the children were playing.

This night as Dagon was telling Claudius and others of the men he hired to transport the army across the River Toba, Ashley and the boys walked up to the group.

"The way you three are grinning something is up," Thaos said to the boys. "Ashley what did they get into?"

"The boys have a surprise," said Ashley. "Do all of you have just a couple of minutes?"

"Of course," said Claudius.

Marty and Logan ran to Gideon and each handed him a homemade card. Cassidy ran to Claudius, Stephan and Thaos and handed each of them a homemade card. But before the men could read them Cassidy burst out, "Ashley is teaching us to read and write. We've only been doing it for a couple of days so I didn't have a lot to say but I want to write letters to Bella, Amy and the others."

"This is very good son," Claudius said warmly. "I am proud of you." Claudius hugged Cassidy.

"We are proud of you too," said Stephan. "Come here." Stephan and Thaos both hugged their little brother.

Gideon was beaming with pride and hugged both of his sons. "They are eager to learn but we need supplies," explained Ashley. "When we stop at the next village, I will need to buy a few things."

"What do you need?" asked Claudius.

"Paper, pens, ink and they really need something to write on. I packed all of my books away, they are on the ship so I need a book so they can look at the letters and practice reading."

"I think we can scrounge up what you need," said Edward. "At least until we get to the next village."

"Ashley, Chasity wants to go to school with the boys. Would that be a problem?" asked Joao as he sat near the fire with Chasity on his lap.

"Of course not. Actually it gives me something to do too, while we travel," Ashley said.

"You know there are a lot of children with us," said Sorren. "If we could put together some tables and things would you consider teaching more of them?"

"Of course. But even if the children just had a piece of slate or something that they could put in their laps to write on; it would help," said Ashley.

"We'll figure out something," said Claudius. "And we appreciate you doing this."

Renya was sitting up in bed reading when Sudfad entered their chambers. "I just checked on the children," he said and chuckled. "They all pretended to be asleep until I said 'good night', then they all said 'good night' to me and giggled."

"Are Peter and Nathaniel still in there?" asked Renya.

"Yes, all eight children and six dogs were lying on the floor together."

"Now that Angelina and Matthew are back, Shara doesn't need the boys to help with the babies. They were so excited when I told them about the campout."

"Besides that the children are having fun, this may help the girls from being scared at night."

"We can only hope," said Renya. "And if it works we should let the children do this more often."

"Of course this is just the first day but doesn't Petra seem happy to have sisters?"

"It may be like with Margarit, he's not the baby anymore. Now he can be someone's big brother."

"Isn't it amazing how our lives have changed?" Sudfad asked as he slid under the covers. "We always wanted a lot of children and for so long this castle seemed empty and now..." he turned and kissed Renya.

As in any kingdom there were dozens of tiny fishing villages along the rivers in Zorta. Villages so small that many of them didn't exist on maps.

Dagon, Koby and a small group of Rualas had visited several of these villages until they found one named New Flounder. In this village they hired a man named Chet who made a living moving logs from the lumberjacks to the mills. He moved the timber on the waterways with his tiny fleet of barges.

Dagon had given Chet a small pouch of gold as a sign of good faith in their verbal contract. Chet would meet the army at a designated location at midmorning of the following day.

Claudius had continued to double the perimeter guards during the night. Leaders walked up and down the perimeter to check on the welfare of their soldiers. The hundreds of campfires illuminated the night, not only exposing the vast army but blinding the Rogetts that once again gathered outside of the perimeter.

"Same thing as last night," Thaos announced loudly as he walked up to a fire where many were eating their breakfast and poured himself a cup of coffee. "Those bastards surrounded us but didn't attack."

"Well that means they followed us from Ganz," said Claudius. "I have never heard of Rogetts doing that before. I guess that guarantees someone sent them."

"I find this fascinating," said the Sanuri as he poured more coffee into his cup. "Only a powerful demon can control them. If it is Samael or whoever, why wouldn't they order the attack?"

"Do you think the Angels are stopping them?" asked Dominic.

"I would think the Angels would scare the hell out of those monsters and they wouldn't come back," said Edward.

"Or the Angels would just destroy them," Thor said.

"They are making their presence too obvious," the Sanuri said.

"You think it's a diversion?" asked Stephan. "And if so, to what?"

"I might know," said Erebus as he joined the group. "Last night I was going through my books to see if there was one that Ashley could use for the children. I stumbled upon this." As he spoke, Erebus handed a large thick book to the Sanuri. The book was already opened to a specific page. The Sanuri read the page in silence then reread it. Then he closed the book and examined the cover.

Everyone around the campfire had been watching the Sanuri. "Well, what is it?" asked Sorren impatiently.

"I expected this to be a book of spells," said the Sanuri. "But it is a sort of history of demons. Erebus, I would like to read this book if you don't mind."

"Of course."

"Remember when Gideon told us about the ancient legends of the Shaker Winds? Peoples thought that the earth and water were rebelling against all of the evil that emanated from Marba." The Sanuri did not wait for anyone to answer his question, he continued to speak.

"Well according to this; strange occurrences have been documented after those storms. Whoever wrote this is citing examples of Huta warriors acting disoriented and as this author states, 'like rabid dogs'. The author says that after the Hutas had been running around wildly and acting insane they suddenly fell to the ground and died."

"There are examples of villagers in Ganz, coming out of their shelters from the storm and finding their fields littered with flocks of dead ravens."

"It also talks about Rogetts acting somewhat similarly to the Hutas. It gives one example of a village where Rogetts ran down the main street when the sun was high. The villagers grabbed weapons and prepared to do battle but the Rogetts fell dead in the street. The author doesn't speculate on what killed them."

"That might explain what happened at those miner's shacks," said Calen. "But what about that group that surrounds us every night?"

246

"I'd like to know what is killing them," said Kate.

"Sanuri do you think they sense your presence and that is why they don't attack?" asked Rachel.

"Oh believe me, I have been attacked by Rogetts before," said the Sanuri. "They don't seem to hold back. But this is all very interesting. Erebus would you mind driving the boca so I can read more of this?"

"They're late," growled Claudius as the army waited on the southern shore of one of the tributaries of the River Toba.

"We'll see what is going on," said Calen. He and six other Ruala warriors flew east towards the Village of New Flounder. They didn't have to fly far because within twenty minutes they saw five barges moving upstream.

"Something is wrong," said Sol. "Look at them." When the men on the barges saw the Ruala warriors they started to wave their arms wildly and to yell. The warriors descended towards the barges; they searched the surrounding area with their eyes but did not see any signs of danger. The warriors split up and landed on all of the barges.

"Boys are we glad to see you," Chet said to Calen. "This has been a hell of a morning. Are you and your army alright?"

"Yeah, what is going on?" asked Calen.

"I think you arc gonna have to see it because honestly I don't understand what happened."

"We're running behind, just tell me," Calen said impatiently.

Before Chet could speak one of the oarsman said excitedly, "There's bodies all over downstream; they are sea monsters or something. We've never seen nothing like them before."

"Some of them devils is Rogetts," said another oarsman. "But Chet is right you have to look for yourselves."

"After we found the bodies we warned all the villages that's why we are late," said Chet.

"Tell that to General Claudius when you see him," said Calen. "And tell him that we are going to look for the bodies."

The blonde haired boy walked among the bodies and cursed. "How the hell did this happen?" he yelled out loud over and over. He kicked the body of a dead Rogett as he walked among the dead and cut the medallions off the necks of each of the Stratas. He had already dissolved the bodies of the dead Elods. He suddenly looked up as he heard wings and voices.

"Damn it!" said the boy angrily and hid behind a tree. He watched as the Ruala warriors landed.

"These are the same creatures that Raul sent us pictures of," gasped Risa with amazement as she bent down and examined a giant Strata that lay dead on the ground.

"But where are the riders?" asked Ratri. "They all have saddles and bridles on them."

The boy laughed at the looks of amazement and confusion on the faces of the Ruala warriors.

"Quiet, do you hear that?" asked Calen.

# Chapter XXI
## Evil

After Chet told Claudius about the unusual battle scene they had witnessed, Claudius delayed the river's crossing and led his army to the bodies. Ralf was flying back to the army when he met them on the road. He landed in front of Claudius who stopped the caravan.

"We thought you would want to see it," Ralf said. "There are hundreds of dead Rogetts and just as many creatures wearing saddles and bridles but there are no bodies of riders. Claudius the creatures are the same as the drawings that Raul sent to us of that creature that washed up on shore in Langer. It is pretty gruesome, I am not sure you want the children to see this."

"How far away?" asked Claudius.

"I just left," said Ralf. "A mile, maybe a little more."

Claudius turned to his sons and Sorren who were riding behind him. "Tell the teams and the Sanuri to come forward. Leave half of the men here and the rest of us will proceed forward. Then when we return the others can have a look."

When Claudius and the first group arrived at the scene of the battle they found Sol and Risa drawing pictures of the Stratas and the battlefield. Ratri and Calen realized that some of the Stratas wore different medallions and different bridles. Calen ordered the other warriors to cut these things off from the beasts so they could be studied.

Calen flew off the battlefield and stopped Claudius' group about five-hundred yards from the scene. "Dismount here because we are still trying to figure out what happened."

"What do you mean?" asked Sorren.

"We haven't been able to find any prints of either the Rogetts or whatever those beasts are coming here. It's like they just appeared and fought it out. Tell the others to be careful and to help us search the area."

"Look at the fangs on these things," yelled Thaos as he held open the mouth of one of the Stratas. "What the hell are these?"

"They kind of look like Talmuth but without wings and different colors," said Edward.

"None of the saddles had saddlebags on them," yelled Ratri. "Unless the riders took them."

"And where did the riders go?" asked Thor loudly. "There aren't any foot prints. Do you think they could fly?"

Dominic nudged Gideon and nodded towards the Sanuri who was kneeling over one of the Stratas and humming. Soon others took notice of the Sanuri and now watched him. After several minutes he stood up.

"These are the beasts of war that the Elods breed," explained the Sanuri loudly. "They are called Stratas. I saw bits and pieces of the battle. I did not see how they all came to be here but I did see the genuine shock on their faces when they suddenly found themselves facing each other."

"What happened to the riders?" asked Claudius.

"I don't know but from the fleeting visions I know many of them died," said the Sanuri. "And I saw something else. I felt the presence of evil here. I saw an image of a boy about thirteen years of age wearing a white robe. His hair was white blonde and he emanated more evil than all of the monsters lying here."

Renya awoke earlier than usual because she was concerned about how Nyla, Saran and Nina made it through the night. The Queen dressed and walked down the stairs to Petra's bedroom. Petra's three dogs wagged their tails and the puppies started to whine when she entered the room. All of the children were asleep. Renya's heart warmed as she looked at them.

Renya had not been paying attention to the dogs and now realized that Petra's three German Shepherds had walked across the large bedroom and were all sitting by the open window. The dogs kept looking at the window then back at Renya.

The hair on the back of Renya's neck started to raise. Ever since Petra was kidnapped he never opened his bedroom windows. Renya stepped over Kyra and Peter and quietly walked towards the dogs. She gasped when she saw that the windowsill was covered with fresh blood. Argus, the oldest of the dogs now stood up on his hind legs and looked out of the window at the ground. Renya moved closer and saw two human fingers lying on the ground. It took her a moment to realize what they were because of the amount of blood.

It was then that Renya really looked at the dogs and saw that all three of them had blood on them. She examined the dogs and realized the blood as not theirs. Renya locked the window and quickly left the room. She ran to the front of the castle and told the soldiers there had been an intruder and sent them to the area outside of Petra's window.

She turned and was going to run up the stairs to wake Sudfad when Matthew, Angelina and Shara walked towards her. They were holding Matthew's and Angelina's children.

"Aunt Renya what is wrong?" asked Matthew as he could see the concern on her face.

"I got up early to check on the children. They are all sleeping but Petra's dogs went to the window and keep acting like they wanted me to follow them. The window was open, Petra hasn't opened his window since he was kidnapped. The window sill was covered in fresh blood. Then Argus stands up and looks at the ground and there are two bloody fingers on the ground. I think someone tried to get in and the dogs attacked him. I already sent soldiers."

"Take Jacob," Matthew said to Angelina. "I am going outside."

"I was just going to wake Sudfad," Renya said.

"We're going to stay with the children," said Shara.

Sudfad and Renya were running down the stairs when Raul, Vitomas, Simon and Annabelle entered the hallway with their children. They were walking towards the dining room. Sudfad never stopped moving when he saw his family.

"Sounds like we had intruders and Petra's dogs got them. Soldiers are outside, we are going back to the room," Sudfad said hurriedly.

The two young couples ran into the dining room and set the children in their chairs. Vitomas and Annabelle stayed with the children while Simon and Raul ran outside.

When Sudfad and Renya entered Petra's bedroom all of the children were awake and talking to Shara and Angelina. "Nyla will you hold little Mathas so I can go outside," asked Angelina and handed her baby to the girl."

"I'll hold Alexas if you want," Saran said to Shara.

"That might be a good idea," Shara said and handed her granddaughter to Saran. Then Shara spoke to Renya and Sudfad who were both examining the window. "The children said they were all up late and when they finally went to sleep they didn't hear anything except for Margarit. She thought she was dreaming but heard the dogs growling. She doesn't remember anything else."

"Shara will you take the children to the dining room?" asked Sudfad.

"They better not have hurt my dogs," Petra said angrily as he and Kyra were trying to clean the blood off the German Shepherds.

"I already checked the dogs," said Renya. "They aren't hurt."

"We found a blood trail," Matthew announced when he saw Raul and Simon running up to the soldiers who were outside of Petra's windows.

"Don't touch anything until we get back," Raul yelled to the soldiers and he and Simon both ran to Matthew.

Renya had previously moved Petra to a room that did not have gardens outside of the windows because after he was kidnapped he kept thinking he saw shadows outside at night.

There was a large grassy area under the window that extended to the woods. Two soldiers had originally found the trail and were several hundred feet ahead of the three Princes. Simon kneeled down and was examining the trail. "I wonder if the dogs got more than one of them, look there; someone is being dragged," he said.

"My Lords, we found one," yelled one of the soldiers. The Princes ran to the soldiers who were standing over the body of a man who was covered in blood.

"The dogs tore his wrist open but he's got all his fingers" said the second soldier as he was going through the man's pockets. "He is dead, but still really warm."

"I'll bet Mother is never going to complain about Petra having the dogs in his room again," said Raul sarcastically as he kneeled down and looked at the body.

"We're going ahead," said Matthew as he, Simon and one of the soldiers continued to follow the trail.

"My Lord this is all I found," said the second soldier and handed Raul a folding knife, six gold coins and a blood stained piece of paper."

"Keep the money," Raul said and carefully unfolded the paper but it was too damaged for him to be able to read the writing. Raul and the soldier heard yelling and now ran after Simon, Matthew and the other soldier.

Simon had a man in a headlock with his left arm and had a second man pinned against a tree; Simon had his right hand on this man's throat. Raul immediately ran to this man as the soldier ran to Matthew and the first soldier, both of whom were fighting with men.

The man who Simon had pinned against the tree wasn't putting up a fight. He was covered in blood. "You have to help me," he said frantically. "Those damn dogs tore my fingers off."

"Those damn dogs may be eating you for breakfast," Raul said as he tied the man up. As warriors, Raul, Simon and Matthew always carried fine cord on them for such purposes.

"Don't kill them unless you have to," Simon yelled to the soldiers as he now threw the man he had been holding in a choke hold to the ground and tied him up.

By the time that Claudius' army and those who traveled with them saw the bodies of the Stratas and Rogetts and then were moved across the river it was late in the afternoon. A huge flock of Enrops delivered letters just as the last barge brought men to shore. Claudius decided to make camp on the north shore of the tributary of the River Toba.

Archetenus, Jared and Michael were men who liked and understood each other. Since Michael was spending considerably more time talking with Tally and Drake these five men were bonding. This night they built a campsite together. While they had been waiting for everyone to be transported across the river, Archetenus and Jared told Tally and Drake about their lives. The stories were long and the men continued them as they sat around the fire eating their dinner.

"Have you read your letters yet?" Edward asked as he walked into their campsite.

"No, we were waiting until we were done with the stories," said Jared but pulled his letter out of his pocket as he spoke. "Something's wrong isn't it?"

"We should have a meeting," Edward said. "First of all your families are just fine but there were several attacks in Wetpr and well there is a lot of information. Karzman might have been behind them."

"What! How do you know?" asked Michael as he now grabbed his letters.

"Your little sisters," Edward said. "Some things about the attacks didn't add up and when Raul and his group were talking about them, well your little sisters are the only ones who realized what happened and damn if they weren't right. There's a lot of stuff; we should have a meeting."

Simon had the intruders locked in the dungeons at Fort Salar the morning they were discovered. The Princes returned to the castle and spoke with all of the children who had been in Petra's room; then they spent the day interrogating the five intruders. Simon, Raul and Matthew returned to the castle for meals but did not talk of the interrogations until they were completed.

When the three Princes walked into the family dining room for dinner, Saran asked, "Did Father send them?"

"We don't want to say a lot in front of the little children," said Simon. "But we really don't know. These men were hired as they sat in taverns just like the men who attacked the homes. A man who said his name was Cass walked up to the men while they were playing cards and asked if they wanted to earn some money. He gave them each a small pouch of gold coins and said they would get more after they came back and told him who was in the castle."

"Your father isn't our only enemy," Simon continued. "But Cass hired the men who attacked the homes too. And since you told us about the Juntos it probably is your father behind it."

"Or someone who wants us to think it is Karzman," said Sudfad. "It could be Madeline and Javier."

"I don't remember anyone named Cass from the village," said Nyla.

"I am willing to bet he is a professional killer and a foreman who was hired to orchestrate the attacks," said Raul.

"What I don't understand," said Shara. "Is why didn't the children hear the dogs attacking them? There was a great deal of blood besides the fingers."

"The dogs only got two of the men," explained Matthew. "The others were more worried about their friends alerting the soldiers so they covered the mouths of the guys before they tried to get the dogs off from them."

"Guess Petra is always going to be able to have the dogs in his room now," Raul said with a grin and winked at Petra.

"We've already discussed that," said Renya and smiled. "Thank The Great Ruler those dogs were there."

"Why do you think that Cass is a professional?" asked Nyla.

"Because he is hiring men who can't be traced back to anyone and he isn't giving them any information in case they get caught," said Simon.

"If he is a professional wouldn't you think he would be more careful about these men getting caught?" asked Annabelle. "I mean they have been pretty obvious."

"There might be more that we haven't seen," said Vitomas in a low voice as she glanced at the children's table. Nina was sitting with the children while Nyla and Saran were sitting at the adult's table.

"So where is everyone sleeping tonight?" asked Raul.

"There are soldiers posted outside every window on the ground floor," said Sudfad. "But tonight the children will campout in the chambers next to ours."

"Marie is making us special treats," said Petra happily. "And she got huge bones for the dogs for saving us."

"I am confused," said Margarit. "Saran said 'her father' but Uncle Sudfad aren't you their papa now?"

"We haven't signed the papers yet because we wanted to have a ceremony," Sudfad said. "And besides we want to make sure the girls want us for their parents."

"And we thought that Michael would want to be here," said Renya.

"Are you saying that when those papers are signed that you will be our new mother and father?" asked Nyla.

"Yes," said Raul. "And Karzman can't do anything about it."

Nyla looked at Saran who was sitting next to her then she turned and looked at the children's table. "Nina will you come here?" Nina ran to her sisters. "Nina have you been listening to what we are saying?" Nina nodded her head. "So what do you think?"

"I thought they were already our mama and papa; that's what I put on the pictures," Nina said and all of the adults smiled.

"We want you to be our parents," said Saran.

"Would you be mad if we asked you to sign those papers tonight?" Nyla asked.

"I think Michael would understand," Simon said to his parents. "You can still have the ceremony when he comes home."

"Oh, I think we can manage to have a little celebration tonight," Renya said with a big smile. "I am going to talk to Marie." Renya walked out of the dining room.

"Does that mean you are going to sign the papers?" asked Nyla.

"Yes," said Sudfad. "We will do that right after dinner." Nyla, Saran and Nina all smiled brightly.

"I am going to kill that bastard!" yelled Archetenus at the meeting. "He sends his men after my family."

"You're gonna have to stand in line," said Jared angrily. "We need to get home."

"Sudfad has increased the men guarding your homes," said Claudius. "And soldiers accompany them wherever they go."

"Hell, we still don't know what happened to all the soldiers watching Gabriel's and Erebus's places," Jared said. "That's a lot of men to just disappear. You would think their bodies would turn up if they are dead. And if they are all spies, well that just makes everything worse."

"Archetenus and Jared, we all understand your anger and fear but your families are protected by more than mere men," said the Sanuri. "The Angels as well as Blue Hengers are watching over them. They are safe but don't you wonder why Karzman would go after both of you?"

"Actually I was wondering the same damn thing," said Thaos. "First, we have been told that he doesn't have a lot of money and that he is trying to raise an army to attack Sudfad. That does make sense. But anyone who watches your places for even an hour can see that both of you, Erebus and certainly everyone in Gabriel's house are formidable opponents. There are other ways he could create distractions without garnering so many new enemies. And powerful enemies at that."

"So what are you saying?" asked Ashley.

"Well, we have been told that Karzman sold his soul to a demon and all of us have a hell of a lot of enemies who are demons," explained Thaos. "If one of them isn't pulling Karzman's strings then I would put my money on someone else. Juleta used to do crap like this all of the time when she was trying to get her father's throne. For my money I would be looking at Hector. We still have things that he wants. Now don't misunderstand me; I'm not saying that Karzman isn't an enemy but I just don't think he is behind all of this. Michael, Drake, Tally what do you think?"

"Karzman was always crazy," said Drake. "But after he changed because Teivel died, he got a whole lot worse. So really it could go either way. He might have made a deal with a demon to get help against Sudfad. The guy will stop at nothing to get what he wants. But the girls were right about those Juntos but that still makes no kinda sense."

"What do you mean?" asked Sorren before Drake could speak again.

"Everything the girls said was true but they didn't come with us when we threw those things around," Drake continued. "None of us knew if those things had any kind of power but they sure enough scared the hell out of people..."

"It's the diversion part that doesn't make sense," Tally interrupted. "First, it sounds like all those properties were clearly marked so why would he have to tell his army to look for those damn things in the grass? They aren't that easy to see. And secondly, he already used up his element of surprise because now all those folks are ready for the next attack. He would use those diversion things when the person was like in a city or something where they could be confused with others."

"Now I have a question," said Erebus. "The Angels told us that Samael owns Hector's soul and didn't they tell us a long time ago that Samael bought Karzman's soul after Teivel was destroyed? So Samael could easily be passing information back and forth. But something has been bothering me. Drake you and Tally keep saying how Karzman changed after Teivel died."

"We aren't lying," said Tally defensively.

"Oh, I am not saying you are," said Erebus. "But wouldn't you think that Samael would have restored Karzman back to his old power and strength; especially if he want's Karzman working for him? Samael will only do things to benefit himself so why keep Karzman as a feeble, crazy old man?"

An hour after dinner the entire family, including Marie met in the Great Hall of Sudfad's castle. Sudfad read the adoption papers out loud then he and Renya signed them. He turned to Nyla and asked each of the girls to sign the paper. Lastly he asked the adults of the family to sign as witnesses.

"Good thing he added an extra page," Simon said kiddingly as he and Annabelle signed their names.

After all of the signatures were written, Sudfad led the family in a toast. The adults had glasses of wine and the children had glasses of juice. "To family, may our bonds never be broken," Sudfad said and everyone in the room repeated his words.

"Thank you so much," Nyla said emotionally. "It is so strange but I feel like we are suddenly free."

"Oh, we aren't done," Sudfad said with a grin. "Vitomas and Annabelle will you come forward?"

"Annabelle and I really haven't had time to sit and talk to the three of you but we all had similar lives before we came here to live. Annabelle and I felt like we were in a dream living here. So we wanted to do something to show Sudfad, Renya, Alexander and Laurel how happy and grateful we were. We designed everyone rings and Sudfad liked them so much that they became the official rings of this family."

Annabelle handed Nyla, Saran and Nina each a small box. All three girls gasped when they saw the rings. The large stones in the center are the colors of the Royal Family. The colors are red and dark blue," Vitomas continued. "All of the women's rings have rubies and the men have dark blue sapphires. And all the little stones are everyone's birth stones."

"Michael told us when your birthdays are," said Annabelle. "So we have your stones in them but the sizes might not be right but we can have them adjusted."

"What are these?" asked Saran as she pointed to the golden sword and the golden scroll that were affixed to the bands on either side of the stones.

"They represent our family," Annabelle said.

"I understand the sword but why the scroll?" asked Nyla.

"This home as well as this kingdom follows The Great Ruler," said Sudfad. "When things settle down a little you will start classes to learn about Him."

"Gabriel and Raphael have already been telling us about Him and the Angels too," said Nina excitedly as she put the ring on her finger. "I have never had a ring before."

The girls hugged and kissed everyone in their new family, even Marie. "This is so wonderful," Nyla kept repeating. "Vitomas, we understood exactly what you meant when you said that you and Annabelle thought you were dreaming. That's how we feel too. I never knew people lived like this before."

"And she doesn't just mean with all the things you have," said Saran. "Ever since you saved us; all the people we have met are so very different."

"What do you mean?" asked Laurel.

"No one is afraid and everyone is so nice," Saran said. "You are all looking at me like I am crazy but we were talking, I mean Nyla, Nina and me. And everybody laughs here. We laugh and we can't remember doing that before."

# Chapter XXII
## Family Concerns

Although they had seen the dead army of Rogetts, Claudius was not taking any chances. Hundreds of fires were again built and extra soldiers were put on the perimeter. But this night, Sorren and Gideon had a surprise for Ashley. The two men walked up to the campsite that Gideon and Ashley shared with others. She was climbing out of the back of a boca when she saw them.

"Gideon aren't the boys with you?" she asked frantically. "I thought they were with you."

"They are fine," Gideon said. "Come with us."

It was then that she realized the two men were grinning. "What are you two up to?" Ashley asked.

"Just come with us dear," Gideon said and took her hand.

The large camp was made up of small camps that all were within the established perimeter. The three walked past two small camps before Ashley said, "Oh, my god!"

"It's not a real school, but it's as close as we can make one under the circumstances," Claudius said with a big grin.

"Once we started telling people that you were teaching the boys, everyone wanted their children in class but we knew that would be too much for you to handle. So these are all your helpers," Sorren said and laughed at the look on Ashley's face as she looked at the group of people smiling at her.

"We didn't have time to make enough tables," said Stephan but when we cut the wood for the fires we made pieces for the children to use to write on."

Ashley looked at twenty-two children, who were all sitting in rows with small, thin slates of wood on their laps. Each child had paper and either a pen or a thin piece of coal to write with.

There was a crudely made table in front of the students which held writing supplies and books. "I just don't believe all of this," she said with a big smile.

"The books belong to the Sanuri and Erebus," Gideon said. "They are all history books of some sort."

"More of the children wanted to come," said Risa. "But they were pretty small and everyone was afraid they would be too much of a distraction. I am going to help too. How do you want to start?"

"First let's have everyone tell us the level of education they have had if any. Then I can divide everyone into groups," said Ashley.

"I want to stay with Marty and Logan," Cassidy said.

"That is fine and also why I am doing this," Ashley explained. "Sometimes children learn better in smaller groups with people they feel comfortable with. You three work very well together."

"Can Chasity be with that group if she promises not to act up," asked Dack. "She feels like those boys are her brothers."

"Of course," said Ashley. "Are you going to help?"

Dack and Joao both laughed, "We hadn't really thought about it. Thor should help. He's a natural teacher."

"You are," said Kate to Thor when she saw him laugh at the comment. "Besides it will give you something to do besides mope around about Tanya." Dack and Joao laughed again.

"I don't know what you two are laughing about," Thor said with a grin to Joao and Dack. "You two act like Maxwell since you found Chasity. And yes Ashley; I will help."

"He's right," Calen said and chuckled. "I don't think the two of you have tried to pick up a girl since…"

"What are they saying?" Chasity asked Joao as she held his hand.

"They are just being jerks," Joao said with a mischievous grin.

"Uncle Calen don't be mean to Uncle Joao and Uncle Dack," Chasity scolded. "They are nice."

Everyone laughed loudly. "That's right Chasity. You stick up for us," Joao said and laughed again.

Thaos and Stephan walked the entire perimeter of the camp before reporting to Claudius the next morning. "No signs of Rogetts," Thaos said as he poured two cups of coffee. "While that is good, didn't it seem like there were a hell of a lot more prints than the dead bodies we found?"

"I was thinking that exact same thing," said Claudius. "The riders of those creatures disappeared. I wonder if they took some of the Rogetts with them."

"I may sound paranoid but I think we should keep up the extra defenses until we get home," said Stephan. "Especially with all the children here."

"I was planning on it," Claudius said.

"Speaking of children," asked Thaos. "Where is Cassidy?"

"With Ashley," Claudius replied with a warm smile. "He really wants to write letters to the girls and he doesn't want us to help him."

"Gee, Father another fiercely independent son; didn't you learn your lesson?" Stephan asked kiddingly.

"He does remind me of the two of you," said Claudius. "Thaos is that why you took to him right away?"

"Actually it was the damndest thing. Ashley brings him into the dining room and I felt like I was looking at myself. I knew we had to bring him home."

"Well, I am certainly glad you did and you know your mother is just going to love him," said Claudius.

When the members of Sudfad's family took their seats at the breakfast table they found little homemade cards on each plate. There was a freshly cut flower attached to each of the cards for the adults and a cookie with each of the children's cards.

"Those are from Saran, Nina and Nyla," Petra said as he took his seat.

"Where are they?" asked Renya.

"In the kitchen. We took the card in for Marie and she started crying," said Margarit.

Sudfad read his card then looked at Raul, Simon, Matthew and Angelina and said, "We see what you meant when you said they work their way into your heart."

"Actually Vitomas and I were talking," said Annabelle. "Doesn't it seem like they've been part of the family for longer than a couple of days?"

On the previous day, Sudfad sent riders to the homes of Gabriel, Erebus, Delilah and Zoya with the news of the intruders at the castle. Once again, Sudfad offered for Delilah and Zoya to move their families into the castle until their husbands returned. But both women wanted to stay in their homes.

When the members of Gabriel's household were told all of the details at the morning meeting they became enraged. "Going after us is one thing," said Raphael. "But going after the children is quite something else. We need to stop this before something happens."

"I am of the same mind as you," said Joshua. "But what are you thinking of?"

"I don't know yet," said Raphael. "And we certainly can't imprison the children because of this."

"Most of the time when the children are outside one of us is with them," said Micha. "And the dogs are really protective."

"We need to really think about this," said Gabriel pensively. "Maybe we do need to hire more nurses and make sure someone is always with the children."

"If you ask the children they would suggest another dog," Misha said with a grin. "Which may not be a bad idea either. The children usually stay together but if they do split up for any reason we can say that they need to have at least one dog with them."

"There is a dozen ways we could set up traps," said Joshua but it is too dangerous with the children and pets. While we are on the subject of protecting our families I wanted to share a letter with all of you. I forgot I had it and didn't read it until just before the meeting. The letter is from Chief Duncan. I believe all of you know that about a year ago the Angels told the Venatores to stop hunting demons and stay in their village. This was done for two reasons, the first because Sampson had been turned into some kind of demon animal and was stalking and trying to kill the villagers."

"The second reason was to protect the village during the civil war in Ryed. Then more recently the Angel Daniel transported all of the priests from the monastery at Rubar to the village for protection."

"Joshua before you continue I would like to say that I receive letters from those priests daily," said High Priest Othnial and they can't say enough good about your tribe. They love the people and now they have met those little people the Half-Mans and they are so intrigued."

Joshua smiled and said, "My people feel the same although it is against everything they stand for to stay confined in the village and not hunt demons. Hunting is who we are. But Duncan says that shortly after the priests came, Sampson stopped his harassment of the Venatores. At first he stopped but they would still find his prints outside of the village; now they don't even see those. While no one trusts that this isn't a trick, it appears that Sampson may have left the area."

"Where would he go?" asked Raul.

"The Angels told us that he was turned into..." Joshua paused and looked at Othnial. "I don't know if you know what we are talking about. I will give you the short version and if you want to know more we can talk after this meeting. The Chief of the Venatores has three sons. Two are great warriors and good men. The oldest, Sampson is a powerful warrior but called to demons. He even took the demon Hecate for his wife. After he did that he asked to go through the rites of transformation to turn into a demon." Othnial's face paled as he listed to Joshua.

"Part of the rites required that Sampson kill his brothers. He was going to do this but basically our team stopped him with the help of the Angels. Since Sampson was already transforming he had dangerous side effects. This is a long story so I will just jump to the part where some powerful demon changed Sampson into a demon but he looks and acts like a wolf. He was sent to track down and kill Hecate but apparently he couldn't find her and returned to Ryed and has been trying to kill the villagers."

"How do you know all of this?" High Priest Othnial asked.

"The Angels told us," said Simon.

"What Joshua didn't tell you," said Raphael. "Is that Sampson has always been obsessed with my wife, Vivian. So this letter could be a warning for us."

Claudius and his army traveled the next two days without any signs of danger. While a relief, they all felt as if they were being watched.

That night Harlow finished writing the story of Hector's child trafficking business and how the children were saved from their prison in Leven. He wanted this story to be printed side by side with the story of Thaos' life as an orphan on the streets of Port Friada. When Harlow was satisfied with his writing he walked to the camp of Claudius and his sons.

"I have completed the stories and rechecked all of the facts," Harlow said. "I was wondering if you would like to read them before I send them for print. I am having them printed in both Port Friada and Langer."

Thaos was pale and visibly shaken when he said, "Yes."

Harlow handed Thaos the stories but continued talking to the group that was sitting around the fire. "I made several copies if anyone wants one."

"May I read one?" asked the Sanuri.

"Of course," said Harlow and handed him some copies.

"I think we would all like to read those," said Edward. "That is if Thaos doesn't mind."

"I already told you everything there is to tell," Thaos said in a hoarse voice. As he read a page he would hand it to Claudius who then handed it to Stephan when he had read it.

"Here," Sorren said and walked up to Harlow and handed him a cup of whiskey.

"Ashley is teaching now," said Gideon as he and Edward were reading one of the copies. "Could I borrow one of these long enough for her to read it? She didn't go to the original meeting because she was taking care of the children."

Since there were few copies, people were passing them around the group, which was becoming larger as others joined them. But for the size of the group they read in relative silence since the stories were both disturbing and personal.

"Did I get anything wrong?" Harlow asked when Thaos finished reading both of the stories.

"No. Both of them were very good. But it's like pouring salt into an open wound," said Thaos.

"I don't know who runs the newspapers in Wetpr," said the Sanuri. "But Harlow I think you should send copies to King Sudfad also." Before Harlow could speak the Sanuri now addressed Thaos. "I know this is painful for you and I commend you for speaking out. But these stories are so powerful they need to be read by everyone. People have to understand these atrocities take place in order to stop them. And your firsthand account makes it real for everyone."

Thaos just nodded as Stephan poured more whiskey into his cup. "But even knowing that doesn't mean people are going to do anything about it," said Michael angrily as the stories reflected his own childhood torture.

"While there are those who would stick their heads in the sand and pretend things like this do not exist, it is my feeling that the majority of people will take a stand; even if it is in a small way. Thaos, this information will do so much good," said the Sanuri.

"He is right son," said Claudius. "And actually I think that Harlow made you sound like a hero."

"All of you are heroes," Harlow said. "While this is who you all are you don't see how very different you are from others; the world needs heroes. Heroes give people hope and everyone benefits from hope."

All of the women and children in Sudfad's household were invited to Gabriel's home for a party for the children. Delilah and Zoya were already in the home when Renya and her family arrived. Vitomas walked into the house ahead of the others and said. "I need to speak to a few of you in private."

Emeral, Natasha, Vivian and Hannah met with Vitomas in the parlor. "Is anything wrong dear?" asked Emeral.

"No but the children all have horses now and they brought them so that your children could ride on them. It was Petra's idea since you have allowed him to ride your ponies. The horses are gentle but they are big. Renya told the children not to say anything until I spoke with all of you."

"It will be fine," said Vivian. "Micha and Thomas will be here soon. We can take the children out."

"Then I will tell the others to come in," Vitomas said but before she got to the door all of the boys were running past her yelling.

"Petra's got horses," Christopher yelled and the boys all ran outside.

"How did they even know?" asked Vitomas and laughed.

"We say that a lot around here," Hannah joked as the women quickly followed the boys outside.

"We know you all want to go for rides," said Emeral. "But Natalie and Cassandra have pies and ice cream for you. Why don't you come in and eat first?"

High Priest Othnial was walking down the stairs to the dining room when all of the children ran into the house. He stopped and started to laugh at the commotion. "Join us for some pie and ice cream," Hannah said when she saw him on the stairs.

"Then we are going to ride horses," Adrone said. "You can come with us."

Othnial laughed again. "I think I will just watch all of you." He sat down at the table and said, "I love how much life there is around here. Where I come from you don't hear a lot of laughter."

"Where do you come from?" asked Nyla.

"Ryed. There is a vicious war going on there. And before that the monster Teivel turned that kingdom into a hell world."

When Othnial said Teivel's name Nyla, Saran and Nina all looked at him. They had previously been introduced to the priest. "Karzman, he was our father, worked for Teivel," said Nyla. "Did you know that?"

"Yes and I can't imagine what your lives were like," Othnial said gently.

"No, that is not why I am asking," said Nyla as she continued to stare at Othnial. "I didn't know you were from Ryed. Where did you live there?"

"I was the head priest of the monastery at Rubar. Why?"

Nyla turned to Renya and said, "I need to go home and get something important. I will be right back."

"First tell me what is going on," said Renya. "You look so serious."

"Our Angel gave us something for him," Nina said loudly as she filled her mouth with ice cream.

"The Angel Ruth helped us to escape our village..." Nyla said.

"But we didn't know she was an Angel then," interrupted Saran. "We just thought she was a nice lady."

"Ruth came to us late at night and told us to hurry," explained Nyla. "We grabbed a basket and put bread and apples in it. She told us to go into Karzman's room. I don't call him father anymore. He wasn't home. I walked in there and Ruth came with me because I was scared. There was a book lying on top of his bed. She told me to take it and to give it to the priest from Ryed. We hid it in our basket. It's in our room."

"I will fly her back," said Emeral. "Renya are all of the men still in that meeting?"

"They were when we left," Renya said to Emeral then looked at Othnial. "While the girls were told to give this to you; it may have importance for the missions. Would you mind if we tell the men?"

"By all means tell them. I would anyways. And I am very curious to see what this is."

"Will someone watch my children and I will go with them; just in case..." Cassandra said.

"Of course," said Natalie. "Do you want others to come?"

"No," said Emeral. "But I am just going to grab a weapon. You should bring one too, Cassandra."

# Chapter XXIII
## Tameric

When Emeral, Cassandra and Nyla returned to Gabriel's home all of the men in Sudfad's meeting came with them. The women walked into the house first. "The men are right behind us," Emeral announced as Nyla walked up to Othnial, who was still sitting at the dining room table. She handed him the book that was covered with a piece of cloth.

"No one looked at it," Cassandra said to the high priest.

"Perhaps now would be a good time for the children to go riding," Emeral suggested.

"I would really like to see what that book is," said Vivian.

"Since our nurses are here too," said Vitomas. "I will go out with the children. I love to ride."

Before Vitomas could get out of her chair, Sudfad and the other men walked into the dining room. "Gabriel, perhaps we should take this into your study," said Othnial.

"I was just going to suggest that," Gabriel said.

"The older children are going riding," Hannah said. "If you will give us a few moments, I think some of us would like to join you; if that is alright?"

"Of course," said Othnial who had not removed the cloth covering the book.

"I will bring in some pie and ice cream for all of you," said Natasha.

"Renya, do you want me to stay?" asked Nyla.

Renya looked at Sudfad but it was Matthew who said, "That might be a good idea. You can read Cerfic can't you?"

"Yes," said Nyla.

Ten minutes later the household had divided up between the adults watching the children and the people in Gabriel's study.

Othnial walked to the front of the room and silently prayed over the book before he removed the cloth. The book was very thick with a dark leather cover. There were no pictures or writing on either the front or back covers.

Everyone sat quietly as Othnial looked at the first few pages. "I thought this might be a book of dark magic," he said. "I believe it is some kind of business ledger but I am not sure." The high priest handed the book to Sudfad who paged through it.

"Vivian, you were the one working on the codes with the Patronus, please come up here," said Sudfad and handed her the book. Vivian took the book then walked over to her father and they both looked at it.

"Sudfad, I believe this is the same code that Shanksaw and Deckor used," said Joshua and handed the book to Maxwell. "That means it must be a code that is used by all of the Insidiae. If we can break this, we will be able to translate many documents."

Matthew walked up to Maxwell and Emeral and looked at the book over their shoulders. "Now correct me if I am wrong here," he said. "Deckor used the code to form gibberish words that formed pictures but Shanksaw used the code to form normal language is that right?"

"Yes, but we were only able to translate part of his ledger. He changed the code for the second half..." Vivian said then paused. "We didn't try to line those words up for pictures. Father we need to do that."

"Pictures of what?" asked Othnial.

"Actually they were pictures that formed words," said Gabriel. "It was very difficult to translate."

"Nyla, why don't you look at the book and see if you understand what he was writing," said Sudfad. Nyla hesitated as if she was afraid to touch the book but she walked up to Sudfad who now had the book back in his possession.

Nyla took the book and looked at the first few pages as all of the others had then she turned to the back of the book.

"We saw him writing in this but it wasn't just writing," Nyla explained. "When he would get letters he would open this book and look at these last two pages as he read the letter. I was never allowed to look at this book before but see here this is some kind of key but I don't understand the language. It's not Cerfic. Mother taught us to read and write in Cerfic."

Vivian had put more time into trying to translate the codes of the Insidiae than any other person in that room. She now walked up to Sudfad and Nyla but before she could speak there was a knock on the door then Zoya entered with Natalie.

"I am sorry to interrupt," said Zoya. "But the spirits are talking to me. It is Fiona, Nadia's mother who is speaking."

Nyla gasped and Vivian whispered to her, "Zoya is a seer."

Natalie shut the door to the study as every person now turned and looked at Zoya. "Fiona is very frightened. She says that Nadia has been wanting to thank Sudfad and Renya for taking in her babies but Fiona is afraid for Nadia and won't let her speak."

"Fiona said that Karzman always said he was from Tameric but no one had ever heard of it. She says that now she understands that centuries ago in the shadows of the Rosu Mountain Range in the Kingdom of Marba was a tiny village named Tameric. This is the ground were the castle of the demon Sporos now stands."

"She says that when the first humans called the demons into this world they did more than allow them access; they bred with the demons and sacrificed other humans to them. Tameric was an innocent village until Emeric and Banaka paid them a visit. They had already received their power and rewards for selling out the world. They rode into the village as immortals. Emeric raped many women and his sister helped him. Karzman was a child born from such a rape."

"The young mother and her family were horrified by both the rape and the pregnancy. They believed Emeric to be a demon and they tried many times to kill Karzman when he was a baby. They could hurt him but they could not kill him which made them believe even more that he was a demon."

"They were desperate and went to a witch that lived in the Rosu Mountains. She made a potion to kill the demon in the baby. But there was no demon in him. The potion did not kill Karzman but it greatly damaged him. He was frail, weak and almost blind. He could barely hear. He was a younger version of what he is now."

"He lived and over the years he learned of Emeric and Banaka and the crimes they committed. He still did not know about the potion that his mother had given him. He spent years searching for Emeric. Finally he called out to darkness and sold his soul to the demon Ahriman who owned the souls of Emeric and Banaka. The demon united the three. Emeric was disgusted with Karzman because he was weak and broken. Ahriman told them about the potion and transported them back to Marba."

"Karzman killed his mother and her family and Emeric, Banaka and Karzman killed the entire Village of Tameric. As a reward Ahriman gave Karzman a strong and healthy body. Emeric and Banaka had already invested greatly in Teivel; he was their head lieutenant and they had no desire to replace him so they made Karzman a second to Teivel. Although Karzman worked for Teivel there were many rivalries between them."

"Karzman worshipped Emeric, Banaka and Teivel so when Ahriman was destroyed, Karzman was weakened but he still had his benefactors. But now Karzman is cursed, he lives in the body of his human frailty. He has sold his soul to Samael but Samael was Ahriman's enemy. That code is the language of the Village of Tameric. They had a different alphabet. Be careful the demons are everywhere. She is gone now," said Zoya. "She was talking very fast and sounded so frightened."

Gabriel jumped up and grabbed some paper and pen. "We need to write all of that down before we forget," he said.

Renya walked up to Nyla and put her arm around her, "Are you alright?" she asked.

"I, I think so," Nyla stammered. "I wish I could have talked to Mother."

"Well, perhaps Zoya can help you some time. She is very good," said Renya.

"Zoya, was she saying that all of the Insidiae codes that we have been trying to translate are actually the language of the Village of Tameric?" asked Maxwell.

"That is what it sounded like to me," Zoya replied.

"Does anyone know the name of that language?" asked Luca.

"Erebus is probably our best bet," Raphael said. "We need to get messages to him and the Sanuri."

"Wait, this doesn't make any sense," said Gabriel. "Why would Ruth tell the girls to give the book to Othnial and not to one of us who rescued them? There is more to this."

"And we have some questions too," said Renya as she still had her arm around Nyla.

Gabriel looked at Renya when he heard the seriousness in her voice then he looked up and called, "Ruth would you please join us?"

"We are tagging along," said the Angel Daniel as he, Ruth and Miranda appeared in the study.

"First let Renya ask her question," said Miranda. "For Nyla is consumed with fear."

It took Renya a moment to speak because she always became so emotional in the presence of the Angels. "We know that Karzman is a monster but whatever he is; well is that passed down to the girls?"

"No, they are their mother's daughters. But the sons are the offspring of their father," said Miranda.

"So what exactly are you saying?" asked Sudfad. "Do they have demon blood in them?"

"No and neither does Karzman but there is more to that story," said Daniel. "The Grand Masters sold their souls to Ahriman and other demons at the beginning of time. So they have considerably longer lives than normal humans. But both Emeric and Banaka promised Ahriman the souls of any of their off spring; fortunately they didn't have many."

"So Ahriman owned Karzman's soul from the beginning?" asked Simon. "Is that why they couldn't kill him?"

"That and Ahriman was somewhat protecting Karzman. You see every soul a demon owns makes him stronger as does fear. As a baby and child Karzman caused a great deal of fear in his village. There is no mercy in demons," said Daniel.

"Nadia and Fiona protected Michael and the girls more than anyone realizes," said Ruth. "But Torin and Cabal, the sons of Karzman and Nadia called to darkness at very early ages and they too have sold their souls to Samael now."

"So is one of them running the tribe since Karzman is weakened?" asked Raul.

"Torin is attempting to," said Miranda. "And he is a dangerous man. While he cares for his father, he also desires power. Torin would kill Karzman but Samael will not allow it yet. But Karzman is no fool, he knows his sons are exactly like him so he expects them to try and kill him. So he in turn is plotting against them. While this is a horrible situation they have created and perpetuate it does keep their eyes off from other things."

"So were they behind the attacks against our homes?" asked Gabriel.

"No that was Hectors' doing. He is trying to distract all of you with a war with Karzman," Miranda explained. "But Karzman is also plotting against you and has spies watching you. He has sent hired killers after those he feels betrayed him which include the girls, Tally and Drake. But Hector is just using all of that to his advantage. You will be receiving a letter from Michael soon. He, Thaos, Drake and Tally already figured this out."

"How?" asked Nyla. "I told the truth."

"Yes you did," said Miranda. "But Tally and Drake were soldiers who implemented Karzman's plans and they saw the discrepancies between the way the attacks were carried out here and how Karzman normally handled such things. But you have more threats than them."

"You mean the Elods?" asked Matthew.

"At this point they don't plan to attack you directly. They are trying to obtain information and they will manipulate situations as Hector is doing. We told you about Tresdor before. He is the nephew of Usman. He serves the demon Bertuck. Tresdor is a coward and has failed to fulfill his promises to the demon as had his uncle. Bertuck is punishing Tresdor by making him live in the diamond mines while he awaits orders. Tresdor is terrified there are Rogetts in the mines. He is already promising Bertuck that he will do anything to leave the mines."

"Does he have any special powers?" asked Misha.

"No," said Miranda. "And you are thinking that he is only one man. But a man with no conscious who will do anything for his demon master. He has lost everything; he is a desperate man."

"Unless anyone has more questions about your endless sea of enemies we can talk about the book," said Ruth. "Karzman is not a well-educated man. He can barely read and write but he did learn the basics of the language of the Village of Tameric. The language is called Cheyweg and it was a common language in the lower kingdoms of Opots centuries ago. It is a simple language not flowery like Cerfic. But it is better spoken than written because one word can have different meanings depending on which part is emphasized."

"So in written form it has punctuation over the words to denote the meaning," Ruth continued. "Emeric and Banaka took this basic language, which was also their language and added words and meanings to form a secret code. They left Marba and traveled greatly before they made their home in Ryed. They realized that few kingdoms had ever heard of Cheyweg much less spoken it."

"So that comes back to why I told the girls to give the book to High Priest Othnial." Ruth now turned so she was looking directly at the priest.

"You saved countless lives in Ryed. You provided food, shelter, medical services and so much more to some of the poorest people in this continent. Did you ever ask for payment?"

"Of course not," said Othnial with indignation. "You should know that." He paused and turned red. "I am sorry I did not mean to speak to you like that. Please forgive me."

Ruth smiled. "You are right I do know that but tell us how people would try to repay you and the other priests."

"Well, some people insisted on repaying us so they would bring us food from hunting or from their gardens. They would help us with chores and sometimes they would give us things. We didn't want the items but to refuse them would have been an insult."

"Tell us, what did you do with these items?" asked Ruth.

"We put them in a chest..."Othnial stopped talking and now looked at the Angel Daniel then back at Ruth then at Gabriel and Raphael. "Daniel had me bring the contents of that chest here. Everything is in the Holy Vault. But what is of importance?"

"You saved the life of a young boy after he had been bitten by a snake. His grandmother walked for miles to repay you with an old scroll. It was the only material thing she had of value. That scroll explains the Cheyweg language; it will translate the many documents you have."

"Where is it?" Raphael asked Othnial. "I will get it."

"All those items are still in a pouch sitting on the table with the other items I brought."

"Wait Raphael," said Ruth. "I told you that Emeric and Banaka used Cheyweg for their secret language hundreds of years ago. But as the Insidiae grew some of the members, especially the more intelligent ones like Deckor made some changes to the secret code so that their fellow Insidiae members could not understand all that they read. Thus the pictures that Deckor created with words. Shanksaw used combinations of codes. Vivian, you and the Patronus broke the first code of those ledgers. Cheyweg is the second code."

"If you have problems you will have to call to us because no one among you knows this language," Ruth said and now turned to Nyla. "You were starting to explain something when Zoya and Natalie walked in."

"Karzman would never let us look directly at that book but he had it out often. He used to do work with it on the kitchen table. I am not sure but I think he kept track of his money with it. And when he would get letters he would go to the back of the book and look back and forth between the last few pages and the letter as if he was translating something. I don't really know anything else," said Nyla shyly.

"How did Karzman get his letters?" asked Daniel.

"Do you mean who brought them to the village?" asked Nyla.

"Yes."

"Ravens."

After the Angels left the study, Sudfad, Raphael and Matthew returned to the castle. They found the scroll in Othnial's pouch in the Holy Vault. Raphael and Matthew returned to Gabriel's home with it.

Vivian, Natasha, Natalie and Diana rearranged the tables in Gabriel's study and put stacks of paper, pens and ink on each table. Joshua and Maxwell gathered all of the coded documents and books they had taken from Shanksaw.

Hannah and Emeral brought pots of coffee and food into the study. As soon as Raphael and Matthew walked in, Gabriel and Raphael unrolled the scroll and started to study it.

"The Sanuri has all of Deckor's papers," announced Matthew. "I didn't want to search his chambers but it looks like we have more than enough here to keep us busy without them."

Joshua joined Gabriel and Raphael and in less than one hour the three men figured out the language of the Village of Tameric.

Gabriel addressed the room full of people while Raphael and Joshua made the first copies of the scroll and their notes. "First, this scroll must be what they used to teach their children the language. It is simple once you figure it out."

"Raphael and Joshua are making copies that include our notes; when they are done they will hand them out and whoever gets them please start making more copies until we all have one. And before we start I would like to say a prayer. Great Ruler we believe these documents to be important. It is certainly possible that the lives of people depend on us being able to correctly translate this code. Please help us all in this endeavor."

Nyla and Renya returned to the dining room and walked up to Zoya. "Can you help me talk to my mother?" asked Nyla fearfully.

"I will try," said Zoya. "But Fiona was very afraid of something and adamant that she didn't want Nadia talking to us."

"What is she afraid of?" Nyla asked.

"I don't really know," Zoya said and handed her toddler to Ella. Zoya closed her eyes and stood motionless for several minutes. Nyla and Renya held hands while they waited. Nyla started to speak but Zoya held her hand up for Nyla to stop talking. Other family members started to gather around the three women.

It was several more minutes before Zoya opened her eyes and looked at Nyla and Renya. "Please someone give me a piece of paper and a pen. Melinda ran and got these items and brought them to Zoya. "Nyla before I start I have to tell you that when I speak with spirits more spirits come to me than the ones I call because they are so excited to be able to communicate with a human."

"Nadia came but for just a brief moment. She never imagined that Renya and Sudfad would adopt all of you and she now wishes she would have contacted him years ago. She started to say something else but disappeared and Fiona came forward again. Fiona told me not to call to Nadia again at least for a long time because it is too dangerous then she too disappeared."

"Other spirits started to come forward to talk with me but they were not connected to Nadia in any way. I was almost ready to stop when the spirit of a man came forward."

"He said his name was River and he had been one of Karzman's men but Karzman had him murdered." Nyla gasped loudly and tightly squeezed Renya's hand when Zoya said this. "River says there is a terrifying darkness that the spirits can see but they don't know what it is. He said that is what Fiona is so frightened of. River curses Karzman and has offered to help us. He said that Michael doesn't know this but Drake and Tally stay near him often because they are trying to protect him."

"Karzman hates Sudfad and will attack him but he has learned that Michael was the one responsible for Teivel's death so now Karzman is asking the demons to curse Michael too. I asked him if Tally and Drake knew this and River said they did not; they just know how hate driven Karzman is."

"He said that Karzman is fearful because he is so weakened and he is bartering with demons always. River said that Karzman has put wooden signs all around his house and he painted the same symbol on all of them. I will draw what he showed me in a moment. River said that he is glad that you and your sisters escaped."

Zoya stopped talking and concentrated on drawing. "Do you know River?" Renya asked Nyla.

"Yes and I will tell you but I don't want to have to explain it to the others."

"I am not good at drawing but this is what he showed me," Zoya said as she handed the paper to Renya and Nyla. "Do you know what it is?"

"I don't," said Nyla.

"I don't know what it means but I have seen this before," said Renya to Zoya. "And I can't tell you why but I think this is very bad." Renya now looked at Nyla. "Honey this might be really important. Why don't we go into another room and you tell me who River is?"

Nyla nodded. "Renya take her to our chambers; no one is in there," said Emeral and led the women up the stairs. Emeral opened the door that led to the parlor.

"I'll leave you now; stay as long as you like," Emeral said and turned to leave the room.

"You can stay," Nyla said meekly as tears filled her eyes. Emeral looked at Renya who nodded.

"We have two older brothers, Torin and Cabal and, and they used to have their way with us all of the time. We always fought them but..." tears were streaming down Nyla's face. "One day River and Tally heard us screaming and they pulled them off from us and hit them. Saran and I got away but Torin and Cabal ran and told Karzman. He had Tally and River tied up in the middle of the village and whipped and left them there for three days. No one was allowed to go near them to help them at all."

"When they were cut down, River ran from the village and Karzman sent his demon dogs after him. I don't even know how River could run because he was so hurt. After that no one tried to help us again." Nyla started sobbing and Renya hugged her tightly.

After a few moments Renya said to Nyla, "Honey, I have to tell the others about River since he gave us information. I may have to tell them everything."

"You can; I just don't want to," said Nyla as she sobbed.

"Renya if you want to stay with her I will go downstairs and tell the others," said Emeral. Renya handed Emeral the drawing then led Nyla to a sofa where they both sat down. Renya held Nyla as she cried.

Emeral went to the study and told the group about Zoya's most recent communication with the spirit world. After she repeated the conversations she told the group about the spirit named River. Raul was so angry that he pounded his fist on the table several times. "Where is Nyla now?" asked Simon.

"She and Renya are in our chambers. Nyla is crying and Renya is comforting her. Nyla said that all of you could know this information but she did not want to have to explain it to you. And this is the drawing."

Emeral was standing in the front of the room with Gabriel and Raphael and handed Gabriel the piece of paper. "We have seen this on the plyogram," said Gabriel as he handed the paper to Raphael.

"For those of you who don't know what a plyogram is," said Raphael as he handed the drawing to Joshua. "In ancient times kings used to have secret messages hidden within pictures. These are called plyograms. Maybe a year and a half ago now, Annabelle discovered a drawing that was painted over. The drawing was in the house of a military officer who was bartering with demons. There were great battles that day and the Angels helped us."

"Alexander cut the wall apart and brought part of it here. Annabelle worked for hours and uncovered a meticulously drawn picture under the paint. This plyogram consists of images of dark magics and demons. The Sanuri and Erebus have been trying to translate it. While we have figured out the meanings of some of the symbols we don't understand the message being conveyed. This symbol is on the plyogram."

## Chapter XXIV
## Brothers and Sons

As soon as Raul and Simon got a couple of copies of the symbol that Zoya saw they returned to their home to show it to Sudfad. Simon told Sudfad everything that both Zoya and Nyla had said. It was obvious to Raul and Simon that their father was as angered as they were by Nyla's story.

"Father, Simon and I want to go with you when you attack Karzman," Raul said angrily then he paused. "We know that someone has to stay at the castle; perhaps Matthew can."

"And what if there are more attacks against the family or the kingdom?" asked Sudfad. "We know there are spies around us. If we all leave some of Karzman's hired killers may come for the girls. No, we will stay with the original plans."

"Actually I would feel better if we reviewed those plans," said Simon. "You could be riding into a trap. Make him come to us. And you certainly shouldn't leave until the Sanuri has seen that drawing."

Chaez had volunteered to go to Port Friada with Claudius' army; that was after he received permission to take the time off from his training as a Patronus priest. It helped Chaez greatly that Gabriel and Raphael had also volunteered for the mission. But Chaez was a serious student and studied every chance he could while on the mission. Because of this he spent a great deal of time by himself.

This night after the dinner meal was eaten the Sanuri made arrangements with Claudius to keep Chaez, Dominic, Fennel, Seth, Lawrence and Noah off the perimeter for a few hours so they could attend a meeting.

The meeting was held at the Sanuri's boca. Dominic and his men were surprised that no one else was in attendance when they walked into the campsite but they heard voices from inside of the boca. A few moments later the Sanuri and Chaez walked in front of the group.

"Chaez, we almost forgot you were here," Lawrence said kiddingly. "Where have you been hiding?"

"Actually that is the reason for this meeting," said the Sanuri with a bright smile. "Will you each go to the back of the boca and grab a pile of the books and other materials."

"What is all of this?" asked Noah as he was the first to get his books.

"We will tell you as soon as you sit back down," said Chaez.

"Are these our books for training?" Fennel asked as he sat near the campfire and read the cover of the book on top of his stack.

"Chaez has a gift for you," said the Sanuri.

"Actually Gabriel, Raphael and High Priest Othnial helped," said Chaez. "Everyone knows the only reason you missed the beginning of training was for this mission. And let me tell you the physical training is grueling but the studies are also intense and all of you were getting so behind that we feared you would have to wait until the next class started."

"So those are all of the books, scrolls and things that you will need for this first year, but there are two huge libraries at the Learning Center and one is just for our program. The reason you haven't seen me is that besides studying, I have copied all of my class notes for you. You each have a copy in those leather journals and I got the teacher's outlines of the classes we are all missing and the Sanuri will teach us. Those outlines are also in your journals."

Chaez and the Sanuri smiled as the men paged through their materials with the awe of children. "Gabriel and Raphael were going to help with your training on this mission but you know they took Michael's sisters back to Wetpr. None of you have to worry about the physical training because you are already incredible warriors but we get a lot of homework," Chaez explained.

Dominic was the first to get up and shake Chaez's hand. "I don't know how we can repay you for this."

"You already did by helping me with my training. The first week all of the priests compete on the training field and it is like a battlefield. I never would have passed that before. Of course the Sanuri is our teacher but the studies seem to build on each other so I would suggest that you read my notes and the chapters that I indicated first."

"I would agree," said the Sanuri. "Now, I already spoke with Claudius and unless we are attacked all of you should be able to concentrate on your studies. I would suggest that we meet here every night after dinner even if you just want to read. That way I will be available for questions. And I have another suggestion. Chaez, things have been so crazy that I don't know if you were told about Hilgra?"

"Thaos told me she is dying because of what Juleta did to her but that Dominic is helping her."

"All of you want to become priests," said the Sanuri. "There is no monopoly on who can help Hilgra. I would suggest that all of you talk with her and pray with her; whether it is as a group or individually."

"I will be meeting her shortly," said Dominic. "I will be honest, she will probably be overwhelmed if all of us just show up. Why don't one of you come with me tonight and we will tell her what the Sanuri said. Then let her decide if she wants to meet with us all together or in small groups."

"I would like to go with you," said Chaez.

"For those of us who don't go," asked Noah. "Can we stay here and start our studies?"

"I will put on another pot of coffee," the Sanuri said happily. "And I don't know if you have looked through everything in your stacks but Chaez provided you with every item and instrument you will need. You can store your things in the boca."

This night the new team leaders had a meeting among themselves and afterwards they looked for Edward and Dominic.

"Dominic and Chaez are still with Hilgra," said Ira as he joined the other leaders near the campfire. "But I told him what we wanted to talk about and he gave me a list."

"We should probably invite a few others," Angus said to Edward. "But we wanted to speak with you and Dominic first. While we as team leaders realize we still have a great deal to learn we also have realized the importance of this work and we feel an urgency to form our teams. Since all five of us feel this urgency we have decided it might be a sign and we want to choose the team members now. All of the trainees are here except for the nurses and it is my understanding they are already chosen."

"Edward, since you and Dominic already have some team members you should have first choice as to who will work with your people. What do you think?"

"I too, have a list prepared but before we go into that I just want to make sure we cover all of our bases," said Edward. "For example we aren't just looking for compatible personalities; I want Jason because we look enough alike that we could pass for family. The same for Dominic's team. They want Brit because he and Fennel favor each other so."

"Well, that throws a new stone in all of this," said Maddox. "We have been concentrating on personal strengths, weaknesses and training. We hadn't actually thought about role playing."

"They are all excellent warriors," said Henrich. "I think in the morning we line them all up and tell them what we are doing."

"There is another point," said Edward. "All of the Ruala warriors on my team came to Wetpr as a group because they were transporting Venatores. Sol, told me that the reason Calen and the others on Gabriel's team work so well together is because they had been training as a group since they were young. Then he told me that their group had done the same. So I scooped them all up on the spot. There are so many warriors here that we haven't had a chance to get to know them all. I think we should bring that up in the morning too."

The team leaders walked to the campsite of Claudius and his family and told them the results of their meeting. Claudius sent for Sorren and the Sanuri. Then they called some of the trainees to their campsite and told them to tell all of the other trainees of the subjects for discussion in the morning line up.

"I think it is smart that you are asking them for their input," said the Sanuri. "It is my understanding that many of them did join us in groups."

"And they need to think and function as a group. And believe me that isn't easy for the Venatores," said Edward. "Ask anyone on my team, Kate was so belligerent at first that everyone was afraid to even talk to her. Working in a group goes against all of their training."

"Of course I am not a team leader but I am going to make a suggestion," said Sorren. "These young men and women have left their homes and families for the honor, and that is what they consider it. The honor of fighting with us. I would suggest that you have some sort of ceremony or something to acknowledge their sacrifices."

"That is an excellent idea," said Vincente. "But it will probably have to wait until we get to Wetpr. But let's decide what we will do and announce it tomorrow."

"You know the moment that you choose them they are on the King's payroll," said the Sanuri. "I am sure that will make them feel better."

"I didn't even think about that," said Maddox. "We need to figure this out. Will they get back pay for this mission?"

"Ask Michael," said the Sanuri. "But it would be only fair. Remember many of the warriors come from poor families and could use the money. So if Michael is unsure; your roles would be to ask Sudfad for it."

Henrich left the meeting and returned several minutes later with Michael, Archetenus, Jared, Drake and Tally. "I didn't tell him what our question was," said Henrich with a grin.

"I am not sure that I can speak for Sudfad," Michael said.

"You are the eldest son of the King and even though you don't want to sit on the throne you still have responsibilities," said the Sanuri.

"Oh this sounds damn good," Michael said sarcastically. "Ok, what is the question?"

"We are going to determine our teams tomorrow for two reasons," explained Vincente. "Every one of us team leaders has an overwhelming sense of urgency and also so they can start being paid. Our question is since they all risked their lives on this mission can they receive pay from the time they came to Wetpr?"

"Before you answer that Michael," Archetenus said. "As I tell everyone, I have known Miranda considerably longer than the rest of you and if you are all feeling the same thing, it is the Angels sending you a message and they are probably waiting for you to ask them for clarification. Ok Michael you can talk now," Archetenus said with a grin.

"Actually that is an easy question," said Michael. "Yes they will receive the back pay and if Sudfad doesn't think so, well. I will make it happen somehow."

"So you would fight for these warriors?" asked the Sanuri.

"Of course," said Michael. "Did you really think that I wouldn't?"

"I don't know since you shun all of your responsibilities as a prince," the Sanuri said. "These are the types of responsibilities you should be assuming."

While everyone expected Michael to get angry he didn't. "You are right. I am the most at home being a soldier and I don't like to go out of that role."

Both Archetenus and Jared were grinning. "Michael, you just got spanked by the Sanuri because everyone knows that Sudfad always gives back pay," said Jared. "But he is right."

"Michael, I did not do this to embarrass you," said the Sanuri. "But I agree with Ruth. Karzman beat you down physically and mentally because he feared both your strength and intelligence. And whether you realize it; you seem to believe the lies he told you. Since you are a soldier at heart, why don't you tell Sudfad that you will take over responsibility for the teams? You have worked with them and know the people and the missions. Raul and Simon have a lot of responsibilities, you would also be lightening their loads."

Michael grinned, "I think this is a set-up but I am all for it. But first I would like to speak with the team leaders. Where is Dominic?"

"He was talking with Hilgra but Chaez is also with them so he could come here," said the Sanuri.

"I'll get him," said Jared and quickly left the meeting.

"I still can't get past you not wanting to be king," said Tally.

"Are you kidding me," Michael said. "I have a hard enough time dressing up and socializing at the ceremonies. And wait until we get home. You have never seen ceremonies like Renya puts on. Besides Raul and Simon have trained their entire lives for that role. They would both be excellent kings."

Archetenus looked at Drake and Tally and said, "You will like them, they are men just like us."

"Considering our history, I don't think they will be happy to see us," said Drake. Many of the men laughed at this comment. "What is so damn funny? We were brutal to Michael when he was a boy. And believe me when I say that we damn regret it."

"I was in love with Raul's wife before they married and I kidnapped her but I did bring her back to him. And I am part of the family now," said Archetenus.

"Are you shitting me?" asked Tally. "Why didn't they kill you?"

"Because we needed Archetenus for the missions which was more important than revenge," said the Sanuri. "Archetenus changed his life and proved his loyalty to the Royal Family and the missions. That is something for both of you to think about."

Jared and Dominic walked up to the group. "Since I don't accept any of my responsibilities as a prince," Michael said with a grin. "The Sanuri thinks I should tell Sudfad that I will be responsible for the teams. And I really like that idea but I want to hear what all of you have to say first."

"Why would we be against it?" asked Dominic. "You have been in the trenches with us. You know what we face and what we need to do, even though you are still learning like the rest of us. I think it is a good idea."

"Is there anyone who doesn't want me in this role?" asked Michael. "You can certainly say it, I won't get mad."

"You're voted in," said Edward. "Now write your daddy so he can have the payroll ready when we get home."

That night Gabriel and the members of his household stayed up late working on breaking the codes of the Insidiae. The older children were allowed to campout in the playroom and kept sneaking into the study to spy on the adults.

"With all of that giggling you aren't sneaking up on anyone," Gabriel called out with a grin. The boys all started laughing and ran into the room.

"We can help you," Paul said.

"Actually boys, I may teach you this language," said Joshua. "But tonight we are trying to translate some important papers. And we are still learning this language."

Nicholas crawled onto Gabriel's lap and stared at the sheet of paper that Gabriel was trying to translate. "There's a boat in those words Papa. How come there is a boat? Did you draw that?"

Gabriel turned and looked at his son. "Show me the boat Nicholas." The boy moved his finger around the outline of the vessel. "Nicholas take this pen and draw the outline lightly." Now all of the boys ran to the desk where Nicholas and Gabriel were sitting and the adults stopped their work.

Gabriel's eyes grew wide as he watched his son connect the characters that formed the outline of a ship. "This is amazing," Gabriel said to the group. "I will pass this around, but Nicholas saw the detailed drawing of a ship. Have all of the children look at these sheets. They might be able to see what we can't."

"Ok boys," said Luca. "Everyone take a seat." Vivian handed each child a pen while Joshua handed them each a sheet of paper that was confiscated from the Shanksaw mission.

"I got a horse!" Christopher said excitedly.

"Boys, draw lightly so that we can still see the words," said Natalie.

Within moments all of the boys were drawing while the adults walked around the tables and looked at the boys' work. "Why can they see these and we can't?" asked Misha.

"I think their minds are more open," said Maxwell. "But these pictures form a code too. Tommy's outline is the number seventeen."

"Boys will you keep helping us with these?" asked Raphael.

"Sure," said Paul. "Do you want us to do it tonight?"

"No, you need to get some sleep but tomorrow we would like you to look at these again," Raphael said as he picked up Adrone's outline of mountains. "These are pretty detailed. This is fascinating."

"Well Uncle Raphael," Gabriel said with a sly smile. "Why don't you tell the boys what we are getting them?" Now all of the children swung their heads around and looked at Raphael with anticipation. Many of the adults laughed.

"Petra told you that his dogs protected the children from invaders and while Jasper and Riley watch over all of you, we decided to get you another dog."

The boys all started screaming loudly. Nicholas and Christopher both jumped out of their seats and started jumping up and down.

"Can we help pick it out?" asked Adrone excitedly.

"I don't see why not," said Joshua.

"You know that none of them will get any sleep tonight now," said Emeral to the adults then she turned to the children. "You all go to bed now because if you are too tired we won't go to look for your dog tomorrow."

"Ok Grandma," yelled Joey and he grabbed Tommy's hand and all of the boys ran out of the study.

"Emeral, you have such a way with words," Misha said sarcastically.

"So where are you taking the boys to look for a dog?" asked Emeral.

"Don't have a clue," Gabriel said and chuckled.

"I will tell you what," said Emeral. "Let's start the children on these papers first thing in the morning and I will go into the city and ask around."

"That works for me," Luca said.

"I think that works for all of us," said Gabriel as he lined the drawings side by side on a table. "I think we should still translate the words on these pages. Right now I don't have a clue what these pictures mean."

Renya and Sudfad checked on all of the older children together this evening. The children were once again allowed to have a campout in the chambers next to the King and Queen.

When Sudfad and Renya walked into their bedroom chambers Renya said, "Sudfad if Nadia was anything like her daughters I can certainly understand why you fell in love with her. Those girls are our daughters now by more than a piece of paper. They have stolen my heart and I just want to kill Karzman and his sons myself." Renya started to cry and Sudfad put his arm around her.

The following morning Claudius postponed their departure so that the team leaders and members could meet with the trainees. The Sanuri suggested that some of the people who often worked with the teams should also attend the meeting. This group included Thaos, Stephan, Michael, Archetenus, Jared, Gideon and Sorren. All of the trainees were lined up.

"All of you should have received word last night, of what we will be talking about today," announced Edward. "We know that all of you are fine warriors. But with all of the attacks we haven't had a chance to get to know you as we would have liked."

"Members of the teams will be walking among you; they are looking for similarity of features for role playing. While that may sound strange to you, it is important. And the team leaders are going to be talking to all of you. We want to have the teams picked today. That being said; you will be happy to know that once the teams are picked you are officially getting paid by King Sudfad and you will be paid from the day you arrived in Wetpr for training. I thought that would bring smiles," Edward said with a grin.

The Sanuri too, walked among the trainees for he remembered Miranda's words of warning several weeks earlier. Michael, Thaos and the others took part in the questioning.

Claudius left the perimeter guards in place since so many of the people were involved with the meeting. The trainees felt honored that their opinions were asked on a variety of matters and they enthusiastically responded. After the interviews, the trainees were released and the regular and part time team members and the leaders sat together and compared notes.

At noon, the trainees were called to a meeting again and to their surprise it was General Claudius who was addressing them. "As you know circumstances have delayed the team leaders in choosing their teams. And because of that we aren't prepared for a true ceremony. But we will have one when we arrive in Langer. I have already sent word to King Mathas and King Sudfad and I would not be at all surprised if there isn't another ceremony in Wetpr."

"Chief Sorren will be doing the honors of calling you forward for your teams. I am not surprised that every warrior here was chosen. Be proud of what you have accomplished and the work you will be doing. With that I am turning this over to Chief Sorren."

The pride was evident on the faces of the trainees as they were called forward to stand behind their team leaders. The Sanuri watched the ceremony with mixed feelings of pride and foreboding.

Only Gabriel, Raphael and Maxwell attended Sudfad's meeting this morning as the other members of Gabriel's household were working with the children on Shanksaw's documents.

"Deckor's pictures spelled out words," explained Gabriel as he was briefing the members of the meeting about the children seeing pictures in the documents. "But there were pictures of ships, mountains and swords in these documents. Look for yourselves. We have not finished translating the meanings of the words because we have the children looking for pictures."

"I am surprised how good these pictures are," Sudfad said as he looked at the documents. "We are fortunate Nicholas saw the first one."

"They are getting another dog for all of their hard work," Maxwell said and chuckled. "You can't believe how wild they were this morning. They wanted to work on the documents before breakfast. Emeral is in the city looking for dogs now."

Everyone smiled at this comment except for Raul and Simon who both had been quiet all morning. Now Raul stood up and addressed the group. "Father, Simon and I have not talked to you about this subject and you may become very angry with us for bringing it up first at the meeting. As you know Vitomas and Annabelle spent hours with the girls after they returned home yesterday. Then our wives told us what they talked about."

"Simon and I care about Nyla, Saran and Nina as if they were our own sisters and...and both of us are so damn mad we can barely talk."

Raul had been looking at Sudfad but now he turned to the other members in the room. "As you know Father and Michael are going to attack Karzman. Simon and I support this move but we feel that it is a trap, as does Father. Both Simon and I want to go on that mission, besides for revenge we feel the mission would go better with more of The Seven Sons involved."

"So we would like you to consider something that has never been done before. Maxwell, Gabriel and Raphael if Father permits it would you be willing to train in some of our duties and cover those duties while we are gone? Even if only one of us stays back we will need help. Now Father you can yell at us."

Sudfad sat back in his chair and glared at his sons. "You are right I am angry that you presented this to the group before saying anything to me. This will not happen again. Do you understand me?"

"Yes we do Father and it won't happen again," said Simon. "But this idea does have merit. As Raul and I talked about this we believe, the Karzman mission aside that it would greatly benefit us to train our friends in some of our duties. Our entire family is The Seven Sons and the Angels have repeatedly told us the battles will get much worse. You agonize because you feel chained to your desk and castle. There may be times when all of us are needed on a mission. Mother can run things but she would need help."

Everyone in the room could see how angry Sudfad was. "I believe that I speak for Gabriel and Raphael too when I say we are honored to be considered for such responsibility," said Maxwell. "And while I agree the boys should have spoken with you first, their idea does have merit."

"Let me think about this?" said Sudfad. "I am more angry that you did not address this with me first than I am about your idea."

"Well then let us finish with what we were thinking," said Simon. "Gabriel and Raphael are almost done with training the new leaders. That is seven additional teams. They both want to spend more time in Salar with their families. When we were in Langer we learned a great deal about how Mathas has divided up the duties of his throne."

"And Father they are very practical ideas." Each of the ruling members has a certain amount of responsibility in the kingdom but they are all trained in each other's duties. We understand that Mathas did this initially when his children were small and he did not want his kingdom to fall into chaos if he was killed."

"But with this war with the demons consuming so much of our time, both here and in Lentz there are other issues of the kingdom that are not being addressed. Father it might not be a bad idea to create some new positions and delegate some of the duties. It would certainly free you up more. And perhaps it would prevent us from having another Shanksaw situation on our hands."

"Now we haven't said anything to Maxwell, Gabriel or Raphael about any of this until now either, but we just want to put the ideas out there for discussion."

The anger was draining from Sudfad's face as he listened to Simon speak. He turned and looked at Maxwell, then Gabriel and Raphael. "If we were to consider such changes would any or all of you be interested in assuming a post in the government? Actually I should rephrase that because it sounds to me that my sons are proposing for you to become ruling members of the kingdom. Am I wrong?"

"You are not wrong," said Raul.

Sudfad again addressed Raphael, Maxwell and Gabriel, "Understand that nothing is worked out yet but you would probably be spending more time here than on missions but you would still be allowed to go on missions."

"I think we are all shocked by this," said Gabriel sincerely. "I can tell you our families would prefer we stay home more often. While I would like to say 'yes' now I need to speak with Hannah and I believe that is the same for Raphael and Maxwell."

"That is understandable," said Sudfad. "Before we go any further on this matter I want to show you a letter I received after breakfast this morning. It is from Michael." Sudfad smiled broadly as he handed the letter to Raul. "Michael said the Sanuri spanked and scolded him for shirking his duties as a prince."

"He said that the short time he filled in for Matthew, he started to realize the duties of the throne. He has volunteered to be in charge of all of the teams. He is suggesting that first as that is really what he is most familiar with. He said the teams have been determined and all of the trainees were chosen and he would like them to receive pay from the day they arrived in Wetpr for training. He said he feels he is ready now to accept other duties and wants to speak with us when he returns."

"He goes on to say that leaving his sisters behind was weighing heavily on him and he was planning on going back and getting them on his own. With them here he feels he is ready to move forward."

"I think we are all glad to hear this," said Simon. "And now that we have the girls here; I think all of us can certainly understand how he felt. I for one approve of him taking over the teams." Simon looked now at Gabriel and Raphael. "What that means is he would be responsible for making sure the teams are paid and have everything they need."

"And bringing any issues to our attention if you aren't here," said Sudfad. "Is there anyone who is opposed to this idea?"

"I believe we all approve," said Raphael. "He is a good man."

"Now back to Raul's and Simon's ideas. Honestly the three of you are better qualified to fill in than Michael is. And while he should be here, we all know he doesn't really care how the duties are assigned. He has been so lost that we haven't pushed anything on him. And even though he now says he is ready to move forward, he actually might not be. So all of that being said we will start a discussion on this subject before he returns home. But I will write to him for his input," said Sudfad.

"Matthew and Renya should both be here also. At this time I would like to take a break and resume in one hour with all of our families here. And that means everyone at your household. Bring the children, our nurses will watch them and we will resume in the Great Hall."

"Emeral is in Salar and Hannah is at the orphanage," said Maxwell. "Could we make it in two hours just to be on the safe side?"

"Two hours it is," said Sudfad.

# Chapter XXV
## Changes

Raphael went back to the house while Gabriel and Maxwell searched for their wives. Everyone was in the dining room working on the Shanksaw papers when Raphael told them about the meeting.

"Matthew, Sudfad wants you to go home now because he is meeting with his family first. But just to warn you he was really mad that Raul and Simon didn't talk to him about all of this before they told us. But he is open to the idea. And all of us are supposed to be there in two hours to discuss it," Raphael explained.

"I am not sure that I understand," said Iris. "Is he offering you different jobs?"

"Mother it sounds like he is going to establish ruling families like in Lentz," Vivian said proudly.

"We haven't worked anything out yet," said Raphael. "But the reason he wants all of you there is because these changes will affect all the families."

"What do you mean?" Ella asked.

"Isadore, Bella and Shara have many responsibilities like Renya does here. I would imagine that if we receive new assignments that many or all of you might assume some responsibilities too. Which means we might be spending less time on the missions; although we would still be working missions," explained Raphael.

"Vivian don't frown like that," said Luca. "All you girls want families and to be on missions too. And the reason you want to be on missions is because they do so much good. This way you can stay at home with the babies and still do a great deal of good. That time that just Calen and I went to Langer and stayed with Fahron's family we were surprised at all of the things Isadore was not only involved with but in charge of. And all of you are so intelligent and capable just think of the things you could do."

"We've been waiting for you," Simon said as Matthew walked into Sudfad's study. Raul, Renya, Vitomas, Annabelle, Nyla and Saran were already in the room with Sudfad.

"Did Raphael tell you what we will be discussing?" Sudfad asked Matthew. "Yes and I will say that I am all for the ideas. And not just because my Father runs his government like that. All of us are consumed with these attacks; we can only be so many places at one time. Father is beating himself up that he didn't realize Isabella was a traitor. How could he when we have been almost at constant war?"

"Matthew, Sudfad did explain the ideas to us before you got here," said Renya. "And honestly I like them too. Right now we have enemies on different fronts besides any missions and we have responsibilities to our people. While we haven't decided on job duties or titles, I personally like the idea of making them ruling members. As Raul said, they might as well be family."

"Father, we do want to apologize for not talking with you about this first but we thought you would not give the ideas a chance," said Raul.

"Oh trust me, I knew exactly what you two were doing and when I calmed down I realized you were right," said Sudfad. "And now I am becoming more intrigued with the ideas."

"Sudfad, I agree with Renya," said Matthew. "If they are a ruling member they have more authority not only to fill in for you but to handle other issues, say if you are gone. There might be times when they have to make a split second decision and don't have time to send you a message. A normal government position would not be able to do that."

"I am sorry for interrupting," Nyla said. "But before Matthew got here you were all talking about responsibilities. Do we have responsibilities?"

"You will, but you don't need to worry about that yet," said Renya. "You just need to adjust to your new family."

"What kind of responsibilities?" asked Saran.

"Just a couple of examples," Sudfad explained. "For a long time Renya was the only benefactor for the orphanage here. Which means she personally provided the food and supplies for those children. Vitomas and Annabelle work with the families of the soldiers and Laurel helps them because there is so much work. Emeral has been helping us with the hospitals we are building. There are so many things. But you don't have to worry about them yet."

Saran and Nyla looked at each other and smiled. "We aren't worried," said Nyla. "We would like to help but you will have to tell us what to do."

"You may be sorry you said that," Simon said teasingly.

"Gabriel what are you doing here? Is anything wrong?" Hannah asked as he walked into her office in the orphanage.

"No and you are never going to believe this. Raul and Simon want to make changes to, well basically how the government is set up here. They are suggesting making positions like Claudius, Fahron and Sorren hold and they want me, Raphael and Maxwell for those positions." Hannah had been getting out of her chair and now quickly sat back down. "We have to be at the castle for a meeting in an hour. Say something. What do you think?"

"I am just so shocked. I don't think this has sunk in yet. Are you saying we might be a ruling family?"

"Yes," Gabriel said and smiled because Hannah seemed dazed.

"Oh my gosh," she repeated then got out of her seat and kissed him.

"Honey, you know the responsibilities that Bella and Isadore have. These decisions will affect all of us."

"You are right," she said in a dazed manner. "We aren't going to have to move out of our house are we?"

Gabriel laughed loudly, "I have no idea why you even asked that. You are really in shock aren't you?"

"Actually I think I am. I can't think."

"Can you finish up here and come to the meeting?"

"Oh my god. I am not thinking straight. Of course I will come." Then Hannah laughed. "I certainly can't work in this condition. Gabriel I almost forgot. I hope you don't get mad because you already promised the children." Hannah took his hand and led him to her supply room where two tiny puppies were sleeping on a blanket. "Someone just left them here. The priests have their hands full with the children and don't want homeless animals brought here too. So I said we would take them."

"Why would I be mad? The children are going to love them. But we will need a crate to get them home in."

"Let me empty a few of these supplies," Hannah said and quickly started to take towels out of a crate. "I, I think I am starting to feel giddy."

"Where are the boys?" asked Gabriel as he and Hannah walked into their house.

"In the back with Bekka and Elan," Sam said. "Emeral found a homeless female dog and brought her home. The poor thing is skin and bones."

"Oh no," said Hannah and started laughing. "Gabriel can we still keep them?"

"These two pups were left at the orphanage," Gabriel said and showed the crate to Sam.

"They are really tiny, we are going to have to watch the children with them," said Sam. "Let me get the others, I think we all want to see the children's faces."

Natasha was the first to come into the dining room. "Oh my god!" she squealed and picked up one of the puppies and kissed it. "This is going to be so much fun."

The family gathered and went outside, where Cicely and Cerey were trying to help their brothers wash the newest dog. All of the children were soaking wet.

"Children, please listen up," said Gabriel. "Two little puppies were left at the orphanage and Hannah brought them home but they are very little and you will need to be careful with them so you don't hurt them."

The children all started yelling. Elan hung on to the dog in the wash tub as Gabriel kneeled down so the children could look in the crate.

"They're little babies," said Joey in awe.

The children took turns carefully petting the puppies. "These are little babies," said Natasha. "So they can't eat what the other dogs eat and we all have to be really careful with them."

"Considering all of the new dogs," said Sam. "Why don't Ella and I stay home with the children and all of you can tell us about the meeting."

"We can stay too," said Lana of her and Tanya. "And we can start fixing some food for those pups."

Gabriel, Maxwell and Raphael had warned their family members that Sudfad might be angry about some of the things for discussion. So they were all surprised when they walked into the Great Hall and the entire Royal Family was not only smiling but a huge meal was prepared.

"We just adopted a dog and two tiny pups," Luca said. "So the children stayed home."

"Please everyone be seated," said Sudfad. "You will notice there is paper and pens at every seat. I want your ideas and opinions. But before we start, Maxwell, Gabriel and Raphael did you talk about these positions with your families and if so what are your decisions?"

"Yes, and we would all be honored," said Maxwell.

"And you realize these positions would include extra work for all of your family members?" asked Sudfad.

"Yes," said Gabriel.

"Joshua would you too consider becoming one of the ruling families?" asked Sudfad.

"Me?" asked Joshua in shock. "But I know nothing of running a kingdom."

"But you aren't saying no yet?" asked Sudfad with a broad smile.

"No I am not but I don't know how I could be of service?"

"We will get back to that," said Sudfad. "And of course we will have celebrations later, but today is a work day. Maxwell, Gabriel and Raphael from this day forward you are ruling members of the Kingdom of Wetpr. The girls are handing out lists that include many of the duties that Raul, Simon and I perform. These are the mundane but very necessary duties of running a kingdom. All of you will be trained in them then after the training we will divide up these responsibilities."

"Don't get too excited," Simon kidded. "These are countless hours of boring and often frustrating paperwork."

"But just put those lists aside for now," said Sudfad. "As I thought more of what Raul and Simon were saying, I realized the wisdom in their words. So for the first topic I am going to talk about projects. The Angels have repeatedly warned us of upcoming battles so we have to put resources to both the defense and offense of this kingdom. In addition, I am considering building more forts, hospitals, orphanages and schools."

"Please wait with any comments until I am done," Sudfad said as he saw Gabriel and Elan about to speak. "I have been very intrigued with Mathas' ideas of starting a navy. As you know two of our borders are on oceans. But honestly I want to monitor what Mathas is doing before I make any decisions. After we discovered members of the Insidiae at our forts I want more oversight of them to include more frequent inspections."

"I don't know if all of you are aware that the Angels told Michael part of his destiny was to save his people. Who knows what resources those people will need and we will need a liaison."

"Then there is another matter that I have not previously spoken about and I can't say that I truly understand. When the Sanuri and Miranda were standing on the shores of the Sea of Grevdt she told him that there will come a time when men will destroy all that sustains them because of their ignorance and greed. I asked the Sanuri what she meant. He said that we will poison our land, water and air and the creatures and forests will die as will humans. This is a concept that I cannot even imagine. The Sanuri was heartbroken by these words and asked if there was no hope. She replied that as always men have choices to make."

"These words have disturbed me greatly and I think of them often. Then one day I remembered a story that Joshua told me about the Half-Mans who were irate because humans do not learn from their mistakes and I realized Miranda's words might already be coming true. Wetpr is the largest kingdom in Opots and we are rich in resources. Joshua, my family has discussed this and we would like you to consider the protection of our lands, water and air as your main responsibility."

"You look shocked and confused. We have mining, logging and great industries here besides that our cities are growing. If you choose to accept this responsibility you will have to ask the Angels for guidance because I don't know where you would begin. But you can think about this."

"As you are now understanding, these are all huge projects and all of us will be working together on many of them. I would like my sons to be able to concentrate on the defenses of this kingdom which means some of their responsibilities like the Learning Center will also be put on the table for discussion. And then there are the countless projects that the women of the family work on."

"Right now I would like everyone in this room to write down things they would be interested in working on and if that is nothing, that is fine also. Then in a second column I would like you to write down any ideas you have."

"And you want all of us to do this?" asked Natalie.

"Yes," said Sudfad. "You look confused."

"I understand what you are saying. I guess I just don't know if my thoughts are important," said Natalie shyly.

"You never know, you may bring up something that the rest of us didn't consider. But for all of you, don't feel pressured to take part or to accept any responsibilities. As I said before this is just an ideas meeting."

"Just to clarify something," Raul said. "While many of us assume that Michael may want to be the liaison for his village that may not be the case at all."

"And not only do Michael, Nyla, Saran and Nina have to get used to a new life and family they have to heal from the hell they were living in. So Michael will be trained as all of you but we don't know what he is really ready for yet."

Spirits were soaring among many of the people in Claudius' caravan. The team leaders felt more content having chosen their teams. The team members were elated and enthusiastic. Dominic and his men were grateful that they would not miss their studies and Michael became happier every time he received a letter from one of his sisters. And he felt good about his new responsibility. Overseeing the teams was something he could sink his teeth into when so many of the responsibilities of the throne seemed foreign to him.

Since they had lost half of a day of traveling because of the teams, Claudius was pushing his people hard.

"Alright, so what is bothering you?" Erebus asked the Sanuri as they rode in the front seat of his boca.

"Can't really put my finger on it. Miranda told me to take part in choosing who would be on the teams because some would be tempted. I did not find anything suspicious with any of the members. But I am haunted by her words."

"Do you think you overlooked something?"

"No, it's not that kind of feeling. I can't really explain it."

Enthusiasm was running high in Sudfad's meeting also. "I never realized all of the things you did," Misha said to the Royal Family. "But I have a question. Matthew, Thaos and Stephan are often pulled out of their duties in the military to work on projects like these. Is that what you are thinking for us?"

"Yes," said Sudfad. "And since all of you will still be working on missions, I wanted all of you to be part of this."

"Well Maxwell and Emeral, I think our family should take the responsibility of the forts. We are all in the military and there are enough of us to cover for others," said Misha.

"I think that is a good idea," said Maxwell.

"Well, I can't do anything but take care of babies right now," Diana said and laughed. "But I would like to work with whoever protects the resources and I will tell you right now that Thor will too. But he will also want to work on the Learning Center. He told me one day that he was going to ask you if you wanted some help."

"Can some of us share responsibilities?" asked Raphael.

"All of you work well as a team," said Sudfad. "If you want to share projects that is fine with me and it might be more practical since you will still have the missions."

"Ok now we are going to have to think about this again," said Luca kiddingly. "This really isn't easy. Sudfad would it be alright if we took all of this home and worked on it?"

Sudfad laughed, "Of course. We can talk about it at the morning meeting but that doesn't mean that final decisions have to be made at that time."

After all of the team members left the Great Hall, Matthew said to Sudfad, "I know that change is not easy but I think you will be very happy doing this. You might actually be able to spend some time doing things you like. You work from dawn to dusk."

"Actually that is what I am thinking," said Sudfad. "We were at war and I missed much of Raul's early childhood. And although I was home more after we adopted Simon as you can see I was doing all of these responsibilities myself. I hardly get a chance to hold my grandchildren and now we have three new daughters. I think I would like to spend a little more time being a father and a grandfather."

Joshua called a meeting of his family as soon as they arrived in their home. The spouses of his children were included in this meeting. "If I accept this position I want all of you to realize we will not be returning to Ryed," said Joshua. "And I want you to think about that seriously."

Simultaneously Maxwell called a meeting of his family. "Your mother and I are still reeling from all of this," said Maxwell. "And we hope the significance is not lost on you. While we feel as family with the Royal Family we are Rualas and now we are one of the ruling families in a kingdom of humans. This is a great deal of responsibility and it binds our tribe even more with Sudfad's family and humans in general. None of you will be forced to accept these responsibilities but if you do; we expect the best out of you."

Few people got any sleep that night in the house of Gabriel. The men left before breakfast to meet with Sudfad and they did not return home until the midday meal. All of the women stayed in the house waiting to hear the results of the meeting. They fixed a feast for lunch and had the table set with candles, flowers and wine glasses when the men returned home. The children on the other hand were so enthralled with their dogs and puppies that they paid little attention to the concerns of the adults.

"Well you are all smiling; that's good," said Natasha as the men walked into the dining room.

"Do you want to have a toast first?" asked Gabriel.

"No," said Hannah excitedly.

"Maxwell, do you want to do the honors?" Gabriel asked.

"All of us and Sudfad's family were in agreement that we did not want to divide the duties as rigidly as Mathas does and part of that is because of our work on the teams. So because of that we will all be involved with the defense of the kingdom in some manner," Maxwell explained.

"Our family will be working closely with Simon and Raul with the defenses, the oversight of the forts and the building of new forts. And yes all of these assignments will require a great deal of travel. Sudfad wanted Raul and Simon to be the direct supervision for Fort Nora since it is in hostile territory and Gabriel will be working with them."

"Joshua has accepted the position and will be responsible for protecting the resources of this kingdom which may turn out to be an overwhelming job. We did call to the Angels and they will help all of us. Joshua and Raphael will share the responsibilities of the Learning Center, which Sudfad said has taken on a life of its own."

"Gabriel and Hannah will be responsible for hospitals and orphanages and Gabriel and Raphael will share the responsibilities of building schools and libraries. Sudfad is giving us the flexibility to determine what we will need to accomplish these projects. We will be governing the budgets and hiring people. Of course this is what we are starting out with so assignments my change."

"All of us have received very generous pay increases and Micha and Thomas as well as our sons are on the payroll. Hannah has received a raise although I don't know how much and Emeral, Iris and Vivian are now receiving salaries. With all the babies and children none of the other women in the household have expressed interest in working on these projects but if and when they do they will be compensated. Gabriel do you want to tell the rest?" Maxwell was smiling broadly as he asked this question.

"Sudfad offered to give us all and I mean every member of this household land to build homes and no one wanted to leave our huge, crazy family."

# Chapter XXVI
## The Road Home

A general sense of relief flooded Claudius and the people he led as they crossed the border into the Kingdom of Lentz midmorning. "We crossed the border," Thaos yelled over his shoulder and the announcement was yelled throughout the group.

"This is so exciting," said Ashley as she looked out of the window of the carriage. "Just think we are starting new lives."

Selen smiled and said, "Thank The Great Ruler." She turned and looked at Hilgra who was sitting next to her. Selen squeezed Hilgra's hand. "Everything will be alright. I just know it will."

"I wish I could be as sure as you are," said Hilgra. "But I want to believe it will."

"If we didn't have all of these children I would just push on," Claudius said to Stephan, Thaos and Sorren who were riding next to him. "We will be in Castor by noon. I think we stop. Get supplies and let everyone enjoy the city. We will be in Langer tomorrow. Any thoughts?"

"I agree," said Stephan. "I think everyone could use a break." Stephan turned and rode through the soldiers and civilians announcing they would be spending the day in Castor. This brought smiles to the faces of most of the people.

When Michael heard this he rode forward until he found Rachel, Batina and Kate who were all riding together. "I need a favor," he said.

"Let me guess," said Batina and smiled. "You want help buying gifts?"

"How did you know?" asked Michael but he didn't wait for her to answer him. "Mostly things for the kids. I will pay you to help me."

"Now that is just plain insulting," said Rachel. "We are friends, of course we will help you. And we want to get a few things too."

Edward rode up to one of the bocas. Tally was driving it and Nana was sitting next to him holding baby Amelia. "Nana when we get in the city I think we should talk for a few minutes," said Edward.

"Is it about the baby?" she asked.

"Yeah, you look like you've gotten pretty attached to her. Calen said that if you wanted to adopt her that you could leave her at their house when you are on missions. Ratri told me you were considering going home and honestly I would hate to lose you."

"I haven't decided anything yet," said Nana and the emotion was heard in her voice. "I am very conflicted about this. Calen told me the same thing but I am not sure if that is a good way to raise a baby and on the other hand I love being on the team."

"Well, all I am trying to say is if you decide to adopt her we will figure something out."

"Thanks Edward, I really appreciate that. This really isn't easy."

"Apparently it is harder for you than it was the baby's grandparents," said Tally.

"That was a different situation," said Nana. "I can understand how they felt. You never met Bruno and Morgan, they were animals. When those people looked at Amelia all they would have seen was the death of their daughter. They actually gave her a chance by taking her to the monastery."

Claudius sent Enrops to King Mathas and to Bella telling them of anticipated arrival times. "Sorren, I know you are planning on checking on things at your village but since your family is in Wetpr why don't you just stay with us?" asked Claudius. "I would imagine Mathas is going to hold a lot of meetings and Bella will have at least one celebration."

"Thanks, I think I will. Hate to say it but the house is pretty quiet with everyone gone. When all the kids were home there were times that Shara and I would dream of a little peace and quiet." Sorren laughed loudly at his own comment. "Besides I really want to see Bella's face when you introduce her to Cassidy."

"So what is the plan when we get to Castor?" Drake asked Michael.

"You guys can do whatever you want. The girls are taking me shopping for toys," Michael said with a huge grin.

"Are you shitting me?" Tally asked then laughed loudly.

"Well, besides my sisters and a little brother, I am uncle to eight kids then there are the ones at Gabriel's house," said Michael. "Actually the kids are great. I got along better with them than I did with the adults at first."

"Ok, I can understand family but why are you buying gifts for Gabriel's kids?" asked Drake.

"There are more than his kids. His entire team lives in a house that is so big I can't do it justice. Apparently they worked together for years and that was all they did. Then Calen gets married and everyone else did the same. They all wanted families and adopted a lot of kids. Most of these kids are orphans because of the damn Hutas. But they are great kids."

"The way you talk, you should have a family," said Tally.

"Don't think I am ready for that," Michael said. "Why didn't you guys ever settle down?"

"And bring someone into Karzman's camp," Tally said. "You know he would rape other men's wives."

"I will kill that bastard some day," Michael said. "But now you don't have to worry about that."

"Michael, before we get to Langer we should talk," said Drake.

"We can talk now."

"We were serious about coming home with you."

"Ok, I know there is more to all of this shit," said Michael. "Spill it."

"First we haven't lied to you," said Drake. "Me and Tally feel like real horses' asses that we treated you so poorly in the camp. By rights you should kill us but you have been more than decent. In fact, you treat us like family. You gave us a second chance. I know we don't talk about it but Michael you've gotta know that Karzman has a bounty on you, your sisters and your father. Maybe you're whole damn family."

"Now maybe you don't want to spend time with us, but we feel like we owe you. We understand how that bastard thinks. We'd like to repay our debt."

"What are you saying you want to be my body guards or something?" Michael chuckled.

"Michael think about it," said Tally. "He hates you more than anybody else in this damn world. He hasn't been able to beat you so how the hell is he going to get to you? Through your family that's how. That would hurt you more than physical pain. Haven't you thought about that?"

"No," Michael said in almost a whisper. "But you are right."

"Hell, boy," said Drake. "You need us around just to keep your head on straight."

Michael motioned to the Enrops that were flying overhead. He gave them the verbal message that Tally had said and sent them to Sudfad and Mathas.

After nights of camping the people traveling with Claudius were grateful to take hot baths and sleep in beds. The soldiers did not stay in hotels but at Fort Castor.

"I couldn't sleep all night," said Bella excitedly as she sat down at the breakfast table with her family. "Ryan, they should get to Mathas' about midmorning. We are going to be there to greet them. Why don't you have Artis and Ralph watch the shop and join us?"

"Actually I was thinking the same thing. I made a wagon for Cassidy. I will need to get that from the shop."

"You mean a toy?" asked Ingr.

"I guess it's a toy but it is big enough for him to ride in. I thought the boys could pull each other around."

"I think that is a wonderful gift," said Bella. "I was just thinking. After the girls and I set up the treats, why don't you ride back with us?"

"You just don't want me riding by myself, admit it," Ryan said.

"You are right," said Bella. "And it's just not you. I don't want any of our family members riding alone. There are just too many threats."

When Claudius arrived at Mathas castle the majority of soldiers returned to Fort Langer but the soldiers who had adopted children stayed with the caravan as their families were at the castle. The caravan rode through the gates of the wall that surrounded the King's castle. The children were wide-eyed as none of them had ever seen a castle before. Soldiers stood at the front door and blew trumpets as the group approached them. The front door of the castle opened and people poured out of it to meet the caravan.

Mathas had previously notified Hugo at the Nordes Village of Tyger as to the arrival time of the group. Hundreds of Nordes people were now at the castle waiting for their friends and family members.

"I'll get Cassidy," Thaos said to Claudius as they rode up the stone roadway to the castle. Thaos turned and rode back to the Sanuri's boca where Cassidy, Logan and Marty were riding.

"Cassidy come with me now; Marty, Logan, Gideon will come for you."

"I'm kinda scared," said Cassidy once he was seated on Thaos' horse.

"That's understandable," Thaos said. "But I'll bet it doesn't last long."

By the time Thaos rode to the front of the caravan, Claudius had stopped the group and they were dismounting. Claudius lifted Cassidy from Thaos' horse and walked up to Bella, who was smiling warmly.

Amy was screaming, "Papa, Papa" and ran to Thaos. Nikki and Ingr both flew to their husbands.

"Bella, I would like you to meet Cassidy," said Claudius proudly. "Cassidy this is my wife and your new mother."

"Hello My Lady," Cassidy said shyly as Claudius held him.

"Can you give me a hug?" Bella asked and held out her arms to the boy. Cassidy went to her and they hugged tightly. "And you can call me Bella, mother or mama but not my lady," she said and laughed.

After Claudius' family had greeted each other Gideon walked up to them with Ashley, Logan and Marty. "Bella, I'll bet you never thought that I would come back with a family," he said with a big smile and hugged her.

"Ashley, I feel like we already know each other," Bella said and the two women hugged. "Boys," Bella said to Logan and Marty. "We've got all kinds of surprises for you at home."

As soon as everyone entered the castle, Rosa and Isadore escorted the guests to their chambers. Thaos set Amy down as his mother-in-law handed him Titus. Nikki was carrying James. Thaos hugged his sons and wife over and over. "I am so glad to see you," he kept repeating.

"Thaos, I know this isn't the place to talk but I have been so worried that you are mad at me for telling about your past."

317

"I'll admit I was at first but everyone kept telling me the good that could come from it. Harlow even did a story on me and the children we saved in Leven."

"Wickfield was waiting for all of you to return before he prints it. I think he has some questions. I, well we all were surprised you did that."

"So was I." Thaos said and kissed Nikki again.

Wickfield, Mayor Tetly and their wives arrived at the celebration minutes later. "I am damn glad to see you," Wickfield said as he first shook hands with Harlow then they hugged. "That whole damn business sounded awful. Are you alright?"

"Yes, and you never will believe half of what I am going to tell you," Harlow said.

"First you are staying with us. Elizabeth has chambers prepared for you and I have an office set up for you at the paper. We'd like you to move here. In fact, Elizabeth has already been looking at houses for you."

Harlow laughed loudly, "And if I know her she is already trying to set me up with someone."

"I wouldn't put it past her," Wickfield said and laughed heartedly. He was overjoyed to see his old friend again.

After Michael, Tally and Drake put their gear in their chambers they walked down the stairs to the Great Hall where the homecoming celebration was. "I just can't get used to this kinda life," said Drake. "Don't get me wrong; I like it. But everywhere we go it's a damn party." Michael and Tally laughed loudly.

"There's Archetenus and Jared," Tally said and nodded at the men.

"First, let's talk to Mathas," said Michael.

They found the King speaking with Sorren and Claudius. "Michael!" Mathas said happily. "Good to have you home."

Michael smiled. "Later can we have a few minutes to talk business?"

"We can talk now," Mathas said. "Do you want to talk in private?"

"No, they already know what I am going to ask," Michael said and nodded at Sorren and Claudius.

"Then now is as good a time as any," said Mathas.

"You got my letters," said Michael. "Drake and Tally have been pretty much filling me in on my life. I didn't believe them at first but the Angels said it was the truth. While they appreciate the jobs you gave them they want to come home with me and help us fight against Karzman. And I think that would be a good idea."

"Sorry to interrupt but Michael doesn't seem to want others to know that there is a bounty on his head too," said Drake. "We done him wrong when he was a boy and we want to make it right now. He's been more than fair with us."

"First, I believe all of us assumed there was a bounty on Michael," said Mathas. "And I too think Drake and Tally could be of great service to Sudfad. They can leave with you."

After Rosa heard about the children who were rescued and later adopted by the warriors and soldiers she turned one of the banquet rooms into a giant playroom. In addition to toys there were gifts for the children.

"Can I show Cassidy the playroom?" Amy asked as she looked at both her parents and grandparents.

"We should take Marty and Logan too," said Bella. "Where are they?"

"Looks like Gideon is introducing his family to everyone," said Claudius. "Cassidy run over there and ask if the boys can go with you."

Cassidy looked at Amy and grabbed her hand. "Come on," he said and the two children ran the short distance to Gideon's family.

"Well, those two have already made friends," Ingr said with a big smile.

"Where did Ryan disappear too?" asked Stephan. "I barely got a chance to talk to him."

"He made toys for the boys and he is putting them in the playroom as a surprise," said Nikki. "We should probably go in there too."

"Then we should tell that to Gideon," Claudius said. He quickly walked up to Gideon and stopped the children from running to the playroom. "You can go but we are going with you," Claudius said to Amy, Cassidy, Logan and Marty. Claudius' family now joined them.

"Thaos is just checking," Nikki said.

"Checking on what?" asked Cassidy.

"Your Uncle Ryan has some surprises for all of you," Bella said. "We don't know if he has had time to bring them all in."

Cassidy, Logan and Marty all looked at each other and their parents excitedly. "Is he our uncle too?" asked Marty.

The adults laughed. "In a way he is," said Stephan. "He is Thaos' and my brother and he is a great carpenter. He owns a shop in the city."

A few minutes later Thaos walked up to the group with a big smile. "Just wait until you see this," he said. "Did you know all of the carpenters are here?"

"No," said Bella with surprise. "I wonder why? I only knew of..." she stopped talking and looked at the boys. "I don't want to spoil the surprise."

Rosa was gathering all of the families with children and they now entered the playroom. She walked to the middle of the room and announced, "Children, we have a special surprise for you today. All of you know General Claudius. His son Ryan is a carpenter and when all of the men in his shop heard about you they got together and well I will let them tell you the rest."

Ryan looked embarrassed to speak in front of the group. "All of the men in the shop wanted to do something for all of you. Because we have so many projects we had to work on the toys after the shop closed. These are the men who provided the gifts for you." Ryan waved his hand to a group of twenty men who were standing in front of a thick red curtain. Everyone in the room applauded.

Two of the men pulled the curtain back and the room became silent as the children, many of whom had spent their lives living on the streets saw wagons, rocking horses, doll furniture and many other gifts. The children were in awe.

"I will admit I didn't expect this response," Ryan said with confusion.

"Most of these children didn't have food or shoes to wear," said Thaos. "They have never dreamed of such wonderful toys."

"The toys are for you," Ryan said to the children. "Come up and take them." Suddenly the children started screaming, laughing and running towards the toys.

While the carpenters were handing out the toys, Ryan walked up to his family. "Artis and Ralph are crying," he said.

"They aren't the only ones," said Bella with tears in her eyes. "Ryan that was a wonderful thing that all of you did. Tomorrow we will talk business."

"What do you mean?" asked Ryan.

"Did these men get paid for this work?"

"No, we did it after hours."

"We will pay them all and a bonus for their charity. And perhaps we need to figure out if you have enough staff. You just keep getting more projects."

Ashley too was crying and waited until Bella was finished speaking before she hugged Ryan. "That was wonderful," she said. "You made those children so happy."

A few minutes later Cassidy, Marty and Logan ran up to their families who were still standing in a group. Cassidy was pulling a wagon. Amy and Chasity were sitting in the wagon and each girl was holding a piece of doll furniture. The wagons that Marty and Logan pulled each had a rocking horse in them. Joao and Dack were walking behind the children grinning and carrying two more rocking horses.

"Ryan, we can't walk into our house with just one rocking horse," said Dack. "We want to place an order for all of the children."

When the children started screaming everyone else from the celebration either entered the playroom or stood in the doorway. Calen, Koby and Dagon now joined Ryan and the others. "We want to order some toys," said Calen.

"We are already getting all of the children rocking horses," said Joao.

"Then we will order wagons and some of that doll stuff," Koby said.

"Michael, this is what you should get the kids," Dagon said as Michael walked up to them.

"I was just thinking the same thing," Michael said and grinned.

Claudius had a proud look on his face as he spoke, "Bella tomorrow morning start putting up notices that we are hiring. I will meet all of you at the shop after the morning meeting and we can decide if we want to add on to Ryan's shop or buy one or two more buildings." The entire family smiled as Claudius spoke. "We might want to consider buying up part of a block." Ryan was speechless.

"Ashley, Gideon will be at the meeting," said Bella. "Why don't you and the boys come with us and we can look around the city?"

After the toy ceremony the Sanuri and Selen walked up to Mathas. Selen was very nervous as she curtsied before the King. "Mathas this is Selen, I have written to you about her."

Mathas smiled broadly and said, "Oh yes, I am so glad to meet you. Let me get Rosa she wants to meet you too. You are staying here at the castle aren't you?"

"Dominic said that Hilgra, Deborah and I can stay with them at their team's house. But I don't think any of us want to stay there after the team returns to Wetpr, so I will be looking for a home tomorrow."

"Please consider staying with us for at least a couple of days. We would very much like to talk with you about Juleta and Sarah."

Selen looked uncomfortable as the King spoke. "My Lord, I don't know if you would like some of the things I would tell you."

"I don't know if you could tell us anything that is worse than what we already know. But you have to understand that our daughter was lost to us so long ago that we are still trying to understand her and what happened. Besides the Sanuri told us how you prayed for Sarah. Those prayers may have been what saved her."

"Rosa, I know you are planning a feast," Dominic said. "Do we have time to take all the new teams to our house and show them around?"

"You have an hour before we eat," Rosa said. "And I hope you know that all of you can stay in the castle too, especially with all of the guests here."

"Thank you, I will tell the others."

As Fennel, Seth, Lawrence and Noah were gathering team members, Dominic made an announcement. "We are leaving now to show people the wonderful home that King Mathas as provided for our team. Anyone is welcome to join us but we need to be back in an hour for the meal."

"Ashley will you watch Chasity so we can go?" Dack asked.

"Of course," Ashley said and smiled warmly. "Besides I don't think you are going to get her out of that wagon for a while."

Calen and his brothers joined Dack and Joao. As the group was leaving the castle, Lawrence pulled Deborah aside. "Have you decided if you are staying at the house or the castle?" he asked.

"I don't really know yet," she said shyly.

"Stay at the house it is huge; you can have your own room. I would like us to have a little time alone to talk."

"About what?" she asked fearfully.

"I know Ashley offered you a job in Langer but we will be returning to Salar soon and I was wondering if you wanted to come with us. We have another big house there too, but it isn't as fancy as this one. Dominic said that he would hire you to work at our house if you wanted or we could help you get a job in the city."

"Why are you doing this Lawrence?"

"I like you and I know you like me but we really haven't had time to get to know each other. I am afraid that if I leave you here we might never see each other again. We work in Lentz a lot so if you don't like it in Salar I can bring you back here."

"Actually I was thinking the same thing. I was afraid you wanted to say 'goodbye' to me. I will go to Salar with you. Let's find Ashley," Deborah said with a big smile and squeezed his hand.

# Chapter XXVII
## New Beginnings

The celebration at Gabriel's home did not last long as most of the people returned to Sudfad's castle to work out job duties and training schedules. Hannah, Emeral, Vivian and Iris met with Renya the following day to learn about their new responsibilities.

"I thought we could talk first," said Renya then I will invite Annabelle and Vitomas to join us. Fortunately all of us here have worked together on so many projects that you do have some idea of what you are getting into. I've made a list of the normal duties of our positions. While these do take time, I believe for all of you it will be the special projects that will monopolize your time and energies."

"Remember you can hire people to help you, whether that is family, friends or strangers. You don't have to do everything yourselves. Vitomas, Annabelle and Laurel work with the families of the soldiers and that is extremely time consuming. I was so grateful when they took that task. They don't want to give it up but they want to train all of you in what they do and sometimes they will need help."

"While I am going to explain the duties we already perform, remember these are newly created positions. You have the flexibility to do what you want but of course you may have to run the ideas past Sudfad and the others. When you are new at this you don't always realize how things can affect others."

"I'll admit that I am very nervous about all of this," said Iris. "Will you give us an example of what you are talking about?"

"Well, the simplest example but a very important one is to know who all the, I guess I will call them players are before you make a move. And when I say move that can be something as simple as a dinner celebration. Say for example, Sudfad wanted to gather the leaders of the people we work with but he forgot to invite King Manu. Well, that could cause all kinds of political problems. People usually won't consider it an oversight they will turn it into a conspiracy and who knows; it could end up with tensions or worse between our kingdoms."

"In your cases you will be dealing with businessmen and local politicians but the issues are the same. But of course we will help you with all of that. Iris, I believe that for you and Joshua you will be doing a great deal of research at first. But I really don't know."

After the feast, most of the guests at Mathas' castle were taken on tours. Rosa did not schedule a lot of activities because she realized everyone would be exhausted. It was early evening when Claudius' family and guests arrived at his castle. The women, children and nurses had been riding in two carriages. Cassidy, Logan and Marty jumped from window to window with excitement which made the women laugh. But the boys were silent as they entered the castle and tried to take in their surroundings.

"Gideon, I hope you don't mind but I moved you to a larger chambers since you have the boys now. You still have a study, library and a safe. But your documents and money are still in the safe of your old chambers." Bella said as she led their guests up the large staircase. "Sorren, you come too. I fixed up different chambers for you also."

"Stephan's and Thaos' families have different wings. This is the center wing where Claudius and I and Ryan have chambers. Cassidy your room is up here also. We were thinking for tonight that all of the boys could stay in Cassidy's room and give Gideon and Ashley a little time alone."

"We appreciate that," said Gideon with a grin.

"Gideon, Ashley these are your chambers," Bella said as she opened the door to a beautifully decorated parlor. Stephan suggested we put the boys in one room but there is an extra bedroom too."

"This is beautiful Bella, thank you so much," said Ashley as they walked through the rooms.

"Marty, Logan," Nikki said and opened the door to their bedroom. Nikki smiled as the boys stood in the doorway and stared at the room that was decorated in shades of blue and filled with toys.

"Mama, Papa you have to see this," Marty gasped.

"Bella let me pay you for all this," Gideon said when he looked into the room.

"You will do no such thing," Bella said. "We were just pleased that you adopted the boys."

"Well, we will work out something," said Gideon. "I am going to start bringing in our things before it gets dark."

"I'll help you," said Sorren.

"Wait, Sorren you're chambers are in this hallway too," said Bella and led the group to another newly remodeled chambers. "You have a study and library in here and this will be yours permanently. So you will always have a home with us."

"Lawrence thank you for bringing my things in," Deborah said as she looked around her room in the house of Dominic's team. "I can't believe this. I feel like a princess here."

Lawrence smiled, "Well it was built for royalty. Do you think Hilgra is coming?"

"I doubt it. The King asked Selen to stay in the castle so she could tell him about his daughter. She is really upset because you know Juleta was a monster and Selen doesn't want to tell her parents that. Hilgra is staying with her."

"Did you ever meet Juleta?"

"No, but I had heard a lot about her before I met all of you; although I didn't believe what I heard. But Selen told Hilgra, Ashley and me about her and the truth was worse than the stories I heard."

"Are you tired?"

"No, why?"

"Do you want to go downstairs and have a glass of wine?" Deborah smiled and nodded. As soon as they walked into the hallway Lawrence pointed at a door. "That is my room, in case you want to know," he said and grinned.

"So you are right next to mine," she said and smiled shyly.

"Yeah, imagine that. I did promise to watch over you. So tell me what did you and Dominic talk about?"

"He is so nice. He hired me as a cook and housekeeper but he said that when we get to Salar that he will hire more staff so I can decide if I just want to cook or take care of the house. I will have a room there and he is paying me." Lawrence smiled. "Why aren't you saying anything?" Deborah asked as they walked into the kitchen.

"I am just happy that you are coming with us but I have to explain a few things," Lawrence was pouring wine into two glasses and now handed one to Deborah. "Besides working on the missions, you know that we are all studying to become priests. Chaez brought us our books and assignments because we have already missed so many classes because of this mission. I am telling you this because even though we will be living in the same house, I will be busy a lot."

"I know and I think it is wonderful that you want to become a priest. Are you saying that we won't be able to spend any time together?"

"No, I am saying we won't be able to spend as much time together as I would like." Lawrence bent down and kissed her on the lips.

"I feel like we are on our wedding holiday," Ashley said as she and Gideon walked into their bedroom chambers and found flowers, a bottle of wine and two glasses. "And there is even a fire going." Gideon was grinning as he opened the wine and poured it into glasses. "Gideon did you do all this?"

"No, I think it was Stephan."

"Stephan!"

"As we were leaving the parlor he said he was making up for interrupting us so many times," Gideon said and laughed.

"Well that is sweet and embarrassing at the same time." Ashley took the glass from Gideon and tasted her wine. "I knew I was going to like Bella from her letters but the entire family treats us like family. I really didn't expect that. It is very nice."

"Those were my exact same thoughts when I first came here. I had heard rumors about Claudius, rumors about the battles he led and won. But I had no idea of what to expect when I volunteered to come here. I was just following Miranda's voice. I certainly never expected to find people who I could so closely bond with. You didn't get much of a chance to talk with Mathas, Rosa, Fahron or Isadore today but they took me into their families too. I really like it here and I am glad that you like the people too."

"Do you think you can take a little time off and meet us tomorrow when Claudius does? Bella is going to show me some of the properties she told us about. It would be nice if you could come with us."

"Actually I was planning on it. And Mathas told me that our ship is in dock. He hired the entire crew and put them to work already. So I want to stop at the docks tomorrow too."

"What does he have them working on?"

"He gave them copies of the papers I drew up for the broad ideas and is having them come up with ideas as well as specifications for a naval yard. Mathas has also had them looking for property. But enough of work my lovely lady. Let's take advantage of our time alone." Gideon took the glass from Ashley's hand and set it on a small table. She giggled when he picked her up and carried her to their bed.

329

"Stephan this is so romantic," Ingr gushed when they walked into their bedroom. "When did you have time to do all of this?"

There were dozens of lit candles in the room besides a fire in the hearth. There were four bouquets of freshly cut flowers and a small table set up with a bottle of wine, a tray of fruit and a tray of cheeses.

"When you were bathing Matty."

"Well you must have had help or you work really fast," Ingr said. They kissed passionately for several moments.

"Honey, I want to talk with you about some things," Stephan said. "Can we talk first?"

"You are worrying me. What is it?"

"Nothing to be worried about. Let me pour some wine first. You might either laugh or get mad at me."

"This isn't sounding good," Ingr said and laughed as she took a seat on the small sofa in front of the hearth.

Stephan handed her a glass of wine and sat down next to her. "I am trying to think how to start this without sounding like a total ass," he said and chuckled.

"Just say it because you are really starting to worry me."

"Now don't get mad until I am done telling you everything. You know that I dated a lot before we got married but none of those girls were my friends. In fact, I never had any good friends that were girls until I started working with the teams. Well, Kate was asking us all how she could surprise Edward with a proposal and Ashley was kind of doing the same. Ashley and Gideon plan to get married but they didn't want the official proposal in Port Friada when we were getting attacked."

"So Kate and Ashley got a bunch of us talking about ideas then Rachel asks some of us how we proposed. Well, when I told them about how we started out all of the girls ganged up on me and told me I was a jerk." Ingr laughed so hard that she spit her wine onto the carpet.

"Oh my god, let me clean that up before you say anything else." Ingr kept laughing as she ran to get a rag and cleaned up the wine. "Ok, go on now."

Stephan was laughing too. "Then after they give me hell, and believe me they did, Rachel and Batina tell us how Dagon and Ratri proposed. And then others joined in. I mean, I know I screwed everything up but I didn't realize how much until I heard everyone talking. Even Thaos gave me a hard time. So I thought we could just do it over."

Stephan got off the sofa and kneeled on one knee before Ingr. He handed her a small velvet covered box. "Ingr, I love you; will you marry me?" She stared at him and tears filled her eyes. Stephan opened the box which contained a huge ruby ring that matched her wedding rings. "Say something," he said with a grin.

"I can't," Ingr said as she cried harder. She took the ring from the box and put it on her finger. Then she threw her arms around his neck and kissed him.

"I know our wedding was a nightmare because of the attack. I told the girls how upset you get every time you think about that day and they all told me how unfair that was to you. So I thought we could have a second ceremony. What do you think?" Ingr cried harder and Stephan put his arms around her. "I am afraid to ask. Are these good tears?" Ingr nodded.

"Well, everyone is all smiles this morning," Claudius said kiddingly as the people gathered around the breakfast table. Stephan and Ingr were the last to walk into the dining room. As they were putting their children into chairs, others at the table saw how Thaos and Nikki were grinning and looking at their friends.

"Ok, so what did she say?" asked Thaos with a huge grin. "The anticipation is killing us." Nikki laughed as did Stephan and Ingr.

"I said yes," Ingr said and now looked at Bella. "Stephan got down on one knee and proposed to me last night. He never did that the first time. Look at this ring."

Ingr walked around the table and showed everyone her new ring.

"That is beautiful but I don't understand," said Bella.

"We want to have another wedding ceremony," Stephan said. "Something small but we want to wait until Matthew and Angelina come home."

"Sorren, you and Ashley are grinning too. What is going on?" asked Claudius.

"Let me tell it," said Thaos. "When we were in Port Friada, Ashley wanted to get a gift for Gideon and Kate was trying to figure out how to propose to Edward. Well, the two of them are asking all of us questions and one thing leads to another and pretty soon they are asking all of us how we proposed and about our weddings." Sorren now laughed loudly. "Well, when Stephan tells everyone how he and Ingr started off those girls jumped on him and kicked...well you know where I am going. Honestly I couldn't believe he just kept talking when we could all see how mad they were getting."

"Believe me, I knew I had screwed things up," said Stephan and laughed again. "But when all the guys started to say how they proposed and the girls were saying how their husbands proposed, then I really realized how bad I was. So I decided to do it over and fortunately Ingr said yes."

"This really makes me happy," Bella said.

"So you are getting married again?" asked Marty. "Why?"

"Because it will be fun," said Nikki.

"Speaking of proposals," Gideon said. "Ashley and I might need someone to watch the boys one of these nights. I didn't want to formally propose when we had Hector and Moses breathing down our necks. In fact, we might need some suggestions of places in the city."

"First of all don't ever think twice about the boys," said Bella with a big smile. "We can always watch them and I already have some suggestions but under one condition."

"What is that?" asked Gideon with a huge grin.

"That you allow us to throw you an engagement party."

"Might as well," said Thaos sarcastically to Gideon and Ashley. "You've had enough practice by now."

This morning Mathas held his morning meeting in the Great Hall since all of the team leaders and some of the team members were also in attendance. As the people were taking their seats a large flock of Enrops were allowed to fly into the hall to deliver letters.

Mathas was just entering the hall when Calen said loudly, "Are you shitting me? Everyone open your letters from Gabriel, Raphael or Maxwell you are never going to believe this."

"What are you talking about?" asked Mathas as he took his seat and noticed a small stack of letters addressed to him."

Calen stood up. "I may have to reread this but Raul and Simon talked Sudfad into restructuring his government like yours and Maxwell, Gabriel, Raphael and Joshua are now ruling members." Calen looked at Koby and Dagon. "We are a ruling family in Wetpr," he said in disbelief. "My letter has the division of duties if anyone wants to hear them."

"This is important news," said Mathas. "Everyone read your letters and we will resume the meeting when you are done."

Bella, Ashley, Ingr, Nikki, Cassidy, Amy, Logan and Marty were already in Langer when Mathas started his meeting. They went to Ryan's shop first to set up the coffee and treats. The children ran through the shop and were intrigued with the many projects that the carpenters were working on. "Ryan, we aren't staying now since we will be returning in a few hours," Bella explained. "I want to show Ashley some properties."

"If it would help you can leave the kids here," Ryan said. "They can paint toys."

"Oh, could we?" Logan asked excitedly.

"Only if you promise to do what Ryan tells you," said Ashley.

"We promise," said Marty. "Can Cassidy and Amy paint too?"

"Cassidy can stay," said Bella.

"Amy do you want to stay with the boys or come with us?" asked Nikki.

"I want to stay. I'll be good."

Nikki smiled. "Alright."

The women had been driven to the city in carriages with a military escort. Now as they returned to the carriages Ashley said, "I am not sure I like all of this fanfare. I understand it today since I am carrying so much money but I hope that Gideon doesn't demand this every day."

"We know exactly what you mean," said Nikki. "But after so many attacks all of our husbands make us take some soldiers with us although there are a lot more today."

"Some of those men in Ryan's shop are soldiers," said Ingr. "They just don't dress like it."

"I hope that Gideon doesn't put soldiers in my shop," said Ashley. "I want to build another system here to help women and having men in the shop may scare them away."

"You should hire some of the women from our tribe then," said Ingr. "They are warriors and they can help you with the work besides guarding your shop."

"That is a wonderful idea," said Ashley. "When I get the building I will have a better idea of how much staff I will need. Then how do I do it? Do we put up notices or go to your village?"

"We were planning on taking you to the village anyways," said Nikki. "We can do it then."

"You know Nikki's mother is a great seamstress," said Bella. "I don't know if you need a seamstress but if you do you might want to talk to Gladys."

334

"Actually I plan to hire several seamstresses," Ashley said. "Nikki, do you think your mother would be interested?"

"The other kids are getting bigger so she might be. We can certainly ask her."

"Why are we stopping?" asked Bella.

A soldier walked up to the carriage door and said, "My Lady, we put up all of the notices and people are already asking about the jobs. The notice says you will interview tomorrow but some men would like to talk to you today. My Lady the reason I am telling you is that these men don't look like no carpenters to me. They look like thugs. And now I think you need to have some men with you when you do the interviews."

"Thank you Corporal Jackson. I appreciate this. If they continue to ask, all of the interviews will be held tomorrow and we will be extra vigilant today," said Bella.

Four hours later, the women returned to Ryan's shop where Claudius, Gideon, Stephan and Thaos were waiting for them. "Oh my, I hope you haven't been here long," said Bella as she walked up to Claudius and kissed him.

"No, just got here and we have been examining this building," said Thaos. "Claudius wants to look at the buildings next door too. How did you fare?"

"I found a shop and a house thanks to Bella," said Ashley with so much excitement she could barely talk."

"Did you buy them?" asked Gideon.

"I didn't want to until you saw them but I put some money down on each one until you could see them today."

"Claudius do you mind if we look at those properties before lunch?" asked Gideon.

"I think that is smart," Claudius said to Gideon then he turned to the entire group. "We decided we can't build onto the back because of the alley but we can build onto the side. I need to find out who owns the buildings next door."

"I can do that," said Ryan excitedly. "If you want to look at the properties."

"Take a couple of soldiers with you," said Claudius. "And we will come back and get you before we eat."

It took the men half an hour to examine the buildings that stood between Ryan's shop and the house that Bella bought for Artis and Ralph.

"Are you really going to buy all three?" asked Ingr.

"We might as well do it now," said Claudius. "The way the business is going he will need them."

"Bella, maybe you should tell Claudius what Corporal Jackson said," suggested Nikki.

"The Corporal was posting our notices and said some men who looked like thugs wanted interviews today. He thinks I should have soldiers with me when I do the interviews."

"We'll do better than that Mother, Thaos and I will do the interviews with you," said Stephan.

"This is a good piece of property," Claudius said as they all walked up to the shop that Ashley wanted to purchase. "This is the main business district."

"Gideon, Ingr suggested that I hire women from their tribe to work here because they are trained as warriors. I really don't want soldiers in here; it will scare off the women who need help."

"It's a good idea," said Thaos as he was examining a large staircase in the front foyer.

"I like it too," Gideon said to Thaos. "Ashley, is the owner meeting us here?"

"He is in the building next door," said Nikki. "I can get him."

"This place looks pretty sound," yelled Stephan. "Father is in the cellar. You might want to wait until he comes back up."

A few moments later Claudius yelled, "Boys come down here. Leave the children there."

It was almost fifteen minutes before the men returned. "There is a tunnel that leads under the street and to the docks," explained Gideon. "It looks like an escape route. But that means someone could use it to get in here."

"Gideon, that is perfect. I may need it to help women escape. Show it to us," said Ashley.

"It's dirty down here," Amy said with disgust as they walked through the cellar.

"Do you want to ride on my back?" asked Logan and squatted down so Amy could climb on.

"I think Amy has some brothers here," said Stephan jokingly.

"I really like this," said Ashley as they all walked out of the tunnel into the sunlight.

"I am going to secure that door better from the inside," said Gideon. "This tunnel needs a little work but I don't want workmen down here, knowing about this. I will do it."

"We can help you," said Thaos. "Actually you don't know when something like this can come in handy."

Gideon was pleased that the owner had already drawn up the papers when they met with him. Gideon paid for the building with cash and the transaction went quickly. Ten minutes later the group was walking into the front foyer of a beautiful old mansion near the ocean.

"One of the reasons I like this house is because it is both close to the shop and the docks," said Ashley. "I assume you will be working near the docks, when you aren't in meetings. It is on a hill in case there is flooding from storms and it has twenty-five acres of land."

"So far I am impressed," said Gideon. "Ashley and I both want to help with the teams so, well actually we didn't know what to expect but in Port Friada my house was filled. So we wanted to get a large house here."

"We do have the castles here," said Claudius as he was examining a door. "But that is good thinking. A place this big you will need staff. Let us help you with the hiring."

"Appreciate that," said Gideon.

"Aren't they living with us?" Amy asked.

"Honey for just a little while," said Ashley but you and Cassidy can come here and play with the boys and I will bring them to visit."

"Good," said Cassidy.

Twenty minutes later everyone met in the kitchen of the house. "So what do you think?" asked Ashley.

"It needs a few repairs but they are minor," said Thaos.

"It's a nice home," said Stephan.

"Is this the one you want?" Gideon asked Ashley. She smiled and nodded. "Then let's buy it today." She jumped into his arms and they hugged and kissed. "Now I have another matter. Claudius would you, Thaos and Stephan be available next week to look at properties for the Adam's Homes? Since Bella is interviewing carpenters tomorrow I thought I would join her and hire some men to work on all of the properties."

"Of course we will," said Claudius. "But let's talk about that with Mathas. You certainly don't have to purchase those properties."

"And we want to help," said Bella with a coy smile. "I may have a few properties in mind."

# Chapter XXVIII
## Hiring

The following morning Mathas walked into the Great Hall and stood before the many men and women who were present for the meeting. "Several things have recently come to my attention so you will be glad to know I am canceling the meeting; unless someone has something of urgency to discuss." No one spoke.

"For those of you leaving for Wetpr you can now get an early start. The cooks are packing up food for you and my men are getting water and feed for the horses. Michael pack your things and go home with this group. I know you want to see your sisters. Take Drake and Tally with you."

"Really? Thanks," said Michael with such excitement that many laughed.

"Claudius with your concerns; why don't you and the boys leave now?" said Mathas.

"What are you talking about?" asked Edward.

"Yesterday Bella had soldiers putting up notices that we would be hiring carpenters today. One of the soldiers warned her that some men who looked like thugs wanted to be interviewed a day early. We want to be with Bella during this and Gideon is looking to hire men also," explained Claudius.

"Do you want us to stay?" asked Dominic.

"No go home, you have to get back to school," said Claudius. "But we appreciate the offer."

Sorren stood up. "If there is anyone not going to Wetpr, Nikki, Ingr and I are taking Ashley, Hilgra and Selen and the children to the village. Anyone is welcome to join us."

"If you can wait until we say goodbye to Chaez, Isadore, Benny and I will go with you," said Fahron.

"We can wait," Sorren said.

When the people walked out of the Great Hall Ashley was waiting for Archetenus. She walked up to him with a large pouch. "Archetenus, here are a few things for you, Delilah and the babies. We are going to Wetpr for Luca's wedding so we will see you in a couple of weeks."

"Plan on staying with us," said Archetenus. "Delilah will be so happy. We are just a few miles from the castle and Gabriel's house so you won't miss anything."

"Thank you we will. I will tell Gideon."

Bella had originally planned to interview carpenters in the front of Ryan's shop. But now that Claudius, Stephan, Thaos and Gideon were joining her they needed more room. They decided to hold the interviews on the first floor of one of the buildings that Claudius had purchased the previous day. Soldiers had escorted Bella and Ryan into the city and helped her set up the area for the interviews. All of the soldiers were wearing civilian clothing. Claudius expected trouble so he had extra soldiers in Ryan's shop and these men too were dressed in civilian attire.

Ryan was concerned for Bella and didn't leave her side until Claudius, Thaos, Stephan and Gideon walked into the building.

"Why are you so early?" asked Bella. "Is anything wrong?"

"No, Mathas cancelled the meeting because so much was going on," said Stephan.

"As you can see, I set up different tables and have paper and pens at each. Please write down the names of anyone you hire. And of course anything else you want to write down. Ingr made two signs. Gideon, I will put one in front of the table you want. It says you are hiring for property projects and the other says we are hiring for the shop."

"Bella, you are so organized," said Gideon with a grin and took the sign from her.

"I'm going to be disappointed if we don't have any trouble," said Stephan kiddingly.

Thaos was standing near the front door. "There's a good line out front. Let me know when I should let them in."

"What are you doing?" asked Bella when she saw Claudius and Stephan rearranging the tables.

"Just preparing for trouble," Claudius said.

"I don't understand," said Bella.

"They have better views of the room with the tables that way," explained Thaos.

"It's really quiet without all of those children," Erebus said as he rode in the front seat of the Sanuri's boca.

"We still have a couple and I am sure they will make their presence known," said the Sanuri with a smile. "Changing the subject; I am surprised that Hilgra isn't coming back with us."

"She's coming for Luca's wedding. She wanted to stay and help Selen with some things. Besides Selen is upset at having to tell Mathas and Rosa about Juleta."

"Where is Hilgra staying when she comes to Wetpr?"

"I hadn't thought about it. She could certainly stay with me. Why?"

"Erebus, I know you like to live dangerously but have you not noticed that Hilgra is quite taken with you, as is Gala? You might want to think about this."

Erebus stared at the Sanuri for several moments then he laughed. "I have never had two women interested in me before. I must say this is something new."

"Remember Hilgra is coming to Wetpr to work with the other healers, so you can't keep your girlfriends separate." Erebus laughed louder at the Sanuri's words.

"You are right and I will have to think about this. In a way it seems so, I don't know, silly I guess."

"I bring it up because I think you have more to think about than you realize," said the Sanuri. "While I believe Hilgra is a good person I also believe she would get her dark powers back if she could and I believe she would encourage you to do the same. And you already know that Gala will leave you if you get your powers back."

Erebus was silent for a moment before he spoke again. "If that is true than are Hilgra's prayers working? She is praying to be healed."

"I cannot answer that question but I do feel that if you choose to have a relationship with her you can influence her to live without those powers. But you will have to decide who is going to be the biggest influence on who." Erebus looked at the Sanuri but did not say anything else.

Job seekers were surprised when they walked into the building and saw Claudius, Stephan and Thaos conducting interviews. Most of the men did not know Gideon. The interviews were short, basically Claudius and the others wanted to weed out any terrorists or hired killers. And most of the decisions were made by how the men carried themselves and acted.

The line of applicants was steady for the first two hours then there was a lull. "I never realized there were so many men looking for work," said Stephan.

"I know," Claudius said. "Keep the lists of names because I am going to give them to Mathas. He will need workers for the orphanage."

"I am thinking ahead to the naval buildings," said Gideon. "So far I am willing to hire everyone I've talked to."

"Since we have a break," said Bella. "I am going to run next door and get us some coffee and treats."

As soon as she walked out of the building Thaos said, "I didn't realize what this was like for Bella; there must have been two hundred men here. I think at least one of us needs to help her with this from now on; just for her own safety."

"Oh, trust me I thought about that as soon as you opened the doors," said Claudius. "While your mother is not trained as a warrior she does have that mindset. I can't remember the last time she was afraid for herself."

"What do you mean?" asked Stephan.

"She worries about all of you. She is very protective of her family."

"I am going to check on her," said Thaos but to his surprise he saw Bella walking back to the building with Zeke, Johnny, Carl and Sam. Sam and Zeke were carrying plates, Carl was carrying cups and Bella held a pot of coffee. Thaos held the door open for them to enter; as Zeke walked past Thaos he gave him a knowing look. Thaos understood that something was wrong.

"Why, thank you so much. And please help yourselves to some cookies," said Bella as she poured coffee into cups.

"Boys, why don't you stay here a minute while I talk with the boss," said Zeke. Stephan and Claudius both were alerted by the tone of Zeke's voice but they did not want to scare Bella.

"Think I will stretch my legs too," Stephan said and walked onto the sidewalk with Thaos and Zeke.

"Boss, you gave us the day off so we came to town and went to the Lady's Slipper to play cards. Since its morning not many people are in there. About twenty minutes ago six men walk into the place and sit at a table near us. None of them says a thing until a seventh guy who was already standing at the bar brings a bottle and glasses to the table. He asks 'what's going on?' and one of them other fellas says, 'hell, the whole damn family is in there with her. We didn't expect that'."

"Then the guy who was at the bar says 'whatya mean?' And one of the others says all your names. Well, we looked at those fellas real good so we could remember their faces and we decide to walk to Ryan's shop. That's where we thoughts you was. We met your mama in there and she told us yous was hiring carpenters."

"Do you think they recognized you?" asked Thaos.

"Don't know hows they could; its done the first time we's come to town."

"You did real good," said Thaos. "When we get home, I'm giving you all a bonus."

"Boss, your family is good to us; we don't want to see nutin happin to any of yous."

"Do you see any of those men on the street now?" asked Stephan.

"I've had my eyes peeled whiles we's be talking and I don't."

The three men walked back into the building and closed the door. "The interviews are over," Stephan said. "Zeke and the boys were playing cards when a group of men said they came here but didn't expect to find us with Mother. They called us by our names. They might still be at the Lady's Slipper."

"How many are there?" asked Claudius as he shot out of his chair.

"Seven that the boys saw," said Thaos.

"Sergeant Manhure we need you out here," yelled Claudius. There were a dozen soldiers in an adjoining room all dressed in civilian clothes. "We just became aware of a threat. Take Bella to the shop and guard everyone there. You might want to close the shop up."

"I'm going with you," said Gideon. "I love a good fight."

The Lady's Slipper Tavern was two blocks south of Ryan's shop. Like most taverns it served breakfast and the morning crowd was considerably quieter than the men who gathered there at night. Zeke, Sam, Johnny and Carl walked into the tavern first and saw that the men were still sitting at the same table. Sam and Carl walked up to the bar while Zeke and Johnny sat at a table near the men.

Claudius and Gideon walked into the tavern through the front doors. Zeke and his men didn't have to point the hired killers out because Claudius and Gideon saw the men stiffening up as they entered the tavern.

While the seven men stared at Claudius and Gideon, Thaos and Stephan entered the tavern through the back kitchen door. They immediately saw the men who Claudius and Gideon were staring at. Even though no words were spoken all of the other patrons and staff knew there would be a fight and moved out of the way. Many of them hiding in the kitchen or behind the bar.

"Who sent you?" asked Claudius gruffly as he walked up to the table.

One of the men grinned and said, "Can't say that I know what you are talking about."

Thaos quickly knocked the man's hat off and grabbed a fist full of hair with his left hand; pulling the man's head backwards. Then Thaos pressed a knife against the man's throat with his right hand. Simultaneously, Stephan grabbed a bottle of whiskey from a nearby table and hit one of the men over the head; knocking the man out. Gideon stepped to a man who was getting out of his chair. Gideon punched the man in the jaw, then the stomach, then another uppercut to the jaw then Gideon slammed that man's head on the table and threw him to the ground.

"Answer the question," said Claudius. "And tell your boys to stay seated because we're just warming up."

Thaos pressed the knife harder against the man's throat and blood was starting to run down his neck. "Deckor sent us," the man choked out.

"Deckor's dead," bellowed Claudius. "Try again."

"He sure didn't look dead to me," said the man fearfully. "Honest the guy told us he was Deckor."

"What did this guy look like?" growled Claudius.

"Big guy, dressed fancy and had his hair greased back; honest that is the only name he gave us."

"What did he pay you to do?"

"He wanted us to scare your wife and give her; there is a note in Jackson's pocket."

"Which of you is Jackson?" demanded Stephan.

"The one on the floor," said one of the men.

Gideon grabbed the man who he had beaten unconscious and rolled him onto his back. "Right front pocket," said one of the men.

"Got it," Gideon said as he pulled a piece of paper out of the pocket and handed it to Claudius.

"Do you know what he meant by this?" Claudius asked.

"No, we didn't even read it," said the man who Thaos held.

"Zeke, bring the soldiers in here," ordered Claudius.

Zeke left the tavern and got the platoon of soldiers who were standing on the sidewalk waiting for orders. The soldiers quickly entered the tavern. "Take them to the dungeons and put them in separate cells," barked Claudius.

As soon as the soldiers had dragged the men from the tavern, Stephan, Thaos and Gideon gathered around Claudius to read the note which read, *You have something I want.*

"If Hector isn't behind this then Juleta made a clone of Deckor," said Thaos with disgust.

"Boys, we are going to interrogate those men together but first I am sending a message for the Sanuri to return," said Claudius.

Amy was already at the Nordes village when Nikki and the others arrived. Ashley, Hilgra, Selen, Isadore and the children rode in a carriage while the others rode on horseback. When Fahron opened the carriage door to help the women out Cassidy said excitedly, "Amy wants us to find her."

"Ashley do you want to see the training area?" asked Nikki as she dismounted. "We can take the children there first."

"We are going to visit Otis," said Fahron as he, Isadore and Benny left the group.

As Nikki, Ingr, Sorren, Ashley, Hilgra, Selen and the boys approached the training field a young man with a big smile walked up to them. "Amy is really excited that you are coming today. Her group is learning how to track this morning. I can take you to her."

"Andrew, this is Cassidy, Bella and Claudius adopted him," said Ingr. "And this is Ashley and her sons Logan and Marty. And Hilgra and Selen." Ingr turned to her guests and explained, "This is Andrew; he is one of the trainers."

"It is good to meet you," said Andrew. "Please follow me. And you don't have to be afraid of scaring away any animals, today we made the tracks ourselves."

"Ashley the children learn many things besides fighting," explained Ingr. "They learn how to survive in the wilderness and how to read the terrain around them. And they learn to respect nature. If the boys are interested they could be trained also."

"Really?" asked Marty excitedly.

"The training starts early every morning," said Sorren. "It's a two hour ride from Langer which means two hours back again for you and Gideon. But he could always have soldiers bring the boys out."

"When do the children go to school?" asked Ashley.

"There is a school at the village," said Nikki. "But Bella just hired a tutor for Amy and Cassidy. She didn't want to overwhelm Cassidy his first week with us so they start their studies next week. And of course there are schools in the city. But I am sure that tutor could handle four kids. They could all train together then go to our home for their lessons."

Ashley looked at the excited faces of the three boys. "I will have to speak with Gideon about this. Is that something you boys would be interested in?"

All three boys nodded their heads and said, "yes".

Andrew motioned for everyone to stop talking as they walked through a wooded area. They saw ten children squatting or kneeling on the ground as they looked for tracks. There were three Nordes warriors with the children. Amy looked up and smiled then waved.

Andrew now looked at Cassidy, Marty and Logan and asked, "Would you like to see what they are looking at?" The boys nodded excitedly. "Then walk behind me. Step in my steps." The adults laughed as they watched the boys clumsily follow Andrew.

After a few minutes, Sorren yelled. "Boys do you want to stay and train?"

"Can we?" yelled Cassidy.

"You stay with the instructors and we will be back for you," said Nikki.

Sorren escorted the women around the village and as he made introductions he told people that Ashley was looking to hire workers and anyone who was interested could meet with them in the Great Hall. An hour later when Sorren led the women into the Great Hall there were two dozen villagers seated in the room.

"Where is Mother?" asked Nikki. "She just told us she would be here." A few moments later Gladys ran into the hall holding a basket of fabric.

"I thought she might want to see samples of my work," Gladys said when she saw the disapproving look on Nikki's face.

Sorren stood before the group and spoke first. "Ashley ran a very successful clothing shop in Port Friada and is opening one here in Langer. But she ran another enterprise too. She established an underground system to help women and children escape from the kind of men who stole Amy, April and Sally."

"Ashely was so good at this work that her life has been threatened many times yet she wants to build the same system here. So besides looking for seamstresses and other skills she needs warriors."

"She prefers female warriors because the women who would come to her for help would come to her shop and many of them were terrified of men. I will let her tell you the rest."

"In Port Friada, I did not have warriors for protection. Secrecy and elaborate planning were the main ways I was keeping those women and children safe. But there were several savage attacks against my home and shop and Sorren and others have convinced me that I need to hire protection. I wanted you to know this before we start to talk about the jobs because I want you to understand that at times you might be in a dangerous position. But on the bright side I do pay very well. If any of you are no longer interested in hearing about the jobs you are free to leave."

Sorren, Nikki and Ingr all smiled when no one left the room.

Enrops can travel considerably faster than horses. Within an hour a small flock circled the Sanuri's boca. He stopped and took a note from the beak of one of the giant birds. The Sanuri was driving at the rear of the caravan. He now called to a soldier who was riding just ahead of him. "Go to the front and stop everyone," the Sanuri said. "I will follow you."

"What is going on?" asked Erebus.

The Sanuri handed Erebus the note and grabbed the reins to the team of horses.

Archetenus was leading the small army and teams. Many of the team leaders were riding near him as was Jared who now yelled for the Rualas to return to the group. The Sanuri drove his boca to the front of the caravan. "You can all read this," as he spoke the Sanuri handed the note to Archetenus. "Claudius and his sons had a situation in Langer and when they questioned the men they swore that a man named Deckor hired them; and they described him. Claudius said they are going to give the men the truth potion."

"The men were ordered to give Bella a note that Claudius thinks was actually from Hector but he is concerned that Juleta may have made a clone of Deckor. He wants me to return and I am going to. The rest of you go ahead."

"Are you sure you don't want us to go with you?" asked Edward.

"No, but take that note and show it to Sudfad and the others," said the Sanuri then he turned to Erebus.

"Don't think you are getting rid of me that fast," Erebus said sarcastically. The Sanuri smiled and turned his boca back towards Langer

.

# Chapter XXIX
## Moving In

The Sanuri and Erebus arrived at Fort Langer midafternoon. Claudius, Gideon, Thaos and Stephan were interrogating the seven men who they had taken prisoner. The interrogations were being done in pairs, one man asking the questions and the second taking notes. The Sanuri and Erebus first walked into the room where Claudius and Gideon were interrogating a man. Gideon was taking notes and handed some pages to the Sanuri, who quickly read them and handed them to Erebus.

"If either of you have any questions; be my guest," Claudius said to the Sanuri and Erebus.

"Actually I would like to look into his mind," said the Sanuri and walked up to the man who was tied to a chair.

"What the hell are ya doing?" yelled the man.

"It won't hurt," said the Sanuri as he put the palms of his hands on either side of the man's head.

"Get him the hell off from me," yelled the man.

"He might be saving your life," said Claudius. "Just sit still."

"This man is a criminal but he doesn't know anything about Hector or Juleta. He didn't see the man who claimed to be Deckor," said the Sanuri after a few minutes.

"We already interrogated the leader of this bunch," said Claudius. "His name is Tanner and so far he is the only one who has said that he saw and talked with Deckor. The rest are pretty much telling the same story." Claudius walked to the door and called two soldiers into the room. "Take this one back to his cell and bring Tanner back in here," ordered Claudius.

Tanner was still under the influence of the truth potion and walked and acted as if he was drunk when he entered the room. He laughed when the soldiers tied him to the chair. "More questions General?" he asked.

"Actually I want to look into your mind," said the Sanuri.

Tanner stared at the Sanuri with confusion. "What did you say?"

"It won't hurt."

"I know cuz you ain't gonna do it."

"Tanner, your life may be in great danger and I am not talking about us. This person claiming to be Deckor may be a demon from another world. It would most certainly be in your best interest to cooperate now," said the Sanuri.

Tanner looked at Claudius and asked, "Is this guy serious?"

"He is a very powerful holy man and he is serious. You would be wise to do as he says."

"Alright then, but don't change nothing that you see." Both Gideon and Erebus laughed when Tanner said this. The Sanuri stared into Tanner's mind for several minutes. "What do you see?" asked Tanner fearfully.

"Just be quiet," said the Sanuri to Tanner. A few moments later the Sanuri addressed Gideon, Claudius and Erebus. "These men are from Stordt and they answered an ad in a newspaper." The Sanuri turned back to Tanner. "When did the King of Stordt allow newspapers and reading?"

"Don't really know. We hire out so we travel a lot. We were in Stordt maybe six months when we hear talk about this ad. We found it and came here. Hell, I've still got the ad in my pocket if you want to read it. We had to show it to the bartender of the Anchors Inn to talk to Deckor. And even after that he made us wait for three damn days. But he gave us gold when he hired us and promised more when the job was done."

"Which pocket?" asked Claudius.

"Left, shirt, under the vest," said Tanner.

Claudius unfolded a tattered piece of paper and showed it to the Sanuri. "So how did you eventually meet Deckor?" asked the Sanuri.

"We hung around that damn bar for three days. We was just about to leave town when the bartender comes up and taps me on the shoulder. He didn't say a word he just nodded. Well, me and the boys all started to stand up then he says, 'No, just you'. So I follow the guy into a back room. It was real dark. If there were windows they were covered and just one candle on a table. Deckor was sitting at the table."

"He already knew that we had been waiting to meet him for three days and gave us some extra money for our troubles. He asked me questions about my gang then he tells us who is running this kingdom and that he wants the ruling families watched. So we watched them for a couple of weeks but Deckor wasn't real interested in what we had to say until some of them came back from Port Friada. Then he wanted every little detail that we saw and heard."

"Then yesterday morning he says that he wants us to scare the boy Ryan or his mother. Deckor said not to go near the other women cuz they were warriors and would likely kill us. We thought that was funny but hell he is paying us good so we follow orders. He says we should just scare them then leave that note that Jackson was carrying. Then no sooner do I leave Deckor but a soldier is posting a notice that Ryan's mother is going to be interviewing men to hire. We tried to get her to talk to us yesterday but the soldiers wouldn't let her."

"Why did you decide to scare Bella and not Ryan?" asked the Sanuri.

"There's a lot of men in that shop and some of them look like fighters. So we decided it might be easier to go after her."

"You obviously don't know Bella," the Sanuri said and smiled. "Go on with your story."

"So this morning I sent the boys to Ryan's shop. They come back a couple of hours later and tell me there was a line of guys down the block waiting to be hired. Well, they weren't gonna start nothing with all those men there. So they are waiting for the line to go down when they hear a couple guys talking that a general and an admiral are talking to everyone. So Howie looks in the windows and see's Claudius and his sons."

"So they came back to the Lady's Slipper."

"Did you tell Deckor that you didn't deliver the message?" asked the Sanuri.

"Hell no. We were figuring what we were gonna do next when they all came in and beat us up."

"When are you supposed to meet Deckor?"

"I am supposed to leave a note with the bartender at the Anchors Inn. But Deckor said he was gonna be outa town for a couple of days. He said to have the message to him by Friday."

"Give these men aplewort we might need them," the Sanuri said to Claudius.

Before Claudius had gone to the fort to interrogate the prisoners he made Ryan close the shop for the day. And he had soldiers escort Bella and Ryan home.

It was midday before Sorren, Nikki, Ingr, Ashley and the children returned to the castle. Bella immediately pulled the adults aside and told them as much as she knew about the incident which had occurred in Langer. She told them that Claudius and the other men were going to interrogate the prisoners at the fort. Sorren left the castle to join the men. He told the women to stay inside of the castle until they figured out what had happened.

Claudius, Thaos, Stephan, Sorren, Gideon, Erebus and the Sanuri entered the castle at dinner time.

"Do you want to have a meeting or a drink before dinner?" asked Bella.

"No, none of us have eaten; we're starving," said Claudius. "We can have a meeting after the children go to bed."

Cassidy, Amy, Logan and Marty were still ecstatic about their experience at the Village of Tyger and all talked at once at the table. "Papa can we go to school here with Cassidy and Amy so we can go to training?" Logan asked Gideon.

"Honey, I haven't had a chance to talk to Gideon about that," Ashley said.

"You can tell me now," said Gideon.

"It was my idea," said Nikki. "All three boys were so excited to join Amy's training. And it is great training. It teaches the children how to survive, how to track and fight. It teaches about birds and animals and to respect nature. But the training is early in the morning and a two hour ride from your house. Sorren said that perhaps you could have soldiers take Logan and Marty to training. Then I suggested they could come back here with Cassidy and Amy."

"Bella hired a tutor who will start next week. I would think the tutor could handle four children. But I realize I should have talked this over with all of you before I said anything to the boys."

"How do the children get back here from the village?" asked Gideon.

"One of us gets them," said Thaos. "But someone from the village would bring them here if something came up."

Gideon looked at Ashley, "What do you think?"

"I was very impressed with the training," said Ashley. "And after talking with Ingr and Nikki it might be safer for the children to have a tutor than to go to school."

"Claudius, Bella how do you feel about this?" asked Gideon.

"It's the first that I have heard about it," said Claudius. "But I think it is a fine idea. Sorren's training is top notch. I am glad to hear that Cassidy wants to go too. And there isn't any reason the children can't have lessons together."

"I agree," said Bella. "I have a classroom set up. I will just add a few things. And after today, well..."

"That is exactly what I am thinking," said Gideon. "Ashley and I will be working a great deal. I have been thinking we should hire a nurse," he paused and looked at Ashley.

"I know we haven't discussed any of this but after working with the teams I now understand why Gabriel hires warriors."

"Sorren, I know the appeal for your warriors to work for Gabriel is that they are also trained for the teams. Do you think someone would work for us for just pay? Or should we offer something else too?"

"Gideon, you aren't a ruling member but you are about as close as you can get," said Claudius. "It would be appropriate for you to have soldiers or sailors stationed at your home. Have you considered that?"

Gideon looked genuinely surprised. "No. If I was living by myself it wouldn't be a consideration but now that I have a family, well..." Gideon paused and looked at Ashley then patted her hand. "What would I have to do to get that done?"

"Just tell Mathas what you want," replied Claudius. "Then you will have to provide housing for them, which I am sure that Mathas will pay for. You can also decide if you want a wall around your property."

"As I said, Ashley and I haven't talked about any of this but today did open my eyes. First I would like the boys to go to the training and schooling here, at least for now and I will pay half of the salary of the tutor. I have to think about this a little more, but can I pay you to allow us to stay here a little longer until I have the house secured?"

"You can stay here for as long as you like," said Claudius. "And to pay us would be an insult. We don't know what the future holds so personally I would station troops there and build a wall."

"I know you run the navy but so far you have a handful of sailors," said Stephan. "I would suggest you station soldiers at your home and if you want to replace them with sailors later that is up to you."

"Ashley, we can talk about this in private but do you have any thoughts on the matter?" asked Gideon.

"While part of this sounds like too much to me, we do have children. I agree with what you are proposing but I also don't want to be an imposition to this family."

"You are no imposition," said Bella. "We have more than enough room and we enjoy your company. This is changing the subject but why don't you tell the men about some of the things we discussed."

"I love the old building that we bought for my shop and today Bella and I were talking and came up with some wonderful ideas. Ryan, I know you are so busy but I would like to hire you to do some work in the shop."

"Sure," said Ryan. "Claudius are we opening tomorrow?"

"Yes, but I am having more soldiers stationed there. We can discuss that more after dinner. Besides we told all of the men we hired to start tomorrow. I figured we could use some of them to start working on the buildings we bought. So we need to discuss that tonight too. I'd have to look at the lists but we hired about seventy-five men, I think."

"One hundred and twenty-five," Bella said. "I added up the lists while you were at the fort."

"One hundred and twenty-five!" Ryan gasped.

"Well, the ones you can't use can work on the orphanage," said Claudius. "There were a lot of good men there that needed work."

"I think I hired everyone you didn't," said Gideon. "We are going to need a lot of men to build the naval yard so there will be plenty of work to go around. Ashley did you hire anyone from the village?"

"Twenty-four. Five of them will be full time seamstresses, which includes Nikki's mother," Ashley smiled at Nikki then continued. "The others are going to help with the shop duties, supplies and deliveries. I am meeting some of them at the shop tomorrow to start the cleaning and buying paint and things."

"Mother is so excited," Nikki said and looked at Thaos. "Ingr and I want to help Ashley get setup."

"You said that like it was a question," said Thaos with a grin.

"Do you mind?"

"No but keep your eyes open. We will discuss that after dinner."

"Ashley tell them the rest," said Sorren with a huge grin.

"Sorren, Ingr and Nikki took us around the village and introduced us to many people, so we were taken into their homes. Gideon, you won't believe the things these women make. They are true pieces of art. I bought some of the baskets and weavings to send to Port Friada. I have two friends who are shop owners and I think they will be very interested in selling these items. These pieces are both beautiful and unique."

"And I told the women they could sell their work in my shop. If enough of them are interested I am thinking of building a separate room for them." Ashely was talking very fast and obviously excited by her discoveries. Gideon was grinning and winked at Sorren as Ashley spoke. "Gideon, I am very serious about this."

"I know you are Honey. I'm not laughing, I just love how passionate you get about things," he said.

"So you really think people will want to buy those things?" asked Thaos.

"I not only think they will sell but I think they will go for very good prices; that is why I want to help the women negotiate the sales so they make the money they deserve."

Thaos looked at Sorren and said, "If Ashley is right this could be a great thing for your tribe."

"I know," said Sorren proudly. "My people have been making these things for hundreds of years. We don't look at them in the same way that Ashley does."

"Ashley had a well-earned reputation in Port Friada as a savvy business woman," said Gideon. "I would listen to her."

Vitomas loved horses and loved to ride. Now that all of the older children at the castle had horses she started to give them lessons every day. She taught them to care for the animals, to ride and how to talk with the animals. The children were enthusiastic students. Even though Nyla, Saran and Nina knew how to ride they attended the classes with Petra, Kyra and Margarit.

All six of the children started to bond during these classes both with each other and with their horses. Vitomas enjoyed the classes as much as the children did and realized she had given up something she loved because she was busy caring for her own babies.

This day Petra's three dogs were allowed to accompany the class as they went on a ride on the royal grounds. It was a warm and sunny morning and the children talked and laughed as they rode. Suddenly the three German Shepherds started to whine then they ran ahead of the riders. Vitomas stopped her class. "All of you stay here and if something is wrong you ride back to the castle." She pulled a sword from the sheath on her saddle.

"Vitomas, we aren't going to leave you," said Petra.

"Petra, you may need to warn the family besides protecting the girls. Now stay here until I tell you to come forward." Vitomas watched as the dogs ran to a spot about two hundred feet in front of her. The dogs stopped and were smelling the area. Vitomas rode forward; all the while looking around for any sign of attack. The dogs had come upon a campsite.

Vitomas dismounted and walked up to the remains of a campfire; the ashes were still warm. She looked around then mounted her horse. She called the dogs back and rode to the children.

"There is a fresh campsite back there and no one should be on this land. Turn around, we are going home," said Vitomas.

"But we are learning how to track," said Margarit. "Maybe we can find prints."

"No. I can't explain it; I just have a bad feeling. We are going home."

Sampson, son of Chief Duncan of the Clan of Gesmal walked out from behind a tree and watched Vitomas and the children leave. He put his knife back into its sheath. Sampson was no longer in the form of a demon dog. Samael had plans for Sampson and restored him back to the human form he had before he was injured in the botched rites of transformation. Sampson was once again a strong man filled with vitality and hatred.

As if planning two wedding celebrations was not enough added stress and excitement in the household of Gabriel, now their worlds had been thrown into a tizzy with the new promotions.

High Priest Othnial enjoyed the energy and controlled chaos of Gabriel's home. It was so different from the life he had led in Ryed. Othnial realized and verbalized that Ryed was a kingdom consumed with death whereas Wetpr seemed brimming with life. He very much enjoyed his new home and his new responsibilities.

He felt blessed to have the honor of working with the projects in the Holy Vault as well as the chapel at the Learning Center. And every afternoon he taught the men who were studying to become Patronus priests about The Great Ruler.

But now High Priest Othnial was filled with excited anticipation. It had been over a year since he had seen Dominic, Fennel, Seth, Noah and Lawrence. These men were the sons that he never had. Othnial's heart was broken when he learned of the deaths of Asher and the other young men who followed Dominic. These men died saving the citizens of Ryed from monsters after the fall of the Dictator Teivel.

Years earlier peasants of Ryed had told Othnial and other priests at his monastery about a group of young men who were saving people from the brutality of Teivel's soldiers and demons. These young men were risking their lives to save total strangers; something quite unheard of in the dark Kingdom of Ryed.

Dominic and his small band of followers soon became local heroes of the people but their acts of courage and compassion put bounties upon their heads. Teivel's armies searched for the young men who would give hope to a lost land.

Villagers started to see past their fears and helped to hide and feed these men. One day a villager arrived at the monastery. At great risk to his life the man had traveled by himself from his Village of Zurlag.

He told the priests that the Freedom Fighters were hiding in his village and that one of the young men had been seriously wounded in a fight with Teivel's soldiers. The villager had no money to pay the priests but he begged them to come to his village and save the young warrior.

Under the cloak of darkness, Othnial and six other priests returned the peasant to his village. They traveled in a large boca that was filled with food for the villagers. The boca also contained extra priest's robes and medical supplies.

It was not unheard of for the priests of Rubar to visit villages so their presence did not alarm Teivel's soldiers who they encountered along the roadways. When the priests arrived in Zurlag they were all surprised at how young this group of heroes were. Asher and Seth were children. The handsome young warrior named Noah was near death. As the priests cared for his wounds and prayed over him, Othnial spoke with Dominic and his brother Fennel.

These two young men were not delusional. They knew they stood against terrible odds but they refused to stand by and watch innocent people slaughtered in the name of darkness. They prayed to The Great Ruler for guidance and while they didn't know if they received it they certainly believed that the heavens were protecting them.

Othnial had seen so much cruelty and pain in his kingdom that at times he too felt hopeless. He prayed every day for The Great Ruler to help his people. The Angel Ruth had performed missions in Ryed over the centuries. The Great Ruler sent her there as a permanent assignment in answer to Othnial's prayers. But it would be decades before Othnial would learn this.

Othnial's heart went out to these young men who stood for everything that was right in the world. That night Othnial promised The Great Ruler that he would protect these young freedom fighters with his life.

Dominic and his men dressed as priests and were taken to the monastery at Rubar which became their home and headquarters for many years.

The lives of these men changed forever when High Priest Gabriel entered the monastery and said that Angels had sent him and others to help the people of Ryed. But by time Gabriel came to them the hearts of Othnial and Dominic had been broken by all of the tragedy they had seen. They had given up hope that The Great Ruler would help them.

But like many who are overwhelmed with the cruelty that man can inflict upon his kind, these two courageous and faithful men failed to understand that little lights had already been ignited in the darkness of that kingdom. Lights that would burst into flames to dispel and denounce the darkness. Lights that would change the lives of many.

# Chapter XXX
## Family

Sampson had left the area by time Raul, Simon and Matthew found the remnants of his campsite. They had been in almost constant meetings the previous day so it wasn't until Raul went to bed that night that Vitomas told him what she found. He got his brothers and they rode out before breakfast the following morning.

"Whoever it was knows what he is doing. He wiped away any signs of a trail," said Simon as he searched the ground.

"But he left the campfire," said Matthew.

"Vitomas said it was warm when she found it. I'll bet he was watching her and the kids and came back later and wiped the trail. He probably didn't bother with the fire because it had already been seen."

"From what I know of Madeline, I certainly can't see her living off the land," said Matthew as he too was searching the area around the campsite. "This has to be someone else."

"What I don't understand," said Simon. "Is he was probably hiding in those trees, in fact there are a number of places to hide here but he builds his fire in the open. Either he didn't know he was on our land or he wanted us to find it."

"Or he could be stupid," said Matthew.

"The way he has destroyed his trail, this guy knows exactly what he is doing," said Simon.

The three Princes returned to the castle just as the Royal Family were taking their seats at the breakfast table. "So what did you find?" asked Vitomas.

"We think whoever it was; was watching all of you from the trees," said Raul. "And came back and wiped away his trail after you left. Whoever it is knows what he is doing."

"I hope you aren't going to tell us we have to stop the lessons," said Vitomas.

"No," said Raul. "But at least one of us will go with all of you from now on."

"Do you think it was someone that Karzman sent?" asked Nyla.

"We don't know," said Simon. "But we are wondering why he made his camp in the open when there were so many areas there to hide. Either he didn't know he was on our land or he wanted us to find his camp."

"Perhaps you should take some soldiers on these rides," said Sudfad. Petra, Margarit and Kyra all frowned and shook their heads from side to side. "What is the matter?" asked Sudfad with a grin.

"It's not fun with the soldiers. We like it with Vitomas; she is teaching us a lot," said Petra.

"Uncle Sudfad did you know that when Vitomas talks to the horses they listen to her just like people?" asked Margarit.

"I have seen her do some remarkable things," Sudfad said. "Is she teaching you to talk to them like that?"

"We are trying but they rather listen to her," said Kyra.

Sudfad looked across the table at his sons, "All of you go with them. We can work on these new positions and fill you in when you return."

Everyone in the group that was returning to Wetpr was anxious to get home so they were taking little rest. There were only two children in this group, Chasity and Amelia and both were healthy and well behaved so they didn't slow down the caravan.

This morning Archetenus sent Enrops ahead to tell the families that the group would be arriving considerably earlier than at first anticipated. Sudfad's family received their notice while they were still eating breakfast.

"It's from Archetenus," Sudfad said as he read the letter. "They expect to be here late afternoon."

"You mean today?" asked Renya. "Or tomorrow?"

"Today. He says everyone is so anxious to get home that they are riding hard," said Sudfad and turned to Saran, Nina and Nyla. "Girls, Michael will be home this afternoon."

Nyla looked at her sisters and said excitedly. "Let's move our things in the chambers next to his. And we have to finish wrapping his gifts."

"I got to draw him a picture," said Nina with a big smile.

"Do you still want to go on the riding lesson?" asked Raul.

"I think we should cancel it for today," said Vitomas. "We had everything planned for tomorrow so we have a lot to do."

Sampson waited in the trees for two hours without seeing Vitomas and the children. He now wondered if finding his campsite had scared them. Sampson cursed and moved closer to the castle.

Archetenus led his group straight to Sudfad's castle. He had considered breaking the formation in two and having the soldiers return to the fort but he had received a note from Renya just before entering the City of Salar. The Queen told Archetenus that the families of the soldiers and team members were at the castle.

It was midafternoon and citizens lined the streets and hailed the returning forces. While the soldiers were accustomed to the patriotism of the citizens the team members were not and were surprised, embarrassed and proud of their reception.

Trumpets were blown when Archetenus started to lead the caravan through the gates of the castle wall. The courtyard was filled with people, tables and chairs. Musician's resumed playing after the trumpeters stopped.

"I can't see him," said Nina with such frustration that she was almost crying. Raul picked her up and put her on his shoulder.

365

"Michael! Michael!" she screamed as she got a glimpse of her beloved brother.

Nyla and Saran were going to run forward when Simon told them to stay where they were until the caravan stopped. Within moments Archetenus stopped the formation in front of the Royal Family. "Go to your families," he ordered and cheers rang throughout the courtyard.

Michael jumped off from his horse and ran to his sisters who were running towards him. Renya cried as she watched the reunion of her children. Michael, Nyla, Nina and Saran were laughing, crying and all talking at the same time as they hugged and kissed.

Most of the members of Gabriel's home were standing together. The children were not only excited for their family members to return but they were excited to meet Chasity. Joey started to scream Joao's and Dack's names and soon all of the children joined in. The two young Ruala warriors landed in front of their family and friends. Calen, Koby, Dagon, Ratri and all of the Ruala members of Edward's team landed just behind them.

"Chasity," screamed Joey and Tommy and ran to their sister. Joao set her feet on the ground and she ran to her brothers.

"I think I am going to cry," said Dack but he was only partially kidding as he watched the small children hugging and kissing each other. Other members of the family were not as restrained and the tears flowed as they watched these lost children reunite.

Calen and Koby were embracing their families as Joao introduced Chasity to Elan and Cassandra. "Chasity this is my sister Cassandra and your new mother and this is Elan your new father."

Chasity had a big, sweet smile. "Uncle Joao and Uncle Dack told me all about you. We bought you presents."

"Can I hug you?" asked Cassandra but she was crying so hard she could barely speak. Chasity jumped into her arms and the two hugged tightly.

High Priest Othnial walked through the crowd until he found Dominic, Fennel, Seth, Noah, Lawrence and Deborah, who were searching for him. Tears came to Othnial's eyes as he embraced each of the young men and they in turn were overwhelmed with emotions.

Delilah and Zoya were standing together and both flew into their husband's arms. Misha and Diana laughed as they watched Thor jump from his horse and run towards Tanya who was already running to him.

Sally and April were standing with Lana searching the crowd for Chaez. The two young girls kept screaming their brother's name until he found them in the din. The entire family hugged as one.

Sampson sat in a tree watching the homecoming and wondering if the troops had been at war. With all that he had been through, Sampson had lost a great deal of his memories. But when he saw Vivian he was flooded with emotions. He saw her from a distance and on some level did not recognize her although his being was filled with conflicting feelings of desire and revenge.

Sampson did not recognize Joshua's family or Diana since they were dressed in the clothing of the people of Wetpr. But he did recognize the warrior's uniforms of his tribe which the returning Venatores were wearing. Although Sampson had grown up with every Venator he now watched in the courtyard, he did not remember them. He was both confused and curious when he saw Wetprian soldiers, Ruala warriors, Venatores and priests celebrating together. To him this union seemed very unnatural.

After an hour the crowd in the courtyard was ushered inside of the castle to the Great Hall. It was here where Nana brought baby Amelia to Emeral and Maxwell.

"I didn't want to bother you while you were greeting your family," said Nana. "But the Sanuri said that I should bring Amelia here for you to meet."

Emeral smiled warmly and took the toddler. "She's a beautiful little girl. The boys wrote to us about her. Dagon in particular was concerned that Misha might be upset at seeing her. But I don't think that will be the case."

As Emeral cuddled Amelia, Maxwell spoke to Nana, "The boys said you have become very attached to her. Are you going to adopt her?"

"I am very torn about that," said Nana. "She has stolen my heart but I am not sure that I am ready for a family and I don't know if she would be better off with two parents."

"Well you certainly don't have to make any decisions right away," said Emeral. "And if you do adopt her we will help you."

"You two have been smiling like a cat with a mouse," Dagon said to Horace and Zelda. "What is going on?" They looked at each other and smiled but it was Zack who spoke.

"They found you a boy," Zack blurted out. "We all helped to pick him. He is really nice."

"What!" said Rachel and laughed.

"Well, you did tell us to keep our eyes open for a child," said Zelda. "And he is such a sweet boy. His name is Cody and he is seven. He has dark hair and brown eyes just like both of you."

Dagon and Rachel looked at each other and laughed, "Well, this is something. We are glad to hear about Cody but we were going to talk to all of you tonight. We are considering adopting the baby Amelia; that is if Nana doesn't and Misha doesn't hate her," said Dagon.

"That is wonderful," said Zelda and clapped her hands but then her demeanor changed. "Does that mean you aren't interested in Cody?"

Dagon and Rachel looked at each other and smiled again. "No it doesn't. Let's meet Cody in the morning."

"But Mother and Father if we adopt any of these children you know you will have to watch them when we are on missions," said Rachel.

"That is what we are counting on," said Horace with a big grin.

Drake and Tally stood together and watched the crowd. There was no one to greet them and all of the friends they had made were now with their families. Once they entered the Great Hall they walked up to a table that contained bottles of whiskey, wine and glasses. Drake poured whiskey into two glasses and as he was handing one to Tally, Michael walked up to them. Nina was riding on Michael's shoulders and he was holding hands with Nyla and Saran.

"All of you certainly look happy," Drake said and smiled.

"Join us," said Michael. "I'll introduce you to the family."

"We don't want to interfere with anything," said Tally and paused. "Michael, I know you are always saying that you feel like a fish out of water but I got to tell you this really does seem like your home."

"It is," said Saran happily and squeezed her brother's arm.

"Join us," repeated Michael. "And later Nyla has something to tell you. You know that Jared's wife is a seer. Well she talked to River's spirit."

Both Drake and Tally looked shocked. "Are you s..." Tally did not finish his sentence. He stared back and forth between Nyla and Michael then said. "Actually I wouldn't mind hearing about that right now."

"Saran why don't you and Nina get some of Michael's gifts," said Nyla. Michael took Nina from his shoulders and set her on the floor. As soon as the two girls left the men gathered around Nyla.

Sampson remained perched in the tree for several hours until his muscles were cramping. He dared not get any closer to the castle because of the soldiers. He climbed down from the tree and hid in some bushes but he couldn't see very much from this new position. After an hour he left to make a camp.

Both Tally and Drake were still shaken from Nyla's story when Michael introduced them to his family. Now the men's eyes widened when they met Raul and Sudfad. "How could Karzman not know who your daddy was?" asked Tally. "All three of you look exactly alike."

"Actually we suspect that he did and that is why he tortured Michael so," said Sudfad. "I understand the history you have with all of our children. We will start with a clean slate. Renya has prepared chambers for you. Every morning I have a meeting of my leaders. Tomorrow I would also like the two of you to attend so we can discuss Karzman."

"We're staying in the castle?" Drake almost gasped.

"It was that or the barn," Michael said sarcastically. "Sudfad is going to hire you as soldiers. We can discuss the details tomorrow."

"You look shocked," said Simon and grinned.

"We are," said Drake. "Michael has every right to kill us and you bring us into your home."

"We also know what happened to Tally for helping our daughters. Nyla if Michael does not know that story you should tell him," said Renya. "As Sudfad said, we are starting with a new slate."

"Just so you know, Renya can fight as well as you guys," Michael said with a grin then laughed when he saw the looks on the faces of Drake and Tally.

"We've never heard of women warriors before we hooked up with Michael," said Drake. "Now everyone is."

"Michael we are training too," said Saran.

"Training for what?" he asked.

"We are training with the Venatores at Gabriel's house," Saran said proudly. "They teach all of the kids there. And Vitomas is training us in riding and animals and we've got a teacher that comes here for our other lessons."

Michael looked surprised. "Are all of you training with the Venatores?"

"Yes," said Nyla. "Why are you mad?"

"No, I guess I just didn't think you would want to do that."

"We love it," said Nina. "We have a lot of fun and afterwards they give us treats." Everyone laughed.

Dagon, Rachel, Horace and Zelda worked their way through the crowded room until they found Emeral and Maxwell. "We want to know if you want to come with us to the orphanage tomorrow morning when we meet Cody," Dagon said with a big smile.

"We would just love to," said Emeral and hugged Dagon then Rachel.

"We have to find Hannah," said Dagon but there is something that we should tell you." As Dagon spoke Emeral and Maxwell saw the smiles on the faces of Zelda and Horace. "We are considering adopting Amelia too but we don't know yet if Nana is going to and we don't want Misha to hate her."

"Your mother and I are happy about this but we just spoke with Nana a few minutes ago. She is really conflicted, I would suggest that you and Rachel speak with her soon."

"And although I don't think Misha will be a problem you should talk to him too," Maxwell said.

Rachel turned to her parents, "Do you want to come with us when we talk to Nana? You haven't met Amelia yet."

"Yes," said Horace.

They found Nana talking with a group of team members. "Can we speak with you for a moment?" Dagon asked then led Nana from the group to his family.

"Is something the matter?" asked Nana.

But before anyone could answer her question Zelda gushed, "Look at her; what a beautiful baby. May I hold her?" Nana handed Amelia to Zelda.

"We know you haven't made up your mind yet," said Dagon. "But if you don't adopt Amelia, Rachel and I would like to. Of course I still have to speak with Misha."

"I didn't know you were interested in her?" said Nana. "Is that why Rachel kept offering to take care of her?"

"Yes," Rachel said. "We talked about it a lot because of Bruno's history with this family."

"Honestly I feel both sad and relieved by this," said Nana as tears filled her eyes. "I love her but I am not sure if I am ready for a family. And then I wonder if she would be better off with two parents."

"Nana, you have been a wonderful mother to her," said Rachel. "And if you decide not to adopt her you certainly can spend time with her."

Nana didn't say anything. She watched Horace and Zelda hugging and playing with Amelia. Nana looked at Dagon, "Why don't you talk to Misha."

Dagon was holding Amelia as he and Rachel walked up to Misha, Diana, Thor and Tanya. Diana and Thor were holding babies.

"Is that Amelia?" cooed Diana. "She's beautiful. Tanya will you take Maximus so I can hold her?"

"I can tell something is up from the look on your face," Misha said to Dagon. "You want to know if I am going to go nuts or something don't you?"

Dagon laughed. "We would like to adopt Amelia but we don't want to bring her into the home if it will distress you. And we will understand if it does."

"Misha hold her," said Diana and handed the toddler to him.

Misha took Amelia and looked at the little girl. "Maybe if you would have asked me this before we had our children my answer would be different. But like I told the others, this is like someone hating our babies because of something I did. I'm not going to hate her. If you need my blessing you have it and I appreciate you asking."

As Dagon and Rachel walked away, Diana turned and smiled at Tanya and Thor who were holding the twins. "That's a good look on you two," she said kiddingly. And to her surprise both Thor and Tanya just smiled at her.

Dagon and Rachel returned to Nana, Zelda and Horace. "He gave us his blessing," said Dagon as he handed Amelia to Nana. "The rest is up to you. But we don't want to pressure you."

"Can I just have a little time to think about this?" asked Nana emotionally.

"Of course and Rachel just reminded me that your house has been empty for a while so Edward will need to buy food and supplies. Why don't you and Amelia stay at our house tonight? You don't have to make a decision right away but we have food."

"Thanks I think I will. She didn't sleep much this afternoon so she will need a nap soon."

Zelda and Horace were so excited they could hardly contain themselves. The family walked through the crowd until they found Hannah and Gabriel. "Hannah, we would like you to go to the orphanage with us tomorrow when we meet Cody," said Dagon with a big smile. "And we might adopt Amelia too."

"Oh this makes me so happy," Hannah said and hugged Dagon then Rachel.

"That's a big step going from no children to two but we did it and have never regretted it," said Gabriel as he shook Dagon's hand and hugged Rachel.

After the feast, people quickly left the castle as most of them wanted to spend time with their family members. Elan and Cassandra had been proudly introducing Chasity to everyone. Now they walked up to Sudfad and Renya. "We're going to leave so the children can get adjusted," Elan said. "Unless you need us for anything."

"No, since it is still so early I was thinking of having a drink with Tally and Drake and hearing about Karzman, but no one has to join us," said Sudfad. Elan looked conflicted. "Elan go home, any information we learn I will tell you tomorrow."

Gabriel, Raphael, Joshua, Maxwell and the team leaders decided to join Sudfad and his sons as they talked with Drake and Tally. Most of the team members remained at the castle while the families went to their homes.

Drake and Tally were talking about their time as soldiers for Karzman when Renya entered the room and sat down. This surprised the two men and they stopped talking. "Is anything wrong?" asked Drake.

"Renya is joining us," said Sudfad. "Let me tell you that my wife has led men in battle and now that we have adopted the girls she wants to kill Karzman herself." Many men in the room laughed at the looks on Drake's and Tally's faces.

"We just started," said Drake. "We'll go back to the beginning."

Sampson made a camp deep within the forest on land that bordered the lands of Sudfad. Instead of cooking food he pulled a bottle of whiskey from his saddlebag and started to drink it down. He was often frustrated that he had such problems with his memory and after seeing Vivian and the uniforms of his tribe he felt like he was missing something that was right before his eyes; something of great importance.

Sampson didn't know that the demon Samael now owned his soul. All he remembered was waking up one morning in Hecate's lair. He remembered Hecate, at least bits and pieces of her. Sampson remembered his family and his village. But much of the time that passed after he started the rites of transformation was lost to him. Sampson did not realize that he didn't remember almost two years of his life.

He did not even realize that Samael had sent him to Wetpr. Sampson just knew that he had an overwhelming feeling that he had to get to the castle of King Sudfad. He watched the castle although he did not understand what he was looking for. But Sampson never had been the type of man to question why he did or felt things, even before he sold his soul to demons.

Sampson was feeling very frustrated and he didn't know why. So he drank until he passed out. He never saw Vivian leave the castle.

# Chapter XXXI
## Cody

Zelda, Horace and Zack went to Gabriel's house after the reception at the castle. The family had gifts for Chasity and to prevent jealousies they bought gifts for all of the children. Many members of the household were surprised at how quickly Chasity fit into the family.

"This is amazing," said Bekka as everyone was gathered around the dining room table watching the children opening their gifts. "You would think she has always lived here."

"Well, all of you wrote to her and she would ask us to keep reading the letters to her," said Calen as he held both of his children on his lap. "So really she has already met you."

"I can't stop crying," said Cassandra. "Every time I think of the three of them running to each other." Elan put his arm around her and smiled.

"Can Chasity sleep with Tommy and me?" asked Joey.

"Chasity," said Elan. "We have you and Cicely sharing a room but if you want to sleep with Joey and Tommy tonight you can." She looked at Elan and nodded then opened another gift.

Emeral looked across the table at Dagon and Rachel and asked, "Have you been in your chambers yet?"

"No, why?" asked Dagon.

"They already have a room set up for Cody," Misha said and chuckled.

"Well, you did tell all of us to look for a child for you," said Emeral with a loving smile.

"Thank you, we appreciate that," said Dagon sincerely.

"Dagon are you going to get Cody tomorrow?" asked Christopher.

"We are going to meet him tomorrow," said Dagon. "Do you want to come along?"

"Sure. Don't we?" Christopher asked as he looked at the other boys at the table. "When he comes home can we all camp out in the playroom?"

"Well, we have to meet him first," explained Dagon. "He might not want to be our son."

"He wants to," said Adrone. "We told him about you and Rachel."

"And we drew pictures of you and showed him," said Nicholas.

Dagon and Rachel laughed loudly. "If we bring him home you can all camp out and Rachel and I will get you ice cream."

The boys grinned and looked at each other excitedly. "Can Chasity too?" asked Paul.

"If she wants to," said Elan.

"She'll want to," Joey said.

"Ok, we have talked about everything except for all of us becoming ruling families," said Koby. "So tell us what is going on."

"I'll make some coffee," said Hannah. "This will take a while."

A few minutes later Nana walked into the dining room with Amelia. "I took a nap with her," Nana said. "Didn't realize I was so tired."

"All of the children got gifts," said Natasha. "We have a doll for her too."

"That was so considerate of you," said Nana. "Thank you." Nana walked around the table until she got to Natasha. Amelia smiled and hugged her new doll.

Hannah walked back into the dining room with a tray. "Nana, I have clothes that Cere has outgrown. There is nothing wrong with them if you would like some things for Amelia."

"I can adjust them for her wings," said Ella. "It won't take long."

"Thank you. I didn't exactly get a chance to buy her many things," said Nana and paused. "Did Dagon and Rachel tell you that they want to adopt her?"

"No," gasped Natasha and looked at Dagon and Rachel and smiled.

"I have gotten so attached to her," explained Nana. "Guess she has stolen my heart but I didn't plan to have a family yet. Calen said I could leave her here when I go on missions but I am not sure that is...I am not saying anything bad about leaving her here. I think she should have more of a family than just me. So Dagon and Rachel if you still want to adopt her..."

"Yes," said Rachel quickly. "But Nana you still should be part of her life. Dagon and I both believe that."

Nana was crying when she walked around the table and handed Amelia to Rachel.

The following morning as Sudfad's meeting was starting, Luca explained that Maxwell and Dagon had gone to the orphanage.

"Well that is good news," said Sudfad. "Tell us if they adopt the boy. You know Renya will want to buy gifts."

Archetenus stood up and walked to Sudfad. "I feel like a horse's ass," said Archetenus. "I was so excited to see my family that I forgot to give you this." He handed the letter that Claudius had sent to the Sanuri to Sudfad. "The Sanuri and Erebus went back to Langer because some men were hired to scare the hell out of Bella and give her a note."

"Zeke and his boys found out about it and as you can imagine, Claudius, Thaos and Stephan weren't happy. The men were hired killers who swore up and down that Deckor hired them and they even described him. So the Sanuri is going to try and figure out what is going on."

"The Sanuri said the note sounded more like Hector sent it than Deckor," added Edward.

Sudfad read the letter and handed it to Simon. "Well, that is disturbing. But before we discuss any of that further I would like to cover a few things that Tally and Drake told us last night. I told them to join us in twenty minutes. Is there anyone in this room who did not believe them or feel that we can't trust them?"

"We know what they did to Michael," said Jared. "But honestly they have been decent and straight shooters. I know they like Michael, now at least and feel bad for what they did."

"While part of me doesn't trust them and maybe never will," said Michael as he stood up. Nyla told me something that I didn't know before." Michael repeated the story of Tally and River helping Nyla and Saran. The men sat in silence and listened.

"Cody wanted to sit on the front steps and wait for you," said Padre Octavos as he led Rachel, Dagon and their families to the playground. Hannah and most of the children from the house were with them. The boys and Chasity now ran ahead of the adults. Paul opened the door to the yard and immediately all the boys started to yell Cody's name.

"I don't want to pressure you," Hannah whispered. "But they will all be so disappointed if you don't want Cody."

"We want him," said Dagon with a grin. Zelda was carrying Amelia and couldn't stop smiling.

A boy with dark hair and huge brown eyes ran up to Christopher who now yelled, "I found him! I found him!" The children from Gabriel's house ran to Cody and Christopher then they all turned and ran to the door leading into the building.

Dagon and Rachel were the first two adults to walk into the yard and saw the excited children running towards them. They both smiled and Dagon squatted down. "This is Cody," Adrone said breathlessly. Cody looked at Dagon and Rachel with a mixture of anticipation and fear of rejection.

"We've heard a lot about you Cody," said Dagon as he shook hands with the boy. "I know you haven't had time to get to know me and Rachel but the family told us they have been talking to you a lot. We would like you to be our son but what do you want? If you need time to get to know us that is alright."

"I want to be your son," Cody said shyly. Rachel hugged him tightly then Dagon hugged him. Cody got a big smile on his face.

"We've already got your room ready," said Joey to Cody.

"Boys why don't you take Cody to the boca while we take care of the paperwork," said Dagon.

"Actually everything is taken care of except for your signatures," said Padre Octavos. Dagon and Rachel looked at Hannah and their parents, who were all smiling at them.

After the morning meeting, there was a family celebration at the home of Gabriel in honor of the recent adoptions of Cody, Chasity and Amelia.

"Where have you been?" asked Joao as Melinda and Jason walked into the dining room with armloads of packages.

"Gabriel gave me a couple of days off," said Melinda happily.

"I know that. I mean where have you been?" teased Joao.

"With Jason," said Melinda and glanced at the children to see if they understood the significance of her statement but they were engrossed with their treats.

"I am trying to talk her into transferring to our team," Jason said.

"Is that something you would consider?" asked Cassandra.

Melinda's demeanor became more solemn, "I promised Gabriel that I would be a nurse until everyone completed their schooling."

"Melinda, with all of the new babies and adoptions most of the family has put their schooling on hold," said Natasha. "You aren't expected to wait around to see if they will go back and complete their studies. If you want to be with Jason, just talk to Gabriel and Edward. Hannah what do you think about this?"

"I agree with Natasha, you helped us when we really needed it. No one wants you to give up your life to work here. Besides, if you go to Edward's team we will still see you all of the time."

"You don't think that Gabriel will get mad?" asked Melinda.

Hannah laughed, "I can't even remember the last time I saw him mad."

Misha walked into the room and heard the conversation. "Melinda, Hannah and Natasha are right. And if you go to Edward's team that doesn't mean you can't come back here if you change your mind. My only suggestion would be that you make a decision soon since all the teams are now training their people to work together. It would be better for you and the other members if you started with them."

Melinda now looked at her brother and sister and asked, "What do you think?"

"Melinda we just want you to be happy," said Cassandra. "And like everyone is saying, unless you are on a mission we will still see each other all of the time."

"I agree," said Joao with a grin. "Besides you will get really grumpy if Jason leaves and you are here. I hate being around you when you are grumpy."

Melinda turned and looked at Jason who was smiling broadly. "Let's talk to Edward and Gabriel today," he said.

Lana was listening to the conversation. "Melinda, you aren't leaving because of Tanya are you?"

"Honestly no. And I feel so foolish for how I acted before. I should talk to her and Thor."

Gideon had considered taking a few days off from work so he could situate his family. But instead he had the carpenters who he hired working on the new house and building a barracks for soldiers. Gideon also hired men to build a wall around his property. These two projects alone took him an entire day to organize.

Ashley was shocked that the men and women she hired brought friends and family members along to work on her shop. They told her they didn't expect her to pay them. The people volunteered because they were so excited that Ashley wanted to help them sell the baskets, pottery and weavings they made. When many of these people arrived at the shop they had wares to show her.

This first day Ashley had planned for the work crew to just clean out the huge building but by midmorning she and several of the male Nordes warriors had determined a location and size of a room that would be dedicated to just their tribe. The men said they could build the room and Ashley gave them the money for supplies.

The shop was located in the center of a block in the busiest section of the business district. Between the Nordes warriors and some carpenters from Ryan's shop there was a great deal of commotion in and around the building. Curious citizens started to stop in to inquire about Ashley's business. So many people walked into the shop that Ashley gave some of the carpenters money and had them return to Ryan's shop to buy some tables and chairs.

Ashley had the workers help her clear out an area near one of the front windows. She planned to set up tables of coffee and treats as Bella did in Ryan's shop. She told some of the Nordes women to bring in tablecloths and pottery to display on the tables.

The excited energy of the workers and Ashley was contagious and the people who stopped into the building become excited about the new business also.

Midafternoon Bella, Nikki and Ingr walked into the shop. "We are taking you shopping," Bella announced.

"I can't believe all of the work that's been done," gasped Ingr as the women walked around the first floor of the building.

"Everyone is so excited about selling their work that extra people came from the tribe to help. That room they are building will be just for the art and crafts of your tribe. And Bella, I stole your idea. I just bought those tables from Ryan and I am going to set up coffee and treats. You can't believe all of the people who have walked in here to hear about the business. And the women are going to decorate the tables with their cloths and pottery."

"Gideon shipped those pieces to my friends this morning but it will probably be a couple of weeks before we hear from them," Ashley was clearly excited as she spoke. "As soon as we get things cleaned and painted here, Gideon will have my goods brought here from the ship. Then I want all of you to come back and look at some of my materials. I already have ideas of dresses I want to design for you."

Adding to the chaos, Luca announced that he and Natalie wanted Cody and Chasity in their wedding also. Emeral immediately took Rachel, Cassandra and the two children to the dressmakers and then shopping. The wedding was less than a week and a half away.

To Shara's disappointment, Sorren decided to stay in Lentz with Mathas since Claudius, Fahron and Gideon were taking their families to Wetpr for the wedding. Rosa intended to travel with Fahron and Isadore so she could see Margarit in the wedding. It was planned that Matthew's family and all of the medical students would return to Lentz after the wedding.

While the Sanuri wanted to remain in the Kingdom of Lentz to figure out the mystery of the appearance of a second man claiming to be Deckor, he still had Juleta's spell books. It had been agreed that Hilgra should go to Wetpr and meet with Gala, Shara and Angelina to see if this group of powerful healers could translate the books. The Sanuri decided to return to Wetpr with Claudius and the others and he would bring Hilgra with him and Erebus.

Sampson may have lost some of his memories but he did not lose his skills as a Venator. This afternoon he realized he was not the only one spying on Sudfad's castle. He found a trail and followed it until he saw two men hiding in the brush.

"I can't see shit from here," said one of the men to his companion. "We have to move."

"Well you better damn well think about this because there are damn soldiers everywhere. Something is going on."

"You don't know that. Maybe they are normal patrols."

"Whether they are normal or not, we can't get any closer right now. We'll have to wait until it gets dark…" the man died before he could finish his sentence. He fell forward with one of Sampson's knives lodged in his back. Sampson jumped on the second man before he realized he was being attacked.

"Who do you work for?" growled Sampson as he held a knife to the man's throat. But before the man could answer, Sampson heard horses and peered through the brush.

"Damn good idea," said Tally. "What is going on anyways?"

"Luca's wedding is soon and the castle will be filled with guests," explained Simon. "And you haven't seen anything until you have been to one of Mother's celebrations. She will have dances every night and all kinds of entertainment and competitions during the day."

"She usually sets up three or four things going on at the same time so you can have a choice. Like she might have competitions and a horse race at the same time," said Raul. "And the castle just gets crazy preparing for these things."

"Told ya," Michael said to Drake and Tally. "You thought the celebrations in Port Friada and Langer were something."

"Do we have to get dressed up too," asked Drake. "Because we saved the clothes that Ashley gave us."

"You will for the dances," said Simon then he grinned. "Let me guess are they rolled up in your saddlebags?"

"They were," said Tally. "They're in our rooms now."

"Take them to Laurel when we get..."Simon stopped talking as all of the men heard crashing through the brush. They stopped their horses.

A man covered in blood stumbled out of the bushes and fell dead to the ground. Raul and the others looked around for any sign of attack before they dismounted.

"That's one of Karzman's men," said Tally as he looked at the face of the body that Raul rolled over.

"There's another one back here," yelled Michael.

"He works for Karzman too," said Drake as he watched Simon searching the man's pockets.

Michael searched the ground for tracks then looked up into the trees. The men searched the area around the two bodies without finding a trail.

"I'm not sorry that they are dead," said Simon. "But I wonder who killed them. If it was one of our people we would have been told."

"I think it's the same guy who was watching Vitomas and the kids," said Raul. "It's like he is a ghost."

"Well, these two left a good trail," said Drake as he and Tally returned to the Princes with two horses. "We haven't looked in the saddlebags yet."

Raul and Michael walked over to the horses and untied the saddlebags. "You might want to dump those before you put your hands in them," said Tally. Both Princes now unfastened the bags from the saddles and dumped the contents on the ground. Raul jumped back when a snake hit the ground hissing and lunging. Drake threw a knife and cut the snake's head off.

"It's a Karzman warning," explained Drake.

"To keep people out of the saddlebags?" Simon asked.

"No, think of it like a calling card," said Tally. "Karzman likes to create fear in people."

Other than the snake there was nothing of importance in either the saddlebags or the pockets of the dead men. "What are you doing?" asked Raul as he saw Drake and Tally pulling the boots off from the corpses.

"You can't trust anyone when you work for Karzman," said Drake. "So most of the guys get creative in hiding things."

"Like this," said Tally as he unfolded a piece of paper that he found in the bottom of a boot. "It's a map to your castle," he said and handed the paper to Simon who was standing the closest to him.

Drake pulled out his knife and pried the heels off the boots he was searching. "This guy was hiding his money but nothing else."

"You two can keep the money," said Raul as he watched Tally tearing the heels off the second pair of boots.

"This guy must have been the boss of the two," said Tally and handed another piece of paper to Simon. "He's carrying all of the information."

"It's another map," said Simon. "But I am not sure..." All the men now gathered around Simon and looked at the map. "It's part of Wetpr," Simon continued after a pause.

"It's from Karzman's village to here," said Michael. "Whoever drew this must not have traveled this way much because it is missing a lot of information. Maybe these guys drew it as they rode."

"But what are those dots for?" asked Raul. "I don't see any type of pattern and there aren't any villages or towns in those areas."

"If I had to guess," said Tally. "They stashed something in those places. Maybe there are buildings or caves to hide in or they have weapons hidden or even men. They probably don't have money hidden there just because one of them would steal it."

"Let's grab the bodies and take all of this stuff back to the castle," said Raul.

Sampson watched Raul and the others from a distance. He couldn't see what they found but it was obvious to him that something had their attention. Now Sampson wondered what he had missed. He killed Karzman's men before he had a chance to learn who they worked for.

Sampson didn't hear Samael's voice in his head or any other voices for that matter. He didn't know that Samael owned his soul which allowed the powerful demon to see through his eyes. Even though Sampson had no understanding as to why he was in Wetpr or why he was watching the castle he now wondered if there were threats against him in this new land.

The two men who Sampson had just killed looked like soldiers but they were dressed poorly. But the men who stood around the corpses were huge, powerful men like Sampson himself. To see five men of such build and demeanor made Sampson curious. He was not close enough to see their faces or to realize that he had met Simon and Raul before.

# Chapter XXXII
## Secrets Unfold

Sudfad asked Annabelle to make multiple copies of the map that Karzman's soldier was carrying. The map and a letter of information was sent to the Commanding General of Fort Nir as well as High Priest Nicholas of the Patronus Headquarters at Philiste. The route indicated on the map was close to both of these institutions. Sudfad requested that the leaders have their men check the areas indicated by the dots on the map.

"Do you want to come with us?" Raul asked Drake and Tally. "We are taking a map to Gabriel's house and we need to pick up the kids from their training."

"Sure, might as well," said Tally.

"You think the castle is crazy," Simon said. "All of Gabriel's team members and their families live in a huge mansion. The place is filled with kids and dogs and everyone gets along. Father offered to give some of them land but they all wanted to stay together."

All of the older children were outside playing when Raul, Simon, Michael, Drake and Tally rode to the front door. Dogs and screaming kids greeted the visitors.

"You have to see our puppies," Christopher yelled as the men dismounted. "They're inside cuz they are too little to play with us."

The men laughed when Paul said, "This is Cody, he's new too."

"Cody it's nice to meet you," said Raul and ruffled the boy's hair.

"They're all princes," Adrone said to Cody.

"Really?" Cody said and his eyes widened.

"Well, not all of us kid," said Tally and chuckled.

Lana and Tanya walked up to the men. "Let me guess more beautiful warrior women," said Drake.

"And they are spoken for too," Michael said with a grin.

"Aren't there any who are single?" asked Drake.

"I'm not sure," said Simon then he turned to Lana. "Is Gabriel or Raphael inside?"

"No, they are at the training field that is between Edward's and Dominic's houses. But Luca and Misha are inside. Can we help you with anything?"

"We found two bodies on our land. We don't know who killed them and we found a couple of maps. First, be careful and second, we brought some copies of the maps," said Raul.

"We always assume someone is watching us," said Lana. "Come on in. Petra and the girls are inside."

"Why? Is anything wrong?" asked Michael.

Lana laughed, "Luca's wedding is getting so big..." she didn't finish her sentence because Nyla, Saran and Nina all ran up to them.

"Can we be in the wedding too?" all three girls asked simultaneously. The men were laughing as Emeral and Luca walked up to them.

"How many attendants are you having?" asked Raul kiddingly. "The chapel may not be big enough."

"Right now we have equal numbers of girls and boys for attendants so we thought the girls could walk ahead and throw flower pedals," said Emeral. "I need to take them to the dressmaker's today if you say yes."

The girls were jumping around anxiously. Michael looked at Simon and Raul. "I don't see why not," said Simon. "Everyone else is in the wedding."

"Oh thank you, thank you," said the girls excitedly.

"We'll bring them home after the fittings," said Luca.

"Where's Petra and the other girls?" asked Raul.

"Ella and Iris are doing the finishing touchups on the clothes that Petra and Margarit are wearing," explained Emeral. "And since Kyra was so upset about Petra walking down the aisle with Margarit we got her a dress too and she is being fitted."

Raul looked at Tally and Drake and explained, "Besides the adult attendants Luca and Natalie are having all of the children pretty much in both our homes being attendants. This wedding is going to be huge."

"But afterwards we are having competitions, a pig roast and a dance," said Luca. "So plan on coming. You can come to the wedding too if you want."

"Thanks," said Tally. "Not sure about the wedding but we're good for the rest."

"Luca, I'm getting so big they have to adjust my dress again," Natalie said with frustration as she walked into the parlor. Then she laughed when she realized they had company.

"We kept putting off the wedding until everyone came back from the missions," Luca said to Drake and Tally as he put his arm around Natalie. Then he introduced the three.

"Nice to meet you," said Drake. "From the way everyone was talking on the mission I think they are all coming for your wedding."

"I think that is one of ours," said Natalie when she heard a baby crying and left the parlor.

"Girls, why don't you go with her," said Raul to Nyla, Nina and Saran. After the girls left Simon handed copies of the map to Luca and Emeral.

"We found two of Karzman's men dead on our property this morning," said Raul. "Whoever did it didn't leave a trace so we are thinking it's the same guy that was watching Vitomas and the kids. There was a live snake in one of the saddlebags and Drake and Tally tell us that is a typical calling card of Karzman. Then they found these maps hidden in the boots of the dead men."

"This one is to your place," said Luca. "But what is this other one?"

"It's a map from Karzman's village to Salar," said Michael. "But as you can see it is piss poor. We are wondering if the guys drew it as they rode here. But we don't know what those dots are for so Sudfad is having the soldiers and Patronus priests in that area check them out."

"We figure they could be hiding spots or areas where weapons or men are stashed," said Tally.

"I am more concerned about this mystery man who is roaming our place than I am about Karzman's men right now," said Simon.

"Understandably," said Emeral. "You know this house is filled with warriors, I think we should discuss this during dinner. Someone might have some ideas."

"Can we go in now?" asked Paul from the hallway outside of the parlor.

"Can the boys come in now?" Lana called to the people in the parlor. "They want to show off the pups."

"Yes," said Raul and chuckled.

Paul and Zack were holding opposite sides of a large crate that had blankets and two little puppies in it. "We have to feed them all the time cuz they don't eat much," explained Joey as all of the children entered the parlor.

"Grandma got us another dog too," said Nicholas proudly. "But she's outside playing."

"Those are some fine looking pups," said Simon.

"We know," said Christopher. "We love them."

Emeral gave Drake and Tally a tour of the home and grounds while the Princes waited for Petra, Kyra and Margarit. "I've never seen a house this big before," said Tally.

"It wasn't this big to start with. We keep adding on," said Emeral. "A lot of us, well I guess all of the parents in the house came to visit and never left." Emeral laughed after she said this. "Maxwell and I had a house full of children too and after they were grown and on their own, well it was just too quiet. And I don't know if you know that all Rualas are trained to be warriors. We had a good life but we were feeling rather useless then we came here. We never imagined how our lives would change."

"Bekka's parents live here too now and so do Vivian's and Rachel's live in a house on the property. So we have three generations here and everyone is busy all of the time."

"You all sure seem happy," Tally said. "And everyone just seems like one big family; I mean all of you not just those that live in this house."

"Actually we all feel like family. For many years Gabriel, his sister Natasha and our sons were the only team that hunted demons. It is a very dangerous life and these people were very dedicated. They didn't have outside lives because they didn't want distractions. So, after a while they became a family. Well, our son Calen and Natasha were the first of the group to get married. After three days mind you. Then one right after another all of the members married. And it was the same thing; they all got married after a couple of days."

"Was there a reason for that?" asked Tally.

"They won't admit it but I think they were all so lonely; I mean they had given up everything in their lives for the missions. Maxwell and I have other children besides the boys here and they are very different from us. I just keep talking. Do you already know all of this?"

"No," said Drake. "But it's interesting."

"Natasha got pregnant and she and Calen were going to come to the Ice Caves to have the baby then this horrible mission came up and they needed to stay here. So they invited Maxwell and me to come and stay with them until the baby was born."

"We were so excited but we didn't know what to expect. The Ice Caves are like another kingdom and we hadn't been out of them very often. We came here and found this family and they stole our hearts. They also needed a great deal of help so we decided to stay longer then they didn't want us to leave."

"In case you haven't figured it out there is a reason I am telling you all of this. The world you come from is very different too. These people are very accepting and are bringing you into the families. I don't really know you gentlemen but you will find out that Renya and I are as protective of our families as a lioness. I hope for your sakes you are who you present yourselves to be."

Mathas released Tanner and his men so they could return to the Anchors Inn with a note for Deckor. Soldiers dressed in civilian attire were already in the tavern and on the streets when Tanner and his small gang rode up to the front door. While Mathas did not tell Tanner that men would be watching them, Tanner was not stupid and assumed as much.

Mathas and the other leaders were well aware that many people had seen Claudius' family confront Tanner and his men and arrest them. If Deckor learned of this he might not show up for his meeting with Tanner.

These hired killers had good incentives to go along with Mathas' plan; their freedom and their lives were at stake. Mathas promised to pardon the men if they helped him capture Deckor. These mercenaries had no bond with Deckor, only Tanner had even met the man who was paying their salaries. They agreed to turn on their boss without hesitation.

Tanner and his men walked into the Anchors Inn and looked at the faces of the men in the room. Tanner walked to the bar while his men sat around a table. "I'll have a bottle and seven glasses," Tanner said loudly. "Then he pushed a piece of paper at the bartender and said in a low voice, "Tell Deckor to watch out."

"I heard you boys was in the dungeons," said the bartender skeptically.

"We was. They think some guy named Hector sent us and they want us to help catch him. Don't even know who Hector is," said Tanner and gulped a glass of whiskey.

"You know you are probably being watched," said the bartender.

"Figured as much. Can understand if the boss don't want nutin to do with us but now that the King thinks we are helping them, wells we kinda got a free pass to the castle. Thought the boss would be interested in that."

After an afternoon of rigorous training, Jason and Melinda met with Gabriel, Raphael and Edward.

"I think we can all understand your request," Gabriel said to the couple. "But I think we all have the same concerns also. Melinda you got too emotional when you learned that Thor was interested in Tanya and there really wasn't a relationship between the two of you. From what you and Jason just said you do have a committed relationship. I am going to pose a question to you and I don't want an answer today. I want you to really think about this and talk about it together."

"Jason will be playing roles. What if that means he has to flirt with another woman?" Melinda started to speak but Gabriel held his hand up for her to be quiet. "If you get as jealous as you did with Thor, you could compromise the mission and get people hurt."

"Now Jason, Melinda is a beautiful woman and it has been difficult for members of my team at times, me included, when our wives work with us. I think you understand what I am saying. Both of you are courageous and well trained warriors but you seriously need to realize whether you can keep control of your emotions."

"I want you to take a couple of days to think about all of this and if you come back to us and say you can't keep your emotions under control we won't be sending you home. We will assign you to different teams for a while."

"Jealousy isn't the only emotion you have to consider. All three of us sitting before you have our wives working with us and we know this is a difficult thing. It is natural to worry about the safety of someone you care about. Do either of you have any questions at this point?"

"No but I want to say that Melinda and I are already discussing these things. Her behavior over Thor and Tanya scared her and she is trying to come to terms with all of that. But I want you to know that both of us consider being on the teams a great honor and we don't want to compromise anything. We already decided that if we were on the same team and felt we couldn't be professional that we would ask to be reassigned," explained Jason.

"I think we are all glad to hear that," said Edward. "In the meantime I would like both of you to train with my other members. The type of training we are doing now is to teach everyone to work together. Every warrior here is an independent person. And most have very strong personalities. While this makes great warriors it can hamper the dynamics of a team."

"Melinda, I hope you already understand that you are a permanent member of our family," said Gabriel. "If you decide you don't want to be on a team, you will always have a home with us."

"What took you so long?" asked Michael as he and Raul walked out to the horses with Drake and Tally. "Simon already took the kids home."

"We'll tell ya as soon as we start out," said Drake.

"Did something happen?" Raul asked.

"Not really sure," said Tally with half a grin. "Emeral takes us on a tour and the whole time she is telling us about her family here then as soon as we get in a place where there ain't any other people she pretty much tells us that she and Renya will kick our asses if we are conning all of you."

Raul and Michael roared with laughter. "Don't you laugh because believe me they could do it," said Raul.

"Oh we weren't laughing," said Drake. "Because she no sooner says that than she starts talking about Michael and his sisters. Michael it ain't our business but why didn't you and the girls come here before? I mean besides your blood family, those people in that house would go to war to protect all of ya."

Michael didn't say anything he just stared at Drake, who continued talking. "I mean all of you are so much better off here. It's a damn shame they didn't take all of you in before this."

Michael sounded emotional when he spoke. "Mother didn't tell me or the girls about Sudfad until she was dying. And she never told him about us. I was so full of hate that I didn't even think about the girls; I rode straight here to kill him. I hated him because he was powerful enough to save us and he never did." Michael now tried to joke, "I charged into the castle and they were all eating. You should have seen all of our faces when we saw each other." Michael stopped talking and glanced at Raul.

"So what happened?" asked Tally.

"I didn't believe Sudfad at first when he said he didn't know about me but he claimed me on the spot and Renya told me I was home. Then I don't really know what happened to me. The only reason I survived Karzman was I refused to die at his hands. My rage kept me alive and it was like it all drained out of me in that dining room. Honestly it was like I didn't know who I was for a while. Ask Raul if you don't believe me."

"It was an adjustment for us all for different reasons," said Raul. "But what surprised Simon and me was how much a like we all are. Michael fit right into the family."

"Michael, we know there is a lot you never knew but your real mama and her mama got hurt a lot trying to protect all of you. She was desperate to get all of you away from Karzman; why didn't she tell you about your real daddy sooner?" Drake asked.

Both Michael and Raul stared at Tally and Drake. "I don't know," said Michael in a hoarse whisper.

After dinner that night Raul, Simon and Michael met with Sudfad in his study. It was Raul who repeated Drake's and Tally's words because Michael was clearly upset. "Both Michael and I believe them," said Raul. "But there was just something about them saying how desperate Nadia was. Father is there more to all of this than we know? I mean she sounds like she would have done anything to protect her children. Wouldn't you think she would have found a way to contact you?"

Sudfad poured each of his sons a glass of whiskey and did not speak until he returned to his seat. "It is difficult for me to talk about Nadia in front of Renya. I really loved Nadia and she broke my heart when she sent me away. But we never had any type of falling out. We certainly didn't harbor any bad feelings for each other. And it breaks my heart too that she didn't contact me. Michael, you don't have to believe this but I would have come for all of you."

"I know," Michael said in a whisper.

"I have no idea why she didn't reach out to me," said Sudfad sadly. "I hope she didn't think that I had turned into a monster and would not protect her and her children."

"Father, I wasn't there," said Simon. "So I didn't hear it but both Michael and Raul are haunted by those words. I know all of you are emotional but I think we should call to the Angels. I mean I understand why Michael and you are upset but look at Raul he is so upset too. I know there is more to this." Sudfad nodded.

"Angels..." was as far as Simon got with his sentence before Adam and Ruth appeared.

"This is the Angel Adam," said Michael. "He took my place in many fights when I was a kid; to save me."

"We hate to bother you," said Sudfad but Ruth interrupted him.

"On the contrary we all feel you should call to us more often," said Ruth. "Sometimes when you fail to call to us we have to give you little reminders; like a strange or overwhelming feeling. We have been listening to you talk. Sudfad first, Nadia never stopped loving you and she was terrified that Karzman and his demons would destroy you. She never though you would turn your back on her; she felt she would be leading you into a trap."

"But I am the King, my armies greatly outnumber anything that Karzman has. She was a very bright woman; certainly she understood that."

"She understood more than you realize," said Adam. "But before we get into that I find it curious that no one ever talks about Michael's half-brothers."

"Because we want to kill them for what they did to the girls," said Raul emotionally.

"But they are a part of all of this," said Adam. "You have all been thinking that we forced that entire family to be tortured to fulfill a prophesy." Every man in the room now looked guilty. "We did not. Tally and Drake did not join Karzman when he first conquered Nadia's people. While they have been honest with you there is much they do not know. And while I am on the subject of Drake and Tally, they have never been good men but they have changed greatly since they become involved with all of you. Michael, like you they are experiencing a new life and they are accepting it without hesitation. Something for you to think about."

"Nadia knew terror from the moment she met Karzman, she saw the demon in him. He raped her and brutalized her from their first night together. She knew she was pregnant with Sudfad's baby and didn't want Karzman to hurt it."

"When the spirit of Michael's grandmother showed Zoya unholy altars there was a reason. Like many abusers, Karzman felt powerful when he saw fear in the eyes of others. He would torment Nadia and others in front of her. We spoke to her but she dismissed our voices."

"Michael one night in order to save your life she agreed to denounce The Great Ruler. She prayed for forgiveness but she was so filled with guilt that she was afraid The Great Ruler would punish her and her family. She would never listen to our voices again and she never prayed or called us in. Like many victims Nadia started to believe that she was worthless and deserved the treatment she was getting but she always knew that you were special. You were her only child who was created out of love. All of the others were conceived after rape."

"As soon as both Torin and Cabal were born, Karzman took them from their mother and placed them as offerings to Ahriman. This was a price he had to pay for power. Although Nadia did not know what Karzman had done she could instantly see the darkness in her sons and it terrified her. She believed she was giving birth to demons which made her even more fearful that she would be punished by The Great Ruler. She never told any of you to call to us because she was afraid you would suffer for her sins."

"Then when I would replace you in the cage and kill the hell beasts he sent after you, Nadia was afraid that you too was cursed by Karzman's darkness; even though we kept whispering the truth to her. Nadia loved her children and the people of her village. She sacrificed greatly for everyone else. But after a while she was so broken and hopeless that she could not think of anything more than to survive one more day. There was not a plot for her not to contact Sudfad. It never occurred to Nadia. And if it had, she might have been too ashamed to let Sudfad see her."

Sudfad and his sons continued to stare at Adam even after he stopped speaking. "There are several reasons that Adam told you this," said Ruth. "First, you can never believe that we let atrocities happen to fulfill prophesies. Secondly, even though Raul and Simon never met Nadia all of you are filled with guilt. Ask The Great Ruler to help you let go of this guilt because it can cripple you. It certainly crippled Nadia. And the final reason is that you have not even attempted to identify Torin and Cabal as powerful enemies."

"You were told that Torin would kill his father for power but Samael would not allow it. There are other ways to have Karzman killed. They are plotting how to have you or your soldiers kill their father. Samael is keeping Karzman weak and desperate for now as both a game and a punishment. But that will not always be the case. You already know that many demons would destroy you and here they have three men who are begging to do their will. Don't you think the demons would use them?"

"Sudfad, you plan to attack Karzman and your sons have wisely warned you that you will be riding into a trap. They know your army is powerful so how do they believe they can win?" asked Adam.

"With the help of demons," said Simon.

"Keep going," said Adam.

"Karzman will do something to weaken Sudfad or to throw him off his game," said Michael. "Is that why his spies are here?"

"We will talk about the spies in a moment but Michael continue with that line of thought," said Adam.

"He knows we are expecting him to attack us," said Raul.

Michael was deep in thought when the blood suddenly drained from his face. "You said he feels powerful when he sees the fear in the eyes of his victims. He will go after the defenseless until Sudfad comes for him. But it will have to be big enough attacks to get Sudfad's attention. Do you know who he is going after and when we leave will the spies go after my sisters?"

"Michael, you understand the mind of the beast," said Adam. "That is why you are such a danger to him. He will act as a coward and kill innocents if you don't stop him first. As we speak he is sending his spies out to gather information."

"How much time do I have?" Sudfad asked anxiously.

"How much time do you need?" asked Adam. "You know there will be powerful demons there."

"We heard about you and Miranda in Ganz. Will you ride with us?" asked Simon.

"You will have the time you need now," Adam said. As the Angel spoke Miranda and Daniel appeared in the room."

"As you have been speaking," said Miranda. "Sampson, son of Chief Duncan has been systematically killing all of Karzman's men on your land."

"What!" yelled Raul. "Is he still a demon?"

"No, Samael saved him from that fate and returned him to the human form you are familiar with, then Samael sent him here. Sampson had sold his soul to other demons and does not currently remember that or know that Samael now owns him. He does not hear the demon's voice but Samael can see through Sampson's eyes. He doesn't even know why he is here or who any of you are. He just knows he must watch you."

"He knows us," said Simon.

"He has lost a great deal of his memories," continued Miranda. "But he did recognize the uniforms of the Venatores that were here a few days ago."

"Vivian!" said Raul.

"He saw her but did not recognize her."

"I don't know this guy but I have heard enough about him," said Michael. "Why would he help us by killing Karzman's men?"

"In his paranoia he believes they are also watching for him," Miranda said. "You would be wise to go to Gabriel's house tonight with this information. Then call together all of the Venatores from the teams. They are the only ones qualified to hunt one of their own. Because of Sampson the threats against your families have been greatly reduced."

"You pleased us all when you chose ruling families," said Daniel. "Your kingdom will be safe in their hands and of course Renya will be helping them. The Sanuri will be returning to Wetpr for the wedding. There will be many guests at your castle and celebrations. That will be a lot of people for spies to watch. Leave Wetpr late at night on the day of the wedding. Since you have asked us along the Sanuri should remain here."

"Will you protect our families while we are gone?" asked Sudfad.

"Yes," said Ruth. "But my sons, you were in Ryed; isn't there something you should be asking?"

"How do we kill Karzman?" asked Raul. "Do we need the Scroll of Imari?"

"No but he and his sons will be more powerful than any humans by time you get there so do not act in haste. Miranda and Adam will ride with you."

"I should be the one to kill that monster," said Sudfad passionately.

"And perhaps you will be," said Ruth. "But what is it that your sons know that you do not?"

"We must ask the Angels to touch us with their holiness," said Simon.

"We know you have many questions and you should be including us in all of your meetings for this mission. But it is getting late and you should go to Gabriel's house. Put Joshua in charge of finding Sampson," said Adam and the Angels vanished.

# Chapter XXXIII
## Listen To Your Son

Thor and Tanya were sitting on the front porch when they heard approaching horses. They both jumped up and grabbed weapons. "It's us," yelled Simon. "We need to have a meeting."

"Is something wrong?" asked Thor as he and Tanya walked up to the riders.

"Yeah, the Angels sent us," said Raul. "And none of you are going to be happy. We are sorry it is so late but they told us to come tonight."

"Everyone is in their chambers," said Thor. "Go into Gabriel's study and we will wake them."

"Thor we know that Vivian and Diana have babies but they need to be there too," said Raul. "Sampson is here."

"What!" said Thor angrily.

"We'll explain everything in the meeting," said Raul as they dismounted.

"Who is Sampson?" asked Tanya.

"I will tell you but we must wake everyone now," said Thor.

Candles were lit all over Gabriel's house so Michael, Simon and Raul easily found their way to Gabriel's study. "I'm going to start pouring drinks because they will need them," said Simon.

"Where are all the dogs?" asked Michael. "They just let us walk in."

"First of all the dogs know you and they sleep with the children," said Gabriel as he entered the room. "Hannah is making coffee."

"We are taking the liberty of pouring drinks," said Simon. "You will need them."

"And we apologize for the time," said Raul.

In less than five minutes all of the adults except for the nurses where in the study. And many of the parents were carrying sleeping children and babies. "Should we wait for Hannah?" asked Simon. "She is making coffee."

"Calen take the baby and I will help her," said Natasha and handed Johnathon to him. Rachel and Batina also left the room. Within minutes all of the women returned with trays.

"I think we should start at the beginning but we will shorten that part up for now," said Raul. "Yesterday we were here and Emeral had a talk with Drake and Tally." Emeral gasped which caused others to smile. "Emeral, you didn't say anything wrong but you made them question a few things then they asked us questions we couldn't answer. We met with Father after dinner and Simon called to the Angels."

"Adam and Ruth came first then Miranda and Daniel. We have to attack Karzman or he is going to butcher villages to get us to ride into a trap. But that is not why we are here. Michael was asking about everyone's safety here when we leave. And Miranda tells us that Sampson is killing all of Karzman's men on our land because he thinks they are watching him too."

"Samael owns his soul but apparently he doesn't know that," explained Simon. "He is back in the form of the man all of you knew. But he doesn't remember a lot. He doesn't even know why he is here. Apparently Samael can see through his eyes and that is something you need to remember. The Angels said that we should meet with all of the Venatores on the teams tomorrow and that Joshua should lead them in searching for Sampson. They said you were the only ones qualified."

"They are right about that," said Joshua. "Is he looking for Vivian?"

"I asked that," Raul said. "Apparently he saw her at the castle and didn't recognize her or any of you but he recognized the clothing of the Venatores. So far Samael has him here to spy on us."

"I know what the Angels said," said Luca. "But Natalie is seven months pregnant. I will go in her place."

"I agree," said Joshua. "And Vivian is pregnant too."

"Oh no you don't," Vivian said. "I'm part of this."

"Then I am going too," said Raphael.

"That might be a problem because all of you are going to be running the kingdom. Of course Mother will help you. Miranda and Adam are riding with us against Karzman and they want us to leave the night of Luca's and Natalie's wedding," said Raul. "We are sorry about the timing of that too."

"Are Micha and Thomas still at Erebus' house?" asked Simon. "I feel strongly that they need to be here."

"We'll get them," said Ratri then he, Dagon, Koby and Misha quickly left the study.

"Does Duncan know any of this?" asked Joshua.

"We don't know," said Simon. "And from what the Angels said it sounded like Sampson has only been watching us. We should have asked them more questions about Sampson but honestly we were focused on Karzman."

"We will call to them," Maxwell said. "So let me understand this. Sampson looks the same but he doesn't have any memories?"

"We don't really know what he does remember," said Raul.

"Miranda!" Vivian said loudly.

Miranda and Ruth appeared. "The others will be here shortly," said Ruth. "We can wait to talk about Sampson when they arrive. When Raul said that you will be running the kingdom fear filled all of your hearts. You will do fine and know that you can call upon us for help. Even if it seems like something minor."

Micha, Bianca, Sasha, Thomas, Dagon, Ratri, Koby and Misha were almost running into the study but slowed down when they saw the Angels.

"Please take your seats," said Miranda.

"We filled them in," Koby said.

"Joshua, you are a dear friend of Duncan's so it is appropriate that you remove the cancer in his family. You should lead the Venatores in this hunt. Sampson has always been a dangerous and powerful man but he is a puppet of Samael's now. All of you need to remember that because you may need our help in destroying him," Ruth explained.

"Wait," said Misha skeptically. "Wouldn't you already know if he can be killed by humans?"

"Timing," Miranda said. "As you know Sampson was greatly damaged when he was going through the rites of transformation. Then the demon Ael turned him into a low level beast. All of these transformations were exceedingly difficult on Sampson. His brain has been damaged. He thinks more like an animal now than a human and that makes him even more dangerous than before. If he gets his memories back before you find him, he will probably call to darkness and in that case he will become a more formidable foe. And Samael may want to save his puppet from you and protect him."

"Will you help us destroy him?" asked Diana.

"Yes," Miranda said.

"You said that Joshua should lead the hunt but does it matter which one of us kills him?" asked Thor.

"No but don't underestimate him," said Ruth. "He may have learned some new tricks from the demons. And if you try to reason with him, remember he was eager to kill his brothers and that was before his mind was damaged."

"Does he know where we live?" Gabriel asked.

"Not yet, but Samael does," said Ruth. "While all of you would die for each other, there is no loyalty among demons. Samael may allow you to kill Sampson just for entertainment. Or at any time he could give Sampson his memories back, or any other information."

"There is more to this; I can tell," Misha said. "Are they going to be fighting Sampson or Samael?"

"Now that is the question," said Miranda. "You are all so emotional about this. Micha, Thomas, you entered Baal's domain. What did we do so you would be able to fight the powerful demons?"

"You touched us with holiness," said Micha. "And we will need to ask for that now."

"Venatores never ask for help," Miranda said. "Joshua listen to your son in this matter."

Since few people could sleep in Gabriel's house after the meeting, Joshua, Thor, Micha and Thomas left several hours before dawn to gather all of the Venatores from the teams. They were all brought back to Gabriel's home. They held a meeting in the dining room until the women needed to set the table for breakfast. The meeting was then moved to Gabriel's study. Edward had accompanied Kate and now he remained in the dining room drinking coffee. Natasha was telling him about the meeting the previous night as she set the breakfast table.

"Did they say if the teams are going with them after Karzman or protecting the kingdom?" asked Edward.

"Honestly it sounded like they just started a meeting with the Angels then were sent over here. They couldn't answer a lot of our questions and when we called to the Angels we just talked about Sampson." Natasha set down a stack of plates and walked very close to Edward. "I don't know if you know the history of Sampson," she said.

"I know the bastard was going to kill his brothers to become a demon."

"He tried to rape Vivian when she was a small child and he has been obsessed with her since. He tried to kill Raphael after they were married. And right after Diana's and Thor's parents were murdered he dragged Diana into the forest and was attacking her when Thor found them. Apparently Thor was only ten but he almost killed Sampson. Joshua stopped them."

"So that is why everyone is so emotional about this. I am glad you told me. I am going to offer our help."

"He is a savage murderer and rapist. And from what I heard last night he has extraordinary skills as a Venator."

As soon as the sun rose Sampson made a fire. The morning was cold and his body was cramped from sleeping in the arms of a tree. He had stolen the possessions of the men he had been killing so he had a large supply of food. He filled a pan with bacon and set it on the fire then everything became black before his eyes. Sampson grabbed his head and collapsed on the ground.

Sampson the fierce warrior and terror of his people lay on the ground and cried as the pains in his head caused his body to spasm. He suddenly remembered his mother before he lost consciousness.

All of the Venatores ate breakfast at Gabriel's house then accompanied Gabriel's team to the castle for the morning meeting. Against their husband's wishes Diana, Vivian and Natalie were with this group and they all brought their babies to the meeting.

Sudfad asked the adult members of his family to attend the meeting as well as Tally and Drake. When Sudfad spoke about the meeting at the breakfast table he did not mention either Karzman's or Sampson's names but it was clear to the family that Sudfad was concerned about immediate threats.

Nyla demanded to attend the meeting. "All of the men at this table look so serious. If this is about Karzman I need to be there. I can help you." Sudfad didn't say anything to Nyla immediately which angered her. "I am going whether you give me permission or not," she said and crossed her arms over her chest in a defiant manner.

Sudfad grinned and said, "You have only been Renya's daughter for a couple of weeks and already you act just like her." Everyone at the table grinned.

"I take that as a complement but don't change the subject. Saran, Nina and I haven't been children for a long time. We love all of you and don't want to see anyone get hurt. We can be of help."

"Not that it's any of my business," said Tally. "But she makes a good point."

"I agree," Matthew said.

"Alright, you can come this morning then we will see after that," said Sudfad.

Michael was staring at his sister during the conversation. "When did you get that fire in you?" he asked with a grin.

Without hesitation Nyla said, "I see things very differently since we escaped. None of us realized there was another world outside of our prison. This world and this family are worth fighting for."

Renya was sitting next to Nyla and now put her arm around the girl and kissed her on the cheek. "That is exactly how we felt when we came here," said Vitomas. "She never had hope before."

The morning meeting was held in the Great Hall. Sudfad started the meeting by telling everyone about their encounter with the Angels the previous night. "We have several issues to discuss and this meeting my run all day. Sampson is our most immediate threat and I will call Joshua up here in a moment. I will be leading troops to attack Karzman in a little over a week and the newly appointed ruling families will be running the kingdom because Simon, Raul and Michael are coming with me. Of course Renya is the Queen and will be in charge."

"I would also like to go," said Matthew.

"While I would love to have you with us," said Sudfad. "We can't discount the fact that there could be attacks against our kingdom and families during this time."

"I would like us to work out as many strategies as possible then I will ask the Angels to join us. And we will ask them about taking all of you on one mission."

The Venatores had the floor of the meeting first. Raul provided them with maps of the royal lands. After a great deal of discussion Joshua asked his group of warriors if any of them thought they could not kill a member of their own tribe.

"He stopped being one of us a long time ago," said Micha. "We saw him in Baal's world. We saw what he chose to become. To me he is just another demon."

Sampson awoke because the pan of meat he had on the fire had burst into flames and smoke was billowing. His first reaction was to grab the pan. He cursed when he burned his hand. He grabbed one of the extra blankets, which he had stolen and used it to protect his hand from the searing handle of the pan. He dumped the meat and grease into the dirt and stomped it out. Then he immediately climbed a tree to see if the smoke had alerted anyone to the location of his campsite.

As Sudfad predicted the meeting ran for hours. The midday meal was served to the attendees in the Great Hall. Mothers would have to periodically leave the room to care for their babies but no one left the castle.

When Sudfad was satisfied with the work that had been accomplished he called to the Angels. Adam and Miranda appeared together. Moments later Ruth and Daniel appeared. As was normal for the Angels they told the men and women to brief them about what they had been discussing and their plans. Then they told the people to ask their questions. The Angels listened to the questions without answering any of them. Then they simply disappeared.

"What the hell!" said Jared. "That was strange. I've never seen them act like that before."

"If they want us to rework things they always tell us," said Edward. "What is different about all of this?"

Suddenly Sudfad jumped in his chair, "That is the key. What is different? He walked to the window and called to some Enrops who were in the garden. "I will be sending messages to all of the forts and Patronus Headquarters in just a few moments and I need a flock to spy on Karzman of the Kozach Tribe. We believe he is going to start attacking farms and villages."

When Melinda heard about Sampson being in the area she returned from her team's house and volunteered to help watch the children at Gabriel's home. The children were glad to see their friend as were Lana and Tanya because these three women feared that Sampson might try to weaken the family by going after the children. Bethany and Marina were teaching medical classes so that Hannah could spend the day at home.

Once the sun warmed the land the children wanted to go outside to play. None of the nurses wanted to let the children out until they heard from the people who were attending the King's meeting. The children were irritated and whining when Elan and Cassandra walked into the playroom.

"We have a project for you today," said Elan with a big grin. "First you have to change into your work clothes. Cassandra and I just moved all of the furniture in Cicely's and Chasity's room. We have different colors of paint and you can all paint pictures on the walls. Then after the paint dries we will have a party in there."

The children cheered and jumped around. "I don't know if I have work clothes," said Cody shyly.

"That is what we call the clothes that has holes in them," said Adrone.

"We have some you can wear," said Paul and the boys ran out of the playroom.

"Well, you certainly win the prize today," Natasha said to Elan and Cassandra. "I'll start making treats for the party."

"Are you going to watch the children?" asked Lana. "Because Batina and Rachel are searching the property for any sign of intruders and if this Sampson is as bad as they say, Tanya and I would like to help them."

"Go," said Cassandra. "And be careful."

Sampson was not aware of the beautiful young warriors who were hunting him on Gabriel's lands. If he had seen them he would have been both amused and intrigued.

When he was convinced that no one was coming towards his campsite, Sampson climbed down from the tree. The ground was covered with his vomit. He kicked dirt over it and put some more bacon in the frying pan he had stolen. Sampson was starving."

The meeting ended late afternoon. Every man and woman in the meeting understood that the unusual behavior of the Angels meant they had work to do. And that possibly they were looking at the situations with Sampson and Karzman from the wrong points of view. So they discussed every issue in detail but by the end of the meeting they were again convinced they would be fighting two soulless monsters.

The following morning King Mathas read Sudfad's letters in the morning meeting. "I will need to return to Wetpr," said the Sanuri. "Has Tanner been contacted by Deckor yet?"

"We may have spooked him off when we made that scene in the Lady's Slipper," said Thaos. "Don't wait around here if you're needed in Wetpr. We will call to the Angels if we need help."

"I really feel that I must leave at once," said the Sanuri. "We'll take Hilgra with us so she can study Juleta's books with the other healers. Then perhaps one of you can bring her back after the wedding."

"Do you think it's safe for us to bring our families to Wetpr now?" asked Gideon.

"I believe the Angels would have warned us. They keep stressing the importance of everyone getting to know and trust each other. They have said we will need that strength to face the days ahead," said the Sanuri.

An hour after Mathas' meeting ended the Sanuri, Erebus and Hilgra started their journey to the Kingdom of Wetpr. The Sanuri prayed to the heavens for protection since he was carrying the books that Hector would kill for.

The commanding generals of the forts in Wetpr had not yet received their letters from Sudfad which detailed the expected terrorist attacks by the Kozach Tribe. But fortunately for the villagers of Bransong a company of soldiers were preforming a routine patrol near their village.

Fort Serpha was one of the newest forts to be built in the kingdom. Commanding General Farnsworth was a superior soldier and an old childhood friend of Sudfad's. Farnsworth not only commanded Fort Serpha but was responsible for its construction.

He choose the location so he could guard the northern border of the kingdom and be near the lands owned by the Kozach Tribe. Even before Michael's identity was revealed, Karzman had a reputation as a murderous barbarian. While it was normal to send platoons on routine patrols, Farnsworth sent entire companies. He knew it was just a matter of time before Karzman caused serious trouble in the area.

Since Farnsworth was a close family friend, both Sudfad and Renya wrote to him often. He knew that the Royal Couple had adopted Michael and his sisters and he knew that Karzman was seeking revenge and threatening a war with Sudfad.

Farnsworth made sure his patrols communicated with the local citizens. This was done to make the people feel safe and to obtain information. Word of Karzman's threats against the King were spreading through the northcentral communities like a wild fire.

It was common knowledge that Karzman did not have an army large enough to support his threats. For Karzman to increase his military he would have to hire mercenaries or abduct local citizens. Karzman decided to do both.

Bransong was an extremely large village. It sat on the eastern border of the lands of the Kozach Tribe. It was a community of loggers and miners; the kind of men who did not roll over easily for an insane tyrant.

The citizens of the northcentral areas of Wetpr welcomed the construction of Fort Serpha and the soldiers, not only for the protection they provided but for their contributions to the local economies. The logging operations of Bransong provided all of the lumber for the construction of the fort.

Lieutenant Murphy was leading his company of men south along the eastern border of the Kozach lands when he saw huge dark plumes of smoke billowing in the air. He sent two men back to Fort Serpha to get reinforcements then he turned his troops west and they rode hard to the Village of Bransong.

Torin, the eldest son of Karzman was leading the attack against the village. He was so accustomed to intimidating people that he was not prepared for the active resistance of the citizens of Bransong. They had anticipated an attack and had built towers outside of the village. The people manning the towers could see for a long distance and would warn the villagers of advancing troops.

Torin never considered attacking under the cloak of darkness. He had an inflated ego like his father and expected the citizens of Bransong to bow before him. In his arrogance he never sent scouts ahead to survey the village. And when his army rode past the towers he never considered their significance. Torin had no element of surprise but the would-be victims did.

Torin led his men over many fallen trees and piles of dried brush as they neared the western boundary of the village. He ordered his men to charge as soon as they were within sight of Bransong.

Once the mercenaries entered the village, arrows rained down upon them from every window of every building. Loggers ignited a ring of trees and brush to prevent the escape of the soulless army. The same trees and brush that the invading army had ridden over.

Miners and loggers attacked Torin's men with axes, hatchets and other tools of their trades. Horses were rearing and screaming as volleys of arrows were shot at their riders. Torin was hit in the left shoulder and the right thigh. He never considered the villagers would actually fight back. He momentarily panicked and turning he saw a wall of fire that blocked his men from returning to their village.

In the din and chaos of this battle the Horn of Cass was blown over and over by the soldiers to let the villagers know they were not alone. Murphy gave the order and his men separated; two thirds of them surrounded the village as he led another group straight into the fight. Torin's men were outnumbered three to one now and many of them tried to escape from the village. While most of the villagers were on foot the soldiers were on horseback and chased down the mercenaries.

When the battle was over, Murphy had his soldiers and the villagers search the buildings. Another dozen of Torin's men were found hiding. Torin was found in a barn. The soldiers didn't know his identity when they dragged him down the street to their Lieutenant.

Many of the villagers yelled and cursed when they saw Torin. They wanted to burn him alive. But Murphy saw the value of Torin as possible leverage against his father.

Two companies of soldiers arrived with orders from Farnsworth to stay and protect the village. This move was radical for Farnsworth to make since Bransong was within the boundaries of the lands of the Kozach Tribe. He sent Enrops with a note for Sudfad. *The war has started with the Kozach Tribe. I will send more details after this battle in the Village of Bransong has ended.*

## Chapter XXXIV
## A Sky Filled With Stars

Sudfad was not the only one who Farnsworth sent messages to. He alerted the other forts, the monasteries and the Patronus priests of Torin's attack on Bransong.

Lieutenant Murphy had the prisoners locked in the dungeons. He provided them with medical care because he didn't know if any of them would be useful. Then Murphy reported to Farnsworth.

"At ease Lieutenant," said Farnsworth as he handed Murphy a glass of whiskey. "Take a seat and tell me what happened."

"First I should tell you that we have twelve prisoners in the dungeons, including Torin. The villagers were tearing his men apart when we arrived. We found him hiding in the hay of a barn. The villagers wanted to burn him alive and the bastard shit himself. Honestly I don't think he believed anyone would stand up to him. I'll say I give those villagers credit. They planned and executed an assault and even prevented Torin's army from escaping. This ought to open Karzman's eyes that the world isn't made up of victims."

Commanding General Farnsworth believed in The Great Ruler. After his meeting with Lieutenant Murphy, Farnsworth prayed for more Enrops. He prayed that the Enrops carrying his messages would have safe and speedy journeys and lastly he prayed for The Great Ruler to give him what he needed to protect the citizens of Wetpr. Then Farnsworth left his office to supervise the interrogations of the prisoners.

None of Torin's men returned to their village. Karzman assumed they were delayed because they were plundering Bransong. But after two days he knew something was wrong and sent some men to that village.

Karzman could not believe his ears when his men told him the Village of Bransong was intact and filled with Wetprian soldiers.

"Did you find any bodies?" yelled Karzman.

"We couldn't get that close. There were hundreds of soldiers everywhere we looked," said one of his hired killers.

There were not feelings of concern for his son or his soldiers that prompted Karzman's question. Karzman was fearful that if any of his men were alive they would betray him. He marched to his unholy altar.

Samael hated humans. He believed they were created for the amusement of the demons. He watched Torin's pitiful defeat and cursed him for being a coward and an idiot. Samael was enraged not because he had believed that Torin would be a better soldier for him but all of the men he had put into positions of power were weak and disappointing.

Samael knew he needed a leader among the humans to stand up against the Kings of Wetpr and Lentz and against The Seven Sons. Samael poured himself a drink and sat down to reevaluate his strategies.

After two days of intense hunting Joshua and his Venatores found no signs of Sampson other than three more bodies of Karzman's men.

"I am beginning to wonder if Samael is hiding him from us," said Joshua with frustration.

"Well, on the good side he is killing these other bastards," said Kate.

"Father, I keep telling you that you have to use me as bait," said Vivian.

"He doesn't remember you," said Thor. "So it's a useless plan until he does."

Hilgra, Erebus and the Sanuri were all crowded into the front seat of the boca. "I may be paranoid," said Hilgra as she looked around. "But does anyone else feel like we are being watched?"

"Yes," said Erebus. "And I know that he does too because he keeps looking up at the Enrops."

The Sanuri smiled at Erebus's observation. "I think on some level we are always being watched. If we travel straight through we will reach Salar by nightfall. I would assume if we are going to be attacked they will want to get us before we reach our destination." The Sanuri looked up at the Enrops again and moments later eight of them left the flock that was flying over the boca and sped ahead.

"What just happened?" asked Hilgra.

"I asked them to tell Sudfad to send troops to meet us," replied the Sanuri.

Although Sudfad had been meeting with his leaders almost constantly over the previous two days he had not called to the Angels to join them. During that forty-eight hours Sudfad had received numerous notes from General Farnsworth which he shared at his meetings. Renya and Nyla attended all of these meetings.

"I am surprised that our men couldn't get more information from those soldiers," said Simon. "Perhaps we should send them some truth potion."

"Karzman is a very paranoid man and he has gotten worse over the years," said Tally. "He doesn't share any information with his soldiers until just before he needs them to do something. Those men probably don't have much good information."

"But wouldn't you think Torin would?" asked Matthew. "And from the way Farnsworth describes him, it sounds like all Torin is, is a big mouthed coward."

"The Angels did say that Torin wants his father's power," said Raphael. "So Karzman probably keeps him in the dark too."

Nyla looked destressed when she spoke, "If they want Torin to talk they should scare him with spiders."

"What?" asked Raul.

"Karzman used to lock Torin and Cabal under the porch to punish them. There were huge spiders under there that bit them. They both got sick from spider bites but he kept punishing them that way. Torin is terrified of spiders."

"I never realized he punished them too," said Michael.

"He punished everyone," said Nyla with tears forming in her eyes.

Several Enrops flew into the room. "We have a message from the Sanuri, he, Erebus and Hilgra are just hours away and are asking that you send soldiers to meet them. They carry the books that Hector wants and they sense that something is wrong." Raul, Simon and Matthew jumped out of their seats and ran out of the room. In his haste Matthew knocked over his chair.

Nyla picked it up and asked, "Why did they run like that?"

"Because the Sanuri never asks for help," said Gabriel. "He has faced armies of demons by himself. They knew it must be bad for him to ask for soldiers."

"How does he fight all those demons?" asked Nyla.

"He prays for help," said Raphael.

"Well maybe he did and that's why our brothers are going," said Nyla.

Karzman did not hear the voices of demons, at least not with his ears. Every day he prayed at his unholy altar and offered sacrifices and every morning he awoke in the same feeble and broken body. Because he didn't get any of the things he bargained for, Karzman believed the demons did not hear him.

As much as Karzman had always hated Teivel, he could count on Teivel to provide him with what he needed. Karzman now sat in his kitchen and gulped down several glasses of whiskey.

Cabal entered the kitchen and sat down at the table, "Give me that," he said, indicating the bottle of whiskey. Karzman handed his son the bottle and Cabal filled one of the filthy glasses that was stacked on the table. "This place is a pigsty since those girls left," he said with disgust.

"And just how the hell did they escape?" growled Karzman. "You and your worthless brother would kill me for my position and you can't even watch your sisters. Neither of you will ever be able to rule these lands."

Cabal was enraged by his father's words but said nothing for several minutes. "Are we going after Torin?"

"You mean attack the fort? You really are crazy," yelled Karzman.

"Aren't we going to save him?"

"First, we don't have the manpower and second, he got what he deserves. He is a worthless fool; you both are."

"You've never given a shit about any of us, but aren't you at least a little concerned that he will talk?"

"And what would the pussy say? I know he wants to overthrow me so I don't tell him jack."

"You know what your problem is Father? You always underestimate us. Torin isn't stupid; he knows a lot more than you think."

"Well apparently he doesn't know how to lead a damn battle. From what I heard the villagers were kicking his ass before the soldiers even got there. So tell me, how is he so damn smart?"

Cabal wanted to spit the answer into his father's face but he stopped himself. He did not want to give Karzman any advantage in his rivalry with Torin. Cabal stared angrily then smiled, "You will see Father, you will see."

Unlike his older brother Torin, Cabal still feared his father, even in the shape Karzman was currently in. Although he hated Karzman he followed in his father's footsteps. Cabal was a cruel and hateful person. A man without a conscious, a man who sold his soul.

Cabal was a large and powerful man who could easily have beaten his father in Karzman's weakened condition but on a subconscious level he still saw Karzman with the eyes of a child. Karzman beat and terrorized all of his children although he was considerably worse to his stepson Michael.

Torin too hated his father and fantasied about killing him. But something always stopped Torin, something he did not understand; that something was the demon Samael.

Samael was punishing Karzman by not returning him to his former vigor and power. Samael did this for a couple of reasons and one was his own amusement. The other reason was that Samael understood that Karzman was a headstrong ego maniac and Samael wanted to teach him who was boss. Samael planned on returning Karzman's vitality, he just hadn't figured out the timing that would be most beneficial to him.

But now Samael was scrutinizing Karzman more closely as he was Sampson and several other men who he owned. Samael wanted a strong and invincible leader to take charge of his human forces. At first Samael thought that person might be Hector but he had disappointed Samael several times.

As the great demon thought about the humans he was considering he started to smile and then to laugh. "I need to have them compete for the position. Perhaps I should hold a Gefrey Game of sorts."

Raul, Matthew and Simon rode fast and hard. They led one thousand soldiers eastward and crossed the border into Lentz before noon. Once they crossed the border Matthew called to Enrops to lead them to the Sanuri.

Emeral walked into the dining room after the rest of the family and team had started to eat their midday meal. "Where have you been?" asked Maxwell. "We were starting to worry."

Before she answered the question Emeral glanced over at the children sitting around their smaller table. "Good Lord, they are covered in paint." The children giggled.

"Don't change the subject," Maxwell said with a grin.

"Well, I don't really want to say in front of all these little ears. I was shopping with Alexander. He came up with some clever ideas of things he wants to build for the children for the wedding reception. But since time is short he wants Sam and Horace to help him. So I stopped at the house and told Horace before I came home."

"Does he want me at his shop?" asked Sam.

"Yes and wait until you find out what he wants to build. He is also going to need a few people with artistic talent to help him," Emeral said with a sly smile.

"I'll go with Sam and find out what Alexander needs," said Joao. "Then I will let the rest of you know."

"This all sounds so mysterious," Natasha said with a grin. "And speaking of mysteries; any sign of Sampson?"

"No," said Joshua with disgust. "He is still killing Karzman's men so we know he is on the lands but either his skills have greatly improved or that demon is helping him."

"I don't really understand how all of that works," said Hannah. "I mean with the rites of transformation and whatever else happened to Sampson. The Angels said that he looks like he did when he lived in your village but is it possible he isn't totally back to his old self?"

"I'm not saying this well. But perhaps he isn't totally in his human form or he can't hold it at times. Remember what the Sanuri told us about Roch when he returned from Ahriman's hell? You could be seeing his tracks and not realizing it. Are all of you looking at me like that because you think I am crazy or on to something?"

"Actually we think you are brilliant," said Misha. "Everyone including the Angels have been telling us how emotional we are; I think our emotions may be hindering us."

Raphael was sitting between Vivian and Hannah and now leaned over and kissed Hannah on the cheek then said with a grin, "Sorry Gabriel."

"Gabriel, we may all be kissing her," said Joshua. "But a lot of us were not on that mission. Tell us about Roch."

"Roch was pulled into Ahriman's hell world. If you want to know why that is a very long story that I can tell you later tonight. He was tortured and at some point Ahriman asked Roch if he would align with the demons and become the torturer. Well, apparently he jumped at the chance. It is my understanding that he excelled in this area and made some big promises to Ahriman who dumped him back into this world. But Ahriman didn't do Roch any favors."

"Roch had no memories, he was naked in the forest and his body literally kept changing forms. Sometimes he looked human, other times he was almost transparent and yet other times he appeared as the demon that he finally transformed into."

"How do you know this?" asked Thor.

"The Angels told us some of it," said Raphael. "But Zoya had a vision that he was back so the Sanuri sent flocks of Enrops to look for him. The Enrops and other creatures told the Sanuri."

"If I remember right I think some spirits told Zoya that too," said Elan.

"So how long was he like that?" asked Thomas.

"Six or eight weeks," said Gabriel. "When we first found him he looked like a human but Ibula spied on him one night and he appeared as a demon then changed back to human form. She spoke to him and he didn't realize he had been in a demon form."

"Why did she talk to him?" asked Batina.

"Gabriel devised this ingenious plan to basically drive him crazy enough to expose himself," said Calen and chuckled. "Ibula and Hannah dressed in the same clothes as Vitomas and all three women would show up then disappear. He thought he was seeing ghosts."

"How did they disappear?" Rachel asked.

"Most of the time it was one of us grabbing them and flying away," said Koby and laughed.

"That is the mission where Elan got hurt," Cassandra said. "I thought he was going to die. If you don't mind I am going to change the subject. The more you talk about Roch the more probable it seems that Sampson could be going through something like that too. Was there anything else?"

"Apparently when he was almost transparent his body wouldn't hold him up so he had to crawl on the ground," said Dagon.

"We need to really look at this with new eyes," Thor said.

"We are glad to see you," said Raul with relief when they met the Sanuri on the road.

"We're glad to see you too," Erebus said. "Some strange things have been happening."

"Have you been attacked?" asked Matthew.

"Not by humans," the Sanuri said. "Twice the ground opened up before us. But no demons came out. Then a flock of some kind of birds that weren't from this world tried to fly inside of the boca. I think someone suspects I have something they want or know where it is."

The Princes were well aware that the Sanuri did not mention the books specifically.

"Do you think something could be listening to us?" asked Simon.

"Anything is possible," Erebus said.

"If you're listening and you want to fight, we're here!" yelled Raul.

"Why did I know he was going to do that?" the Sanuri asked with a grin. Everyone waited but no response came from the demons.

"That's what I thought," yelled Raul sarcastically. "You're cowards."

"And you are a fool," said an unfamiliar voice.

Everyone quickly looked around suspecting an army of demons would appear but instead a young boy materialized on the ground at the front of the boca.

"Who are you? What are you?" asked Simon.

"My name is Thot and I am an emissary of The Great Ruler."

"Are you an Angel?" asked Matthew.

The boy smiled, "No, I am another version of the Sanuri."

"What do you mean another version and where do you come from?" Raul asked.

"While those questions have merit we don't have time for social conversation. Great wars are going on in other worlds because of what is happening here. And eyes that never cared to watch you before now study what is happening in Nunc so they can prevent it in their worlds. I recently learned something and the Angel Adam has helped me to transport to different worlds so I can help."

"Everyone talks about the demons watching you from other worlds or even hell worlds in Nunc. But they don't have the abilities to see through time and space as Angels do so they can't see you in the manner you think. They can't see you as you and I see each other now." Thot could see the looks of confusion on the faces of the men.

"They have put spells upon you so they can be aware of your locations. Think of a sky filled with stars. Some are larger and brighter and some fall. That is how they see you. And the books you carry have that spell on them also. The Angels have been protecting you. But this was found in a cave in my world."

Thot was wearing the robe of a priest and now pulled a piece of flat rock out of his pocket. Matthew was the closest to him and dismounted and walked up to Thot. "This is a purification rite that will cleanse you from those spells. It takes away their power to see you but it doesn't keep them from you. You and your people would be wise to perform this rite once a week. The Sanuri can translate it for you. Once you are cleansed it is like a sky without stars."

"What has happened to the Sanuri?" gasped Erebus. "Is he in a trance?"

"He is alright," said Thot. "I can't explain it but he and I are somehow connected and it affects time when we both appear in the same spot. Tell him what I have said."

"Is this your only copy?" asked Matthew as he looked at the strange markings on the stone.

"No, the Angels have made more. You are surrounded by demons but the Angels are blocking them from reaching you. Adam is waiting for you to call him." Thot disappeared and in that instance the Sanuri came out of his trance.

"We have a lot to tell you," Simon said to the Sanuri but we have to call to Adam first."

"Adam!" yelled Raul.

"Before any of you say a word," said Adam as he appeared. "Only the most powerful demons can send creatures from other worlds or open the doors to hell. These are not the kind of demons you can fight, at least not without our help."

"Wouldn't the Sanuri know that?" asked Erebus.

"He does and he prayed for protection," Adam said. "But he sensed that another emissary was coming. One all of you needed to meet."

"So are Thot and the Sanuri the same person?" asked Raul.

"No," said the Sanuri. "But it is very difficult to explain. Although I was basically unconscious I did hear everything that was said. Please show me the stone." The Sanuri's facial expression changed several times as he translated the language. Then he looked at Adam. "Is this from our future?"

"No," it is from the past of a world that was very similar to Nunc. That world lost its fight with the demons. Before all of the holy men were killed they buried the holy objects to keep them out of the hands of the demons. Thot has been living in caves and is finding these treasures. As soon as he realized the importance of that tablet he called to me to spread the message to others. I decided it might be time for you to realize that what we keep telling you are not wild stories."

"Is he from the past?" Erebus asked.

"No, The Great Ruler is always sending little lights into the darkness. Thot is a light. Now tell me, do you want me to unleash the demons that surround you?"

Both Raul and Simon looked at Adam as if they thought it was a trick question. Adam laughed. "While we want to say yes, what would you suggest?" asked Raul.

"I am impressed," Adam said. "I would say your message would have more of an impact if I hurled them back to the demon that sent them."

"You can do that?" asked Hilgra.

Adam smiled but did not answer her question. "What is your answer?" he asked Raul.

"What you think is best."

Suddenly all of the soldiers grabbed their swords as thousands of demons appeared around them. As soon as they were seen the demons were blown away by a tremendous wind that did not affect the humans.

"You used wisdom here and you were not blinded by pride or your emotions. Remember that, for you will be in such situations again," the Angel said and disappeared.

# Chapter XXXV
## Torin

General Farnsworth was pleased that Sudfad supported his decision to keep troops stationed in Bransong and the citizens of this village were overjoyed. Everyday villagers would walk up to the soldiers and give them things to eat and drink as well as to invite them into their homes. And the soldiers liked and respected the villagers especially after their defiance of Torin and his men.

Farnsworth was not a man to torture his prisoners but he was getting frustrated with the lack of information his men were obtaining from Torin and his men. Farnsworth thought hard about the letter he had received from Sudfad that told of Torin's fears; finally the General decided to give it a try. He called one of his sergeants into his office.

"Sergeant McAvoy, I need some spiders, some big ass spiders," Farnsworth said with a grin.

The Sergeant wasn't sure if his superior was joking with him. "I am not sure that I understand Sir."

"Torin's sister said that he is terrified of spiders and he will tell us anything to avoid them. Got any ideas?"

"There are caves about ten miles from here, towards the ocean with spiders like no man has ever laid eyes on."

"Can you catch some?"

"Sir, the spider webs are bigger than horses. I think we will need to take the prisoner there. I'm not afraid of spiders and when I saw the web that crosses the front entrance I'll tell you a chill ran down my spine. I don't think we have to show him a spider, the web will do just fine."

"Just how damn big are these spiders?"

"I haven't seen one but some of the men have and they claim they are about fifty pounds. Of course I thought they were exaggerating but the locals will tell you the same story."

"I am coming with you; I want to see this."

Karzman was pacing around the kitchen of his small house. He had been drinking all night and was still drunk in the early morning hours. He had waited until Cabal left the house then he searched his son's room. Karzman was convinced that Torin and Cabal had something of importance that they were going to use against him; Karzman just had no idea what it could be. The search of the room did not uncover anything of importance or even of interest.

Karzman had planned on leaving Torin to his fate but now he considered helping his son to escape; or having Torin killed so that he couldn't talk. Either idea was a dangerous and an almost impossible feat to accomplish since Torin was in the dungeons of the huge and well protected fort.

The Sanuri, Hilgra and Erebus were already seated in the Great Hall when the other people arrived for Sudfad's morning meeting. As soon as the last person entered the room the Sanuri stood up and began to pray over them all. While the prayers only took a few minutes the men and women in the room felt a change in the energy as well as a slight change in themselves.

"What did you just do?" asked Gabriel. "Something actually seems different."

"That was a purification rite and I will be teaching it to all of you," said the Sanuri. "We learned that the demons can't see us from a distance like we were thinking. They put spells on us so they can track us. This rite destroys those spells but it has to be performed on a regular basis. I would suggest you say the prayer everyday perhaps at your morning meal. Now you are going to want to fill those cups with coffee because we have a great deal to tell you."

Karzman sent some of his soldiers to spy on Fort Serpha. This handful of men were supposed to identify any weaknesses that they might be able to exploit to get to Torin.

Torin had no illusions that his father would try to help him escape and at first this revelation filled him with anger. But as he sat in his cell, Torin realized that if the situation was reversed he would allow his father to rot in prison.

Torin was both surprised and suspicious when soldiers came to get him. Normally two soldiers would escort him to the room for the questioning but now there were five. "Am I to be executed?" he asked with a hoarse voice.

"Actually we're taking you for a ride," said one of the soldiers with a grin.

"A ride," repeated Torin. "Where? Why?"

"You ask a lot of questions," said the soldier who had unlocked the cell door. "We are gonna tie your hands; for your sake don't try anything."

Torin did not trust the soldiers and was surprised when he saw a company of men mounted on horses, waiting for him outside of the dungeons. Torin's arms were tied behind his back so two soldiers put him on top of his horse. Another soldier maintained the reins of the horse. "Are you taking me to my father?" Torin asked but no one answered him. Torin's village was west of the fort. As soon as the soldiers exited the gates they headed north and Torin had no idea why.

Karzman's men had just hidden in the forest surrounding the fort when they saw the company of soldiers leave. They saw the Commanding General and they saw Torin; the men knew something unusual was happening.

"I don't know what the hell is going on," said Dillon the leader of this small band of men. "But Trace ride back and tell the old man. And does anyone have a clue why they are traveling north?"

Trace mounted his horse and left to tell Karzman. Dillon and the others followed the soldiers.

After the first hour of Sudfad's meeting Erebus and Hilgra left. They went to the reinforced barn where Sudfad stored items he didn't want brought into the castle. Gala, Shara and Angelina were waiting outside of the building.

"The books are inside," said Erebus as he met the women. After he introduced them all he said, "We need to say a protection prayer."

"We already did," said Shara. "You should before you even go in there."

Hilgra looked surprised but she too prayed for protection. The group went into the building and lit candles. The windows were covered so no sunlight entered the barn. "This is really nice," said Angelina with obvious surprise. "This is a study. I will start a fire in the hearth."

The group had left the door to the building open to give them some light. "I have a tray for you from Marie," said a soldier who appeared in the doorway. Hilgra was the closest to the door and walked up to the soldier.

"Hilgra stay back!" yelled Erebus and stared at the soldier as he was walking towards him. Angelina and Shara didn't know what was wrong but they could clearly see that the soldier was looking nervous and sweating so they walked towards him too. The soldier threw the tray at them and turned and ran.

"Stay in here!" yelled Angelina and took chase. But two other soldiers quickly grabbed the fleeing soldier and wrestled him to the ground. "He may be a spy," said Angelina.

Erebus ran up to them and stared at all of the soldiers before he spoke. "The one who ran has an aura as black as night. Touch him with your crystal."

The soldier yelled and fought harder against the two who held him. Several more soldiers ran up to them. Angelina took off her crystal necklace and touched the forearm of the man. His arm started to smoke. "Someone get the Sanuri," she ordered.

"We're already here," said Sudfad loudly. "What is going on?"

Shara ran up to the group. "Someone should check on Marie. There is an unusual smell to that coffee he brought us." Simon nodded at two soldiers who now ran to the kitchen door.

"The building was too dark for us to see initially," explained Erebus. "We left the door open so we could find the candles and this man suddenly appeared in the doorway with a tray that he said Marie sent us. I could see how black his aura is. As we walked towards him he threw the tray and ran."

"Smoke came from his arm when I touched it with my crystal," Angelina said as the Sanuri walked up to the man.

"He is one of our soldiers," said Raul.

The man struggled to get away from the Sanuri who placed the palms of his hands on either side of the man's head. The man looked at the Sanuri fearfully. The Sanuri did not speak. The man collapsed.

"Is he dead?" asked Edward.

"No he passed out from fear. He is not a demon," replied the Sanuri who now looked at the other soldiers standing around them. "This man drinks always at the same tavern in the city. Does anyone know its name?"

"That would be Hancock's My Lord, it's near the river," said a soldier. "A lot of us go there; they have great food. Why?"

"How many men here go to that tavern?" the Sanuri asked.

Four men raised their hands. "Have any of you been approached by a man named Cass?" asked the Sanuri.

"Does playing cards count?" asked one of the soldiers. "A man by that name joined four of us last Tuesday night. We were in Hancock's playing cards."

"Come closer," said the Sanuri. "You aren't in trouble. Did he ask any of you questions about the King's family or anything to do with the castle?"

"Not that I remember but he did ask if any of us were interested in making some extra money. Right then a couple of fellas started fighting and one of them landed on our table. I don't know what happened to Cass after that."

"Was this soldier with you?" the Sanuri nodded at the man on the ground.

"Gilmore, no. Why is he in trouble because of Cass?"

"We aren't sure yet. Do you mind if I look into your mind?"

"Will it hurt?"

"Not at all. And rarely does anyone pass out."

"Ok," said the soldier and walked closer to the Sanuri.

"I saw the face of the man who told you he was Cass but it wasn't the same man who told Gilmore that was his name," the Sanuri said to the soldier after a few minutes.

Marie the lifelong head cook of the Royal Family marched out to the group with two soldiers behind her. "Where's that tray?" she demanded and Raul and Simon started to grin.

"It's here Marie," said Shara. "He threw it at us then the room filled with a strange smell." The women walked inside of the barn. "You better come in here," Shara yelled to the people outside. "No Marie don't touch that!"

"What is it?" asked Matthew as he was the first to enter the building.

"That silver coffee pot is green and whatever was in it burned a hole in the carpet," Shara announced loudly.

"Gala!" yelled Dominic and ran to the woman who was lying unconscious on the floor.

"Bring her into the fresh air," said Shara. "Angelina get our medical bags!"

As soon as Dominic carried Gala outside she started to cough and she kept coughing. Dominic placed her on the grass. The Sanuri and Shara were kneeling on either side of Gala when she jolted to a sitting positon. She was coughing violently. The Sanuri placed his hands upon her and started to hum.

"I think I know what that was," said Erebus as he now kneeled beside Gala too. He stopped talking when he realized the Sanuri was healing Gala. Erebus stood up and walked over to a group of men and women who Marie was talking too.

"My Lord; that soldier Gilmore said he needed a tray of coffee for Erebus. I poured the coffee myself into the serving pot. One of the other cooks put the cups on the tray," Marie explained.

"We never asked for coffee," said Erebus. "And that soldier is still passed out. He should be awake by now."

One of the soldiers kneeled down by Gilmore and started to shake him. "I think he's dead," said the soldier.

Angelina was running towards the group with two medical bags. She saw that the Sanuri was with Gala so she ran to Gilmore. After a moment she yelled. "He is dead but I don't know what killed him. I can't find any marks."

Gala's coughing was lessening as the Sanuri healed her. A few moments later he stopped and walked over to Gilmore's body. He held his hands over the corpse and again started to hum. After a couple of minutes the Sanuri stood up. "I believe this man died of fright."

"How can that be?" asked Sudfad.

"I don't think that Gilmore was a bad person but he hired on with one of the men who claimed to be Cass. From what I could see before he passed out, Gilmore was supposed to find out what is in that barn. I couldn't see anything else. But he was filled with guilt and shame," the Sanuri explained. "Erebus do you know what was in that coffee?"

"I am pretty sure it is an herb called halrut. If you put it in boiling water it creates a vapor that will put others to sleep. Something strange occurred when he mixed it with the coffee."

"I am very familiar with that herb," said Hilgra. "It grows commonly in Stordt. Healers make tonics to help calm people and to make them sleep. I have never seen it burn through anything like it did that carpet."

Shara helped Gala walk to the group. "I am fine," Gala said. "We heard you; that is why I wanted to come over here. I have used halrut many times. In fact, I gave it to both Raul and Simon when they were wounded. I have never heard of a reaction like that. It might have been mixed with something else besides the coffee."

The Sanuri quickly walked inside of the barn and opened one of the vaults. He examined the books that were locked in there. "Old Friend is it safe for the healers to study these?"

The Lion did not appear but the Sanuri heard his voice. "It is safe, we have disabled the evil attached to them. It would be wise for your friends to review them inside of the castle. A barn that is surrounded with soldiers peaks curiosities. Some of the soldiers have talked about it and that is how word got out."

"Now I have a question for you," said The Lion. "What did you do today that was different?"

"The purification rites."

"Yes and the demons are panicking. Using Thot's example their sky went black. Do not be surprised if they try to seduce more people into spying on everyone."

"But won't they just say another spell?"

"It is considerably more complicated than that. The spells require great resources and time. If nothing else you will keep them busy as they keep having to recreate the windows to see into your world. But you have a key to that window."

"The key that High Priest Othnial put into the vault?"

"No, the plyogram. All of you think of that as something to read like a book. It is considerably more than that. Which is why the Old One Molach was guarding it himself."

"The symbols on it with thirteen eyes in a group. They appear thirteen times on the plyogram. Do those symbols have anything to do with the windows into our world?"

"Yes, gather your high priests, others may watch. As you perform the Rites of Purification over the plyogram have the priests pour blessed water on each symbol of the eyes. You will need to perform the rites thirteen times, once over each symbol."

"Have your healers watch the ceremony and that includes Hannah. The family of King Manu will be arriving here in a few days for Luca's wedding. Show them the plyogram and teach them the purification rites. You question whether Hilgra should be part of this. Why?"

"I feel she will turn to darkness at the first opportunity. Then are we giving her too much information?"

"She is like a leaf that is blowing around. She has never had any roots to hold her to the ground. No roots to give her strength or to steady her. She has been blowing around aimlessly with no sense of direction. She clings to whatever she is blown up against. You sense that and that is why you are concerned. But watch her as the healers study those books. Her roots are already starting to spurt out. This little leaf just might turn into a mighty oak someday."

"Now speaking of healers, all of you want Shara, Angelina, Gala and Hilgra to study Juleta's ledgers. Why would you not consider asking the exceptional physician that we sent you?"

"Hannah? I just, actually I don't know why."

"The spell books are part of the mystery but so are the ledgers. Ledgers that contain information about very complicated medical procedures. It would not be a waste of anyone's time for her to join that group. And again, when Manu's family arrives, ask Gael, Hadar, Ibula and Lakin if they too would like to join the group. You will have some of the most powerful healers in your world sitting around that table and they all are followers of The Great Ruler; don't you think miracles can happen?"

The Sanuri called everyone but the soldiers to come into the barn. This group now consisted of all the people who had started out in Sudfad's meeting except for the Venatores who were hunting Sampson. He told them the words of The Lion.

"Where should we perform the ceremony?" asked High Priest Othnial. "In the chapel?"

"That thing holds such darkness; you don't want to take it to the chapel," said Ira.

Suddenly the Sanuri smiled. "The Lion just said, where else would you take an object of great darkness but to a place where The Great Ruler's Spirit has been called in. The Light will always dissolve the darkness."

When Trace told Karzman that the soldiers were taking Torin north, Karzman himself led a group of men towards those soldiers. As they rode Karzman made Trace repeat his story several times.

"That doesn't make any damn sense," Karzman yelled over and again. "Why would the Commanding General ride with them and why are they traveling north?" Suddenly Karzman became quiet as his paranoid fears took control. "What if Torin was taking the soldiers to show them whatever it was that Torin held against him?" This question filled the tyrant's mind as he spurred his men towards the fort.

Farnsworth was not a stupid man. He knew that Karzman would have spies watching the fort and he knew they were probably following his company northwards. Having Torin out of the protection of the fort would give Karzman an opportunity to orchestrate an escape.

Major Iders had soldiers dressed as lumberjacks in the forest watching for Karzman's men. He was briefed that eight men were following the soldiers but that one lone rider was riding towards Karzman's village at a fast pace.

Within an hour Karzman and one hundred of his soldiers rode past the disguised soldiers traveling north. Iders' soldiers quickly mounted their horses and sped towards the fort.

Loyalty was not a concept that Karzman understood. Hatred and obsession with power were his driving forces. Karzman was consumed with desires to kill Sudfad and Michael. He fantasied about how he would torture his daughters who he felt betrayed him. Revenge was his. He sped northward.

Sudfad immediately canceled the remainder of the meeting so the priests could focus on purifying the plyogram. Calen, Koby, Misha and Elan took to the skies to find Joshua and the other Venatores. Ratri and Dagon flew to Gabriel's house to tell every one of The Lion's words and to bring Hannah to the castle.

Renya prepared a room that would be designated for the study of Juleta's books. Raphael sent Enrops to the Cisero Headquarters of the Patronus priests telling them to come to the chapel at the Learning Center. Archetenus rode to the Learning Center with the same message for the priests and trainees there.

Commanding General Farnsworth was not only a childhood friend of Sudfad's but like Commanding General Craven, Farnsworth was an adopted uncle to Sudfad's children. Farnsworth had not yet met Michael or his sisters but that did not lessen his sense of family towards them. Sudfad and Renya both wrote to Farnsworth and Craven on a regular basis.

The King and Queen were more open with their feelings and fears with these two old friends than they were with other people. There was more than a sense of duty that drove Farnsworth to stop Karzman, there was a sense of family.

"This is it Sir," Sergeant McAvoy said to Farnsworth who stopped the company of soldiers in an area of stark rock formations.

Farnsworth stared at the rocks. "What is this place? These rocks aren't natural to the surroundings. They almost look as if they were put here, but how could that be?"

"Sir, some of these rocks have strange carvings on them. There's a few of us who have wondered if this is some ancient ceremonial site," said McAvoy.

"I will have to come up here another time and study all of this," said Farnsworth.

"The cave is back here," McAvoy said. He and Farnsworth dismounted and walked about fifty yards before turning left and walking around one of the huge rocks that looked very unnatural in its setting. Immediately behind the rock formation was the opening to a huge cave.

A spider web partially covered the opening. Several birds were stuck in the web and struggling to get free. Both soldiers looked at the strange footprints that covered the ground and led into the cave. "This is damn incredible," said Farnsworth. "Call the men." Within moments half of the company of soldiers arrived at the entrance of the cave. Torin was with them.

Torin had been cursing the soldiers and calling them names but now he stood mute as he gazed upon the incredible spider web. "I'm freeing those poor birds," announced McAvoy as he climbed up the side of the hill that housed the cave. "If that bastard is hungry he can eat Torin."

"What is this?" gasped Torin.

"Torin, you are a murderous little prick with a big mouth," said Farnsworth and the soldiers laughed. "You raped your own sisters who are my nieces. You tortured your stepbrother who is my nephew. You are only alive because I want information." Torin started to sweat profusely as Farnsworth talked. "Your sisters said you are terrified of spiders. So we found the biggest damn spider in the world and you are going to be its lunch if you don't start talking."

"You can't do this," Torin yelled.

"You sold your soul to a demon. You have no value in this world; it will be a better place without you. The choice is yours."

"What, what is my choice?" stammered Torin fearfully.

"Give me Karzman or dance with the spiders."

"If I do will you let me go?"

"Now that depends on a couple of things," said Farnsworth. "The value of the information you give me and you. If I free you it will not be to continue the life you have led. Rapists, murderers and demon lovers have no place in this kingdom."

"I will leave Wetpr, I promise. What do you want to know?"

"How many fighting men does your father have?"

"Two thousand."

"Two thousand! How is he paying them?"

"I am not really sure."

"I find that hard to believe. I heard you wanted to take over the tribe."

"I do, I mean I did. All the time we grew up he kept saying he had no money yet he always paid his soldiers. And now that he is crippled he seems to have a lot more money. We have been trying to figure out where he hides it."

"Your village can't be that damn big."

"It isn't that's why me and Cabal think he is hiding it with dark magics. But, well, ok I am just going to say it. Father has always prayed to demons. And now he is obsessed with it. But he is asking to get his old strength and body back. And the demons haven't done that so why would they give him money?"

"Don't you talk to demons?"

"Yeah, but you don't think they talk back do you? I mean it's not like talking to a person."

"There are demons who materialize and also assume human form you moron. You probably have demons in your camp."

"Well, we used to have the devil dogs but they disappeared when Teivel died. And Father can't get them back."

"Ok, more about the soldiers, where is he getting them from?"

"He has put word out somehow because groups of men ride into the village to get hired. And he is giving them all new weapons. He never leaves the village anymore so I don't know where the weapons are coming from or where they are stored."

"You're his oldest son aren't you?"

"Yes but he doesn't tell me much because he doesn't trust us."

"How can you be his right-hand man and not know these things?"

"I'm not his right-hand man, Korbin is."

"Who the hell is Korbin?"

"He was one of Teivel's lieutenants. He came to the village after Teivel was destroyed and he is the only one who Father trusts."

"I still don't understand how he can keep so much from you when you live under the same roof. Something isn't adding up here. If you truly are planning on taking his spot you have to have something of strength or are you all talk?"

"The soldiers work for him but some of them are coming to my side."

"Either you are more of a fool than I thought or you aren't telling me everything. So far you haven't said enough to save you from the cave."

"Father has a lot of enemies."

"No shit." Again the soldiers laughed at their commander's comments.

"You don't understand, there are some like the King of Stordt who have been waiting for Father to weaken because they did not want to attack when he was aligned with Teivel, Emeric and Banaka. Father has always been paranoid but now he has reason for that. Last week they caught two men spying on the village. Father tortured them and they said they worked for the King of Stordt."

"And every time he sends men after Michael and the girls they are killed. None of the men he has sent to spy on King Sudfad have returned. Then some of the men who came to the village to get hired said they heard there were attacks in Salar and everyone thinks Father is behind them. He wasn't so now he thinks powerful demons are behind all of this and he is desperate. He sold his soul to Samael after Teivel died but Samael doesn't seem pleased with him. In two nights he is planning a raid on the Village of Kaffa. He is going to steal people to sacrifice on the full moon. He thinks that will please the demons."

"Well boy, you may have just earned your freedom."

Suddenly they heard the Horn of Cass being blown and the men ran from the cave to the other soldiers who were holding their horses. Torin was thrown on top of his horse and Farnsworth led this company of soldiers towards the sounds of battle.

Major Iders and three companies of men were fighting with Karzman and his hired killers. The battle was savage. Farnsworth ordered one of his soldiers to blow their Horn of Cass announcing their arrival. Iders heard it as did Karzman who was too frail to fight and sat on his horse watching the battle. He rode into the forest when he heard Farnsworth's men coming.

Karzman hid behind trees and cursed. Then he saw his son sitting on top of a horse with his hands bound behind his back. Torin was now unattended. "Torin," Karzman gasped. He rode deeper through the forest until he was in a position parallel to Torin. Karzman waited until all of the soldiers around Torin were embroiled in battle then he raced his horse across the battlefield.

"Father!" yelled Torin. "Untie me."

As Karzman rode towards Torin he pulled a sword out of its sheath on his saddle. Torin quickly looked around him to see if any of the soldiers would try to stop his father. Karzman stopped his horse alongside of Torin's and yelled, "Samael this one is for you!" Karzman ran his sword through Torin's heart and as he pulled the sword out of his son's body he could feel himself getting stronger.

# Chapter XXXVI
## The Voices of Demons

Hannah felt both proud and a little out of her element to be included with the healers in trying to translate Juleta's ledgers. Renya had fixed up a chambers instead of a meeting room for the women. Trays of food and beverages were brought to the room as well as paper and writing instruments. Although the Sanuri said the books were no longer dangerous neither Hannah nor Angelina wanted to bring their children into the chambers, so the King's nurses cared for them.

It took several hours for all of the priests to gather in the chapel of the Learning Center. Ten minutes before the ceremony was to start, Gabriel sent for the healers to join them. In the meantime the Sanuri sent lengthy messages to the children of King Manu. He told them about Thot, about the plyogram and about the words of The Lion. And the Sanuri prayed to the heavens to give the Enrops a speedy journey in delivering the messages.

Sudfad and his family also sat in the chapel which was filled past capacity. People stood in every open spot between and around the pews. Yet for all of these people the chapel was silent until the Sanuri started to chant the Rites of Purification. Many high priests stood in the front of the chapel with the Sanuri. These priests were broken into groups and each group was to pour blessed water on one of the symbols of the thirteen eyes on the plyogram.

Gabriel, Raphael and Othnial were part of the first group who poured the blessed water into each of the thirteen eyes of their symbol. Intense smoke rose from the plyogram causing many to cough and choke. First the plyogram then the building began to shake. Then screams were heard from outside of the chapel. Several of the priests went outside to check on the soldiers who were guarding the chapel; they were not screaming. The sounds were coming from the hell worlds. When the ceremony was over each of the symbols of thirteen eyes was literally burned out of the plyogram.

Karzman would never realize how the Rites of Purification would affect his destiny. Samael was out of his mind with rage. The simple yet powerful ceremony shook the hell worlds to their foundations. Great quakes opened the grounds. Volcanos exploded, intense lightening and tremendous winds took form and for the hell worlds that had bodies of water, flooding over took the lands.

Samael had long wanted to destroy the followers of The Great Ruler, now he declared war on them. As Karzman rode west towards his village his body and mind were restored to his former strength and power. And now for the first time Karzman realized that he was hearing the voice of the great demon. A voice he heard with great clarification. A voice that told him to go to the villages and cities and to destroy all places of worship.

Not only did Samael want to show The Great Ruler the power he had but he wanted to sever the connection between The Great Ruler and His children.

Karzman never thought to help any of his men who were losing their battle with Farnsworth's soldiers. He never felt even a moment of remorse for murdering his defenseless son. He only felt elation for finally pleasing the demons.

The people who filled the chapel prayed during the entire ceremony of the Rites of Purification and they all felt the need to continue praying after the ceremony was completed. As the last prayer was said, the Angel Adam appeared in the front of the chapel with the Sanuri and the high priests.

"What you have done has never before been accomplished in this world. These rites have not been performed since ancient times. The power of The Great Ruler and your prayers have not only closed the windows into many worlds besides your own, but have created havoc in the hell worlds."

"But Samael has now declared war on all followers of The Great Ruler. Moments ago, during a battle between Commanding General Farnsworth's soldiers and some of Karzman's men, Karzman murdered his eldest son Torin as a sacrifice to Samael and the demon is rewarding him greatly."

"Karzman now hears the voice of Samael and is receiving orders. His first orders are to gather his men and to attack the places of worship in every village and city."

Sudfad jumped up and asked, "Will you deliver this message to all of my forts and the Patronus while I ready my army?"

"I will certainly deliver the message but there was a reason that we told you to start out on the night of Luca's wedding. And we will remain with that plan. That gives you four days to prepare. Any messages that any of you send now will be delivered without the confines of time in your world. Use these four days wisely." Adam disappeared.

"Othnial do you have paper and pen here?" asked Sudfad. As Othnial left to get these items, Sudfad now walked to the front of the chapel. Since we are all here, we might as well hold a meeting now."

"What kind of monsters burn places of worship?" Emeral asked loudly. Her voice betrayed her horror and disgust.

"Those who choose to listen to the voices of demons," said the Sanuri.

Not only did Adam deliver the messages, he did it in person. Farnsworth was still on the battlefield when time seemed to stop. He shook his head, thinking there was something wrong with his mind. When Adam appeared before him, Farnsworth could feel the intensity of the holy energy and instantly fell to his knees and started to sob.

"Rise my general," said Adam. But Farnsworth was too overwhelmed. "We have work to do; would you like me to help you control your emotions?" Farnsworth nodded.

A second later General Farnsworth stood up and listened to the Angel speak. "You have not yet realized that Karzman murdered Torin while you were in the midst of battle. He did this as a sacrifice to Samael and the demon is rewarding him greatly. Karzman can now hear the demon's voice and his first orders are to burn all places of worship. Sudfad will be leading an army here in four days but he has asked me to give this message to all of his commanders and the Patronus. You have no time to waste."

Karzman was not the only monster to receive gifts from the great demon. In the Continent of Opots there were fifty men who gained in power and strength. And in the World of Nunc there were two hundred and thirteen men.

Sampson was one of these men. Earlier in the morning he had taken to the concealment of a tree as he watched a group of Venatores hunting him. Although he had grown up with these men and women he did not recognize their faces.

Sampson was climbing down from the tree when the pains in his head overwhelmed him and he fell. He was cut and bleeding from the branches he hit during his fall. He was already unconscious when his head hit the ground.

Messages were sent to the kings of all kingdoms that were not ruled by demons. Messages were sent to all of the churches, temples and monasteries. Sudfad was particularly concerned about the City of Nora where he had given permission for the people to build places of worship although the kingdom itself was ruled by darkness.

Messages were sent to the Ice Caves, to the ruling families of Lentz and to General Amundsen in the Kingdom of Ganz. All of these messages warned of Karzman's plans but a few of the messages also told of Sudfad's plans.

Since the Angel Adam was stopping time as he met with the Commanding Generals of each fort in Wetpr and the High Priests of the Patronus, he was able to deliver the messages simultaneously. Each general reacted immediately in dispatching troops to safeguard the places of worship.

Commanding General Colter of Fort Nora did not believe that Karzman had influence in the Kingdom of Stordt. But Colter had seen too much to underestimate the demons. And he was well aware that a demon sat on the throne of Stordt. Colter dispatched troops to protect the newly built temple and monastery in the City of Nora.

While there are some people who become terrified when they hear the voices of demons there are others who are exhilarated as the voices fan the flames of hatred and prejudice that are already burning inside of those humans. It is as if the demonic voices give those people permission to release the monsters inside of them.

Almost as soon as Samael declared war upon the followers of The Great Ruler gangs and crowds formed in every community in The World of Nunc and attacked all places of worship. Some claimed they attacked in the name of religious beliefs others attacked because of fear and prejudice but for whatever reasons they proclaimed; they all attacked out of hatred.

Innocent people were murdered and altars desecrated. Ignorance too fueled the flames of hatred as now entire city blocks were going up in smoke.

The peoples who made up these crowds wore many faces and came from different social classes and ethnic backgrounds. The hatred they shared broke down their normal social and racial barriers and for a moment in time they all danced with demons.

Sampson moaned loudly and sat up. He clutched his head as pains surged through his body then he puked.

He held his head tighter and closed his eyes as everything was spinning. Suddenly images and memories were bombarding his mind. He felt as if he were watching a play as his life unfolded before him.

Sudfad's meeting in the chapel was interrupted by dozens of Enrops that were announcing the chaos and riots that had erupted throughout the kingdom. Men jumped from the pews and started to run out of the building. When Renya heard the Enrops speak she was consumed with anger and disbelief.

While others were running out to help the soldiers, Queen Renya ran to the front of the chapel and grabbed a bowl of blessed water and threw it on the entire plyogram. Smoke filled the chapel. "Adam, Adam, you get back here now!" she screamed.

The Sanuri was the first to run to Renya. He tried to pull her away from the plyogram but she fought him. "Which one of these is the symbol for chaos?" screamed Renya. Sudfad was almost out the door but now turned and ran to his wife. "Adam get back here!" she screamed. Renya grabbed a dagger from her husband's belt and lunged at the plyogram when the Angel appeared.

"Adam stop this, or tell us how to stop this madness," yelled Renya. "If people are listening to the demons can't we stop them from hearing the voices?" Adam did not answer Renya which added to her anger. "All of you Angels are always telling us about free will and freedom of choice. Well I choose to be the conduit to stop this. What do I need to do?"

"Do you understand what you are asking?" asked Adam.

Renya's demeanor softened greatly. "Actually I probably don't but I am still asking. The Sanuri has told us that sometimes it takes but one voice to say no to darkness. I will be that voice."

"Renya," gasped Sudfad.

"This is my choice," said Renya to her husband. Then she turned back to Adam.

"I know that The Great Ruler and you are strong enough to sever this connection between Samael and those who are doing all of this. What I don't know is what you need from us. Now I will ask you again, what do you need me to do?"

Adam smiled and said, "Take my hand." As soon as Renya touched Adam's extended hand they both disappeared.

"Sanuri what is going on?" shrieked Sudfad. "Will she be alright?"

"I honestly don't know where they are going or what they are going to do," said the Sanuri. "But your wife and my dear friend is taking a journey with a warrior Angel. Personally I would be more worried about the demons."

Sampson rolled around on the ground as the memories of his life were forced upon him in a matter of moments. The images were moving so quickly that at times he didn't understand what he was seeing. His emotions were in turmoil. He started to scream loudly although he did not understand why.

"Hecate, where is my wife and child?" Sampson yelled. Then he saw the images of his journey to Wetpr. "Vivian!" he yelled and shot up to a sitting position.

Shara and Angelina were both in the chapel when Renya disappeared. The two women called to Miranda almost simultaneously. The Angel Miranda appeared to the stunned warriors.

"Miranda will she need help?" asked Angelina frantically. "Can we go with her?"

Miranda smiled, "This is a journey she must take alone," she said to Angelina. Then Miranda looked at the other faces in the chapel. "Do not let Renya's choices deter you from your duties." Her words brought the people back to the reality of the situation. The warriors left the chapel.

Raul, Simon, Michael and Matthew had already left the chapel before Renya called to the Angel Adam. Miranda now turned to Sudfad who had a look of horror on his face. "Sudfad, you can do no more in here today. I would suggest you prepare for your attack against Karzman."

"What is this place?" asked Renya as she and Adam appeared on the cliff of a stark mountain.

"Some call it Motfer."

"I have heard that word before. In ancient legends it was a place where warriors would go when they died. Adam am I dead?"

"No and this is a world between worlds. A place where the time limitations of your world do not exist. Renya, you are the Queen of the most powerful kingdom in one of the most powerful continents in a world that is experiencing a pivotal point in time. The choices and actions of the people of your world right this very moment affect worlds and futures you can't imagine."

"You come from a family of kings. Almost every member of your family has asked to walk with or fight alongside of the Angels. And yet you barely speak with us when we give you the gift of seeing us and hearing our voices. You are a woman of phenomenal strength and courage. You have great faith in The Great Ruler and you ask Him for help and guidance but when He sends it, you don't take advantage of His gifts."

"I don't understand what you mean."

"He has sent us to you and your family and close allies in answers to your prayers. Renya your husband, sons and daughters are pillars of strength and yet it is you who holds them all up. You are the glue, so to speak, in your family. A family that needs to remain strong for the sakes of many. Tell me, why do you not call to us?"

"I guess I don't have a good answer for you."

"Renya, you can do better than that."

"I am not a passive wife and I understand my responsibilities but I don't, well I guess I don't feel it is my place to question my husband. I did call to The Lion once when I was taking over the command of the castle."

"And yet in four days you will be taking over command of the kingdom. While that does not bring fear to your heart, the ruling members are terrified of their new roles. Every one of them feels more comfortable on the battlefield; so here too you will be holding them up."

"Renya, Angels have an advantage of seeing things from different points of view than the humans who are in the midst of their battles. We are not all knowing as The Great Ruler and we too have our journeys to take. I am on such a journey because I had lost faith in many things outside of heaven. I am being allowed to work with all of you now to help me see the goodness and integrity in people again."

"Renya, I can't believe that it is a coincidence that you and Sudfad rule Wetpr at this important time in the history of so many worlds. You are a leader and an inspiration in your own right. And while you say you don't want to question Sudfad, in the very near future he will need you to help carry his load."

"Is something going to happen to him?" she gasped.

"Many things are happening in your world. Did you know that the ruling families of Lentz tell everyone that their warrior wives look to you as the example of how they strive to become; as do your own daughters. These wives of leaders and future queens are walking in your footprints. Tell me Renya, where will those footprints take them?"

"Adam, I am not sure I understand what you mean. I believe you are telling me I have choices to make but I don't know what the choices are."

"This is not a trick question and I want you to carefully think about your answer. Do you really want to become a conduit between the heavens and the people of your world?"

"I realize there is a lot more to that than I understand but you said it like you thought I was going to become afraid. Adam just tell me what you are getting at."

"I do not think you are afraid but I don't know if you are ready to see this kind of darkness either. Your brother Mathas and Gabriel have been to Motfer. They fought demons in battles to strengthen their faith and understanding. Simon and Natasha too, have been here. You Queen Renya have fought demons with great courage and faith outside of Motfer."

"There is an abstractness about the concepts of both Angels and demons that many humans experience. They expect Angels to be good and demons to be bad. Yet when they see these same traits in their own kind they can react very differently. There are some who fear the darkness in man more than the demons. And there are some men who are far worse than some demons. Renya for you to be a conduit you need to understand your world so that you can understand the role you have asked to play. Are you willing to take that walk with me?"

Renya smiled. "I am beginning to suspect that we may have somewhat different definitions for some words or that perhaps my mind cannot comprehend your meanings. So I have one question for you. When I made the request it was to do good in this world. To stop the darkness and to perhaps bring The Great Ruler's Spirit in. Tell me, after this walk will I be able to do these things?"

Adam held out his hand and smiled warmly, "My Queen, we do have the same definitions."

# Chapter XXXVII
## Just Call My Name

Visterle himself ushered Nada, their babies and nurses into a special room in the center of his castle. "You will be safe here. Do not come out until I tell you," he said.

"Visterle what is happening?" asked Nada as she was comforting one of their babies. The loud noises outside of the castle were scaring the children.

"I really can't explain it now."

"Are we under attack?" asked Nada. "If so, I need a weapon."

"We are not under attack in the sense that you think. I will explain later."

"Please tell us something, can't you see how frightened the nurses are."

"Alright but I will not go into detail now. Over the centuries demons have put many things into place and emissaries of The Great Ruler are destroying them," he said and ran out the door.

When Visterle said 'The Great Ruler', Nada was consumed with fear and guilt. Her people had entered into an ancient covenant with their God, swearing their allegiance to Him. Nada had been raised to believe in Him, but as she chose to listen to the voices of demons, she pushed that belief to the far regions of her mind. She had always gotten so much pleasure from listening to the demons that she found ways to justify turning against her people and her God.

Nada turned to her nurse, midwife and confidant. "Ada do you know what he is talking about?"

"Not exactly. I believe the kinds of things he is referring to can only be accomplished by the most powerful of demons."

"I can understand a battle but it seems like we are being attacked by storms."

"Nada, I cannot give you a good answer. I have never seen anything like this before and I am hundreds of years old. But tell me why are you so frightened? Is it because of the children?"

"No," Nada said in a whisper. "I'm afraid The Great Ruler will find out that I am here."

By the time Karzman reached his village he had the body and strength that was his before Teivel's demise. He jumped from his horse and ordered every member of the village to come to the center of the village. He wanted everyone to know he was back to his old glory.

Cabal as well as most of the soldiers and villagers were shocked when they saw Karzman. Even the most naïve among them understood that the dictator must have done something of great horror to have his powers restored.

Cabal stood with the crowd; not next to his father. Before Karzman addressed his people, Cabal yelled out, "Where is Torin?" Karzman looked for his son in the crowd and when their eyes met a chill ran through Cabal's body. In that instant he knew his father had murdered his brother.

"He is dead," said Karzman smugly. "He will not be taking over my position."

In another community the people may have been shocked by what they heard. But these people were the victims of demons; they expected only the worst.

"I want half of my men to saddle up now!" yelled Karzman. "We ride in ten minutes!" The dictator said no more to the crowd. He gave no explanation of Torin's death or why the men who had left with him in the morning did not return to the village. Neither did he explain his plans to attack the places of worship in Norge. He saw Korbin smiling at him in the crowd. "Korbin, let's have a drink to celebrate."

Norge was a small village on the southernmost tip of the lands of the Kozach Tribe. It was used to suffering from the brutality of Karzman and his sons, but never before had its own citizens raised up in anarchy.

There was one small building that served as a place of worship for all faiths. Outwardly the building was disguised as a store so that the demon worshippers would not know it was a church. But Norge was a small community and every villager knew what that building really was. Just as every villager knew who the demon worshippers were even though many sought to hide their faces from their neighbors. But the sacks, sheets and blankets they put over their heads did not hide the hatred or the human masks they wore.

Because of the help from the heavens, Enrops were given incredible speed in delivering their messages. The commanding generals from each fort and the high priests of the Patronus were sending each other messages as they determined where they were sending troops.

Farnsworth himself led troops into the huge City of Serpha. Troops were already stationed in Bransong. More troops from Fort Serpha were riding to Norge and the large City of Landmar which was west of the lands of the Kozach Tribe.

In every community in the World of Nunc citizens fought against each other. Neighbors against neighbors, fathers against sons. Samael had declared war on the religions that did not listen to demons. People fought, screamed, cried and prayed.

The kingdoms of free men and women had more places of worship than the dark kingdoms. The armed forces in these kingdoms could barely address all of the areas that were under attack. The troops were spread out too thin, dangerously thin and Samael savored the moments. The fear and hatred that filled the worlds gave him great strength and power. He fed off these emotions and like many other demons, Samael was always amazed at how easy it all was.

Renya's knees buckled as Adam took her on a spiritual tour of her continent. "Can we not stop this?" she asked as tears ran down her face.

"You are horrified by this but the darkness you see here is nothing compared to what awaits this world if all of you surrender to the demons. My Queen are you prepared to see what you are really fighting against?"

"I don't know," Renya said in a whisper. Then she straightened herself up and took a deep breath. "Are these the things that my family and the warriors who fight with them have seen?" Adam nodded. "Then I trust you will give me the strength I need," as Renya said this she reached out and grasped Adam's hand.

Karzman stopped his men and took pause when they rode into the Village of Norge. People were fighting in the streets and buildings were burning. Karzman had wanted to cause this type of chaos but no one even noticed him and his band of mercenaries. They rode down the main street and still no one took notice of them. No one saw that the demonic dictator was back in his glory. No one cared.

Karzman was dumbfounded and disappointed. He stopped his men again and they watched the citizens tearing each other apart.

The soldiers of Fort Serpha blew the Horn of Cass as they raced towards the Village of Norge. Karzman was momentarily torn; if he battled the soldiers he would lose more men, which he could not afford to do. He turned his men around and they retreated from the village.

Michael, Matthew, Simon and Raul all returned to the castle individually that night. Each man was both exhausted and disgusted with what they had seen. And each man was met at the door by all of the adults in the family. One by one the Princes were told that Renya had disappeared with Adam and still had not returned to the castle.

"I've been waiting for everyone to come home," said Sudfad. "Now that Raul is here we can have a meeting. We might as well have it in the dining room so you can eat."

The group entered the dining room and while the others took seats Raul closed the door and stood with his back against it. "Ok, I know the girls were in the parlor so everyone was being careful about what they said. But where is Mother? And why did she leave with him? Did she go willingly?"

"Sudfad, would you mind if I tried to explain something?" asked Shara. "Because I don't think any of you really understand what Renya asked for. And honestly Angelina and I don't think she understood what she said."

"I for one want to hear what you have to say," said Sudfad.

"Raul, I will start by telling you what we told your brothers," said Shara. "While everyone was running out of the chapel, Renya ran to the front and attacked the plyogram and the entire time she was screaming for Adam to come back." Shara stopped speaking when Marie knocked at the door.

Raul opened the door and stepped aside as she carried a large tray into the room. The Sanuri walked into the dining room behind her. It was obvious to everyone that Marie had been crying.

"Marie why are you crying," asked Angelina.

"I am just worried about My Lady. You let me know when she comes home and I will fix her something special."

"Shara what you have to say, can Marie hear it too?" asked Simon.

Shara looked at Angelina then Angelina said, "Yes, but Marie if we get to certain information we will have to ask you to leave."

"Do you know where My Lady is?" asked Marie hopefully.

"No," said Shara. "Raul, you should close that door again. As I said Renya ran to the front of the chapel and attacked the plyogram with blessed water. She fought both Sudfad and the Sanuri when they tried to stop her."

459

"Then she grabbed Sudfad's dagger and was going to stab the plyogram when the Angel Adam came back."

"Wait, that doesn't sound like Mother at all," said Raul. "Does anyone know why she was acting like that?"

"Every man and woman in this room has a limit as to how much horror they can tolerate in this world," explained the Sanuri. "Your mother is always so gracious in the face of adversity that, well, that perhaps you and I mean all of you don't realize how much this affects her too. Like all of you she was enraged and disgusted that people were forming mobs and attacking places of worship. But while all of you were going to battle the mobs your mother decided to challenge the heavens."

"Shara why don't you finish what you were going to say," said the Sanuri.

"When Adam appeared she demanded to know what could be done to sever the connection so people wouldn't hear Samael's voice. Adam didn't answer her. Then she said she knew that The Great Ruler and the Angels had the power to do that but she didn't know what they needed us to do. Adam still didn't say anything which was making her madder."

"Then she says that the Sanuri has often said it only takes one voice to stop the darkness and she said she wanted to be that voice. She said she wanted to be a conduit between the heavens and this world. Adam asked her if she understood what she was saying and Renya said probably not but she was still asking. Adam told her to take his hand and they disappeared."

"Then Mother and I called to Miranda to see if we could go with Renya," explained Angelina. "But Miranda said it was a journey that Renya had to take alone."

"Adam will protect her if that is what you are all worried about," the Sanuri said.

"Oh, I think we are worried about a lot more than that," said Simon. "So what exactly is a conduit?"

"I could be wrong but I think that is what the Sanuri is," said Shara. "What Renya asked for is very powerful and it could change her greatly."

While the Princes of Wetpr and their troops were able to quell the rioting and chaos in the City of Salar; that was not the same for the rest of the kingdom. The soldiers and Patronus priests arrested so many people in each community that they had to turn buildings into makeshift jails. Then they had to leave some of their men behind in each community to guard these jails. All of this continued to deplete the ranks of the forces.

Karzman figured that Farnsworth would not dare to invade his lands any farther than the border towns so Karzman attacked his own villages in the interior of his lands. But every time he rode into a village he found the same chaos he had seen in Norge. Karzman didn't want to stand back and watch the riots; he and his men joined in.

"Now My Queen do you understand?" asked Adam.

Renya was wiping the tears from her face. "Actually I don't understand it at all. I don't understand why the people call to those monsters and why they allow themselves to be victimized like that. Don't they ever fight back?"

"I too have asked those same questions for hundreds of years. In some cases they have lived such lives of hopeless despair that they know nothing else. They don't call to us; in fact, they don't want us in yet they...well, I could talk about that all night and I am sure that your family is worried about you."

"Adam, Sudfad, Mathas and my sons have told me some of this, but I could not really understand what they were talking about. I think that is because what you showed me is unimaginable. How, how can we stop this?"

"As I said before, the actions of your world, your kingdom will affect other worlds and other times besides your own. Decisions need to be made carefully because the demons also understand the things that are happening and will try to sabotage all that is done."

"When you asked to be a conduit between worlds what did you think you were asking?"

"Honestly I don't even know. I just know we have to stop this madness. You asked me at the beginning of this why I never call to the Angels and I have been thinking about that question as we have traveled. I hope you don't think that I have been trying to shirk my duties. It's just that I am not sure what my duties are. I am the wife, the mother and the friend of The Seven Sons of Prophesy and I don't really know what that means."

"I have always understood my role as a Keeper of the Scrolls. Adam what should I be doing? You said that it wasn't a coincidence that Sudfad and I are King and Queen of Wetpr in this time. Have you been trying to tell me that I have a destiny too?"

Adam smiled, he truly enjoyed Renya. "First, people get confused about that word destiny. The Great Ruler has a, I will use the word 'plan' for everyone. But humans have freedom of choice so you may or may not follow that plan. Now take the Sanuri and Thot; they realized this and asked The Great Ruler to exceed the plans He had for them."

"I am not sure I understand what you are saying."

"I don't think it is an easy thing to understand so," Adam paused for a moment. "Let's say that The Great Ruler's plan for the Sanuri was that he would be a very good and pious person who helped others. But we all know that the Sanuri is an extraordinary human who has surpassed the limitations of his existence because he asked The Great Ruler to use him as an instrument of His hand. That is one way a person can change their destiny. Of course people can go in the opposite direction too like Roch."

"I am not defending that beast but he was created in a way by the Insidiae."

"And because of that The Great Ruler sent him Angels, that he could see and hear his entire life to help him. Even the Sanuri was sent to him. Roch cursed them all and sent them away. He made his choices with full knowledge of what he was doing."

"Knowing that is even more disturbing," said Renya with a shudder.

"Renya when you asked to be a conduit you were asking to exceed your limitations. The Great Ruler and I know you didn't really understand what you were asking which is why I have been allowed to show you these things."

"Did the Sanuri understand when he asked?"

"He had a much better understanding then than you do now."

"So what are you really saying?"

"You should think about it then call to me again."

Renya stared at Adam in disbelief. Then she got angry. "I am actually offended. Adam, I know I am not a Sanuri or Thot and perhaps I don't really want to be. But you wouldn't have taken me on this journey unless I could be of some kind of help. I really doubt that you do this sort of thing often just because someone yells at you."

Adam laughed. "You are right with everything you said but..."

"But how can I make a choice if you don't tell me what my choices are or explain to me the ways I can help. I understand the horror you showed me. But it's like you are playing a word game about everything else. So young man will you please be more specific." Renya paused and stared at Adam. "Is this some kind of test?"

"Renya you are truly the first human I have met who talks to me like you are my mother," he laughed again.

"Well, I am sorry if I offended you but I find this very frustrating. I have worked on behalf of The Great Ruler for, well since Sudfad and I were married."

"And I have gone on this journey with you and seen all of these horrible things and you talk like I am a child and you are going to send me home to my parents. I don't know what I can do but I want to do more than I am. You are looking at me like I am crazy."

"No, not at all."

"Then why aren't you saying anything?"

"Renya, I am going to take you home now."

"You will not! Not until I have an answer of some kind."

"Renya, I do enjoy talking with you which is why I am smiling and I am telling you this because I think it is making you angry. You act like I am going to give you a description of a job when the real question is what are you willing to do? You are a politician, a warrior and a queen. You are a Keeper of the Scrolls. You do many impressive things on your own but to do more for the heavens you will have to let The Great Ruler work through you; you will have to let Him take charge."

"And you will have to call to us for guidance so you understand what the heavens want you to do. All of these things will require you to change your behavior which is not easy for humans to do. I can't give you a regimented list right now. The Great Ruler doesn't even give us regimented lists. That is why I am telling you to think about this."

Renya stared at Adam and for a moment he thought she was going to cry but then the Queen got on her knees and prayed. "Great Ruler, I will admit I don't understand how this works but if there is anyway at all that you can use me to stop the violence against the places of worship; to silence Samael's voice which is inciting this madness; please use me. Let me know what you need me to do. And if I need help doing it please give me that also."

Renya had closed her eyes when she prayed, when she opened them she and Adam were in the dining room of her home. Adam held his hand out to the Queen to help her to a standing position as her family stared at them both.

"Mother are you alright?" Raul asked as he jumped out of his chair.

"Yes, I am fine; just frustrated and probably in some kind of trouble for yelling at an Angel."

Adam laughed loudly, "Your mother speaks to me like I am one of her sons." Now everyone grinned at that comment.

"I take it you passed your test," the Sanuri said to Renya.

"I have no idea," she said and looked at Adam. "I wasn't sure if I was being tested."

"It wasn't me who brought us here," said Adam. "I would take that as a good sign."

"You don't really explain much do you?" asked Renya.

The Sanuri laughed loudly. "That's why they call it faith."

"I'm confused," said Vitomas. "Why was Renya being tested?"

"When people are in a certain point of their spiritual evolution they know it's time; she demanded it," said Adam. "I will tell you what I told Renya. Angels are not all knowing but we can see much more than humans. I am here with all of you now because I had to be reminded there is goodness, integrity and faith in people. And as I have been watching all of you, I feel that every one of you is here, in this place and at this time because you are needed."

"Renya now understands what most of you have already known. She knows the hope this world is bringing to others and she knows what a dangerous position that is for all of you. And she has seen what will happen if this world falls. Most of you in this room are Kings and Queens of the most powerful kingdoms in this continent, in this world. Of a world that is greatly influencing the futures of countless other worlds."

"All of you have important roles to play. Roles that will not succeed unless you allow The Great Ruler to work through you."

"Sudfad, I know you share a great deal with Renya but a time will come soon when you will need her to help you with more of your responsibilities. I would suggest it would be wise if Vitomas, Annabelle and Angelina attended more of your meetings also."

"I am sure that Renya will have many questions for the Sanuri. And she may certainly tell you about the journey we took. Do you understand that anyone can do as Renya did?"

"Are all the journeys the same?" asked Vitomas.

"No, and I am not the one who determines the path you need to travel but I will volunteer to walk with you on that path when you are ready. Just call my name."

"How many can go on a journey?" asked Matthew.

"One," replied Adam.

"Can I?" asked Annabelle as she jumped out of her seat. "But I have to be back in time to feed babies."

"Annabelle!" said Simon.

"I'll take care of the babies," Vitomas said.

"Actually I think it would be more fitting if I was the next one to walk with Adam," said Sudfad.

# Chapter XXXVIII
## Eyes Below

Like many people who pray to make a difference in the world, Renya never found out if her prayers were answered. She was never told that The Great Ruler used her prayers to stop the hordes of demons that were flocking to Opots to rekindle the riots that had been quelled. No one knew that the heavens had stopped a massacre.

The chaos and madness of the riots exhilarated Karzman. Although he did nothing more than to help destroy his own villages he returned to his village feeling like a conquering hero. He kicked in the door of his own house and with his right arm he pushed all of the filthy glasses and dishes stacked on the kitchen table onto the floor. He stepped on the broken pottery as he walked to the only cupboard in the kitchen and grabbed a bottle of whiskey. He drank straight from the bottle. After several long gulps he threw the empty bottle against the wall. It smashed and the glass littered the floor.

Karzman grabbed another bottle of whiskey from the cupboard and sat down at the table. As he raised the bottle to his mouth he saw that Cabal's bedroom door was partially open. This in itself was not unusual but there was a thin column of smoke working its way from the bedroom into the kitchen. At least Karzman thought it was smoke because it did not have an odor.

The hair on the back his neck started to rise. Karzman set the bottle on the table and walked to the bedroom door. He stood outside of the room and listened for several moments. Silence. He pushed the door open but did not enter the room immediately.

The first thing that Karzman noticed was that the floor was clean. Both of his sons habitually threw their clothing and belongings on the floor. He then looked at the bed and saw that the blankets were missing, exposing the soiled and tattered mattress.

Cabal did not have a hearth in his room. There was but one candle and it was not lit but that thin column of smoke floated around Karzman as he stood in the doorway. He pulled a knife from the sheath on his belt and entered the bedroom. He heard something dripping and looked behind the door.

Karzman yelled and cursed as he jumped to the middle of the room. A dead goat was hanging from a noose behind the door. Cabal had cut the goat open and placed dolls that looked like Karzman inside. There were also dolls hanging from small nooses and dolls with pins and nails stuck in them. Karzman stared at this scene for but a moment, he quickly looked at the walls that had been blocked from his view by the door and saw curses written in the blood of the goat.

Karzman turned and ran out of the room. His fears consumed him. His head was spinning and he was gasping for air. Karzman collapsed in the doorway of his home.

Adam and Sudfad returned to the castle just in time for the meeting the following morning. Everyone was already seated in the Great Hall when they arrived. Sudfad looked exhausted and as if he had been crying. Renya jumped out of her chair and hugged him.

"Honey sit down and I will get you a meal," Renya said and quickly left the room.

"Adam, I have an unusual request for you," said Gabriel and the members of his team all smiled. "We were talking about you taking Renya on a journey and Chasity overheard us. She got so excited and told the family how you saved her and those two boys. So now all of the children have made you things that they want to give you and everyone wants to meet you. Would you mind coming to the house?"

Before Adam answered Raphael said, "Most of the children have met Miranda and Daniel. And some of the children feel particularly close to Miranda because she healed them. We told them you were Miranda's brother and that made them more excited to meet you."

"I would be honored," Adam said with a big smile.

"Well, I hope you have some pockets in that robe because they drew you a lot of pictures," Calen said with a grin.

The ruling families of Lentz led a caravan towards Wetpr for the wedding of Luca and Natalie. They left Langer before sunrise. Only King Mathas and Sorren stayed to run the kingdom. One thousand soldiers of Lentz escorted the caravan, which stopped in the Village of Tyger to gather the members of the Nordes Tribe who were also attending the wedding. All of the children who were to be in the wedding were excited and all spoke at once.

Ashley talked Selen into coming with them since everyone she called a friend was going to Wetpr. These two women started out riding in a boca that was filled with noisy children.

Claudius and Fahron led the caravan, which consisted of people on horseback, bocas and carriages. Three bocas were filled with furniture and toys that Simon, Raul, Gabriel, Raphael and others had ordered. Ryan was driving one of these bocas and he too was very excited because he wanted to see Nyla.

Sudfad's meeting was halfway over when the Great Hall filled with Enrops carrying notes. "Is something wrong?" asked Sudfad when he saw the number of birds.

"No, your friends from Lentz are coming," said one of the Enrops.

"We will take a break now," said the King as the letters were being distributed.

"Ryan is coming," said Nyla excitedly then she quickly looked at Michael.

"Michael, we need to talk after the meeting," Simon said and winked at him.

"Talk about what?" asked Michael suspiciously.

"Ryan and Nyla have crushes on each other," said Raul. "We talked to the boy and he has never been on a date or even kissed a girl, so you don't have anything to worry about."

Everyone thought that Michael would get mad but he turned to his sister and grinned. "You have a crush on Ryan? Honestly I had my money on Joao or Dack." This comment brought a great deal of laughter and Nyla blushed. "I didn't mean to embarrass you. Ryan is a nice kid."

"So it's alright if we dance together?" Nyla asked.

Michael grinned again and said, "Maybe we should talk after the meeting."

"We're going to change the subject here," said Raul. "But it is still talking about Ryan. We knew he was a talented carpenter but when we were bringing the girls home we stayed at Claudius' castle. Bella redesigned his study and Ryan made all of the furniture. It was impressive. So Father and Mother, we ordered all of the furniture for your new study. And Mother before you gasp, Bella helped us because it was clear we didn't know what we were doing."

"It's from all your sons," Simon said. "And I said it that way because our wives are always telling us we never do anything for you."

"I feel embarrassed," said Michael. "I didn't know about this."

"That's because you were too busy fighting demons," Simon said. "And be thankful you didn't have to look at all those fabric samples."

"What all did you get?" asked Renya.

"Everything Bella could think of," said Matthew and chuckled. "We were so grateful that she helped that we took everyone out for dinner."

"I don't know what to say sons," said Sudfad emotionally. "Thank you."

"Oh my god!" said Renya and quickly stood up. "Girls, we have to finish that room."

"Mother, Bella sent material for you to choose from for the drapes," said Simon.

"Really?" asked Renya with disbelief.

"We actually got everything except the carpets, "Raul said.

"Annabelle and I know the colors," said Vitomas. "We will just need to check on the painters and buy carpets." The women left the meeting.

"Now that they're gone," said Raphael to Sudfad. "Between your sons and our team we have a boca filled with gifts and toys too. So we will need a place to set all of that up."

"Well, with all of this going on. Let's end the meeting early so we can work on these other things," said Sudfad. "Besides I could use a little sleep."

Gideon was riding a horse next to Thaos and Stephan and the two brothers grinned as they listened to him talk. "I'll tell you, now that I have a family I worry about every little thing. When I was single I didn't care if I had furniture. Hell, I didn't worry about food half the time. Now I am consumed with making the property safe enough for Ashley and the boys."

"Believe me, we understand you," Stephan said. "But we were lucky; Mother just went ahead and built our homes for us. Father finally told us what was going on since she didn't ask for any of our input."

"Stephan is kind a making that sound bad," said Thaos. "When we saw what Bella was doing none of us changed a thing."

"I never thought I would be this way," said Gideon. "Actually I never really planned to settle down."

"You're just protective and there is nothing wrong with that," said Thaos. "And honestly you have reasons to be worried as we all do."

Unless Madeline and Javier were heavily involved in a mission they usually went back to their home in the Kingdom of Inferus once a month to report to their superiors. This brother and sister team led a clandestine group of spies that worked in a variety of kingdoms. Occasionally some of their people would return home with them as was the case of the most recent trip.

There was so much going on in the kingdoms of Wetpr, Lentz and Ganz that this group of spies was spread out thinly. Because of the volume of information that needed to be discussed with their superiors, Javier pulled two men assigned to each of the three kingdoms to join the meeting.

While all of these Elods were watching the actions, attacks and gatherings in Lentz, Wetpr and Ganz; they had little inside information. So they speculated on the political motives. For the first time in years they didn't have any contacts in either the royal families or the militaries of these kingdoms.

Some of the Elods who were watching Sudfad's castle discovered three of Karzman's men also spying on the Royal Family. The Elods captured these men and tortured them for information. So as Javier and Madeline were beginning to understand the connection with the ruthless dictator of the north and Sudfad's family; Sampson appeared in the picture.

The Elods were intrigued by Sampson because they could see the darkness in him. They watched him spy on Sudfad's castle and kill others who did the same. Javier and Madeline did not understand who Sampson was or why he was spying on the castle.

Then just days before they left for Inferus, Javier and Madeline saw groups of Venatores hunting on Sudfad's land. But these warriors were not hunting for food. Javier suspected the Venatores were looking for Sampson but this was confusing to him and Madeline because Sampson was dressed as a Venator.

Thousands of years earlier after the Elods chose to live in the bowels of the World of Nunc they built passageways to enter and escape from the world above them.

They also devised ways to watch this world for they still feared it. When the Rites of Purification were performed over the plyogram, the hell worlds were not the only ones affected.

Great quakes, storms and flooding also occurred in the Kingdom of Inferus but unlike the powerful demons of old, the Elods had no idea what was causing these disruptions.

That evening before dinner, every member of Gabriel's household was in the huge dining room of the mansion. The children awaited with excited anticipation as Gabriel called out to the heavens. Within a moment the huge, powerful warrior Angel Adam appeared.

"Adam!" screamed Chasity and ran to him. All of the children followed her and screamed his name. Even the smallest of the children were now hugging his legs and robe. Adam picked Chasity up first and she hugged him tightly. "Adam, you have to meet my new family."

To the surprise of the adults in the room, Adam took the time and spoke with every child who hugged and kissed him. Hannah walked up to him. "Adam, thank you for coming. I guess, well it may sound silly; we have never seen an Angel eat. But we would be honored if you would join us for dinner. We made a feast in your honor."

Adam laughed, which too surprised some of the people who had been with him in the Kingdom of Ganz. Adam carried himself with the presence of a commanding general. His bearing was so prominent that for many it distracted them from the holy energy he emitted. To the people who fought with him in Ganz, Adam seemed powerful, confident and very angry.

"Yes, Angels eat too," said Adam. "It is I who would be honored."

"Gabriel will show you to your place," said Hannah. "We will bring the food out."

Most of the women quickly walked into the kitchen. "I hope I don't go to hell for this," said Natasha with a grin. "He is so handsome."

"Natasha!" Vivian said in a scolding tone then laughed loudly as did the other women.

"I mean all of the Angels we have met are beautiful even Ruth in the form she portrays but boy is Adam handsome," Natasha continued.

"Natasha do you have a crush on an Angel?" Vivian kidded.

"I might," Natasha said and giggled.

As the women spoke they were unaware that Raphael had walked into the kitchen and was listening to them. "You do know that he is probably aware of everything you just said," he said and laughed as Natasha turned bright red.

"Oh my gosh, you are right," Natasha said as the others continued to laugh. "Now I will be too embarrassed to go out there."

"Well you can't very well stay in here," said Iris while she was still laughing. "Just pretend like you don't know that he can read your mind."

"Read my mind, oh no now I am really in trouble," Natasha said and laughed again.

"As handsome as he is you are probably not the first human to have a crush on him," said Diana and giggled.

"You girls," said Emeral in a scolding manner but she too was laughing. "I don't know what I am going to do with you."

"I am changing the subject for a moment," Raphael said. "Do you know where High Priest Othnial is? Did he know about the feast for Adam?"

"I know he is with Dominic," said Hannah. "He told me this morning that he would be spending the day and perhaps the night with that team. That was before we found out that Adam would be coming."

Maxwell and Sam poured their best wine as Gabriel introduced Adam to everyone in the household. The children would not leave the Angel, it was as if they were mesmerized by him.

"Adam after dinner I would like to ask you a question," said Elan. "It's about the rest of Chasity's brothers and sisters."

"Of course," said Adam. "But the children will not join us for that conversation." Cassandra gasped and tears started to fill her eyes.

"You two have shown great love and compassion with the family that you are building," said Adam. "The worlds would change if everyone acted in such a manner."

Elan put his arm around Casandra and nodded his understanding to Adam. Elan too was upset as he understood that the words that Adam would tell them were not the words they wanted to hear.

"What do you mean we can't get out?" shrieked Madeline.

"The tunnels are collapsing from these quakes," Javier said.

"It's worse than that," said Ivan who was the direct supervisor of Javier and Madeline. Ivan had just walked into Madeline's chambers since Javier had left the door open.

"What do you mean?" Javier asked.

"I don't understand how any of this can be happening but our windows into the world above have closed too," said Ivan. "The Abuckto are holding an emergency meeting to try and figure all of this out. They are reviewing the prophesies for what good that will do."

"Do you really think those lunatics know what is happening?" yelled Javier. "They are the reason we want to take over the world above. And I will tell you sometimes those people seem a lot more sane than ours."

"Javier, keep your voice down," warned Madeline. "You know there are spies everywhere."

Ivan had closed the door when Javier was yelling, now he walked closer to Javier and Madeline and lowered his voice as he spoke, "Our men tell me that the world above was not experiencing these whatever you want to call them, feats of nature but suddenly riots broke out all over the world, then our windows closed."

The women in Gabriel's home filled the table with delicacies. Zelda, Horace and Zack were also at the dinner table. "Adam, there are many different groups represented at this table and the women have fixed you the finest foods of their people. I don't know if they told you that," said Horace.

"They did not and I do appreciate this. It has been a long time since I sat at a table in your world."

"Well, you are certainly welcome to join us at any time," said Emeral. "Your presence here is a great honor for us."

"You are an unusual group of people in more ways than you realize," said Adam. "As Horace said there are different peoples represented here and yet you don't have to be an Angel to feel the love in this room. You may be surprised to hear this but many people fear Angels and some curse us yet you bring all of us into your family. Even for an Angel this is surprising."

"Well, we are really glad that you are here," said Hannah.

"Where is Natasha?" asked Gabriel. "We are ready to say Grace." Suddenly all of the women started to grin. "Something is up. What is going on?"

Batina glanced at Gabriel then at Adam and said, "She is still in the kitchen." Adam smiled and all of the women broke into laughter.

"What is the joke?" asked Gabriel as he saw that Raphael was also laughing.

"I'll get her," said Calen as he too was wondering why everyone was laughing.

"Tell her she isn't going to hell," Adam said with a grin. And the women roared with loud laughter. Vivian was crying she was laughing so hard.

"What is so funny?" asked Thor.

Vivian started to speak but couldn't stop laughing.

"I'll tell you later," Diana choked out as she was laughing.

"Tell us now," said Joao.

Calen and Natasha walked into the dining room. Calen was laughing and Natasha was blushing. Her face was a deep red and she took her seat without looking at anyone.

"Is someone going to tell us what is going on?" asked Maxwell.

"Apparently my wife has a crush on Adam and he heard what she said." Calen laughed loudly as he spoke.

"Calen!" Natasha scolded and now everyone in the room laughed again.

"Well Adam, I guess you are part of the family now," Misha said with a grin.

"What caused the riots?" asked Javier. "This all has to be related."

"We don't know yet," Ivan said. "But I agree and I want to resume our meeting. Perhaps something you or your people saw or heard can shed light on these most unusual happenings."

"While I agree with everything you have said," Madeline said anxiously. "I am more concerned with us being trapped here."

Ivan stared at Madeline for a few moments before he spoke, "Madeline you look scared. Is there more to this? More that you know?"

Madeline didn't speak for a moment then she said. "We spend so much time in that world that I feel more at home there than here. There are many more freedoms above. I never realized how repressed we were until I entered that other world."

"And I know if I said these words in front of the wrong people here that I could be killed but that is exactly what I am talking about. If I said these words in Lentz, Wetpr, Ganz or other kingdoms it would simply be a topic of debate."

"Javier, I know you understand what I am saying. I sometimes wonder about what we are doing?" Madeline continued.

"What do you mean?" growled Javier as he realized the seriousness of his sister's statements.

"Our sect was formed because we felt imprisoned in the bowels of this world," said Madeline. "We wanted and still do want to reclaim our lands in the world above. But I have realized that it isn't the boundaries of our kingdoms that imprison us but our own way of life. If we take over the world above and bring the same civilization there that we have here we will still be in a prison; don't you see that?"

After the evening meal the women in Gabriel's home were clearing the table while Gabriel and Elan were lining up the children so they could give Adam his gifts. Raphael and Maxwell were pouring wine into everyone's glasses. Once the meal had started everyone felt more at ease with Adam in their presence and asked him many questions which led to long discussions.

"Adam, I don't think I am the only one at this table who is surprised at how this evening has gone," said Luca.

"Luca!" scolded Emeral.

"No, I mean it in a good sense. I think that we are always so awestruck when we are in the presence of Angels that it forms a barrier in a way. Tonight it is as if you have really become part of our lives," Luca continued.

"He's right," said Raphael. "But I don't know if that is good. I mean we should never lose our reverence."

Adam smiled. "Inviting the heavens into your lives is always a good thing. And while this dinner has been an unusual but very pleasant event for me too, I do not feel that any of you have lessened your reverence."

"Adam are you ready?" Gabriel asked as he entered the dining room. Everyone could hear the excited chatter and giggles of the children.

"Yes," Adam said warmly.

Chasity was the first to run to Adam. Each child presented him with something they had made for him, a drawing, a letter, a bracelet or other item. Since some of the children had made more than one gift they would go back in line for another presentation.

The adults watched with amazement as the powerful warrior Angel truly seemed touched by the love the children were showing him. He carefully opened his gifts and hugged each child. Tommy gave Adam the last of the gifts. It was a drawing that was so unusual the Angel took pause.

Adam picked Tommy up and set him on his lap, while he studied Tommy's colorful drawing. Then to the surprise of all Adam put his hand on Tommy's forehead and closed his eyes in prayer. No one made a sound in the room.

When Adam opened his eyes Cassandra quickly asked, "Is something wrong?"

"On the contrary." said Adam. "All of you have been given a gift for the love and mercy you have shown by taking in all of these children; children which others threw away. Tommy is a seer. Which would explain the trauma you said he experienced. It is very difficult for people much less children to understand what they are seeing. Did anyone look at this picture?" Adam handed it to Gabriel who was sitting the closest to him.

"I didn't. But there is something familiar about this," Gabriel said and handed the drawing to Raphael.

"You saw that world briefly," said Adam. "That is the Kingdom of Inferus. When you performed the Rites of Purification you not only closed the windows of the demons into your world but also the windows and passageways of the Elods. That is what Tommy drew."

Both Cassandra and Elan ran over to Raphael who had the drawing. "There are more," said Elan as the color drained from his face.

"I'll get them," Cassandra said in a whisper and ran out of the dining room.

"Does it hurt him when he sees these things?" asked Emeral.

"Not in the physical sense, although some things can scare him," Adam said to Emeral then turned to Tommy. "Tommy when you get scared you should pray to The Great Ruler and ask Him to surround you with His Light."

"We already do," said Christopher. "Miranda told that to Natalie and Natalie told us."

"Good," Adam said and smiled again. Then he addressed the adults. "Many times parents rationalize that children have vivid imaginations when they draw or talk about things they could have no knowledge of. This is a gift. Do not make Tommy feel like there is anything wrong."

"Are you saying he is like Zoya?" asked Zack.

"In a way. But seers can have different abilities and Tommy is very young yet."

Cassandra walked into the room and handed a small stack of drawings to Adam. "He always draws but he started drawing these a couple of weeks ago," Cassandra said. "Elan and I thought that perhaps he had overheard some of the people talking about missions."

"Tommy these are very good drawings," Adam said gently. "Tell me when you see these things do you ever hear the people in your pictures talking?"

Tommy was surprisingly eager to talk about his artwork. "Sometimes and sometimes I know things."

"Can you give me an example?" asked Adam as he spread the drawings on the table in front of him.

"That pretty lady is scared a lot," said Tommy as he pointed to a woman that was in several drawings.

"That is Madeline," said Adam and people started to get out of their chairs and gather around the drawings. "Do you know why she is scared?"

"No," said Tommy. "But I heard all this noise. But I don't think that is what scared her."

"And that boy is very bad." Tommy pointed to a boy with white blonde hair who was wearing a white robe."

"His robe kinda looks like the Sanuri's," Christopher said.

"Is that Thot?" asked Raphael.

"No and Tommy is right about him."

"That's one of the creatures we saw in Langer," said Gabriel. "A beast like that was washed up on shore."

"They are called Stratas. They are one of the beasts that the Elods breed. I will explain more after the children have gone to bed."

"We saw this man when we went on the journey with Angelina," Gabriel said with concern and pointed to a man riding a horse. "Tommy do you know anything about him?"

"Bad man," Tommy said nonchalantly. Then Tommy climbed on the table and picked up one of his drawings. "This is my friend Anka she shows me these pictures. She said she saw me in a dream." As Tommy spoke he held out a drawing of a little girl with long curly red hair.

"How do you hear her talk?" asked Elan.

"In my head not my ears," Tommy said. "She is really nice."

"Tommy what have you shown her?" asked Maxwell. The concern in his voice was echoed in the minds of all the adults.

"I don't think I have shown her anything," Tommy said.

"Adam will you help us with this?" asked Gabriel.

Adam closed his eyes for several moments. He sat motionless then he started to smile. "Miranda join us."

Miranda appeared in the room and the children ran to her. "We should have invited you to dinner too," gasped Emeral. "We are sorry."

"Perhaps another time," said Miranda. "This was a gift for Adam in more ways than you realize. But you want to know about Anka."

"Children why don't you go to the playroom and draw pictures for Miranda," said Emeral. The children quickly left the dining room.

"As we have told you the Elods are a race of extremely intelligent and advanced people. So intelligent that many of them feel superior to The Great Ruler and have abolished Him from their lives. We told you about the sect of powerful seers that calls itself the Abuckto and some of the political sects such as the Charto that Madeline and Javier belong to," explained Miranda.

"But in the darkness there is always some light. One of the secret sects of that society is called the Credo. They are followers of The Great Ruler and have prayed to Him to prevent the other Elods from realizing their secret. Many people of that race are seers, very powerful seers as is Anka and her father Benedict. Benedict is a leader of the Credos and because of this he is very scared about letting his children play with others."

"Anka prayed for The Great Ruler to send her a friend. And that is why Adam called me. I went to Anka. She is a brilliant and sweet child who lives in a repressive culture. Even if she didn't believe in The Great Ruler she would live in fear. She is very lonely and welcomed me greatly."

482

"I told her I would help her find a friend closer to her age but she should tell no one about him. I knew Tommy was a seer too."

"Since I brought Anka and Tommy together I am monitoring their friendship. The flame of faith is so tiny in Inferus that it needs to be fed. Anka, a courageous and faithful child now has a special friend who she can talk with about anything. There are few freedoms in Inferus. One has to be careful of what they say for fear of being put to death."

"Tommy has not sent her anything that would be a threat to you and I will make sure that he doesn't. But I am allowing Anka to send him images of her world."

"Does that child know about all of these people in these drawings?" asked Emeral.

"Of course not," said Miranda with a smile." But it is an open door and I am using it."

# Chapter XXXIX
## Doors

Miranda and Adam stayed late into the night and talked with the members of Gabriel's household. Raphael took careful notes of everything that was said.

"I have one more question before you go," said Maxwell. "That boy in the picture wearing the robe. Of course I haven't meet Thot but that boy looks exactly the way the Sanuri described him. All of you tell us not to believe in coincidences so what is the significance?"

"That is an excellent question and one that Adam should answer," said Miranda.

"The boy in the picture is named Andrac and he is as evil as Thot is good. They are not related although you would not believe that if you saw them both. You know we get assignments and I have been working with Thot. I do not know why The Great Ruler created those two to look alike, but trust me there is a good reason. You have experienced the same thing with Ibula and Vitomas."

"We have heard that everyone has a twin somewhere," said Koby. "Is that true?"

"No," said Adam. "That is why you should understand there is significance when you come across such things."

"I am sorry that we ask so many questions," said Hannah. "But you never finished saying what Madeline was afraid of."

"Inferus is a repressive society that controls its members by fear," said Adam. "But you should understand also that nothing is totally black and white. While spies are sent here with the task of retrieving information and setting things into motion so they someday can regain their lands here, they are seeing a new way of life. Which makes them then look at their lives in Inferus with new eyes."

"The Elods are a strange combination between extreme intelligence and savage brutality. Like the Hutas, they teach their children to hate."

"The various sects are sending more of their people into this world with the idea of destroying it but this action is starting to become self-destructive."

"I don't understand what you mean," said Rachel.

"He means some of the Elods like it here," Misha said.

"Some of them are becoming involved with men and women in this world and not just to obtain information. They are developing relationships as friends and lovers which could result in them being put to death in Inferus," said Miranda. "That is a race that has many choices to make."

"Father, tell them," Vivian said to Joshua.

"When Gabriel and the others saw that creature that washed up on the shore in Langer, Ingr drew pictures of it. Diana and Natasha copied the picture and I sent one to Chief Duncan. I remembered seeing something like that pictured in an ancient cave drawing."

"I received this before dinner and haven't had a chance to show everyone yet," Joshua explained as he unfolded a piece of paper and handed to Miranda, who was closest to him. "One of the warriors copied a couple of the drawings from that cave. There seems to be a great similarity between the beasts that are being ridden like horses in the cave drawing and the drawing from Ingr."

"Those are Stratas with Elod warriors on their backs," said Miranda as she handed the drawing to her brother.

"Then how long have they been coming into this world?" asked Dagon.

"For centuries," Adam replied and handed the drawing to Gabriel.

"Then why are there so many more coming now?" asked Luca as he was handed the drawing.

"It could be that you are just aware of them now," said Miranda and smiled. "They are an ancient culture."

The following morning the members of Gabriel's household arrived earlier than usual for Sudfad's morning meeting. They understood that since the King had shortened the meeting the previous day this meeting might last longer and they wanted to make sure they could tell him everything about the visit with Adam and Miranda.

When Gabriel and the others entered the castle the Royal Family were still eating breakfast. Sudfad invited everyone into the dining room and the King's family sat spellbound as they listened to the highlights of the previous evening.

"I am going to stop you there Raphael," said Sudfad. "Because we should bring Zoya here and show her the drawings."

"Actually that was one of the reasons we came early," said Gabriel.

"I'll get them. Jared is probably on his way," said Koby and left the castle.

"I think everyone needs to hear what you have to say," said Sudfad. "And I don't want you to have to repeat it all."

"We didn't know what you had planned for the meeting and wanted to make sure we could tell you about all of this," said Gabriel. "Raphael was just giving you the highlights."

"Well, this certainly will be the main topic of the meeting," Sudfad said.

"While we wait," said the Sanuri. "I am curious how did the social aspect go with Adam?"

Everyone from Gabriel's household started to grin. "You know how Miranda is all business; well we kind of expected Adam to be the same. He really surprised us," said Dagon.

"How so?" asked the Sanuri.

"Well, first he seemed really touched by the attention of the children. He spent time with each of them and made them feel that he really appreciated their gifts," said Maxwell and started to smile.

"Oh let me tell the rest," said Calen and laughed loudly. "Well as you can imagine everyone in the house is on their best behavior because we are entertaining an Angel." As Calen spoke others started laughing. "Well, all the women go into the kitchen and my wife starts shooting her mouth off saying she is probably going to hell because she thinks Adam is so good looking she could get a crush on him and he heard her."

"Oh my god!" said Annabelle and covered her mouth with her hand.

"Actually he teased her and when we all got done laughing, it was kind of like he was just another guy at the table." Calen continued.

"We had very interesting dinner conversation," said Gabriel. "And as Maxwell said he was very gracious with the children."

"Oh, I think he was more than gracious," said Luca. "Michael remember when you first came here? You didn't feel comfortable with all of us but you poured your love into the kids. That's what he reminded me of last night. Actually as I am saying the words I realize I am not explaining this well. You expect Angels to love kids but am I the only one who felt that Adam seems a little lost? I think that is why he reminded me of Michael in the beginning."

"I am certainly not an expert on Angels," said the Sanuri and chuckled. "But I have often thought about their roles and I don't think I could do their jobs."

"What do you mean?" asked Renya with great surprise.

"Renya if any one of us in this room was riding down the street and saw someone who needed help we can make the choice whether to help them or not. Can you see any of us standing by while great acts of horror are being committed?"

"You know the Angels would save everyone they could and clean up these worlds but these worlds belong to men and women who have freedom of choice. All of that is a very complicated matter and I am not sure I could explain it adequately. But because Adam is such an incredibly powerful Angel he volunteered for some awful assignments that seem to have taken a toll on him."

"He is working with us to help him heal. So Luca you may have been right in your observations. That and you put him in a very unnatural setting having him as a guest in your home and treating him like part of the family. Tell me, did he enjoy that?"

"He said he did and when Miranda appeared Emeral apologized for not inviting her to dinner too," explained Raphael. "Miranda said that the night was more of a gift for Adam than we realized."

"Now I kind of feel bad," said Michael. "In Ganz we got into some pretty heated arguments and I blamed him and Ruth for a lot of things that weren't their fault. I need to apologize to them."

"Michael!" Saran said sharply. "Are you saying you were mean to Ruth? She saved us. We love her. You better apologize."

Michael looked at his three sisters who were all glaring at him and started to laugh. "Boy, all of you have really changed. You're all so feisty now..." he didn't complete his sentence because Koby, Jared, Zoya and Archetenus walked into the room.

"I told them the part about Tommy on the way in," said Koby.

"We should move this into the other room now," said Sudfad and stood up. "I know it is still early; did all of you eat breakfast?"

"No," said Archetenus.

"I'll have three breakfasts brought in," said Renya. "Does anyone else want one?"

"We never turn down food," said Misha.

The meeting was moved to the Great Hall. Raphael and Elan were rearranging the tables and chairs while Thor and Dack lined up all of Tommy's drawings.

Archetenus picked up one of the drawings and stared at it. "I wonder if Miranda helped him with this because it is really good for a little kid; you know she did that with me."

"Cassandra and I wondered that too," said Elan. "His other drawings are much more childish."

"The reason I bring this up," continued Archetenus. "Is that if she helped him then we need to make sure we really study the details."

Platters of food were brought into the room before the door was closed. "Since Zoya is eating should we just start telling about last night?" asked Gabriel. Sudfad nodded.

"At the risk of sounding paranoid, this trip has been too easy," Claudius said to Fahron as they were leading their caravan towards Salar.

"I think we live in a time when we always need to be a little paranoid," Fahron said. "Which in itself is a sad thing to say." He paused. "I will tell you I am anxious to see the children. I wish that Chaez and Lana could return with us and the girls."

"Perhaps you can work something out. Do the priests get any breaks from their studies?"

"I think he took his break when he went on that mission with you. I never thought any of my children would become warriors; I am so proud of that boy and the girls too."

Karzman was feared and hated by the villagers and his soldiers. No one went to his house because no one wanted to be near him. He lay in the front doorway half in the kitchen and half in the dirt of the yard. His body was stricken with convulsions. His vomit was filled with his blood. He suffered delusions and these delusions were filled with monsters.

Sampson sat in a tree and stared at the lands of Sudfad. For the first time in days he did not see any sign of another person; no spies, no troops, no hunting parties of Venatores. And this absence made him paranoid.

He had not slept in days as his memories were returning to him. He was filled with extreme ranges of emotions. He remembered everything now, even becoming the hunting dog for the demon Ael. Sampson was always a proud man and he felt the demons humiliated him. On some level he heard Samael's voice but it was in the regions of his mind. Now that Sampson was strong and had his memories back he felt in control, confident and confused. He had no idea why he was spying on the castle of Sudfad.

The people attending Sudfad's meeting remained quiet as Zoya studied the drawings that Tommy had made. Several long tables had been pushed together and the drawings were lined up in two rows. Suddenly people started to jump out of their seats as their coffee cups and glasses started to explode.

"What the hell!" yelled Jared and ran to his wife who looked like she was in a trance.

"Leave her," said Miranda as she appeared in the Great Hall with Daniel. "We are protecting her."

"What is happening?" asked Jared fearfully.

"We will tell you in a moment," Daniel said and moved closer to Zoya. Daniel place his hand on her right shoulder and she came out of her trance-like state. Zoya quickly swung around and looked at the Angels first.

"I have so much to tell you," Zoya said. "Jared, I am alright; you look so scared. But that was the most incredible journey. I am not sure I really understand it all."

"Then let us start to explain," said Miranda. "But first I am going to tell you again that you have to call to us. All of you in this room not only put Zoya but everyone in great danger. You will not do that again without speaking with us first."

"I told most of you last night that a door opened and I worked with Anka and Tommy to connect. All of us have told you that the Kingdom of Inferus is made up of incredibly powerful seers. Don't you think they have been spying on you and trying to connect with you? Just because Zoya uses her gift with integrity does not mean that all seers do."

"As Zoya studied Tommy's drawings she walked through the door, so to speak that Tommy and Anka communicate through. Zoya is so powerful that the seers of Inferus knew they had an intruder and went searching for her. Think of it as you are on patrol on a dark night and you see a flame in the distance."

"We have been closing doors to protect you from the Elods and basically you sent Zoya into battle by herself. The other seers ran to that flame in the darkness and tried to attack her. They also tried to gain entrance through the door she had walked through, which I had to close. We prevented them from hurting her or getting into her mind. When Daniel touched her shoulder he sent energy into that world. It did not hurt them but it has surprised and confused them."

"Never before has a seer from any world been able to infiltrate their defense system. And part of that is because few know that the Elods exist. The good thing about this is that they are all scrambling to figure out what happened."

"Zoya, we are so sorry," said Gabriel.

"I wasn't hurt but I saw their world and I saw some of them. The powerful seers dress as priests and I could feel their power which was incredible. Their cities look like ours, like Salar but they have strange creatures everywhere. People ride them and use them as farm animals. And the people I saw seemed to look like people in this world." Zoya paused and looked around the room. "Where is the Sanuri?" she asked frantically.

"He is..." Sudfad said. "He was just here. Where is he? Does he need help?"

"Oh yes," said Daniel. "He jumped through the door that Zoya opened."

"He's in Inferus?" asked Erebus.

"Yes," said Miranda. "And I will speak with him too. He saw an opportunity and took it. He is looking for the Credo to give them hope."

"He will need help," said Raul. "Can you send some of us? We went there before."

"That was a different thing all together," said Daniel. "That was a journey of the spirit into different time dimensions."

"Can't we help him?" asked High Priest Othnial.

"Wait a minute," said Edward. "Just how is he planning on giving them hope?"

"I believe he is planning on helping them to escape," Daniel said with a smile.

"So that is why you didn't stop us," said Archetenus with a grin. "How are you going to get us in there to help him? Does Zoya need to open the door again?"

As Sampson sat in the arm of a large oak tree he kept reviewing his life. He had been raised to hate demons yet they gave him great pleasure. But they betrayed him and humiliated him every chance they had. Sampson realized how he had been used and was consumed with anger.

Sampson also realized he had betrayed his family and his tribe yet they never betrayed him. Sampson had not suddenly become a good man. He was however learning from his mistakes and he was focusing on new enemies.

As powerful as he was, Sampson knew he could not get revenge on the demons without help. He climbed out of the tree and ran towards the castle.

"The Elods have been watching all of you for a very long time," said Daniel. "You will be recognized and will hinder the Sanuri's efforts."

"Then disguise us," said Gabriel. "This is insane that we can't help."

"We didn't say you couldn't help," Daniel said.

"Have they been watching us?" asked Drake. "Cuz, well you know we are kind of bad guys. So they may not be interested."

"Would you risk your lives to help the Sanuri get those people out of hell?" asked Miranda.

"Sure," said Tally. "Can we take weapons?"

Fighting and yelling was heard outside of one of the patio doors to the Great Hall. "Let him in," said Miranda.

"Who?" asked Sudfad.

"Sampson!" gasped Vivian as he kicked open the door and walked into the hall. Every man in the room pulled out a weapon.

"I do not come to fight you!" yelled Sampson. "The Sanuri is calling me."

"What?" asked Joshua through clenched teeth.

Sampson had not initially seen the Angels and now he stopped in his tracts and looked terrified.

"You may enter," said Miranda and walked towards him. But Sampson did not move. "You dance with demons; tell me are you afraid to speak with Angels?"

Now everyone in the Great Hall watched in silence as the giant Venator fell to his knees before the Angel. "We have been talking to you for years why now do you listen to our voices?" asked Miranda.

Sampson was crying and did not speak but shook his head from side to side. "Oh come now, you had a loud enough voice when you cursed The Great Ruler and all His followers."

"What is going on?" asked Micha. "Is he good now?" No one answered his question.

"You heard his question," said Miranda sternly. "Tell us Sampson, are you good now?"

"I don't think so," he answered as he tried to control his emotions.

"Then why are you here? To attack us?"

"No."

"To serve your master Samael?"

"He is not my master!"

"He owns your soul."

"What? No he does not. No one owns my soul."

"He does and he brought you to Wetpr to spy on his enemies. And his enemies are the followers of The Great Ruler."

"What? How can he own my soul?"

"Because you have been a puppet of darkness for so long that you lost all control. They pass you around as any other toy. But you just realized this didn't you?"

Sampson nodded.

"I asked you a question. Answer me."

"Yes. For so long I couldn't remember things and a few days ago I, I started to remember and..."

"Finish your statement."

"And I realize that I betrayed everyone who cared about me and I rode with the demons and all they did was make a fool out of me."

"And what did you do when you realized this?"

Sampson was kneeling at Miranda's feet and had been staring at the floor. Now he looked up at her. "You mean when I declared war on the demons?"

"Then what happened?"

"I heard the Sanuri calling for help." Sampson now composed himself. "The Sanuri needs help."

"And you would help him? You who defied and cursed him?"

"Yes."

"Why?"

"I guess, I don't, because he needs help."

"He is in a very dangerous place. A hell world. A place where you should feel at home. He is trying to save innocents. How would I know that you would not betray him and dance again with the demons?"

"I don't know, honestly. But I will go there. You are right I am familiar with hell worlds. I have traveled in many."

"Stand before me!"

Sampson slowly rose to his feet.

"You look into my eyes and you listen very carefully to my words. I do not play games as the demons do. You could be of great help to the Sanuri but there is not a man or woman in this room who trusts you because you have betrayed all trusts. So you who have walked with the demons. You swear to The Great Ruler now that you will not betray the Sanuri and those he is trying to save."

Everyone could see the terror in Sampson's face.

"Does the mission scare you?" asked Miranda sharply.

"No, The Great Ruler does."

"You can walk out that door and return to your demons. They desire playthings. Or you could try to become the man you once were; a proud and powerful Venator. But your journey out of darkness will not be easy, for you have dug a tremendous hole."

Joshua walked next to Miranda. "Son, do the right thing."

Sampson looked at the faces around the room. "Why are so many of our tribe here?"

"Because we are doing the right thing," said Kate harshly. "And we are all sick of being ashamed of you."

"If you are sending him to help the Sanuri," said Thomas. "We will not trust him but we will fight alongside of him." Soon one by one every Venator in the room stood near Miranda.

It was not hatred that made Sampson hesitate, it was humiliation and fear. "Sampson, we don't have all day," said Thor. "Make your choice."

Sampson looked at Daniel then back again at Miranda. "I give my oath to The Great Ruler that I will help the Sanuri on this mission."

"If I were you I would ask Him to help you keep that oath," said Miranda.

Sampson looked sheepish and said out loud, "Great Ruler help me to keep the oath I just made to you."

Raphael walked up to the Venatores. "Vivian, you can be mad at me but you aren't going into a hell world when you are pregnant. Miranda, I will go in her place."

"Very well," said Miranda.

"Now just wait..." yelled Vivian.

"Listen to your husband," said Joshua.

Vivian was enraged but would not dishonor her husband or father in public. She marched up close to Sampson and said angrily, "It is not just The Great Ruler you will fear if you betray them."

"I won't Vivian," Sampson said without his typical anger which greatly surprised her.

"Ok, Sampson is coming," said Raul. "How do we get in and out?"

"We are serious that not all of you can go," said Miranda. "You will draw the attention of the seers. They have you marked in a sense."

"Do you need those of us who have been in hell?" asked Archetenus. "Because it seems to me like time is wasting."

"I wouldn't make Miranda mad," Simon said kiddingly to Archetenus.

"Is someone with the Sanuri now?" asked Dominic.

"Adam is," Daniel said.

"Then I will go," said Michael. "Let it be my turn to help him fight demons. If you need to change something about me to get the mark off; have at it." Michael walked up to the group of Venatores and Drake and Tally followed him. Miranda looked at them.

"We can't let the boy go by himself," said Drake. "He gets in trouble."

"It appears that you are sending everyone who understands the demons most," said Jared as he and Archetenus joined the Venatores.

"Well, if living in the world of darkness is some kind of qualification, I should be at the head of the class," said Erebus and stood with the group of Venatores.

"You are marked," said Miranda.

"Actually I assume we all are so please do whatever you have to do." Miranda and Daniel stared at Erebus. "The Sanuri is my friend and he would do the same for me." Daniel smiled.

"Wait!" said Gabriel. "You told us that Samael can see through Sampson's eyes. Can he still?"

"By praying to The Great Ruler Sampson closed that door and we will make sure it stays closed during this mission," said Miranda. "Now you should have questions of us."

"How many Elods are coming?" asked Sudfad. "We will need to prepare."

"They are still making their choices," said Daniel. "Perhaps a couple of hundred. And they may be pursued. Those who do not come should be prepared for a battle."

"Then where is the door they will enter from?" asked Sudfad.

"Where would you like it to be?" asked Miranda with a smile.

# Chapter XXXL
## Inferus

The Sanuri found himself in the thick jungles of the Kingdom of Inferus. He initially felt disoriented and needed to momentarily steady himself. He felt a presence and turned. The Angel Adam materialized before him.

"Next time you decide to jump into hell you might want to tell one of us," Adam said and smiled. "You will have help coming and trust me you will be surprised who some of them are. So what is your plan?"

The Sanuri chuckled. "Actually I didn't have one. I suddenly saw a door open in my mind's eye and decided to jump through. I figured one of you showed it to me. Are you blocking the seers from seeing us?"

"Actually their fear is blocking them since they realized they had an intruder. But that too means they will be looking for you."

"But they would be expecting an attack of some kind. I am planning a rescue mission. How do we find the Credo?"

"I believe you have a drawing in your pocket. You will need it." The Sanuri pulled out Tommy's drawing of Anka. "Put your hand on it and speak to her with your mind."

Joshua and the group he led never realized they left the castle of Sudfad. They were listening to the Angels speak then they were in a thick jungle. It was very humid and insects attacked them as soon as they materialized.

"This doesn't look like a hell world," said Sampson. "Where are we?"

"In a kingdom in the center of the world," said Joshua. "Apparently there are different kinds of hell."

"And different kinds of creatures," said Jared as he pointed to enormous footprints in the moist earth.

"I'm not sure I want to find out what made those," said Archetenus.

"Quiet!" snapped Kate.

Everyone stood motionless as they now heard movement. Joshua motioned for everyone to hide; which was easy for them because of the dense foliage. The ground started to shake slightly and they heard voices in a language they could understand. The group remained silent as the voices grew louder and the shaking became more prevalent.

Anka ran into the Temple of the Abuckto. Men wearing priest's robes were in groups of eight to ten and searching the temple and courtyard.

"Child this is no place for you," growled one of the men and grabbed Anka's arm roughly.

"I need to find my father. Do you know where he is?" Anka was terrified that the man would read her mind.

"Why do you look so scared?" demanded the man.

"I heard someone say we are under attack. Are we? Is my father alright?"

The man stared at her for a few moments. "The last I saw of Benedict he was meeting with the other elders. They are in the Hall of Knowledge."

"Thanks," said Anka and ran down a long marble hallway. "Please Miranda help us, please Miranda help us," repeated the child.

Normally the temple was a place of tranquility but now it was loud and chaotic. Men were running in all directions.

"Where are you going girl!" yelled a voice that frightened Anka. She knew the voice well and the sorcerer who owned it.

"Miranda please," whispered the girl as she turned and faced Andrac.

"If you have to know I am looking for my father and why do you speak to me in such a manner?" Anka looked at Andrac challengingly all the while her knees were shaking.

Andrac laughed. "I love the fire in you. Tell me did Benedict tell you of our last conversation?" He moved closer to her as he spoke.

Anka held her ground. "No, why would it be of importance to me?"

"It is of great importance to you. I have asked for you to become my wife."

"What! But, but I am not old enough to take a husband."

"You will be ten on the red moon."

"What did my father say?" Anka asked in a fearful voice.

"He has not yet given me an answer but how can he refuse?"

Although her heart was sinking, Anka put her hands on her hips and stomped her right foot on the marble floor. "Well, I do not want you for a husband. And you can't make me."

"Oh but there you are wrong," he said with a grin. Suddenly he stopped walking towards her and looked dazed.

"Andrac what is it? What is wrong?" Anka was terrified that the powerful sorcerer knew she had been talking to an Angel.

"We have more intruders," he said. "Go in there, you will be safe." Andrac pointed to the doors leading into the Hall of Knowledge and turned and ran in the other direction.

Anka opened the heavy doors to the hall and ran inside. Her intrusion stopped a meeting of the leaders of the Abuckto, the most powerful seers of her people. "Anka what is the meaning of this?" asked Benedict as he did not like his daughter around the men in the room.

"Father, I have to talk to you."

"Anka, you know you can't interrupt me when I am working."

Anka was trying to think of a way to separate her father from the other men. "Andrac said there are more intruders and he told me to come in here for protection."

"More intruders? When? When did he say this to you Anka?" asked Baruk the leader of the Abuckto.

"Why, just moments ago. How could he know about the intruders and not you?"

"Excellent question," said Baruk angrily. "Where is he now?"

"He told me to come in here and he ran out of the building."

All of the men in the room ran out of the building except for Benedict. He was a powerful seer and was now seeing things he did not understand. "Father it is important that I talk to you." Anka said and ran to him. "We must speak privately."

"What is going on daughter?"

"Privately Father."

Benedict took Anka's hand and hurried her out of the Hall of Knowledge. They ran out of the building and into the jungle. When they were sure that no one was listening, Anka started to speak in a low voice. "Father, I have much to tell you and you will be angry but wait until you know everything."

"I have been praying for The Great Ruler to send me a friend and a few weeks ago the most beautiful Angel came to me. Her name is Miranda. She visited me every day and we had long talks. I told her about our world, everything Father, but I think she already knew. She told me she would find me a friend who was closer to my age. Then she did something. I don't know how to describe it. She opened a window to the world above and introduced me to a boy named Tommy who is a seer too."

Benedict listened to his daughter in silence. He was filled with both admiration and horror.

"Tommy is really nice and we talk all of the time. Just a little while ago another person came to the window. He said he is the Sanuri and he is an emissary of The Great Ruler. He wants to help all of us escape. Father he is here, in this world."

"My daughter what have you done?"

"Father, I am telling the truth. The Sanuri wants to talk to you."

"I can tell you are speaking the truth but this is all so unbelievable. Where is he?"

"I don't know," Anka said when she suddenly pulled a drawing from the pocket of her dress. "This is Tommy's picture. This is how I open the window." She put her hand over Tommy's face. "Sanuri, I need to talk to you." Instantly she smiled. "Father, he is answering. Here, put your hand on Tommy's face."

Benedict quickly took the drawing and placed his hand on the picture. The face of the Sanuri filled Benedict's mind. "Benedict, you must listen to me. I am an emissary of The Great Ruler and he has allowed me and others to help all of the Credo escape. We will take you to a place of freedom where you can worship Him without fear. But I do not need to tell you the dangers. I am with the Angel Adam. If you lose that drawing you call his name."

"We will not force this upon you. You have a choice, all of you do but I would suggest you make those choices quickly."

"I desperately want to believe you," said Benedict. "How do I know you are not a trick of the Abuckto?"

"Because I am Miranda."

Benedict turned and instantly fell to his knees. "This is a miracle, thank you, thank you."

"Benedict rise. We do not have time to waste; people from another world are risking their lives to help you. Do you want to escape to a world of freedom?"

"Yes, oh yes."

"Then gather your people. They will not believe you so call my name and I will come wherever you are."

"Thank you Miranda," Anka said and hugged the legs of the Angel. "I love you."

"As I do you child, but you must hurry. Have your people take only the basics of what you need. People are already preparing lodging for you." Miranda disappeared. Benedict grabbed his daughter's hand and they ran.

Joshua and his group tensed for battle as six Stratas walked past them. The creatures were enormous as were their riders. Men who looked like warriors of old with massive muscles, long hair and long beards. They all wore helmets, breast plates and bracers made of metal. The men talked and laughed as they rode their beasts in a leisurely manner.

Thor heard a sound and turning he saw a strange bird watching him. It was the size of an Enrop but its feathers were the color of the rainbow. "Miranda is that evil?" Thor whispered.

"No, he is no threat."

"Good," said Thor. The bird seemed very curious by these strange intruders and kept nodding its head back and forth. Thor smiled and held out his arm. It only took a moment for the bird to fly to Thor. He stroked its feathers and gave it some bread he had in a pouch on his belt. Thor was surprised at how tame the bird seemed. It ate out of his hand. "You are so beautiful; I wish you could come home with us," Thor whispered.

Joshua made a low whistle and the warriors understood the danger had passed. They regrouped. "Diana, Kate look," said Thor in a low voice as he walked up to them with the bird sitting on his shoulder. "Miranda said he wasn't a threat." Both women got big smiles and quickly walked up to Thor to pet the bird.

"He kind of looks like an Enrop but with different colors," said Micha. "Can he talk?"

"I don't know," said Thor.

"Can you talk you pretty boy?" cooed Diana as she petted the bird.

"Who is your leader?" asked the bird.

"Joshua," called Thor in a low voice.

As Joshua approached Thor, the bird flew to Joshua's shoulder.

"The Angel Adam has a message," said the bird. "You are in great danger. The seers know of your presence although they cannot see into your minds. It is a diversion so the Credo can gather. Although Adam and Miranda are blocking the seers there are many sorcerers here. I am to take you to the Sanuri."

The bird flew in the opposite direction of the road they were standing near. It flew low and stayed within sight of the warriors. Although Raphael, Michael, Jared, Archetenus, Drake and Tally were experienced warriors and woodsmen they were amazed at the way the Venatores moved in the jungle. These warriors seemed to move without disrupting the foliage or leaving tracks. It was as if they became one with the jungle.

Erebus on the other hand was out of his element in the jungle. He walked clumsily. Diana and Thor kept Erebus near them. But Erebus could do something the others could not and that was to sense the darkness.

Joshua kept Sampson close to him as the other warriors spread out. Sampson knew that no one trusted him and he understood that for he wasn't sure that he trusted himself.

The bird suddenly turned and flew back to Joshua. "There are soldiers coming. You must stay down wind of the Stratas. Follow me."

If the sun had the same bearings in this underworld, the warriors knew they had been traveling southeast. Now the bird changed their path sharply to the east. The warriors who did not hear the message understood this change in course was to protect them and followed the bird.

The air was very humid and all of the warriors were sweating. "We didn't bring any water," said Drake. "Damn shame cuz I could use some right now." Kate stopped walking so Drake could catch up with her and she handed him her canteen. "Much obliged," Drake whispered.

"Hand it to the others," whispered Kate then disappeared in the vegetation.

"How do people live in this?" asked Tally as he tied his bandana around his forehead because sweat was running into his eyes. He kept walking as he adjusted his bandana and lifted his leg to step over a fallen tree when Michael threw Tally to the ground and jumped in front of him.

"Holy shit!" said Archetenus when the men realized the log was actually a monster of a snake.

Michael grabbed his sword and struck the snake in an attempt to sever its head. But even with all his power Michael only injured the beast. Archetenus and Jared both struck the snake which lunged at the men. The fangs of the serpent were eight inches long. The men kept dodging the tail and the head of the snake. Tally jumped to his feet and he and Drake also attacked it.

Raphael and others heard the battle and ran to their friends. It took the five incredibly powerful men over thirty-six blows to kill the snake.

"Everything seems larger in this world," said Joshua when he saw the dead snake. "Be careful. And we may not have been the only ones who heard you."

"Where is the bird?" asked Thor.

Benedict and Anka first ran to their home. "Cyrene, Cyrene," called Benedict. His wife ran out of the kitchen and was frightened when she saw the looks on the faces of her husband and daughter. "I don't have time to explain. Anka can tell you. Pack up the boys, we are leaving this place."

"What? Where are we going?" asked Cyrene.

"Please, there is no time. Just do as I ask and Anka will tell you." Then Benedict turned to his daughter. "Perhaps you should take the drawing."

"No Father, keep it. Miranda will come if I call her."

Benedict kissed his wife and daughter and ran out the door.

As soon as the Sanuri had finished speaking with Benedict, he and Adam started to create distractions to keep the eyes of the seers from the Credos. Powerful winds were created. Buildings collapsed and fences were destroyed. The Stratas that were property of the army were now free to roam. They understood their freedom and ran wildly in every direction.

The Credos had many secret signals in a world of seers. But for extreme emergencies they had a plan to set a tower on fire. The tower was high enough to be seen for miles. The followers of The Great Ruler knew that if the tower was set ablaze they were to meet in the ancient catacombs. It was to this tower that Benedict ran.

The winds grew in intensity. Thunder roared and lightning struck trees and buildings. There was no loss of life but utter chaos in the streets.

The storms did not affect the warriors from Wetpr. In fact, they didn't even realize the storms were occurring. "Is this bird leading us to the Sanuri or are we a distraction for him?" Sampson asked Joshua. "Because if we are to be a distraction perhaps we need to do more to make our presence known."

Joshua did not respond to Sampson but searched the skies. They had not seen the bird that was to be their guide since the battle with the snake. "Something is wrong," said Joshua. "I can feel it." He made the sound of a yellow bird to warn the others of possible danger.

"There he is," said Diana and pointed to the sky. "What is that behind him? He looks hurt."

"Diana save the bird," said Thor. "I will get that monster."

The brother and sister ran forward. Because of the thick vegetation most of the other warriors could not see Thor and Diana. Then they heard her scream.

"Come to us!" "Come to us!"

The bird dove towards the ground and now other warriors ran to that area. Thor stepped in front of Diana and took aim with his bow at the flying beast that was chasing the bird. This creature was over ten feet long, it had a flat head which was covered with horns. Its tail appeared as spikes. Its wings seemed more leather-like than feathers and it was quickly gaining on the brightly colored bird.

Thor did not take his eye off the creature when Sampson stood next to him, although he was aware of Sampson's presence. "Now!" yelled Thor and the bird dropped from the sky into Diana's arms. The flying beast could not maneuver as quickly. As it dove closer to the ground Thor and Sampson shot it with arrows.

The beast fell to the ground but continued to move. Sampson and Thor ran towards it. "Don't let it touch you with its horns, they are poison," said the bird weakly.

"The horns are poison!" yelled Diana.

Sampson and Thor both circled the injured beast. It lunged at Thor and Sampson jumped on its back and drove his sword into its brain.

"Have you been poisoned?" Diana asked the bird.

"No, it bit me."

"Where are the wounds?"

"Under my wings."

"What can I do to heal you? Will our medicine work on you?"

"I don't know." The bird was getting weaker as it spoke.

"Adam help us save this creature," called Diana.

"He said to put your crystals in the wounds and bind them," said Raphael as he ran up to Diana. He and Diana tore off their crystals and put them into the wounds.

Raphael prayed over the bird as he took his shirt off. He was wearing a lighter shirt underneath. He took that shirt off and handed it to Diana who tore some strips for bandages. Then she tore the rest of the shirt in half and tied the ends together making a sort of sling. She put the sling on and placed the injured bird inside.

"You're going to carry that bird?" Sampson asked with a sneer.

"Oh Sampson just shut up or I will punch you," said Diana. Sampson laughed and they joined the other warriors.

When they all regrouped Raphael called out, "Adam, we have lost our guide. Where do you want us?"

"I can see that," said Adam as he materialized in the midst of the warriors. "Tell me Diana are you going to carry that bird into battle?"

"Yes. I will protect him," she said defensively.

"Good," said Adam and smiled then he turned to the others. We have set several distractions into motion which are now protecting you also. Soon you will see a light in the distance. That fire is a signal to the Credos to meet in an emergency. You will see the light to the east. But their meeting place is in the catacombs under the city which is southeast, the original direction you were traveling. There are few warriors among the Credos. They are families with many small children. They will not be of help in a battle."

"Where do you want us?" Joshua asked. "Near the catacombs or out here as a distraction."

"Right now as a distraction. I will tell you when to head towards the catacombs. They are under a heavily guarded city. A city that does not get strangers."

There are many dangers in this jungle, including quick sand. You must be wary." Adam said then smiled. "But for the mercy you have shown to Azu, his entire flock has volunteered to help you."

"They're so beautiful," said Kate as they saw a large flock of brightly colored birds flying overhead. "What are they called?"

"They are Florines," explained Adam. "They are a distant relative of the Enrop, which you might have guessed. But this is a different world. Anka was the first to call the Angels in. The Credo believe in The Great Ruler but no one works on His behalf here. I had to remind the Florines of the covenant their species made with Him. They will be returning to Wetpr with us."

Benedict was a man in his forties and although he was in good health he was not athletic. His chest ached and his head pounded as he ran to the tower. But he was elated for he had spoken with an Angel and soon, very soon they would be free.

Benedict crashed through the thick vegetation. He was gasping for breath so loudly that he did not initially hear the soldiers on the road ahead of him. A road that he must cross. Now he slowed down and tried to get his breathing under control. He slowly moved forward. Soldiers riding Stratas were rounding up several dozen Stratas that were running free.

He started to panic, which had never been a normal response for Benedict. He was a seer of the highest order in the Kingdom of Inferus. He did not fear harm from the soldiers but to be in this area when there were intruders in the kingdom would draw suspicion.

Benedict waited a few minutes but the soldiers appeared to be having difficulty rounding up the beasts. Suddenly a Strata ran towards Benedict but was herded away by a soldier. Benedict took Tommy's picture from his pocket and as soon as he placed his hand on Tommy's face he was seeing the Sanuri. Benedict explained the signal and meeting place of the Credo. Then he described the scene on the road and his fears of drawing suspicion. He asked the Sanuri for advice and a moment later one of Sampson's arrows impaled one of the soldiers.

The soldiers were never under attack in their own land and were taken off guard. So much so that the sound of the thud as it entered the neck of the soldier did not draw attention. They did not realize their comrade was hurt until he fell to the ground. By that time arrows were flying out of the jungle. The eight soldiers fell dead without knowing who was firing upon them.

The Stratas were spooked by the arrows and ran from the area, one was dragging its rider.

"Benedict walk to the road now. Those are the people who will help you escape," the Sanuri sent this message to Benedict with his mind.

Fearfully Benedict stood up and walked to the center of the road. "I am Benedict."

"And we are here to help," said Archetenus with a grin as he ran into the road and grabbed Benedict by the arm. "Didn't mean to scare you, just want to get you out of sight."

"Yes, yes I understand," said Benedict as Archetenus led him to the others. Benedict stared at the men and women before him wearing their different uniforms and he was overwhelmed. "I can't believe this, I…"

"We don't mean to be rude," said Joshua. "But there are soldiers everywhere. The Sanuri said you need to light a fire. Where?"

"Yes, yes it is a tower; it is very close. The fire will be seen for miles," said Benedict. He felt so anxious and giddy that he was having difficulty thinking.

"Lead the way," said Joshua.

"Erebus why are you staring at him like that?" whispered Diana.

"His aura is such a strange color. I have never seen one like that before. It is greenish."

"Is that bad?" Diana asked

"I have no idea." Erebus replied.

The group walked about a quarter mile and saw a huge wooden tower. It was several hundred feet in the air. "How do you start the fire?" asked Micha.

"There is a container of oil up there," explained Benedict as he pulled an instrument out of his pocket. "And this."

511

"What is that?" asked Joshua.

"You probably won't recognize our name but if you press this button it produces a spark, see."

"I like it," Micha said. "I'll climb up there." Micha and the others in their group felt that Benedict was not in the shape to climb that tower and escape the flames. The warriors immediately spread out and hid in the foliage. Joshua told Benedict to stay with him.

Micha quickly climbed the tower and found the crock of oil. He poured the oil on the hay and wood. He was about to start the spark when he looked around. He was now above the trees and in every direction he looked he saw soldiers.

# Chapter XLI
## The Terror was within Them

Anka and her mother Cyrene knew they could not pack much without drawing suspicion. They took few items from their home, food, water and a pouch of diamonds which was the currency of the Kingdom of Inferus. These items were put into two baskets.

Cyrene made Anka repeat her story several times as they packed and dressed Anka's brothers. Santi was seven years old and Linus five. Cyrene and Anka each carried a basket and held the hand of one of the boys. They walked quickly down the old stone streets.

"We are surrounded by soldiers and you know they will come here to investigate the fire," said Micha as he ran to his group.

"Come," said Benedict and walked quickly past the burning tower. They walked through the jungle and onto a road. After a little more than ten minutes they came to a pond that was partially surrounded by a rock formation. "Follow me," said Benedict. He stepped into the shallow water.

Benedict walked to the rock formation. He moved several small rocks then turned a lever which opened a door. "Quickly, everyone in." All of the warriors walked through the door before Benedict so he could close it and conceal their path.

There were lit torches on the stone walls of the narrow passageway. "Benedict come up front," said Joshua. "What is this place?"

"Credos have been persecuted since the beginning of time. This is a meeting area. We can't get to the catacombs from in here but we can hide out for a little while." The passageway opened to a large chamber that had tables and chairs. "There is food and wine in here if anyone is hungry," said Benedict as he walked to a wooden cupboard. "The supplies are replenished daily."

"I think we all could eat something," said Joshua and helped Benedict put loaves of bread, cheese and apples on one of the tables.

"Where does this other passage go?" asked Thor.

"That is how we will leave," said Benedict. "It will take us on the far side of this hill. We will be closer to the catacombs."

"I am going to check it out," Thor said.

"I'm coming with you," said Thomas.

"As am I," said Kate. "Three should be enough," she added when she saw Sampson start to walk towards Thor. The three Venatores disappeared into the tunnel.

Diana carefully took Azu out of the sling and placed him on the table. She poured some water from her canteen onto a plate and broke some pieces of bread for him to eat. "I'll take care of you until you are well," Diana said to the bird. "But I hope you like kids because we kind of have a house full but I won't let them bother you."

Raphael laughed as he listened to her talk. He sat down at the table next to Diana. "He may wish he was back in the jungle when he meets our family," Raphael joked.

Diana leaned close to Raphael and whispered, "Don't turn your back on Sampson this all could be a trick." Raphael nodded.

Erebus could not contain his curiosity any longer and walked up to Benedict. "I have to ask; I can see people's auras and I have never seen one the color of yours before. Are you human?"

Benedict stared at Erebus, not because of the question but because of the energy he transmitted. "You too are different, there is a strange...you were a very powerful sorcerer and you gave it up for The Great Ruler." The shock was evident on Benedict's face.

"Stranger things have probably happened," said Erebus.

"But you give off great energy which will be picked up by the sorcerers here. How can it not?"

"We are supposed to be a diversion for your people," Raphael said. "And I think the Angels are blocking a lot."

"Back to my question if you don't mind," said Erebus.

"It is a good question. We were humans and maybe still are but something has changed within us living in this world. Tell me, what is it that you see?" asked Benedict.

"As you know an aura is nothing more than energy. When I see it, normally it only expands a couple of inches around the person but yours is considerably wider and it is a greenish brown color which I have never seen."

"I am a seer but I have never been able to see auras," said Benedict. "I cannot give you an answer to your question. But I find this all very interesting."

"Can you tell us how your people changed living here?" asked Raphael.

"Understand we left the world above shortly after the demons were called in and it took generations for our people to dig to this world. One theory is that we have become a part of the world in a small sense."

"We had heard that at times your people smell like earth so that would make sense but why don't you cast shadows?" asked Raphael.

"How do you know these things?" asked Benedict.

"Because Javier and Madeline are causing a lot of havoc in our world," replied Raphael.

"They are members of the Charto. It is the most radical group in Inferus. Their goal is to reclaim our former lands but who even knows what they were after all of these centuries. They are dangerous people. They are here, you know. Everyone has been trapped here because all of our passageways closed."

"They are here? Are you sure?" asked Michael.

"Yes, they return every month or so to bring back information."

Michael, looked at Drake and Tally and said, "Those are the two who gave the information to the demons that attacked Lentz."

"Do you want to look them up since we are here?" Drake asked.

"They are very dangerous people," Benedict repeated. "Not only for their capacity for violence but they are Etos."

"What does that mean?" asked Raphael.

"There are many in my world who experiment with genetics both with animals and the people. The Etos are the results of centuries of experimentation. They are bred to be seductresses both the men and women. At first that was for the pleasure of the Abuckto but then their true value was seen as spies for the Charto. No one can resist them, not even demons."

"Well, that isn't really true," said Kate as she, Thor and Thomas entered the chamber. "Madeline put it to Michael and he didn't fall for her and neither did other members of our group."

"Really? Is this true?" Benedict asked Michael.

"Yeah, but then I don't know what I am doing around women anyways," he joked.

"Do you think your Angels are protecting you from them?" Benedict asked.

"That is a good question," said Raphael. "Do you know where we could find them?"

"Why would you put yourselves at such risk?"

"Because we don't really know what they have put into place in our world. They have endangered many people," said Raphael.

"When we get close to the catacombs there is a meeting place of the Charto but that is a very dangerous thing you propose."

"You are a powerful seer," said Erebus. "Is there a way you can get one of them to go to an area where we can find them?"

The city streets were more congested and chaotic than usual. The storms had momentarily stopped and people were leaving their shelters. This reprieve in the storms allowed the Credo to travel to the catacombs.

Anka's family lived in a culture of spies. Some of the seers could read minds and people would be punished for their thoughts. Both Cyrene and Anka tried to maintain calm demeanors all the while feeling terrified.

"I'm changing the subject for a minute," said Thor. "That tunnel is about a mile and a half long. Benedict can you draw us a map so we know exactly where we are?"

"Certainly," Benedict said and turned to the cupboard to get paper and a pen.

"I think we have to talk about all of this," said Joshua. "Our mission is to help these people escape. If we go after Javier and Madeline we might get a lot of innocent people hurt. Perhaps we could ask the Angels to help us come back another time."

"I agree with Joshua," said Diana. "Adam told us these are families with children and babies. We can't risk getting them killed."

As they walked down the street both Cyrene and Anka saw other members of the Credo who were also going to the catacombs. The blazing tower was seen for miles. These people did not acknowledge each other they just kept walking. But unlike Anka and Cyrene these other members of the Credo had no idea why they were going to the catacombs.

The plan had always been that if there was an emergency the members of the Credo would gather their families and meager belongings and go to the catacombs. These people never thought about an escape from their way of life. They only dreamed about freedom. Almost everyone going to the catacombs thought they had been exposed as followers of The Great Ruler and would be put to death. Many, many people cried as they walked.

"Sudfad have you heard anything?" asked Renya as she walked into a meeting in the study.

"No but it's only been six hours. We were planning on calling to Miranda soon," he replied.

"Well, I need to speak to her now," Renya said to her husband then looked upwards and called, "Miranda would you please join us?"

"Renya that is the first time you have ever called to me," said the Angel as she materialized.

"I will do better. And thank you for coming. I sent staff to buy food for the Elods but do they eat our food. Do I need to get special things?" asked Renya.

"The food is basically the same. Where are you housing them?"

"In the castle unless you think they would prefer some other place. Chambers are already being prepared. Actually can you tell us a little about them?"

"They are mostly families with children. They live in a world where even the wrong thoughts are against their laws. They have risked their lives to worship The Great Ruler and this will be a terrifying act for them. Have you decided where you want us to open a door?" asked Miranda.

"We were thinking in the courtyard," said Sudfad. "That way we can get them into the castle and if they are being followed, we will have soldiers outside to do battle."

"That idea will work."

"Miranda is there something you need us to do?" asked Sudfad.

"As I said, this people are risking everything to have freedoms and to be able to worship The Great Ruler. They have never known other ways of life. It would comfort them to know that all of you too are follows."

"And you should have Gabriel's family bring Tommy here at some point. He will be the only familiar face even if it is only for one child. These people have known only terror; they will be grateful for any little thing you do for them."

"I know what you are thinking," continued Miranda. "Claudius and Fahron have pushed their people greatly and will arrive tonight instead of tomorrow. You will be receiving a message soon with that information. Do not change any of your plans for them but inform them of what is happening. You may need their assistance."

Miranda disappeared. "I need to get more staff in," said Renya and quickly left the study as Sudfad wrote a note for Claudius. The new ruling members as well as the Princes were preparing the defenses for an attack by the Elods. Sudfad sent Alexander to Gabriel's home to tell the rest of the team members Miranda's words.

"Bekka will you watch my children?" asked Hannah. "I should go to the castle and prepare for wounded. Who knows what shape those poor people will be in."

"Vivian instead of being angry that you couldn't go, come with me to Salar and we will buy clothing and toys. Those people are running for their lives they can't be bringing much," Emeral said.

"Well, if you are going to do that stop at the castle first," said Alexander. "I am sure that Sudfad will want to pay for those things."

"If someone will watch my babies I would like to go too," said Natasha.

"Go," said Ella. "Of course Sam and I will watch them."

Elan and Cassandra walked out of the house and to the back yard where the children were playing with the nurses. "We need to talk to all of you," Elan said. "But I am not really sure how to start." Everyone now gathered around them. "Miranda helped Tommy to talk to a girl from another kingdom," Elan said and Tommy interrupted him.

"Anka, she's my friend and she's really nice," Tommy said proudly. "We talk with our heads."

Elan and Cassandra smiled. "Yes Tommy. Well, Anka lives in a very bad place, a place where no one can talk to Angels or The Great Ruler. So the Venatores and others have gone to that bad place to bring them back here. They will all go to Sudfad's castle and Miranda said that we should take Tommy there to meet Anka. Do the rest of you want to come too?"

"Yes," yelled several of the children.

"There is one thing," said Cassandra. "We can't take the pups, at least not at first because it sounds like they don't have dogs in that kingdom and the pups might scare them. These people are already afraid of the bad men in their kingdom."

"No dogs!" said Paul.

"What kind of place doesn't have dogs?" asked Zack.

"I don't know," said Cassandra. "But I do know that a lot of children are coming so you will make new friends."

Every mother who was entering the catacombs was wondering how she was going to feed her children. And every father was wondering how he was going to protect his family. These terrified people huddled together under the city. No one from Benedict's family had yet arrived to explain what was happening.

Benedict led Joshua and the group through the passageway. When they arrived at the exit, Sampson and Thomas went outside and searched the area for soldiers. Several minutes later they returned. "It's clear," said Thomas. "But what happened to those birds that were supposed to help us? Are they in trouble too?"

"Azu do you know what happened to your flock?" Diana asked. The bird's condition was improving as the crystals were healing his wounds.

"Wait," he said. "Let me try to talk to them." The bird was motionless for several moments. He had been lying in the sling and now he straighten up as he listened to a voice the others could not hear. "Show me that map. Where are we?" asked Azu. Joshua walked up to Diana and showed the bird the map. Azu appeared to study it then was quiet for a few moments. Then he looked at Joshua.

"My flock has been searching for us. They didn't know about these secret passages. They said that many of the soldiers went to the burning tower and are searching around that area. I told my flock where we are now and that we need to get to the catacombs. They said to stay here until they search the area. They said there are sorcerers searching for us too."

"There is something I should tell you while we wait," said Benedict. "There is a very, very powerful sorcerer here and he wears the body of a thirteen year old boy although I do not understand why because he is very old. He wants to marry my daughter Anka. He may try to come after us."

"Wait, isn't she a little girl?" asked Raphael.

"She will be ten at the next red moon and that is the earliest she can take a husband. Anka wants nothing to do with Andrac. That is another reason I am so thankful you are here but we may be putting you in even more danger."

"We are kind of used to that," said Michael with a grin.

"Sounds like a man after your heart," Kate said hatefully to Sampson. The two Venatores stepped towards each other in a challenging manner.

"That is enough!" yelled Joshua. "If you two fight it will be after this mission do you understand!"

"Yes," said Kate and backed down.

"What is she talking about?" asked Drake.

"Sampson tried to rape both Vivian and Diana when they were small children," Kate spat.

"Kate drop it!" yelled Joshua. "Whatever crimes he committed in the past; he is helping us now so shut your mouth."

Tally leaned towards Michael and whispered, "Does she really think she can take that big guy?" Michael shrugged his shoulders and grinned.

"Something is happening," said Azu. "My flock says the soldiers are running back to where you were hours ago. They said we should leave here now and they will watch for soldiers."

Andrac barged into the meeting room of the Charto Sect.

"What is the meaning of this?" demanded Benix, the highest ranking member in the room. Andrac had forced the door open with his magics. When the door flew open everyone in the meeting room jumped out of their chairs.

Andrac walked into the room and stared intently into everyone's faces. "Did you have anything to do with that signal fire?" he asked challengingly.

"What are you talking about?" asked Javier. "Or is this just an excuse to intrude where you aren't wanted?"

"Interesting choice of words," Andrac said. "You know we have reason to believe that there are intruders here?"

"Yes and that is why we are meeting?" said Benix. "Has anyone been attacked?"

"We found some of our soldiers dead on a road with strange arrows in them," said Andrac. "Then a short distance later that wooden tower that has been standing for years was set on fire."

"Well that blows our theory," Ivan said.

"What are you saying?" asked Andrac.

"Take a seat," Benix said. "You know that we have spies all over in the world above and very few people know we exist. And the ones who do have no idea how to get to us."

"And even if they did all of the passageways have been destroyed, so how would they enter? We thought it was demons but demons wouldn't use arrows."

"Unless they wanted us to think it was someone else," said Madeline. "Andrac, I thought the first intruder was a seer or sorcerer is that true?"

"That is what the Abuckto said."

"So now we think we actually have beings of some sort here?" Madeline asked.

"It certainly appears that way," replied Andrac. "You act like you don't believe that. What are you thinking?"

"We are all thinking it," said Javier. "Why would outsiders invade us and not create a war? It is not like we are a close neighbor to anyone. This is not a boundary issue as are problems above. How does an army travel down here? And why would they and not attack? Have you considered the idea that there aren't any intruders?"

Andrac stared at Javier suspiciously but leaned back in his chair. "Go on."

"The facts would indicate that intrusion is almost impossible. So would anyone benefit from creating this type of a diversion?" asked Javier. "That is what we were asking ourselves when you came in."

"That is an interesting question," Andrac said.

"And there is another thing," said Madeline. "We are spies and very good at what we do so trust me when I tell you that if there are intruders who are walking in this kingdom without being seen they have to have help and spies here. But how would they communicate with anyone here?"

"You think the Abuckto are behind this don't you?" Andrac asked.

"They would be powerful enough but how would this benefit them?" asked Benix. "They already have all the power here."

"Not all," said Andrac and stood up. "You have made some excellent points here." He walked out of the room and shut the door.

"Do you think he was trying to set us up?" asked Madeline.

"I did at first," said Benix. "But he did seem very interested in what we had to say."

"That doesn't mean he won't use it against us," snarled Javier.

"Do you think you would recognize those arrows if we got one?" Ivan asked.

# Chapter XLII
## Traitors among Us

When Claudius received Sudfad's letter he stopped the caravan and had a meeting with the leaders. Among the leaders was Hugo, Sorren's brother. Hugo's youngest daughter Patris was going to be in Luca's and Natalie's wedding. Claudius read the letter out loud and no one spoke for several moments.

"Do you think our families will be safe around those people?" asked Gideon.

"It sounds like the Credo are all desperate families," said Claudius. "But who knows what will be following them."

"That's what I don't understand," said Thaos. "If the Angels are opening a door for our people and the Credo don't you think they would shut it and keep the others out?"

The catacombs ran under the entire city but the area where the Credo were gathering was close to the meeting room of the Charto. Andrac was leaving the meeting room when he saw Cyrene and her children walking down the street.

"I thought I told you to stay in the Hall of Knowledge," Andrac said sharply as he walked up to Anka. Both Anka and her mother were filled with fear.

"First of all you don't own me," Anka said. "And secondly they didn't want me in there. And why are you here? I thought you were looking for the intruders."

Andrac laughed because he liked Anka's spunk. "I still am."

"Do you think they are near here?" Cyrene asked with concern. "I didn't want to leave the children while I shopped. But is it more dangerous here?"

Javier and Madeline had left the meeting room and were walking down the street when they saw Andrac approach Anka and her family.

"That poor little girl," said Madeline. "That monster wants to take her for his wife."

"It is not our concern. Besides if he is dealing with her he is not looking at us."

"Javier, sometimes you make me so mad."

"It isn't our concern and there is nothing that we can do about it anyways. We have more to worry about."

"All we ever do is turn away. We talk all the time about how we want to stop the monsters and we never do anything. I am going down there."

"Why? What are you going to do?"

"I don't know. But I get sick of always watching. I'll catch up with you later."

"Andrac is powerful don't piss him off."

Madeline laughed and walked towards Cyrene's family. Andrac had his back to Madeline but Cyrene and Anka were facing her and Madeline could see the fear in them.

"Andrac can I speak with you for a moment?" asked Madeline sweetly and took his arm. Then she whispered into his ear, "It's important." Madeline winked at Cyrene which added to the woman's fear.

"Certainly," said Andrac and turned and walked a few steps with Madeline.

"Ivan is wondering if any of our people will be able to recognize the arrows you talked of. Javier is getting our group but we don't know where the arrows are, do you?"

"Yes, but the soldiers have them. Let me speak with Ivan." Andrac walked towards the meeting room and Madeline walked up to Cyrene.

"Go to wherever you are headed; he will only be distracted for a short time," said Madeline.

"You did that to help us?" asked Cyrene with surprise since she feared Madeline too.

Madeline didn't answer Cyrene's question but looked at Anka. "You do know that by our laws you don't have to marry that monster."

"I told him that and he said that I still do."

"You don't and don't let him intimidate you."

"Thank you but we must be going," said Cyrene and walked towards the business section of the city.

Madeline was not afraid of intruders but she was feeling anxious, very anxious. She had been feeling that way since the passages to the world above were closed. She stood on the walkway for a few moments as she was trying to decide what to do. She decided shopping might make her feel better and turned towards the business district.

As she walked a family walked past her. They too were carrying baskets like Cyrene and the mother was crying. While Madeline took notice of this she didn't think it that unusual until she walked past another family that was carrying baskets and the man and woman looked terrified. Madeline was not a seer but her gut was telling her that something was very wrong. She turned and followed the two families who were walking in the same direction.

Madeline was surprised when she saw the families enter the catacombs. She hid behind some large rocks and watched the entrance. She watched family after family enter the catacombs. Madeline stood up and was going to walk to the entrance when she felt a presence behind her. She quickly turned and gasped.

"Michael what are you doing here?"

"Can't really talk here. I would suggest you come willingly."

"Do you know how dangerous this is? You can't be seen here. There are soldiers everywhere."

"I know and don't think about calling to any of them." Michael grabbed Madeline's arm and quickly walked her into the catacombs. To his surprise she didn't fight him.

"How did you get here?"

"You really ask a lot of questions."

As soon as they entered the catacombs Madeline stopped and stared at Sampson. "I know you," she said. Then she looked at Micha, Thomas and Thor. "I know who all of you are. What are you doing here?"

"Just keep walking," said Michael and led her down several passageways. They approached the meeting room of the Credo where Drake and Tally guarded the entrance.

"She is a looker," said Tally with a grin.

"Aren't all of you enemies?" asked Madeline. "This makes no sense at all."

Michael and Madeline walked into the room as Benedict was telling the Credo that they would be escaping to the world above. Madeline was stunned as were most of the people in the chamber. As soon as he finished speaking to the group. Raphael, who was standing with Benedict called to Miranda.

People gasped and fell to their knees when the beautiful Angel appeared before them. Michael could feel Madeline shaking with fear. Miranda spoke to the frightened people. Then she called to Michael. "Bring the others in here and this is a mission of mercy we are not taking prisoners this day."

"Guess it's your lucky day lady," Michael said and let go of Madeline's arm. He started to walk past her but Madeline grabbed his shirt, then both of this arms.

"Michael, take me with you. I mean it. Really. I could be a lot of help to you."

"Why would you leave here? You have a bounty on your head."

"I am sure what I can tell your people will be worth my freedom. Take me please."

"Tally, Drake get in here," Michael called. When the men walked in he said. "Take her to Miranda. Miranda can decide if she comes with us." Michael left the cavern to get the other members of his group.

Many people were frightened when they saw Tally and Drake lead Madeline to the front of the room. Madeline stood speechless and shaking with fear before the Angel. "She has something to tell you but apparently she ain't talking," said Drake.

"What do you have to say to me?" asked Miranda.

Madeline summoned up all of her courage. "Please take me with you."

"You have spied on and betrayed the world above why do you think you would find a home there?"

"I know a lot of information and I could be very useful to them."

"So now you want to betray your people?"

"I don't want to live in this world. I want to live in the world above."

"How could we ever trust you? Did you know that Isabella is dead? She sold her soul to Samael so that she could be reunited with your brother."

"She what?" Madeline seemed genuinely surprised. "I warned her." Madeline paused. "I would think that as an Angel you could tell if I was lying but what must I do?"

"Raphael, she may be a great deal of work; perhaps more than you want to deal with but she does possess important information. And for this small moment in time she is telling the truth. You are a ruling member of Wetpr; do you want her in your kingdom?"

"Yes," said Raphael. "But I do not trust her. Drake, Tally watch her."

"Gladly," said Tally with a grin and grabbed Madeline's arm.

Erebus walked up to Madeline and stared at her aura which was considerably darker than those of the other Elods in the room. "Tell me did you orchestrate the attack on my home?" he asked.

"No but we saw it. It was Hector's men."

"So you stood by and watched them attack unarmed men?" Erebus asked with disgust but before she could answer Michael reentered the chamber.

"We might have a problem," Michael announced. "Does anyone know where Archetenus and Jared are?"

"They are checking out the tunnels down here," said Joshua. "But I would have thought they would be back by now." Joshua turned to Benedict and asked, "Are there more coming?"

"I really don't know," Benedict said to Joshua then he said loudly to all the Elods. "Please look around you, are we missing anyone?"

"Coming in! Coming in!" yelled Jared and the Venatores ran to the entrance. "We've got soldiers behind us!"

Jared was carrying a wounded man as he ran into the cavern. Archetenus was behind him holding two children and a woman was running next to him. Both men had blood on them.

The Venatores formed a line and blocked the entrance into the cavern. The soldiers were too close to Archetenus and Jared for the Venatores to use their bows so they attacked the soldiers with swords and knives.

Jared and Archetenus ran to Miranda and put the people they were carrying at her feet then they turned and ran back to the entrance.

"Erebus watch her," Tally said and pushed Madeline at him. They turned and followed Michael to the entrance.

"Miranda, we might want to leave now," yelled Archetenus.

Miranda was healing the wounded man; she did not respond.

The people inside of the cavern gathered closer to the Angel.

"Miranda, I feel a powerful sorcerer," yelled Erebus. "Do you want me to find him?"

"No. Raphael you will need to carry him," Miranda said of the man she was healing. She walked towards the entrance as the group of Elods parted for her.

The warriors had not allowed the soldiers into the cavern, they were fighting in the crowded passageway which now smelled of sweat and was slippery from blood. The flock of Florines had entered the catacombs and were attacking the Elod soldiers.

"Into the cavern," said Miranda loudly as she walked into the passageway. The light emitted from her grew brighter which blinded the soldiers. The warriors from Wetpr turned and ran into the cavern. Archetenus stood next to Miranda. "You too Archetenus. Those people in there need help."

"Andrac forward!" ordered Miranda.

The powerful sorcerer pushed his way through the soldiers who were frightened by the Angel. But Andrac approached her with a smug look on his face. "You have no right to be here," he said.

"The heavens have claim to all of the worlds. I show you my form so you do not accuse others of being your intruders and murder more innocents. The Great Ruler knows the man you are and that you persecute His children. Change your ways. I tell you this but once."

"I curse you and The Great Ruler; you have no right..." Andrac did not finish his sentence because he fell to the ground screaming in agony. And in that instant Miranda, the warriors and the Credo disappeared.

"Adam why are we here?" asked the Sanuri as he and the Angel materialized in a cave.

"There is something you must see," said Adam and led the way down a long tunnel. There were lit torches affixed to the stone walls. Unusual yet pitiful sounds and smells were becoming prevalent as they walked.

They entered a large cavern and tears came to the Sanuri's eyed. "What is before us?"

"These are the creatures and people that the Elods experiment on," said Adam with disgust.

The cavern was filled with cages of mutilated people and animals. The largest animals were not in cages but chained to the walls.

"Can we heal them?" asked the Sanuri. "And set them free."

"Yes, but there will only be others."

"Adam perhaps you should leave now," said the Sanuri angrily.

"Why?"

"Because I believe cages were built to contain the real monsters. You probably shouldn't be a part of this."

"Oh, I strongly disagree," said Adam.

The loud clanging of chains filled the cavern as they fell to the stone floor. "Do not be afraid," said Adam loudly. "The Great Ruler has sent us to help you. You are healed. Leave this place quickly."

The animals as well as the people understood the words of the Angel. Their pain ceased as their limbs and organs were restored. People fell at the feet of the Angel; thanking him and crying. The animals too gathered around Adam.

"This is a world that does not call to The Great Ruler or His emissaries," said Adam. "Remember this day for The Great Ruler has allowed many miracles to take place. He will protect you. Pray to Him. But now you must leave."

As soon as the last of the victims left the cavern the room was filled with screaming and cursing as the men and women responsible for the experimentations found themselves in chains and cages.

"Who are you to defile the children of The Great Ruler?" asked Adam loudly. The intensity of his presence and voice silenced and frightened the Elods. "You preform experimentations of great horror for your own egos and amusement. I hold up a mirror to you; may the horror and darkness you have sent into the world be reflected back to you." The screams of these butchers were heard well beyond the cave.

The Horn of Cass was blown by soldiers at Sudfad's castle to alert the others. Sudfad ran down the hallway to the door that Renya had already opened. Raphael was running up the steps carrying the wounded man. Thor was carrying Micha and Joshua was carrying Sampson both of these wounded warriors had multiple wounds.

Hundreds of people had suddenly appeared on the front courtyard of the castle. "Are you being followed?" yelled Raul.

"I don't think so," said Michael. "But we are all wounded."

Sudfad and Renya stood on the top steps of the castle and a horn was blown again. People fell silent.

"I am King Sudfad and this is my wife Renya. You are in the Kingdom of Wetpr. A Kingdom that bows only to The Great Ruler. We have prepared chambers for all of you. Please enter and you will be taken to living quarters then we have food prepared. I will need to speak with your leaders."

"We have physicians inside for the wounded," Renya said and ran down the steps to Michael.

The stunned Elods did not move. "Please come into our home," said Sudfad.

Simon walked up to a terrified family. He took one of the baskets the husband was carrying and picked up one of the children. "You are safe here," Simon said and led the family inside.

All of the members of Gabriel's home were at the castle and helping to take the refugees to their chambers. The children from Gabriel's home as well as Sudfad's home were in the family dining room watching the people walk into the castle.

"They all look so scared," Margarit said. "Are they scared of us?"

"I think they came from a place where they are always scared," said Nyla and walked forward to help a woman who was carrying two small children.

"Anka!" yelled Tommy as he looked through the crowd. Soon all of the children from Gabriel's house were yelling her name. "Anka, Anka,"

The Elod families looked with wonder at these children who were yelling for Anka.

"Father, Mother do you hear that?" asked Anka excitedly. "It must be Tommy and his family. Can I go in now?"

"You should wait for us," said Benedict.

Tally led Raul to Benedict's family, "This is Benedict, he is the leader of the Credo and this is Prince Raul, the son of King Sudfad."

Raul extended his hand to shake with Benedict. "Please, come forward in line so I can introduce you to my parents," said Raul. Benedict and Cyrene were each holding one of their sons as Anka stood in front of them. "Are you Anka?" Raul asked.

"Yes," she said with a big smile.

"There are a lot of children in the dining room waiting to meet you. It is the first door to the left as soon as you walk in. I will show you."

Raul escorted Benedict's family into the castle. Sudfad and Renya were standing at the entrance. As soon as they entered Tommy yelled, "Anka" and ran to her as did all of the children. The adults smiled as they watched Anka and Tommy hug.

"Let's all go back into the dining room so we can make room here," said Casandra and led the excited children out of the hallway. Tommy proudly introduced his friend to all of the children.

"Prince Matthew we have a present for you," said Drake as he and Erebus escorted Madeline.

"Madeline!" Matthew said.

"Matthew, Miranda told us to leave her behind but she begged to come. She knows there are bounties on her head but she wants to help us in exchange for her freedom," explained Erebus.

"You were responsible for the deaths of thousands of our people," Matthew snapped.

"Matthew, Javier and I were not responsible for that armada attack," said Madeline. "But I have much to tell you. Javier does not know I came here. I am prepared to betray my kingdom."

"Why would you do that?" asked Matthew angrily.

"Because she comes from a kingdom of barbarians," said the Sanuri with disgust as he walked up to them. "Let's take her inside."

"Sanuri! Sanuri! yelled Vitomas as she ran into the courtyard. "We need you. We have wounded." The Sanuri and the people with him all ran into the castle. They ran past the family dining room which was filled with children.

Cassandra had distracted the children so they did not see the wounded warriors carried into the castle but now they saw Vitomas and the others running down the hallway.

"Wounded who's wounded?" asked Paul loudly. When Cassandra did not answer Paul and Adrone feared the worst for most of their family had gone to the Kingdom of Inferus.

"Father!" yelled Adrone and both boys ran out of the dining room and down the hallway.

"Where is Diana?" yelled Misha as he ran into the castle. In the chaos no one answered but he saw Paul and Adrone running and followed the boys.

Renya always had wounded put into the first floor chambers in the central wing of the castle because these rooms were close to the kitchen, study, family dining room and family parlor so the patients could get more attention.

The people from Lentz would be arriving in a matter of hours and this would be the first time that any of them would see the homes that Renya had built for them within the castle. Between the guests coming for Luca's wedding and now the Elod refugees the castle would be filled within a matter of days. So Hannah was putting two wounded warriors in every room instead of one.

Diana and Kate shared a room; both women had minor wounds. The door to their room was open and they saw Paul and Adrone run past it. Both boys looked distressed.

"Paul, Adrone come in here," yelled Diana. She did not want the boys to see the other wounded family members. The boys stopped, turned and ran into the room. Misha was relieved to hear his wife's voice.

"Come here," said Diana. "I need you to take care of Azu because he is wounded too. Adrone you hold him and Paul help me take off this sling." The boy's eyes widened as they saw the beautiful bird. "He is a cousin to our friends the Enrops and his entire flock came home with us. They can talk too. You will have to find Petra and tell him the birds need to be fed."

Misha laughed as he walked to the bed. "You are more worried about that bird," Misha said and helped Paul remove the sling from Diana.

"He got hurt helping us," said Diana and kissed Misha.

"I'll wear the sling," said Paul and Misha tied it on him.

"How come no one is in here with you?" asked Misha as he helped Adrone put the injured bird into the sling.

Kate glanced at the boys then said, "Gala was but our wounds are nothing compared to the others. Misha, Sampson pushed me aside and got stabbed instead of me. Tell that to the others will you?"

"Yes and since you weren't being followed, Edward is coming in. He was behind me."

Vitomas led the Sanuri to the room shared by Micha and Sampson both of these men had more serious wounds than the rest of the warriors. Drake, Erebus and Madeline followed the Sanuri into the room, where Hannah and Marina were desperately trying to stop the bleeding of both men.

"Madeline do your soldiers put poisons on their weapons?" asked the Sanuri as he ran to the area between both of the beds.

"Madeline!" gasped Hannah and looked at the woman.

"No," Madeline replied. "We never have attacks against us in our world."

The Sanuri stood between the beds and started to hum. He grew brighter and lighter and his light extended to both of the wounded warriors. Everyone in the room became quiet as they watched him. The bleeding of both men quickly slowed then stopped but the Sanuri remained in his state of light for several minutes. When he returned to his normal appearance he turned to Hannah and said, "Take me to the others."

"Erebus will you watch them?" Hannah asked as she turned to leave with the Sanuri.

"I will help," said Madeline and walked towards the bed.

"Sanuri can we trust her?" Hannah asked loudly.

"For the moment, yes," he replied and followed Hannah out of the room.

"Since you are all in here," said Marina. "Help me change this bedding it is covered in blood. I will show you how."

# Chapter XLIII
## Spies

"Drake you're bleeding," said Marina. Drake and Erebus had rolled Sampson on his side as Marina changed the sheet underneath him.

"It's nothing," said Drake.

"The front of your shirt is all blood," said Marina. "Sit in that chair and let me look at you. Now!"

"Erebus and I can finish this," said Madeline to Drake. "Do what she says."

Drake sat down and unbuttoned his wet shirt. "It's been a long time since I had two beautiful women bossing me around," he said with a grin.

"Men are the same no matter what world they come from," said Madeline and smiled.

"Erebus when you are done there tell Hannah we will need another room and tough guy here might need some help getting into bed," Marina teased. "Madeline can you come here?"

It took only a moment for Erebus and Madeline to roll Sampson back onto clean bedding. Erebus quickly left the room and Madeline knelt down by Drake's chair. "Hold these crystals in place," said Marina.

"Why do you put crystals in his wound?" asked Madeline as Marina removed her hands from the injury.

"They are blessed by The Great Ruler with healing energy," responded Marina then she looked at Drake. "I am going to have to cut your shirt off. If you think you are going to pass out let me know."

"Do what you've got to do," Drake said with his normal grin but both women could see that the color was draining from his face.

"Madeline, later will you tell me about the medicines of your people?" asked Marina.

Madeline was surprised by this question. "I am not a healer but I will tell you what I know. But you do understand that I might be a prisoner here."

"You can still have visitors," Marina said with a smile. "Besides I have a feeling you aren't going to be chained in the dungeons."

Matthew, Raul and Simon followed Erebus into the room. "I'm not quite done," said Marina. "But he looks like he could pass out any minute even though he says he is fine."

"We've got a room ready," said Raul. "We'll put him to bed."

"Can't one of these beautiful ladies put me to bed?" Drake asked and winked at the men.

"I'll be in to check on you," said Marina who finished bandaging the wound. "He's all yours now."

"Madeline, you should come with us," said Matthew.

"Can she stay here a little longer? I could use the help. Actually I could use a couple of you to roll Micha over so I can change his bedding," said Marina.

"We'll be back," said Simon and the three Princes helped Drake to his bed.

While Renya helped Cyrene settle into their chambers, Benedict met with Sudfad. "I am so sorry that your people were injured helping us. I would very much like to see them," Benedict said.

"I will take you to their rooms but the medical staff may not let us in," said Sudfad.

The two leaders visited every patient and Benedict prayed over each one of them. As Sudfad and Benedict were leaving the last room they saw Cassandra in the hallway.

"Where is Anka?" asked Benedict with concern.

"My husband is with the children. They are feeding the birds that came with you. Some other children from your group are with them," said Cassandra with a warm smile. "You should see them all; they act like they have been friends forever."

"I think we could learn a great deal from our children," Benedict said sincerely. "I never thought to ask The Great Ruler to send us help and as soon as Anka asks these miracles happen. I must admit I feel like I am in a dream."

"I think you will probably feel like that for some time," said Sudfad. "Let's go into my study and talk."

Renya waited until Benedict left Sudfad's study before she entered. She closed the door and walked up his desk, where he was still seated. "Sudfad are you still planning on attacking Karzman in three nights? I think you should postpone it. We have wounded as well as all of these Elods here."

"I was thinking the same thing. It was Adam who told us the night they wanted us to leave. I was going to call him as soon as Benedict left the study." Sudfad called to Adam twice without a response. Then he called to Miranda, she did not respond. Sudfad called out to Ruth, Daniel and The Lion and none of these Angels spoke or appeared to him.

"This is very unusual," said Sudfad.

"What are you going to do?" Renya asked.

"Leave the plans in place for now and find the Sanuri."

Paul and Adrone took their new responsibilities very seriously. They showed Azu to the other children but would not let anyone pet him yet. "Diana says we have to let him rest so he can heal," Paul said to the children who surrounded him.

"Diana said he got hurt helping us," said Adrone as he stood guard next to his brother.

Christopher and Joey ran up to Paul with a saucer that contained grain and cut fruit. "Azu are you hungry?" Christopher asked.

"Thank you," said the bird weakly.

"How do you eat?" asked Paul.

"Set the plate on the ground and set me next to it. I can't fly with the bandages."

Adrone carefully took Azu out of the sling and set him on the ground.

"Nica's here," announced Zack.

"Nica, Diana said that Azu is your cousin," said Christopher. "We are going to take care of him until he can fly."

"Good," said Nica as he landed near the children who moved so the birds could see each other.

"Azu this is Nica he is the leader of the Enrops here," Paul explained.

The children stood in silence as the two great birds spoke in a language they did not understand. After a few minutes Nica spoke with the children. "We are pleased to have our family here," said Nica. "Tell me, where will you take Azu, your home or the castle?"

"Our home," said Adrone. "So you can come and visit."

Renya and Sudfad split up and searched for the Sanuri. When Renya found him she sent the Sanuri to Sudfad's study and sent a soldier to find the King.

The Sanuri was sitting in the study drinking coffee when Sudfad entered. "Renya told me," the Sanuri said.

"Well, what do you think it means? Have I done something to displease the Angels?"

"I don't see how that could be," said the Sanuri. "But I agree that it is unusual that none of them responded to you. Their silence may be significant."

"Actually I thought about that but I couldn't figure out how. Do you think they are unhappy because I want to ask about changing the time of the attack?"

"You have several very good reasons to consider changing the time. If I had to guess, some things are in motion that would affect the answers they give you. I would suggest you try calling to them later and keep calling until one of them responds."

"Sanuri do you think we should expect to be attacked by Elods who are coming after the Credo?"

"While that is a valid question I don't know how they would get here since their doorways are closed."

"What do you think about these people?" Sudfad asked. "For one I am surprised that we speak the same language and look alike. And for the little time I have spoken with Benedict he seems like an intelligent and compassionate man."

"Unfortunately I haven't had much of a chance to speak with him but I can feel the terror within all of them. It took great faith and courage for them to come with us. I would not be surprised if these people were a little lost for a while."

Within the hour a meal was served in the Great Hall of the castle. Benedict and his family sat at the head table with the Royal Family and the Sanuri. High Priest Othnial said Grace over the food and Sudfad and Benedict both stood up.

"We are pleased to have you here," said Sudfad. "And I am sure there is anxiety among you for your futures. You are guests in the castle for as long as you like but I have to tell you that we are expecting a great many other guests also. They are coming to celebrate a wedding. I am telling you this so you won't be frightened. They are all followers of The Great Ruler."

"So in three days we will have a huge wedding here and you are all invited to attend. I want you to know that you are safe here; now Benedict has some things to say."

"I know this does not seem real yet to me and I am sure that many of you feel the same," explained Benedict. "King Sudfad showed me a map of this world. We are in the Kingdom of Wetpr which is the largest kingdom in a continent called Opots. Sudfad has offered us land to build homes on. We have the choice to make our own community or to blend in with the people who live here."

"He tells me that few people know of our world below and it is up to us if we want to share that information. His generosity is beyond belief. I want all of you to think about these things and we will have a meeting in a few days."

"Also the brave men and women who saved us are all wounded and need your prayers. We owe these people everything. Sudfad said that as soon as we all feel settled, people will start to take us on tours of the area so we can discover this new world."

"May I speak?" Cyrene asked Sudfad.

"Of course."

Cyrene stood up and felt nervous as she looked at the room of people staring at her. "I do not think that I am alone in my amazement at how similar things are here. Our entire lives we were told these people were monsters but instead they are generous and gracious. They have gone to great work to make us feel comfortable and I believe we should repay them. Especially now that we learn they will be having a wedding here. After the meal I would like to meet with the women and we can form groups to help with the cooking and work."

While none of the Elods felt comfortable to speak in front of the group the adults nodded their heads in agreement with Cyrene's words. One of the men looked around the room then stood up. "I believe we would all be willing to help. Let us know what needs to be done."

"Renya is rather in charge of all that; I am sure she welcomes the help," said Sudfad.

Madeline too was in the Great Hall although she was not free to walk around. She sat between Matthew and Raul. At the end of the meal Raul turned to her and said. "Father wants you to join us in a meeting after we eat." Madeline nodded.

Besides all of the chaos and work from taking in over three hundred refugees and preparing for hundreds of wedding guests, the medical students would be returning to Lentz after the wedding. In addition, all of the physicians who Matthew had hired would be traveling to Lentz with this group. Angelina, Shara and Matthew were overwhelmed with the arrangements and the finalization of classes.

Gala and Hannah were helping but now they needed to stay at the castle with the wounded.

Because the Great Hall was full, Sudfad held the meeting in his new study which had just been painted so all of the windows were opened. The ruling members as well as the team leaders were in attendance besides members of the Royal Family, Erebus and the Sanuri. The room was full when Raul and Matthew escorted Madeline in. She showed the nervousness which she felt.

"Madeline since you have been spying on all of us for some time I won't bother with introductions," said Sudfad sarcastically. "I have been told that you came here on your own accord to help us or to escape your world but I believe you will understand that none of us trust you."

"Within the next few hours the ruling families of Lentz will be arriving and I promise they will have many questions for you. But first, since you are in my home which is filled with children I want the Sanuri to look into your mind."

"King Sudfad, I understand all that you have said but I promise you I am not a danger to any of you especially the children. Sanuri what do you need me to do?" asked Madeline.

"It won't hurt," the Sanuri said as he walked up to her and placed the palms of his hands on both sides of her head.

Although Madeline was frightened she would not admit it. She wanted to maintain the upper hand with bargaining information and now she didn't know if the Sanuri was going to ruin that for her.

After many minutes the Sanuri took his hands from her head and spoke to Madeline first. "I saw why you were frightened and that was not my purpose. When I see things they are often fragmented pictures that flash quickly before my eyes. I saw some very disturbing things and many faces. I also saw something very curious."

The Sanuri now turned to Gabriel. "Please bring some of the children in here. It is safe. I just need to ask them a question."

Gabriel left the study. "Sanuri what did you mean disturbing things?" asked Madeline fearfully.

"Let's just say for now you have had a colorful life. But I also saw things that you have seen in this world and in yours. I have many questions."

The Sanuri turned to Sudfad. "She was frightened that I would expose the information that she wants to use as bargaining chips. I don't know if I even saw any of that. As far as Madeline goes she appears to be telling the truth now but she has led a life built on deception. She is safe to have in the castle. But I saw a very strong connection between her and Javier and I would not be surprised if he doesn't come looking for her."

Gabriel entered the study with Christopher, Nicholas, Joey, Tommy, Adrone, Paul, Zack and Cody.

"Thank you for coming boys," said the Sanuri warmly. "I would like you to tell me if you know this lady and if you do from where?" The Sanuri looked at Madeline and said, "Please turn around."

"I know her," said Tommy. "She is in my pictures."

"Very good," said the Sanuri. "How about the rest of you?"

"I don't know her," said Christopher. "Why?"

"I will tell you in a minute but I want the other boys to answer my question."

"Me neither," said Adrone. "Are we supposed to?"

"Do any of you boys know her?"

They all shook their heads from side to side except for Tommy.

"Sanuri why are you asking this?" asked Madeline.

"Because some months ago a man and woman who said they were you and Javier tried to lure the boys from their home."

"Boys this is the real Madeline," said the Sanuri. "Do any of you think you remember the other woman enough to have Annabelle draw a picture?"

"She kinda looks like that other lady," said Christopher.

Simon stood up, "Boys come with me and we will find Annabelle."

"Sanuri can you heal our friend?" asked Adrone. Paul walked up to the Sanuri and showed him Azu.

The Sanuri smiled and placed his hands on the bird. He closed his eyes and started to hum. After a few moments the Sanuri said, "He will need a lot of rest but he will be just fine."

"Thank you," yelled Christopher loudly and the boys left the study with Simon.

"Gabriel will you close the door?" asked the Sanuri. "Madeline why would someone pretend they were you?"

"I don't know," she said as the color drained from her face. "Is that why you thought I would hurt the children?"

No one answered her question but Raphael said, "A woman who fit your description went to Erebus' home and spoke with the workmen was that you?"

"No," Madeline said as she now stared suspiciously at the men in the room. "How do I know you are telling me the truth? And what did that boy mean when he said I was the person in his pictures?"

"We are telling you the truth," said Gabriel. "Obviously we have much to discuss and neither of us trusts each other but these sightings that we speak of were done days before attacks on those same properties. In both incidents the woman we thought was you made sure her presence was known. We thought that was a scare tactic. Do you have any ideas of who would frame you like that?"

"Not off the top of my head but I will have to think about that. First let me explain some things and if the Sanuri needs to do something to let you know that I am speaking the truth then do it."

"Go ahead," said the Sanuri.

"I expect that we will have discussions for days if not weeks but to start at the beginning you need to understand Inferus. While there are many beautiful things about that kingdom it is filled with darkness. I heard what Cyrene said and it was true. We are raised to hate everyone in your world. We are told that you drove us out of your world and that we would be tortured and killed if we returned. So do you understand what a test of faith it was for Benedict and the others to come here?"

"You have many enemies and from what I have heard I don't believe you were always in this position so this is new for you. In Inferus no one is trusted. You have tribes here; in Inferus we call them subcultures. While many of your tribes are basically the same as you, in our world they are physically different. And they were bred that way."

"The Abuckto are powerful seers that are the ruling party of Inferus. Benedict is an Abuckto so it is a wonder that he could block the others from knowing that he is a Credo."

"Before you continue," said Sudfad. "How do you know about the Credo and Benedict?"

"I am a spy and a very good one. I belong to a group called the Charto. We are desperate to leave Inferus and we are enemies of the Abuckto but let me get back to that. I want you to understand what I am saying."

"The Abuckto are so powerful that they can read people's minds at times. People will be dragged off the streets and executed for their thoughts. Those of us in the Charto knew about the Credo and were fascinated at how they could block the Abuckto from knowing about them. We never found out."

"You are wondering how we block the Abuckto from knowing we hate them. Well we don't but we have such specialized skills that they need us; so we all operate with certain agreements. Many of the members of the Charto are Etos like myself and Javier. We are bred to be irresistible to other beings which helps us to gain trust and information. I would assume that your Angel is blocking me from all of you because of the way that you act around me."

"Members of the Charto are also highly intelligent and most of us are trained as warriors. We, not the Abuckto have the guts to come to your world. We agree to give the Abuckto information and they do not persecute us. There are many members of the Charto who are like me. We have found that your world is a considerably better place to live than Inferus. I have to tell you that my brother does not share my feelings on this matter."

"Before I go any farther I want to say that I know I will be repeating all of this when the people of Lentz arrive so right now I am just giving you an overview so you have a better understanding of all of us who you have brought into your home."

"The original mission of the Charto was to find ways to reclaim our lands in your world although no one knows exactly which lands were ours. As we spied on you and when I say this I mean your world not necessarily you as individuals we have seen many changes over the centuries and that brings me to you."

"While humans cannot tell us apart from them, the demons can differentiate us. And yes sometimes we have worked with them and often we get information from them."

"But we have become aware of many powerful demons who are now watching your world and even coming here. They have contacted us to try and get information."

"We found it curious that a handful of people could garner the attention of so many. You are both hated and feared. We started watching you to try and figure out why. The members of the Charto are wise military leaders and at any given time have multiple charts in the works with strategies on how we can take over our lands."

"And one strategy has always been to let all of you battle it out and we fight the last ones standing. And you may not believe this but we don't want to live in a world that is owned by demons. Don't you see that defeats our purpose for leaving Inferus?"

"Prince Matthew, I am sure Isabella told you by now that she and Javier were having an affair. That is true and he and I both asked her for information which she was eager to give us. But that information was for us, not the demons."

"Don't get me wrong I am not saying that the humans and Elods are allies but we are not allies with the demons either. In fact, we left when we heard demons talking about a great attack on Lentz. You may not want to hear this but Isabella was, I am not sure how to say this, like a volcano that was ready to erupt. Javier opened doors in her that she became addicted to. He took her places and introduced her to things that she found exciting and fulfilling."

"We usually return to Inferus once a month to brief our superiors in the Charto about our findings. Of course Javier did not explain to Isabella where we were going. She started to go to the places he frequented by herself. At first it was to look for him but she met many people and many more demons in these places."

"I understand that this may be an emotional subject but please look at it from the point of view of a spy. Isabella was like the icing on a cake for us."

"She opened doors and was more than eager to give us anything we asked for. Did she tell you that Javier broke it off with her?"

"Yes," Matthew said in a hoarse voice.

"Think about it. Why would any spy give up their most valuable asset? It certainly wasn't because we got all of the information that we wanted from her. It is because our people who would frequent the Catacombs, do you know what I am talking about?"

"Yes," Matthew said.

"They saw her in, shall I say compromising situations with many others. We; that is the members of the Charto that were in Lentz had huge arguments about what we should do with her because we felt she was heading for trouble and would expose all of us. That is why he left her. Isabella was an intelligent woman but in some ways she was like a child always trying to get attention and a pat on the head. She never took the time to question anything. If she thought she could do something to get praise or a thrill she did it; no matter who it was with."

"There are ways besides us; that the sorcerers and the Abuckto have of spying into your world. And I will show you some of these. We watched your battle. We saw your Angel on the shores. The same Angel that allowed me to come here."

"I have never been a Credo and I am not saying that I am one now. But watching all of you I have seen things which I could not believe. But not all the Charto felt like that because our world is filled with dark magics. We all have seen many things that we can't explain. And you should know that the sorcerers are very, very powerful. They do not work with the Abuckto and some like Andrac seem to be enemies of that group. The sorcerers certainly don't work with us. They are powers unto themselves and they are very dangerous."

"For me to show you some of the ways we can spy into your world we will need to saddle some horses. These windows were somehow closed so we can wait if you want the people from Lentz to join us. But first I am very curious. Why did that boy say I was in his pictures? Certainly he wasn't spying on us."

The men in the room looked at the Sanuri because they weren't sure they wanted to answer Madeline's question. "Like Anka, Tommy is a seer. They found a way to communicate and became friends and that is how we learned of the Credo. Tommy drew many pictures of your world and you were in some. In the pictures you weren't doing anything unusual but Tommy told us you were scared a lot," explained the Sanuri.

Madeline's face became white. "I don't understand how that could happen in itself much less how those children were protected from the Abuckto."

"Our Angel," said Gabriel. "Now I have a question for you. Drake said you know there is a bounty on your head but you want to give us information for your freedom in this world. Is that true?"

"Yes and I don't expect you to believe me. But I am hoping that as you get to know the members of the Credo and listen to their stories you will understand why all of us want to escape. Gabriel, for all that I am and all that you think I am; I am not naïve nor am I trusting. Under the circumstances you should not trust me, yet. I know I have to prove myself."

Simon had reentered the study while Madeline was speaking and was standing in front of the door. "Ok, just say that we all work out an agreement that gives us all what we want. Won't your people put a bounty on you for what you are doing?"

"Eventually. In my world a spy would be tortured and executed immediately. If you do not treat me in such a manner the other members of the Charto will think I am simply working. But you have to understand I am not alone in wanting to live in your world. Some of our members have families, friends and lovers here. They too would seek asylum. But that brings me to my next proposal."

"I was trained and some could even say that I was bred as a spy. That really is all I know. Gabriel, I have watched your team in action. You could use someone with my skills. So that is something I would like all of you to think about."

"So you are saying you would spy on your own people?" Edward asked.

"I could spy on anyone you wanted," Madeline said and smiled. "Isabella would tell us how difficult it was for Matthew, Thaos and Stephan at first to be married to women warriors."

"Although I will say those women fulfil the roles of wives and mothers because that is how they were raised. I was never raised like that. I know nothing else but being a soldier and I think that some of you can understand that."

"My biggest threat would be Javier. We are twins and can read each other well. He is so bitter and angry that I don't know if he would ever understand how I feel about being free."

"Madeline, I will be honest," said Gabriel. "I don't trust you, not yet anyways. But I am intrigued by your proposal."

It was evening when Korbin found Karzman lying in the doorway of his house. While Korbin was not a demon or darklord he had been employed by Teivel for decades. As soon as he saw the leisons and boils that now covered Karzman's body, Korbin knew the dictator had been cursed by powerful dark magics.

Korbin was no fool, he understood how these types of curses were executed. He knew the curses were alive in Karzman's house. Korbin grabbed Karzman's arms and pulled him into the yard. Karzman was in and out of consciousness. He was whinning, cursing and yelling.

Korbin left Karzman lying in the dirt and ran to a group of soldiers. Within minutes they returned with bottles of whiskey and lit torches. "Burn the place down," ordered Korbin. "And don't anyone touch him." The soldiers stared at Karzman with disgust and horror. He had ozzing sores and he was covered with pus and vomit.

Karzman's home was little more than a shack which was quickly enveloped in flames. All of the soldiers now gathered around Korbin who was standing near Karzman's head.

Korbin started chanting in a language the soldiers did not understand. They kept looking back and forth between Korbin and Karzman.

All of the men jumped as there were explosions in Karzman's home. Flames with strange colors now shot into the sky. Some of the men thought they saw images in the flames. Karzman screamed and thrashed around on the ground.

"Do not touch him," Korbin ordered again. Then he resumed chanting.

# Chapter XLIV
## Veils

The people in Sudfad's study were interrupted when several Enrops flew into the room and handed Sudfad a note. He quickly read it. "It's from Claudius, they will be here within the hour. I propose we resume the meeting when they get here." Now Sudfad looked at Madeline.

"I am considering you a prisoner until we sort all of this out. My sons will get you chambers within the castle and assign escorts for you. At this point, I do not want you roaming around the castle by yourself. Do you have any questions?"

"No, that is more than generous. If I might suggest, Marina asked if I could come back and help her with her patients. Of course you can verify that with her. While I am not a healer I would rather be doing something than sitting around."

"Sudfad, I would feel better if we kept a close eye on her until Claudius and the others get here," said Matthew.

"Fine, Raul, Simon and Matthew she will be your responsibility. Work out what you think is best," said Sudfad.

"Wait, before you leave," said the Sanuri. "I have a question. The Angel Adam took me to a cave where there were people and animals in cages and chains. Limbs were cut off them all and sewn onto different species. These poor beings were mutilated and in great agony. Who was responsible for such horror?"

"I have not seen the place you speak of but I have heard about it. There are rumors that some of the members of the Abuckto are working with the sorcerers. And I have heard that they are responsible for these things," said Madeline. "But understand too that many believe they are just wild rumors."

"What is the purpose of such depravity?" asked the Sanuri.

"Our people are always experimenting with breeding. That is how they have developed many of the creatures they use such as the Stratas."

"It is rumored that some of the Abuckto want to create powerful soldiers to send into your world for battle. Benedict may know more about this than I do."

When Cabal left his village he rode straight to the cave where he and Torin had hidden some of Karzman's treasure. Torin was the only member of Cabal's family who he had any feelings for and now that Torin was dead Cabal felt lost.

Cabal cried as he rode although his tears were the results of fear more than grief. He knew it was a matter of time before Karzman sent men and possibly demons after him. Cabal jumped off his horse and ran inside of the cave. He quickly dug up the two sets of saddlebags that held riches. He ran out of the cave, mounted his horse and started his journey to Stordt.

Cabal knew he had to get out of his father's lands as quickly as possible. To ride south would have been a more direct route to Stordt but he would have to travel the length of Karzman's lands. Cabal headed east. He rode as if the devil himself was chasing him.

Marie, the head cook of the Royal Family was very territorial and at first overwhelmed when dozens of Elod women offered to help work in the kitchen. It wasn't that the kitchen was not large enough to hold all of these women it was that Marie was used to doing things in a certain manner. But to her surprise she found the Elod women more than accommodating and helpful. Although they did not know the recipes they followed Marie's instructions to the smallest detail.

These women were still consumed with fear and the reality of their situation had not yet hit them. They wanted to stay busy and they wanted to show their gratitude to their rescuers.

After several hours, Marie had so completely changed her attitude about the Elods that she spoke with Renya. The two women met in the hallway outside of the kitchen.

"My Lady, I know this is not the right time. But these women are hard workers and very pleasant. We are still several positions short on staff; perhaps you and My Lord would consider hiring some of them."

"Marie, you never want anyone in your kitchen," Renya said with a smile. "Honestly I don't know their customs yet. I don't know if offering them a job would be a good thing or an insult but I will speak with Sudfad about your idea."

The women were interrupted by the sound of trumpets announcing the arrival of the people from Lentz. Renya ran to the front door of the castle to greet her guests.

The next couple of hours were chaotic as the guests moved into their chambers and the soldiers were assigned quarters. Renya personally escorted Bella and Claudius to their new home.

"Renya, I don't know what to say," said Bella. "Thank you so much. This is lovely and very practical."

"I fixed up rooms for Cassidy and Ryan but I will be honest I couldn't decide at first if I should build a bigger home for all of your family. But Sudfad suggested that Thaos and Stephan might enjoy their own homes."

"They all have studies in them. Please let me know of anything that you would like. Raul and Matthew are helping Stephan's and Thao's families move in. They are on either side of you. Fahron's, Mathas' and Sorren's families are just down the hallway. When you are settled I can take you on the tour."

Simon and Ryan were having all of the furniture moved from the bocas into Sudfad's new study. Many of the Elod men offered to help with this project. Simon pulled Ryan to the side and spoke with him. "Michael was injured helping the Elods to escape. Nyla and the girls are with him. I will take you to his room. He knows that you and Nyla like each other and he is alright with that. But don't be surprised if he gets a little over protective at times."

"Thank you. I wondered if something had happened when I didn't see them."

"Ryan everyone in the family is fine with you and Nyla seeing each other. But I have to tell you all of those girls have changed a lot just since we found them. I guess I am just trying to say that you may have to give her some time to completely adjust to everything."

Although Angelina showed Rosa the new home for her and Mathas, Angelina and Matthew wanted Rosa and little Sarah to stay in their home. This made Rosa happy since she greatly missed her children and grandchildren.

Lana, Chaez, April and Sally pushed through the crowd until they found Fahron, Isadore and Benny. They were all elated to be reunited. Chaez and Lana escorted his parents to their new home in the castle. Renya had allowed Fahron's family to help with the decorating and the children had surprises for their parents.

After Raul and Matthew finished moving Thaos' and Stephan's families into their homes, they joined Simon in the new study. Vitomas and Annabelle were already in the room helping to set it up.

Renya had a reception planned in the Great Hall for the guests but her children planned a special reception in the new study for all of the leaders. Besides setting up the furniture the Princes and Princesses were also setting up refreshment tables.

Nyla and Ryan walked into the study, "Oh my, this is so beautiful," said Nyla as she started to walk around the huge room.

"And your boyfriend made it all," said Raul kiddingly.

"Raul!" Nyla said and blushed as the others laughed.

"I really love it," said Annabelle. "Ryan, we know that Bella was sending material for drapes but with all of the spies we have around here we had some made. Renya can replace them later."

"What can we do?" Ryan asked.

"Honesty can both of you go in the hallway and keep people out of here?" asked Simon. "I can't tell you how many times someone has walked in here thinking it was the Great Hall."

"We can do that," Ryan said with a grin.

"The cooks can bring food in and Bekka and Cassandra are bringing the flowers," said Vitomas. "But no one else and that means Sudfad and Renya either. And Ryan you did a wonderful job, they are just going to love this."

"Which reminds me," said Raul. "Here's three bags of coins, let us know how much more we owe you. And I mean for everything."

"Now that sounds suspicious," Annabelle said and smiled.

"There is a lot more besides this," Simon said with a glint in his eyes.

Korbin continued calling to the dark worlds for help healing Karzman, who lay on the ground screaming in pain. Korbin did not want to say anything to the soldiers but he started to fear that Cabal had paid powerful demons to inflict the curses. As Korbin chanted his mind was racing as he tried to figure out what was really happening.

Korbin knew that Samael owned Karzman's soul and that Samael was the most powerful demon in the World of Nunc. It did not make sense to Korbin that Samael would restore Karzman's power only to take it away a matter of hours later. So who was defying Samael by attacking Karzman?

Korbin also knew that the types of curses that were inflicted upon Karzman came at a great price and he wondered how Cabal was paying for them.

It never dawned on Korbin that someone else could be responsible for the curses. He stopped chanting and looked at the horrified soldiers who were standing around Karzman.

"Some of you find Cabal and the rest of you raid the Village of Kaffa," ordered Korbin. "I am going to need sacrifices to get the attention of the demons."

Korbin then ordered the remainder of the soldiers to watch over Karzman as he went to his home, which was little more than a shack. As soon as Teivel was killed, Korbin was contacted by Hector, who now employed him. Hector sent Korbin to Karzman's village to monitor him. It was to Hector that Korbin now sent a message. A very long message that not only explained the unusual occurrences surrounding Karzman but Korbin's ideas about healing him. Then Korbin asked for help from the powerful dark lord.

Emeral, Laurel, Natasha, Alexander and Vivian had been shopping in Salar and now led a small caravan of bocas into the front courtyard of the castle. Soldiers were driving the bocas.

"Let me see where Renya wants this set up," said Emeral and walked into the castle.

It took Emeral a few minutes to find the Queen. "Where do you want us to set up?" she asked.

"All of the Elod families are in the southern wing. I thought we could set things up in the large meeting room there," replied Renya then she stepped closer to her friend and said in a lower voice. "Did anyone tell you that Madeline is here too? Sudfad said that the Sanuri looked into her mind and it wasn't her and Javier who were at your house but imposters."

"Maxwell came into the city and told us. But I would still like to speak with her myself."

"She's helping Marina with the wounded and Erebus is watching her. She will be in one of the chambers in this hallway."

Emeral found Madeline in the room where Jared and Archetenus were patients. Both men were injured but sitting up in their beds and drinking whiskey.

"Well, you two look good," Emeral said to the men as she walked into the room.

"Emeral, you should hear them," Marina said and laughed. "Delilah and Zoya just left here. And these two clowns made it sound like they were really suffering then as soon as their wives leave they sit up and pour some drinks."

Emeral laughed then looked sternly at Madeline. "May I speak with you in the hallway?"

"Sounds like you're gonna get scolded," Jared said and laughed. "We're too injured to help ya."

Both Emeral and Madeline laughed as they walked into the hallway. "I am Emeral."

"I know who you are and I suspect you want to know if I am a threat to your family. I am not. I assure you," said Madeline as she looked boldly into Emeral's eyes.

"I didn't realize you are a seer too," Emeral said sarcastically.

"I am not but everyone is concerned that I am going to hurt someone. I do not lie when I say I haven't yet figured out who impersonated us. Emeral your tribe and your family take great pride in being warriors. I am a soldier and a spy, which I take great pride in. I do not kidnap or hurt innocent children. You can have the Sanuri look into my mind again if it will make you feel better."

"I will admit you are not what I expected," said Emeral as she was staring at Madeline. "I like someone who speaks their mind. My husband told me what you said earlier and if you were telling the truth that takes great courage. Madeline, you have a second chance here; not many people get one. I hope you think about that seriously."

561

Emeral turned and opened the door to Archetenus' and Jared's room. "Marina if you don't need Madeline's help any more she can help me with a project."

"That's fine but Erebus will have to go with you," said Marina.

"Good, he can help too," Emeral said. When Erebus joined the women in the hallway Emeral led them towards the southern wing. "A few of us have been shopping all day. We brought back bocas filled with clothing, shoes and toys for the Elods. The soldiers are setting up tables in the meeting room of the south wing. We need to put all of the goods on tables so people can pick out what they want."

"That is very generous, I am surprised," said Madeline sincerely.

"I have a feeling many things will surprise you here," Emeral said. "Madeline, you too are welcome to take anything you want. I doubt if you will be free to go shopping. Since all of you will be here for the celebrations we purchased a variety of things. The first reception starts in an hour."

Emeral was surprised that the meeting room was filled with soldiers who had already emptied the bocas. Laurel and Vivian were directing the men in setting up the tables while Natasha and Alexander were organizing the goods.

"Who paid for all of this?" asked Erebus. "I'm impressed."

"Maxwell and I were going to but Sudfad demanded to. Well, let's get to work."

"Girls, I have to make sure everything is ready for the reception," Renya said as Nina and Saran dragged her and Sudfad down the hallway. Sudfad was laughing.

"Raul said you would say that," Saran said. "He said to tell you this comes first."

"Is it the study?" asked Renya. "Is the new furniture here?"

"We aren't supposed to tell you," Nina said. "But you will like it."

When they got to the door of the new study, Saran knocked on it and Gabriel opened the door. The room was filled with people, candles and flowers. Both Sudfad and Renya looked shocked when they saw the rich furnishings.

"This is absolutely beautiful... Michael what are you doing out of bed?" Renya gasped.

"He has to be here," said Simon. "Petra you're up."

"Papa this is from all us boys," said Petra proudly and took Sudfad's hand. "This is your new desk and all of the drawers lock. Here's the keys."

"This is beautiful, thank you so much," said Sudfad as he admired the fine workmanship.

Petra led Sudfad around the room and showed him the special features like a hidden safe and an escape tunnel.

"And Papa, when you move this wall there are all your maps," Petra continued. When the tour was finished everyone applauded.

Raul stood in front of the room, "Ryan made all of this furniture and Bella; god bless you for helping us because it never would have turned out this good otherwise."

The door opened and Emeral, Erebus and Madeline entered. "Sorry we are late," Emeral said.

Claudius and Fahron stared coldly at Madeline. "We have much to discuss with you," Claudius snarled.

"Claudius, you certainly do but now is not the time," said Emeral. "Sudfad, Renya we have everything set up. All of the Elods are in the Great Hall is Benedict here?"

"Benedict will you and Cyrene come forward?" Sudfad asked.

"What is happening?" asked Benedict as he and his wife walked up to the King and Queen.

"Emeral, Laurel, Natasha, Vivian and Alexander have been shopping since before your people arrived. We understood that you would be escaping with only the clothes on your backs. We would like you to lead your people to the meeting room in the south wing. The room is filled with clothing, toys and other items for your families. Please help yourselves."

Benedict stared at Sudfad for several moments. "We cannot; why would you do this?"

"First of all you can take these things and secondly all of you need them. And of course Emeral apparently picked out a great deal of fancy clothes for the celebrations," Sudfad said with a big smile.

"Madeline, you stay with me," said Emeral and took her hand. "You need to try on a few things."

The group in the study walked to the south wing, while Benedict and Cyrene gathered their children and their people.

"These are for all of you," Sudfad announced to the Elods. "There are all different sizes so pick out what you want. And I am told that Emeral picked out clothing for you for the celebrations we will be hosting over the next few days."

Like Benedict, his people were in shock and simply stood in the room staring at all of the gifts.

"What are you waiting for?" Adrone asked loudly and everyone laughed.

"We'll help you," said Nyla and took a woman by the hand and led her to a table.

"Anka, Santi, Linus come on!" yelled Christopher as he and Amy pulled their new friends towards the toys. Slowly the families walked forward and sorted through the shoes and clothes.

Emeral had not made up her mind about Madeline but she had decided to give the young woman a chance to prove herself. The people from Lentz looked at Madeline with hatred. So Emeral decided to keep her close for a while.

"I put aside a few things that I thought might fit you," Emeral said to Madeline then she looked at Erebus and smiled. "I know you have to watch her but I will take her into the changing room."

"I won't argue," Erebus said with a grin.

"Emeral why are you doing this?" asked Madeline as the two women walked across the room.

"Doing what?"

"You know what I mean."

"Madeline many of us were outsiders when we first came here. We all had to prove ourselves. And you know you have more to prove. You could have a very good life here. But if you betray us...well...I guess I don't have to explain."

Emeral opened a door. "These things looked about your size, but tell me if you don't like them."

Kaffa was a medium sized village that was south of the lands that Karzman owned. It was east of the Farth River and directly north of Fort Nir.

It was late in the day when two hundred of Karzman's soldiers left for Kaffa. They pulled a dozen caged wagons which slowed their pace. They knew they would have to travel all night. What they did not know was that all of the commanding generals of the forts as well as High Priest Nicholas of the Patronus had been previously warned by Sudfad that Karzman would attack communities to abduct people.

Besides the additional patrols, soldiers and Patronus priests were also stationed in every village and city in the northcentral section of Wetpr.

The soldiers and priests were stationed in these communities for protection as well as for keeping the peace after the recent riots.

Because of the reception in the new study and the gifts for the Elods, the original grand reception started two hours late. The refugees from Inferus and the people from Lentz and Wetpr were intrigued with each other. Barriers were broken down and veils were lifted as these two cultures talked, laughed and danced.

"Emeral, you don't have to babysit me," said Madeline. "Enjoy yourself."

"Oh my dear, I always enjoy myself," Emeral said with a smile. "Maxwell would you dance with Madeline? I will be right back."

"I would be honored," Maxwell said and led Madeline to the dance floor.

"Bella may I dance with your husband?" Emeral asked.

"I have to warn you he loves to dance," Bella said. "One may not be enough."

Claudius and Emeral walked to the dance floor. "Claudius, I want to talk to you about Madeline. While all of you have every reason to hate her I think you need to listen to what she has to say."

"We plan to," he said angrily.

"No, I mean really listen instead of letting your anger take control. I challenged her earlier and I have spent time with her. I will say she wasn't what I was expecting. She has been helping me today and we have been talking. I don't know all of the crimes she has committed in your kingdom but I believe she really wants to escape from Inferus. I am not telling you to trust her or even to like her. I am asking you to listen to her."

After the dinner meal, the leaders returned to Sudfad's study while the other guests remained at the celebration. Many of the wives of the leaders also joined the meeting.

Raphael had taken notes of the first meeting with Madeline. Bekka and Cassandra had made copies of the notes and were now handing them out in this meeting.

Erebus addressed the group first. "I am one of the few people who went to Inferus who is not injured so Sudfad asked me to tell you about the part of the mission that I experienced, which includes Madeline joining us. Then the Sanuri will tell of his experience since he was not with the rest of us. Then Madeline will speak."

With all of the activities of the day most of team members had not heard the details of the mission. The people listened intently to Erebus and to the Sanuri. Benedict was not in the meeting. Madeline was the only Elod. She walked to the front of the room.

"The Sanuri looked into my mind once today. If it would make any of you feel better he should now do it again. Because I promise you that I am going to be saying things that you will not like hearing." No one spoke so Madeline continued. "I have much to tell you but for you to really understand any of it you need to understand Inferus so I will repeat some of the things that I said at the earlier meeting."

The meeting lasted for hours. "I know you have many more questions for Madeline but it is late and all of you look exhausted," said Sudfad. "Renya has many activities planned for tomorrow but I would like to continue this meeting. If any of you are interested we will resume after breakfast."

"I think most of us will be back," said Claudius. "Madeline, you have given us a great deal of information but understand that we will need to verify it."

"Of course. I don't know what all of you have planned but I would like to take at least some of you to the areas where the sorcerers have opened windows to watch you. Sudfad there are six such places on your land. Gabriel there are two on yours and Erebus there are two on your property also. Of course there are other windows in Salar. They are closed now, I assume your Angel did that so they are not a threat."

"Can we destroy them?" asked Gabriel.

"They were created by dark magics," replied Madeline. "I don't know how to destroy them. Perhaps the Sanuri or Erebus can do that. I assume I will be returning to Lentz with you. I will show you the windows there. I will also take you to our meeting places."

"Claudius and Fahron, there is something that I want you to think about. Matthew told me that you closed down the Catacombs and I can understand why. My brother has many addictions and frequented those businesses nightly. I found them repulsive. But they were a great place to get information. There is an advantage to keeping all of your enemies in one area and where you can watch them. We have gotten some of our most valuable information there."

"Are you suggesting we allow those businesses to reopen?" asked Fahron.

"What I am suggesting is that you turn the tables on your enemies. You are always being watched and attacked. I am sure that everyone in Langer knows you don't approve of those businesses. So they would never expect you to be running a few or at the very least have your own spies working in them. That is how Javier learned of the armada attack. He heard about it weeks before it happened. None of us believed it at first but after we got more information we returned to Inferus before the demons landed."

Thaos stood up. "Claudius, Fahron, I know that you and Mathas really were disturbed by those businesses. But I have to agree with Madeline on this one. When I worked for Juleta, I got most of my information in taverns. The problem would be who we would get to work there. We should give this idea some serious thought."

"I like the idea too," said Gideon. "You will have to bring people in that nobody knows. We could get sailors or others from Port Friada."

"Since the windows and passageways were closed, our spies in this world cannot communicate with Inferus. You have four members of the Charto operating in Langer and six in Castor. About half of these spies desire asylum. Think of the possibilities you have."

"Claudius it is worth talking about," said Dominic.

"There are many things which we will need to talk about before we return to Langer if for no other reason than how we present Madeline. If she returns as a prisoner or a spy or both. Madeline, Gabriel told us that you offered to work with us for your freedom. But what exactly do you want?" asked Claudius.

"My freedom is my main concern. I left Inferus with nothing. Emeral just gave me some clothing. The reason I tell you this is that if I work for you I will need the proper disguises just like your teams use. I do have some things still in Langer. That is if my house is still there."

"Madeline, I have found this night very interesting," said Thaos. "For so long we thought of you as a woman hunting wealthy men and I believe we are all realizing how intelligent and shrewd you are. I would imagine you are holding many cards up your sleeve to bargain with. Are you planning on showing us your hand if you get your freedom?"

"I assure you that you will be shocked at the things I will tell and show you Thaos. But I am no fool either. Just as you need assurances from me I will need some from you and then I will show you all of my cards."

# Chapter XLV
## Second Chance

After the meeting Madeline was escorted to her chambers. Two soldiers stood guard outside of her door. She opened the balcony doors and saw that two soldiers stood beneath the balcony. Madeline did not plan to escape, at least not this night. She was exhausted and emotionally drained. She drank a glass of wine and went to bed. Sleep did not come easily for her and for the first time in a very long time, Madeline wondered what she was doing.

The moon seemed to disappear as Karzman's soldiers traveled southward. One of the wagons hit a huge boulder and the axle broke. After a considerable amount of cursing, Sean the leader of the men decided to leave the wagon. They continued their journey to the Village of Kaffa.

Renya was sitting up in bed reading when Sudfad walked into their bedroom chambers. "I checked on the children," she said. "Were you able to speak with any of the Angels?"

"No," Sudfad said as he was disrobing. "And I am getting a really bad feeling about all of this."

Madeline was escorted to breakfast in the Great Hall. She immediately noticed the change in her people. They were laughing and talking. The children were running around with the children from Sudfad's and Gabriel's homes. There was considerably less fear in everyone's faces. Madeline hoped that she too would feel like that.

Arrangements were made for all of the children and pets at Gabriel's home to spend the morning at the castle. This was done so that all of the team and family members could be shown the windows the sorcerers had opened on their land.

Hannah walked up to Madeline during breakfast. "I brought you some riding clothes and boots. There are several sizes so hopefully something will fit."

"Thank you," Madeline said. "You are very kind." Although she had spent years as a spy in this world, Madeline had always had the upper hand. This was a new experience for her. Her identity was exposed and people were helping her. Both of these things made her feel very uncomfortable.

Korbin had continued to chant over Karzman during the night. Now that the sun was rising Korbin could see there was little improvement in Karzman's condition. Korbin had thought that the curses would have been broken when the house was burned down; but Karzman seemed to be suffering more after the house was destroyed.

Korbin had forbidden the soldiers from touching Karzman for fear the effects of the curse would be transmitted. Now, in the early hours of the morning Korbin was clearly exhausted. He needed to get food and sleep but he didn't want to leave Karzman lying in the dirt. Korbin ordered some soldiers to move Karzman to a vacant shack. When the men rolled the dictator over onto his back they all jumped back from him.

Karzman's stomach had broken open and hundreds of insects that looked like huge beetles were running around on the ground. The soldiers started to stomp on the insects with their boots. The soldiers and Korbin watched in horror as the same insects were crawling out of Karzman's mouth. Karzman groaned and coughed and dozens of the insects were expelled from his throat.

Hannah helped Madeline change into riding clothes after breakfast. As the two women walked to Sudfad's new study they suddenly heard loud screams. Madeline immediately grabbed her belt as if she was going for a weapon, but there wasn't one. Then she heard the laughter.

"It's the children," explained Hannah. "Your people are meeting all of our dogs and puppies. Apparently you don't have them in Inferus."

Madeline laughed and relaxed. When they entered the study, she was not surprised to see all of the team members dressed in riding clothes but she was surprised to see Renya, Vitomas and Annabelle also wearing riding clothes.

"One of the windows is near the camp of Sampson. You might want to bring his things since his injuries will keep him in bed for a while," Madeline said.

"Madeline do all of the windows look the same?" asked Annabelle. "Because perhaps I should draw them."

Madeline walked over to one of the windows in the study. "Think of them like this. Say this is a window in a tree, there will be a veil over it to look like bark. A similar window in a rock will have a veil to look like stone."

"So they are inside of objects?" Erebus asked.

"Ours are but I know that demons have different ways of spying on everyone and I believe their windows are different," Madeline said. "Before you ask, the Abuckto will tell us where they have created windows and when we get to the general area we can feel the energy which is very strong. After you know what you are looking for, all of you should be able to recognize the energy also."

"But there are drawbacks in that one's sight is limited in the windows. For example, even though there are six on the royal grounds none of them are close to the castle. Several of our members, including me have spied on your gatherings the old fashioned way. But that is difficult because your soldiers and your dogs prevent us from getting too close."

"But that reminds me of something I should tell you. As I said last night the demons can tell us from humans. We can also tell most demons from humans. It is similar to Erebus seeing auras. And perhaps it is auras that we see but the ones we see have, I am not sure what a good word is to describe this."

"For lack of anything else let's say they have signatures so we can tell who the demon is if we recognize the signature. Of course I am talking when they are in disguise as humans."

"Javier and I were watching all of you, almost two years ago. You had days of celebrations. I don't know what the celebrations were for but I do remember Diana and Nada competing. You not only had the demon Hecate walking through the crowds but the demon Visterle. He was dressed as a nobleman. He is a notorious demon and actually Javier and I became more interested in him than all of you."

"I don't know if you realize that he is a king of a world. To have someone of his statue spying on a group of humans is very unusual. But he wasn't interested in any of you. He was spying on Hecate. Then when he saw her watching Nada, well Nada caught his eye. I have heard that he stole her and made her his queen."

"This is disturbing for everyone here," said Erebus. "But I too was at those celebrations and I had my powers then but I didn't pick up on their energies. How can that be?"

"Those two demons are so powerful and so rich," explained Madeline. "That if they can't do something they can pay to have it done. Do you know there were many rumors in the underworlds that Hecate was a traitor? Many were saying that she was responsible for the fall of several Old Ones; which included Moloch. Visterle was Moloch's head lieutenant. And for all that Visterle is he was very loyal to Moloch. I suspect that Visterle was hunting Hecate for revenge."

"Madeline do you know that Nada is Misha's mother?" asked Emeral.

"Yes."

"Do you know if she or Visterle are any threat to Misha's family?" Madeline could hear the fear in Emeral's voice as she asked this question.

"I have never heard anything but I don't have all the answers either. But I will tell you that he is waging wars in Nunc for Molach's hell world and on his planet of Sidus because others are trying to take his world. I can't image that he even has time to worry about any of you."

"I did hear that he and Nada had twin sons. First, never has a Ruala been the mate of a demon and secondly, demons don't conceive as easily as humans and they rarely have multiple births. Visterle held celebrations for over a week in his world to celebrate. He is very proud of his new family, which rather surprised me because he is so vicious."

"Madeline, Diana and I have twin boys and Diana had some strange visions about Nada. We don't know if she is a threat to our children. If you hear any information will you tell us? I will pay you well," said Misha.

"Misha, I would not take your money but you must realize that the only way I will hear information is to go back to work. I am not a seer. But I work very hard."

"I just want to revisit something you said earlier," said Sudfad. "You were sure that Visterle was only interested in Hecate and Nada?"

"When Javier and I realized that all of you were unaware that you had demons walking among you, well we came out of hiding and joined the celebration too. That is how we heard that Nada was Misha's mother. Honestly the only thing of interest to us at that celebration was why two notorious and powerful demons were attending your celebration. I am sure that the Sanuri and Erebus will back me when I say that is almost unheard of."

"The truth is that the Charto started spying on all of you because we become aware of the demons watching you and we were wondering why. I don't mean to insult you but in the scheme of things you are a small group of seemingly ordinary people. But now that I see that you work with an Angel, I understand a little more."

"Madeline, all of us have a long way to go before we trust each other," said Sudfad.

"But as you earn our trust we will give you more information also. But not yet."

"That is understandable. But are you beginning to understand how eyes are upon you and of course they will see me with you now also."

"It is our understanding that windows in all worlds were closed," said the Sanuri. "At least temporarily."

A large group of people followed Madeline to the rear of the castle; they stopped at the tree line near the back wall. Madeline dismounted and walked directly to a large spruce tree. She started to look around the base of the tree. "I need something to stand on," she said.

"How about a boost," Edward said and lifted her into the air.

Madeline laughed, "Move about three steps to your left." She reached up and appeared to be clawing at the bark but within moments she had something that appeared to be net-like in her hand and all could see a small cloud attached to the spot that was uncovered. "That is the energy I told you about. But it isn't as strong now that the window is closed. All of you should feel it. Perhaps you can ask your Angel to turn it up so you know what to look for."

Edward set Madeline on the ground and she handed him the piece of net.

"Miranda would you join us?" asked the Sanuri as he walked closer to the tree.

"We both will," said Adam as he and Miranda appeared near the tree. "Madeline why do you look so frightened?"

"I am not used to seeing Angels. And I have done a lot of things that I am sure you aren't happy about. But can you help them so they know what to look for. This energy is so weak I don't think they can feel it."

"Madeline, you are doing well," said Miranda. "Stay on this course. Your brother realizes you are gone. He thinks you were taken by the intruders."

"Do any of them know what really happened?" Madeline asked.

"I allowed Andrac to see me so he would not kill innocent people trying to learn of the intruders. But he is not sharing that information freely."

"I suppose it is a witch hunt there now," said Madeline.

"Actually Adam and I both left Inferus with things to think about. They are planning their actions very carefully right now. Since you are starting on a good path I am going to give you a gift of sorts. All of the people here believe that you and Javier captured Harlow and gave him to Hector."

"Are you talking about that reporter in Port Friada? Why would they think that?"

"Because two people fitting your descriptions did just that," Miranda said.

"So Hector is responsible for the imposters; that swine. I should have killed him when I had the chance. But why?" Madeline paused. "Is he using us as a distraction?"

"Sudfad, having a spy among you could be an asset. Like Erebus she sees much more than the goodness in people," Miranda said. "Madeline why do you think he would use you as a distraction?"

"There could be a number of reasons. He is weakened because he is undergoing the transformation into a demon, that's one. And when he took over Juleta's enterprise he had to almost sell shares like businesses here do to get support. Juleta was hated even among the demons and only a few dark lords would back her. Dieter and Zane are the only two that I know about."

"Zane?" repeated Claudius loudly. "What do you know about him?"

"You will not like some of this," Madeline said. "There were many more similarities between Juleta and Isabella than most realized or would admit."

"Both were desperate and needy women who would do anything for recognition and acceptance. I am a spy and I will tell you that male or female, a person with those characteristics is ripe for the picking. Both of those women had many lovers, humans and demons and in my opinion they all took advantage of them. Juleta became more bitter but she never learned from her mistakes. Isabella became more needy."

"Isabella screwed demons?" Stephan asked in disbelief.

"These were some of the cards I had up my sleeve," Madeline said.

"You can tell them about Zane later but continue with your thoughts on Hector," said Miranda.

"He is more in the shadows than most dark lords I am aware of," said Madeline. "Which means it is harder to get information on him. All I know is that we were always hearing people and demons laughing at Juleta. They said she had a lot of wild ideas that she was trying to sell to others. She really wanted to become a big shot in the Insidiae and from what I heard they barely let her become a member."

"I don't know what all of her schemes were but when she started changing people's appearances, well then others were taking her seriously. One rumor I heard was that she and the dark lord Dieter, from Port Friada, were trying to create an army of sorts. But as you know the Insidiae have always been trying that."

"All I ever heard was that she had a lot of big ideas, then she was destroyed. There are rumors that she kept meticulous notes and I know for a fact that many beings are searching for them right now."

"If I had to guess; that is probably why Hector grabbed that reporter. He had a, is he still alive?"

"Yes," said the Sanuri.

"He has a reputation of finding out things that no one else can. I'll bet Hector thinks that Harlow found something. Harlow might not even realize he has it."

"If that man isn't being protected you should have him guarded. Because if Hector grabbed him and the guy got away others will find out about it and they will go after him too."

"There are still many choices for all of you to make," said Adam. "We were listening to your meetings. And while they are being conducted in an orderly and logical manner for your world. There are some things that all of you need to discuss now."

"Madeline has a great deal to prove to all of you and she trusts you less than you trust her. But while she does not have all of the information which you need, she has a great deal and she sees things differently than most of you do and that is because of her life experiences."

"Miranda and I will not tell you what to do. But it is clear to us that it could take months and even years for all of you to trust each other and honestly a lot of lives will be lost during that time. So we are suggesting that you figure something out soon."

"I just opened this window," Adam continued. "It will be interesting to see how the Abuckto and sorcerers react when they realize you can see them. You should test the energy now. Of course if you don't want them to know that you know about the windows you don't have to participate."

"Calen lift me up," said Natasha.

"You just want to be near Adam," Calen teased as he picked up his wife.

"Calen! I can't believe you said that." Natasha blushed deeply as many roared with laughter.

"Can you see anything?" Vivian asked.

"Just darkness but I can feel all this energy," Natasha said. "If you can hear me we are watching you," she yelled into the window then laughed.

"Well, that should make their day," said Edward with a grin.

As all of the members of the group examined the window, Madeline walked closer to Miranda and Adam and said, "I want to teach them how to find these. So I will take them to the spots and let them search. Will they be able to feel the energy?"

"Yes," said Adam.

"Ok, you are probably both reading my mind. I will be honest; I don't know anything about The Great Ruler and I won't pretend that I do. I do however understand that you are Angels and work for Him. And I come from a world of darkness. Why did you help me escape?"

"I think the real question is what are you going to do with this second chance?" asked Miranda.

Madeline looked around to see if anyone was listening to her. "I always know what I am doing and I pride myself on being at least one step ahead of the game. I don't know what I am doing now and that is a frightening feeling. But I will honor my word with these people. I will tell them what I know and I hope they will allow me to live here as a free person."

"All of the Elods who are at this castle feel scared and confused," said Adam. "But you have one big advantage in that you know a great deal about this world. Your people could use your help now. They fear you because you are a member of the Charto. Perhaps it is time for all of you to get to know each other. Right now they are starting to trust these people more than they do you. Isn't it time to stop the fear?"

As the people were examining the window in the tree, Sudfad walked up to Adam and Miranda. Renya and the Sanuri saw this and followed him.

"I will let you talk," Madeline said and walked towards the group who were inspecting the window in the tree.

"Before you say anything Sudfad," said Adam. "You have not done anything wrong. We did not respond because many, many things are in motion that would affect the answer we would give you. As we speak soldiers from Fort Nir and Patronus priests are embroiled in a battle with an army of Karzman's hired killers. Karzman's lieutenant sent the army to Kaffa to get people to sacrifice."

"You told us that was Karzman's plan in an effort to get the demons to restore his powers," said the Sanuri. "But his powers were restored so why the sacrifices? To show his gratitude to Samael?"

"No, to persuade the demons to heal Karzman. Cabal knows that Karzman killed his brother and the fear and hatred in him is overwhelming. Before his death, Torin had contacted Zieman, the demon King of Stordt to collaborate their efforts in destroying Karzman. While Cabal was aware of this, he had little to do with it because of his fear of his father's retribution. But after Torin's death, Cabal summoned Zieman and the two placed living curses inside of Karzman's house," Adam explained.

"Cabal is on the run now and Karzman is suffering a fate much worse than death. Samael has not yet become involved because he is under attack by the Old Ones of this world who have collaborated with powerful demons of other worlds. Zieman is powerful but he is nothing compared to Samael and Zieman knows it is just a matter of time before Samael turns his eyes upon him. Zieman is a strategist and has been aligning himself with many of the Old Ones."

"While demons do not have the same types of bonds as humans do they do have alliances. Samael is an outsider who has done nothing but attack and humiliate the demons of this world since he conquered Ahriman's domain. The Old Ones want to drive Samael from this world which would greatly benefit everyone in Nunc."

"So should we attack Karzman now when he is weakened?" asked Sudfad.

"While that would sound logical you should not," Adam continued. "The curses that were set upon Karzman are extremely powerful and contagious. Zieman wants to destroy Karzman's empire."

"Korbin, Karzman's lieutenant has been so focused on Karzman that he has not yet realized that many of the soldiers are deserting and the villagers are running for their lives."

"When the citizens of Bransong not only fought against but won the battle with Torin and his men, the news spread like a wild fire. And people who had lost all hope are now energized and they realize they have choices to make."

"Where are the villagers going?" asked Sudfad. "Because I should alert my commanders."

"Write your letters now and we will expedite their journeys," said Miranda. "I expect the people will run to the forts for protection."

"Sudfad, you will be going there soon just not as soon as we had originally planned," said Adam. "These curses will not kill Karzman because death would be a reprieve. If Samael removes the curses Karzman could come out of this more of a monster than he already is. Samael has been looking for a strong leader among his followers."

"Well that is all the more reason for me to attack him now," Sudfad said. "Or am I not understanding something here?"

"The innocents are escaping and the demons will be fighting this one out and no matter what side the demons are on they all expect you to attack Karzman while he is weakened. This is a trap for you," explained Adam. "Do not play into their hands."

"Sudfad, you will have your chance soon enough," said Miranda. "When you write to your commanders and the Patronus tell them to help the refugees but under no circumstances should they go into the lands to attack Karzman and his men. We will tell you when such attacks can take place."

"It would be wise for your soldiers to be situated around Karzman's lands and help the villagers as they cross the borders."

"What about Bransong?" asked Sudfad. "We have troops in that village. Certainly you don't want us to desert those people."

"As we speak a group of citizens from Bransong are traveling to Fort Serpha to present General Farnsworth with a decree. They are declaring their independence of Karzman's rule and are requesting to live under your rule."

"You see Sudfad as badly as you want to run in there and save everyone, choices must be made. Those people are just realizing the power they have to denounce the demons that control them," Miranda said.

The rest of the morning Madeline had the members of the group searching for windows and each time they found one they made their presence known to the Elods who were on the other end. Adam and Miranda remained with the group and destroyed each window when the exercise was over.

Vivian and Bekka had retrieved Sampson's few belongings from his campsite. As the group was walking back into the castle, Bekka said, "This stuff is filthy, we should wash it for him."

"Tell him first or he will think you are stealing it," Vivian said.

"Stealing these rags?" Bekka said with disgust.

"Those rags are all he owns," said Vivian. "Doesn't look like he profited from serving the demons."

Madeline was listening to the women talk. "You know he has been killing all the men who spy on you. I thought he was your enemy too."

"He is," Vivian said.

"He fought alongside you and now you care for him; I really don't understand," Madeline said.

"Second chance," said Raphael. "Although he is likely to cut our throats when he feels better."

"Then will you give him another chance?" asked Madeline.

"Then we will kill him," said Raul.

# Chapter XLVI
## Starting Over

The group returned to the castle in time for the midday meal. Several competitions and a horse race were scheduled to start in the early afternoon. But the leaders wanted to continue to meet with Madeline. They decided to have a short meeting with Benedict first to verify some of the information that Madeline had given them. Then Claudius wanted to discuss what they should do with her.

"I don't like not having Mathas' input into this," said Fahron.

"I feel the same but am I the only one who felt the Angels wanted us to expedite this process? My feeling is that Madeline possess knowledge that we need to learn soon," Claudius said.

"I think most of us feel the same way," said Maxwell. "But she is smart holding out until we agree to her terms. I would do the same in her shoes."

Although Joshua and Michael were wounded they both attended this meeting. "Some of us haven't been at all of the meetings," said Michael. "What exactly are her terms?"

"Not to be put into prison or executed," said Fahron. "But in addition she says the only thing she knows is how to be a spy and she has offered to work for us. She didn't ask for pay just the disguises she would need for the missions."

"Michael and Joshua, we will go over the fine details later," said Stephan. "But we learned that she and Javier did not commit some of the crimes that we originally believed and the Sanuri, Adam and Miranda have verified this. Personally, I wanted to execute her yesterday. Now I think we should hire her."

"I feel the same," said Thaos. "I worked as a sort of spy in my former profession and I for one am impressed with this woman. I would work with her. Now that doesn't mean I totally trust her. Gabriel, I am interested in hearing what you think."

"I would consider her at the same level of experience as Natasha and me. I don't think we can afford not to give her, her freedom. And I think we would be fools not to hire her."

"She knows we don't fully trust her and will be watching her. So say we hire her and she betrays us, well then we deal with it then. I also feel that Miranda and Adam rather went out of their way to tell us all to work together. That being said, which King will hire her and which team will she be attached to?"

"We all agree we don't trust her and we all agree that she has information that we need," said Sudfad. "Is there anyone in this room who disagrees with those statements?" No one spoke. "Like her or not, I believe we are all realizing we could benefit from her training and experience. If anyone does not agree with me, this is the time to speak up." No one spoke.

"This is what I am thinking," Sudfad continued. "I will hire her but she will be on loan to Lentz. I think that will be easier considering all of the emotional issues involved. Gabriel, you will be her supervisor but that responsibility will fall on Dominic when she is in Lentz. Does anyone want to discuss what I have suggested so far?"

"I think they are wise decisions," said Claudius.

"I am prepared to write up a contract spelling out our obligations to each other," Sudfad continued. "She will be granted her freedom and treated as any other team member. She will be paid and receive extra money for the clothing and other things she will need. Once again Gabriel will oversee all of that."

"Even though those windows are closed now, that doesn't mean that other people and demons will not recognize her. Which means we don't want her seen spending too much time at the castle or Gabriel's house unless it can be worked into part of her disguise. Gabriel and Raphael I will leave that to you and the team members but I agree with Claudius that we must make some decisions soon."

"Sudfad, I am in agreement with everything you said, but I think we need to be part of that discussion about her disguise," said Stephan.

"We have somethings to say," said Nikki as she, Ingr and Angelina all stood up.

"We are in trouble now," Thaos said kiddingly.

"First, we are in the exact same mindsets that all of you are," said Ingr. "But while you have been in meetings with her we have been talking with the other Elods."

"That culture is repressive of both the men and women and I think that is one reason those people fear Madeline too," said Angelina. "She is a warrior in a culture that does not allow woman warriors. I believe that tells us she is very good at what she does. And we think she should be included with the discussion of her disguise. She may have better ideas than all of you. Also, Nikki, Ingr and I will volunteer to watch her if you want."

Koby walked into the room that was shared by Sampson and Micha. Vivian and Bianca were sitting next to Micha's bed. Sampson appeared to be sleeping. "I have some things for Sampson," Koby said as he held up two pouches. "I will just put them next to his bed."

"I'm awake," Sampson said and painfully raised himself to a sitting position.

"Were you pretending to sleep so you could listen to us talk?" asked Vivian accusingly.

Sampson did not answer her but watched Koby as he walked towards him. "We found your camp and my wife Bekka tried to wash your blankets and they basically fell apart. So we got you a couple of new ones and another jacket."

"Why would you do such a thing?" asked Sampson suspiciously.

"Because they are good people," Vivian snapped. "Something you wouldn't know anything about."

"Is she always that mean to you?" Koby asked with a grin.

Sampson chuckled and said, "Yeah. Thanks, I owe you."

"You don't owe us anything," Koby said. "Bekka put your old stuff in one bag and the new in another." As he spoke, Koby opened both pouches and put them next to Sampson. "But I can't imagine you still want that old stuff."

Koby turned to walk out of the room when Sampson said, "Wait. Who are you?"

"Koby."

"He's part of our new family," Vivian said in a nicer tone of voice.

"Guess you weren't spying on our place or you would know that," Koby said sarcastically. Sampson started to laugh then grabbed himself in pain.

Raul found Madeline with Marina. They were changing the bandages on Tally and Drake.

"When you are done there we want you in the study," Raul said.

"Did you decide my fate?" Madeline asked seriously.

"Yes but you should be happy," said Raul.

"Good," Drake said and grinned. "Then she can keep being our nurse."

"Thanks to the Sanuri you are healing quickly," said Marina. "You won't need nurses soon."

"Tally, guess we are going to have to find a way to get hurt again," Drake joked.

"Will we be well enough to go to the wedding celebrations?" asked Tally.

"If you're careful," said Marina. "And I mean that."

"Well would you two ladies save us a dance?" Tally asked with a grin.

Marina and Madeline looked at each other and smiled. "We could do that," Marina said.

Raul escorted Madeline to the front of the study where Sudfad was sitting at his desk.

"Madeline, we originally wanted King Mathas to be part of this decision but today we all felt that the Angels want us to hurry this along. We have written up a contract." Sudfad handed the paper to her as he spoke.

"You will be granted your freedom from any crimes that occurred before today. But in exchange you will give us information. Then, I would like to hire you to work with Gabriel's team. He will be your supervisor but when you work in Lentz, Dominic will fill that role. You will receive a good wage in addition to expenses. Please read that then tell me what you think."

"I am pleased with this," said Madeline and picked up a pen to sign the contract. "You will not regret this."

"I believe we will all benefit from this collaboration," said Sudfad. "But because we are always being watched it may not be safe for you to remain in the castle. Gabriel will take over the next discussion."

"You probably already know that our teams travel all over," said Gabriel to Madeline as he walked to the front of the room. "So you may be working in any kingdom but most assuredly you will be in Lentz for a while. We need to develop your cover now. It would be advantageous if it was something that allowed you to mingle with the royal families. We want your ideas on this matter."

Madeline looked at Claudius and asked, "Was my identity exposed in Langer?"

"Do you mean as an Elod and a spy?" he asked.

"Yes."

"No, only the members of teams and the royal families know the truth."

"I said that I was a woman of means from Port Friada. Having wealth opened many doors for me. I told everyone that Javier was my old friend. I believe that cover is still effective. Also the members of the Charto are used to Javier and me disappearing for weeks at a time. If I suddenly appear in my old role they will not be suspicious. And if you are considering opening businesses like in the Catacombs that identity will get me in doors."

"It did get her invited to our castle many times," said Matthew.

"We will keep that identity in place then," said Gabriel. "Would it be believable that you would travel here with the ruling families?"

"No," said Stephan and grinned. "But we thought she was chasing Michael. We could say she is visiting him."

"Stephan is right, that would work. But Michael was so uncomfortable around me that you better talk to him about this," Madeline said.

"I'll get him," Simon said and walked out of the study.

"Michael was supposed to keep you distracted while we searched your place," said Thaos.

"Well he certainly isn't a very good actor," Madeline said. "And which place did you search?"

"The mansion by the ocean. Have you got more than one?" asked Thaos.

"I have three. I will show you when we get there. It allows me to have more secrecy from men who want to follow and watch me. Remember the Angels are blocking you from me. Most men follow me around like puppies."

When Michael and Simon entered the room many of the men were grinning at them. "Why do I have a feeling this isn't good?" Michael asked sarcastically.

"Madeline is on the payroll and working on our side now. We've decided to keep the same identity she used in Langer. But we need to find a believable story for her being here," explained Gabriel.

Michael laughed. "Am I the bait again?" he asked.

"It is a good story," Gabriel said. "But Madeline said you were too uncomfortable around her. You would have to act like you were at least interested in her."

"I think I can handle that now because I know her," said Michael. "What do you need me to do?"

"Starting tonight she will be your date at the celebrations," said Gabriel. "Walk around together and talk with people and dance."

"I can do that but Madeline you should know that I only recently learned to dance," Michael said and continued to grin.

"Michael isn't going to be able to dance," said Ingr. "He can make an appearance then go back to bed and Madeline can sit with us."

"That would work," Madeline said. "Is there anyone at the celebration tonight that you want me to get information from?"

"I would say just keep your eyes open," said Gabriel. "You may recognize a spy or a demon."

"And you should know that Michael has a bounty on his head by the dictator Karzman," said Raul. "So that could put you in danger."

"We captured a couple of his men who were spying on you. We tortured them. They were looking for Michael and his sisters but they didn't say they were supposed to kill them."

"I am sure that Karzman wants to kill us himself," said Michael.

"Sudfad, we will need to get Madeline some gowns and some jewels," said Gabriel.

"Whatever you need," said Sudfad.

"Madeline since the ball starts in five hours you will have to borrow somethings for tonight. I will have Hannah work on that," Gabriel said.

"That is fine."

Sudfad ordered an hour break in the meeting so Madeline could obtain some clothing for the ball. Sudfad, Claudius and Fahron wrote a very long letter to Mathas during that time. Claudius had previously sent a short note telling Mathas that Harlow was in danger, now these men explained the details of all their meetings in a letter.

Joshua and his son Thomas shared the same room. While they both were injured from the battle in Inferus, they were healing quickly because of the Sanuri. All of Joshua's family was in the room visiting them, except for Micha and Bianca. Micha's wounds were more serious and he could not yet get out of bed.

"I really don't like this idea Father," Vivian said.

"I am not suggesting we bring him home," said Joshua.

"Well in a way you are," Vivian said. "If you let Sampson come to the wedding."

"I want him close so we can watch him," Joshua continued. "I am not suggesting this because I think he has changed any."

"I agree with Father," said Thomas. "Sasha said his injuries will slow him down, even after the Sanuri healed him; which means he won't be as much of a threat. And we can take turns watching him. Otherwise he will be spying on us and who knows what."

"We can watch him too," said Paul.

"I think you have enough with watching your bird," Joshua said with a smile and nodded at the sling that Paul was wearing.

"We can do both," Adrone said.

"Alright, you can help," said Joshua. "But if you see Sampson do anything suspicious you find one of us; you don't take any action with him. Do you promise?"

Both boys nodded and smiled.

"Are you awake?" Luca asked as he and Natalie walked into the room shared by Micha and Sampson.

"Yeah," Micha said as both men were sitting up in bed.

"We brought you some pie," said Luca and handed a plate first to Micha then one to Sampson who was staring at Natalie's very pregnant stomach.

"Sampson this is my husband Luca," Natalie said. "I think you met before." Sampson looked at Luca and nodded. "Wedding ceremonies are different here. We celebrated as is the custom of our tribe months ago but day after tomorrow we will be celebrating in the manner of Luca's tribe. We will have a wedding ceremony then competitions, a feast and a dance. We came here to invite you."

"Why would you want me there?" Sampson asked with genuine confusion.

"What else are you going to do?" Luca asked with a grin. "If you rather stay in bed that is fine too."

Natalie was surprised that Sampson laughed at Luca's words. "You have a point," Sampson said. "I will come."

Natalie sat down on the edge of the bed. "Sampson, there is a lot of history between all of us. And I am not here to start a fight but I want to tell you that this is a very good place to live. We are all happy here. I don't know how many people you have met but we are all warriors and families with many children. I am asking you to respect that and not start anything at the wedding."

"I don't think I could if I wanted to," Sampson said and grinned. Then to everyone's surprise he said, "It has been a long time since I have been included with other people, I appreciate the offer."

The meeting resumed and Madeline had the floor. "The Charto has sent spies into your world for centuries. Most of the time we are sent to a kingdom then move on. But when Javier and I first went to Lentz we were fascinated with all of the things we were hearing so we decided to establish more permanent identities. That was over five years ago. We only became involved with Isabella a little over three years ago."

"Three years? Her husband didn't think you knew each other that long," said Claudius.

"Josef worked all of the time and I believe part of that was just to get away from Isabella. I am not telling you anything new when I say she had a grating personality. Isabella had a secret life that she kept from all of you. I think she started it as soon as they moved out of Mathas' castle."

"I first met her at a party. She was drinking and flirting with Mayor Deckor which I found interesting. Then Juleta walks in and looks around the room. That woman always looked angry. She saw Deckor and Isabella dancing and marched up to them. Deckor stopped dancing and walked out of the room with Juleta. Isabella looked both angry and humiliated so I walked up to her. That was our first contact. But, I can tell you more about her later."

"Javier and I had been working in Port Friada before we went to Langer. Javier spent a great deal of time in Joy City; that is an underground city similar to the Catacombs. He overheard demons and members of the Insidiae talking about Welpr, Lentz and Juleta. We became curious and started to investigate these rumors and that is what brought us to Langer. I am telling you this only so you understand that over five years ago Juleta was the talk of other cities."

"This means that she was already establishing her empire and was becoming a notorious dark lord. Only in her case she was becoming famous for what many considered her insanity. Like I already told you; most people were laughing at her and her ideas but many others thought she had such a big mouth that she would bring unwanted eyes upon them."

"The Insidiae prides itself on its secrecy. But all the members drink and do drugs which means they talk. And if you know the right places to go you can learn a lot. Many were talking about Juleta not only because of her wild ideas but like Isabella she was having sex with about anything that would breathe. Once I started watching Juleta I realized for the most part that she was attracted to men who shared certain physical characteristics. She liked men who were large, muscular with dark hair and features."

"As you know that describes Stephan and Thaos, it also describes Javier and we used that to our advantage. Javier had an affair with Juleta. It was brief because she was such a hateful person that she repulsed him and after a while scared him. He stopped seeing her when she asked him to bring her children to sacrifice to demons."

"My brother and I are criminals by your standards but no member of the Charto worships demons. Nor do we ever involve children in our work. It may be difficult for you to believe but we have standards. Juleta was furious when Javier broke it off with her and tried to curse him. He too became furious and struck her, more than once."

"Well, I am not really sure about your standards," Stephan said. "But I kind of feel sorry for your brother. He romanced two women who no one could stand to be around. He must be dedicated to his work." Many in the room chuckled at this statement.

"Many parts of our work are distasteful. But I told you we were bred to be spies. Here your children for the most part have choices for their futures. In Inferus you are bred for your purpose which is why Benedict is an Abuckto. He is nothing like the rest of those monsters. In your world he would have become a priest. But let me finish my story."

"Javier told me he slapped Juleta across the face when she started cursing him. Then she tried to claw his eyes so he slapped her again. Then he started to tear her apart with words. As he yelled he picked up one of the statues in the parlor and threw it against the wall. Juleta started screaming at him when he picked it up and tried to take it from him."

"When the statue hit the wall it started to move. That is the wall moved. There was a doorway and stairs. Juleta became frantic so Javier knew something was wrong. He ran down the stairs and found people chained to the walls around an unholy altar. Do you know what those are?"

"Yes, and we have been in that room," said the Sanuri. "I am finding this very interesting because of a vision I had. Please continue."

"Javier has an explosive temper and he went crazy when he saw what she was doing. Now you have to understand that we have as much disdain for demons as you do. And the thought of her sacrificing those people to demons well; he told me he went crazy. He picked up an axe and broke the chains of the prisoners. He told them to go to the top of the stairs and he would get them out of there."

"Then, Sanuri perhaps you can explain what he did because he said he didn't understand it. You see we know nothing of your god. He is forbidden in Inferus. Well, Javier said he walked towards Juleta and was calling her names. Then he says something such as, 'You would curse me with darkness. You are a fool. I call The Great Ruler here to cleanse this place and this witch.' Javier told me it was like he was hearing the words come from someone else's mouth."

"As soon as he yelled to The Great Ruler they heard the roar of a lion. He said it was so loud it sounded like the lion was in the room with them. Then the altar and the snakes burst into flames and Juleta started to scream. Javier had no idea of what was happening so he ran up the stairs and got the people. He had traveled to the castle in a carriage. He squeezed all of the people in the carriage and took them to their homes. That was the last he ever saw Juleta."

"Javier returned to Langer. He traveled all night and came straight to my home. He was still shaken when he told me what happened."

Everyone in the room was silent for moments then the Sanuri spoke. "When Angels come to any world they do not portray the forms they have in heaven and that is because we are not ready for such holiness."

"The most powerful warrior Angel takes on the form of a lion in these worlds. He answered Javier's call. And as to why Javier called, well, sometimes The Great Ruler uses us in most unexpected ways."

"Madeline, understand I believe everything you just told us but I also work on behalf of The Great Ruler. It is highly unusual for Him to use someone who calls to darkness. But nothing is impossible with Him. Is it possible that Javier has called to the heavens before?"

"He has never mentioned such things to me. From the looks on your faces you are surprised but not stunned by this story. You have heard such things before?"

"We have experienced such things before," said Gabriel. "And I too am wondering about Javier now. Madeline, you have said many times that you and your brother are criminals, which you may be. You have not yet showed us that side and I was thinking that was because you were negotiating your future. Up until this story I thought of Javier as a monster. But what he did took courage and mercy."

Angelina stood up. "Madeline this is somewhat changing the subject but when did this all take place?"

"Two, two and a half years ago. That must be important from the looks on your faces."

"Would you be able to tell if a child was Elod or human?" Angelina asked.

"Yes. Matthew your face…wait did Juleta have a child?" No one answered her question. "She did, I can tell from your faces. And you think it is Javier's? Does it look like him?"

Matthew was upset and looked at the Sanuri for guidance. "Tell her," the Sanuri said.

"I will," said Angelina. "It is too difficult for Matthew. She had a baby girl that has dark curly hair. She put the baby in a monastery and we found out later Juleta was trying to hide the baby from her father. The Sanuri brought the baby home."

"We have been thinking that either Hector or Zane were the father and we don't know what kind of a threat they would be to her."

"Matthew is that the child that your mother carries?" asked Madeline.

"Yes."

"I would have to get closer to the child to tell but my question to you is do you really want an answer to that question? If the child is Javier's I would doubt that he would claim her especially as much as he hated Juleta."

"Their concern is that the real father, whoever he is, will show up and try to take Sarah or hurt her," said Claudius. "Mathas and Rosa have adopted the child and love her as their own."

"If my brother is the father of that child he will not hurt her; that I can promise you. But think about what you have told me. She was a witch and dark lord and she hides her baby in a monastery. She would do that because demons and dark lords will avoid the places of your god. For all she knew Javier worshiped your god. Just because of that I would doubt if the baby is his. But I will look at her. But understand too that Juleta had many lovers."

"I don't know if that news would bring comfort to Mathas and Rosa or not," said Claudius. "But I would like the Sanuri to explain the vision he talked of."

"Each time I have been in that castle I have seen fragments of that torture room but I see it as two rooms side by side and divided by a thick wall. Once The Lion cleansed that room that Javier was in, Juleta would not be able to call demons into it. So there are two such rooms. Which makes me wonder if we need to return to that castle."

# Chapter XLVII
## The Image

The castle was filling with guests for the ball when Sudfad received a note. The Ruala families and warriors who were coming for Luca's wedding were traveling together and were being delayed by storms.

Madeline was in her chambers when she heard a knock at the door. She no longer had soldiers guarding her. She answered the door and saw Michael. He was dressed for the ball and looked sheepish. Madeline stepped to the side so he could enter her parlor.

"Michael, you are handsome as ever but you are also white as a sheet. Are you going to be able to do this?"

"I am afraid I won't be able to do more than make an appearance so I hope that will be enough for your cover. And Renya sent these."

Michael handed Madeline a large velvet covered box. "These are perfect," she said as she looked at the fine jewels. "Seriously Michael sit down while I put these on. You really don't look good."

Michael sat down in an over-stuffed chair. "Madeline, I have to tell you that I haven't done much of this spy stuff."

"Really? I would never have guessed," she said sarcastically. "Just follow my lead. And the way you are looking I think we talk to a few people, perhaps have a dance then I am putting you in bed."

"There is a little more to it," Michael said. "Gabriel talked to me and I think I need to tell you somethings so that we can..."

"Can what?" Madeline was putting on her jewels as she listen to him speak and now turned and looked at him.

"Can work around me I guess."

"Michael if you are interested in men that is fine because this is just an act."

"I don't even know what that means."

"Are you going to tell me you don't like me because this isn't a real date?"

"Will you just let me talk? For what I know of you I like you but you may not like what I have to say. And honesty the way I feel it is getting harder to talk so will you just shut up and listen to me."

Madeline heard the seriousness in Michael's voice and sat down on the arm of the chair he was sitting in. "Madeline, we may need to change your cover. First, do you know anything about me?"

"I know that you are Sudfad's son but that he didn't know about you until recently."

"My real mother was named Nadia and she and Sudfad fell in love when they were young. She sent him away when she was pregnant with me because she told him she was promised to someone else. But the truth was that the Warlord Karzman demanded she marry him or he would butcher her tribe."

"Without going into details he is a monster. He beat and raped my mother and my sisters and he beat me and kept me in a cage most of my life."

"Michael," Madeline said softly and touched his hand.

"The reason I am telling you this is most of my life I had all I could do to survive. I certainly didn't go to parties and I have never had a girlfriend. I know how to fight. I am a soldier too but I feel like a fish out of water at these celebrations. Chances are real good that I won't do something that I am supposed to."

"We can work with this. Do most of the people here know about your past?"

"Yes."

"Then they will understand if you feel a little awkward. But that isn't your main concern is it? Michael have you ever kissed a girl or held hands?"

"I don't see how if I have never had a girlfriend," he said with frustration and Madeline laughed.

"Michael, you are such a handsome man; I can only imagine that many women are attracted to you. May I ask why you haven't had a girlfriend since you came here?"

"Besides that I have been working on almost constant missions, I had things to work out. It is hard going from being treated like an animal to all of this. And I was angry at everyone for no reason."

"Michael this is all an act so you don't need to feel pressured about anything and I will take more of a lead. But we should at least hold hands and kiss once in a while."

"That is what Gabriel said which is why I am telling you this."

"I have never seen a man so nervous about kissing me before," Madeline said and smiled. "Ok, we are going to do a little training." She stood up then sat on Michael's lap. "Tell me if I hurt any of your wounds." Madeline put her arms around his neck and softly kissed his lips. After a moment she smiled. "Michael, you need to kiss me back. Just do what I do."

Michael and Madeline walked into the Great Hall which was filled with people. "We should get drinks and walk around," she said. Michael took Madeline's hand and led her to a table where a server was pouring drinks.

"It's about time you two got here," Raul said as he and Vitomas walked up to Michael and Madeline. "Is everything alright?"

Michael grinned which caught Raul's attention. "We were training," Madeline said and took a sip of her wine.

"Training for what?" asked Raul.

"To be her date," Michael said and was still grinning.

Raul roared with laughter. "I don't understand," said Vitomas.

"I'll tell you later," Raul said to his wife then he turned back to Michael. "The Rualas are going to be late because they ran into some bad storms. There's people here from the city, the college and of course the Patronus."

"Michael, you are really pale, are you sure you should be out of bed?" asked Vitomas.

"That's what I told him too," Madeline said.

"I'm feeling better," said Michael.

Madeline looked at him and laughed. "Remember if you start to pass out I can't catch you. So we are doing one walk around the room then you go back to bed."

"Yes, My Lady," Michael said teasingly and took her hand. They disappeared into the crowd.

"Would you like to dance My Lady?" asked Raul.

"Why yes My Prince," Vitomas said. As soon as they were on the dance floor she asked. "What was Michael talking about that you thought was so funny?"

"You know what his life was like. He's never had a girlfriend. And I am not sure about this but I don't think he has even kissed a girl before tonight."

"So you think they were kissing?"

"I'm not sure what they did but he doesn't look uncomfortable anymore."

Erebus walked up to the Sanuri who was watching the dancers. "I am going back to work. Do you think Sudfad will let me in his study?"

"No one else is working," the Sanuri said with a grin. "Would this have anything to do with both Gala and Hilgra being here?"

Erebus grinned. "I have never been in a situation where I am interested in two women and they are also interested in me. And to basically have us all under the same roof; well I will have to admit I feel uncomfortable."

"Perhaps you should make a decision then instead of working?"

"I am much more attracted to Gala but I feel sorry for Hilgra with all that she is going through and I don't want to add to her distress."

"Well, it certainly sounds to me like you have made your decision. I believe it is time to talk with them. It is only fair to them."

"Do you think I should talk to them together?"

"You really don't know much about relationships do you?" asked the Sanuri and chuckled.

"It's that obvious?"

"I would suggest you speak with Gala first since she is the one you have chosen. She is a very compassionate person and might give you some insight with Hilgra."

"Wish me luck," Erebus said and walked across the dance floor.

Gideon's family had been staying at the home of Archetenus and Delilah since their arrival in Salar. Archetenus and Jared had improved enough that they moved to their homes earlier that morning. Now all three families walked into the ball together. Gideon had attended every meeting that Sudfad held and continually briefed these families about the information.

"I want to meet Madeline," Ashley said as the group found a table.

"I know the girls told you that she was after me but it was her job," Gideon said as he was a little concerned about the two women meeting.

602

"I understand that," Ashley said. "But I have never met a professional spy before. Honestly, I think it is kind of exciting."

Jared laughed loudly at this comment. "Not that I really know her but I don't think she looks at it as exciting but I could be wrong."

"Order me a whiskey and I will find Michael and Madeline," Gideon said and left the table. He didn't have to walk far as the couple were talking with instructors from Cisero College.

"I am sorry to interrupt," Gideon said. "But our wives would like to meet Madeline."

"It was lovely talking with you," Madeline said to the two men from Cisero then she and Michael walked away with Gideon. "Is this a good or bad meeting with the wives?" she asked and both Gideon and Michael laughed loudly.

"I have been telling them about our meetings and they think it must be very exciting to be a spy." Now it was Madeline's turn to laugh.

When they approached the table Ashley said with obvious surprise, "We know each other. She has come into my shop many times."

"And you are the woman who has that underground system. I must say what you do for those women is impressive," Madeline said as Michael held out her chair.

"So were you in my wife's shop as a customer or spy?" asked Gideon.

"Oh, as a customer. She has the finest dress shop in Port Friada."

"I sold it and am opening another in Langer, you will have to come."

"I certainly will. I expect I will be returning there with all of you."

"We know each other too," said Delilah. "You were at one of Dieter's parties."

"I wasn't sure if I should say anything," said Madeline. "I heard you were killed during that Rogett attack and I thought it was better than living with that monster."

"I agree with you on that," Delilah said. "Ashley helped Archetenus and me to escape. We are married now."

"And you look so happy. I am glad for you," said Madeline and looked at Zoya. "You must be the seer I have heard so much about. Is it true that you invaded Inferus? You must be very powerful."

"Actually it was kind of an accident that I intruded," Zoya said modestly.

"Zoya, if you could have seen what we did," said Archetenus. "I don't think it was an accident at all. I think Miranda set it up."

"Do you really think so?" Delilah asked.

"Oh yeah," said Jared. "What Zoya did was a distraction so we could get to the Credo."

"Delilah, you look so happy now and so do my people. I have never seen them like this," Madeline said.

"And what about you Madeline?" asked Ashley. "Are you happy?"

"I am happy to be out of Inferus and I am very happy with my agreement with King Sudfad. But this is all very unsettling at the same time. I was talking with Diana and Kate while I changed their bandages and they told me about their tribe and the transitions they made moving here."

"Like the Venatores we are trained to always work alone. Although at times we may have several people in a city we basically operate alone. And I try to be at the very least one step ahead of the game. But here, I am exposed and I wasn't in control of anything for a few days. All of you are the first people in this world who know me and not a false identity and I have found that a little frightening."

"Actually it sounds like a lonely way of life to me," said Delilah.

"I don't really know if you can make that comparison if it is the only life you have ever known," said Madeline.

Anka and her brothers were immediately adopted by the children in Gabriel's home and became inseparable in the short period of time. Amy, Batina's little sisters Ana and Daisy, as well as Sasha's little sister Patris and Bianca's little sister Callie added to the mix.

All of these little girls from the Nordes Tribe were going to be in Luca's and Natalie's wedding and because of this their families were staying at Gabriel's home.

Gabriel and Hannah were sitting at a table with Benedict and Cyrene when Anka ran up to them. "Father, Mother can we stay at Tommy's house tonight? They are going to do something called camping out and they said it is a lot of fun."

Hannah laughed and explained, "We have an enormous playroom for the children. We call it camping out when we let them sleep in the playroom instead of their beds. Of course they talk and giggle all night instead of sleeping. The dogs sleep with them and we check on them all night."

"And they eat lots of treats," Gabriel added. "They are more than welcomed to stay. We will watch over them and bring them back here in the morning."

"Please can we go?" asked Anka.

Cyrene and Benedict looked at each other and smiled, "All right," Benedict said. "But you have to do whatever the parents tell you and don't go anyplace on your own."

"Oh thank you," Anka said and hugged both of her parents then ran from the table.

"Anka seems like a child again here," said Benedict. "In Inferus she had to become an adult."

Madeline and Michael spoke with Gideon and the others for almost half an hour before Michael said, "I am really sorry but I think I need to go back to bed."

"You're looking pretty white there," said Jared. "Want some help?"

"I'll take him," said Madeline. "And if he falls I will come and get one of you."

Michael took Madeline's hand as they walked out of the Great Hall. "Michael, I can feel you shaking; are you sure you can make it? Where is your room?"

"Yeah, it's close." A few minutes later they entered his chambers. They walked through the parlor and into his bedroom.

"Sit on the bed and I will help you undress," Madeline said.

"I can get it."

"And would you like to bet money on that?" she said sarcastically. "Now sit!"

Michael laughed then grabbed his side in pain. "I'll check that bandage too before I leave."

"If I didn't know better I would think it was Renya talking to me," Michael said with a grin as Madeline helped him take off his jacket and tie.

"Well, I am certainly not your mother," she said as she started to unbutton his shirt. "Michael, you are bleeding through your bandage. This might not be good." As Madeline took Michael's shirt off from him she saw how his body was covered with scars. "Oh Michael, did Karzman do that to you?"

"Yeah."

"I hope you kill him."

"Plan to."

"I am going to take your shoes off now; then I want you to stand up so I can get the trousers."

606

"The pants stay on."

"Michael, you won't be the first naked man I've ever seen and you are too weak to fight with me." As she spoke, Madeline removed his shoes. "Now stand up." She helped him off with his trousers and pulled the blankets back. "Lie down. Michael there is a lot of blood coming from that wound on your side. I am going to get Hannah. You stay right here and don't think about getting up."

"Yes Mother," he said teasingly. Madeline laughed and quickly left his chambers.

Less than ten minutes later Madeline returned with Hannah and Renya. Hannah pulled back the blankets and looked at the bandage. "Renya, I will need some hot water and towels and why don't you bring a bottle of whiskey." Before Hannah finished speaking Sudfad, Simon and Raul walked into the room.

"Do you need anything else?" asked Raul as Renya left the chambers.

"No, but one of you might want to stay here. If Michael passes out he is too big for me and Madeline to move."

"Madeline, he probably did this to get out of dancing," Simon joked.

Michael started to laugh then grabbed his side again. "Don't make me laugh!"

"He keeps telling me that I talk to him like his mother," Madeline said and smiled as she watched Hannah removing the bloody bandages.

Vitomas, Annabelle and Renya walked into the room with a bowl of hot water, towels, a bottle of whiskey and glasses.

"What were you two doing that you broke that open?" Raul asked Michael with a grin.

"Not what you are thinking," Madeline said to Raul then paused. "Michael how did you get all of these scars?"

"Karzman used to tether me to a stake and whip me."

"He's a barbarian." Madeline was standing on the opposite side of the bed as Hannah. "Have any of you ever looked at these scars?"

"Actually none of us have seen him without clothes on before," Simon said and started to walk towards Madeline. "Why?"

"Raul would you bring a candle closer?" asked Madeline. "We can't roll him on his side until Hannah is done but look at his right shoulder and it looks like it goes onto his back."

"What are you talking about?" asked Renya.

"It looks like these scars are covering a large tattoo," said Simon as he was studying Michael's shoulder.

"I don't have any tattoos," said Michael.

"You sure do," Raul said. "Why would Karzman tattoo you?"

"I think a better question is why did he try to hide it with the scars?" said Madeline. "Whips tear people's flesh but this tattoo is intact. Michael could he have been trying to cut this off you?"

"I have no idea."

"Annabelle would you give Michael some of that whiskey?" Hannah asked as she worked on his wound. "I have seen people whose flesh was ripped from their bodies by whips. And from what I can see of these scars; I would expect the same. I can't believe anything could have survived those whippings."

"Can you see what it is?" Michael asked as all of the men in the room were now examining his skin.

"I think it looks like a map," said Sudfad. "I think we need to get the Sanuri in here."

"I'll get him," said Vitomas and left the room.

"Is there any reason that Nadia might have tattooed you?" Sudfad asked Michael.

"If she did, I don't remember it and she never talked about it. Now you've got me curious. I want to see too."

"Michael don't you dare move now," scolded Hannah.

"Annabelle come over here," said Simon. "You found that plyogram under that painting. Tell us what you see."

Simon held the candle up as Annabelle examined Michael's shoulder. "Well it's not a birthmark because there are different colors, although they are really faded. It has to be a tattoo. And from what I can see it looks pretty detailed."

"Where is it?" asked Michael.

"It starts at the top of your right shoulder," explained Madeline. "And it looks like it extends down your back."

Vitomas, Erebus, Gala and the Sanuri entered the room and walked to the side of the bed opposite of where Hannah was working. "Look, see the colors," said Annabelle as she ran her fingers around the outline of the tattoo."

"I told them everything all of you said as we were coming here," said Vitomas who was trying to look at the tattoo also.

"I don't feel any energy coming from it," said Erebus.

"Do you have any idea how strange this feels?" asked Michael with a grin as he was starting to feel the effects of the whiskey.

"Ok, you can roll him over now but be very careful," said Hannah. "Raul, Simon come on this side of the bed and roll him towards you."

"This goes almost across his back," said the Sanuri. "I am going to ask for help." Everyone became quiet as they watched the Sanuri praying.

"Oh my god!" gasped Annabelle then she covered her mouth with her hands as she thought she should be quiet while the Sanuri prayed.

"What is happening?" asked Michael.

"It's like the picture is moving in front of the scars," Raul whispered.

Two minutes later the Sanuri spoke, "I prayed for help seeing the image clearly, if it was important. Michael, you have a huge and detailed map on your back but I have no idea of what it represents. There are small words in places but I don't know the language."

"Michael tomorrow when you are feeling better we will have you sit up and I will copy that map," said Annabelle. "Unless the Sanuri thinks we need to do it now."

"I believe tomorrow will be just fine. And Michael you have no memory of this?"

"No, in fact I thought Madeline was wrong when she first saw it."

"No, don't roll him back yet," Madeline said to Raul and Simon. She was scrutinizing the tattoo. "I have seen something similar to this but right now I can't remember where. But whatever this place is it is not in Opots. I think we need to bring Gideon in here."

"We'll roll him back for a minute then," said Simon.

"I'll get Gideon," Annabelle said and left the room.

"I didn't realize the party had been moved in here," Jared said jokingly as he, Zoya, Archetenus, Delilah, Ashley and Gideon walked into Michael's bedroom a few minutes later.

"Boy, for a guy who never wants to be the center of attention this must be killing you," Archetenus said to Michael and they both grinned.

"Thanks," Michael said and Raul and Simon rolled him on his side again.

"Annabelle told us everything," said Gideon as he now examined Michael's back. "This is fascinating." After a few moments Gideon said, "I am pretty sure I have seen this map before and so has Michael. It is in that scroll I brought back from the Continent of Porto."

# Chapter XLVIII
## Sampson

Simon found the scroll from Porto in the parlor of Michael's chambers. He brought it into the bedroom and handed it to Gideon. "There are several images drawn in this scroll," Gideon said as he carefully unrolled it. Vitomas and Annabelle were bringing more candles into the room to increase the light.

"Here," Gideon said after a few moments. "I think it is the same but the map in the scroll is much smaller. He walked over to Michael, who once again was rolled on his side. Gideon held the map near the tattoo and the people stared at the two images.

"It's the same damn thing," said Archetenus. "Michael have you had that your entire life?"

"Didn't know I had it at all."

"Ok, what I am getting at," Archetenus continued. "There is so much small detail in your tattoo and your back is huge. Think if you were a baby, how would anyone be able to see well enough to draw that?"

"Ruth wanted me to translate that scroll and another," said Michael. "I started them but then got busy with missions and forgot about it. The scrolls are written in Cerfic."

"Michael, I don't read that language as well as you do," said Erebus. "But since you are injured, do you mind if I start working on them tonight? And a lot of the words on this map aren't Cerfic."

"Simon that table you found the scroll on, there is a pouch on the floor next to it. Will you bring it in here? It's all scrolls I was working on."

"Michael, I didn't realize you were doing this work," said Renya. "I think we should move you to a set of chambers that has a study."

"That would be nice but the girls are next door."

"Well we can certainly move them too," Renya said. "It's not like we don't have the room."

Simon carried a huge pouch into the bedroom and next to the bed. "Sorry but you are going to have to take the scrolls out and show me," Michael said.

"Who is Ruth?" asked Madeline.

"Another Angel," said Sudfad.

"I am convinced that I have seen something similar to this map before but I don't remember where. Gideon how did you get that scroll?" Madeline asked.

"You probably know I was a pirate hunter. Short version, we were chasing down a slave ship that had left Porto and was heading for Opots. We boarded it and all of the slaves were from a small village on the northern coast of Porto. When we returned the prisoners the village held a big feast for us."

"There was a shaman who was married to a seer in the village. The seer held my hands and said I was the one so they gave me that scroll and a necklace. The seer said she had been having visions about that scroll being hidden in a cave. Some of the men found it and now I can't remember if she said she heard a voice or saw a vision that told her to hang onto the scroll until the right person came along."

"The other scroll I was supposed to study is from Ryed and both of these scrolls are so similar that it appears they were written by the same person. But they were found in different parts of the world," said Michael as he sorted through the scrolls. "Here it is."

"Sudfad, I don't want to take these out of the castle," said Erebus. "Would it be alright if I worked on them in your study?"

"Of course or we can certainly put you in a chambers. That way you could get some sleep," said Sudfad.

"You could study them in here too," said Michael. "Then I could help."

"You need to get some rest," said Hannah in a scolding manner.

"Actually I am going to give him some more healing energy," said the Sanuri.

"Erebus, I can't read that language but is there any way that I can help you?" asked Madeline. "This is intriguing."

"There are maps and pictures in both scrolls," Michael explained. "Since they are so similar, I spread them out side by side and study them together."

"Then I believe I will have to work in your study Sudfad but I may also take you up on that chambers," Erebus said.

"Simon, I would like to study the artwork and maps," said Annabelle.

"I think that is a good idea. I will be in to check on you later," Simon said to his wife then he looked at Michael. "Do you want anyone to stay with you?"

"No, besides the girls usually come in a couple of times during the night," Michael said.

"He really should have someone at least checking on him," said Hannah. "If he starts bleeding again come and get me."

"We will take turns," said Raul.

"You have families and he is pretending to be my boyfriend. I will watch him tonight. But I would like something to work on," said Madeline.

"Why don't all of you just work in my parlor? I have that big table in there to spread the scrolls out on," Michael said. "And if I have another glass of whiskey I will be asleep anyways."

Erebus, Gala, Annabelle, Madeline and the Sanuri moved to the parlor in Michael's chambers. They carefully unrolled both scrolls. Erebus was the only one of the group who could read Cerfic. The others were studying the illustrations.

After a while the Sanuri said, "Erebus is right. The scrolls themselves appear to be written in Cerfic but the words on the maps and pictures are another language and perhaps more than one language. I would like to ask Joshua and Hilgra to join us. Perhaps they can translate those words."

"I was just going to get us all coffee," said Gala. "I will bring them back."

"I am going to close Michael's bedroom door so we don't wake him," Annabelle said and quietly walked across the parlor.

"I'm not a sleep," Michael said loudly. "I want to join you."

"I don't think that is a good idea," said Annabelle as she now stood in the doorway of the bedroom.

"Gala and the Sanuri are both in there; if I start to bleed I am sure one of them can do something about it."

Annabelle looked at the Sanuri. "I'll help him out," the Sanuri said and got out of his chair. Annabelle walked into the bedroom with the Sanuri while Madeline prepared a chair for Michael.

"You are certainly stubborn," Madeline said to Michael with a smile as he entered the parlor. "Good thing you really aren't my boyfriend or we would be fighting all of the time."

"No, you mean you would just be bossing me around," Michael said and chuckled as he sat down at the table.

"Are you two starting to like each other?" Annabelle asked with a coy smile.

Michael wasn't sure why he felt relieved that Gabriel and Raphael entered the room. Neither Michael nor Madeline answered Annabelle's question as the group was explaining about the tattoo on Michael's back and the scrolls.

Over the next few hours more people gathered in Michael's room. Renya had dinner served to them in Michael's chambers. Nina walked into the room and climbed onto Michael's lap. She listened intently to what was being said. "Why are you looking at those pictures?" she asked after almost twenty minutes.

"Because I didn't know that I have a tattoo and it is the same picture," Michael said.

"Where?" asked Nina.

"On my back," Michael replied. He was not wearing a shirt. Nina got off his lap and looked at his back.

"I'll be back," she yelled and ran out of the room. No one paid attention to the little girl when she ran back into the room. She stood next to Michael's chair. "Here," Nina said loudly and handed Michael some tattered and dirty pieces of paper that looked like they had once been pages in a book.

"What is this?" asked Michael.

"Grandma Fiona had them buried and Mama told us to dig them up just before she died. Look at the pictures," Nina said and now everyone stopped talking and watched as Michael placed each fragile page on the table.

"Nina are there more of these?" Michael asked.

"I don't know but these are the ones she buried," Nina said and climbed onto her brother's lap again.

"I don't know what language these pages are written in," said Michael. "But I recognize one word. Karzman always told everyone he was from Tameric which I never saw on any maps. That word is on these pages in several places. Didn't the Angels say he was born in Marba?"

"Michael, you weren't here when the Angels told us that Karzman was born in a small village in Marba that was named Tameric. It doesn't exist anymore because Karzman, Emeric and Banaka killed everyone who lived there," explained Raphael.

"I am sorry, I think the pain medicine is effecting my head," said Michael. "I do remember Sudfad writing to me about that. But why would Fiona bury these pages? And there is a map here that looks like the one in the scroll that you say is also on my back. There has to be more to this than the murder of those villagers."

615

Shortly after sunrise the front courtyard of Sudfad's castle started to fill with hundreds of Ruala warriors. The Elods ran outside to witness the splendor of watching these ancient warriors fly.

Inferus was such a controlled society that most of the people had little knowledge of the world outside of their kingdom. And what knowledge they did have was fed to them by the people in power. The Abuckto and the sorcerers could see into the world above but the Charto, the spies, got to experience life in other kingdoms and this taste of freedom burned within them all.

The Elod children were losing their fears much more quickly than their parents and now ran to the landing Rualas. Sudfad had been sending constant messages to King Manu who was leading the Rualas so they were aware of the Elods. The Rualas were just as fascinated to meet this ancient race who lived in the bowels of the world.

"There are few things that have taken my breath away," said Madeline as she stood in the courtyard. "What an incredible sight."

"Wait until you see them up close," said Annabelle. "They are supposed to be the most beautiful people in the world."

Sampson too was in the courtyard and although he would not admit it he found the sight spectacular. He also found life at the castle confusing and intriguing. While Sampson was intelligent he had never been one to question the world or his own actions for that matter. Since he had been in the castle he saw powerful warriors both men and women from different tribes. Now for the first time he was also seeing Shettees as they landed with the Rualas and all of these people welcomed each other. To Sampson all of these people acted as if they were from the same tribe.

Per Joshua's request all of the Venatores on the teams were keeping a close eye on Sampson. Thor now walked up to him. "I had the same look on my face the first time too. I have flown with them and it is like nothing you can imagine. You should ask one of them to take you up."

"Why would they do that?" asked Sampson.

"They just do," said Thor. "But I have a question for you and I don't want you getting all pissed off."

"Everyone thinks I am going to get mad all of the time."

"Well, that may be because you always do. But just listen to me for a minute. Last night we realized that Michael has a huge map tattooed on his back..."

"Wait, how could he not know this?"

"Because it was covered with scars, now let me finish. We have found the same map in a scroll and a book but we are trying to figure out the languages they are written in. You've been in hell worlds haven't you?"

"Yeah," Sampson said suspiciously.

"You always act like everything is a challenge. Would you look at the map and the words and see if you recognize them. We think it might be a map of some kind of hell."

"Sure but I don't know languages like Joshua does."

"Even if you recognize one word that would help. It will be a while before breakfast because all of the Rualas and Shettees will be shown to their rooms first. Come on," Thor said and turned towards the front door of the castle. "Madeline come with us. Do you know where Michael is?"

"In his chambers with the scrolls," she answered.

As the three walked to Michael's chambers Thor explained to Madeline why Sampson was with them.

"You don't act afraid; you should," Sampson said in an intimidating manner. He greatly admired Madeline's looks and was consumed with lust.

"Why would I. First, I come from a hell world and second, you are just another man. But I suspect you like women to fear you, am I right?"

"She's already figured you out," Thor said to Sampson and grinned. "Sampson all the women are warriors here so don't pull that crap with them." Sampson was angry and embarrassed so he did not speak.

They found Michael, the Sanuri and Erebus still sitting around the table in Michael's parlor. "Sampson's been to hell worlds so I asked him to look at the maps," said Thor. "It's worth a shot."

"The tattoo is the biggest and easiest to read," said Madeline and walked towards Michael who was not wearing a shirt.

Sampson winced with pain as he squatted down to examine the tattoo. He stared at it intently without speaking for several minutes. "Why would you have this?" Sampson asked Michael.

"Hell if I know, that is what we are trying to figure out," Michael said. "And for all I know it just showed up last night. Do you know what it is?"

"I can't read the words but I know what that is because well; this is going to sound unbelievable to you," said Sampson.

"Hey this giant map shows up on me and it is in ancient texts too; I would believe just about anything right now," Michael said.

"You may know this but I defied my people and married a powerful demon. I was going through the rites of transformation when many of you interrupted them and Hecate pulled me out."

"You are married to Hecate?" gasped Madeline.

"Do you know her?"

"I know of her and I have seen her; we aren't exactly friends."

"I will talk to you later," Sampson said and turned back to Michael. "Understand I had lost my memories for a long time so some things are still unclear. Hecate kept me drugged because of my pain but I would still hear things. The demon Visterle stole me and the Ruala Nada and took us to Sidus. He thought Hecate would bargain for us but she never did. Visterle did not give me the drugs and I was in horrible pain."

618

"Then the demon Ael turned me into his dog and sent me to the hell worlds to find Hecate. I searched for her for what seemed like years. I stopped hearing Ael's voice in my head and went back to Ryed. Sometime later I was turned back into a man and found myself here. Then I got my memories back and you know the rest."

"And I thought my life was bad," said Michael. "So what is it?"

"That is Tameric, the hell worlds of Nunc. I can show you how they are divided among the demons but I don't want to draw on your back."

"I'll get Annabelle," said Madeline and quickly left the room.

"Annabelle is our artist," said the Sanuri. "Tell me Sampson have you seen this particular map before?"

"In my head. Ael would send me pictures of where he wanted me to go. But your map doesn't have the boundaries of the kingdoms that is why I didn't recognize it right away. But why is it on Michael's back?"

"That is a very good question. You have done well Sampson," said the Sanuri.

"I would like a copy of that map," Sampson said. "I mean to go back there and kill Ael."

"How would you get there without the help of the Angels?" asked Erebus.

"Grab a demon and make him take me back. They go back and forth all of the time," Sampson replied.

"Never thought of that," said Thor.

When Madeline and Annabelle entered the chambers many others were with them. Sampson repeated his words as Annabelle skillfully drew the map that was tattooed on Michael's back.

Sampson liked having these warriors interested in his words. It made him feel powerful again. Raphael was in the room and the two men stared at each other.

Vivian had begged Raphael to stay away from Sampson but Raphael would not agree to her requests. This was the first time that Raphael saw Sampson well enough to leave his bed.

"It is time we talked," said Raphael.

"I agree," Sampson said. "Where?"

"In the back," replied Raphael.

"You two are not going to fight!" said the Sanuri in a commanding voice and stood up. "The hatred in both of you will have to wait. Every person in this room and perhaps this castle is here for a reason right now and that takes priority!"

While both men wanted to tear each other apart they both respected the Sanuri. Everyone in the room was quiet as they could feel the tension between the men. "Raphael, you are a priest," continued the Sanuri. "You should know better than to let that darkness control you."

"And you, Sampson have committed unspeakable crimes and have gotten away with them. That will no longer be the case. For whatever reasons The Great Ruler is giving you a second chance and we are respecting that. But we know you are a rapist and murderer and that you victimize children and the weak like a Rogett. You are being treated with respect here and you will act like an honorable warrior for there will be no more chances."

Both men stared angrily at the Sanuri. "Now let's get back to work," said the Sanuri and sat down. Sampson was furious and was about to leave the room when Annabelle spoke to him.

"Sampson can you draw on this map while I make another copy?" Annabelle asked. Sampson glared at her. "Do you need different colors for the different kingdoms?"

"That would help," he snapped and grabbed the map. He walked away from the group at the table and sat at the desk in the parlor. He had his back to the others as he worked on the map.

"I'll get more colors," said Annabelle and left the room. Raphael too left the chambers.

When Annabelle walked into the hallway she turned around and motioned for Madeline to come out to her. Madeline walked up to Annabelle who pulled her farther down the hallway.

"You are probably the only one in there who doesn't know what is going on here," said Annabelle. "Besides who knows how many others, Sampson tried to rape Vivian and Diana when they were small. He was stopped both times but became obsessed with Vivian. He tried to murder his brothers so he could complete his trials to be a demon. I know he wants to talk to you but be careful. You are beautiful and I am sure he is attracted to you. You should take someone with you when you talk to him."

"Thank you, Annabelle but I assure you I can take care of myself. I have met monsters like him before. But I don't understand why you allow him to walk among you."

"The Angels gave him a chance and we didn't understand it but look; he just gave us that information about the map and maybe there will be more. Just be careful."

"You and your Angels are a very curious lot," Madeline said with a smile. "Understand I am not insulting you. I have spied on so many of you and I think living among you, well, I am still trying to figure you out."

"I will take that as a good thing," said Annabelle. "Remember be careful."

Raphael did not return to Michael's chambers that morning. Sampson was sullen and pouting but he outlined the hell domains of the Old Ones on the map and explained it to the people in Michael's parlor. Sampson also indicated which domains were being fought over.

Once again, Madeline said, "I know I have seen that somewhere but...now I remember. Andrac, the sorcerer that tried to stop the Credo from leaving has such a map. We need to speak with Benedict."

"We will discuss all of this at the morning meeting," said the Sanuri and stood up. "It should be time for breakfast now."

"Madeline, I want to speak to you," Sampson said. "Come with me."

"What I have to tell you about Hecate can be said here," said Madeline.

"It is my business."

"Sampson everyone in this room already knows the information I have for you and perhaps they can add to it."

"Alright," Sampson said angrily.

"You already know that Hecate declared war on most of the people in this castle right now," Madeline said. "She set traps for them and sent armies against them and always lost. I know this because I am a spy but Gabriel and the others can give you more details."

"Five Old Ones were vanquished by Angels in one day and rumors were spread through all the worlds that Hecate had betrayed them."

"Sampson it was the Grand Masters Emeric and Banaka who started the rumors. They did this as a distraction because they were selling this world out to demons from other worlds," said Erebus.

"After the rumors started, many demons put bounties on Hecate and sent death squads after her. Before you mentioned Nada the Ruala," said Madeline. "Well, about two years ago there were great celebrations at this castle and my brother and I were spying on them. We didn't care what they were for but just as today the castle was filled with warriors from many tribes, which we found interesting."

"Javier, that is my brother and I saw Hecate at the celebration. She made appearances for several days and she was very pregnant. We recognized her even though she wore an appearance that was similar to Vivian's. Then we recognized Visterle, the demon who stole you. He wore the disguise of a human, a nobleman. And he was watching Hecate who was watching Nada. That is how Visterle learned of Nada."

"Visterle made Nada his queen and they have twin sons. That is all I can tell you."

"I don't understand how you could recognize them," said Sampson.

"All Elods can differentiate between humans and demons by the energy around them. And the energy is different for every being, kind of like a signature. We had seen them before and recognized their signatures."

"I heard Visterle say that Nada would take care of me while Hecate was with her demon lover. Do you know who he is?"

"Sampson, truly I told you everything I know. Are you aware of how rich she is? Hecate can afford anything. She is probably paying someone well to hide her, that is if she is still alive," said Madeline.

"You said all Elods can tell the difference?" asked Sampson. And immediately Madeline regretted telling him that.

"Yes, but you have to be familiar with a signature to recognize it," said Madeline. "Sampson don't get any ideas about kidnapping any of the people here. They have never been out of Inferus before and will not recognize any signatures."

"But you have. If you help me find her I will split her riches with you."

"Sampson, I am not going with you. You should just drop it and get on with your life."

Sampson glared angrily at Madeline. Michael stood up and walked next to her. "Sampson, you are a guest in our castle and Madeline is my girl. If she sees Hecate here she will tell you but she is not traveling with you anywhere. And from now on if you want to talk to her you come to me."

"When did she become yours?" Sampson asked suspiciously.

"Last night."

Sampson stormed out of the chambers.

"Michael, your acting is improving," Madeline said and kissed him on the cheek. "We should join the others for breakfast. I'll get you a shirt."

When Michael turned around Annabelle was smiling at him and winked, "You did good," she said.

"He is going to start something, I just know it," said Gabriel.

"Then we will kill him," Thor said. "He already tried to intimidate Madeline and he couldn't. I think he likes the easy victims."

"And there are many at this castle right now," said the Sanuri.

# Chapter XLIX
## Andrac

Introductions were made during the breakfast feast. Afterwards Sudfad held a meeting in his new study, which could barely hold all of the participants. The leaders of the Rualas and Shettees were in attendance as was Benedict and Madeline.

"We have a lot to cover so I will get right to it," said Sudfad. "I have been sending King Manu and King Neputa messages about the things we have been covering in our meetings but of course there are many details to fill in. But first we need to talk about what occurred last night."

"Michael was injured in Inferus and one of his wounds broke open so Madeline put him to bed. As you know her cover story for being here is that she and Michael are seeing each other. While Hannah worked on Michael's wound, Madeline saw a tattoo under the scars that Michael has from Karzman's whippings. She got others and the Sanuri prayed for clarification and the tattoo became visible to us all. Michael, I don't want to embarrass you but will you show them the tattoo?"

Madeline helped Michael take off his shirt and he walked around the room. "As you can see that map has incredible detail. Archetenus brought up a very good point. If Michael was given that when he was a baby or young boy, how could anyone draw such detail on a small back?"

"In addition, that same map is in an ancient scroll that the Angel Ruth told Michael to translate and in pages of an old book that Michael's grandmother had hidden. I will let him tell you the details of all of that but Thor had an excellent idea. He asked Sampson if he had traveled in hell worlds. Sampson had so Thor asked him to look at the tattoo. Sampson said it is a map of the hell domains of Nunc."

"Obviously I have only given you an overview. I would like those who were working on the tattoo and scroll to come up here and fill in the details. Then Joshua, you or Thor fill everyone in on Sampson's background."

"Madeline, Annabelle told me that she considers Sampson a threat to you. I want you and Michael to tell us all about those issues."

The audience listened intently to the speakers and as soon as they were done Hugo, brother of Sorren, shot out of his seat. "There are so many disturbing things here but at the foremost for me is the threat that Sampson poses. Joshua, I know you are having him watched but now that he can get out of bed I will have our warriors watch him too. I don't mean any disrespect but most of your warriors are wounded and this castle is filled with children. If he touches one, my people will show no mercy."

"Actually I was just going to say the same thing," said Claudius. "We should alert all the adults in the castle."

"I agree," said King Manu.

Stephan stood up, "I'm not an expert on Sampson but I have seen him in action before this. Does anyone realize that Madeline has the looks of the type of woman he is attracted to, besides her value as an Elod? Madeline, I know you said you can take care of yourself but he is a huge and vicious man. We will be watching over you too."

"Maybe she should move in with Michael," Jared said with a grin then laughed when he saw the look on Michael's face.

Renya stood up. "Michael and Madeline we do not want to impose on or embarrass either of you but Jared might have a point."

"What! Mother I can't believe you are saying this!" said Raul.

Renya smiled, "Let me finish. I told Michael last night that I wanted to move him into larger chambers with a study and library. Those chambers have two, three or four bedrooms, whereas Michael currently only has one. They could each have their own room with extras for the girls when they have nightmares."

Renya now turned to Madeline, "I don't really know you but you carry yourself as a warrior and I mean no disrespect."

"I have been hearing about Sampson for years and honestly I am horrified to have him under our roof. I will not go against the Angels but I think we need to take every precaution. If he is still so focused on Hecate, he will try to steal you; there is no doubt in my mind."

"I agree with Renya and I like her idea," said Sudfad. "But Michael, you and Madeline talk it over. If you try it and then feel too uncomfortable, she can always move back to her other chambers and say you two got into a spat."

"I will move to the larger chambers and would like the extra rooms for my sisters since they still have so many nightmares but Madeline and I have to talk about the rest," Michael said.

"While I agree with what everyone is saying, none of you know of my world. The Sorcerer Andrac is considerably more of a threat to everyone than is Sampson," said Madeline. "When I realized that I had seen that same map in his possession my blood ran cold. I would like Benedict to come up here and the two of us can give you more information about Andrac."

Benedict walked to the front of the room and everyone could see how uncomfortable he was with speaking to this group of royalty. "Madeline is correct in her fears about Andrac. Since many of you are new here I feel that I need to explain a little about our culture to help you understand our concerns."

"Your world is so very different from ours. Our people originally tunneled through the world to escape the demons in your world. Our history says that when the humans first called the Old Ones into this world it was like a hell domain. Our ancestors had ancient prophesies that foretold of a promise land which is why they dug into the world. It took them generations but they came upon a world that was not unlike the world here. It is rich with plants and animals of every sort."

"Our original clan was known because of its powerful seers, who would warn our people of the dangers of the demons. I do not lie when I say I don't understand what happened because the Elods too called the demons in."

"I will be honest in that I am still learning of your world. But in Inferus the people are bred to fulfill certain roles. Our society is divided into races and subcultures all of which are bred for specific purposes and these groups all are suspicious and hateful of each other."

"The Abuckto are the ruling people, of which I was one. They are powerful seers and some can read the minds of others and this has caused great fear among my people. In our world a person, adult or child, can be arrested, imprisoned or executed for the wrong thoughts. Can you imagine the fear and paranoia that this creates?"

"My young daughter Anka is also a powerful seer and with the help of the Angel Miranda was able to connect with Tommy, son of Elan and Cassandra. It was the friendship of these children and their faith to talk to the Angels that resulted in my people being rescued."

"We; that is those of us who worship The Great Ruler are called the Credo. We too have been around since the beginning. We of course must live in great secrecy because to worship Him is punishable by death."

"Madeline and her brother Javier were bred to be Etos. People of such extraordinary beauty and sexuality that no one could resist them. They were originally bred to entertain the Abuckto and the sorcerers but it became apparent that they had great value as spies. The Charto is the name of a group that is responsible for monitoring your world. They bring the information back to the Abuckto and sorcerers. This group has become more radical over the years and has wanted to reclaim our lands in your world; although no one even knows where those lands are."

"Queen Renya referred to Madeline as a warrior and that is what all the Charto are. They are the only ones besides the sorcerers who are allowed to leave Inferus. They are both feared and admired by the people of Inferus. Madeline and I rarely spoke before we came here. I was more than surprised to recently learn that she helped my family to get away from Andrac so they could gather in the meeting place to leave. You see such things, well no one stands up to the sorcerers."

"I should also tell you that Andrac wants my nine year old daughter as his wife and this may put all of us in greater danger. Andrac is a very old sorcerer but he wears the disguise of a thirteen year old boy. He appears with white blonde hair and always wears a robe."

"The sorcerers are a subculture and are greatly feared. They hold slightly less power than the Abuckto but there have been rumors that some of the Abuckto and sorcerers are collaborating and that is why both Madeline and I are fearful now that we know that Andrac has a map of the hell worlds. Why and how he got it; I have no idea."

"In ancient times the Abuckto were our spiritual leaders now they wield only darkness. For them to collaborate with the sorcerers will bring more suffering to my people and I am sure to your world. While the Charto walk in your world, the Abuckto and sometimes the sorcerers can see into your world."

"Andrac is cunning, intelligent and feared even among the other sorcerers. Please do not underestimate him."

Most of the Elod soldiers who were in the tunnel of the catacombs when Miranda appeared were so horrified by their experience that they told everyone they met about it. Miranda only appeared as a blinding light to the soldiers but to Andrac she appeared in all of her glory.

The soldiers told of hearing Andrac's screams and his transformation into a monster. They did not help the sorcerer but fled in fear. The soldiers never realized that the cavern they had been but feet from, was filled with the members of the Credo.

Storms of such power and ferocity struck Inferus that it was days before anyone realized that over three hundred people had disappeared.

On the day that the Credo gathered in the cavern in the catacombs, Javier had been looking for the arrows left by the intruders. Word came to him of a great commotion in the city. He arrived as terrified soldiers were filling the streets. Javier ran into the catacombs and heard Andrac's screams. He pulled his sword and followed the sounds until he found the sorcerer writhing on the ground.

Javier did not recognize the being that Andrac was turning into but he did recognize his clothing since the two had met just hours before.

"Andrac is that you?"

"Help me. Help me."

"What can I do?"

"Take me home."

Javier was repulsed by the monster as he helped Andrac to his feet. "What happened to you?"

"An Angel cursed me. I will kill her!"

"An Angel are you sure?"

"I have seen her before. She fought with the people from Lentz."

Javier too had seen Miranda on the shores of the Sea of Grevdt when the demon armada attacked the Kingdom of Lentz. He was in Inferus but watched through the windows the sorcerers had created. Javier did not speak of Miranda as he took Andrac home. Javier was a strategist and was playing scenarios over in his mind as he considered what would bring an Angel into Inferus.

The storms created by Adam prevented the people from doing anything besides seeking shelter. Javier and Madeline had known about the Credo for years but never told anyone else. Now, Javier wondered if they were the reason an Angel would descend into hell.

Javier had great difficulty getting to the home he shared with Madeline because of the storms but he did not want to stay with Andrac any longer than he had to. Javier changed into dry clothes poured himself a whiskey and waited."

Sampson had not joined the others for breakfast after he stormed out of Michael's chambers. He did not believe Michael when he said that Madeline was his woman. But Sampson did not feel he was in a positon of power to challenge Michael with so many others present.

Sampson walked into the forest and screamed. He was infuriated with what Madeline told him about Hecate because he realized some of Hecate's lies. She told him she was traveling to the hell worlds trying to find ways to help him. And she never told him about her riches. Sampson grew up poor. Hecate lived in a cave; he never thought to ask her about money. Now he reflected on many things she had said to him.

Andrac had not been seen in public since the Angel Miranda held a spiritual mirror to him so his darkness would be reflected back to him instead of being directed towards others.

The storms were still raging in Inferus. Few left their areas of shelter. The Abuckto and sorcerers had heard some of the stories of the soldiers but did not believe them. No one yet realized that over three hundred people were missing. No one went to the experimental caves to discover the victims had been healed and freed and the cages contained the monsters who claimed to be healers. And no one checked on Andrac because no one cared if he died.

Only Javier realized that his sister was missing and assumed she was not alone. But why would an Angel take her? Was it to punish her? And if so why wasn't he taken also? Javier sat in his home, drinking whiskey and pondering these questions.

The leaders stayed in meetings all day, finally Renya ordered them to stop. She was hosting the pre-wedding ball for Luca and Natalie and didn't want anyone to miss it.

Renya had Michael's things moved to a large chambers on the second floor. The chambers had four bedrooms but his sisters still wanted their own chambers so Renya moved them across the hallway from him.

Michael felt too uncomfortable to talk to Madeline about sharing a living space. She sensed this and simply told him she was not planning on moving.

Gabriel's household was electrified with all of the excited energy. Lakin, Zada and their children were also staying at Gabriel's since Isla was in the wedding.

Luca and Emeral not only bought all of the children clothing for the wedding but also for the pre-wedding ball. All of the little girls were incredibly excited about their new outfits while the boys were considerably more reserved.

Amy and Margarit spent all of their time with the children from Gabriel's house and were surprised when they received outfits for the ball also.

Earlier that morning Hannah invited Logan, Marty and Cassidy to spend the day at the house. Now, an hour before the ball was to start these boys had made friends they would have their entire lives.

News traveled quickly among the teams and guests that Sampson was a rapist and victimized children. Parents made sure they knew where their children were at all times. The warriors worked out a rough schedule of who would be watching Sampson. It was Dominic's team who discovered that no one had seen him since before breakfast. This news was not received well by anyone.

Sampson had not gone far, he sat in the forest that surrounded the castle and watched the people who were playing in competitions. He did not feel a part of these people yet they were the first to include him in their lives in several years.

For all the hatred in him, Sampson missed the camaraderie of his tribe. He sat by himself and watched hundreds of warriors from different tribes competing and playing games. Then he saw a movement out of the corner of his eye.

Madeline had just walked into her chambers to prepare for the ball when there was a knock on the door.

"Michael is that you?" she asked as she walked towards it.

"It's Drake and Tally. Let us in," said Drake.

As soon as Madeline opened the door both men burst into her chambers and started to search it. "Sorry about this," said Drake. "Thaos sent us. No one knows where Sampson is."

"I just got here. I haven't searched anything," she said.

After the men searched the three rooms and the balcony they returned to Madeline who was standing in the parlor. "We're supposed to stay with you and escort you to the ball," said Tally. "So, well I guess you can do whatever you need to do and we will watch the doors."

Madeline looked at both men and laughed. "Can I trust the two of you?"

"You're one of our favorite nurses," Drake said. "We wouldn't do anything bad."

"Alright," she said. "There is whiskey and wine on that table. I am going to take a bath."

"Madeline," Tally said. "We've never met women warriors until we come here and Lentz. We are still getting used to it and we have found out that all of you seem insulted if we try to protect you. But we've found out a lot more about Sampson."

"Well, I guess I am just saying that you can get mad at us if you want but there are a lot more than me and Drake watching out for you."

"Actually I think it's very nice of you," she said and walked into the bathing room.

Sampson sat motionless and listened. He had seen a movement but he did not know what caused it. He was wondering if more of Karzman's men were in the area. He pulled one of his knives from its sheath and slowly moved his position. He saw movement again about two hundred feet to his right. Sampson crept through the forest. After a few moments he heard muffled voices.

The competitions and games were ending as people left the field to prepare for the ball. A war cry came from the forest and every man and women on the field stood still.

"Where did that come from?" yelled Stephan.

Ruala warriors took to the skies then another war cry was heard and warriors ran from the field towards the forest.

Sampson had smelled whiskey before he saw the five men watching the competitions. They stayed together as a group and were passing around a bottle of whiskey.

"There's too damn many of them. We can't go down there," said one of the men. "What the hell was Cass thinking?"

"How could he have known there was a damn celebration going on," said another man then took a gulp from the bottle.

"Well, what do you want to do? Wait until they are all asleep?"

Sampson threw his first knife and grabbed a second before the men realized someone was behind them. His first knife struck a man in the back, killing him. The second knife that Sampson threw hit a man in the chest as he turned towards his attacker.

Sampson pulled a third knife from a sheath and yelled the war cry of the Venatores as he ran towards the three remaining men.

Sampson was a savage fighter but the wounds he had received in Inferus had not healed. He was not wearing a shirt just a leather vest that exposed his bandages.

Sampson kicked the man to his left in the stomach, then grabbed the man directly in front of him and used him as a shield. Sampson kept moving as the man who was originally on his right repeatedly tried to stab him. Sampson yelled a second war cry just as the man who he had previously kicked in the stomach stood up and grabbed a tree branch. That man deliberately hit Sampson on the side where he was bandaged. Sampson let go of the man he had been using as a shield. This man turned around and punched Sampson.

The men running towards the forest saw four Ruala warriors dive towards the ground. "This way," yelled one of the men who was running. The first Rualas to find the intruders did not know Sampson but they did recognize him as a Venator. Sampson had fallen to the ground after he was punched. The man who punched him kicked Sampson in the side twice and was pulling his leg back to kick Sampson in the head when he was jumped by a Ruala warrior.

Several more Ruala warriors joined the fight before the warriors on foot reached the area. Sampson was lying on the ground, all of his bandages were covered with blood as were his mouth and nose. He was conscious and angry. Sampson was not used to losing fights.

"What happened here?" yelled Matthew as he ran up to the Rualas who were tying up the three men.

"They were beating this guy up," replied one of the Ruala warriors.

"Sampson what happened?" asked Calen as he ran forward and helped Matthew pick Sampson up.

"I was pissed so I was in the forest thinking," Sampson stopped talking and spit a mouthful of blood on the ground.

"Then I see these guys. They said someone named Cass sent them. They didn't expect all of you to be here and wondered if they should wait until after dark to do something. That's when I attacked them."

"I'm taking him in to Hannah," Calen said and ascended into the sky with Sampson.

"Someone grab my knives," Sampson yelled.

A large group was forming around the intruders. Ratri retrieved Sampson's knives while others searched the men. Raul and Simon were in the castle when they heard of a problem. As they were running to the forest they saw Calen flying towards them with Sampson. "Intruders, Hector's men," Calen yelled as he passed the Princes.

Simon and Raul were almost to the site when the group was returning to the castle. "Where do you want these guys?" asked Matthew.

"Would one of you gentlemen be kind enough to button the back of my dress?" Madeline asked and walked up to Drake and Tally.

"As soon as I can breathe again," Drake said. "Damn if you aren't the prettiest woman I have ever seen."

Madeline laughed. There was a knock at the door. "It's Michael."

Tally opened the door as Drake was still buttoning the dress. Michael walked in and shut the door behind him. "Calen just brought Sampson in. He's all beat up. Said he was in the woods trying to cool off when he found five men spying on us. He attacked them all and lost but killed two. The others are bringing those guys in and they think they are Hector's men."

"Why would they think that?" asked Madeline.

"Because Sampson heard them say Cass sent them. There have been multiple attacks against all of us and Cass was behind them. Actually there might even be two men using the name of Cass."

"They tried to make some of the attacks look like Karzman's men did them."

"What are you doing with those men?" Madeline asked.

"Raul is taking them to the dungeons to be interrogated and Simon is leading troops in searching the grounds."

"I would very much like to see those interrogations," said Madeline.

"If you walk into the dungeons looking like that all those damn men will go wild," said Drake seriously.

"Michael would Vitomas or Annabelle have a cape I could borrow?" Madeline asked.

"I would think so, come on."

"We'll come too," said Tally.

# Chapter L
## The Ball

No one told Luca and Natalie about the intruders because no one wanted to spoil their night. Emeral and Maxwell made sure that Luca, Natalie and their children were the last to enter the Great Hall. Luca carried Hunter, Natalie carried Emma and Christopher walked between them holding their hands.

The doors to the Great Hall were closed so that Luca and Natalie would be surprised when they entered. Maxwell and Emeral walked behind them and they all walked on a long red carpet that covered the area from the door to the head tables. The room was extravagantly decorated and all the guests clapped as Luca and his family entered.

All of the Elod families were in attendance and were very excited about the celebration although most of them hadn't met Luca or Natalie yet.

"Sampson what were you thinking attacking five men, especially in your shape?" scolded Hannah as she and Gala were trying to stop the bleeding in his wounds.

"Guess I wasn't," he tried to joke. But he could see how much blood he was losing.

"The only reason you could even get out of bed is because the Sanuri was healing you. I told you to take it easy," Hannah continued. She paused. "Gala, please get the Sanuri."

Michael told Madeline about the truth potion that was used for interrogations. He explained the procedures and the effects. "In Langer they used it on two of your men and they got really sick and died," Michael said. "Nana was trying to save them and one of the guys said the potion was hitting them like that because they weren't human."

"I didn't know about that. Do you remember their names?" she asked.

"You'll have to ask Dominic and Edward about that," Michael said as they entered the dungeons. A soldier escorted them to the area where the interrogations were being conducted.

Michael, Tally, Madeline and Drake entered the room and stood against the wall. Raul was asking the questions and Thor was writing down the answers. Raul looked at Madeline and said, "The potion forces them to tell the truth but you have to know the questions to ask."

Raul asked questions for another ten minutes then walked up to Michael and the others and said in a low voice. "It's the same story; some guy walks into a tavern, says his name is Cass and asks drunk men if they want to make some money. Then he has them attack us. These guys don't know anything about him and we have gotten different descriptions of him."

"It would seem that Cass wants these men to be discovered," said Madeline. "But why?"

"Cass sent these guys here to find out who was at the castle," said Raul.

"Ask him what Cass smelled like," Madeline said.

Raul grinned and said, "Ok." And turned back to the prisoner who was tied to a chair and acting drunk.

"Do you remember what Cass smelled like?"

"What?"

"What he smelled like. Try and think about it."

The prisoner was quiet for a few moments, "Hell, now that you mention that; he did have a peculiar smell. Hank mentioned it too. I am trying to think what it was like."

"Was it like a forest when it rains?" Madeline asked.

The prisoner didn't seem to notice that he was hearing another voice now. "No, it was real bitter and strange. Almost made your eyes water."

"Did you touch him at all; to shake hands or anything?" asked Madeline.

"Well we kinda touched when he handed me a pouch of coin."

"How did your skin feel afterwards? Did his smell come off on you?"

"Now that you mention it my hand was sticky and it did stink. Why was that?"

"Because he was a demon," Madeline said.

"A demon! He didn't stink like no demon."

"There are different kinds," Madeline said.

Raul walked up to Madeline and asked in a low voice, "Do you know who it is?"

"I know what it is. It is a Rappal demon. They have very slimy skin and difficulty keeping it from seeping through their disguises. Less powerful demons usually can't disguise their forms but Rappal demons can. They are a lower level demon which means they are cheaper to hire. But they can't totally mask their smell and they can't hold a disguise for long periods of time; which may be a reason he spends so little time with these men."

"Although they are disgusting, Rappal demons are smart. He is very deliberate in what he is doing." Madeline was thoughtful for a moment. "You know these attacks are basically distractions but for what? Michael just told us that Hector thinks some of you may have something he is searching for. Have you considered that he may have spies inside and that is why the distractions are out here?"

"We already thought about that," Raul said. "But the homes of Gabriel, Jared, Erebus and Archetenus were attacked too."

"So that attack we saw on the carpenters at Erebus' home was orchestrated by this Cass?" Madeline asked. "I would like to return to the castle and observe the people in the ballroom."

"Michael do you feel up to that or perhaps Drake or Tally could escort me."

"You look awful pale boss," Drake joked and winked.

Michael laughed. "I'll go back with you now and if I need to go to bed these two can fight over you."

There were two huge tables at the front of the room for the royal and ruling families and the adults in the wedding party. These two tables were set at angles with a third table between them for all of the children in the wedding. Because Luca and Natalie wanted their children to be part of the wedding celebrations, everyone had their children at the ball which added another level of noise and excitement.

"Gala, go to the ball," Hannah said. "Enjoy yourself. Besides, I shouldn't say anything but Erebus has a little surprise for you."

"Are you sure?" Gala asked. The two women were in Sampson's room while the Sanuri was healing him. Hannah was cleaning up the bloody linens.

"Yes, now go."

"I have to go home and get my dress."

"I think you might want to find Erebus first," Hannah said and smiled.

"He didn't buy me another dress did he? I keep telling him not to spend money!" Gala turned and left the room.

Hannah heard familiar voices in the hallway before Calen and Natasha appeared in the doorway. They both stopped talking when they saw that the Sanuri was praying. Hannah walked out into the hallway to meet with them.

"I brought your dress and things," Natasha said. "I had to guess at your jewelry. The kids are dressed and with the family. And Gabriel just got called to another meeting but he said it wouldn't take long."

Calen was watching the Sanuri while the women were talking. "It's kind of ironic," he said. "We keep saving Sampson's life but one of us will probably end up killing him anyways."

"He is in bad shape," said Hannah. "Even with the Sanuri's healing he won't be getting out of bed for a while."

"That is just as well, everyone is afraid to have him around their children," said Natasha.

"I can't stand the guy but I have to give him credit for going after five guys," Calen said.

"He's a fool," said Hannah. "I told him to be very careful or this would happen. Those men not only opened all of his knife wounds but made them worse. Do you think he was trying to get himself killed?"

Jugglers and acrobats were preforming in the Great Hall when Michael, Madeline, Tally and Drake arrived. "I need to walk around this room and look at the people," Madeline said to the men. "If there isn't a demon in here I will buy you all a drink."

"I just keep liking you more and more," Drake said.

"Do you always have so many children at a ball?" asked Madeline.

"No, it's what Luca and Natalie wanted," Michael said.

"If I see a demon or dark lord I will find a way to get them out of the ball then you can grab them. It is too dangerous to do it in here," she said. "So just play along."

"Sounds like a plan to me," said Tally.

"I'll start introducing Madeline to people," Michael said. "You two keep an eye on us."

Raul finished the interrogations and had the prisoners locked in separate cells. He returned to the castle and held a short meeting in Sudfad's office.

Raul told the leaders about the interrogations and the information that Madeline told him. He also said that Madeline suspected there was a demon in the castle and she was on the hunt.

"I will say she has turned into a pleasant surprise," said Fahron.

"I agree," said Claudius. "I now understand why Miranda helped her escape. But I am still questioning Sampson."

Bethany the Ruala healer volunteered to watch Sampson so Hannah could go to the ball. Hannah and the Sanuri were leaving Sampson's room when Gabriel walked in and told them about Raul's meeting.

"This just gets more disturbing," said Hannah.

"Honey it will be alright," Gabriel and kissed her on the forehead. "Do you need me to go home and get your things?" Gabriel could see that Hannah's nice dress was covered with Sampson's blood.

"Natasha brought them. But I will need help with the back of the dress."

Bethany was one of the instructors for the medical classes at the Learning Center. She had brought a large stack of work with her and now sat at the small table in Sampson's room and started to read. She had her back to the window.

Gideon rejoined Ashley and the boys in the Great Hall. He told Ashley about Raul's meeting. "And I thought Port Friada was bad," she said in a low and angry voice. "This is making me mad. It's just constant threats."

"I am sorry I brought you into all of this," said Gideon. "Perhaps I should have told you more about my job before I asked you to marry me."

"No, there were plenty of monsters in Port Friada too. I think it is different when you have children to protect."

"And all of these families here, well everyone seems so nice. I like these people. It is too bad they are stalked by darkness because they are good people."

Sampson started to moan and move around. Bethany watched him. Then his moaning became louder and his movements more pronounced. She went to the side of his bed and checked him for a fever.

"Sampson are you having a nightmare?" she asked and checked his bandages. "Sampson, it's Bethany and I am taking care of you. You are safe. Can you talk to me?"

Bethany knew Sampson's history and what a dark soul he had. This did not scare her but made her consider that more might be going on with him then his physical wounds. She took a blessed crystal from her medical bag, said a prayer and put the crystal into the palm of his left hand. "Sampson hang on to this it will protect you," Bethany said and the shadow moved away from the window.

While everyone appeared to be enjoying the entertainment, many eyes were on Madeline as she and Michael walked through the crowd.

"You tell me if you need to sit down," Madeline said as she surveyed the room with her eyes.

"Don't worry about me," Michael said and chuckled.

"Michael do you know those men standing near the fifth set of patio doors. They are looking over here so don't let them know we are talking about them."

Michael took her hand and they walked up to Misha and Diana who were talking with a group of Ruala warriors. Michael positioned himself so he could look at the men by the door.

"I don't know them. Is one of them a demon?"

"No, but they don't look like they are comfortable in their clothing and they aren't socializing with anyone else. They don't fit in with the rest of your guests."

Diana had her back to the men. "How many are there?" she asked.

"Six, and they don't have escorts," said Madeline.

"I want to play too," said Diana. "Emeral and Maxwell have the boys."

"You aren't going to be able to kick in that dress, it's too tight," Misha said with a grin as he glanced at the men near the door.

"Oh Honey, I will think of something," Diana said with a sly smile.

"I think I will take a walk outside," Misha said and the four Ruala warriors went with him.

"Michael, let Diana and me talk to them first then you come up with some drinks," said Madeline. "I would like to get them outside."

Michael walked away from the women and nodded to Raul and Simon as he walked past them. Diana and Madeline talked and laughed for a few moments then they walked up to a table of Ruala warriors and Diana introduced Madeline to the group. Thor saw his sister with Madeline and became suspicious. He and Tanya walked up to the table also.

The group chatted for a few moments then Thor asked. "Where are you heading?"

"The six men by the fifth door," Diana said. "Tanya do you want to join us?"

"Sure," she said with a smile.

"I am making introductions," said Diana. "Just follow our lead."

The three women walked towards the men but they stopped and spoke with several people on the way.

"Hello, I am Diana, Misha's wife and this is Madeline and Tanya. I am sorry I don't know your names?"

"I am Elliot," said one of the men and took Diana's hand and kissed it. He did the same with Madeline and Tanya. "You are the most beautiful ladies in the room."

"Aren't you sweet," Madeline said flirtatiously. "I am from Langer and don't really know anyone here. Tell me Elliot what do you do?"

"I'm afraid I can't tell you pretty lady," Elliot said with a smile. "We are here on business; I can say nothing more."

"Well that sounds suspicious," said Raul as he and Michael turned around and faced the men. They had been standing close to the women. "You carry yourselves like hired fighters."

"Well we should because we are, but we are no threat to you. We work for King Friada. I have paperwork in my right jacket pocket."

"I'll get it," said Madeline and took a sealed envelope from the inside pocket of Elliot's jacket. She handed it to Raul."

"This is addressed to the Sanuri," Raul said. "Elliot, so why didn't you just deliver this?"

"Perhaps we should meet with the Sanuri and discuss that matter. But first, why did you pick us out from the crowd?"

"You look uncomfortable in your clothing and your setting," said Madeline. "You don't have escorts and you aren't socializing."

"We will do better next time," Elliot said with a grin.

Misha and the other Rualas were able to hear the conversation and now entered the ballroom through the patio doors. Raul, Michael, the six men, the five Rualas, Madeline, Diana and Tanya now walked up to the Sanuri who was talking with Claudius and Bella. Thor joined the group.

"Gideon, I know that man with Raul; he works for King Friada," Ashley said and nodded to the group that was approaching the Sanuri.

Gideon and Ashley were sitting with Archetenus, Delilah, Jared and Zoya. "Excuse me," Gideon said. "But I think I will find out what is going on." He left the table and walked up to the group who was now leaving the Great Hall.

Simon, Matthew, Gabriel, Claudius and Raphael joined the group, Michael left to find Sudfad. The men entered the King's study and Simon poured glasses of whiskey and wine for everyone. "We should wait for Father to get here before we begin."

By the time the last person had received a drink, Sudfad and Michael entered the room.

"Michael why don't you start," said the Sanuri.

"I don't know if Raul has told you yet about the interrogations tonight but Madeline suspected we might have a demon or dark lord here. She wanted to walk through the crowd and she saw this group of men who looked suspicious. I will let her tell the rest but she has a very good eye for such things."

"They looked uncomfortable in their clothing and surroundings," said Madeline. "They did not have escorts and they didn't socialize; they watched the crowd. Diana and Tanya came with me. We approached the men, while Misha and others waited outside. If we believed the men to be a danger we were going to find a way to get them out of the Great Hall since there are so many children in there."

"This man said his name is Elliot. Elliot this is King Sudfad. I believe it is your turn to explain yourself."

"My men and I were hired by King Friada to deliver a letter to the Sanuri which he now has in his possession. Prince Raul said we look like hired fighters and we are. We work for the King but we are not in his military which affords us more latitude especially when we are crossing borders. Also our actions do not come back to haunt the King."

"I would request that the Sanuri read the letter now and I will answer any questions after that," Elliot said.

"Do you know what the letter says?" asked Sudfad.

"Yes."

"King Friada and I are close friends," said the Sanuri as he opened the letter. As soon as he finished reading it the Sanuri looked at Elliot and asked, "Have you seen these creatures?"

"Yes but we know little of them except that they exist."

"King Friada is well aware of our concerns and dealings with Hector. He has General Amundson and Admiral Wainburst ever vigilant," explained the Sanuri. "As you know there was a war in Port Friada between different sects of the Insidiae when we left that last mission. The fighting went on for days. Hector's compound was destroyed but there has been no sign of Hector or his lieutenant Clev since."

"Shortly after that battle, strange ships were found in the docks of the city. They contained no markings or flags and appeared deserted. The people of Port Friada are all on alert because of all their dealings with dark lords. In particular are the men who work on the docks and ships as their ranks were often kidnapped."

"People were suspicious of the first ship they found but night after night more unmarked ships pulled into the docks. Members of the navy as well as citizens who worked near the docks started to spy on these ships. Friada believes his city has been invaded by creatures that are described as shadows. These figures can be seen if they are in the light but they disappear in the darkness."

"He says they walk on two legs like a man but seem to be outlines of a person. They wear what could be war paint on their bodies which is usually white and can be seen very well if they are directly near a light. For lack of anything better Friada says his men call them the Shadow Men."

"I thought you would believe me to be a liar if I told you that story," said Elliot. "My men and I believe these creatures have invaded more than Port Friada."

"As you know it is a long journey and we have gotten glimpses of these creatures as we traveled here. One was near one of our campfires and the rest were in cities where we took lodging."

"Do you think they followed you here?" asked Sudfad.

"Perhaps the one near our campfire but the others appeared to be watching other people. So far we know of no attacks and we certainly don't know how to kill them," said Elliot. "King Friada fears that all of you might be the targets of who knows what with these creatures. That is why we joined your celebration. We walked around the outside of your castle twice before these lovely ladies spotted us."

"Is there any other way to recognize them?" asked Gideon. "A smell or footprints?"

"Not that I am aware of but we left Port Friada several weeks ago. We have sent messages to King Friada about our sightings. These creatures move so quickly that people have thought their eyes were playing tricks on them at first."

"Can they be seen during the daylight?" asked Claudius.

"We have not heard of any sightings."

"I don't want to spoil the night for Luca and Natalie," said Sudfad. "Raul, Matthew and Simon why don't you circulate through the crowd and send more of our people in here. Elliot, I would like you and your men to stay here at the castle. Would you brief some more of our people tonight then again in the morning at my daily meeting?"

"Of course," said Elliot. "I should tell you that King Friada is very paranoid about spies, which is why he sent us. In our normal clothing we don't look like we are messengers for a king."

"Sudfad, we will help bring people in here too," said Misha. "The wedding is in the morning. I don't think we should tell Luca and Natalie until afterwards. Let them enjoy their day."

"I think we all agree with you," said Sudfad. "Michael, you aren't looking well. Perhaps you should go to your chambers. But I would like Madeline to continue to work the room."

"Work the room?" repeated Elliot. "Were you looking for spies?"

Madeline did not answer but smiled and turned to Michael. "Your father is right you are really white. I will walk you to your chambers."

"Actually this is just getting interesting," Michael said with a grin. "I think I am going to try sitting down for a little while but I don't want you alone. I'll get Drake and Tally."

"I haven't had any fun in a while," said Diana.

"What!" said Misha and laughed.

"You know what I mean," Diana said and laughed too. "I will stay with Madeline until Emeral and Maxwell get sick of the babies."

"Mind if Tanya and I tag along too?" asked Thor.

"Thor if I need to, can I ask you to be my dance partner?" Madeline asked.

"I'm not the best dancer," Thor said then looked at Tanya. "Do you mind?"

"No and he is a good dancer. Actually this is fun," Tanya said.

"I don't think you girls get out enough," Misha joked. "I think we will all be keeping an eye on you too."

"Sanuri, King Friada said you would want to look into my mind to see if I was telling the truth," said Elliot. "Do you want to do that now?"

"Actually I could already tell that you are speaking the truth," the Sanuri said and smiled. "Perhaps I will take you up on that offer later. Right now I think we need to get this information to the others."

# Chapter LI
## Destinies

"I don't think I have ever been happier," Luca said as he and Natalie danced close.

"If I get any bigger we won't be able to dance like this anymore," she said and smiled. "I too am very happy."

"Well, then my dear. Maybe we should dance the night away."

Small groups of people rotated in and out of Sudfad's study to be briefed about King Friada's letter. Tally and Drake joined Madeline until the meal was served then she and Michael sat at one of the head tables together.

"Are you feeling better?" Madeline asked.

"Yes and I want to apologize. I haven't been much help with all of this."

"Michael, Hannah didn't want you out of bed. Your wounds are serious, you shouldn't even be doing this."

"It's hard to pretend we are a couple if we don't spend time together."

"Well don't worry, I will be out of your hair soon; then you can get some rest."

"Do you mean Langer?"

"Yes. Claudius said I will be returning with them and we will leave in a week. I didn't know this but Dominic and his men are training to become Patronus priests. High Priest Othnial volunteered to go to Langer with them and conduct their studies. I will be working with that team."

"Actually I kinda like having you in my hair," Michael said and smiled. "Why do you look so surprised?"

"Because half of the time I don't think you even like me."

"I am sorry. I guess I really am not good at these sort of things."

"What sort of things," Madeline asked with a coy smile.

"I told you I've never had a girlfriend; well I've never been on a date before either."

"Michael are you even aware of all the women who have been watching you tonight? I'll bet every single woman and half of the married ones in this room would like to be your date."

Michael blushed. "Guess I was too busy looking at all of the men who were watching you."

Toast after toast was given then an extraordinary feast was served. After the meal when Luca and Natalie danced the first dance, Christopher and Amy went on the floor with them and danced which brought smiles to everyone's faces.

"They have been practicing for the last two days," Emeral was heard proudly saying.

Nikki laughed loudly and said, "Thaos, they are just dancing!" Michael and Madeline looked down the table at Thaos and they too laughed.

"I think he is a protective father," Madeline said.

"He and Nikki adopted her, I think two years ago. He and Stephan were working on a mission and got information about someone selling little girls. When they tracked the guy down he had killed one girl and had three others. Amy was one of them. Fahron's two daughters are the other two. The girls were starved and covered in bruises. Thaos and Stephan killed the guy on the spot and brought all of the girls home."

"Good for them," said Madeline seriously. "Actually Isabella told me they adopted Amy but I didn't know the whole story."

"So what is your story Madeline? Angelina said you were a warrior in a kingdom that didn't allow women warriors."

"Perhaps life in Inferus is more like the life you led then it is like life here. Etos were bred to be the sex toys of the Abuckto and sorcerers. I have just the one brother and our parents of course were Etos too but they..."

"They what?" asked Michael.

"Our father was murdered at an early age and Mother was the very definition of an Eto. She was a slave to the powers who owned her. She never considered rebelling; in fact, she didn't believe she was complete unless she was the property of someone. After a while it was like she was so lost and broken that she didn't know herself anymore and committed suicide."

"Javier and I are quite the opposites of our parents and we have done everything we could to change our destinies. We joined the Charto right after Mother died. We were ten. We have earned the respect of the monsters who would try to own us."

Madeline paused for a moment. "Javier and I both threw ourselves into our work. But he worries me. He has become so bitter. I think he tries to escape from life in his addictions. I guess I escape in my work. Did I tell you that the Angel Adam told me that my people, the ones who are here in your home, need me right now? He said they are terrified and I have the advantage that I know this world."

"Makes a lot of sense to me," Michael said. "You know sometimes when you talk you sound bitter too."

"Imagine that," she said sarcastically. "And this from the man who only survived by his anger."

"It's the truth and I'll admit it is difficult to change. People tell you to stop being angry like it is as simple as drinking a cup of coffee," he paused. "Did any of the family tell you about when I first came here?"

"No."

"My mother tells me who my real father is moments before she died. I loved my mother dearly and I went crazy when I couldn't stop Karzman from hurting her and the girls."

"When she told me that King Sudfad was my father I went exploded. All I could think of was that he was powerful enough to save us and he never did."

"I rode straight here and stormed into the castle. I planned to kill him and believed I would die in the process and I was alright with that. Of course the soldiers grabbed me but I had already made it into the dining room and they were all eating breakfast. When I saw him I couldn't even talk. It was like looking in a mirror. Then I looked around the table and saw Raul. His baby daughter called me papa and that's when I saw all of the babies."

"Of course they were all shocked. Sudfad claimed me on the spot. I never expected that. Then Renya told me I was home. I started to cry and right then all of the anger left me. The anger was all I ever had that was my own. I understood what you said when your mother was so lost she didn't recognize herself anymore. That is how I was for a long time."

Madeline squeezed Michael's hand. "In a small way we are alike. We are both strangers in this land and sometimes we are strangers to ourselves."

The dance floor soon filled with guests. Michael and Madeline danced around the outside of the floor so she could look at the people who were not dancing. "I may owe the three of you drinks tonight," she said.

"Don't sound disappointed. It's a good thing. Luca and Natalie have had hard lives. Everyone is happy they are getting married and wants the best for them. They don't need this shit," Michael said then grinned. "I suppose that if we are pretending to be seeing each other I should come and visit you in Langer."

"Michael, you are full of surprises tonight. I would like that."

"Good."

Gabriel and Hannah returned to the head table after several dances. As soon as they sat down Chaez and Lana walked up to them. "Do you have a moment to talk business?" Chaez asked. "I am sorry to interrupt you."

"That is fine," said Gabriel. "And I have a feeling I know what you are going to ask."

"I just heard that High Priest Othnial is going to Langer to preside over the training of Dominic's team. I too am on that team and wondered if I could return to Lentz. You know I will keep up on my studies."

"Chaez, Othnial made the offer just a few hours ago and yes, you are part of that team so that does include you. So the real question here is does Lana want to go home with all of you? She is also a member of that team besides your relationship."

"Gabriel, I would like to but I don't want to leave you short-handed, especially with all of the threats," Lana said. "But you should know that Tanya wants to stay here. And I hope you don't get the wrong idea because I adore the children. But as soon as Chaez told me this I spoke with Melinda. I don't know if any of you realize how much she misses the children. She loves Jason but she would come back as a nurse in a heartbeat. She is just afraid all of you don't want her back because of how she acted when Thor and Tanya first got together."

"That is very good to know," said Hannah. "She is part of our family and the children love her."

"I don't know if you have talked to Marina and Bethany about what they want to do after the classes finish, but they really like it here" Lana continued. "I didn't ask them but I will bet you anything they would stay on as nurses."

"Lana, you have saved us a great deal of work," Gabriel said. "We will miss you but go home and have a happy life."

"Thank you, we really appreciate this," said Chaez and shook hands with Gabriel.

Hannah and Gabriel watched as Chaez and Lana walked up to Fahron and Isadore and told them the news.

"They are all so happy," Hannah said warmly. "Do you think we should talk to the other girls now?"

Gabriel and Hannah held hands as they walked through the crowded room. They found Melinda and Jason sitting with the rest of Edward's team. "Melinda could we speak with you privately?" Gabriel asked.

"If you want to know if she will return as a nurse, the answer is yes," Jason said with a grin. "We were all just talking about that."

"Good," said Gabriel. "I guess the next question is do you and Melinda want a chambers in our house or do you want to live at Edward's house? It really doesn't matter where you live and both houses are fairly close."

"Gabriel that is so generous," said Melinda then she turned to Jason. "The chambers are a home instead of the bedroom we share."

"Edward how do you feel about it?" asked Jason.

"Take the chambers," Edward said. "You would be a fool to turn down an offer like that."

Jason stood up and shook hands with Gabriel and Edward. "Thank you both."

Gabriel and Hannah left Edward's team and walked through the crowd looking for Marina. After a short time they walked up to Joao and Dack. "Do you know where Marina is?" asked Gabriel. "I saw her with you a while ago."

"She was going to relieve Bethany as Sampson's nurse," said Dack. "Why is anything wrong?"

"We are going to ask them to stay on as nurses and healers," Gabriel said. "How do you feel about that?"

"Good idea," said Joao. "They are good and everyone likes them. Of course some more than others." Joao looked at Dack and winked.

"Now boys, I thought they weren't wild enough for you two," Hannah teased.

Both Dack and Joao roared with laughter. "When we knew them before all they did was study. So we are getting to know them better now," said Dack.

"And which one do you like?" Gabriel asked with a grin.

"He can't make up his mind but it looks like Marina is in the lead," Joao said and they all laughed.

"How long has he been like this?" asked Marina as they both examined Sampson.

"The crying just started," said Bethany. "Earlier he acted like he was having nightmares so I prayed over a crystal and put it in his left hand. That calmed him for a long time. He is still holding onto it. I didn't want to leave him but I think we should get Hannah and Lakin."

"Why?" asked Hannah as she and Gabriel entered the room.

"I'll get Lakin," Marina said and quickly left.

"Sampson is unconscious and crying," Bethany said. "This just started. But right after you left for the ball he acted like he was having nightmares so I prayed over a crystal and put it in his hand. That calmed him until just a few moments ago. Hannah, I don't think these reactions are because of his physical injuries."

"Which hand is the crystal in?" asked Gabriel as he walked closer to the bed.

"His left. He has been clinging to it," Bethany said. "Actually I was thinking about putting one in his other hand."

"Gabriel, blood is coming from his hand," said Hannah.

Gabriel tried to open Sampson's fist but couldn't. "Don't take it from him," said Lakin as he and Marina ran into the room. "That might be the only thing that is saving him. I think the demons are trying to take him."

"Girls, do you have your medical bags here?" asked Lakin. "I need crystals and blessed water. Gabriel would you start to pray over him?"

"We packed his wounds with crystals," said Hannah and reached for one of the bandages.

"No, Hannah don't touch him right now," Lakin said. "This isn't like when the demons tried to take Gabriel. They once owned Sampson and perhaps still do but he seems to be fighting them," Lakin explained as he poured blessed water over a handful of crystals. He then prayed silently for a moment.

"Sampson, I am putting another crystal in your right hand," said Lakin. "It will help you." Sampson did not respond but his body started to convulse. "Girls quickly place these crystals on his body," Lakin said as he tried to open Sampson's right hand.

Marina and Bethany prayed as they placed the crystals. Lakin was a strong man and was able to open Sampson's clenched fist just enough to insert a crystal.

Other people were gathering outside of the doorway. "If he's fighting those bastards he will need this," said Jared as he pushed his way through the crowd and placed a sword on Sampson's chest. "It would help if we could get his hand around the hilt."

Shara ran into the room. "How are they connected to him?" she asked.

"He sold his soul," said Hannah.

"There might be something else too," Shara said and pulled the covers off from Sampson.

"Don't touch him Shara," Lakin said.

Archetenus now pushed into the room and looked at Sampson who was going through convulsions. "Miranda surround him with holy light," he yelled.

Sampson's convulsions worsened and green foam started to come out of his mouth and nose. "There's got to be a connecter," Shara said loudly. "Some of you look around the room."

"What are we looking for?" asked Micha.

"Anything unusual," Shara replied.

Hannah, Gabriel, Lakin, Bethany and Marina were all praying over Sampson. "Fight those bastards," Jared yelled.

"There is something on the windowsill," said Bianca.

"Don't touch it," Shara said and grabbed a bottle of blessed water.

"It looks like an herb," Bianca said and pointed to a small stem with five leaves.

Shara prayed then poured blessed water on the cutting which immediately burst into flames. Sampson screamed and blood gushed out of his mouth.

"Stand back," yelled Lakin and pushed Bethany away from the bed. Blood flowed from Sampson's eyes, ears and nose. His skin started to crack. He screamed, agonizing screams then slumped on the bed. The sword clanged as it hit the floor. Everyone stared at him; Sampson did not move. Lakin kept everyone away from the bed for a few more moments then he walked forward and checked Sampson for signs of life.

"Is he dead?" asked Raul.

"Yes."

"But how can that be?" asked Hannah. "We were doing everything right."

# Chapter LII
## The Wedding
## (Part I)

The wedding was scheduled for midmorning. No one told Luca or Natalie about the events of the previous night. Bekka, Cassandra and Hannah each took one of Luca's and Natalie's children for the night so the wedding couple could sleep in. When Luca and Natalie walked into the dining room they found the breakfast table filled with gifts and flowers.

Gabriel led a toast. The children were given glasses of juice so they could take part in the toast and this excited them all. The additional house guests only added to the festivities. Gabriel announced that Lana would be returning to Lentz with her team which upset the children but they brightened up when they were told that Melinda was returning.

Cassandra and Joao were particularly excited to learn that their sister was moving into her own chambers with Jason. Gabriel was still standing when he turned to Bethany and Marina. "You too have become part of this crazy family. We were wondering if you would like to stay and work as our nurses and healers. Of course we will pay you. You don't have to make a decision now but know that if you decline you will always have a home here."

The chapel at the Learning Center was standing room only for the wedding. Many of the Elod families also attended the ceremony. All of the doors of the chapel were open so that the people who could not make it inside of the building could still see and hear the service.

Luca led his attendants to the front of the chapel. Gabriel was the best man. He was followed by all of Luca's brothers, Ratri, Elan, Joao, Dack, Thor, Micha, Thomas and Edward. As soon as the men were lined up Christopher led the boys out and each one stood in front of one of the men. The boys wore suits that matched those of the adults.

Vivian and Diana were both maids of honor and walked down the aisle next to each other. They were followed by Kate, Hannah, Natasha, Rachel, Batina, Bianca, Bekka, Casandra, Sasha, Tanya and Marina.

Amy led all of the little girls out and they each stood in front of one of the women. The dresses of the women were dark pink and the dresses of the girls were light pink. Everyone in the chapel smiled as they watched the excited children.

Nyla, Saran and Nina came next. They sprinkled rose petals on the red carpet. They were followed by Natalie who was walked down the aisle by Joshua, who was as proud as if she was his own daughter.

Raphael preformed the ceremony and his words touched the hearts of all. The ceremony was long and some of the children had difficulty standing still which brought smiles to many.

Madeline was surprised when Michael asked her to go to the ceremony with him. There were four aisles of pews in the chapel and all of the front pews held royal and ruling families.

Because of the threats of spies and terrorists, Sudfad had soldiers guarding the chapel. But fortunately for all no darkness marred the ceremony. There were lines of carriages waiting outside of the chapel to take everyone to the castle where the grounds were set up for games and competitions. Lunch would be served in the Great Hall and in the evening there would be a pig roast and a dance.

The reception activities were originally planned to be held at Gabriel's home but with the addition of the Elod families everything was moved to the castle.

Luca had asked that everyone go to the back of the castle as soon as they returned from the chapel. The guests found poles with huge drapes that secluded a large area. Sudfad had soldiers pull down the drapes and every child screamed with delight. A large area was set up just for the children. There were toys of all manner; some to climb, some to crawl through, some to swing from.

There was a merry-go-round, giant forts and giant doll houses, sand boxes, live ponies to ride and tables set up with treats. Horace had a stage set up for puppet shows.

Many of the Elod women wanted to help and volunteered to watch the children so others could enjoy the festivities. Renya had four sets of musician's playing in different areas of the grounds.

"Even for Mother this is something," Raul said jokingly as he put his sons on the merry-go-round.

"Perhaps we should have had the kids change their clothes first," Luca said with a grin as he held Hunter on one of the wooden horses on the merry-go-round.

"It is too late to think about that," Raul said as they watched hundreds of children in the play area.

But with all of the laughter and excitement, soldiers constantly patrolled the grounds. Groups of Ruala warriors would take turns patrolling from the air.

Sampson's body had been buried before the sun came up. Joshua sent a mournful letter to his dear friend Chief Duncan explaining the actions of Sampson the last days of his life. Joshua hoped that Duncan would get some peace knowing that his son did several good things before he died. But Joshua also had to describe the manner of Sampson's death. He knew this news would bring grief but also a sense of relief since Sampson had been such a threat to his family and his village.

Hannah had been greatly disturbed by Sampson's death. Not because she cared about him but because so many people were trying so hard to save him. She did not understand why methods that were successful with others failed with him.

Shortly after the festivities at the castle started Hannah and Gabriel found the Sanuri walking among the crowd.

"I am sorry to bother you," Hannah said. "But can you explain why Sampson died when we were all praying over him. Archetenus asked Miranda to help him and there were so many others. Did we omit something or do something wrong?"

"Understand I cannot give you an exact answer," explained the Sanuri. "But even in such situations there are always choices to be made. While both Archetenus and Jared were men with dark souls they still owned their souls whereas Sampson willingly sold his soul to more than one demon."

"But even with this, the Angels would have helped him if he would have asked. Archetenus and Jared fought their demons and won. Who knows what choices Sampson made? He did want to kill Ale; perhaps he thought he had a chance if he let them take him. He was very isolated in this world because of his choices and actions and while he would have made the same choices again he was lonely. Perhaps he felt more at home in a way with the demons."

"But he looked terrified and in pain," said Hannah.

"I am sure he was. He may have made a decision that he quickly regretted."

"Gideon this is such a wonderful reception," Ashley said. "I am getting all sorts of ideas." Gideon laughed loudly as they watched Logan, Marty and Cassidy riding ponies. "Oh Gideon, I just realized we have no idea when the boy's birthdays are. I will ask them today. I want to have parties for them every year."

"I think that sounds like a wonderful idea My Dear," Gideon said. "But at some point you and I need to plan out our wedding or did you forget?"

Ashley laughed, "No, I didn't forget. But we are all so settled; doesn't it seem like we are already married?"

"I've actually been thinking a lot about it," Gideon said. "I like that Luca and Natalie had their children in the wedding. I would like to do the same with our boys. What do you think?"

"You and I have been thinking the same things," she said with a warm smile.

"What do you think about asking Bella and Claudius to be our best man and maid of honor? Or did you want someone else?"

"I think that is a wonderful idea. But I should tell you that I already told Kate, Rachel, Nana, Risa and Batina they would be in the wedding too. And I think I should ask Nikki, Ingr and Delilah as well."

"Actually that is one reason I am bringing this up. I thought you had asked the girls when we were in Port Friada. We have a week left here and I think we should make the most of it. I brought extra money with us for wedding preparations. I think we should start fittings while we are here, at least for the people who live in Wetpr."

"Do you think it will be rude if we talk to people about this at Luca's wedding reception?"

"No, besides I would like to take everyone shopping tomorrow to get started on this. We just don't seem to find the time when we are home. And I have another idea. You and I already have so much that I was thinking instead of wedding gifts we could ask people to help sponsor the building of Adam's Homes."

"I love that idea," Ashley said and kissed Gideon on the lips.

After lunch Gala, Hilgra, Shara, Angelina, Hannah, Lakin, Gael, Hadar and Ibula met with the Sanuri to start their review of Juleta's medical logs. The Ruala healers had not previously been a part of this group.

"You can certainly enjoy the ceremonies," the Sanuri said as he brought the books into the chambers that Renya had prepared for the healers. "Don't feel that you have to do this now."

"We are very anxious to see these books," said Lakin. "And while we can stay for a while, we just heard that Shara, Angelina and Hilgra are returning to Lentz in a week. We want to make the most of our time here."

"You are dedicated people; I am proud to be your friend," said the Sanuri. "The Angels are protecting you from the evil these books contained. Renya has paper and pens in here besides refreshments. Don't hesitate to let us know if you want anything else."

"Most of us brought reference books," said Hannah. "Do you think we can leave them in these chambers?"

"I don't see why not," said the Sanuri. "But I would like to make a suggestion. All of you are incredibly powerful and experienced healers. Do you think that some of your, say top students, would benefit from doing research with you?"

"Until we have an idea of what we have here," said Hadar. "I don't want to bring a lot of students in. But are you thinking of anyone in particular?"

"Bethany, Marina and Nana have all been involved with healings from dark magics. They have performed well and showed no fear in the face of darkness. And they are all dedicated and intelligent. I think they will be very strong healers someday. For now, they may not have much to offer you in this research but they would benefit from the experience. But the decision is yours. I am merely making a suggestion."

"Sanuri, I agree with your assessments," said Ibula. "But I also agree with Hadar. I think we need to look at these books before we bring anyone else in and possibly put them in danger."

"Benedict, I am sorry to pull you away from the festivities," said Sudfad as the two men met in his study. "But things have been so crazy that I thought we could use this opportunity to talk."

Sudfad poured them each a small glass of whiskey. "As you know I don't understand the customs of your people so I hope that what I am about to ask is not taken as an insult."

"I am sure it won't be," said Benedict. In the short time he had known the King, Benedict both liked and respected Sudfad.

"As you know we have had problems with spies and about a year ago some spies who were employed as our cooks tried to poison us. Marie, our head cook was always very finicky about who she would allow into her kitchen but after the attempts to kill us, she is much worse. She is impressed with some of the women who are helping her and would like to hire them. What are your thoughts on this matter?"

"Without knowing the specific women I believe they would welcome the employment. Just so you understand, my people here are very loyal to you and your family not only for saving us but you have treated us all with such honor. And you allowed us to partake of these wonderful ceremonies. To say we never expected such gracious treatment would be a great understatement."

"Madeline and I had a long talk yesterday," Benedict continued. "I told her about your offer to give us land to build a settlement. She doesn't like that idea because she is afraid we will isolate ourselves here. She suggests that if we decide to do that; that we all work within the City of Salar so that we can socialize and learn your ways. I think she makes a good argument but I have not presented it to my people yet."

"She also thinks that we should not tell others about Inferus. She says people everywhere are afraid of what they do not understand."

"I think she has given you some wise suggestions," Sudfad said. "If your people are interested in employment, speak with Simon and Raul. "We have multiple projects going on and I am sure they are aware of employers in Salar who need help."

"Now to change the subject," Sudfad continued. "I know the boys took you on a tour of the Learning Center. And I believe they told you our reason for building it. We have an entire building prepared for students but so far only some of our children and the children from Gabriel's house attend classes there. If you would like to send your children to the school, let me know and we will hire more teachers."

"That is a very generous offer which I believe all my people will be pleased with. We come from all walks of life and possess many skills. There are also teachers among us. I think this could benefit both of our peoples."

The happiness on the faces of both Luca and Natalie were evident to all. The wedding couple did not participate in the competitions but walked among their guests and socialized.

All of the Elod families were at the reception ceremonies. Although weddings were different in Inferus it was still traditional to give gifts to the wedding couple. Cyrene and a group of women walked up to Luca and Natalie. After they all congratulated the couple Cyrene said,

"We have never seen a wedding as beautiful as yours and this," she waved her arm at the events on the field. "Is beyond anything we have seen before. We brought nothing with us when we fled our world and feel awful that we have nothing to give you as gifts."

"We don't care about the gifts," said Luca. "We just want everyone together to enjoy this day."

"We want to do something for you so we decided to offer our services," Cyrene continued. "We can help with your housework, cooking and the children. And the men can help with other things around your home."

"Now that is a great gift," said Luca with a warm smile.

Claudius and Bella were honored to be asked to stand up for Gideon and Ashley. Bella immediately offered to help with the preparations. She went with Gideon and Ashley as they spoke with the other men and women they wanted to be attendants. Everyone they asked was married except for Nana and Risa. Gideon asked Joao and Dack to walk down the aisle with these two women.

"Sure, we love weddings," said Joao with a big grin. "This will be fun."

"Did you ask them if they would walk down the aisle with us?" Dack asked and both young men laughed.

"I know there is more to this," Gideon said with a grin. "What are you talking about?"

"When we were in Port Friada they told us we were immature," Joao said and grinned. "We agreed with them but told them we weren't going to change. So you might want to run this past them."

Gideon, Ashley and Bella all laughed heartedly at Joao's comments. "Well, you are in the wedding whether they want to walk with you or not. If they don't we will just ask a couple more girls."

"Thanks," Dack said.

"Tomorrow morning right after breakfast we are all going into the city for fittings and whatever else we can get done. Ashley and Bella are already making lists," Gideon said and laughed loudly. He was very happy and wanted to share his happiness with others.

"You look like you really want to join some of those competitions," Madeline said to Michael with a smile. They were walking around the field. Madeline was searching the crowd for intruders.

"I do. I hate being laid up," Michael chuckled. "Renya and Hannah both told me not to exert myself today. I didn't think they knew me that well."

"Michael, as you know I spend a great deal of time watching people. If you would not have told me your story I would have thought that you lived in this family your entire life. I understand there have been difficulties for all of you but honestly what family doesn't have difficulties and even a stranger can tell how much all of you care about each other. I have to admit I am a little jealous. I would have loved to have grown up in a family like yours."

"I would have too," said Michael sarcastically then he softened his voice. "You really would think we have spent our lives together?"

"Yes, why would I just say that? Did you see Renya's and Sudfad's faces that night that your wounds broke open? They love you as their son. Tell me Michael do you feel the same about them?"

"I do care about them."

"But what?"

"How did you know there was a 'but'?" Michael asked and laughed.

"I am waiting for your answer; you aren't getting out of it."

"Don't laugh but sometimes I feel like I am going to wake up and find out this is all a dream. And I will find myself back in that cage dreaming about having a real family."

"So that barrier you built is because of fear then instead of anger?"

"I didn't realize I had built a barrier."

"Michael are you telling me the truth? Are you really that unaware?"

"When I was in Langer, Maxwell talked to me because everyone felt like I was avoiding them and I was but I didn't understand why. Everyone has been great to me since I became part of the family. Well, Maxwell said that seeing happy and loving families made the horror of my past more real to me. I thought he was full of it at first but the more I thought about what he said; I think he was right. But I have been trying to correct that."

"I have been working in your world for twelve years and this is the very first time I have not played a part or worn a disguise. While trust was understandably an issue at first, everyone here has been so accepting of me. I can't tell you how exhilarating it feels to be myself. I am telling you this because that wall you built keeps you in a prison as well as keeping them out."

"You have a chance to be really happy here don't let your fear ruin that for you." Michael was quiet for a couple of minutes as he thought about her words. "Are you mad at me now?" Madeline asked.

"No, I think you are right but I don't know how to change it. I mean, well what do you think I should do? Madeline, I am not stupid but... well... you know how difficult it is for me with people sometimes."

"Michael, I would never think you are stupid. I think you should just tell Renya and Sudfad what we have been talking about. They have everything; they don't need gifts but I will bet it would mean the world to them if you told them you cared about them."

"I think you are right," Michael said and paused.

"If you would like, I will come with you but you have to do the talking."

"Alright, I would like that," he said with half a smile. "Madeline, why are you helping me?"

"I told you that you and I are alike in some ways but I am realizing that you and Javier have more similarities. Being with you makes me understand him better and I don't want you to turn out like him, and you easily could. Michael, you have such a chance here; you would be a fool to throw it all away. These people really love you. Sometimes I wish Javier could have escaped with me so he could have met all of you."

"Maybe we can go back and get him."

"Even if we did, he is so full of darkness right now. I don't know what he would do."

As Michael and Madeline talked they searched the crowd for the King and Queen. "There they are," Michael said and nodded towards a group of people. "But they are with others."

"They won't mind being interrupted for this," Madeline said warmly. "Trust me."

"Can I speak to the two of you in private?" Michael asked as soon as they approached Sudfad and Renya.

"Certainly, is anything wrong son?" Sudfad asked.

"I'm not sure how to answer that," Michael said with a sheepish grin. "It won't take long."

"Now you have me worried," said Renya.

"There is no need to worry," Madeline said reassuringly.

The four walked a ways from the guests. Michael was the first to stop and looked at both Sudfad and Renya for a moment before he spoke. "I am trying to think how to start this, so I am just going to tell you what we were talking about. Madeline said I am very fortunate to have such a loving family. And if I wouldn't have told her about my past she would have thought we had always been together. Then she asked me if the wall I built to keep all of you at a distance was out of anger or fear."

"I realize now that I love all of you and I want this family so much that I am always afraid that I am going to wake up and find out this is a dream and I am back in that cage. I used to dream about having a real family and now that I do, it doesn't seem real. I am sorry I don't let you in."

Renya was crying too hard to talk so she hugged and kissed Michael. Then to Madeline's surprise Renya hugged her too.

"You can't believe how happy this makes us son," Sudfad said emotionally and he too hugged and kissed Michael.

Vitomas and Annabelle cried also when Sudfad and Renya told them, Raul and Simon, Michael's words. "I feel kind of bad now," Raul said. "I thought he was just being a jerk sometimes."

"Raul!" Vitomas said with a scolding tone. "How many times did I tell you that you should talk to him about something besides missions and horses?"

Simon looked at Annabelle and said, "I know; you told me the same thing." Simon paused for a moment.

"You know there is a horse auction tomorrow. It's just outside of Salar, maybe just Raul and I should take Michael there. We can make a day of it. Unless you want to come along too, Father."

"I think that is a good idea," Sudfad said. "And let me think about that invitation. While I wouldn't mind going it might be better for you boys to spend some time together."

"Well do you feel better now?" Madeline asked Michael as they resumed their trek around the grounds.

"I'm not really sure but I was shocked to see how emotional they got. I wasn't expecting that."

"See, you should listen to me," she said teasingly.

"I will admit I was skeptical but you were right. Do you want to stop for a minute? They stopped at a wrestling competition. Archetenus was wrestling with a Nordes warrior and both men were equally matched.

"Michael, want to place a bet?" Jared yelled.

Michael laughed and guided Madeline to Jared. He placed a bet on Archetenus then he and Madeline moved to an area where they had a better view of the fighters.

"You really look like you want to get into that ring," Madeline said as she looked at Michael's face.

"That obvious huh?"

"You are being smart by sitting these out now. From the sounds of it there are a lot more weddings coming up; you will have plenty of chances to compete. You are a very social group," she said and smiled.

"A lot of the people thought about cancelling or postponing some of these celebrations because of all the threats but Miranda said they should all be held. She said that all of the team members and people that we work with should also be invited so they could bond. She said we would need that strength for the dark days ahead."

The little boy was crying
He was lost in this place
So many people passed him by
No one ever saw his face

Dirty and shivering
They were busy, they were late
The little boy stood crying
They never cared about his fate

He went into a building
Dark as it was cold
No one lived there
The building was so old

His head he buried
In his wet and torn sleeves
He cried for his parents
Why did they ever leave

An Angel's Touch

By Sandra J Yearman © 2011

# Glossary of Characters

**Aaron:** an escaped prisoner from Wetpr

**Aaryan:** a male Grand Master of the Insidiae

**Abaddon:** an ancient demon/one of the Old Ones

**Abella:** daughter of Prince Lakin and Princess Zada/Ruala

**Abigail:** sister of Marie/ nurse for grandchildren of King Sudfad

**Abraxas:** the demon that Hector sold his soul to

**Ackley:** hired fighter for Mayor Deckor of Langer

**Ackly:** an arms dealer in Ryed

**Ada:** demon midwife to Nada

**Adam James:** a notorious pirate

**Adam:** an emissary of The Great Ruler who takes on the disguise of a human man

**Adam:** Nordes child/brother of Celia

**Adi:** son of Elen and Batya/ Ruala

**Adin:** male Ruala warrior

**Adrone:** youngest son of Joshua and Iris/younger brother of Vivian/Clan of Gesmal

**Adwell:** Prince/ son of King Zachariah and Queen Noella of New Samona/husband of Nada/father of Misha/ Adwell was killed in battle leaving Nada to raise ten children/Ruala/

**Ael:** an ancient demon/ one of the Old Ones

**Aetes:** Shettee warrior

**Agnes:** owner of the Midnight Tavern in Stoba Lentz/wife of Bert

**Agnus:** a captain in the covert organization The Guardians

**Ahriman:** an ancient demon/ one of the Old Ones

**Aiden:** five year old Ruala boy/son of Artis and Jenna/nephew of Ratri

**Akasha:** former king of Ryed/grandfather of Nehmota

**Alexander:** former servant of King Roch's parents/ father of Annabelle

**Alexander:** one of the twin sons of Simon and Annabelle

**Alexandras:** King of Wetpr/brother of Jaretta/uncle of Sudfad and Roch

**Alexas Rose:** daughter of Matthew and Angelina

**Alexis:** son of Usman, the leader of the Valdore Tribe

**Alice:** and her husband find Jorge near death in Nora

**Aloeus:** Shettee warrior

**Amelia:** baby Ruala girl

**Amiee:** sister of Marie/ nurse for grandchildren of King Sudfad

**Amundsen:** Commanding General of Fort Friada in the Kingdom of Ganz

**Amy:** a young girl who was kidnapped by Sal

**Ana:** eleven year old Nordes girl/daughter of Edgar and Cora/younger sister of Batina

**Ana:** Princess/daughter of Zeman and Oda/niece of King Manu of New Samona/Ruala

**Anda:** one of Chief Romogi's three wives/Huta

**Andrac:** a powerful sorcerer and seer in the Kingdom of Inferus/Elod

**Andrea:** female Ruala warrior/ sister of Bekka

**Andres:** Princess of Ryed/daughter of Oren and Astrel/ has twin sister Jorga

**Andrew:** jeweler in Salar

**Andrus:** father of Rabi/Ruala

**Angelina:** daughter of Sorren, Chief of the Nordes Tribe/female warrior

**Anka:** Elod child

**Annabar:** daughter of King Sharonne

**Annabelle:** handmaid and best friend to Queen Vitomas of the Kingdom of Stordt

**Anthony:** one of the twin sons of Simon and Annabelle

**April:** a young girl who was kidnapped by Sal

**Arca:** Enrop leader who protects King Mathas' family

**Arches:** a Patronus priest

**Archetenus The Brave:** Captain in the Taperian Army

**Arianna:** daughter of Simon and Annabelle

**Ariel:** daughter of Raul and Vitomas

**Arlene:** housekeeper and cook for Erebus/wife of Theodore

**Armstrong:** soldier and scout in the army of Wetpr

**Arthur Marcus:** father of Hannah

**Artis:** an old sailor from the Navy of Ganz

**Artis:** male Ruala warrior/oldest brother of Ratri/husband of Jenna

**Asgar:** an Old One on the planet Filsum

**Asher:** male Ruala warrior

**Asher:** youngest of three brothers who formed the Libertas in Ryed

**Ashlee:** young female Nordes warrior

**Asmodeus:** an ancient demon/ one of the Old Ones

**Astar:** General in the Military of Ryed who tries to take over the kingdom after the fall of Teivel

**Astrel:** former princess of Ryed/daughter of Akasha and Norah

**Atomos:** Elder of the Centras and Keeper of the Box of Itifer

**Augustus Endleson:** a wealthy businessman who owned part of the City of Nora

**Ava:** twin of Benjamin/daughter of Archetenus and Delilah

**Axel Sam:** a notorious pirate

**Baal:** an ancient demon/ one of the Old Ones

**Babu:** Enrop

**Bac:** male Ruala warrior

**Bachnenus:** warrior guarding refugees/Shettee

**Bali:** Enrop leader of the flock that does battle at Juleta's castle

**Balin:** Prince of Norkv/son of Thaddius and Omara/grandson of Benjeman and Esther

**Balius:** Shettee warrior/brother of King Neputa

**Banacus:** General in the army of King Tobias of Puntd

**Banaka:** a female Grand Master of the Insidiae

**Barak:** Prince of Norkv/grandson of Benjeman and Esther

**Barak:** Prince/son of King Neputa and Queen Tiara/Shettee

**Barid:** Prince of Ogg

**Barid:** Prince of Ryed/son of Nehmota and Vasart

**Barnabas:** a member of the wealthy and elite in Ryed

**Bart:** male Ruala warrior/ married to Bekka's sister Andrea

**Bartholomew:** alias used by Raphael in Ryed

**Baruk:** the leader of the Abuckto Sect in the Kingdom of Inferus/Elod

**Barush:** a major in the Military of Ryed

**Bastra:** Huta captain

**Batina:** young female Nordes warrior

**Batya:** wife of Elen/Ruala

**Beatrice Endleson:** wife of Augustus

**Becca:** Princess of Norkv/daughter of Thaddius and Omara/granddaughter of Benjeman and Esther

**Behtay:** Princess/daughter of Segal and Cahina/niece of King Manu of New Samona/Ruala

**Bekka:** female Ruala warrior

**Bella:** wife of Claudius and mother of Stephan

**Benedict:** leader of the Credo in Inferus/father of Anka, Santi and Linus/husband of Cyrene/ Elod

**Benedict:** Prince of Norkv/son of Benjeman and Esther

**Benix:** boss of Ivan/ from the Kingdom of Inferus

**Benjamin:** twin of Ava/son of Archetenus and Delilah

**Benjeman:** vicious rebel leader who overthrew the government of Samona

**Benny:** adopted son of Fahron and Isadore

**Benson:** a Private in the Wetprian military

**Bentra:** an ancient demon/ one of the Old Ones

**Bert:** owner of the Midnight Tavern in Stoba Lentz/husband of Agnes

**Berta:** cook at Racing Horse Tavern

**Berta:** Queen of Stordt/wife of Micha/grandmother of Roch and Sudfad

**Bertha:** an elderly woman from Nora

**Bertuck:** the demon who Usman sold his soul

**Bethany:** female Ruala healer

**Betsy Sarbush:** wealthy socialite in the City of Langer in the Kingdom of Lentz

**Betty:** a woman from Nora

**Betu:** male Ruala warrior

**Bianca:** young female Nordes warrior

**Bill:** owner of a butcher shop in Stoba Lentz

**Black Jack:** a regular patron at the Ghost Ship Tavern in Port Friada

**Blackjack:** works for Hector

**Bode:** Shettee warrior

**Boris:** a general in the Military of Ryed

**Botis:** a demon

**Brandon:** Nordes child/son of Marsha and Kyle/nephew of Jasmine

**Bremmer:** an arms dealer in Ryed

**Brent:** a soldier from Lentz who fights in the Gefrey Games in Ryed

**Brik:** son of Prince Lakin and Princess Zada /Ruala

**Brina:** Princess of Norkv/daughter of Valor and Cai/granddaughter of Benjeman and Esther

**Brit:** male Nordes warrior

**Bruce:** male Nordes warrior/eldest son of Edgar and Cora/older brother of Batina

**Bryce:** male Ruala warrior

**Cabal:** son of Karzman and Nadia

**Cacu:** Enrop leader that joined Raul and Simon on a mission

**Cade:** son of King Pergo and Queen Vinus/ Kingdom of Gandt

**Cadi:** daughter of Prince Hadar and Princess Paj/ granddaughter of Manu/Ruala

**Cadmus:** the demon that the Dura Tribe worships

**Cael:** Shettee boy who is adopted by Thedes and Ibula

**Cage:** male Ruala warrior

**Cahina:** Princess/ married to Segal son of King Zachariah and Queen Noella of New Samona/Ruala

**Cai:** Princess of Norkv/wife of Valor who was the son of Benjeman and Esther

**Calen:** male Ruala warrior/cousin of Luca/son of Maxwell and Emeral/

**Calla:** female Ruala warrior

**Callie:** Nordes child/younger sister of Bianca/daughter of Tyler and Dora

**Calus:** a dark lord/member of the Insidiae

**Calvin:** a desk clerk at The Captain's Retreat Hotel in Port Friada

**Campbell:** one of the spies at the Castle at Wetpr

**Canton:** Cisero's second in command

**Cara:** Princess of Ogg

**Carl:** a drifter/travels with Zeke, Sam and Johnny

**Carlsman:** a Lieutenant in the Army of Lentz

**Carlson:** Sergeant in the Wetprian Army

**Carlton:** alias used by Archetenus in Ryed

**Carson Dormors:** a wealthy landowner in the Kingdom of Ganz

**Carston:** member of the governing body of Nora

**Casey:** male Ruala warrior/father of Melanie/husband of Tasha

**Cass:** one of Hectors' men

**Cassandra:** female Ruala warrior

**Cassidy:** homeless boy

**Cates:** alias used by Sorren in Ryed

**Cedrick Teivel:** a ruthless, powerful man in the Kingdom of Ryed

**Celia:** Nordes child/sister of Adam

**Celo:** Prince of Ryed/son of Oren and Astrel

**Cere:** daughter of Tristt/Shettee

**Cerephus:** General in the Taperian Army

**Cerey:** orphan girl/sister of Nicholas/adopted daughter of Gabriel and Hannah

**Ceria:** Princess/daughter of Gunnel and Uma/niece of King Manu of New Samona/ sister of Elan/Ruala

**Chaez:** son of Fahron

**Chaladrone:** an ancient demon/ one of the Old Ones

**Chalice:** hired fighter for Dieter

**Chalta:** daughter of King Pergo and Queen Vinus/ Kingdom of Gandt

**Chance:** works with the Patronus

**Chara:** three year old Ruala girl/ daughter of Orin and Rene/niece of Ratri

**Charlene:** a woman from Nora

**Charles Moses:** a violent and abusive man

**Charles:** Father of Cassandra, Joao and Melinda

**Charles:** hired farmhand of Arthur Marcus

**Charter:** Colonel in the Military of Ryed

**Chasity:** missing sister of Joey and Tommy

**Chet:** owns a company of barges in the Village of New Flounder in the Kingdom of Zorta

**Chief Romogi:** leader of the Hutas/ Kingdom of Marba

**Christopher:** six year old boy who Luca saves from the Hutas/brother of Lila

**Ciao:** female Ruala warrior

**Cicely:** adopted daughter of Elan and Cassandra

**Cisero:** a member of the Insidiae

**Clair:** a woman from Nora

**Clair:** female Ruala warrior/mother of Ratri/wife of Joseph

**Claudius:** General in the Army of Lentz

**Clay:** the manager of the Teivel Manor Hotel in Ryed

**Cleo:** a man who works for Cicero/a vessel

**Cleta:** female Ruala warrior who fought in Ryed

**Clev:** Hector's head lieutenant

**Clifford:** a general in the Military of Ryed

**Cobren:** Prince of Norkv/son of Grace and Makalo/Grandson of Benjeman and Esther

**Cody:** orphan boy

**Collins:** Lieutenant in the Army of Ganz

**Compro:** Taperian soldier injured at Wall of Dorath

**Conrad:** father of Jasmine/husband of Leta/Nordes Tribe

**Cora:** mother of Batina/wife of Edgar/Nordes warrior

**Corina:** young female Nordes warrior

**Corsa:** female Nordes warrior/healer

**Corwin:** son of King Fahra and Queen Sitha of Zorta

**Crater:** a Sergeant in the Wetprian army

**Crater:** a soldier in the army of Wetpr

**Crispus:** a guard at King Roch's castle

**Crocell:** a demon

**Cronn:** a demon

**Cronos:** Shettee warrior

**Curtis:** male Ruala warrior who fought in Ryed

**Cyrene:** wife of Benedict/mother of Anka, Santi and Linus/Elod

**Daceron:** a demon from the world of Balterak in the Mensor Galaxy

**Dack:** male Ruala warrior

**Dacron:** former prince of Ryed/is murdered by his younger brother Nehmota for the throne

**Dael:** an ancient demon/ one of the Old Ones

**Dafney:** a witch

**Dagon:** a male Ruala warrior

**Dagor:** son of King Fahra and Queen Sitha of Zorta

**Dai:** son of Gael, grandson of Manu/Ruala

**Daisy:** nine year old Nordes girl/ daughter of Edgar and Cora/younger sister of Batina

**Damas:** an ancient demon/ one of the Old Ones

**Danar:** a man created to be a vessel for demons

**Daniel:** an emissary of The Great Ruler who takes on the disguise of a human man

**Danilla:** mother of King Mathas

**Dano:** seven year old Nordes boy/son of Edgar and Cora/youngest brother of Batina

**Darius:** Prince of Samona/son of Thomas and Rewel/brother of Varden

**Darla:** young female Nordes warrior

**Darlah:** sister of Marie/ nurse for grandchildren of King Sudfad

**Dea:** Nordes warrior/mother of Adam and Celia/wife of Vilem

**Deborah:** a servant of Charles Moses

**Deckor:** mayor of Langer, the capital city of the Kingdom of Lentz

**Delilah:** wife of Dieter

**Delilia:** Queen of New Samona/mother of Ibula, Lakin, Gael and Hadar/ wife of King Manu/Ruala

**Demanko:** a demon

**Demetries:** a demon

**Denise Froush:** wife of Martin who is a wealthy ship builder in Port Friada

**Denks:** a soldier in the army of Wetpr

**Denton:** one of the spies at the Castle in Wetpr

**Derek:** friend of Thaos

**Derlock:** Huta warrior

**Desavo:** the demon who leads the Armada of the dead

**Diana:** a Venator/sister of Thor

**Dieter:** member of the Insidiae

**Dillion:** one of Karzman's hired fighters

**Dion:** Princess of Samona/wife of Yorggi who was the son of Thomas and Rewel/brother of Varden

**Dixon:** a Taperian soldier

**Dixon:** Chief Seaman of the Falcon

**Dominic Petlov:** was the senior High Priest at the monastery at Malga before he was murdered

**Dominic:** oldest of three brothers who formed the Libertas in Ryed

**Dora:** Nordes warrior/mother of Bianca/wife of Tyler

**Dorme:** Prince of Ogg

**Doros:** works for High Priest Meekos

**Douma:** King of Ogg

**Dr. Theodore Jackson:** head of the medical school at Cicero College in Salar

**Drake:** worked for Karzman

**Dresden:** a Sergeant in the Wetprian army

**Duncan:** Chief of the Clan of Gesmal in Ryed/ husband of Liza

**Duran:** father of Nikki/Nordes Tribe

**Durst:** Colonel in the Military of Wetpr

**Dymas:** Shettee warrior

**Eachann:** Shettee warrior

**Edgar:** father of Batina/husband of Cora/Nordes warrior

**Edith:** wife of Lloyd a banker in Nora

**Eilig:** male Ruala warrior

**Elan:** male Ruala warrior/son of Gunnel and Uma/

**Eldridge:** works with the Patronus

**Elen:** son of Andrus and Naomi/ brother of Rabi/ Ruala

**Elexas:** a female Nordes warrior

**Elizabeth:** wife of Wickfield

**Ella:** female Ruala warrior/mother of Bekka/wife of Sam

**Elliot:** a hired fighter who works for King Friada of the Kingdom of Ganz

**Eloise:** a store clerk in Salar

**Eloise:** female Ruala warrior/oldest sister of Bekka/wife of Tony

**Elsa:** female Ruala warrior/mother of Mia/wife of Tyron

**Emeral:** mother of Calen/Ruala

**Emeric:** a male Grand Master of the Insidiae

**Emma:** daughter of Luca and Lila

**Emmet:** worker for Gabriel

**Emon:** a male Grand Master of the Insidiae

**Enzo:** male Ruala warrior

**Erebus:** sorcerer from Ryed

**Erwat:** a member of the Half-Man's Tribe who helps the Clan of Gesmal

**Esser:** Prince/son of Segal and Cahina/nephew of King Manu of New Samona/Ruala

**Esteban:** a member of the Insidiae

**Esther:** Queen of New Norkv/wife of rebel leader Benjeman

**Fabron:** Prince of Ogg

**Fadil:** a male Grand Master of the Insidiae

**Fahra:** King of Zorta

**Fahron:** General in the Army of Lentz

**Fairoot:** demon/ lieutenant for Salzar

**Fala:** female Ruala warrior

**Farnsworth:** General in charge of building Fort Serpha in Wetpr

**Fatima:** Prince of Ryed/ son of Oren and Astrel

**Fatronas:** an ancient demon/one of the Old Ones

**Felistine:** a member of the wealthy and elite in Ryed

**Fengu:** Enrop leader who helps Gabriel and his group against Omnibus

**Fennel:** one of three brothers who formed the Libertas in Ryed

**Ferguson:** a Sergeant in the Army of Lentz

**Fiona:** mother of Nadia/grandmother of Michael

**Fraisier:** a businessman and member of the Insidiae in Nora

**Frank:** a villager in Telmark

**Frankie:** Nordes child/younger brother of Jasmine/son of Conrad and Leta

**Fred Stapleton:** a farmer in Wetpr

**Fred:** a bartender at The Treasure Chest Tavern in Port Friada

**Friada:** King of the Kingdom of Ganz

**Gabriella:** sister of Marie/nurse to grandchildren of King Sudfad

**Gad:** male Ruala warrior

**Gael:** Prince/son of King Manu and Queen Delilia/Ruala

**Gala:** a healer from the Kingdom of Stordt

**Galen:** male Nordes warrior

**Geobel:** General in the Military of Ryed who tries to take over the kingdom after the fall of Teivel

**Geof Thurstand:** ship owner/husband of Linda

**Geoff:** Prince of Lentz/son of Princess Isabella and Captain Josef

**Geoff:** Prince of Norkv/son of Benedict and Sasaha/grandson of Benjeman and Esther

**Georganson:** an arms dealer in Ryed

**George:** an advisor for King Fahra of Zorta

**George:** middle son of Chief Duncan and Liza of the Clan of Gesmal in Ryed

**Gideon:** Admiral in the Navy of Ganz

**Gilder:** a dark lord from the Kingdom of Inferus

**Giles:** hired fighter for Mayor Deckor of Langer

**Gilmore:** a Wetprian soldier

**Giovani:** Rachel's older half-brother

**Gita:** wife of Hadi/ Ruala

**Gladys:** member of Nordes Tribe/ mother of Nikki

**Glenda:** great, great, great grandmother of Gala/ a healer from the Kingdom of Stordt

**Grace:** Princess of New Norkv/daughter of Benjeman and Esther

**Gracie:** cook for the Arthur Marcus family

**Grady:** worker for Gabriel

**Great Ruler:** God

**Gregory Bancar:** a wealthy landowner in the Kingdom of Wetpr and member of the Insidiae

**Greta:** older Ruala woman/friend of Emeral's

**Greta:** wife of Hugo/mother of Sasha/ sister-in-law of Sorren

**Gunnel:** Prince/ son of King Zachariah and Queen Noella of New Samona/husband of Uma/father of Elan/Ruala

**Gunter:** Seaman in the Navy of Lentz

**Gus:** husband of Penelope/ killed for trying to help Nadia and Michael escape from Karzman

**Gus:** owner of Racing Horse Tavern

**Haas:** a Lieutenant in the Wetprian military

**Hadar:** Prince/son of King Manu and Queen Delilia/Ruala

**Hadi:** son of Andrus and Naomi/ brother of Rabi/ Ruala

**Hadi:** son of Andrus and Naomi/brother of Rabi/Ruala

**Hadu:** female Ruala warrior

**Halsal:** Sergeant in the Military of Lentz

**Hamon:** one of the members of the Nordes Tribe who was injured in an attack at Snakes Crossing

**Hamond:** General of the Taperian Army who declares himself king

**Hanger:** one of the spies at the Castle at Wetpr

**Hangered:** Wetprian soldier

**Hannah:** physician in Nora/ Roch murdered her sister

**Harlow:** an investigative reporter for The Port Friada Gazette

**Harold:** husband of Berta/part owner of the Racing Horse Tavern

**Harold:** owner of the general store in Nora

**Harriet Marcus:** mother of Hannah and Laurabelle/wife of Arthur

**Harris:** male Ruala warrior who fought in Ryed

**Harrison:** Lieutenant in the Military of Lentz

**Harvard:** President of the Port Friada Bank

**Hatus:** General in the Army of Lentz/on loan to Sudfad

**Hazel:** housekeeper at Erebus' mansion in Salar

**Hector:** fighter hired by Juleta

**Hector:** Prince of Samona/son of Varden

**Henry:** and his wife Alice find Jorge in Nora

**Henry:** husband of Noreen/father of Jacob

**Hermanas:** second in command to Archetenus at Wall of Dorath

**High Priest Aaron:** member of the Patronus

**High Priest Alfonso:** a member of the Patronus

**High Priest Amos:** a member of the Patronus

**High Priest Barnabas:** most Senior High Priest of the monastery at Leven

**High Priest Caleb:** member of the Patronus

**High Priest Ephraim:** a member of the Patronus

**High Priest Gabriel:** member of the Patronus/demon hunter

**High Priest Gideon:** a member of the Patronus

**High Priest Gregory:** member of the Patronus

**High Priest Henrich:** a member of the Patronus Priests

**High Priest Ira:** a member of the Patronus Priests

**High Priest Joseph:** member of the Patronus, in charge of the Cicero Headquarters

**High Priest Josiah:** member of the Patronus

**High Priest Maddox:** a member of the Patronus Priests

**High Priest Meekos:** priest at the monastery at Malga

**High Priest Nicholas:** most Senior High Priest of the monastery at Philiste and most Senior High Priest of the Patronus

**High Priest Norbert:** Senior High Priest at the monastery at Casum in NW Wetpr

**High Priest Othnial:** Senior High Priest of the monastery in Rubar in the Kingdom of Ryed

**High Priest Paulas:** member of the Patronus

**High Priest Phanuel:** member of the Patronus

**High Priest Philetus:** member of the Patronus in charge of Malga Headquarters

**High Priest Pravis:** priest at the monastery at Malga

**High Priest Raphael:** a leader of the Patronus

**High Priest Rueben:** member of the Patronus in charge of Nora Headquarters

**High Priest Silas:** a member of the Patronus

**High Priest Tenebrae:** priest at the monastery at Malga

**High Priest Timothy:** was murdered by Meekos, Pravis and Tenebrae

**High Priest Tyrus:** a member of the Patronus

**High Priest Uriel:** member of the Patronus

**High Priest Vincent:** assigned to the monastery at Malga before he was murdered

**High Priest Zophar:** priest at monastery at Malga/ trained as a healer

**Hilgra:** a witch

**Hobart:** a man who works for demons

**Horace:** father of Rachel and Zach/husband of Zelda/freedom fighter in Ryed

**Hores:** son of Chief Romogi and Anda, Kingdom of Marba/Huta

**Horta:** Prince/son of Gunnel and Uma/nephew of King Manu of New Samona/brother of Elan/Ruala

**Howie:** one of Deckor's hired fighters

**Hugo:** younger brother of Sorren/father of Sasha/husband of Greta

**Hunter:** Prince of Samona/son of Varden

**Hunter:** son of Natalie and Troy/Clan of Gesmal

**Ian Maxwell Luca:** son of Koby and Bekka

**Ian:** husband of Mia/ brother in law of Calen/ Ruala

**Ibula:** warrior princess and healer of the Ruala Tribe/daughter of King Manu and Queen Delilia/

**Iden:** warrior guarding refugees/Shettee

**Igor:** brother of King Sharonne

**Ike Ferguson:** elderly neighbor of Gabriel and Hannah

**Imad:** a male Grand Master of the Insidiae

**Ina:** daughter of Mia and Ian/ Ruala

**Ingr:** female warrior of Nordes Tribe

**Inon:** one of Cisero's men/a vessel

**Ipos:** an ancient demon/ one of the Old Ones

**Iris:** mother of Vivian/wife of Joshua/Clan of Gesmal in Ryed

**Irit:** daughter of Hadi and Gita/ Ruala

**Isabella:** Princess of Lentz, sister of Mathas, Renya and Tasha, married to Captain Josef

**Isadore:** wife of Fahron

**Isla:** daughter of Prince Lakin and Princess Zada/Ruala

**Isla:** female warrior of Nordes Tribe

**Ivan:** boss of Javier and Madeline/from the Kingdom of Inferus

**Ivan:** youngest son of Chief Duncan and Liza of the Clan of Gesmal in Ryed

**Jace:** husband of Oda/ brother in law of Calen/Ruala

**Jack:** member of governing body of Nora

**Jackson:** a private in the Army of Lentz

**Jackson:** an escaped prisoner from Wetpr

**Jackson:** Corporal in the Army of Lentz

**Jackson:** one of Deckor's hired fighters

**Jacob:** boy who Angelina found in the woods

**Jacot:** son of Prince Lakin and Princess Zada/ grandson of King Manu/Ruala

**Jaden:** Sergeant in the Army of Lentz

**Jago:** son of Elen and Batya/ Ruala

**Jake:** hired fighter for Mayor Deckor of Langer

**Jake:** works for Talverson Transport Company in Port Friada

**Jakiv:** Prince/son of Segal and Cahina/nephew of King Manu of New Samona/Ruala

**Jama:** Enrop leader who protects Chief Sorren's family

**James:** Taperian soldier

**Jana:** female Ruala warrior

**Janja:** Princess/daughter of Gunnel and Uma/niece of King Manu of New Samona/ sister of Elan/Ruala

**Janson:** Wetprian soldier

**Jared:** hired fighter

**Jaretta:** King of Stordt/husband of Queen Lillian/ father of Roch and Sudfad

**Jarrod:** works for Pravis/leads attack on castle in Wetpr

**Jarvis:** a farmer who is killed by escaped prisoners

**Jasmine:** young female Nordes warrior

**Jason:** male Nordes warrior

**Jasper:** a large white dog that Gabriel brings home

**Jasper:** Prince of Lentz/son of Princess Isabella and Captain Josef

**Jatu:** Enrop leader who protects Fahron's family

**Javier:** a spy from the Kingdom of Inferus/brother of Madeline

**Jeb:** friend of Thaos

**Jeb**: one of Cisero's men

**Jela:** Queen of Samona/wife of Varden

**Jenna:** female Ruala warrior/married to Ratri's oldest brother Artis

**Jenny:** secretary of Mayor Deckor

**Jeremy:** cousin of Andrew the jeweler in Salar

**Jerik:** a male Grand Master of the Insidiae

**Jess:** a soldier of Wetpr

**Jillian:** Queen of Ogg/wife of King Douma

**Jinn:** an ancient demon/ one of the Old Ones

**Joao:** male Ruala warrior

**Joe:** works for Hector

**Joey:** adopted son of Elan and Cassandra

**Johnny:** a drifter/travels with Zeke, Sam and Carl

**Jonas:** Captain in the Taperian Army

**Jonathan Gabriel Maxwell:** son of Calen and Natasha

**Jonathon Blackmoore:** a physician who attended college with Hannah

**Jonathon:** a waiter at the Calla Lily Restaurant in Teivel Ryed

**Jorga:** Princess of Ryed/daughter of Oren and Astrel/ has twin sister Andres

**Jorge:** a cook who is kidnapped from Endleson Hotel in Nora

**Josef:** Captain in the Lentz military/ married to Princess Isabella, sister of King Mathas

**Joseph:** male Ruala warrior/father of Ratri/husband of Clair

**Joseph:** nine year old Ruala boy/son of Artis and Jenna/nephew of Ratri

**Joshua:** father of Vivian/husband of Iris/Clan of Gesmal in Ryed

**Josie:** an escaped prisoner from Wetpr

**Juleta:** cousin to Raul and Simon/daughter and oldest child of King Mathas and Queen Rosa

**Kadin:** a member of Valdore Tribe

**Kagen:** a man who kidnaps and exploits children

**Kalee:** female Ruala warrior/married to Ratri's older brother Quinn

**Karin:** wife of Mayor Deckor of Langer

**Karl:** two year old Ruala boy/son of Artis and Jenna/nephew of Ratri

**Karta:** male Ruala warrior

**Karzman:** leader of Kozach Tribe/ stepfather of Michael

**Kasper:** Prince/son of Zeman and Oda/nephew of King Manu of New Samona/Ruala

**Kata:** Princess/daughter of Gunnel and Uma/niece of King Manu of New Samona/ sister of Elan/Ruala

**Kate:** a Venator from the Clan of Gesmal

**Khryriss:** an ancient demon/ one of the Old Ones

**Kiana:** Princess/daughter of Gunnel and Uma/niece of King Manu of New Samona/ sister of Elan/Ruala

**Klass:** Lieutenant in the Wetprian Army

**Koby:** male Ruala warrior

**Koh:** son of Prince Gael and Princess Mada/grandson of King Manu/Ruala

**Kora:** Princess/ married to Raphael son of King Zachariah and Queen Noella of New Samona/ mother of Luca/ Raphael and Kora were killed in battle when Luca was a small boy/Ruala

**Korbin:** one of Teivel's lieutenants

**Korth:** son of Tristt/Shettee

**Kraus:** hired fighter and intended vessel, works for Dieter

**Kretcher:** Commanding General of Fort Polta in Wetpr

**Krister:** Princess of Samoan/daughter of Thomas and Rewel

**Kyle:** Nordes warrior/older brother of Jasmine/son of Conrad and Leta/husband of Marsha/father of Brandon

**Kyra:** young sister of Marie/ friend of Petra

**Laban:** Prince of Samona/son of Yorggi and Dion/grandson of Thomas and Rewel

**Lael:** daughter of Nina and Rhea/ Ruala

**Lakin:** Prince/son of King Manu and Queen Delilia/husband of Zada/Ruala

**Lala:** Princess/daughter of Adwell and Nada/niece of King Manu of New Samona/ sister of Misha/Ruala

**Lana:** female Nordes warrior

**Lana:** female warrior of the Nordes Tribe

**Lana:** Princess/daughter of Segal and Cahina/niece of King Manu of New Samona/Ruala

**Lance:** Nordes warrior/older brother of Jasmine/son of Conrad and Leta

**Lani:** daughter of Mia and Ian/Ruala

**Lara:** one of Usman's wives

**Larson:** a fighter hired by Juleta

**Laurabelle:** Hannah's sister who was murdered by Roch

**Laurel:** Annabelle's mother and former servant of King Roch's parents

**Lawrence:** a member of the Libertas

**Lazo:** fighter hired by Juleta

**Lea:** Princess/daughter of Adwell and Nada/niece of King Manu of New Samona/ sister of Misha/Ruala

**Leith:** four year old Ruala boy/son of Quin and Kalee/nephew of Ratri

**Leo:** Prince of Samona/son of Darius and Rebek/grandson of Thomas and Rewel

**Leon:** Captain in the Military of Ryed/ a member of Teivel's inner circle

**Leta:** mother of Jasmine/wife of Conrad/Nordes Tribe

**Lieutenant Tarp:** Lieutenant in the Wetprian Army

**Lila:** seventeen year old girl who Luca saves from the Hutas/sister of Christopher

**Lilian:** female warrior of the Nordes Tribe

**Lillian:** Queen of Stordt/wife of Jaretta/ mother of Roch and Sudfad

**Lily:** daughter of Calen and Natasha/Ruala and human

**Linda Thurstand:** wife of Geof/lover of Mayor Deckor

**Linus:** Elod child

**Liza:** wife of Duncan the Chief of the Clan of Gesmal in Ryed

**Lloyd:** banker in Nora

**Loftus:** Commanding General of Fort Styls

**Logan:** boy stolen by Hector's human trafficking ring

**Lordes:** Seaman in the Navy of Lentz

**Louie:** works for Talverson Transport Company in Port Friada

**Luca:** male Ruala warrior

**Lucene:** male Nordes warrior/oldest son of Hugo and Greta/older brother of Sasha

**Lucifer:** an ancient demon/ one of the Old Ones

**Lucile:** a member of the wealthy and elite in Ryed

**Lucky:** Sally's puppy

**Luque:** Prince/son of Segal and Cahina/nephew of King Manu of New Samona/Ruala

**Mab:** a female Grand Master of the Insidiae

**Mable:** a servant in the castle of King Nehmota of Ryed

**Mabon:** warrior guarding refugees/Shettee

**Mada:** Princess /wife of Prince Gael/Ruala

**Madam Bular:** owner of a dress shop in Port Friada

**Madeline:** a friend of Princess Isabella

**Madix:** General in the Army of Ryed/member of Teivel's first inner circle

**Maggie:** elderly store owner in Salar

**Maggie:** Mayer Tetly's wife

**Mahon:** son of King Neputa

**Makalo:** Prince of Norkv/husband of Grace who was the daughter of Benjeman and Esther

**Malana:** daughter of King Neputa

**Malard:** Captain in the military of Wetpr

**Mali:** Princess of Norkv/daughter of Makalo and Grace/granddaughter of Benjeman and Esther

**Maligma:** an ancient demon/ one of the Old Ones

**Malik:** member of the Insidiae

**Malus:** sorcerer from Ryed

**Mandrake:** Taperian soldier

**Manhure:** Sergeant in the Army of Lentz

**Manu:** King of New Samona/The Chief of the Grand Council made up of Rualas and Shettees/ father of Ibula, Lakin, Gael and Hadar/husband of Delilia

**Manutu:** King of the Gants

**Marcia:** friend of Hannah's/ Roch's men murdered her family

**Marcus Stephan:** son of Stephan and Ingr

**Margarit:** daughter of King Mathas and Queen Rosa of the Kingdom of Lentz/ cousin of Raul and Simon

**Margerie:** female cook of King Mathas and Queen Rosa

**Margo:** a young girl who was kidnapped by Sal

**Margolia:** girl from Nora who was sacrificed to a demon

**Marie:** a cook for King Sudfad and Queen Renya

**Marina:** female Ruala healer

**Markus:** a soldier in the Army of Wetpr

**Marla:** High Priest Meekos' housekeeper

**Marsha Jarvis:** a sixteen year old girl who is raped and killed by Timothy

**Marsha:** wife of Charles Moses

**Marsha:** Nordes warrior/wife of Kyle/mother of Brandon/sister-in-law of Jasmine

**Marshal:** Captain in the Military of Lenz

**Marshal:** Major in Army of Lentz

**Martha:** a cook for Cerephus

**Martha:** hotel owner in Telmark

**Martin Froush:** wealthy ship builder in Port Friada/husband of Denise

**Martin:** a member of the Libertas

**Marty:** boy stolen by Hector's human trafficking ring

**Mary:** Jared's young wife who was brutally murdered by Hutas

**Mata:** Igor's wife

**Mateo:** Chief Healer of the Ruala Tribe

**Mathas Sorren:** son of Matthew and Angelina

**Mathas:** King of Lentz/ brother to Queen Renya

**Matilda:** one of Usman's wives

**Matthew:** son of King Mathas and Queen Rosa of the Kingdom of Lentz/ cousin of Raul and Simon

**Matty T:** son of Stephan and Ingr

**Max:** one of Hector's men

**Maximus Bartholomew Joshua:** twin son of Misha and Diana/brother of Thor Adwell Gabriel

**Maxwell:** father of Calen/ Ruala

**Maxwell:** infant son of Nina and Rhea/grandson of elder Maxwell/Ruala

**McAvoy:** Sergeant in the Army of Wetpr/stationed at Fort Serpha

**Melanie:** female Ruala warrior/daughter of Casey and Tasha

**Melina:** mother of Thaos

**Melinda:** grandmother of Misha

**Melinda:** older sister of Cassandra and Joao

**Mia:** daughter of Maxwell and Emeral/ Ruala

**Mia:** female Ruala warrior/daughter of Tyron and Elsa

**Mica:** Princess of Norkv/daughter of Benedict and Sasaha/granddaughter of Benjeman and Esther

**Micha:** oldest son of Joshua and Iris/older brother of Vivian/Clan of Gesmal

**Micha:** son of King Sharonne/ grandfather of Sudfad and Roch

**Michael:** ancient king of Wetpr/father of Queen Sumona

**Michael:** son of Sudfad and Nadia

**Milo**: male Ruala warrior

**Miranda:** daughter of Raul and Vitomas

**Miranda:** emissary of The Great Ruler who takes on the disguise of a human seer

**Miriam:** a friend of Hannah's/works at Endleson Hotel in Nora

**Misha:** male Ruala warrior/lieutenant

**Molach:** a member of the Insidiae

**Moloch:** an ancient demon/one of the Old Ones

**Moraine:** Captain in the Navy of Lentz

**Morgan:** Sergeant in the Wetprian Army

**Morris:** member of governing body of Nora

**Morton:** Cedrick Teivel's original name

**Muhar:** Shettee warrior

**Murdock:** Major in the Wetprian Army

**Murphy:** Lieutenant in the Army of Wetpr/stationed at Fort Serpha

**Myla:** wife of Rex, the owner of the Dragons Inn in Salar

**Naal:** warrior guarding refugees/Shettee

**Nabi:** male Ruala warrior

**Nada:** Princess/ married to Adwell son of King Zachariah and Queen Noella of New Samona/ mother of Misha/ Adwell was killed in battle leaving Nada to raise ten children/Ruala

**Nadene:** a member of the wealthy and elite in Ryed

**Nadia:** wife of Karzman/mother of Michael

**Nana:** female Ruala warrior

**Naomi:** mother of Rabi/ Ruala

**Napo:** Enrop leader who protects Claudius' family

**Nash:** a soldier of Lentz

**Natalie:** female Venator/wife of Troy/mother of Hunter

**Natasha:** sister of High Priest Gabriel

**Nathaniel:** Sorren's oldest son/ Nordes Tribe

**Nebula:** son of Chief Romogi and Anda/ Kingdom of Marba/Huta

**Negal:** a demon

**Nehmota:** King of Ryed

**Nelpus:** Shettee warrior

**Neputa:** leader of the Shettee Tribe when it was conquered by the Hutas

**Nestor:** a demon that specializes in procuring things for a price

**Nethers:** one of Karzman's hired killers

**Nica:** Enrop leader who protects Sudfad's family

**Nicholas:** orphan boy /brother of Cerey

**Nicolas:** Prince of Puntd/son of King Tobias and Queen Tasha

**Nieatzae:** an ancient demon/ one of the Old Ones

**Nigel:** Chief Seaman in the Navy of Lentz

**Nikki:** female warrior of Nordes Tribe

**Nina:** daughter of Maxwell and Emeral/Ruala

**Nina:** youngest daughter of Karzman and Nadia

**Nita:** Princess/daughter of Adwell and Nada/niece of King Manu of New Samona/ sister of Misha/has twin brother Waed/Ruala

**Noah:** a member of the Libertas

**Nobel:** former prince of Ryed/son of Akasha and Norah/father of Nehmota

**Noel:** a cook at the Teivel Manor Hotel

**Noella:** the first Queen of New Samona/wife of King Zachariah/mother of seven sons/Ruala

**Norah:** former queen of Ryed/grandmother of Nehmota

**Noreen:** mother of Jacob/ wife of Henry

**Norge:** Private in the Wetprian Army

**Norris:** hired fighter and intended vessel, works for Dieter

**Novack:** Corporal in the Wetprian Army

**Nyla:** oldest daughter of Karzman and Nadia

**Oda:** daughter of Maxwell and Emeral/ Ruala

**Oda:** Princess/ married to Zeman son of King Zachariah and Queen Noella of New Samona/Ruala

**Odam:** male Ruala warrior

**Odell:** one of the spies at the Castle at Wetpr

**Oliver:** a member of the Libertas

**Omar:** Prince/son of Zeman and Oda/nephew of King Manu of New Samona/Ruala

**Omara:** Queen of Norkv/wife of Thaddius who was son of Benjeman and Esther

**Omnibus:** an ancient demon/ one of the Old Ones

**Omoria:** former queen of Ryed/wife of Nobel/mother of Nehmota

**Opago:** an ancient demon/ one of the Old Ones

**Oran:** son of Visterle and Nada/twin brother of Verto

**Orcus:** Shettee warrior/brother of King Neputa

**Oren:** former prince of Gandt who marries princess Astrel of Ryed

**Oriah:** name used by the Grand Master Banaka

**Orin:** male Ruala warrior/older brother of Ratri/husband of Rene

**Otis:** Nordes Warrior/first adopted father of Benny

**Ottillia:** Princess of Lenz/daughter of Princess Isabella and Captain Josef

**Otu:** son of Hecate and Sampson

**Padre Augustus:** a member of the Patronus

**Padre Bartholomew:** survives the massacre at the monastery at Avaide

**Padre Bishop:** assigned to the monastery at Leven

**Padre Cornelius:** a member of the Patronus

**Padre Darius:** a member of the Patronus

**Padre Dibon:** a priest at the monastery at Malga

**Padre Dominick:** priest at monastery at Malga

**Padre Edgar:** member of the Patronus

**Padre Edward:** a member of the Patronus

**Padre Finn:** Patronus priest assigned to the Cicero HQ

**Padre Francis:** priest at monastery at Malga

**Padre Joram:** member of the Patronus

**Padre Lucas:** a member of the Patronus

**Padre Markle:** a Patronus priest

**Padre Nebat:** alias for Dominic leader of the Libertas

**Padre Octavos:** runs orphanage in Salar

**Padre Philip:** a member of the Patronus

**Padre Philip:** a priest at the monastery at Malga

**Padre Simpson:** priest at the monastery at Malga

**Padre Sorben:** a member of the Patronus

**Padre Sornce:** Patronus priest assigned to the Cicero HQ

**Padre Stephens:** priest at monastery at Malga

**Padre Thomas:** priest at the monastery at Malga

**Padre Tobias:** a member of the Patronus

**Padre Xavier:** priest at monastery at Malga

**Paj:** Princess/wife of Prince Hadar/Ruala

**Pallas:** Shettee warrior

**Pata:** daughter of Chief Romogi and Trina/Huta

**Paterson:** a Private in the Wetprian military

**Patrick:** owns a company of mercenaries/ a member of the wealthy and elite in Ryed

**Patris:** six year old Nordes girl/daughter of Hugo and Greta/younger sister of Sasha

**Paul:** third son of Joshua and Iris/younger brother of Vivian/Clan of Gesmal

**Paulas**: a man who works for Cicero/a vessel

**Paulas:** Sergeant under Archetenus in Taperian Army

**Paullo:** works for High Priest Meekos

**Paxel:** Major in the Military of Lentz

**Pearl:** eldest daughter of King Tobias and Queen Tasha of Puntd

**Penelope:** wife of Gus/ killed for trying to help Nadia and Michael escape from Karzman

**Pergo:** King of the Kingdom of Gandt

**Peter:** Sorren's second son/Nordes Tribe

**Peters:** member of the governing body of Nora

**Petorus:** an ancient demon/one of the Old Ones

**Petra:** peasant boy from Ort who saves Padre Bartholomew

**Phifer:** nine year old Nordes boy/ son of Hugo and Greta/younger brother of Sasha

**Philip:** Prince of Puntd/ son of King Tobias and Queen Tasha

**Phillip:** Court Physician to the Royal Family of Wetpr

**Polgate:** one of the men who kidnapped Petra

**Potomas:** warrior guarding refugees/Shettee

**Powell:** a lieutenant in the Military of Lentz/stationed at Fahron's castle.

**Prescott:** a hired killer

**Quin:** male Ruala warrior/older brother of Ratri/husband of Kalee

**Rabi:** male Ruala warrior

**Rachel:** member of the freedom fighters in Ryed

**Radnor:** a male Grand Master of the Insidiae

**Rael:** Prince of old Samona/husband of Krister who was the daughter of Thomas and Rewel

**Rafa:** an Enrop

**Rahi:** a female Grand Master of the Insidiae

**Rakio:** Prince/son of Adwell and Nada/nephew of King Manu of New Samona/brother of Misha/Ruala

**Rako:** a male Ruala warrior

**Ralf:** male Ruala warrior

**Ralph:** an old sailor from the Navy of Ganz

**Raphael:** Prince/ son of King Zachariah and Queen Noella of New Samona/husband of Kora/Ruala/father of Luca/ Raphael and Kora were killed in battle when Luca was a small boy/Ruala

**Ratri:** male Ruala warrior

**Raul:** Prince/son of King Sudfad and Queen Renya of the Kingdom of Wetpr

**Raum:** an ancient demon/ one of the Old Ones

**Rebek:** Princess of Samona/wife of Darius, who was the son of Thomas and Rewel

**Rebke:** six year old Ruala girl/ daughter of Orin and Rene/niece of Ratri

**Remi:** an Enrop

**Rene:** female Ruala warrior/married to Ratri's older brother Orin

**Renya:** Queen of Wetpr/ wife of Sudfad

**Rewel:** Queen of Samona/wife of Thomas/mother of Varden

**Rex:** a notorious pick pocket in Port Friada

**Rex:** owner of the Dragons Inn in Salar/husband of Myla

**Rhea:** husband of Nina/ brother in law of Calen/ Ruala

**Richard:** third husband of Madeline

**Ridon:** General in the military of Wetpr

**Riftca:** male Ruala warrior

**Riker:** a scout in the Wetprian military

**Riley:** an abused dog that Luca saves

**Risa:** female Ruala warrior

**Risha:** a witch who deals with potions

**River:** one of Karzman's soldiers who he murdered

**Roch:** King of the Kingdom of Stordt/brother of King Sudfad

**Rogers:** one of the men who kidnapped Petra

**Rolif:** son of Chief Romogi and Silva/ Kingdom of Marba/Huta

**Romale:** member of the Insidiae

**Romos:** an elder of the Centras

**Rosa:** Queen of Lentz/wife of King Mathas

**Rosalie:** a dressmaker in Nora/wife of Peters

**Roy:** owner of the Pirates Flag Tavern in Langer

**Ruth:** emissary of The Great Ruler who takes on the guise of a frail old woman

**Ryan:** grandson of Jeb/friend of Thaos

**Rybkin:** Warlock who worked for the dictator Teivel

**Sabot:** member of the Insidiae

**Sahil:** a male Ruala warrior

**Sal:** a murderous pedophile/also goes by the name Tyrone

**Sally:** a young girl who was kidnapped by Sal

**Salzar:** powerful demon on Sidus

**Sam:** a drifter/travels with Zeke, Carl and Johnny

**Sam:** male Ruala warrior/father of Bekka/husband of Ella

**Samael:** a demon as powerful as Ahriman who rules the hell world Xibalba

**Samara:** wife of Tristt/Shettee

**Samat:** son of Chief Romogi and Silva/ Kingdom of Marba/Huta

**Samos:** Prince of Norkv/son of Thaddius

**Sampson:** oldest son of Chief Duncan and Liza of the Clan of Gesmal in Ryed

**Sampson:** Sergeant in the Taperian Army

**Samuel:** a high priest at the monastery at Malga who was murdered

**Samuel:** Prince of the original Samona/grandson of Thomas and Rewel

**Samuel:** second son of Raul and Vitomas

**Santi:** Elod child

**Sanuri:** a holy man/emissary of The Great Ruler/warrior

**Sar:** an Enrop

**Sar:** male Ruala warrior

**Sara:** daughter of Usman

**Sarah:** baby granddaughter of Mathas and Rosa

**Sarah:** housekeeper for Claudius and Bella

**Saran:** daughter of Karzman and Nadia

**Sasaha:** Princess of the original Samona/granddaughter of Thomas and Rewel

**Sasha:** young female Nordes warrior

**Sasha:** female warrior of the Nordes Tribe/wife of Galen

**Satan:** an ancient demon/ one of the Old Ones

**Satter:** male Ruala warrior

**Sattleman:** a Sergeant in the Wetprian army

**Sauer:** male Ruala warrior

**Sauer:** Nordes warrior/older brother of Bianca/son of Tyler and Dora

**Saunders:** a Taperian soldier

**Saxton:** powerful lieutenant who works for Teivel the dictator of Ryed

**Schroeder:** man who works for Insidiae leader Dieter

**Schuester:** Commander of a special unit of Teivel's government/identifies betrayers

**Sean:** one of Karzman's hired killers

**Segal:** Prince/ son of King Zachariah and Queen Noella of New Samona/husband of Cahina/Ruala

**Seguna:** former princess of Ryed/daughter of Akasha and Norah/ committed suicide

**Selen:** house keeper for Juleta

**Seth:** a member of the Libertas

**Sez:** male Ruala warrior

**Shanksaw:** mercenary

**Shara:** wife of Sorren/Nordes Tribe

**Shard:** Captain in the Military of Ryed/ a member of Teivel's inner circle

**Sharon:** one of Mayor Deckor's lovers

**Sharonne:** King of Stordt; great, great, grandfather of King Roch and King Sudfad

**Sheba:** a female Nordes warrior

**Shon:** son of King Fahra and Queen Sitha

**Shone:** Princess/daughter of Zeman and Oda/niece of King Manu of New Samona/Ruala

**Sicily Bella:** daughter of Stephan and Ingr

**Sila:** Princess of Ogg

**Silva:** one of Chief Romogi's three wives/Huta

**Simmons:** Commanding General of Fort Nir

**Simon:** adopted son of King Sudfad and Queen Renya of the Kingdom of Wetpr

**Sinclair:** King of Lentz/father of King Mathas

**Sirius:** works for High Priest Meekos

**Sitha:** Queen of Zorta

**Smoking Joe:** a regular patron at the Ghost Ship Tavern

**Sol:** male Ruala warrior

**Sonja:** female warrior of the Nordes Tribe

**Sophie:** cook and servant of King Roch

**Sorren:** leader of the Nordes Tribe

**Soto:** male Ruala warrior who leads first death squad for criminals

**Spooner:** an architect in Lentz

**Sporos:** priest turned demon

**Stephan:** Captain in Army of Lentz/son of Claudius and Bella

**Stiller:** a fighter hired by Juleta

**Stolas:** an ancient demon/one of the Old Ones

**Stone:** an alias used by Dominic during the mission in Ryed with Gabriel's team

**Stone:** hired fighter and intended vessel, works for Dieter

**Strait:** Lieutenant in the Army of Ganz

**Stranton:** Colonel in the Military of Wetpr

**Sudfad:** King of the Kingdom of Wetpr and brother to King Roch of Stordt

**Sudfad:** little Sudfad is grandson of King Sudfad

**Sumona:** Queen of Wetpr/wife of Alexandras/aunt of Roch and Sudfad

**Swenson:** one of Shanksaw's hired men

**Syrius:** a Bakken hired by Juleta

**Tabeth:** daughter of Fahron

**Tabith:** son of Tristt/Shettee

**Tabitha:** Princess of Lentz/daughter of Princess Isabella and Captain Josef of Lentz

**Tadeo:** Prince/son of Adwell and Nada/nephew of King Manu of New Samona/brother of Misha/Ruala

**Tafer:** a warlord who drove the Hutas out of the Kingdom of Norkv after years of wars and rebellions

**Tahira:** a female Grand Master of the Insidiae

**Tahira:** Princess of Samona/granddaughter of Thomas and Rewel

**Tal:** son of Oda and Jace/ Ruala

**Tally:** worked for Karzman

**Talmai:** Shettee boy who Thedes and Ibula adopt

**Talon:** a male Ruala warrior

**Tambor:** male Ruala warrior

**Tamour:** General in the Army of Lentz/on loan to Sudfad

**Tanner:** a Lieutenant in the Wetprian army

**Tanner:** a Sergeant in the Army of Lentz

**Tanner:** one of Deckor's hired fighters

**Tanya:** a female Nordes warrior/younger sister of Lana

**Tapster:** a demon who works for Meekos

**Tarig:** a lieutenant in the Huta army

**Tarin:** son of King Neputa and Queen Tiara/Shettee

**Tarla Grey:** wealthy socialite in the City of Langer in the Kingdom of Lentz

**Taron:** Prince/son of Adwell and Nada/nephew of King Manu of New Samona/brother of Misha/Ruala

**Tasha:** female Ruala warrior/mother of Melanie/wife of Casey

**Tasha:** Queen of Puntd/ married to Tobias/ sister of Renya and Mathas

**Tate:** a Lieutenant in the Wetprian Army

**Tatterd:** a Sergeant in the Wetprian military

**Tavin:** son of Prince Lakin and Princess Zada/Ruala

**Ted:** one of Karzman's hired fighters

**Teddy:** male Nordes warrior/son of Edgar and Cora/ older brother of Batina

**Teddy:** owner of a general store in Stoba Lentz

**Teddy:** works for Hector

**Tega:** housekeeper for the cabins of the captains of the Taperian Army

**Tegman:** soldier of Wetpr

**Tehtfote:** a Lieutenant for Dieter

**Temark:** villager of Neva

**Tetly:** a mayoral candidate in Langer/ Kingdom of Lentz

**Tetro:** Huta warrior who was a captive in Ogg

**Thadddius:** Prince of the new Kingdom of Norkv/son of Benjeman

**Thaddies:** member of Nordes Tribe/ father of Ingr

**Thanatoes:** an ancient demon/ one of the Old Ones

**Thaos:** a hired fighter

**Thatcher:** Prince/son of Zeman and Oda/nephew of King Manu of New Samona/Ruala

**Thatus:** Taperian soldier

**The Lion:** emissary of The Great Ruler who takes on the appearance of a lion when he is in the world of man

**Thedes:** warrior guarding refugees/Shettee

**Theodore:** handyman for Erebus/husband of Arlene

**Theodore:** the physician at Fort Stanus in the Kingdom of Wetpr

**Thomas:** King of the original Kingdom of Samona/father of Varden

**Thomas:** second son of Joshua and Iris/older brother of Vivian/Clan of Gesmal

**Thomas:** the young husband of Zoya who was murdered in Taperia

**Thompson:** Wetprian soldier

**Thor Adwell Gabriel:** twin son of Misha and Diana/brother of Maximus Bartholomew Joshua

**Thor:** a Venator/brother of Diana

**Thot:** an emissary of The Great Ruler

**Thronson:** one of Meekos hired killers

**Tiara:** Queen of Shettee Tribe when it was conquered by Hutas/wife of Neputa

**Timothy:** son of Fahron

**Tina:** Mother of Cassandra, Joao and Melinda

**Tito:** member of Valdore Tribe

**Titus Derek:** son of Thaos and Nikki

**Titus:** a lieutenant in the Taperian Army

**Tobart:** a member of the Nordes Tribe

**Tobey:** a carriage driver in Ryed who helps Gabriel's team

**Tobias:** King of Puntd.

**Tomas:** works for High Priest Pravis

**Tome:** a businessman and member of the Insidiae in Nora

**Tomi:** son of Usman the leader of the Valdore Tribe

**Tommy:** adopted son of Elan and Cassandra

**Toni:** young female Nordes warrior

**Tony:** male Ruala warrior/ married to Bekka's oldest sister Eloise

**Toomback:** Huta warrior

**Torance:** father of Thaos

**Torin:** oldest son of Karzman and Nadia

**Trace:** male Ruala warrior

**Trace:** one of Karzman's hired fighters

**Tratz:** one of the men who kidnapped Petra

**Travor:** Taperian warrior who was injured at the Wall of Dorath

**Tresdor:** nephew of Usman

**Tresdore:** son of King Sharonne

**Trevor:** Prince/son of Zeman and Oda/nephew of King Manu of New Samona/Ruala

**Tria:** daughter of Oda and Jace/Ruala

**Trina:** one of Chief Romogi's three wives/Huta

**Trina:** Princess/daughter of Zeman and Oda/niece of King Manu of New Samona/Ruala

**Trist:** a male Ruala warrior

**Tristt the Horrible:** Shettee warrior

**Tritor:** a powerful demon of Sidus and ex-lover of Hecate

**Troy:** male Venator/husband of Natalie/father of Hunter

**Tye:** Prince of Norkv/son of Princess Grace and Prince Makalo

**Tyler:** Nordes warrior/father of Bianca/husband of Dora

**Tyron:** male Ruala warrior/father of Mia/husband of Elsa

**Tyson:** Wetprian soldier

**Ulger:** a demon

**Uma:** Princess/ married to Gunnel son of King Zachariah and Queen Noella of New Samona/mother of Elan/Ruala

**Umar:** Prince/son of Adwell and Nada/nephew of King Manu of New Samona/brother of Misha/Ruala

**Uri:** an Enrop

**Uri:** son of Nina and Rhea/ Ruala

**Usman:** leader of the Valdore Tribe

**Valdus:** name used by the Grand Master Emeric

**Valerie:** young female Nordes warrior

**Valor:** Prince of the new Kingdom of Norkv/son of Benjeman and Esther

**Vandrew:** Petra's male tutor

**Vania:** Princess of Samona/daughter of Yorggi and Dion/granddaughter of Thomas and Rewel

**Varden:** last king of Samona/he and his family were murdered by rebels

**Vardin:** one of the men who kidnapped Petra

**Vasart:** Queen of Ryed/ wife of Nehmota

**Verto:** son of Visterle and Nada/twin brother of Oran

**Viktor:** an ancient priest in Ryed who tried to stop the Insidiae

**Vilem:** Nordes warrior/father of Adam and Celia/husband of Dea

**Vinca:** Queen of Stordt, wife of Sharonne

**Vincent:** Prince of Ryed/son of Nehmota and Vasart

**Vincente:** a captain in the covert organization The Guardians

**Vinus:** Queen of the Kingdom of Gandt

**Visterle:** a powerful demon

**Vitomas:** Queen of Stordt

**Vivian:** a demon hunter from the Clan of Gesmal

**Voltar:** Prince of Samona/son of Darius and Rebek/grandson of Thomas and Rewel/later becomes King of Wetpr

**Voss:** one of Karzman's hired killers

**Vuall:** a demon

**Waed:** Prince/son of Adwell and Nada/nephew of King Manu of New Samona/brother of Misha/has twin sister Nita/Ruala

**Wainburst:** Commanding Admiral of the Navy of the Kingdom of Ganz

**Wallis:** member of governing body of Nora

**Wanda Ferguson:** elderly neighbor of Gabriel and Hannah

**Wickfield:** editor of the most powerful newspaper in the Kingdom of Lentz

**Wilard:** Captain at Fort Polta

**William:** son of Jared and Zoya

**Willis:** son of King Pergo and Queen Vinus/ Kingdom of Gandt

**Xeni:** a female Grand Master of the Insidiae

**Yara:** daughter of Nina and Rhea/Ruala

**Yorggi:** Prince of Samona/son of Thomas and Rewel/brother of Varden

**Yori:** son of Usman the leader of the Valdore Tribe

**Yuri:** Prince/son of Adwell and Nada/nephew of King Manu of New Samona/brother of Misha/Ruala

**Zac:** one of the men who kidnapped Petra

**Zachariah:** first King of New Samona/husband of Queen Noella/father of seven sons/Ruala

**Zack:** eight year old brother of Rachel

**Zada:** Princess/wife of Prince Lakin/Ruala

**Zadok:** a male Grand Master of the Insidiae

**Zane:** one of Juleta's husbands

**Zede:** an ancient demon/ one of the Old Ones

**Zehmann:** an ancient demon/ one of the Old Ones

**Zeke:** a drifter/travels with Sam, Carl and Johnny

**Zelda:** mother of Rachel and Zack

**Zeman:** Prince/ son of King Zachariah and Queen Noella of New Samona/husband of Oda/Ruala

**Zieman:** a demon

**Zorda:** Taperian soldier injured in battle at the Wall of Dorath

**Zortus:** demon/lieutenant of Visterle

**Zoya:** a seer from Taperia

# Glossary of Terms

**Aboultis:** the calling cards of demons

**Abrax:** the planet that orbits closest to the three suns/ uninhabited

**Abuckto:** a sub race of superior intelligence in the Kingdom of Inferus

**Abyss:** a vast void used to imprison demons

**Acura:** the whispering shadows/are in the inner circle of demons that directly serve the Old Ones

**Adros:** one of five solar systems in the Mensor Galaxy

**Alferto:** a type of grain that is common in Opots

**Amark:** ancient language of The Great Ruler

**Amper Tree:** special wood/forests of these trees are found in the lands of the Valdore Tribe

**Amulth:** means filth in the language of demons/these monsters are made out of the waste of tortured souls from the hell dimensions

**Anewa:** one of seven continents in the World of Nunc

**Aplewort:** an herb when mixed with water purges poisons from a body

**Asherane:** ancient tribe that lived in the northern regions of the Kingdom of Lentz

**Ashta:** a common herb/when the dried leaves are boiled they give off a pleasant scent

**Astras:** the ancient underground city of the Centras

**Astrum:** the solar system that consists of three suns that form a triangle and seven planets

**Backor:** one of the eight worlds in the Naz Solar System in the Mensor Galaxy

**Balterak:** one of the eight worlds in the Naz Solar System in the Mensor Galaxy

**Beltrad:** a species of lower level demons

**Blood rings:** Large red rubies set in silver with markings of the Old Ones

**Boca:** a covered wagon pulled by horses

**Box of Itifer:** a gift to the world of man from The Great Ruler; this gift affects the balance of creation

**Bozie:** a game of skill played by the Nordes Tribe

**Cava plant:** a poisonous plant that grows freely near bodies of water

**Centras:** ancient race of creatures who have the responsibility of protecting the Holy Box of Itifer

**Cerfic:** an ancient language widely spoken among many kingdoms/a language of the masses not royalty

**Chalice of Ascension:** a gift from The Great Ruler, this gift contains unimaginable powers

**Charto:** the most radical political faction in the Kingdom of Inferus

**Cheyweg:** the ancient language of the Village of Tameric in the Kingdom of Marba

**Cicero College:** in Wetpr, outside of Salar, where Raul, Simon and Hannah attended college

**Clan of Gesmal:** a tribe of demon hunters who live in the southern region of the Kingdom of Ryed

**Credo:** a secret group in Inferus who worship The Great Ruler

**Crystal pillars:** in the Ice Caves of Mordv/are blessed by The Great Ruler and filled with spiritual life force

**Cyrus cloth:** an ancient cloth made in Ryed

**Czarsta:** one of seven continents in the World of Nunc

**Daliosis Demons:** an ancient species of demon that lives underground in lairs

**Demalogs:** an inferior species of demons

**Demosa:** a slow acting poison from the cava plant

**Diamond of Cazo:** a gift from The Great Ruler, this gift can unleash powers from the center of the world

**Dirtx:** one of the eight worlds in the Naz Solar System in the Mensor Galaxy

**Discedo Sect:** a radical sect of the Insidiae

**Durisks:** large demonic birds/their elongated beaks contain rows of fangs

**Ekel Beast:** similar to a deer

**Elods:** a race of people who live in the center of the World of Nunc in the Kingdom of Inferus

**Engas:** a wild cat that inhabits the Vandrew Mountains

**Engor:** a small pack animal that lives in trees

**Enrop:** a large species of bird that can speak many human languages

**Epocos:** one of the original tribes in the Kingdom of Ryed

**Eto:** a sub race of beings in the Kingdom of Inferus. They are all seductresses

**Farduth:** a Shettee necklace that symbolizes a male has completed his rite of passage to become a warrior

**Filsum:** the sixth planet in the Astrum Solar System/ two moons

**Florines:** a brightly colored species of bird that lives in the Kingdom of Inferus

**Frebre:** one of five solar systems in the Mensor Galaxy

**Fuln:** one of the eight worlds in the Naz Solar System in the Mensor Galaxy

**Gafet:** an ancient Shettee weapon

**Gants:** large apelike creatures/Watchers of the Caves of Muldun

**Gate of Isula:** the only opening in the great Wall of Dorath

**Gefrey Games:** games of sport where men fight each other and great beasts to the death

**Grand Masters:** the first people to call to the demons and invite them into this world

**Great Ruler:** God

**Half-Mans:** a tribe of creatures that are partially human and partially nature. They are three feet tall and walk on two legs but can change their coloring to match their environment.

**Hall of Antiquities:** a giant hall located in the monastery at Malga/ a sanctuary for holy items and manuscripts

**Hall of Light:** the Great Hall in the Ice Caves of Mordv

**Halrut:** an herb commonly found in the Kingdom of Stordt/used to help people sleep/

**Hengers:** giant blue eagles/ birds of war

**Highland Pass:** the only passage through the Rosu Mountain Range

**Holy Scrolls:** gifts given to each kingdom by The Great Ruler, these gifts contain powers, wisdom and immortality

**Holy Vault:** a secret vault under the King's study in the castle in Wetpr designed to protect holy objects

**Horn of Asher:** a horn used by the Patronus warrior priests to signal each other

**Horn of Cass:** a horn used by the Wetprian soldiers to signal each other

**Horn of Cornwell:** a horn used by Dieter's men to signal each other

**Horn of Eel:** a horn used by the Ruala warriors to communicate with each other

**Horn of Esker:** a horn used by the Valdore Tribe to communicate with each other

**Horn of Ire:** a horn carried by the Taperian soldiers to communicate with each other

**Horn of Shana:** a horn carried by the soldiers of Lentz to communicate with each other

**Horn of Tula:** a horn used by the members of the Nordes Tribe for communication

**Horn of Vamont:** a horn used by the Kozach Tribe for communication

**Horn of Xepoltr:** a horn used by the Shettee warriors to communicate

**Huta:** a race of humans that is driven by hatred and ideas of racial superiority who live in the Kingdom of Marba

**Insidiae:** means conspirators/a highly organized secret group of humans who have sold their souls to demons

**Irtma:** one of the eight worlds in the Naz Solar System in the Mensor Galaxy

**Jacar:** giant leech-like creatures

**Jacept Plant:** a plant that a powerful poison is made from

**Jaze:** one of the eight worlds in the Naz Solar System in the Mensor Galaxy

**Juntos:** Talismans of black magic that Karzman would use to terrorize and weaken his opponents

**Kafer:** a small crescent shaped knife carried by the Beltrad

**Keepers of the Scrolls:** the Royal Family of the Kingdom of Wetpr entered into a covenant with The Great Ruler to protect his gifts until a time when they can be safely given back to the world of man

**Kier:** one of five solar systems in the Mensor Galaxy

**Kinsman:** the capital city of the planet Sidus

**Kozach:** a tribe that lives in the far north central regions of the Kingdom of Wetpr

**Lafz:** one of five solar systems in the Mensor Galaxy

**Lamsman:** an ankle bracelet worn by Venatores/stones in the bracelet signify great feats they had to accomplish to become a demon hunter

**Learning Center:** the first of its kind/a complex educational facility that is open to multiple peoples and guards the students and staff from terrorists

**Leaves of the Talamar plant:** used for food and medicine but also used in black magics to alter people's senses and to create illusions of the mind-in small quantities/ in large quantities can effect time/

**Libertas:** the name of a group of freedom fighters in northern Ryed

**Linges plant:** a plant that grows in damp, swampy regions in Opots/the white berries are used to make the drug Melanwhop

**Lithanize:** an ancient language common to the southern kingdoms of Opots.

**Lynswood:** an herb that reveals tracks that are concealed by black magic

**Mark of Satan:** a coiled red snake with green eyes and a yellow tongue

**Matu potage:** a food staple of the Shettee Tribe

**Mayka:** one of seven continents in the World of Nunc

**Melanwhop:** a drug made from the linges plant, causes lethargy and apathy

**Mensor Galaxy:** is 20,000 light years from the Astrum Solar System/this galaxy contains five solar systems: Adros, Kier, Lafz, Frebre and Naz

**Menzine:** a species of giant snake in the Kingdom of Inferus

**Mordov:** the special place in hell for hypocrites

**Motfer:** the land of the dead

**Muysack:** a huge flying beast from hell

**Naz:** one of five solar systems in the Mensor Galaxy/this solar system has eight worlds: Balterak, Nords, Jaze, Fuln, Backor, Dirtx, Irtma, Puner

**Nefandus:** a secret sect within the Insidiae

**Nordes:** a tribe of fiercely trained warriors who live in the northern region of the Kingdom of Lentz

**Nords:** one of the eight worlds in the Naz Solar System in the Mensor Galaxy

**Nunc:** the world where this story takes place/third planet from the three suns

**Old Ones:** the original demons that came to the World of Nunc

**Opatu bread:** a food staple of the Shettee Tribe

**Opots:** one of seven continents in the world of Nunc/the continent where this story takes place

**Oran:** a tobisk that is filled with a mixture of ramni oil, buruto powder and meno salts, designed to explode on impact

**Orantho:**  the seventh planet in the Astrum Solar System/inhabited/four moons/ large planet/many hell worlds

**Patronus:**  an elite group of men who serve as the protectors of the church

**Pfison screen:**  a type of demonic cloaking devise/it is sensitive and has to be calibrated for the specific individuals it is intended for

**Planteen:**  the fourth planet in the Astrum Solar System/inhabited/two moons

**Plyogram:**  a drawing containing pictures within pictures to hide secret messages.

**Porto:**  one of seven continents in the World of Nunc

**Prophesy of Isto:**  an ancient prophesy of the Elods

**Prophesy of Izera:**  Predicts the downfall of the Teivel regime

**Prophesy of the Blood Moon:**  a demonic prophesy that predicts the doors to hell being opened.

**Propilatry:**  a powerful form of demonic curse

**Prostras:**  an ancient tribe that once inhabited the Ice Caves of Mordv

**Puner:**  one of the eight worlds in the Naz Solar System in the Mensor Galaxy

**Raftifa:**  ancient bat-like creatures that devour human flesh

**Rappal demon:**  a lower level demon with slimy skin and an unusual smell

**Ravens:**  messengers used by the dark lords

**Recupero:**  a sect within the Insidiae that worships the demon Omnibus

**Rites of Purification:**  an ancient ritual to close the windows of the demons

**Rogetts:**  a tribe of humans that have digressed into murderous mutant monsters

**Rualas:**  an ancient tribe of warriors said to be half human and half bird

**Salszar:** one of seven continents in the World of Nunc

**Salts of Envoy:** a sleeping potion

**Schumack roots:** used for food and medicine but also used in black magics to alter people's senses and to create illusions of the mind-in small quantities/ in large quantities can effect time/

**Scio:** a crystal ball

**Scroll of Imari:** a gift of The Great Ruler, a scroll that unleashes the power of The Box of Itifer

**Seal of Natun:** a gift from The Holy Ruler that can open doors to other worlds

**Second Sons:** men bred to become vessels for demons

**Serpents of Satan:** can only be called forth by dark lords and demons, large red snakes with green eyes and yellow tongues

**Seven Sons Prophesy:** an ancient prophesy about seven sons who stand up against the demons and dark lords

**Shadow Men:** creature that can only be seen when illuminated at night

**Shaker Winds:** incredible storms that form when the currents and winds of three oceans converge

**Shesone:** an ancient fighting style of the Shettee Tribe

**Shettee:** an ancient tribe of warriors said to be half human and half lion

**Sidus:** the fifth planet in the Astrum Solar System/inhabited/red fog surrounds the planet

**Solv:** a specific prison within the Abyss

**Song of the Second Son:** an ancient prophesy about an evil that is passed between second son's of a family resulting in a monster that brings terror and darkness to the world of man

**Stratas:** Creatures bred by the Elods

**Sundra Templer:** a gift from The Great Ruler that was stolen by dark lords/an orb with extraordinary powers that can be used in multiple ways such as transporting humans through other worlds

**Tabutu:** an ancient form of fighting developed by the Asherane Tribe of the Kingdom of Lentz

**Talisman:** an object with magical or supernatural meaning

**Talmuth:** giant red dragon-like creatures

**Taluth:** a light weight metal used to make the ancient Shettee weapons called the Gafets

**Tameric:** the place where Karzman claims he came from although it does not exist on any map of Opots/also the name of the collective hell worlds of Nunc

**Tangers:** large wild, grazing animals that travel in herds

**Tansof:** one of seven continents in the World of Nunc

**Tarus demon:** huge, power creatures that walk on two legs but have the head, neck and shoulders of an ox

**Telgras:** a hell beast that looks like it is half wolf and half panther

**Teragon:** death terror/a monster created as a result of diabolical acts

**Terbot bear:** a bear that roams in the northern regions of the continent of Opots

**Tervator:** fourteen foot monster that walks like a man with long dark hair over its entire body and bull-like horns protruding from its head

**Texts of Semalia:** ancient texts about demonic language and rituals

**The Boldface:** Admiral Gideon's ship

**The Book of Horror:** a book that is worshipped by demons/contains prophesies

**The Celebration of Days:** an annual celebration of the Centras

**The Dead Runner:** ship of the notorious pirate Axel Sam

**The Hall of Knowledge:** the primary meeting room in the Temple of the Abuckto in the Kingdom of Inferus

**The Hall of Understanding:** the building in Astras where the history of the Centras is documented in drawings

**The Hunters:** another name for the Shettee Tribe

**The Lion:**  a very powerful messenger of The Great Ruler assumes the form of a lion when he walks in the worlds of man

**The Thirteenth Color:**  not seen in the world of man it is the color of horror/hell

**Timbar:**  ghost dragons/ demons that can fly

**Tinchure water:**  an herbal pain remedy used by the Nordes Tribe

**Tincture of the Redeti Plant:**  Hutas dip the tips of their weapons in this insect infested liquid. The insects lay eggs inside of the victim. When the eggs are mature and hatch, two inch worm-like creatures are produced and will eat the organs of the victim causing a long and painful death

**Tobisks:**  sphere shaped objects, metal and hollow inside that are designed to be launched from a Trebuchet

**Tramor:**  a flying monster in the Kingdom of Inferus

**Traxsor:**  the second planet in the Astrum Solar System

**Trebuchets:**  wooden machines used to catapult objects

**Trimoth:**  a game of skill, strength and speed

**Triolie:**  a Nordes gambling game

**Twanize:**  a language common to the Continent of Porto

**Tygrus:**  a ship that docked in Port Friada

**Unholy altar:**  altar used to worship demons

**Valdees:**  the tribe that lives in the underwater Kingdom of Ogg

**Valdore:**  a tribe of merciless separatists who live in the extreme northern regions of the Kingdom of Lentz

**Venator:**  means hunter in the old language

**Venom of the Atha serpent:**  one of the poisons that Hutas put on their arrows

**Vessel of Darkness:**  a human created from darkness to hold the essence of a powerful demon

**Wall of Dorath:**  a giant wall that separates the Kingdoms of Norkv and Xepoltr from the Kingdom of Marba

**Willimonns:**  small furry creatures that are hunted for food and sport

**Xelope:**  the oneness of spirit with all that lives

**Yellow Jay:**  a bird native to Opots

**Yellow Mandeze**:  a song bird common to Opots

**Zehno demon:**  thin, creature with long red and blue plumes on the back of its head with large eyes and round mouths

**Zendoti:**  demons that are distinguished by the geometrically shaped tuffs of hair that protrude from their heads

# Glossary of Maps

**The maps are displayed in order of relevance**

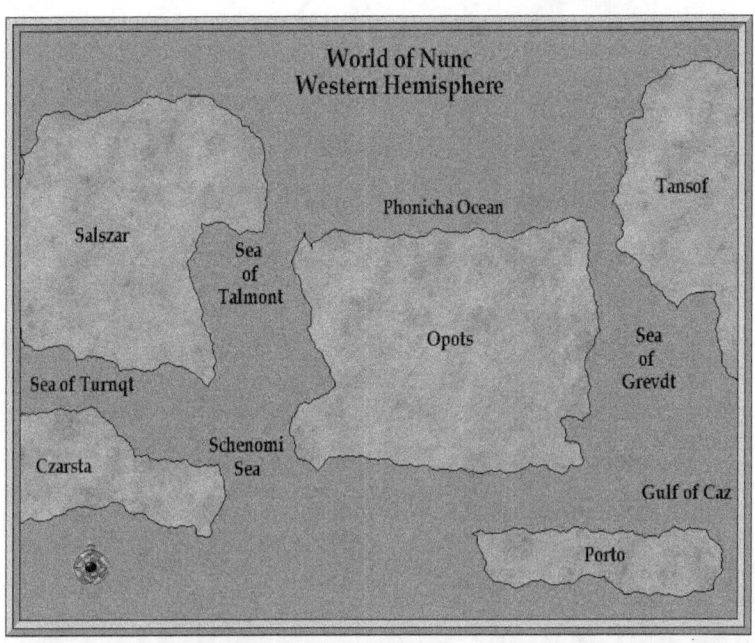

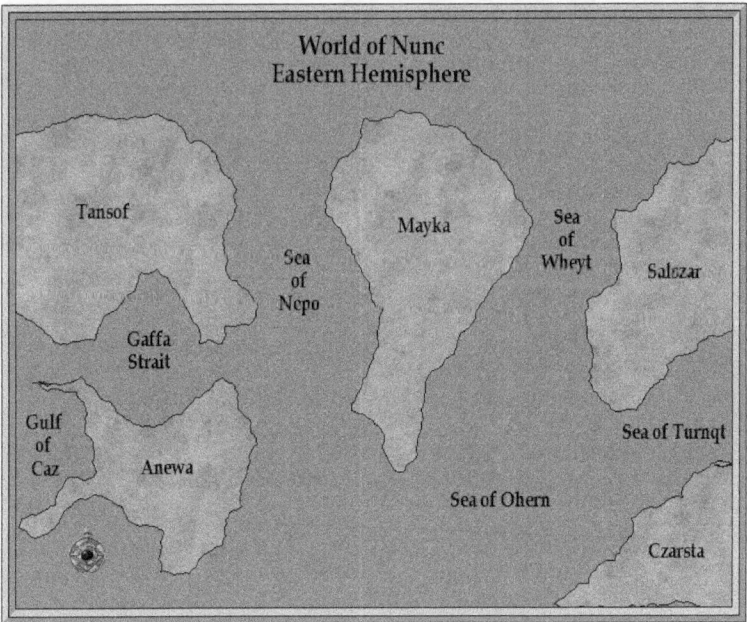

# Continent of Opots
## With new forts

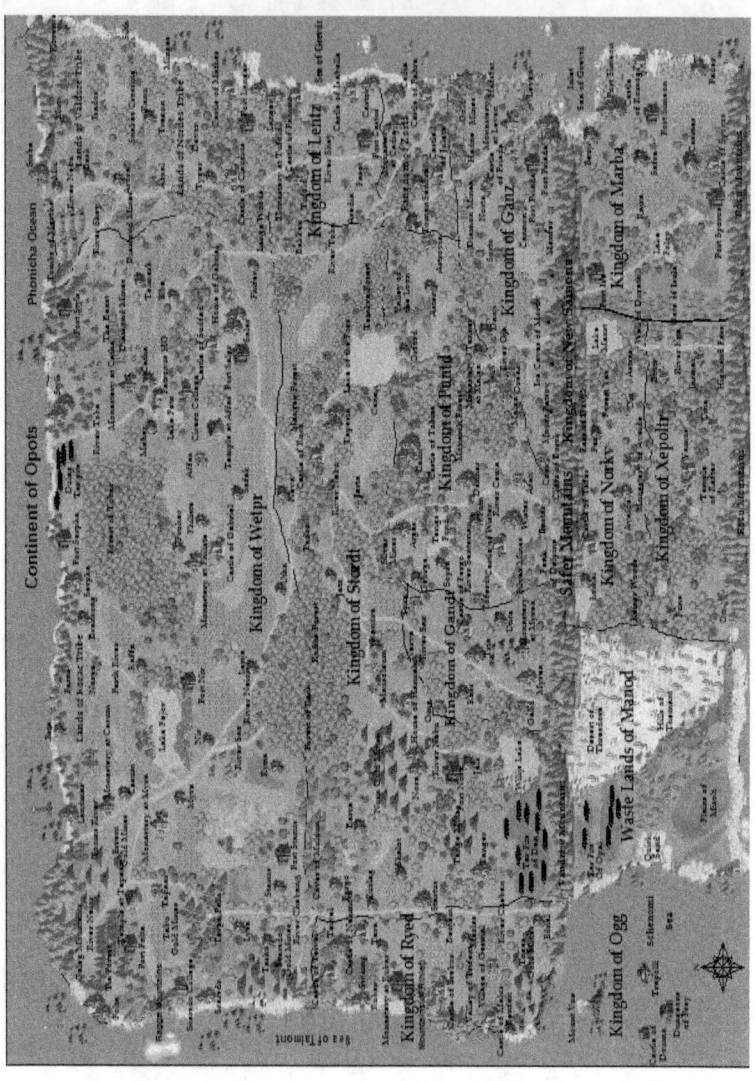

## Western Stordt
## With Fort Nora

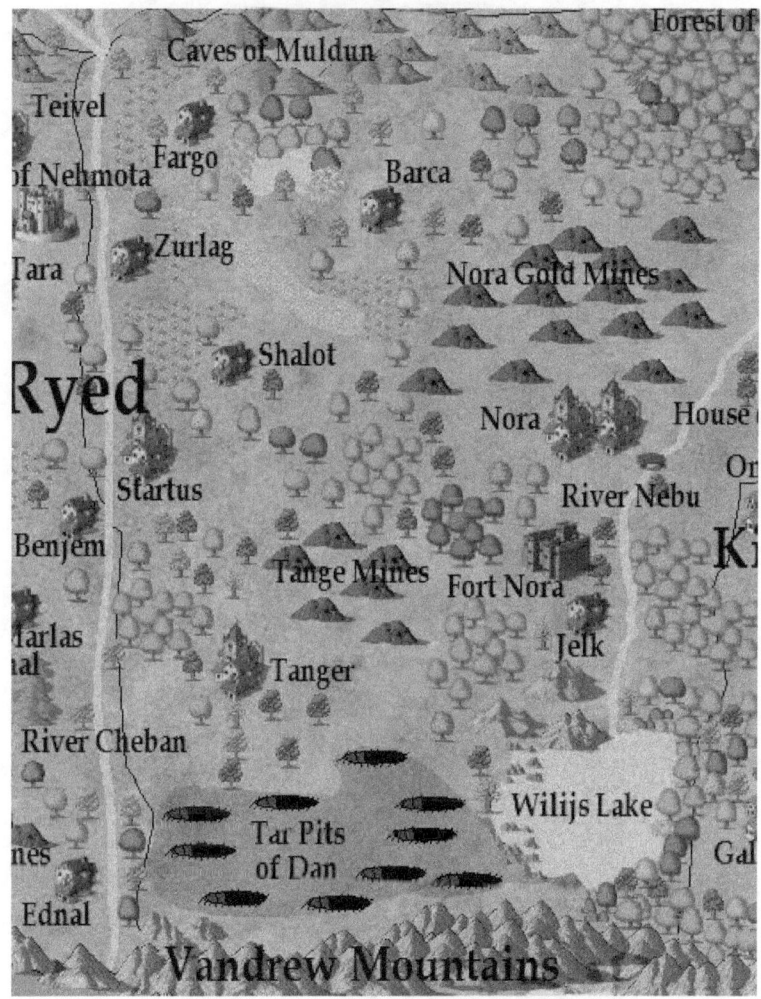

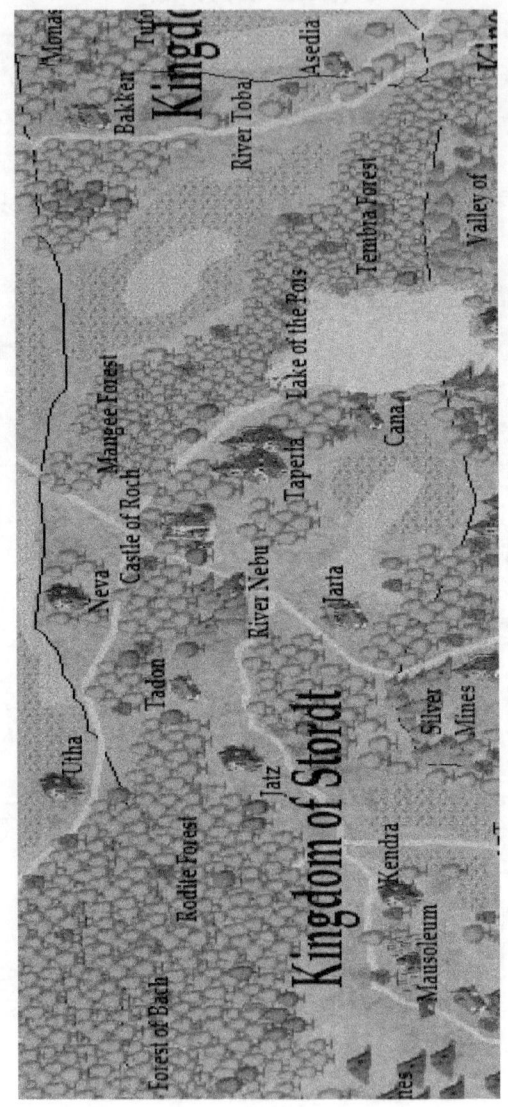

## Western Wetpr
## With Fort Stanus

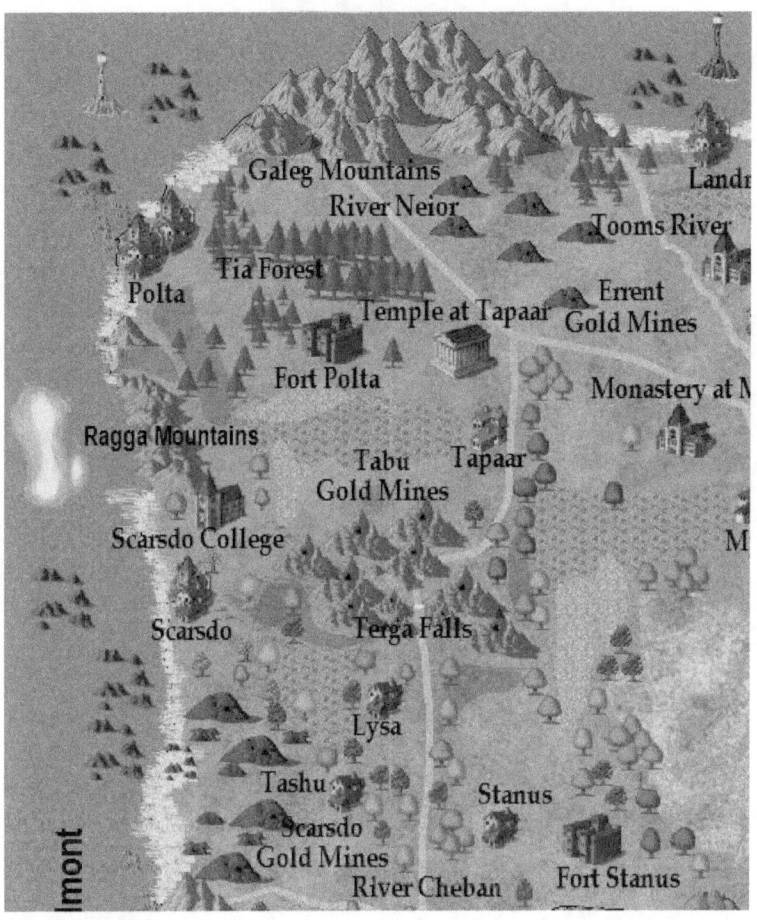

# Marba

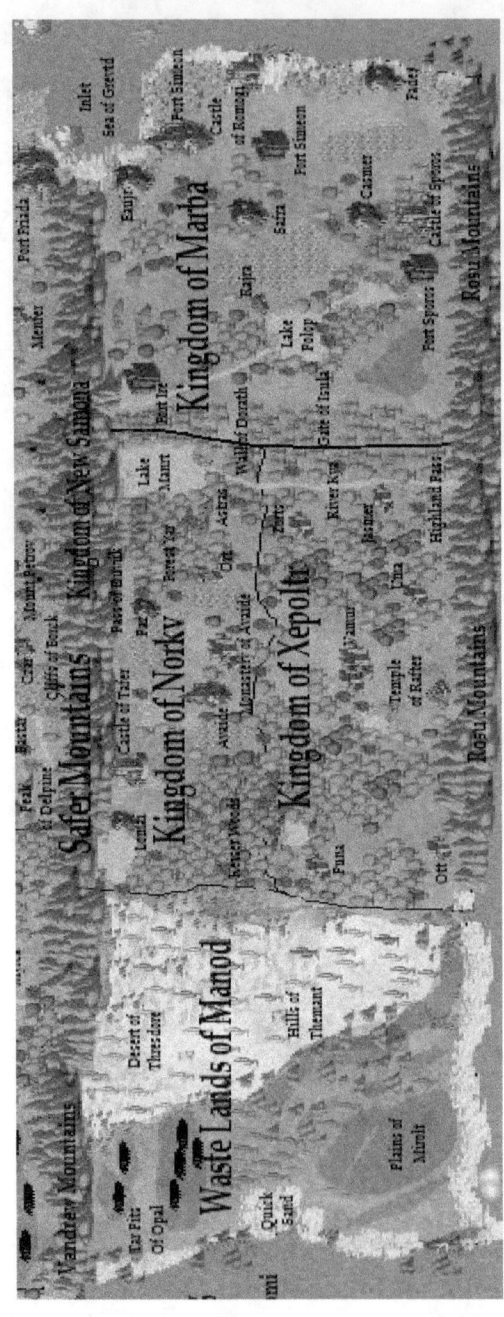

**Puntd**

Kingdom of Puntd
Valley of the Loon
Astrovia
Aster
Orford
Cana
Calix
Castle of Tobias
Monarch Forest
Monastery at Malga
Tanner
Sorto
Danji
River Oja
Oreak
Malga
Mount Petrov
Danner
River Cenja
Potn
Afax
Czar
Wister
Bastar
Terigs Pond
Argas
Silver Mines
Georga
Sopra
River Senterian
Castle of Wister
Toferdt
Silver Mines
Peak of Delpine

# Astrum Solar System

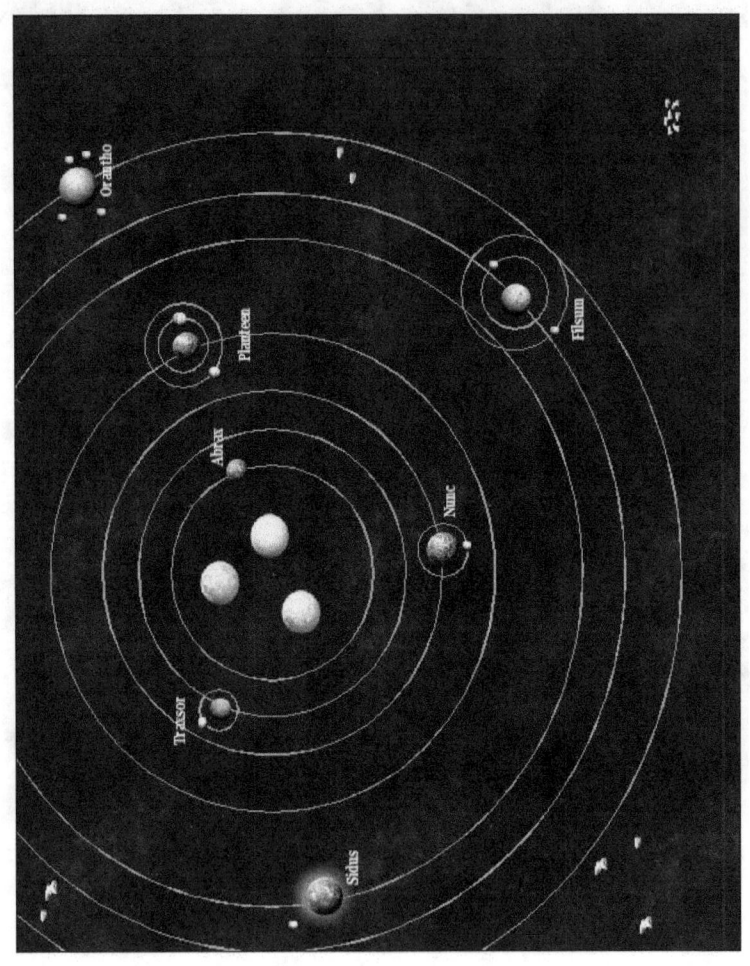